May Agnes Fleming

One Night's Mystery

A novel

May Agnes Fleming

One Night's Mystery
A novel

ISBN/EAN: 9783337027506

Printed in Europe, USA, Canada, Australia, Japan

Cover: Foto ©Andreas Hilbeck / pixelio.de

More available books at **www.hansebooks.com**

NIGHT'S MYSTERY.

A Novel.

BY

MAY AGNES FLEMING,

AUTHOR OF
"GUY EARLSCOURT'S WIFE," "A WONDERFUL WOMAN,"
"A TERRIBLE SECRET," "NORINE'S REVENGE,"
"MAD MARRIAGE," ETC.

NEW YORK:

G. W Carleton & Co., Publishers.

LONDON: S. LOW & CO.

MDCCCLXXIX.

CONTENTS.

PART SECOND.

ONE NIGHT'S MYSTERY

CHAPTER I.

SYDNEY.

" A girl who has so many wilful ways,
She would have caused Job's patience to forsake him,
Yet is so rich in all that's girlhood's praise,
Did Job himself upon her goodness gaze,
A little better she would surely make him."

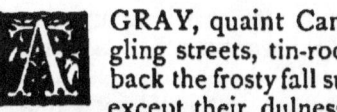 GRAY, quaint Canadian town, a dozen rows of straggling streets, tin-roofed houses that wink and twinkle back the frosty fall sunshine—houses uniform in nothing except their dulness and their glistening metal roofs. Dull, very dull they certainly are ; two-storied, many-windowed, of dingy red brick or gloomy gray stone ; depressing beyond all telling to the eye and mind of the solitary stranger doomed for his sins to drag out a few dreary months in the stagnant— well, let us say—town of Petit St. Jacques. Stagnant—that is the word. · Life long ago lay down for a siesta there, and never woke up. Religion is the only thing that seems at all brisk. Many gilt spires point upward to the blue Canadian heaven ; a full score of bells clash forth each Sunday, and thrice on that day, and thrice each week-day, the great booming bell of the dim old Cathedral de Notre Dame chimes forth the "Angelus Domini," as you may hear in some dreamy, world forgotten town of old France. Beneath its gray stone arches tall pines and feathery tamaracs toss their green plumes in the salt breezes from the stormy gulf, and brilliant-plumaged, shrill-voiced Canadian birds flit among the branches. In the fiercely hot, short-lived Canadian summer grass grows green in the market-places and busiest streets of Petit St. Jacques.

1*

In the summer. But the summer, brief and sweet as a
pleasant dream, is at an end; the ides of October are here.
Shrill October winds whistle down the wide empty streets ; drifts
of scarlet maple and orange hemlock leaves swirl in your face ;
a black frost holds the earth iron bound ; your footsteps ring
like steel over the unpaved sidewalks ; the keen breath of coming
winter sets your blood leaping, your eyes sparkling, and lights
in dusk Canadian cheeks a hue rosier than all the *rouge végétal*
on earth can give.

"And the last of October will be Halloween ! This is the
twenty-ninth—only two days more. Girls, *do* stop whooping
like a tribe of Mic-macs gone mad, and list, oh I list to me.
Friday next is Halloween."

But the speaker's voice was lost in the shrieking uproar of
five-and-thirty school-girls "on the war-path." Afternoon
school was over, the day scholars gone home, and the
boarders, out in the playground for the last half-hour's recess
before evening study, were rending the heavens with the deafening, distracting din that five-and-thirty of those rose-cheeked,
gold-haired, corseted angels alone know how to raise.

If there was one thing besides its churches for which Petit
St. Jacques was famous, it was the establishment of the Demoiselles Chateauroy for young ladies. It stood in the centre of
the Rue St. Dominique ; and if there was anything to choose in
the matter of dulness and respectability among all the dull and
respectable streets of the little town, the Rue St. Dominique
should be awarded the palm. There were no shops, there
were no people ; the houses looked at you as you passed with a
sad, settled, melancholy mildew upon them ; the doors rarely
opened, the blinds and curtains were never drawn ; prim little
gardens, with prim little gravel-paths, shut in these sad little
houses from the street ; now and then a pale, pensive face
might gleam at you from some upper window, spectre-like, and
vanish. The wheels of a passing wagon echo and re-echo
down its long silence ; the very dogs who sneak out to waggle
their tails in the front grass-plot have a forlorn and secret-sor-
row sort of air. Take it for all in all, you might travel from the
St. Lawrence to the Rio Grande and not find another so absolutely low-spirited and drearily respectable a street as the Rue
St. Dominique. Indeed, as Miss Sydney Owenson often and
justly remarked, it was a very poor compliment to St. Dominique
to christen it after him at all. Miss Sydney Owenson was one
of the Demoiselles Chateauroy's five-and thirty boarders ; and

It may as well be stated here as elsewhere, had made the Demoiselles Chateauroy more trouble, broken more laws, been condemned to solitary confinement oftener, been the head and front of more frolicsome offendings, and, withal, been better loved by both pupils and teachers during the past three years than the other four-and-thirty put together.

"Miss Owenson is in disgrace every week of her life," Mademoiselle Jeanne Chateauroy was wont to observe, taking a surreptitious pinch of snuff, "and, if strict justice were administered, would be in punishment and disgrace every day of the week; but, *ma foi !* what would you ? It is only high spirits and good health, after all. She keeps the school in a ferment, that is true ; there is no mischief of which she is not ringleader, but it is innocent mischief, after all; she has the smile and voice of an angel ; it is impossible to be as severe with her as she deserves, and then, Mon Dieu, it is the best heart that ever beat."

This *pensionnat des demoiselles* of the sisters Chateauroy was situated, as has been said, in the centre of the Rue St. Dominique, fronting directly upon the street—its extensive gardens and playground in the rear. A wooden wall eight feet high shut in this sacred inclosure and its angelic "jeunes filles" from the sacrilegious eye of man. In the face of the fierce summer sun, in the teeth of the fierce winter blasts, the twelve green shutters that protected the twelve front windows were kept jealously closed and barred. No prying, curious daughter of Eve might by any chance look out upon the gay and festive dissipations of the Rue St. Dominique—no daring masculine eye might ever in passing glance in. This prison discipline had only existed within the past two years, and a dark and dreadful legend was whispered about through the dormitories in the "dead waist and middle of the night" to all newcomers of the reason why. As usual, it was all Sydney Owenson's fault. Perched on top of the highest desk in the school-room, her eager head thrust out of the window, this daring, ill-behaved girl had deliberately winked at a passing soldier from the dingy old stone barracks outside the town. The soldier had winked back again; then this totally depraved Miss Owenson had thrown him a kiss ; then this dreadful soldier threw *her* a kiss, and grinned, and went by. Next day he came again ; next day Miss Owenson was perched up on the window-sill, like sister Anne on the watch-tower, to see if there was anybody coming. Sent by her guardian-angel, no doubt, at this dreadful juncture, Mademoiselle Chat-

eauroy the elder came into the school-room; Mademoiselle
Chateauroy's horrified eyes beheld Miss Owenson with all the
superior half of her person projecting into the Rue St. Dominique: Mademoiselle Chateauroy's stunned ears overheard
these words:

"I say, Mr. Lobsterback, who *is* that lovely young officer I
saw prancing all you fellows to the English Church last Sunday? All the girls are dying to know, and I told them I would
find out. We're all in love with him. Do tell us his——"

Mademoiselle Chateauroy heard no more. To seize Miss
Sydney Owenson, to tear her from her perch, to slam down the
window, to glare annihilation upon the grinning red-coat, to
confront the offender, livid with horror, was but the work of a
second.

What awful fate befell the culprit no pupil knew—no, not to
this day; her punishment was enshrouded in the same dark
mystery that envelops the ultimate end of the Man in the Iron
Mask. She had not been expelled, that was clear, for that was
two years ago; and when questioned herself, Miss Owenson
was wont to look for a moment supernaturally solemn, and
then go off into a peal at the remembrance that made the
"welkin ring."

It is close upon five on this October evening, when the
thirty-five boarders of the *pensionnat* are disporting themselves
in the primrose light of the dying day, under the watchful and
weary eyes of Miss Jones, the English teacher. It is a French
play, and a very noisy one. "Brother Hermit, can you dance?"
half a dozen tall girls are chanting, in high, shrill, sing-song
French. Shrieks of laughter rend the atmosphere, and Miss
Jones covers two distracted ears, and calls frantically, and calls
in vain:

"Young ladies! Oh, dear me! Young ladies, *less* noise."

The noise grows fast and furious, the chanting rises shriller
and shriller, the screams of laughter wilder and wilder. The
"Brother Hermits" caper about like dancing dervishes gone
mad. In the midst of it all, a tall, dark, handsome girl, with a
double eyeglass across the bridge of her patrician aquiline
nose, comes laughingly up to half-delirious Miss Jones.

"It's more like a *maison de santé*, with the lunatics set loose,
than a decorous young ladies' school," she remarks. "I say,
Miss Jones, where is Sydney Owenson?"

"I don't know. Oh, if the study bell would but ring! Go
and look for Sydney Owenson in the thick of the *mêlée;* you'll

be sure to find her; they never could make half so much noise
without her. Oh, good heaven! hear that."

Another ear-splitting shriek made Miss Jones cover her
bruised and wounded tympanums. The dark damsel laughed.

> "At once there rose so wild a yell
> Within that dark and narrow dell,
> As all the fiends from heaven that fell
> Had pealed the banner-cry of ——"

"Miss Hendrick!" screamed Miss Jones.

"The place unmentionable to ears polite. Don't cry out before you're hurt, Miss Jones. No, Syd isn't there, however they
manage to raise all that racket without her. Where can she be?
I want to tell her that Friday is Hallowe'en, and that Mrs. Delamere has invited all our class who will be allowed to go to a
party at her house."

"Indeed, Miss Hendrick!" Miss Jones, the English
teacher, fixed two suspicious light-blue eyes upon Miss Hendrick's dark, handsome face, and expressed volumes of disbelief
in that one incredulous word.

"Yes, 'indeed,' Miss Jones, and you are not invited, I'm happy
to say. You don't believe me, do you? You never *do* believe
anything Cyrilla Hendrick says, if you can help yourself, do you?
You see, Mrs. Colonel Delamere happens—unfortunately for
you—to be a lady, and has a weakness for inviting young ladies
only to her house. That is why, probably, she is blind to the
manifold merits of Miss Mary Jane Jones. You're name *is*
Mary Jane, isn't it, Miss Jones? I saw it in your prayer-book.
No, don't apologize, please—it's more one's misfortune than
one's fault to be born Mary Jane Jones—'A rose by any other
name,' etc."

All this, with her black eyes fixed full upon Miss Jones's face,
in the slowest, softest voice, an insolent smile on her handsome
lips, Miss Cyrilla Hendrick said.

Miss Jones sprang to her feet, passion flashing from her eye,
her pale, freckled complexion flushing crimson.

"Miss Hendrick, your insolence is not to be borne! I will
not bear it. The moment recreation is over, I will go to
Mam'selle Chateauroy and report your impertinent speech."

"Will you, really? Don't excite yourself, dear Miss Jones.
If you palpitate in this way, something will go crack. Tell
mam'selle anything it pleases your gracious highness; it won't
be the first time you've carried stories of me. Mademoiselle

can get a better teacher than you any day, but first-rate pupils don't grow on every tamarac-tree in Lower Canada. Adieu, dear and gentle Miss Jones! I kiss your ladyship's hands. Sydney! Sydney! where are you?"

She walked away, sending her fresh, clear young voice over all the uproar. Miss Jones, the teacher, looked after her with a glare of absolute hatred.

"I'll be even with you yet, Miss Cyrilla Hendrick, or I'll know the reason why! You have given me more insolence during the past year than all the school together. As you say, it's no use complaining to Miss Chateauroy. You're a credit to the school, *she* thinks, with your brilliant singing, and playing, and painting ; but I'll pay you for your jibes and insults one day, mark my words—one day, and that before long."

"Sydney! Sydney!" the clear voice still shouted. "Now, where can that girl be? 'That rare and radiant maiden, whom the angels call Lenore.' Sydney! Sydney-y! Sydney-y-y-y!"

She stops, expending all her strength in one mighty shout that rises over the wild, high singing of the French Canadians, "Frère l'Hermite, savez vous danser?" It comes pealing to an upper window overlooking the playground, and a girl huddled up cross-legged like a Turk takes two fingers out of two pretty pink ears, and lifts a yellow head from a book to listen.

"Sydney! Sydney Owenson! Oh, my own, my long-lost daughter!" cried Miss Hendricks with ear-splitting piercing-ness, "where in this wicked world are you?"

"Bother!" mutters the girl in the window, and then the yellow head, "sunning over with curls," goes down again, two fingers return into two ears, a pair of gray eyes glue themselves once more to the pages of the book, and Miss Sydney Owenson is lost again to all sublunary things. They may shriek, they may yell, they may rend the heavens with their unearthly cries, they may drive Miss Jones deaf and frantic—Cyrilla Hendrick, the friend of her bosom, the David in petticoats to her Jonathan ditto, may split her voice in her distracted cries for "Sydney," Sydney is a thousand miles away ; nothing short of an earth-quake may arouse her, so absorbed is she.

Yes, something does.

"Miss Owenson!" says the awful voice of Mademoiselle Chateauroy the elder, and Miss Owenson drops her book and jumps as though she were shot. "Miss Owenson, what book is that?"

A small, snuff-colored lady, with a frisette and a head-dress of yellow roses and black beadwork, confronts her—a very small, very snuff-colored lady, with glancing opal eyes—Mademoiselle Stephanie Chateauroy.

Miss Owenson puts her two hands, the book in them, behind her back, and faces Mademoiselle Stephanie *à la* Napoleon the Great. She is a pretty girl—a very pretty girl of seventeen or so, with gray, large, innocent-looking eyes, a pearly skin, a soft-cut, childish mouth, and curls of copper gold down to her slim girl's waist.

" Yes, mam'selle," says Miss Owenson, in a tone of cheerful meekness ; " did you call me, mam'selle ? "

"Why are you not in the playground, Mees Owenson ? " demands, severely, mademoiselle.

"Oh, well ! " responds Miss Owenson, losing a trifle of her cheerful meekness, " I'm sick of 'Brother Hermit' and the other stupid plays, only fit for the babies of the *première* class. Besides, the noise makes my head ache."

Miss Owenson makes this remarkable statement calmly. The open window at which she has been sitting is just three feet over the heads of the rioters, and in the very thick of the tumult. Its utter absurdity is so palpable that mademoiselle declines to notice it.

" Mees Owenson is aware that absence from the playground, in play-hour, is a punishable offence ? " goes on mademoiselle with increased ascerbity.

"Oh, yes," says Miss Owenson, quite cheerfully once more ; "that's no odds. Nothing's any odds, when you're used to it, and I ought to be used to every species of punishable offences in this school by this time."

" Mees Owenson, what were you reading when I entered this room ? "

" A book, mam'selle."

" Mees Owenson, *what* book ? "

"Oh, well—a story-book then, if you will have it, by a person you don't know—a Mr. Dickens. I know it's against the rules, but it was all an accident—upon my word it was, mam'selle."

" An accident, you sitting here in play-hour reading a wicked novel ! Mees Owenson ! "

" It's not a wicked novel. Dickens never wrote anything wicked in his life. Papa has every one of his books in the library at home, and used to read them aloud to mamma. And

I mean it's an accident my finding the book. It isn't mine ; I don't know whose it is ; I found it last evening, lying among the cabbages—honor bright, mam'selle ! I'll pitch it back there now."

And then, before Mlle. Stephanie can catch her breath, Miss Owenson gives the volume behind her a brisk pitch out of the open casement, and it falls plump upon the head of her sworn friend, Cyrilla Hendrick.

There is a moment's pause, and teacher and pupil confront each other. That an explosion will follow, Miss Sydney Owenson fully expects, but what was she to do? Helen Heme's name was on the fly-leaf. Helen Heme was a day-scholar, who surreptitiously smuggled story-books inside the sacred walls of the *pensionnat* for the private delectation of the boarders. Helen had been threatened with expulsion the next time she was caught in the act "red-handed," so to say, and it was much more on Helen's account than on her own that Sydney Owenson was palpitating now.

"I coaxed *so* hard for that ' Pickwick,' " Sydney thinks. "I hope to goodness some of the girls will pick it up and hide it outside. I don't mind mam'selle's flare-up—I'm used to it— but I'd never forgive myself if Nell came to grief through me."

She looks up now into mademoiselle's indignant face, clasps two little white hands imploringly, and begins, with that voice and smile mademoiselle herself declares to be the most charming on earth, to wheedle her out of her just wrath.

"Oh, Mam'selle Stephanie, *don't* be angry, please. I know it's wrong to break rules, but then I am so tired of the stupid old plays out there, and the girls *are* so noisy and rude, and my head *did* ache, and the book was not a bad book—upon my word and honor it wasn't, mam'selle ; not a bit like a novel at all, and I *did* find it among the cabbages last evening, and——"

Mademoiselle Stephanie knows of old that Miss Owenson is perfectly capable of going on in this strain without a single full stop for the next hour. Therefore, without a word, she pulls a letter out of her pocket and hands it to her pet pupil.

"I will overlook your disobedience this once, *petite*," she said, "because it is probably the very last time you will ever have a chance to disobey. Read your mamma's letter, my dear ; I know what it contains, as it came inclosed in one to me. *Chérie*," mam'selle's voice absolutely falters, "you—you are about to leave school."

Sydney Owenson rises to her feet, the great gray eyes dilate and grow almost black with some vague terror. She looks at her letter—a look of absolute affright, the last trace of color leaving her pearl-fair skin—then at mademoiselle.

"Papa," she falters. "Oh, mam'selle ! *don't* say papa is——"

"Worse ? –No, my dear. You poor child, you are as white as the wall. No, papa is no worse—it isn't that—it is—but read your letter, *tres chère ;* it will tell you all about it, and believe me, my dear," and mademoiselle lays two snuff-colored old hands kindly on the girl's shoulders, "no one in this school will regret the loss of its most troublesome pupil more than I shall."

She toddies away and leaves Miss Owenson to read her letter. "Ah," she sighs, "it is the best, the tenderest little heart in the world, after all. I shall never love another pupil so well. Only a baby of seventeen, and to be married in a month ! *Hélas*, the poor little one ! "

Sydney tears open her letter ; it is a lengthy, spidery, woman's scrawl.

"OWENSON PLACE, *October* 25, 18—.

"MY DEAR LITTLE DAUGHTER :—I have written to the Mademoiselles Chateauroy, telling them to have all things ready for your departure on Monday, the third of November. You are to leave school, and for good. Papa is not worse really, but he thinks he is, and he pines for you. He has taken it into his head—you know how hypochondriacal he is—that he will die before the year ends, and he insists that you must be married at once, else he will not live to see it. Now don't worry about this, Sydney. I know how foolish you are concerning poor papa's whims, and it is only a whim. Bertie is here, came by the Cunard steamer from England three weeks ago, and is naturally all impatience *to* see you. It is a *very* absurd whim of papa's, I think myself, this marrying a child of seventeen and a boy of twenty-two ; but what use is it my saying so ? *I* was nine-and-twenty when I married Captain Owenson. Still, I am sure, I hope you will be happy ; and Bertie is so nice and good-tempered and gentlemanly and all that, that any one might get along with him. Rebecca will reach Petit St. Jacques Saturday afternoon, and you and she will start for home on Monday morning. Papa has actually sent to Paris for your wedding-dress, and pearls, and veil, as though good enough could not have been got in New York City ; but it is another of his whims to look down upon everything in *this* country, and

think nothing fit for you that doesn't come from Europe. I'm
sure sometimes I wonder he ever married an American lady, or
that he found a school on this continent fit for his only child.
I know he would have sent you to the *Sacre Cœur* at Paris, only
he couldn't bear to put the ocean between himself and you. But
this has nothing to do with it. So bid the young ladies and
teachers good-by, and be ready to start on Monday morning
: with Rebecca.

" Your affectionate Mother,

" CHARLOTTE OWENSON.

" P.S.—Bertie sends his love and a kiss, he says, to all the
pretty girls in the school. He is as foolish as ever, but very
handsome and elegant, I must say. Christ Church College has
improved him greatly. He wanted to accompany Rebecca,
but, of course, I wouldn't hear of anything so improper as
that.   C. O.

" P.S. No. 2.—By the by, papa says you may invite your
particular friend, Miss Hendrick, if you like, to be one of your
bridemaids. He knew her aunt, Miss Phillis Dormer, in
England, and her mother comes of one of the best families in
Dorsetshire. As if the best family in Dorsetshire mattered in
America.   C. O."

CHAPTER II.

CYRILLA.

HE long, loosely written, rambling letter dropped on
Sydney's lap, her hands folded over it, and she sat
strangely quiet (for her), looking out at the faint opaline
twilight sky. To leave school on Monday—to be
married in a month ! Surely enough to startle any school-girl of
seventeen. Besides being the daughter of the richest man, besides having double, treble the spending money of any other girl
in the *pensionnat*, besides having silks and laces and jewels as
though she were five-and-twenty and " out," besides having
beauty and talent and goodness and grace, Sydney Owenson
had one other and still greater claim to be " queen rose " of

Mlle. Stephanie's "rosebud garden of girls,"—she was engaged!
All and each of the four-and-thirty other boarders of mam'selle—
not to speak of the one-and-twenty day-scholars—looked forward in the fulness of time to a possible lover, a prospective
engagement, and an ultimate husband, but a real lover and a
bona fide engagement none of them had yet attained, with the
exception of Miss Owenson. That heighth of bliss Miss Owenson had reached in her sixteenth birthday. The midsummer
vacation over, the young lady had returned to Canada from her
paternal mansion—a solitaire diamond ablaze on one slim finger, a locket (with a gentleman's portrait and a ring of brown
hair) around her white throat—and calmly announced to all
whom it might concern that she was engaged.

The first stunning shock of surprise over, a torrent of questions poured upon the blissful *fiancée.*

"Oh! good gracious! Oh, Mon Dieu! was she really? Oh,
how nice! *Oh! c'est charmant?* What was his name?
Where did he live? How did it come about? What did he
say? Was he handsome? Was he rich? Did papa and mamma know? Oh, what a love of a ring, and oh, how splendid it
was to be engaged at sixteen! And when, O Sydney! *when*
were they going to be married?"

"There! there! there!" cried Miss Owenson shrilly,
breaking away from fifty-six eager, excited faces. "I am sorry
I told you anything about it! One would think I was the only
girl in the world ever engaged before. If you leave me alone
I'll answer all your questions. Stand off, and let me see. 'His
name?' Well, his name is Albert Vaughan—Bertie Vaughan—
a pretty name to begin with. 'Where does he live?' He lives
at Oxford at present; at least he was on his way back there
when I left home. 'How did it come about?' Well, it didn't
come about; it was always to be, destined from all time, and
that sort of thing. Ever since I can remember anything, I remember being told I was to marry Bertie some day, if I behaved
myself—family arrangements, you see, like a thing in a story.
'What did he say?' Oh, well, he just came to me on my birthday, and slipped this ring on my finger, and said, 'I say, Syd,
I want you to marry me this day twelve months, or thereabouts,
you know;' and I said, 'All right, Bert, I will.' 'Is he handsome?' Handsome as an angel, Helen—brown eyes, brown
curling hair, fair complexion, rosy cheeks like a girl, small hands
and feet, and the sweetest little love of a mustache! 'Is he
rich?' Poor as a church mouse, Cyrilla—not got a sou in the

earthly world; but as I am to have enough for both, that doesn't signify. 'Do papa and mamma know?' Of course they know, goosies! Bertie and I would never have thought of such a thing if papa hadn't told us to think of it. 'And when are we to be married?' Oh, I don't know—not for ever so long. I don't want to be married—it's dreadfully dowdy and stupid. We won't be married for ages—not until I'm old—oh! ever so old—twenty-one, may be. It's nice enough to be engaged, but married—bah-h-h!"

Miss Owenson pronounced her "bah!" with the disgusted look of one who swallows a nauseous dose, and sprang to her feet.

" I say, girls! let's have a game of ' Prisoners' Base;' I'm dying for a romp. Come !"

Miss Owenson had her romp until the pearl pale cheeks glowed like twin pink roses, and the vivid gray eyes streamed with laughing light. But from that hour a halo of romantic interest encircled her.

She had a lover—she was engaged—she would be married in a year. Oh, happy, thrice happy Sydney Owenson! Every month or so came to her a letter bearing the English postmark, dated "Ch. Ch., Oxford"—real, genuine love-letters. Mlle. Stephanie shook her head, and passed them over in fear and trembling to her engaged pupil. She had never had such a thing before, and to a certain extent it was demoralizing the whole school.

Six-and-forty youthful heads ran more on lovers than on lessons, on engagements than on "Télémaque" or "Chopin's Waltzes." Miss Owenson, as a matter of Christian duty, read those epistles of her young Oxonian faithfully aloud to her six-and-forty fellow-students. On the whole, they were rather a disappointment. They contained a great deal of news about boating on the Isis, riding across country, college supper parties, and a jolly time generally, but very few glowing love-passages to his affianced. Indeed, beyond the "Dear little Syd" at the beginning, and "Your affectionate Bertie" at the end, they didn't contain a single protestation of the consuming passion which it is to be supposed possessed him.

"Of course not," Sydney was wont to cry out indignantly, when some of the more sentimental young ladies objected to these love-letters on that head. "You wouldn't have Bertie spooning all the way across the Atlantic, would you? I suppose, Helen, you would like the sort of letters Lord Mortimer

used to write to namby-pamby, milk-and-waterish Amanda
Fitzallan, 'Beloved of my soul!' Ha! ha! I fancy I see Bert
writing that sort of rubbish to me. He wouldn't do it twice,
let me tell you!"

As may be seen, Miss Owenson was not in the slightest sentimental herself—not one whit in love, in the common accepta-
tion of the word, with Bertie Vaughan. "He was the dearest,
jolliest old fellow in the world—Bertie," she was calmly
accustomed to observe; "and since she *must* marry somebody sometime, she would rather marry Bert than anybody else,
but to go spooning as they did in books—no, not while either
of them kept their senses."

She sits very quietly now, the letter on her lap, looking out
at that pale yellow, frosty sky—a little pale, and very thoughtful.

Going to leave school—going to be married! All the old life
to end, and the new to begin. And the old life had been such
a *good* life, such a pleasant life; she was so fond of school and
of all the girls—well, with about three-and-twenty exceptions.
She could never play "Brother Hermit," or "Hunt the Slipper,"
or "Tag" any more—never any more! Married women
never jumped skipping-ropes, never played "Puss in the
Corner," or got people to swing them until their heels touched
the beam in the barn each time! Never! never! It was all dull
and stupid, and dowdy, being married. And great tears rose
up in Miss Owenson's gray eyes and splashed, one by one, down
upon the fatal letter.

"All alone, Syd?" cries a brisk voice, and, with a swish of
dingy skirts, Miss Hendrick is in the room. "And a letter—
another *love*-letter! Happy girl! Well, 'blessed are they
who expect nothing, for they shall not be disappointed!' of
whom I am one. And how is our beauteous Bertie?"

"It isn't from Bertie," answers Sydney, hastily wiping away
the last tear. "It's from mamma, and"—a great gulp—"O
Cy, I'm going to leave school!"

"Happy girl once more! When and why?"

"On Monday, and—to be married."

"On Monday, and be married! Happy, happy, happy girl!
I wish I were going to leave school on Monday, and be married.
I wouldn't sit by myself in the dark and mope, I can tell you.
But what's all the hurry about?"

"Read the letter," says Miss Owenson, placing it in her
hand, and looking out with a woe-begone face at the fast dark-

ening evening sky. One, two, three, four, five more evenings may she watch that little white, cold-looking, half moon float up yonder among the tamaracs, five more evenings may she listen to the discordant shrieks of the thirty-four boarders making day hideous, and then never more for all time. And another large tear comes plump down, at the misery of the thought, in her lap.

Cyrilla Hendrick reads the letter, and throws it back with an envious sigh.

" What a lucky girl you are, Syd ! A father and mother who dote upon you—a *rich* father and mother, a handsome young husband waiting for you, and all the freedom and gayety of a married woman yours, at seventeen. While for me—ah, well ! " with a bitter laugh, " as poor Freddy used to say, ' Life can't be all beer and skittles ' for the whole of us."

" Freddy ! " Sydney exclaimed, looking up at her friend with sudden curiosity, " that is the first time I ever heard you mention any man's name ! Who is Freddy ? "

" Ah, who indeed ? " Miss Hendrick answers with another half laugh. " ' Thereby hangs a tale,' which I'm not inclined to tell at present. But I say again, what a happy girl you are, Sydney Owenson ! "

" What, because I am to be married next month, Cy ! " Sydney cries, opening her great eyes in unfeigned wonder. " You *can't* mean that."

" I mean that, and everything about your life. You are an heiress, you will be a beauty, you have people who love you, you make friends wherever you go. Why, here in school the girls swear by you—even snuffy, priggish, dried-up little Mam'selle Stephanie, in her dreary way, is fond of you. At sixteen you wear diamonds and ' walk in silk array.' While I——" Again she stopped, with a gesture that was almost passionate in the intensity of its envy. Sydney looked at her in wonder. The bitterness of her tone and words was a new revelation ; it was a contrast indeed to the usually cool, almost insolent serenity of Cyrilla Hendrick's manner.

" While you, Cy," Sydney supplemented, " are ten times over better looking than I am, sing better, play better, paint and draw better, speak four languages, and are the cleverest girl, mam'selle says, she ever had in her school. You have an aunt who is fabulously rich, so everybody says, who has adopted you, and whose heiress you are to be. While, as for being married——."

Cyrilla Hendrick laughed, as Miss Owenson faltered and paused, all her easy *insouciance* of manner returned.

"While, as for being married, I have only to walk over to St. Jacques Barracks and ask any of the officers, and they will take me on the spot—is that what you want to say, Syd? And I sing well, play well, paint well, and am a famous linguist? Lucky for me I am, since these accomplishments are my stock in trade, with which, until some man *does* compassionate me, I am to earn the bread I eat."

"I don't understand you."

"Don't you? You never suspected, I suppose, that my brilliant *rôle* in the drama of life is that of governess?"

"Governess! What nonsense, Cyrilla. The rich Miss Dormer's heiress and niece!"

"The rich Miss Dormer's heiress and niece! Sydney, would you like to know exactly *how* much Miss Dormer means to do for her pauper niece, Cyrilla Hendrick?"

"If you please, Cy. You know you and your history are darkest mysteries to Mademoiselle Chateauroy's boarders."

Cyrilla laughed, still standing behind her friend. "I knew it, *chère belle*, and mysteries we all like to remain. Let me unveil the darkness to you a little. I was born in Paris eighteen years ago, in a garret—mark that, daughter of Mammon!—and my mother was the daughter of a baronet; my father was the only brother of the rich Phillis Dormer. My father was one of the handsomest men, one of the cleverest men, and one of the most utterly unprincipled men in Europe—a thorough-paced adventurer, in fact, as Aunt Phil takes care to impress upon my innocent mind every time I see her—an out-and-out Bohemian. Before I was twelve years old I had traversed the Continent from one end to the other, and had a smattering of every European language. No wonder I study them with facility *now*. When I was twelve my father came to England, his native land, and there, in the parish of Bloomsbury, we set up our household gods, and from utter vagabondism went in for moderately respectable Bohemianism. My mother was dead—luckily for her, poor soul!—and I was housekeeper in the Bloomsbury establishment—think of that, Syd—at twelve years old! From that until I was sixteen, I kept my father's house, and I saw more of life—real, genuine life—in those three years than you, mademoiselle—only child and heiress—will ever see in your whole respectable, rich, Philistine existence! Good heaven, Syd! *how* happy I used to be with my handsome, clever, vagabond father and my poor, dear little Fred."

She stopped—passionate pain, passionate regret in her face and voice. Sydney Owenson sat listening with bated breath to this marvellous and rather shocking revelation.

"It was poverty, Syd, but picturesque poverty; that meant truffled turkey and champagne to-day, and a dry crust and a cup of water to-morrow ; a seat in the upper tier of a Strand theatre or Astley's circus among the gods of the gallery, big bearded men to take me on their knee, and kiss me, and pet me; men who wrote books, and painted pictures, who wore sock or buskin, who got tipsy on gin and water or Cliquot, as their finances stood. Men who taught me to roll up their cigarettes, and to light them after. By the way, Syd," Cyrilla broke off her half-bitter, half-cynical tone, ending in a sudden laugh, "*do* you remember the night, after I came here first, that Miss Jones caught me smoking a rose-scented cigarette, a dozen of you standing around in an awestruck and admiring row ? She told Mademoiselle Stephanie, as in duty bound, and got me punished. I vowed vengeance, and the vendetta has waged between us ever since."

"I remember, Cy. And what a superior being you seemed to me, to be able to sit there and smoke off four cigarettes without wincing once ! Go on."

"Oh, well !" Cyrilla said coolly, "there's nothing more to go on about. When I was sixteen, Aunt Phil sent for me, and I bade farewell to old England and my jolly Bedouin life, and came to America, exchanged the tents of vagabondia for the red brick mansion of respectability. She found me half savage, wholly uneducated, according to *her* notions, and knowing a great deal I would be much better without. She sent me here—unfolded something of my antecedents to horrified ma'm'selle, and I had to pledge myself to keep my disreputable history to myself before I could be taken into this spotless fold of youth and innocence. That is three years ago—I am almost nineteen, and at Christmas I am to leave school for good."

"To go and live with Miss Dormer ?"

"To go and live with Miss Dormer, in the dreariest, gruesomest old house in America ; companion to the crossest spitefulest old woman on earth ? Don't be shocked, Syd—she is ! I'm to read to her, write for her, play for her, sing for her, sew for her, feed the birds and cats, and run her errands, all for my clothes and keep."

"And her fortune when she dies ?"

"Not a bit of it ! She has two wills made, unsigned

One bequeaths her hundred thousand dollars to endow an asylum for superannuated maiden ladies ; the other bequeaths that sum to myself, on condition——"

"Well?" Sydney cried breathlessly.

"On condition that I'll swear—swear on the Bible, mind !— to do something she wants me to do. I haven't taken the oath yet, and I believe, oath or no oath, she will never trust me an inch farther than she can see me. ' There is bad blood in my niece Cyrilla' "—Miss Hendrick grows dramatic when she narrates, it is a high-pitched old woman's voice that speaks —" 'all the Hendricks were reprobates—all, every one !' ' Do we gather grapes of thorns, or figs of thistles?' My niece Cyrilla is—fortunately—the last of the tribe, a Hendrick to her finger-tips, and mark my words ! my niece Cyrilla will come to no good end.' "

"Ugh, how horrid !" said Miss Owenson, with something between a laugh and a shudder. " I wonder, thinking that she ever troubled with you at all."

"So do I wonder. She means to utilize me until the final catastrophe comes, and I disappear in the outer darkness to which I was born. It is a wonderful old woman—Aunt Phil ! And sometimes, Syd, sometimes," the handsome, youthful face darkened and grew sombre, " when I think of what my past was, when I think of what my father is, when I think of what my future is likely to be, I rank Aunt Phil among the prophets, and believe, with her, that her niece Cyrilla will come to no good end !"

CHAPTER III.

SCHOOL GIRL GOSSIP.

HERE is a silence for a while. Cyrilla Hendrick has walked away to the curtainless school-room window, and stands looking out at the pale, chill, twilight sky, where a white moon hangs silvery, a few yellow, frosty, sparkling stars near. The tamaracs shiver and toss their feathery green plumes in the evening breeze, a breeze that bears a prophecy of coming winter even now in its breath. Miss Hendrick's handsome brunette face looks darker and sadder than Sydney Owenson has ever seen it before.

2

"Ten minutes and the study bell will ring, and this horrid tumult end, for which *Dieu merci.* Look at them, Syd, 'a motley crowd, my masters, a motley crowd.' Of course, all this I've told you is strictly *sub rosa.* Mademoiselle Stephanie, poor old snuffy soul, would go out of her senses if she thought I was corrupting her favorite pupil by such improper conversation."

She half-turned around, all her gloom gone, the airy ease of manner, so uncommon in a school-girl, and which constituted this school-girl's especial charm, back. Independently of wealth and social position (and no one on earth thought more of wealth and social position than this waif of vagabondia), she liked Sydney Owenson for her own sake.

" I promised not to tell, you know, Syd ; and, reprobate as Aunt Phil thinks me, I like to keep my word. I *have* kept it for three years ; all those noisy girls think, as you thought an hour ago, that my life, like their lives, has been the quintessence of dull, drab-colored gentility. Your papa was a captain in the English navy once, wasn't he, and is a great stickler for good birth and breeding ? I wonder if he would ask the rich and respectable Miss Phillis Dormer's niece to be your bridemaid if he were listening now ? "

" If papa knew you as I do, he would like and admire you as I do," Sydney cried, warmly. "Who could help it ? I never saw a man yet whom you did not fascinate in ten minutes if you chose."

"If I chose?" Cyrilla laughed. "Ah, yes, Syd, the *men* like me, and always will ; let that be my comfort. I shall be one of those women whom other women look upon askance, and know as their natural enemy at sight, but men will like me to the end of the chapter. Only be very sure of this, pretty little Sydney." She took the pearl-fair face between her two hands, and stooped and kissed her. " *You* need never fear me."

"Fear you, Cy ? What nonsense ! What do you mean ? "

"This Mr. Bertie Vaughan is handsome, you say, Syd?" was Cyrilla's inapposite answer. " Let me look at his photo again."

As a rule Miss Owenson wore her lover's picture and locket affectionately in her trunk, but she chanced to have it on to-day. She snatched the slender yellow chain off her neck and handed it to her friend. She had been touched strangely by Cyrilla's confidence, more touched still by the unexpected caress. They had been good friends and staunch comrades dur-

ing the past three years, with the average of school-girl quarrels
and make-ups; but never before had Cyrilla Hendrick been
known to kiss her or any other creature in the school. She
was wonderfully chary of enthusiasm or caresses; set down as
"that proud, conceited thing" by her fellow-boarders, admired
and envied for her superior cleverness and ease of manner, and
dark, aristocratic, high-bred face, liked by a few, Sydney Owenson chief among them, and cordially hated by the many. - Without knowing why, without being able to reason on the matter,
they instinctively felt she was of them, but not like them.

She came into their midst with her pauper head held well
aloft, a sort of defiance in her black, derisive eyes, a sort of·
superior contempt for them and their ignorance of life in her
slight sarcastic smile. Wonderfully reticent for a girl of sixteen,
she yet said things, and did things, besides the smoking of
cigarettes, that proved that she had lived, before coming here,
in a very different world from any *they* had ever known. The
sketchy outline of her life she had given to Sydney Owenson—
the sketchy outline *only*—there were details that might have
been filled in, which would have raised every red-gold hair on
Miss Owenson's pretty head aloft with dismay. She *had* seen
life with her "handsome, clever, reprobate father," as luckily
it falls to·the lot of few daughters ever to see it. Bacchana-
lian nights of gambling, song-singing, wine-drinking, and festive
uproar. There was not a capital in Europe which she and her
doll had not visited at the age of twelve. She had spent three
whole months behind his chair at Baden-Baden, with a pin and
a perforated card, and starved and feasted as he lost or won.
All the jolly outlaws of Bohemia had lounged in the shabby
rooms of "Jack Hendrick," where a perpetual "tobacco par-
liament" seemed to reign. Scions of aristocracy, youthful
sprigs of gentility, deep in the books of the children of Israel,
made it their headquarters and lounging-place, and lost their
last sovereign to their genial host. Clever painters, whose
pictures hung on the line in the Royal Academy, had painted
"Little Beauty Hendrick"—as Cyrilla had been named—
painted her as Cupids, as Undines, as Hebes, as gypsies, as
angels, as everything a plump, pretty, black-eyed rosebud of a
child could be painted. Clever actors gave her orders to their
plays, and coached her in small private theatricals. Old Jean
Jacques Dando, teacher of the ballet of the Princess Theatre,
taught her to dance, and the first violinist taught her to play
the fiddle. She could jabber in five different languages at

twelve, and read French novels by the wholesale. Tall booted
and spurred military swells had carried her aloft on their
shoulders, and taught her to roll and light their cigarettes.
Midnight, as a rule, was this little damsel's hour of lying down,
and noonday her time of rising up.   Then, in the midst of
this jolly, vagabond career, came Miss Phillis Dormer's offer
and its acceptance.

"Will you go, Beauty?" her father said, doubtfully. "It
will be beastly dull without you, but the old girl's rich, and intends to make you her heiress, no doubt. She'll send you to
school, and do the handsome thing by you when she dies.
Will you go?"

"Yes, father, I'll go," Cyrilla answered, promptly. "I'll
pack my trunk and be ready at once. Freddy says there's a
steamer to sail day after to-morrow."

"Ah! *Freddy* says," her father repeated, still looking at her
doubtfully. "Look here, Beauty! I wouldn't say anything
about Freddy, or the rest of 'em over there, if I were you.
Just tell the old girl and the other Philistines you meet that you
came of poor—poor, but honest—parents *you* know.   Mum's
the word about the card-playing and the scampering over the
world, and—the whole thing, in short."

"You may trust me, father.   I know when to hold my tongue
and when to speak.   I haven't lived with *you* sixteen years
for nothing," calmly says Mademoiselle Cyrilla.

"No, by Jove!" Jack Hendrick cried, admiringly. "You're
the cleverest little thing that ever breathed, Beauty!   You
know on which side your bread's buttered.   And you'll not forget the dear old dad, eh, Cy? out there among the purple and
fine linen, and your first taste of respectability?"

So Cyrilla came and was received by Miss Dormer—a pale,
dark girl, tall and slim, quiet, silent and demure.   But Aunt
Phil had the keenest old eyes that ever sparkled in the head of
a maiden lady of sixty, and read her like a book.

"Ha!" the old voice scornfully cried ; "you live sixteen
years with Jack Hendrick and then come to me and try to take
me in with your mock-modest airs !   But I'm an old bird, and
not to be caught with chaff.   You're a very pretty girl, Cyrilla
—you take after your father in that—and you hold your beggar's head well up, which I like to see.   You take that and
your aquiline nose from your mother.   Your mother was a fool,
my dear, as I suppose you know, and proved her folly to all the
world, by running away with handsome, penniless, scoundrelly

Jack Hendrick. She was the daughter of a baronet, and engaged to a colonel of the Guards—Lord Hepburn to-day—and she ran away one night, just three weeks before her appointed wedding, with your father. Ah! well, she paid for that bit of romance, and is in her grave long ago—the very best place for her. But you're a Hendrick, my niece Cyrilla—a Hendrick to the backbone, and a precious bad lot, I have no doubt. I never knew a Hendrick yet who came to a good end—no, not one! and you take care, niece Cyrilla, or you'll come to a bad end, too."

"I dare say I shall," niece Cyrilla answered, coolly, seeing in a moment that perfect frankness was best with this extraordinary old fairy godmother. "My father always taught me that coming to grief was the inevitable lot of all things here below. At least I hope I shall do it gracefully."

"I'm going to send you to school," the old lady pursued, "for three years, and mind you make the most of your time. You are as ignorant as a Hottentot now of all you *ought* to know, and horribly thorough in all you ought *not*. I shall send you to the Demoiselles Chateauroy, at Petit St. Jacques—a very strict school and a very dull place, where even you cannot get into mischief. And mind! don't you go contaminating your fellow-pupils by tales of vagabond life! Don't you offend me, niece Cryilla; I warn you of that."

"I don't intend to, Aunt Phil," the girl answered, good-humoredly. "I shall study hard, and be a credit to you; trust me. I know my ignorance, and am as anxious to shake the dust of vagabondism off my feet as you can possibly be. I shall do you honor at school."

She had kept her word. She was brilliantly clever, and amazed and delighted her teachers by her progress. She was the pride of the school at each half-yearly exhibition; her playing, her singing were such as had never been heard within these walls before. And in the small milk-and-water dramas performed on these occasions she absolutely electrified all beholders. In truth, she did it *so* well that the Demoiselles Chateauroy were almost alarmed.

"She goes on more like a real play actress than a school-girl," they said; "it can't be the first time *she* has tried parlor theatricals."

It was not, indeed. And at one of these exhibitions a little incident had occurred that disturbed Ma'm'selle Stephanie more and more. The rooms were crowded. "Cinderella" had been

dramatized expressly for the occasion, and "Miss C. Hendrick" came on as the Prince, in plumed cap and silk doublet,
acting her part, as usual, *con amore*, and making much more
violent love than ever Mlle. Stephanie had intended to the Cin-
·derella of the piece.   As she came gracefully forward before the
audience, singing a song, a tall, dashing-looking man, an officer
newly arrived from England, had started up.

"It is!" he exclaimed; "by Jupiter, it is!—Beauty Hen
drick!"

Miss Hendrick had flashed one electric glance from her
black eyes upon him, and the play went on.   People stared
the Demoiselles Chateauroy turned pale; pupils pricked up
curious little ears and looked askance at the big trooper.
"He knew Cy Hendrick, and called her Beauty.   What did it
mean?"

The performance over, Major Powerscourt sought out Mlle.
Stephanie, and a low and earnest conversation ensued—the
gentleman pleading, the lady inexorable.

"But I knew her in England, knew her intimately, by
Jove!" said the gallant major, pulling his long red mustache
in perplexity.   "Just let me speak to her one moment,
mademoiselle!"

Mademoiselle was resolute.

"I would be very happy, monsieur," was her answer, polite,
but inexorable, "but it is her aunt's wish that she makes no
new gentlemen acquaintances and renews no old ones.   What
Monsieur the major asks is, I regret, impossible."

"Confound her aunt!" Major Powerscourt muttered
inwardly, but he only bowed and turned away.   "Little Beauty
Hendrick! and here! By Jove! it will go hard with me though
if I don't see her."

See her he did not.   Mademoiselle Stephanie spoke a few
low-toned words to her tall pupil.   Miss Hendrick listened
with downcast eyes and closed lips; then she bowed.

"It shall be as ma'm'selle pleases, of course," she answered,
quietly.   "I have no wish to transgress even the slightest of
my aunt's commands."

With the words she left the parlors, and appeared no more.
Next morning she went for the midsummer vacation to "Dormer
Lodge."   When she returned, the dangerous Major Powers-
court was gone.

Miss Jones, the second English teacher, had been one of the
witnesses of this scene.   Miss Jones set her thin lips, and

drew her own conclusions. She hated Cyrilla Hendrick with an absolute hatred,—hated her for her beauty and that indefinable air of haughty, high-bred grace that encircled the girl,—hated her for her bright cleverness and talent,—hated her most of all for her cool impertinence to herself. There was a long debt standing between these two,—a long debt of petty tyrannies on the teacher's part, of serene, smiling insolence on the pupil's.

"And if the day ever comes, Miss Hendrick," Miss Jones was wont to think—"and I think it will—I'll pay off every affront, every sneer, every scornful smile and innuendo with compound interest."

That day was nearer than Miss Jones dreamed.

CHAPTER IV.

"SO YOUNG, AND SO UNTENDER."

ELL," the sweet girlish voice of Sydney Owenson cried, "have you fallen asleep over Bertie's picture, Cyrilla? What do you think of it?—handsome, isn't he?"

Cyrilla looked up. She had been critically examining the well-looking photographed face of Mr. Bertie Vaughan through her eyeglass, in silence, for the last three minutes. The dark eyes, brilliant as stars, were a trifle short-sighted, black as it is possible for human eyes to be, and consequently the least attractive feature in the very attractive face. She dropped her glass now, and returned the portrait to its owner.

"Very handsome, Syd; but—you won't be offended, will you?"

"Oh, dear, no! Why should I? Go on."

"But rather weak and womanish, rather fickle and unstable, I should say. Not the sort of man to pin your faith to *too* securely. Men with that sort of mouth and these pretty, girlish dimples in the chin are always weak-minded. You don't mind my saying this, do you?"

"Not a bit. Poor, dear old Bertie! I think I like weak-minded men, Cy. If he were stern and dignified, and all that, he might think *me* silly and frivolous, as I am, I daresay, and try to improve me, and not let me have my own way. I should

hate being improved, and I always mean to have my own way.
Yes, Cy, I prefer weak-minded men."

"No, you don't, Sydney.   You may think so now, but you
don't.   You want a husband you can lean upon, trust, and look
up to.   And there *are* such men, for I've met them—glorious
fellows, worth a woman's giving her life for.   That's the sort of
husband for you, *chérie*, while I——"

"Yes, Cy."

"While I want one who will look up to me—not a Bertie
Vaughan exactly—I wouldn't like a fickle man—but a husband
whom I can rule, who will let me henpeck him, in short! I
couldn't love a man I had to look up to—it's dreadfully tiresome,
looking up.   And I wouldn't live with a man I couldn't love.
It would bore me to have a supreme being for my lord and master.
And I never mean to bore myself.   Those are my principles."
Sydney laughed.

"*Mon Dieu!* only hear her!   One would think she had all
mankind by heart.   Have you ever met your small, gentle,
henpecked ideal, Cy?"

Cyrilla Hendrick did not answer at once, but over her face a
smile broke, a smile so soft, so tender, so womanly, that for a
moment it transformed her.

"Yes, Syd," she said, softly ; "I have met my ideal, poor,
dear little fellow, and loved him well, before I ever saw you.
Ah! those were the best days of my life I begin to think; and,
like all best things, they are gone forever."

"You can't tell that.   To a girl as handsome as you are
infinite capabilities lie open, as Carlyle would say.   I predict
that you will make a brilliant match, Cyrilla."

"I mean to, Sydney.   That is why I am here.   Every accomplishment, every one of my good looks, are so many steps
toward that end.   I mean to marry well—that is, a rich man.
He may be old as the everlasting hills, he may be ugly as Cali-
ban, he may be vulgar, he may be absolutely idiotic—I will
twine roses, like Titania, around his ass's head, and bow myself
down, and do homage before him, so that he but possess the
bags of ducats.   Yes, Syd, my aunt may design me for a life of
drudgery in her bleak old house—*I* mean to marry one of the
wealthiest men on this continent before another year ends."

"And henpeck him afterwards?"

"By no means.   *That* is my ideal.   I won't henpeck my
wealthy husband.   I shall simply do in all things as I please.
But if the fortune of war should go against me, Sydney, and I

fail and come to grief, as Aunt Phil says I shall, I wonder if, under all circumstances, I can count upon a friend in *you ?*"

"Under all circumstances, Cyrilla, through good report and evil report, for better or for worse, I will be your true friend always."

"You vow this, Sydney?" She came closer, the black eyes eager, dark, intense earnestness in her face. "It is no school-girl promise, made and forgotten in a moment. You mean this?"

"With all my heart!" Sydney exclaimed, carried away by the moment's excitement, her fair "flower face" flushing. "Your faithful and firm friend to the end."

"Shake hands on that!" Cyrilla said, holding out her own; and the white, diamond-starred hand, and the brown, ringless one met and clasped for a moment firmly and strongly as the clasp of two men.

"It is a compact between us," Cyrilla Hendrick said. "I have a presentiment that one day you will be called upon to fulfil that promise. There goes the study bell at last."

"And you haven't promised to be my bridesmaid. Will you, Cy?"

"Of course. If your father will write to Aunt Phil and ask her. I know she will be delighted to say yes. In common with all virtuous people she has the intensest respect for rich and respectable associations. Apropos of the rich and respectable, we're asked to a small dinner at Mrs. Colonel Delamere's on Friday evening—Hallowe'en, you know. Will you go?"

"Only too glad. Who knows—we *may* see some of the new officers. You've heard that another regiment was quartered at the barracks last week. The colonel may fetch some of them along."

"Ah! pigs *may* fly, but they're unlikely birds!" is Miss Hendrick's more expressive than elegant answer. "No such luck, Syd. Mademoiselle Stephanie, or Mademoiselle Jeanne will be along as usual, to play sheep-dog to us lambs—or, worse still, Miss Jones—and turn to stone any military interloper under fifty with one glance of her Gorgon eye."

The folding doors of the schoolroom flew open and Miss Jones came in, the four and thirty boarders at her heels. Cyrilla sauntered away to her desk, singing as she went:

"Oh, for Friday night,
Friday at the gloaming;
Oh, for Friday night—
Friday's long a-coming."

"No singing in study hours, Miss Hendrick!" cried Miss Jones, sharply, with a flash of her pale eyes.

Cyrilla smiled—the smile that always galled Miss Jones more than words, and went humming on her way unheeding .

> "Oh, for Friday night,
> Then my true love's coming."

"I shall report you to Mademoiselle Chateauroy, Miss Hendrick!" Miss Jones angrily cried.

"What! again? Poor Mademoiselle Chateauroy, to be compelled to listen," Cyrilla answered, mockingly, taking her seat and her books.

Silence fell. Five and thirty girls bent five and thirty heads over five and thirty books for the space of half an hour—then the loud ringing of a bell, then a simultaneous jump of five and-thirty girls on their feet, a hustling of books into desks, doors flung wide, and a marshalling, two deep, Miss Jones at their head, and in strictest silence, down stairs to the refectory.

The meal was eaten, still in silence,—Miss Jones read aloud some drearily instructive book, then back to the school-room —more study—another half-hour's recreation, and then to their rooms for the night. It was one among Miss Jones's manifold duties, to go the round of the rooms and remove the lights. The chamber of Cyrilla Hendrick and her companion was the very last of the row, but to that room Miss Jones spitefully went first. Miss Hendrick was busily writing out to-morrow's German exercise.

"What! so soon?" she cried out. "Antoinette, look at your watch. Miss Jones *must* have made a mistake. It's a good ten minutes yet to nine, and I haven't my exercise done."

"It's nine o'clock, Miss Hendrick," Miss Jones retorted grimly, seizing the lamp. "If you are behind with your exercise it is your misfortune, not my fault."

She paused a moment, lamp in hand, and gazed at Cyrilla's indignant face with ill-concealed exultation.

"You made a mistake this afternoon, Miss Hendrick. I *am* going on Friday night, in charge of you and the others, to Mrs. Delamere's."

Miss Hendrick might be discomfited, never defeated. At a moment's notice she was ever ready to do battle with her foe.

"Are you, Miss Jones? Poor Mrs. Delamere! But she must expect to pay some penalty if she *will* ask school-girls.

For myself, I den't mind, but one can't help compassionating Mrs. Delamere—with her natural dislike of *canaille*, too."

It was a coarser shaft than even Cyrilla was wont to wing. A furious look was her answer. Then, armed with the lamp, Miss Jones had left the room.

"*Mon Dieu !* Cyrilla, how impertinent you are !" the French girl exclaimed. "Are you not afraid she will report you to mademoiselle?"

"Not a bit afraid, Toinette ; the principal amusement of Miss Jones' life is reporting me to mademoiselle. I don't know what will become of her when I leave school at Christmas, and that healthful stimulus is taken from her sluggish blood. Now, then, Toinette—to bed, to bed !"

As a rule, the Demoiselles Chateauroy did not allow their pupils to dissipate their minds by accepting invitations from their friends in Petite St. Jacques.

There were a few exceptions made, however, in the graduating class by the express desire of parents and guardians. The girls were to quit the *pensionnat* so soon and "come out," that to accept a few invitations to innoxious tea-parties and dinners could do no great harm. But even on these occasions one of the Demoiselles Chateauroy or one of the under teachers invariably went along to keep a watchful eye on their charges, and see that the masculine element was not too dangerous. It was an understood thing, particularly when an invitation came from Mrs. Colonel Delamere, that no officer under half a century was to put in an appearance.

On this eventful Friday afternoon, then, destined to make an epoch in more than one of their lives, the young ladies, five in number, with Miss Jones in the *rôle* of guardian angel, set out at four o'clock down the Rue St. Dominique to Nôtre Dame Street, where resided Mrs. Colonel Delamere, Miss Hendrick and Miss Owenson, as usual, walking arm-in-arm, as usual, also, making a very pretty contrast—a fact which the elder of the two at least very well knew. Cyrilla wore her one best dress—Aunt Phil's Christmas gift, a garnet merino—its rich tints setting off well her richer beauty, a ruffle of thread lace at throat and wrists : for ornaments, brooch and earrings of rubies and fine gold. Miss Hendrick had brought these jewels with her from England, and, apart from their intrinsic worth and extreme becomingness to her brunette face, valued them as parting gifts from "Freddy."

"He gave them to me with tears in his eyes, and nearly

ruined himself, poor little dear "—Miss Hendrick always spoke
of this gentleman as though he were seven years old—" to buy
them. As Mademoiselle Stephanie would say, 'Fred is as poo'
as mouses of the church.' "

Miss Owenson, in turquoise blue silk, her drooping, sun-
bright ringlets, tied back into a knot of blue ribbon, falling
loosely over her shoulders, looked by contrast white and pure
and fair as a lily. She wore no adornings, except her shining
engagement ring and her chain and locket.

" I can't quite realize, Syd," Miss Hendrick observed thoughtfully, " that this time next month you will be, as people phrase
it, ' a respectable married woman.' And only seventeen year'
old ! "

"It does seem absurd, doesn't it ?" Sydney laughed ; "it *is*
absurd. I wish poor papa's crotchet had taken any other form ;
but since it has taken this, there is nothing for it but obedience.
I would do much more unpleasant things than marry Bertie to
please poor, sick, hypochondriacal papa."

Cyrilla looked at her curiously.

" You are an oddity, Sydney—half child, half woman ; I
don't quite understand you. Do you love this Bertie
Vaughan ? "

Sydney laughed again, and blushed—that bright, flitting
blush that made her pearl-clear face so lovely.

" Love ?—love, Cyrilla ? " The girl of seventeen pronounced
the incisive word shyly, as most girls of seventeen do. " Oh,
well, that's another thing, you see—something, I fancy, one
thinks more of at seven-and-twenty than at seventeen. Of
love, such as I have read in novels and poetry, I know nothing.
I am not sure I ever want to know. As far as I can make out,
love and misery are synonymous. No, I'm not in love with
Bertie—I'm tolerably sure of that."

"Nor he with you ? "

" Nor he with me. How could we—only boy and girl ?
Since I was ten years old, and Bertie fifteen, papa gave us to
understand we were to marry some day, and we never made
any objections. I like Bertie better than any one I ever
knew—that is enough."

" Enough ? Oh, you poor child ! You like Bertie—yes, and
some day, when you are ten years older, the right man (they
say there is a right man for all of us, if we only wait long
enough) will appear on the scene, and then—and *then*, Syd,
you will wake up and know what love and marriage mean.'

Once more Sydney laughed aloud—her sweet, clear, heart-whole laugh.

"Cyrilla Hendrick turned sentimental! What shall I hear next? Have you been reading French novels lately, Cy?—that sounds like an extract. Oh, no, Cyrilla!"—the girl's face grew suddenly grave—"I am not a bit like one of the heroines of your pet romances. When I am Bertie's wife I will love him—yes, love him with my whole heart; and no man in all this world will be to me what he will. Of love, as you mean it, I know nothing; but that I will be Bertie's true and loyal wife I know as well as that I am walking here."

Cyrilla smiled—the cynical and most worldly smile that often marred the beauty of her Titian-like face.

"We will see!" she said, prophetically. "Meantime, what a romantic old gentleman your papa must be! I thought that sort of thing, affiancing people in their cradles, went out of fashion two or three centuries ago."

"It is simple enough after all," Sydney answered. "I will tell you how it was, Cy, in return for your confidence the other day. When papa was a very young man, and a middy in the British Navy, he was guilty of some youthful indiscretion—I don't know to this day what—but some act that if brought to the ears of his captain would have disgraced and ruined him for life. Mr. Vaughan, Bertie's father, was second officer of the ship, and Mr. Vaughan came to papa's aid, rescued him from his danger, screened him—saved him, in a word. Papa could do nothing then to prove his gratitude, but in his heart his gratitude was deep and strong. Years and years after, when papa had come into a fortune, and was married, and I was a baby, his turn came. Mr. Vaughan died poor, *very* poor, leaving Bertie friendless and alone. Papa came forward, sought him out, brought him here, and adopted him as his son. I was one year old, and Bertie six, but I believe even then, Cy, he destined us for each other. He had married mamma in New York —mamma is American, you know—and finally, when his health began to fail, he came and settled there. The climate agrees with him, and mamma prefers it. Bertie was at Rugby at the time, and finally went up to Oxford. I had not seen him for three years before last vacation, when he came over, and, as I told you girls, gave me this ring, and informed me he intended to marry me next year. Of course papa had told him to do it, and I am sure if I *must* marry, I would rather marry Bertie than any dreadful, strange man. That is the whole story Cyrilla, romantic or not, as you like."

" H'm !" was Cyrilla's comment, her black eyes twinkling; "what a comfort it must be to your papa to possess so dutifu. a son and daughter. I am curious to see this docile Mr. Vaughan, and curious, *very* curious, Syd, to see how this romantic marriage turns out."

" You are welcome," Miss Owenson answered, stoutly. " It will be a modern case of Darby and Joan, I feel sure. When we are married and settled—we are to live at home with papa and mamma, of course—you must come and make me a long visit, and we will look out together for the ugly, old, idiotic, wealthy Bottom the Weaver, you intend to marry."

Miss Hendrick laughed, then sighed impatiently—that look of dark discontent Sydney had learned to know long ago overspreading her face like a cloud.

She glanced up at her, half-wonderingly, half-compassionately.

"Cyrilla," she said, holding the girl's arm a little closer, "what a troubled face you wear!—what a troubled face you often wear, as though you were almost sick of your life."

" Almost !" Cyrilla Hendrick repeated—"almost, Sydney ! Why, there never was a time when I was *not* sick of my life. I have an infinite capacity for discontent, I think—for discontent, envy, and all uncharitableness. I long for freedom, for riches, for splendor, for the glory of the world, more than words can ever tell. And drudgery, and poverty, and meanness have been mine since I can recollect. But, as you say, Syd, I have a handsome face, and the average of brains behind it, and it will go hard with me, if out in the big, wide world I cannot win for myself a place in the first rank."

Sydney Owenson gazed at her in increased wonder and perplexity. Her own life ran on like some clear, shining river; the turbid, restless spirit of her bolder friend she could by no means understand. In all things her life sufficed for her, and had from the beginning; with her niche in the world she was amply content. This craving, never-satisfied longing for the unattainable was to her a marvel.

"We were talking of love a few minutes ago," she said, trying perplexedly to work out the puzzle. "Are you in love, Cyrilla, with Freddy ? "

Cyrilla laughed—the sweetest, airiest laugh was Cyrilla's— the clouds clearing away as if by magic.

"And if I am, Sydney, you don't think, I hope, *that* has anything to do with it! Oh, no! If I were queen of the universe, and all the best and bravest of mankind knelt before me, I would single out little Fred Carew and marry him from among them all, and care for him as greatly as it is in me to care for any one besides myself, and make him most exquisitely miserable for the rest of his mortal life, I have no doubt. But with my chronic dissatisfaction with my lot, Freddy, at present, has nothing to do."

"And yet you are fond of him ? "

"Fond of him? Fond of Fred Carew? Ah ! well, Syd, it's one of those things that won't bear talking about. We have said good-by, and said it for all time."

"Who knows? You will one day inherit Miss Dormer's fortune, marry your Fred, and live happy ever after."

" Never, Syd ! I opened the mysteries a little the other day. Let me open them still more now. I told you Miss Dormer had agreed to leave her money to me on one condition —that I solemnly swear to obey her in one thing—did I not ? "

" Yes—well ? "

"Well—that one thing is, that I am never to marry Fred Carew. Before she signs her will, if I am not already married, I am to swear, in the presence of witnesses, that never, while I live, will I marry poor little Freddy. If I refuse to take that oath, or if I break it when taken, I forfeit every dollar. No more questions, Syd, and get rid of that shocked face. Here we are at Mrs. Delamere's."

CHAPTER V.

"PART NOW, PART WELL, PART WIDE APART."

MRS. COLONEL DELAMERE, a fat, fair, and forty matron with the usual comfortable, placid, stall-fed look, came forward in pearl-gray silk to receive her youthful guests. Miss Sydney Owenson, her especial pet, she kissed with effusion.

"You darling child ! how good of you to come so early ! " she whispered. "And so we are really going to lose you for good ! "

"Who told you?" Sydney demanded, opening wide her gray eyes.

"Mademoiselle Chateauroy—I called yesterday. Told me you were to be married—a little girl of seventeen! My pet, it's a shame!"

"Is it?" laughed Sydney; "but a little bird has whispered through the town that Mrs. Colonel Delamere ran away and was married at sixteen!"

"So she did, my dear, and a precious simpleton she was for her pains," Mrs. Delamere answered, shrugging her ample shoulders. "Sydney, why did you fetch that shrewish Miss Jones? I have a treat in store for you, girls, but it's against orders — three contraband admirers who are dying to meet my pretty *pensionnaires*. Miss Jones will be sure to spoil all."

"Poor Miss Jones! she seems to make enemies on every hand. It is war to the knife between her and Cyrilla. Are you really going to introduce the new arrivals? I heard the regiment had come. How nice of you!"

"They will drop in after dinner—the colonel dines with them at the mess, and will bring them over afterward. You are to have parlor croquet, and a carpet dance, and go home by moonlight. If only that Miss Jones would not tell!"

"How plaintively you speak of *that* Miss Jones," Sydney laughed. "Let the most fascinating of your military heroes make love to her, Mrs. Delamere, give her his arm home, and so seal the dragon's mouth."

Mrs. Delamere looked doubtfully across at Miss Jones.

"Do you think so, pet? But then she is so plain, poor thing, and not so young as she was ten years ago, and though they're all plucky fellows enough, yet I'm afraid they're not equal to it. However, we will eat, drink, and be merry to-night, if we are to die for it to-morrow."

All things went on in a most exemplary way for the next two hours, until the six o'clock dinner ended. Not a red coat, not even a black coat, made its appearance. Games of all kinds, books of all sorts, had been provided by Mrs. Delamere, the jolliest of hostesses, for her young friends. They dined together, waited upon by a solemn, elderly butler, and even Miss Jones was amused and propitiated by Mrs. Delamere's condescending kindness.

"I really want the poor things to enjoy themselves this evening, my dear Miss Jones," she said, confidentially. "You must permit them a little extra liberty, and at least one hour more than usual."

Miss Jones fixed her dull, glimmering eyes upon the colonel's lady, scenting danger afar off.

"My orders are not to allow my pupils out of my sight, madame," she answered, stiffly ; "and to bring them home positively at nine. It is as much as my position is worth to disobey."

"Oh, nonsense ! my dear Miss Jones. I will make it all right with Mademoiselle Chateauroy. Do recollect how little amusement the poor things have, and remember we were once young ourselves."

It was the most unfortunate appeal the good lady could have made. Miss Jones was verging upon the thirties, a period when any unmarried lady may be pardoned for becoming sensitive. Her leaden eyes absolutely flashed.

"Mrs. Delamere is very kind, but my orders were positive, and it is my duty to obey."

She set her thin lips, and looked across at Cyrilla Hendrick.

"The military are coming, and I shall spoil your sport, my lady, if I can," she thought, vindictively.

Miss Hendrick at the moment was the centre of a circle of laughing, eager faces. They had adjourned to the ample grounds in front of the house, and seated under a great scarlet maple, armed with a pack of cards, Cyrilla was gravely lifting the mystic vail of futurity.

"I see here, my pretty lady," she was drawling in true gypsy tone to Miss Owenson, "a sudden journey, and a change in your whole life. Here is a fair man, who is destined to cause you a great deal of trouble. Here are tears, a disappointment, a sick-bed, and—yes—a death."

"Cyrilla !" Sydney cried, her gray eyes flashing indignantly.

"It is on the cards—look for yourself, and very near, too. Here is a dark man, this king of spades, who follows you everywhere, and a dark woman, who is your enemy, and comes between you and the fair man, and——"

She stopped suddenly, as suddenly as if she had been shot. For a voice broke upon them as she uttered the words.

"I never go in for high stakes, myself," said the pleasant, lazy voice ; "say ponies, or monkeys. My exchequer never stands anything higher. My dear colonel, what a charming scene ! a veritable group from Watteau, and sitting on straw, like Marjory Daw ! These are the young ladies Mrs. Delamere spoke of, no doubt."

The speaker raised his eye-glass complacently, and stood surveying the "group from Watteau," as though it had been got up for his especial delectation. He had spoken in an undertone, but in the clear, crisp, still air, every word had reached the ears of the fortune-teller. She did not start, she did not look up, a sudden stillness came over her from head to foot. Then she lifted her handsome, high-bred face, and went coolly on.

"The dark lady is in love with the fair gentleman, and will do her best to part him from you. Whether she succeeds or not is not on the cards, but I see here no end of trouble, disappointment, sickness and tears."

"A very dreary prediction for lips so gentle to pronounce. Fairest fortune-teller, will you not speer my future as well?"

The gentleman whose bets never exceeded "ponies or monkeys" had advanced, bowing gracefully, smiling sweetly upon the fluttering group. The seeress lifted her eyes from the pack, and glanced up at him with the careless indifference of a practised coquette. But Sydney Owenson saw, and Miss Jones saw, that the faint rich carnation her olive cheeks ever wore had deepened to vivid crimson.

"Certainly," she answered, with perfect *sang froid;* "cross the sibyl's palm with silver, my pretty gentleman, and tell me which shall it be—past, present, or future?"

She held out her hand, all present looking on in a flutter of expectation, a startled expression upon Miss Jones' vinegar visage, a bland smile upon Colonel Delamere's.

"The future, by all means," the gentleman answered, making search gravely for the silver coin. He found a sixpence, and dropped it with a second Chesterfieldian bow into the extended palm. She shuffled the cards. "Cut," she said, authoritatively.

The stranger obeyed, a military stranger all saw, though in mufti. Miss Hendrick took up the first "cut," and began to read.

"This is the knave of hearts—you are the knave, monsieur! This means water—you have recently made a long voyage. There is the queen of spades—a dark lady whom you are to meet soon, very soon. Let me warn monsieur against this young dark lady ; she will cause him endless trouble and mischief if he does not cut her acquaintance at once. Here is a blonde lady, the queen of diamonds, immensely wealthy. Look at all these cards that follow her. She will fall in love with the knave if he sets about it properly, and may even ultimately marry him. She will not be young and certainly not pretty, but, as you see, she has a fortune that is immense, and that is much better for the knave of hearts, and much more to his taste than youth or pretty looks. The dark lady is poor, and really will make monsieur no end of worry whenever-she appears. This card certainly means a wedding. Here it all is—monsieur turns his back upon the evil-minded dark lady, marries the queen of diamonds and her money-bags, and lives happy ever after."

She sprang to her feet, bowed low to the gentleman, and turned as if to depart.

"Ha, ha, ha!" boomed out the big bass laugh of the colonel. "By Jupiter, that's good—eh, Carew? If she had known you all you're life, by Jove, she couldn't have hit home better —hey, my boy? Let me introduce you—Miss Cyrilla Hendrick, Mr. Carew of the —th Fusiliers."

"Carew!" The gray eyes of Sydney Owenson opened in swift, sudden surprise. She glanced at Cyrilla, strangely startled, but that young lady was bowing as to one she had never seen before—the gentleman with equal gravity.

Sydney drew a long breath. After all Carew was not such a very uncommon name. There might certainly be two men in the world who bore it. If she could only hear his other.

"Freddy, my boy," cried the colonel's cheerful stentor tones, "here is another. Miss Sydney Owenson, Lieutenant Carew."

Freddy! She flashed a glance of amaze and delight across at her friend, but the face of Cyrilla Hendrick was beyond her reading. She had-turned partly away, with only the usual, half-indifferent, half-disdainful expression on the handsome brunette face.

"Mr. Carew, Miss Jones," says genial Colonel Delamere, and Miss Jones makes a prim, stiffish, little bow. "Mademoiselle Marie Antoinette Desereux, Madamoiselle Angele Garneau."

Twice more does Mr. Carew bestow his graceful court-chamberlain bow and smile on the bread-and-butter school-girls, and then he is free.

"Two more coming, Rosebud," whispers the elderly colonel to Sydney; "two more—good men and true. Fred Carew and I toddled on ahead. How does Carew compare with *le beau* Bertie—eh, little pearl?"

"Mr. Carew is very good-looking indeed, sir ; not very tall,
but that's a matter of taste," answers, demurely, Miss Owenson.

"And a bit of a dandy—eh, my dear? *Regardez vous*, as
they say here, the lavender kids, the shiny boots, the swell
hat, the moss-rose in the button-hole. That coat is one of
Poole's masterpieces; but I suppose you are not capable of
appreciating Poole's *chef-d'œuvres*. But, with all his Dun-
drearyism, he's one of the best and most honorable little fellows
that ever breathed, is my young friend, Fred Carew."

"Indeed, sir."

"Yes, that he is. I've known him since he was the size of
this cigar. May I light it? Thank you, my dear. Miss Hendrick hit him off to the life—ha ! ha ! 'Rich wife—not pretty
—not young—lots of money'—ha ! ha ! ha ! Clever girl, very,
that handsome, black-eyed Miss Hendrick. Couldn't have
struck home more neatly if she had been his mother. Hasn't
a stiver but his pay—Carew hasn't—best connections going,
but no expectations. - Terrible flirt, but no marrying man.
However, that's nothing to you, my dear. *You're* booked.
Lucky fellow, that young Vaughan. I've heard of him. Ah !
you needn't blush—if I were only twenty years younger and a
single man. Well ! you may laugh if you like, but Vaughan
wouldn't have it all his own way. Yes, as I say—as Miss Hendrick said rather—a wife with fifty thousand. down is about
Freddy's figure. The widow, or the orphan, my dear, doesn't
matter which, and the money not selfishly tied up on herself
either."

Thus guilelessly prattled on the colonel, while Sydney laughed
and watched her friend with intense curiosity. At least Colonel
Delamere did not dream that Mr. Carew and Miss Hendrick
had ever met before—no one did except herself. Yes—one
other ! Miss Jones' leaden eyes might be dull, but they were
sharp, and where Cyrilla Hendrick was concerned hatred had
sharpened them to needle-points. She had noticed the first
start, the first flush of tell-tale color ; she had seen for one
moment an expression on her foe's face she had never seen
there before. The fortune-telling, too, had been peculiar. Did
she mean herself by the "dark lady," Miss Jones wondered?
Had they ever met before ? Had they met before—in England,
for example—and was there some reason for keeping that meeting secret ? She would watch, and wait, and see.

Mr. Carew had joined Miss Hendrick, and walked away by

her side. For a moment neither spoke—the young lady looking serenely before her straight into space, the young gentleman watching her with a curious smile. He was the first to speak.

" Well, Beauty ? "

"Well, Freddy ? " Cyrilla Hendrick's black eyes turned from the horizon to his face at last. " It *is* you, Fred Carew, then, after all. How in the name of all that is astonishing do you come to be here ? "

"What ! " Mr. Carew said, lifting his blonde eyebrows, "do you mean to tell me, Beauty, you did not know I was here ? "

" Know you were here ! Good Heaven ! Fred, what a preposterous question. Freddy Carew away from Regent Street and Rotten Row ! Fred Carew out of sight of White's Club House and a Bond Street tailor ! No—the human mind refuses to take in such an antithesis ! I would as soon expect to meet the Czar of Russia in the wilds of Canada as you, Mr. Carew."

" Ah ! " Freddy sighs, plaintively. " You can't feel sorrier for me, Beauty, than I feel for myself. But the fortune of war, my dear child, however cruel, must be accepted by a soldier. Still, since it has brought me to you, I can't say I regret it."

" You knew I was here ?—from papa, I suppose."

" Your papa is improving the shining hours in Boulogne, my dear Cyrilla, and has been for the past year. No ; I knew you were in Canada somewhere, and that knowledge alone made the thought of my exile endurable. I had no idea we were to meet, until this very day, at mess."

" And then——"

" And then our garrulous friend, the colonel—'our old lady,' the fellows call him—let out the blissful secret. ' Capital place, Petit St. Jacques, Freddy, my, boy,' says Delamere to me. ' Yes, *mon colonel*,' I answer. ' Capital place for a man to go melancholy mad or cut his throat, I should say.' ' Not at all,' retorts my superior officer ; ' lots of fun—famous for maple sugar and pretty girls. There's a whole seraglio of beauties down there in the Rue St. Dominique, and you're to meet two of the prettiest at my house this evening—azure-eyed, golden-haired Sydney—black-eyed, raven tressed Cyrilla. Take either, my boy, with my blessing—' you pays your money, and you takes your choice.' Need I tell you, Beauty, I woke up at that —at the sound of your name ? ' Both beauties, both heiresses, my boy,' pursued the doddering old colonel ; ' and an heiress

is just about what you want most, I should say, Freddy.'
'Precisely, sir,' I answer; 'to which do you advise me to lay
siege—belle blonde or brunette?' 'Well, my little Sydney,
Miss Owenson, is bespoken, I'm sorry to say,' Delamere
answers, 'so it must be Miss Hendrick. Eyes like sloes, lips
like cherries, cheeks like roses, and the air of a duchess. Yes,
by Jove!' cries the vagabond old colonel, smacking his lips,
'the air of an empress. *Benedicite*, my son, and go in and
win.' So I came, Beauty—I needn't tell you how I felt, and
you met me as though you had never seen me before. I made
sure you knew all about my being here, and were on guard."

"Not I," Cyrilla answered; "when your voice reached me,
as I sat there telling fortunes, I was struck dumb. But oh, dear
old fellow! *how* glad I am to see you—how good it seems to
meet a familiar face in this desert of Canada."

"Miss Hendrick!" peals forth a sharp-accented voice; and
Miss Hendrick wakes up almost as from a dream at the too
familiar sound. "Miss Hendrick, you are wanted in the drawing-room, to sing."

Mr. Carew's glass goes to his eye; Miss Hendrick turns half
round upon her foe, with her usual air of serene impertinence.

"Couldn't you take my place this once, my dear Miss
Jones?" (Miss Jones has about as much voice as a consumptive
raven.) "You see I am well amused as it is."

"I must insist upon your returning to the house, instantly,"
cries Miss Jones, in a rising key. "My orders are, as you know,
not to let you out of my sight."

She advances upon them. Mr. Carew, his glass still in his
eye, regards her as he might some newly-discovered and wonderful specimen of the British megatherium.

"But, my *dear* Miss Jones," he begins, in most persuasive
accents, with his most winning smile, "there is really no need
of all this trouble. Your natural and affectionate anxiety about
Miss Hendrick does equal honor to your head and heart, but, I
assure you, no harm shall come to her while she is in my care.
I am ready to shield her, if necessary, with my life."

"Mademoiselle Chateauroy's orders were not to let any of
my pupils out of my sight; more particularly Miss Cyrilla
Hendrick—*most* particularly with gentlemen. I shall obey
mademoiselle's orders," is Miss Jones's grim and crushing reply.

"It's of no use, Freddy," Cyrilla says, in an undertone;
"we must go back and part. I don't care for her," motioning
contemptuously toward Miss Jones, "nor for Mademoiselle

Chateauroy either; but I do care for Aunt Phil. To offend her means ruin to me; and the deadliest offence I can give her is to have anything to say to you. Let us go back, and for pity's sake don't speak to me again until you say good-night."

"But, Beauty, this is absurd," says Fred, as they turn to retrace their steps; "don't speak to you again until I say good-night! What ridiculous nonsense! I have ten thousand things to say to you, and I mean to say them in spite of all the Gorgon aunts and grim duennas on earth. When and where will you meet me?"

"I will not meet you at all, Freddy. I tell you it is impossible. I am watched more closely than any other girl in the school, and all are watched closely enough, goodness knows. Miss Jones's basilisk eyes are upon me this moment, and Miss Jones will faithfully report every word and look to the powers that be the moment she returns to the *pensionnat*.

"Hang Miss Jones!"

"With all my heart," says Cyrilla, laughing; "nothing would give me greater pleasure. At the same time I can't afford to have my misdeeds reported to Aunt Phil; and so, sir, let us shake hands and part."

"Never, Cyrilla, you *must* meet me, and at once. Appoint some place and time, here in the town, and I will be there, whether it be midnight or midday."

"Impossible. I am never permitted to stir outside the gates alone"

"Then, by Jove! we shall meet inside the gates. I will scale the wall this very night, and you steal down and meet me in the grounds. Cyrilla, for Heaven's sake, don't say no, as I see you are going to! It is three years since we met. Have you forgotten all that——"

"I have forgotten nothing, Fred—nothing," the girl answers almost with emotion; "better for me, perhaps, if I had. Yes, I will meet you—at least I will try. I risk more than you dream of, but I *will* risk it. If you can get over the wall of the *pensionnat* to-night, I will try to meet you in the grounds."

"My darling"—under Miss Jones' argus eyes, Mr. Carew takes and squeezes Miss Hendrick's hand—"are your windows high? Do you run any risk in coming down?"

"I run risk enough, as I told you, but not of that kind. My room is on the second floor, and there is a tree close to the window, from whose branches I have often swung myself into the playground. Get over the wall about eleven to-night, and, if it be possible at all, I will meet you. But mind—only this once, Freddy; not even you will tempt me to do it again."

"You will write to me, though, Beauty, and allow me to——"

"No letter comes into or goes out of the *pensionnat* that does not pass under Mademoiselle Chateauroy's scrutiny. No, Fred; there can be no writing and no meeting except this one. Fate is against us, as it has been from the first. We were not one iota farther apart when the Atlantic rolled between us than we will be here together in Canada."

"That remains to be seen," Fred Carew answered. "My own opinion is that fate has not brought us face to face in this queer old world-forgotten town for nothing. We shall meet —you and me, 'Rilla, love—and go on meeting, please Heaven, to the end of the chapter."

They had reached the house. Cyrilla went in at once, while Mr. Carew lingered and allowed Miss Jones to join him. The yellow half-moon was lifting her face over the tree-tops, the air was spicy with aromatic odors from the pine woods. Through the open windows came the gay strains of "La Claire Fontaine," the national air of Lower Canada, played by Miss Sydney Owenson.

"Why should we go in just yet, Miss Jones?" says Mr. Carew, in his slow, sleepy voice, with his slow, sleepy smile. "It is a lovely night, a little coldish, but I perceive you have a shawl across your arm; allow me to put it on—you may take cold—and permit me to offer you my arm for a walk."

He removes the shawl as he speaks, and adjusts it as tenderly and solicitously about Miss Jones's angular shoulders as though it had been Miss Hendrick herself; then, still smiling, he offers her his arm.

The temptation is great. Miss Jones is nine-and-twenty, and not even at nineteen was her head ever turned by the flattering attentions of fickle man; and Miss Jones, albeit the milk of human kindness has been somewhat curdled in her vestal breast by a long course of refractory pupils, is human, very human.

"Do come!" says Mr. Carew, sweetly. "It is really a sin to spend such a night in-doors. The young ladies? Oh, the young ladies are perfectly safe. There is no one there but the colonel and Mrs. Delamere. The other fellows said they would come, but they haven't, as you may perceive. All the better for me, Miss Jones, smiles Mr. Carew, drawing her hand within his arm, "since it allows me the pleasure of a *tête-à-tête* stroll with you."

A flush, an absolute flush, rises to Miss Jones's sallow cheeks. Yes, since none of those dangerous military men had come, there could surely be no harm in a little walk with Mr. Carew. She coughed a little cough of assent, and meandered away with her subtle tempter.

"Oh, Cy, look! *do* look!" cries Sydney Owenson, springing from the piano. "Here's richness! Miss Jones and Mr. Carew getting up a flirtation in the moonlight! She nipped yours in the bud, and now she leads him off captive herself!"

"Haw, haw, haw! Yes, by Jove!" booms the colonel; "Carew has trotted off Miss Jones! The wolf spares the lambs, and makes off with the sheep-dog! Fred Carew turns his back on four of the prettiest girls in Canada, and begins spooning with the old maid! What a capital joke for the mess-table to-morrow!"

"A most capital joke," says Cyrilla Hendrick; but her black eyes flash as they follow the two retreating figures. She knows as well as that she stands there that he is doing it for her sake, martyrizing himself to propitiate the dragon, but in her heart she loves this elegant, soft-spoken dandy so passionately well, that the bare sight of him flirting with even poor, plain Miss Jones is hateful to her.

The lamps are lit in the drawing-room; song, and music, and games of all kinds go on. An hour passes, and the truants have not returned.

"You don't suppose Carew can have eaten her, Dorothy, my love?" says the old colonel, with a diabolical grin, to his wife. "Begad! if they're not here in ten minutes, I shall con-sider it my duty to go in search of them."

They enter as he speaks—Mr Carew calm, complacent, list-less, but *not* looking more bored than customary—Miss Jones with a flush, either of pleasure or night air, still glowing frostily on either pippin cheek.

"Mr. Carew asked me to explain the process of converting maple sap into maple sugar," she explains elaborately to Mrs. Delamere; "so we wandered down by the grove of maples, and really I had no idea an hour had passed."

"Pray, don't apologize, my dear Miss Jones," answered Mrs. Delamere, demurely. "I am only too grateful to Mr. Carew if he has helped to make your visit agreeable. What! going so soon? Oh, surely not, Miss Jones!"

3

But it is past nine, and Miss Jones, conscious of having swerved from the stern path of rectitude, is resolute. So the girls flutter up-stairs after wraps, still giggling in chorus over Miss Jones's unexpected flirtation. Miss Hendrick does not giggle, she smiles scornfully, and transfixes her teacher with her derisive black eyes—a glance Miss Jones, for once, does not care to meet.

" Begad, Freddy," says the colonel, when the ladies have left the room, "I expected it would be a case of love at first sight with you this evening, but I didn't—no, by gad, I didn't think it would have been with the old maid."

" Miss Jones is a most intelligent and well-informed young lady," answers Mr. Carew, imperturbably, and with half-closed eyes. " I am going to see her home."

They flutter back as he says it, and he and the colonel rise. Good-nights are spoken while Mr. Carew draws on his overcoat and gloves, looking very elegant and amiable, and a little vibrating thrill of expectation goes through the group of girls. To whom will he offer his arm ? He walks up to Miss Jones as they think it, with the air of its being an understood thing, and once again draws her hand within his coat sleeve.

"*En avant, mon colonel,*" he says ; " we will follow."

The colonel gives one arm to his favorite, Sydney, the other to Cyrilla, and leads the way. The two French girls come after. Mr. Carew and Miss Jones bring up the rear, sauntering slowly in the piercing white moonlight. All the way, along the deathly silent streets, the colonel cracks his ponderous and rather stupid jokes. Sydney laughs good-naturedly, but Cyrilla Hendrick's darkly-handsome face looks sombre and silent. They reach the gates—Babette, the portress, is there awaiting them. Universal hand-shaking and adieus follow. For one second Cyrilla's cold fingers lie in Fred Carew's close clasp, for one second the blue eyes meet the black ones meaningly.

" At eleven," he whispers ; " don't fail."

Then the great gates clang upon them, and Babette, yawning loudly, goes in before into the gray, gloomy *pensionnat.*

CHAPTER VI.

WHY MISS DORMER HATED FRED CAREW.

I.L is still when they enter; the *pensionnaires* are safely in their rooms and in bed. Mademoiselle Stephanie, looking like a snuff-colored spectre, in a loose white wrapper, awaits them. A few questions, a recognized formula, are asked and answered, then they are dismissed with "*bon nuit, mes chéries,*" and bed-room lamps.

"In twenty minutes, young ladies, I will come for the lights," is Miss Jones's valedictory, as she mounts up to her own room.

"Good-night, Cy," Sydney Owenson cries, gayly; "don't dream of that pretty little Mr. Carew if you can help. His mad passion for Miss Jones is patent to the dullest observer."

"*Bonne nuit et bonns rêves, ma belle,*" Cyrilla answers, with rather a forced smile, "we would all be happier if we never dreamed of Mr. Carew or any other of his kind."

'Toinette goes virtuously and sleepily to bed at once, gaping audibly. Miss Hendrick throws off her hat and jacket, draws a volume of Dante, in the original, toward her, with a book of Italian exercises, and sets to work translating. So, the twenty minutes up, Miss Jones finds her.

"Industrious, upon my word!" sneers Miss Jones. She is generally worsted in the fray, but she can never by any chance let her enemy pass without a cut-and-thrust.

"Yes, Miss Jones," Cyrilla replies; "and if I continue to be industrious until I am—well, nine and twenty, say—I may hope to attain the elevated position of fourth-rate teacher in a second-rate Canadian school; I may even aspire to entertain military men, six or seven years my junior, by an hour's dissertation on the art of making maple sugar."

She rises, with a short, contemptuous laugh, and begins to unlace her boots. Another instant, and the door closes behind Miss Jones, and she is alone.

It is a vividly, brilliantly bright night. The yellow moonshine floods the room as Cyrilla raises the window, wraps a shawl around her, and sits down. 'Toinette's watch, lying on the dressing-table, points to ten. Another hour and she and Fred Carew will be together once more. Her pulses thrill at the thought.   She loves this man ; she has loved him since she was ten years old—of al' the bliss l'fe holds it holds none greater than his presence for her.   The mystery and danger of the adventure, too, have their charm.   Life has gone on, for the past three years, so flat, stale, and unprofitable that to-night's excitement and wrong-doing, if you will, possess an irresistible fascination.   If it is ever discovered, if it ever reaches Miss Dormer's ears, all is up with her forever—her last hope of Miss Dormer's fortune is gone.   And she longs for and covets Miss Dormer's fortune, this school-girl of nineteen, as the blind desire sight.   Miss Dormer hates Fred Carew, and all of his name, with a hatred as intense as—even Cyrilla must own—in a retributive light it is just.   The story is this—told with what passionate intensity and vivid fierceness by Miss Dormer herself, the girl remembers well.

Forty years before, the father of Phillis Dormer had died, leaving a fortune, a widow, and a daughter of eight.   Two years passed, and the widow was a widow no longer—she had taken for her second husband good-looking, good-for-nothing Tom Hendrick.   Of that marriage came Jack, the father of Cyrilla. If Mr. Tom Hendrick had expected to possess the late Mr. Dormer's fortune, as well as his widow, he was doomed to be disappointed—the sixty thousand pounds were tightly tied up on Phillis.   And Phillis, even as a child, was not easily to be wronged.

She endured the reckless, riotous life of her step-father's house, the daily insolence of her bold, handsome, half-brother Jack, for a dozen years or more ; then her mother died, and Miss Phillis Dormer separated herself entirely from her disreputable relations, and engaging a *dame de compagnie*, set up for herself as an heiress.   The wife of the member for her native county brought her out, one or two fine ladies took her up, she was presented at court, ran the round of the season, and finished by finding herself engaged to Frederic Dunraith Carew, nephew of the Earl of Dunraith.

She was three and twenty years old, slightly lame, and most pathetically ugly.   Fred Carew of the Blues was handsome of face, graceful of figure, elegant of dress and manner, all that his son was to-day, and more.   He was poor—a beggar absolutely, over head and ears in debt—a rich wife his one earthly hope of salvation from Queen's Bench for life.   The ugly, the rich Miss Dormer fell in love with him.   Mr. Carew was told so, pulled his long blonde whiskers perplexedly, thought the matter over, "more in sorrow than in anger," faced the worst like a man, and went and proposed to Miss Dormer.

She was intensely, infatuatedly, insanely almost, in love with him. Like many very plain people, she had a morbid adoration of beauty in others. Mr. Carew had fascinated her at sight— he continued so to fascinate her to the end. If anything could have made plain Phillis Dormer lovely it would surely have been the perfect, the intense joy, that filled her when Frederic Carew asked her to be his wife. Hers was the perfect love that casteth out fear. She accepted him, she trusted him—in one word, she bowed down and idolized him.

The noble relatives of Mr. Carew were delighted, and made most friendly advances toward the bride-elect at once. It is true the sixty thousand pounds had been made in coal, but the coal-dust did not dim their golden glitter in the least. There had been talk of some penniless girl down in Berkshire, with two blue eyes and a pink-and-pearl face alone to recommend her ; but that was all at an end, no doubt. Fred had come to his senses, and realized that love is all very well in theory—a pretty girl well enough to waltz with, but when a wife is in the question the thing to be looked at is her bank account. Frederic had done his duty ; his noble relatives were quite prepared to do theirs, and accept the coal merchant's heiress as one of the family. The season ended, they invited her down to their country place in Sussex, the accepted suitor dutifully playing *cavalier servante* to a by no means exacting mistress. She gave so much and was satisfied to receive so little, that it was really pathetic to watch them. Frederic was perpetually running up to town, and staying away days at a time, even when the wedding day was not two weeks off. But Miss Dormer asked no questions, gave him wistful glances and smiles at parting, joyful glances and smiles at coming—come when and how he might. In secret she had made over her whole fortune to be his indisputably in the hour that made him her husband. A fool you think her, perhaps. Well, very likely, but a folly none need quarrel with, since it is very far from common.

Three days before the wedding-day there was a dinner-party, given by the Earl and Countess of Dunraith, in honor of the approaching nuptials. Mr. Carew had run up to town as usual, two days before, but had promised to be in time for the dinner. He failed, however, and, to the chagrin and annoyance of host and hostess did not put in an appearance at all. The bride-elect bore it bravely—something had detained Fred ; she missed him sorely, but in all things his lordly will was her law, "The king could do no wrong."

One hour after dinner, as she sat in the drawing-room, listen ing to the song Lady Dunraith was softly singing, looking out at the tremulous beauty of the summer twilight, gemmed with golden stars, and wondering wistfully whereabouts her darling might be, a note was presented to her by a servant. It was from *him*—her heart gave a glad bound. This was to explain satis-factorily his absence, no doubt. With a smile she opened the note; from that hour until the hour she died no smile like that ever softened the hard face of Phillis Dormer.

"Dover, *September* 18*th*, ——.

"My Dear Miss Dormer:—While waiting for the Calais boat I drop you a line. I am awfully sorry to disappoint you; but really, when it came to the point, I was not equal to it. I mean my marriage with you. Besides, I was engaged to another young lady before I ever knew you, and my honor was seriously compromised. She is poor, but we must make up our minds to that, I suppose, somehow. 'Better is a dinner of herbs where love abideth than a stalled ox and contention.' I was married this morning, and we are now on our way to Paris to spend the honeymoon. Regretting once more any little dis-appointment I may have caused you, I remain, dear Miss Dor-mer, very truly yours,   Frederic Dunraith Carew."

"Love not! love not! Oh, warning vainly said," sang Lady Dunraith at the piano. Phillis Dormer crushed the note—the curiously heartless note—in her hand, and listened to the song. To the last day of her life the words, the air, the look of the violet-twilight landscape would remain photographed on brain and heart. She had loved him, words are weak and poor to tell how greatly. She had trusted him with her whole soul. From that hour she loved no one, trusted no one, to the end of her life.

Her song ended, the countess came over to her, as she stood in the bay looking fixedly out at the rising harvest moon.

"Was that note from Fred, tiresome boy? Why was he not here?"

"It was from Fred," Miss Dormer answered. "He could not come."

Lady Dunraith looked at her curiously. "What a livid color her face was! what a black, dilated look there was in her eyes! " Fred is well?" she anxiously asked.

"He is quite well, I think, Lady Dunraith."

Her ladyship moved away, too well-bred to ask further questions. An hour later—without one farewell, without taking a single one of all her trunks or boxes—Phillis Dormer vanished from Dunraith Park forever.

She went straight to London, packed a few things with her own hands, wrote a brief letter to her man of business, sent for a cab, drove to Euston Square Station, and disappeared for all time from London, from England, from all who had ever known her.

Two days after, the truth came out, and all London was laughing over the last good joke. Fred Carew's pluck had failed at the eleventh hour; he had shown the white feather, and fled from the clutches of the ugly heiress. He had run away with a penniless little country lassie, pretty as a rosebud, and poor as a church mouse. His noble relations cast him off forever. He sold out, and with the proceeds lived abroad, and from thenceforth became as socially extinct as Phillis Dormer herself.

Of Miss Dormer no one knew anything. The ground might have opened and swallowed her for all trace she had left behind. Her solicitor knew, no doubt, but he held his professional tongue. Her half-brother, Jack Hendrick, was the only being on earth interested in her, and his interest was chiefly of a pecuniary nature.

"She usen't to be half a bad sort before she fell in with that duffer, Carew," Jack was wont to say. "Would pay a fellow's debts as quick as look, but with the devil's own temper all the time."

A few years later Jack's own little romance came off. The daughter of a baronet eloped with him, of which elopement Cyrilla was, in due time, the result. Then, sixteen years after, came that letter dated "Montreal," and signed "Phillis Dormer," asking curtly enough that her niece should be sent out to her to be educated and decently brought up. "If she pleases me, I may leave her all I possess one day. If she does not, she can go back to you, the better at least for a few years in a good school."

Phillis Dormer had gone straight to Montreal, where some of her property lay, and there buried herself, so to speak, alive.

One year after her coming she read in the *Times* this announce‹
ment :

" At Brussels, the wife of Frederic D. Carew, Esquire, of a son."

The old wound, not even yet seared over was torn open
afresh. In a paroxysm of fury she tore the paper to shreds and
trampled it under her feet, cursing, in her mad rage, the man
who had betrayed her, the wife he had wedded, and the son who
was born to him.
Fifteen years after, and in the same paper, at the same place,
she read the death of Frederic Dunraith Carew. In all these
years no softening had ever taken place in her bitter, desperate
heart. In all these years *that* moment perhaps was the happiest. Now he was as lost to her rival at least as to herself—
the grave held him. Bitter, lonely, wicked, most wretched,
most unrepentant, she lived alone, served in fear and dislike by
all. Suddenly the resolve seized her to send for her niece.
Jack Hendrick's daughter could be no good, but she was the
only creature on earth, except her worthless father, whom she
could call kin. Old age was upon her—a most unlovely old
age—and desolate and forsaken her heart cried out for some
one. At least this girl would serve her faithfully in the hope
of a future fortune, and ask no wages. For avarice had been
added to her other infirmities, and Miss Dormer, once generous,
had grown a miser.
Cyrilla came—a slim slip of a girl, with Jack Hendrick's
dark, thin face, and bold, black eyes, her mother's aquiline
nose, as Miss Dormer said, and that way she liked of holding
her pauper head well up. Cyrilla came, and with the intense
curiosity of a woman hungry for news of that world which had
once been hers, Phillis Dormer plied her with questions—
questions of her father, of her father's friends, of her mother's
family, and their bearing toward herself.
" I know nothing about them," Cyrilla answered. " I desire
to know nothing. My mother's relations have never noticed
me in any way, although my father wrote to them at her death,
and since that time again and again."
" I am quite sure of it," said Miss Dormer, grimly. " Jack
Hendrick is not the man to let any one, who has the misfortune
to be connected with him, alone on the subject of money. If
he had known my address I should ha.'e had begging letters
from him by the bushel."
" Please don't say anything unkind about papa, Aunt Phillis,"

the girl cried, imperiously. "I am very fond of papa, and he was always very good to me. And he always spoke well of *you.*"

Miss Dormer found her niece unpleasantly reticent for a girl of sixteen. Of the life she had led before coming here Cyrilla seemed able to give but the most meagre details.

"Who had given her this very expensive ruby set? Who had given her all these handsome books of poetry, marked with the initials 'F. D. C.'? Oh, a friend of papa's—papa had so many friends, and they all made her presents." The girl of sixteen had heard the history of her aunt's exile, and was on guard. But in an evil hour Miss Dormer swooped down upon her quarry, and learned all.

It was an album that told the story—a gorgeous affair of ivory, purple velvet, and gilt clasps, that her niece kept always jealously locked up, filled with cabinet-sized photographs of her Bohemian friends. The first picture in the book—a finely-tinted vignette of a boyish head and face—made Miss Dormer start and change color. She glanced at the fly-leaf. The murder was out! There was the tell-tale inscription:

"Beauty Hendrick, on her Fifteenth Birthday, from the most Devoted of her Adorers.   FREDERIC DUNRAITH CAREW."

The old woman uttered a shrill, hissing sort of cry, as though she had been struck, her yellow face turned green, her wicked old eyes absolutely glared with fury. After all these years, when the man was dead and rotten in his grave, to be stung by that name! It was winter time; a large coal fire glowed in the grate. Miss Dormer sprang from her chair, and in the twinkling of an eye Cyrilla's elegant album was on the bed of coals.

The girl darted forward to the rescue with a scream of dismay, but warding her off with one hand, Phillis Dormer held it down with her stick, not speaking a word, and glaring, as Cyrilla ever afterward said, like old Hecate over her witches' cauldron. So she stood, holding it mercilessly, until it crumbled upon the coals, a handful of black, charred ashes. And then the storm burst—a very tempest of fury and invective hurled against Cyrilla—"the viper she had warmed only to sting her" —against her father, against the Carews, sire and son. It was a most horrible scene. Even the girl's strong young nerves shrank with a shudder of disgust. But outwardly she stood

3*

like a rock, her lips compressed, her eyes flashing black lightning.   At last, exhausted, the old woman paused from sheer
want of breath.

"This is the sort of ingrate I have taken into my house, is
it?   This is the sort of friends you and your father have made.
My curse upon them—the living and the dead!"

She shook her stick in the air more like one of Macbeth's
witches than ever.   Cyrilla Hendrick spoke for the first time,
her short, scornful upper lip curling.

"You forget, Aunt Lillis, that curses, like chickens, come
home to roost," was what she said.   "I don't think your
anathemas will hurt Freddy Carew very greatly.   You are a bad
old woman, Aunt Phillis Dormer, and you may send me back
to England as soon as you like."

Then she walked out of the room, with her pauper chin
higher than ever, and the air of an outraged *grande dame*.   But
in her own room, with the door locked, she flung herself on her
bed, and cried passionately, cried herself sick, for the loss of
Freddy's portrait.

Miss Dormer did not send her home.   The first outburst past,
even her warped sense of justice showed her that the girl was
not so much to blame.   She could not be expected to feel the
wrongs of the aunt she had never seen very deeply, and no
doubt the son was as fatally fascinating as the father had been.
Only her mind, up to this time undecided concerning the
disposal of her fortune (nearly doubled by judicious investments
during a quarter of a century), was made up.   She would edu-
cate her niece, she would select a husband for her.   If her
niece married the man of her choice she would bestow her
fortune upon her.   If not, it would go to found an asylum for
maiden ladies of fifty.   In any case she must so secure it that
by no possible means could any fraction of it ever come to
Frederic Carew's son.   On their next interview Miss Dormer,
quite calm by this time, proposed to her niece the oath of which
Cyrilla had spoken to Sydney Owenson—the oath never to
marry Fred Carew.   Miss Hendrick promptly and resolutely
declined.

"I am thousands of miles from poor Freddy," she said.   "I
may never see him again.   I never expect to see him again—
all the same, Aunt Phil, I won't take the oath.   I never took
an oath in my life, and I never mean to.   Fred is as poor as a
rat, and always will be.   I don't suppose, if it comes to that,
he will ever be able to marry anybody unless he falls foul of an

heiress. For my own part, Aunt Dormer, find me a rich man, a millionaire, please, and I will marry him to-morrow."

With this Miss Dormer had to be content—the niece had a will of her own as well as the aunt. It was true the ocean rolled between them, it was impossible for them to correspond at Mlle. Chateauroy's *pensionnat*—there was really no present danger. He was poor, as Cyrilla had said, and Cyrilla was not the kind of girl to throw herself away upon a poor man, let her girlish fancy for him be ever so great—not the sort of girl whose heart is stronger than her head—a sort, indeed, that is pretty nearly obsolete—latter-day young ladies having a much more appreciative eye for the main chance than for the exploded "love in a cottage."

Last midsummer vacation Cyrilla had met at her aunt's house a middle-aged, sandy-haired, high-cheek-boned gentleman, introduced to her as Mr. Donald McKelpin. Mr. Donald McKelpin had expressed his pleasure in a pompous and ponderous way, set to a fine Glasgow accent, at making her acquaintance, accompanied by a look of broad, undisguised admiration. Upon his departure Miss Dormer informed her niece that this was the gentleman upon whom she designed her to bestow her hand and fortune, a gentleman in the soap-and-candle line, at whose Midas-touch all things turned to gold.

"Very well, Aunt Phil," had been the young lady's submissive answer, "just as you please. One might wish him twenty years this side of fifty, and with tresses a trifle less obnoxiously fiery, but after all one doesn't marry a man to sit and look at him. Whenever it is Sultan McKelpin's pleasure to throw the handkerchief his grateful slave will pick it up. Whenever he is ready to make me, I am ready to become"—mimicking to the life the broad Scotch accent—"Mistress Donald McKelpin."

   .   .   .   .   .   .

The clock in the steeple of St. James-the-Less, striking loudly eleven, awakes Cyrilla from her reverie. All is still. Moonlight floods the heavens and the earth ; the trees stand up black and nearly lifeless in the crystal light. It is cold, too, but her shawl protects her. As the last sonorous chime sounds a head rises over the wooden wall, directly opposite to where she sits. Her heart gives a leap. It is Carew. The head pauses a moment, reconnoitres, sees that all is safe, and then the remainder of Mr. Fred Carew follows. He poises himself for an instant on the top of the wall, unguarded, in this peaceful town, by wicked spikes or broken bottles, then lightly drops upon the turf beneath. Cyrilla waves her handkerchief to him, and he approaches, takes his stand under the tree beneath her window, and waits. She rises to her feet and listens. The silence is profound—all are in bed, no doubt, and asleep. 'Toinette's deep, regular breathing is like clock-work. A momentary pause, then Cyrilla prepares to descend. Her window is about fifteen feet from the ground—three feet beneath it a leaden spout runs round the house. She lowers herself upon this precarious footing, and then, without much difficulty, swings into the strong branches of a huge hemlock near. It is not the first time Miss Hendrick has, for a freak, reached the playground in this tom-boy fashion. Here she rests a moment to poise securely.

"For goodness sake, Beauty, take care," says Mr. Carew's anxious voice below.

She smiles. "All right, Freddy," she answers.

Branch by branch she descends, with wonderful agility for a girl—the lowest limb is reached. She frees her dress, and leaps lightly to the ground and to the side of Fred Carew.

CHAPTER VII.

"UNDER THE TAMARACS."

"MY dear little Beauty, what a trump you are!" is Mr. Carew's enthusiastic exclamation. "It's is awfully good of you to come."

He tries to embrace her, but Cyrilla resolutely frees herself, and draws back.

"No, thank you, Freddy; 'palm to palm is holy palmer's kiss.' I didn't come here to be made love to; I came for news of papa. There is a bench yonder, under the tamaracs, let us go to it. I believe, with the Orientals, that 'man is better sitting than standing.'"

"'Lying down than sitting, dead than lying down.' Is that your belief, Beauty?"

"No, I am afraid I would not be at all better off dead, particularly while I act as I am doing to-night. By-the-by, Freddy, I wish you would leave off calling me Beauty; it sounds too much as though I were a little woolly King Charles, with a curly tail and pink eyes."

"All right, Beau—I mean Cyrilla." They have found the bench by this time and sat down. "It is rather cruel of you, though, to refuse me one fraternal embrace, seeing we have been parted three years, and after my superhuman exertions to thaw out Miss—what was it?—oh, yes, Jones, and everything."

"You looked as though you rather enjoyed your exertions to thaw out Miss Jones," answered Cyrilla, coolly; "and we will have no tender scenes, if you please, Mr. Carew, either now or at any other time. You see before you the future Mrs. McKelpin."

Mr. Carew's glass goes to his eye instinctively in the moonlight.

"The Mrs.—how much?" he asks, helplessly.

"Mrs. Donald McKelpin," repeats Cyrilla, with unction and Mr. McKelpin's own Glasgow accent. My Aunt Phillis has not only undertaken to provide me with an education in the present, a fortune in the future, if I conduct myself properly, but a husband—a gentleman fifty-one years of age; a tallow-chandler, Freddy, with a complexion like his own soap and candles, and hair and whiskers of brightest carrots. It is well to announce this fact in time for your benefit. I am an engaged young lady, Mr. Carew, and it is my intention to behave as such."

"Engaged!" Freddy repeats, blankly. "Beauty, you don't mean to tell me—you can't mean to tell me that——"

"Well, not positively, but it is all the same. Mr. McKelpin and Aunt Dormer understand each other pretty thoroughly, I fancy. He is worth a hundred thousand dollars, Aunt Phil three times that amount, and you know the proverb, 'He that hath got a goose shall get a goose.' I leave school at Christmas, and I have not the slightest doubt Donald will propose two days after."

"And you will accept him, Cyrilla?"

"Such is my intention, Freddy. Beggars mustn't be choosers I don't know how he managed to ingratiate himself into Aunj Phil's good graces; he isn't by any means a fascinating being but the fact remains—he has. It seems to me sometimes a pity she can't marry him herself, but I fancy she feels bound to perpetual continence by her hatred of your father's memory. After all, Fred, it was a shame for him to treat her so, poor old soul."

"A most heinous shame!" assents Mr. Carew, with considerable energy. "My father is dead, and it may be disrespectful, but I will say, it was the action of a cad."

Cyrilla shrugs her shoulders.

"'Like father, like son.' Are you sure you would not do the same yourself?"

"Quite, Beauty."

"Well, don't be so energetic. You are never likely to have a chance of jilting *me*. What I tell you about Mr. McKelpin is quite true. I mean to marry him and lead a rich and virtuous life; that is, if the last of an utterly reprobate and castaway race can become rich and respectable. How is poor papa, Fred, and when did you see him last?"

"Poor papa is perfectly well, as he always is, Beau——I mean Cyrilla. It doesn't seem in the nature of things, somehow, for jolly Jack Hendrick to get knocked up. It is three months since I saw him, and then he was hanging out at Boulogne, in a particularly shady quarter, among a particularly shady lot. My granduncle Dunraith, who, in an uplifted sort of way, now and then recalls the fact of my existence, had sent me a windfall of fifty pounds. Your poor papa, Beauty, won it from me at chicken-hazard, with his usual bland and paternal smile, and sent me back to Aldershot a plucked chicken myself."

"Ah! poor papa!" says Miss Hendrick, heaving a sigh.

"Ah! poor papa!" echoes Mr. Carew, heaving another. "Papa is one of those people whom it is safer to love at a distance than close at hand. He wept when he spoke of you, and he had not been drinking harder than usual, either. 'Take her my bless-ess-hessing, Freddy, my boy,' sobs your poor papa, wiping a tear out of his left optic; 'it's all I have to send me child.' And then he took another pull at the brandy-and-water. He's a humbug, Beauty, if he is your father! Don't let us talk about him—let us talk about ourselves. When are you going back to England?"

"Never, Freddy. Go back to England! What on earth should I go back for? Your father's noble relatives recall the fact of your existence every once and a while: my mother's noble relatives totally ignored me from the first. By the way, Fred, if your father had behaved nicely, and married Aunt Phil, and pleased the earl and countess, *you* would have been heir to all the Dormer thousands now, and my first cousin. Think of that!"

Mr. Carew does think of it, and the notion so tickles his boyish fancy that he goes off into a shout of laughter that makes the echoes ring.

"By Jove, Beauty ! Your first cousin, and Miss Phillis Dormer's son ! How good, by Jove ! But I am afraid the Dormer thousands would have been beautifully' less by this time if
my father had had their handling. The only genius he possessed
was a genius for getting rid of money, and that has honorably
descended to his only son, only *he* never has any to get rid of."

" Yes," Cyrilla says, gravely. " Mr. McKelpin will make a
much better guardian of the Dormer dollars than you or your
late lamented father. For pity's sake, Fred, don't laugh so
loudly. Miss Jones's window is directly over mine, directly opposite this, and Miss Jones invariably sleeps with one eye
open."

" If Miss Jones's beauteous orbs were as sharp again as they
are," answers Mr. Carew, "she could hardly see us here. But
all this is beside the question. Let us return to our mutton—
I mean to our soap-and-candle man. Beauty, it isn't possible
—it cannot be possible—that you are going to throw me over,
and marry the Scotchman ? "

He takes both her hands in one of his and holds her fast.
Cyrilla resists a little, but Mr. Carew is firm, and maintains his
clasp.

" 'Throw you over, Fred ! I like that ! As if there could ever
be any question of loving or marrying between you and me.
As if I could ever look upon you—a small boy—in the light of.
a lover ! "

" Indeed !" says Mr. Carew, opening his handsome blue
eyes, " a small boy like me ? In what light, Beauty, have you
looked upon me, then, in the past, in the days we spent together
in Bloomsbury ? You see I am deplorably ignorant in all these
nicer distinctions."

" As my very good friend and staunch comrade, always.
Those days in London, spent together, were the best I have
ever known ; the best I ever will know."

" What, Miss Hendrick ! Even when you are the rich and
respectable Mrs. Sandy McKelpin ? "

" Donald, Freddy, Donald—Mrs. Donald McKelpin. Yes,
even then ; although, as far as money will go, I mean to enjoy
my life. And there is no enjoyment, to speak of, in this lower
world, that money will not purchase. For you, Fred, I told
you your fortune six hours ago. You will stear clear of the
dark lady, Cyrilla Hendrick, and you will marry the elderly
blonde person with a fortune. I can't point her out at present,
but I have no doubt she exists, and can be found if you set

about it properly. Seriously, Fred, your father made a fiasco of his life by marrying for love and all that nonsense, and died years before his time in poverty and premature old age. Take warning by him, and do as I shall do, marry for money."

Mr. Carew smiles that peculiarly sweet smile of his that lights up so pleasantly his blonde, boyish face.

" I have never thought much about marriage in the abstract," he says, " in fact I never thought of it at all, Beauty, until *you* put it in my head : but I think I may safely say this : that I will never marry, either for love or money, unless I can call Cyrilla Hendrick my wife."

There is real feeling in his voice, real love in the blue eyes that shine upon her. Cyrilla Hendrick's black ones flash and soften in the moonlight as they meet his.

" Oh, Freddy ! you really are as fond of me as this ! "

His answer is not in words, but it is satisfactory. There is silence for a little.

" And you won't marry the Scotchman, 'Rilla ? " he says, at last.

" Yes, Freddy : I shall marry the Scotchman, but all the same, dear old fellow, you shall be first in my heart—such heart as it is—to the end of the chapter."

" Happy Mr. McKelpin ! Is this the sort of morality they teach in young ladies' seminaries, then ? "

" I never required to be taught, Fred," Cyrilla replies, rather sadly ; "all worldly and selfish knowledge seems to come to me of itself. Besides, it is done every day, and where is the great harm ? I shall marry Mr. McKelpin, and make him as good a wife as he wants or deserves, and you and I shall go on, meeting as good friends, just the same as before."

" No ! " cries Fred Carew, with most unwonted energy, " that I swear we shall not ! The day you become Mrs. McKelpin, or Mrs. Any-body-else, that day you and I part forever. None of your married woman platonic friendships for me ! The hour you are made any man's wife that hour we shall shake hands and separate for all time ! "

" Freddy ! " she says, almost with a gasp, " you don't mean that ! "

" I mean that, Beauty. Mind—I don't say you are not right —if you do marry the Scotchman, I won't blame you. I am poor—I have my pay, just enough at present to keep me in moss rosebuds, cigars, and Jouvin's first choice. I have no ex-pectations ; a poor man I will be as long as I live. No one could blame you for throwing me over for the tallow-man

Only when you marry him our intimacy shall end. My father acted like a scoundrel to your aunt. I won't act like a scoundrel to you."

"It would be the act of a scoundrel to remain my friend—to go on seeing me after I am married?" Cyrilla demands, her cheeks flushing, her eyes flashing.

"It would, Beauty. Your friend I could never be—that you know. The motto of my Uncle Dunraith is, 'All or nothing.' In this matter it is my motto also—all or nothing!"

Again there is silence. On the young man's face a resolute expression, altogether new in Cyrilla's experience of him, has settled. On hers a deep, unusual flush burns.

"You mean this, Mr. Carew?"

"I most decidedly mean this, Miss Hendrick. I will be the happiest fellow in the universe if you will marry me to-morrow. If you will not, I have nothing to say—you know best what is best for you, I am very sure. But stand by and see you married to another man—go on meeting you after, knowing that you were lost to me forever—no, by Jove! " cries Mr. Carew, "*that* I won't!"

"As you please," Cyrilla answers, and she rises resolutely as she does answer. "You will act, of course, in all things, Mr. Carew, as your superior wisdom may suggest. I can only regret, since the proposal is so distasteful to you, that I made it at all. Forget it—and me—and my folly in meeting you here, and good-night."

She turns to go, but before she has moved half a dozen steps he is by her side, detaining her once more.

"Angry, Beauty? and with me? What nonsense! You couldn't be, you know, if you tried. Are you really going to leave me, 'Rilla?" He is holding both her hands once more. "Not at least until you tell me when and where we are to meet again."

"There shall be no more meetings, Mr. Carew. The friendship you disclaim so disdainfully in the future shall end at once. Good-night."

"And once more—nonsense, Beauty! I decline to meet Mrs. McKelpin, but Cyrilla Hendrick I shall go on meeting, and loving, while she lives. If I may not come here again, will you write to me, at least?"

"Have I not already told you no letter can come into the school that is not opened by Mademoiselle Stephanie? Still——"

" Yes, Beauty—still ? "

" Still I think I can arrange it." Cyrilla has relented by this time. " Helen Herne, one of the day-scholars, will smuggle my letters out, and yours in. She and Sydney Owenson are the only two in the school I would trust. Are you stationed here in Petit St. Jacques for the winter ? "

" No, only temporarily ; our headquarters are Montreal. By-the-by, your home, Miss Dormer's rather, is in Montreal. When you leave school we must manage to meet often. Mean-time, 'Rilla,"—he draws her closer to him in the moonlight— 'promise me this—don't take that oath not to marry me."

The handsome face is very close, very pleading. She loves him, and the last shadow of anger vanishes from hers like a cloud, and a smile, Cyrilla's own, too, rare and most radiant smile, lights it up.

" I think I may safely promise that much, Fred—yes."

" And you won't marry McKelpin—confound him !—without letting me know ? "

She laughs, and promises this too. They are out in the open air by this time—in broad, chill, dazzlingly white, midnight moonlight. St. James-the-Less chimes out sonorously, on the still frosty air, twelve.

" Good Heaven, Fred, midnight ! This is awful ! Let me go. No, not another second ! Good-night, good-night ! "

She tears herself from him, and swings nimbly into her friend, the hemlock-tree. He stands and watches her clambering up, hand over hand, sees her reach the lead water-pipe and mount upon the sill of the window. She waves her hand to him, and he turns to depart. With that parting smile still on her face she vaults into the room, and finds herself face to face with— Mademoiselle Stephanie and Miss Jones !

CHAPTER VIII.

" ALL IS LOST BUT HONOR."

RED CAREW'S fatal laugh had done it all—reached Miss Jones's slumbering ear, and aroused her from her vestal dreams. Cyrilla had said Miss Jones slept with one eye open ; she might have added, truthfully, with one ear also. And, as it chanced, on this particular night her slumbers were lighter even than usual.

For nearly an hour after quitting the pupils' rooms with their lamps, she had sat at the window—a very unusual thing with Miss Jones—and gazed sentimentally out at the moonlight. She was nine and twenty, as has been said, and in all these nine and twenty years no man had ever paid her as much attention as Mr. Carew had paid her to-night. A delicious trance wrapped Miss Jones. What if a brilliant match were yet in store for her!—on this side of forty all things seem possible. Mr. Carew had committed himself in no way, certainly ; but he had given her looks, and there had been tones and words that made her unappropriated heart throb with rapture. What a triumph it had been over her refractory, her supercilious pupil, Cyrilla Hendrick ! He had hinted at meeting her again—inquired, with seeming carelessness, her hours for visiting the town, the church she attended on Sunday, and at parting he had squeezed, absolutely squeezed, her hand. No doubt he would be in waiting on Sunday to attend her home after worship. How very handsome and *distingué* he was—heir to a title, it might be—many of these officers were. A vision of rosy brightness—orange blossoms, Honiton lace, half-a-dozen of the girls for bridesmaids—rose before her enraptured vision, and in the midst of it a loud sneeze warned Miss Jones that she was sitting by the open window in a draught, and that the probable result of her roseate visions would be a bad cold in the head to-morrow. Upon this Miss Jones went to bed.

For hygienic reasons, she invariably left her window open, winter and summer. She had dropped into a slight beauty sleep, when suddenly there came to her ear the decided sound of a hearty laugh. In one second of time Miss Jones was sitting bolt upright in bed, broad awake, and listening intently. Yes, there it was again—a laugh, a *man's* laugh, and in the garden. Burglars !—that was her first thought. But no ; burglars do not, as a rule, give way to fits of merriment over their work. She slipped from her bed, went to the window, and strained sight and hearing to discover the cause. There was nothing to see but the broad sheets of moonlight pouring down upon everything ; but, yes, distinctly Miss Jones could hear, in that profound frosty silence, the subdued murmur of voices under the trees.

Was it inspiration—the inspiration of hatred, the inspiration of hope—that made her mind leap to Cyrilla Hendrick ? Without waiting to reason out the impulse that prompted her, she ran from her room, down the stairs ' and noiselessly into

that of her foe.   Yes, she was right !   There stood the bed un-
occupied, the window wide open, the girl gone.   On *her* bed,
'Toinette lay fast asleep ; she, then, was not Cyrilla's companion !   Who could be ?   Even more distinctly than up-stairs
Miss Jones could hear the murmured talk here—one voice, she
could have sworn, the voice of a man.

In an instant her resolution was taken ; in another she had
acted upon it, and was rapping at the sleeping-room of Mademoiselle Stephanie.   At last her time had come.   The prize
pupil of the school, her arch-enemy, was in her power.   Mademoiselle Chateauroy, in a white dressing-gown, opened the
door, and stared in bewilderment at her second English teacher.
People talking and laughing in the grounds !   Miss Hendrick
not in her room !   *Mon Dieu !* what did Miss Jones mean?

"There is not a second to lose, mademoiselle," Miss Jones
feverishly cried, " if we wish to see who the man is !   It wants
but five minutes of twelve—she surely will not stay much
longer.   Come ! come at once !"

She took Mademoiselle Chateauroy's hand, and fairly forced
her along the chill passage to Cyrilla's room.   They were not
a second too soon.   As they took their places at the window,
the two culprits stepped out from under the tamaracs into the
full light of the moon.   The gentleman's arm affectionately encircled his companion's waist.

"*Mon Dieu !*" mademoiselle gasped.

Miss Jones gave one faint gasp also, for in the brilliant light
of the moon she recognized at first glance her false, her recreant
admirer, Mr. Carew.   It all flashed upon her—it had all been a
blind to lead her off the scent, his attentions to herself.   He
and Cyrilla Hendrick had planned this meeting.   No doubt
they had laughed together over *her* gullibility there under the
trees.   She set her teeth with a snap of rage and fury at the
thought.

"You have had your laugh, my lady, with your lover," she
thought, with a vicious glare ; "it is my turn now, and those
laugh best who laugh last."

Then came that hurried parting embrace, extorting another
horrified "*Mon Dieu*" from mademoiselle.   Then Cyrilla was
mounting the tree, then the lead pipe, then, kissing her hand to
her lover, leaped into the room and stood before them !

.   .   .   .

Imagine that tableau !   Dead silence for the space of one
minute, during which judge, accuser, and criminal stand face to

face. One faint cry of sheer surprise Cyrilla had given, then as her eyes fell on the intolerably exultant face of Miss Jones, her haughty head went up, her daring, resolute spirit asserted itself, and she faced them boldly. There was fearless blood in the girl's veins—bad blood, beyond all doubt, but pluck invincible. For her this discovery meant ruin—utter, irretrievable ruin—but since it had come there was nothing for it, with · Mary Jane Jones looking on particularly, but to face it without flinching.

"Come with me, Miss Hendrick," Mademoiselle Stephanie coldly began. "You also, Miss Jones."

She led the way back to her own room, where a lamp burned and a dull red glimmer of fire yet glowed. Spectral and ghostly the two teachers looked in their long night-robes, and a faint smile flitted over Cyrilla's face as she followed. Mademoiselle closed the door carefully, and then confronted the culprit.

"Now for it!" Cyrilla thought. "Good Heaven! what an unlucky wretch I am! Nothing can save me now."

"Well, Miss Hendrick," Mademoiselle Chateauroy began, in that cold, level voice of intense displeasure, "what have you to say? I presume you have some explanation to give of to-night's most extraordinary conduct."

"A very simple explanation, mademoiselle," Cyrilla answered. "I thank you for letting me make it. Nothing can wholly excuse a pupil keeping an assignation with a gentleman in the school-grounds by night—of that I am aware—but at least my motive may partly. I have heard no news of my father for over a year; I went to hear news of him to-night. This evening, at Mrs. Delamere's, I met a gentleman whom I have known from childhood—who has been as a brother to me since my earliest recollection—who was a daily visitor at my father's house in London. I was naturally anxious for news, of papa in particular, and would have received it then and there but for Miss Jones's interference. She would not allow us to exchange a word—she was resolute to make me leave him, and I obeyed. What followed Miss Jones knows. He and I did not exchange another word, but before he left me he told me he had an important, a *most* important message to deliver from my father, and was determined to deliver it to-night. I refused to meet him at first, but when I remembered it was my only chance of hearing from poor papa, that no letters were allowed to come to me, I consented. He came over the wall, and I descended, remained with him a few minutes, and returned. That is the whole story."

She could see the sneering scorn and unbelief on Miss Jones's face, the cold, intense anger deepening upon Mademoiselle Stephanie's. Neither of them believed a word she had said.

" Does 'Toinette know ? " Mademoiselle Chateauroy asked.

" No, mademoiselle. 'Toinette was asleep long before I went."

" Of that at least I am glad. It is sufficiently bad to have a pupil in my school capable of so shameful and evil an act, without knowing that she has corrupted the minds of other and innocent girls. For three and twenty years, Miss Hendrick, I have been preceptress of this school, and in all that time no breath of scandal has touched it. Wild pupils, refractory pupils, disobedient pupils, I have had many—a pupil capable of stealing from her chambers at midnight to meet a young man in the grounds I have never had before. I pray the *bon Dieu* I never may have again."

A color, like a tongue of flame, leaped for a moment into each of Cyrilla Hendrick's dark cheeks. Something in mademoiselle's simple, coldly-spoken words made her feel for the first time how shameful, how unmaidenly her escapade had been. Up to the present she had regarded it as rather a good joke—a thing to tell and laugh at. A sense of stinging shame filled her now—a sense of rage with it, at these women who made her feel it. All that was worst in the girl arose—her eyes flashed, her handsome lips set themselves in sullen wrath.

" I thank Heaven, and I thank my very good friend, Miss Jones," pursued mademoiselle, " that this wicked thing has been brought to light so soon. So soon ! *Mon Dieu*, who is to tell me it has not been done again and again ? "

Once more the black eyes flashed, but with her arms folded Cyrilla stood sullenly silent now. The worst had come ; the very worst that could ever happen. Miss Dormer would hear all, she would be expelled the school, expelled Miss Dormer's house—her last chance of being Miss Dormer's heiress was at an end. Ruin had come, absolute ruin, and nothing she could do or say would avert it now. The look that came over the face of the girl of nineteen showed for the first time the strong capabilities of evil within her.

" What was the name of this young man you met, Miss Hendrick ? " mademoiselle went on.

Cyrilla lifted her darkly angry eyes.

" I have given you an explanation of my conduct, mademoiselle, and you refuse to believe it. I decline to answer any further questions."

"His name was Mr. Carew," said Miss Jones, opening her lips for the time. "Lieutenant Frederic Carew of the —— Fusiliers."

She gave the information with unction, her exultant eyes upon Cyrilla's face. Once more the dark eyes lifted and looked at her—a look not good to see.

"This is your hour, Miss Jones," that darkly ominous glance said. "Mine shall come."

Mademoiselle Stephanie made a careful note of the name.

"That will do, Miss Jones. I will not detain you from your needful rest longer. Of course it is unnecessary to caution you to maintain strictest silence concerning this disgraceful discovery. Not for worlds must a whisper of the truth get abroad or reach the other young ladies. Miss Hendrick will remain in this room a close prisoner until she quits the *pensionnat* forever. She has been, not the pupil I have best loved, but the pupil I have most been proud of. It gives me a pang, I cannot describe how great, to lose her, and thus. I am sorry for my own sake, and sorrier for hers. Miss Dormer told me to watch her closely, for she was not as other girls, and for three years I have. For three years she has offended in no way, and now, to end like this!"

"Then let my three years' good conduct plead for me, mademoiselle," Cyrilla said, boldly. "It is my first offence—it shall be my last. Say nothing to any one ; let me remain until Christmas—not three months now—and quit the school, as I have lived in it, with honor."

But mademoiselle shook her head, sorrowfully, yet inexorably.

"Impossible, Miss Hendrick. You have been guilty of an offence for which expulsion can be the only punishment. How could I answer to Heaven and the mothers of my pupils for the guilt of allowing any one capable of such a crime to mingle with them and deprave them ?"

"'Guilt ! deprave !' You use strong language, mademoiselle. The gentleman I met has been all his life as my brother—I met him to hear news of my father, which I can hear in no other way. And that is a crime !"

"A crime against obedience, against all delicacy and maidenly modesty. But it has been done, and no talking will undo it. Go to your room, Miss Jones, and be silent. You, Miss Hendrick, shall remain with me. To-morrow I will write to your aunt, telling her all.   Until her answer arrives you will remain under lock and key here."

"And the sentence of the court is that you be taken hence to the place of execution, and that there you be hanged by the neck until you are dead."

The grim words flashed through Cyrilla's mind.   She had read them often, and wondered how the miserable, cowering criminal in the dock must feel.   She could imagine now. She did not cower—outwardly she listened unmoved, with a hardihood that was to mademoiselle proof of deepest guilt; but inwardly—"all within was black as night."

Miss Jones, that covert smile still on her face, left the room. Mademoiselle Stephanie pulled out that transparent deception, a sofa-bed, amply furnished with pillows and quilts.   Many pupils had slept out their week of solitary confinement on this prison bed, but never so deeply dyed a criminal before.

"You will undress and sleep here, Miss Hendrick," mademoiselle said; "but first kneel down and ask pardon of *le bon Dieu* for the sin you have done."

"I have committed no sin—I will thank you not to say so, mademoiselle," Cyrilla flashed forth at last.   "Make mountains out of mole-hills if you like, but don't expect me to call them mountains too.   Write to my aunt, expel me when you please, but meantime don't insult me."

And then Cyrilla, flinging her clothes in a heap on the nearest chair, got into the sofa-bed and turned her face sullenly to the wall.

"There goes my last hope," she thought, "thanks to my horrible temper.   I *might* have softened her to-morrow—now there isn't a chance.   Like Francis the First, at Pavia, 'all is lost but honor!'"

CHAPTER IX.

"A TEMPEST IN A TEAPOT."

THE dim firelight flickered and fell, one by one the cinders dropped softly through the bars, one by one the slow moments ticked off on the old-fashioend chimney-piece clock.   Outside, the autumnal wind sighed around the gables, and moaned and whistled through the pines and tamaracs. Broad bars of luminous moonlight stole in through the closed jalousies, and lay broad and bright on the faded carpet. Wiry and long drawn out, Mademoiselle Stephanie's small, treble snore told that a good conscience and a light supper are soporific in their tendency, and that she, at least, was "o'er all the ills of life victorious." And Cyrilla Hendrick lay broad awake, seeing and hearing it all, and thinking of the sudden crash that had toppled down her whole fairy fortune.

Impossible to sleep. She got up softly, wrapped a shawl around her, went to the window, opened one of the shutters, and sat moodily down. In sheets of yellow light, the moonsteeped fields and forest, the Rue St. Dominique wound along like a belt of silver ribbon, no living thing to be seen, no earthly sound to be heard beside the desolate soughing of the October wind. And, sitting there, Cyrilla looked her prospects straight in the face.

To-morrow morning Mademoiselle Stephanie would write a detailed account of her wrong doing to Miss Dormer, giving Mr. Carew's name, as a matter of course. She could picture the rage, the amaze, the fury of the passionate, tyrannical old woman, as she glared over the letter. Other, and even more grievous faults Miss Dormer might condone—this, never. She would be sent for in hot haste—she would be expelled the school—her lip curled scornfully at the thought, for *that* her bold, resolute spirit cared nothing—and she would return in dire disgrace to Dormer Lodge. And then the scene that would ensue! Miss Dormer glaring upon her with eyes of fire, and tongue like a two-edged sword. "My niece Cyrilla comes of a bad stock!" over and over again the old maid had hissed out her prediction; "and mark my words, my niece Cyrilla will come to no good end!"

The end had come sooner than even Miss Dormer had expected.

Well, the first fury, the first tongue-lashing over, Aunt Dormer would send her back, penniless as she came, to her father. No splendid fortune, hoarded for a quarter of a century, for her; no "rich and respectable" Mr. McKelpin to take her to wife. Back again to the nomadic tribes of Bohemia, to the tents and impoverished dwellers in the realm of vagabondia! As vividly as a painting it all arose before her—her father's dirty, dreary, slipshod lodgings in some dismal back street of Boulogne-sur-Mer. She could see him in tattered dressing-gown, haggard and un-

4

shorn, sitting up the night long with kindred spirits over the
greasy pack of cards, fleecing some, and being fleeced by others.
The rickety furniture, the three stuffy little rooms, the air perfumed with tobacco and brandy and water, herself draggled
and unkempt, insulted by insolent love-making, spoken of with
coarse and jeering sneers.   Oh! she knew it all so well—and
her hands clenched, and a suffocating feeling of pain and shame
rose in her throat and nearly choked her.

"No," she thought, passionately, "death sooner than that!
Oh, what a fool I have been this night! to risk so much to
gain so little."

A feeling of hot swift wrath arose within her against Fred
Carew.

"My father ruined the life of your aunt.   I will never ruin
yours."   That, or something like it, he had said to her, and now
—all unconsciously it is true—the ruin of all her prospects had
come, and through him.

"I will never go back to my father," she thought again, this
time with sullen resolution.   "No fate that can befall me here
will be worse than the fate that awaits me with him.   America
is wide; it will go hard with me if I cannot carve out a destiny
for myself."

What should she do?   No one knew better than Cyrilla Hendrick the futility of crying over spilt milk.   What was done, was
done—no repentance could undo it.   No use weeping one's
eyes red over the inevitable past; much better and wiser to turn
one's thoughts to the future.   She would be expelled the school;
she would be turned out of doors by her aunt, all for a school-
girl escapade, indecorous, perhaps, but no heinous crime, surely.
Was she to yield to Fate, and meekly submit to the disgrace
they would put upon her?   Not she!   Her chin arose an inch
at the thought, sitting there alone—her handsome, resolute lips
set themselves in a tight, determined line.   She would take her
life in her own keeping, away from them all.   She would never
return to her expatriated father and his disreputable associates.
"The world was all before her where to choose,"—what should
that choice be?   Two alternatives lay before her.   She might
go to Fred Carew, tell him all, and at the very earliest possible
moment after the revelation she knew he would make her his
wife.   His wife—and she must march with the regiment; both
must live on seven-and-sixpence a day, just enough, as Fred
now said, to keep him in bouquets and kid gloves.   They must
live in dingy lodgings, and appeal humbly in all extremity to the

Right Hon. the Earl of Dunraith for help. Life wou'd drag
on an excessively shabby and out-at-elbows story indeed ; and
Love, in the natural order of things, would fly out the door as
Poverty stalked in at the window. A shudder ran through her.
No, no ! Freddy had acted badly in getting her into this scrape,
but she would not wreak life-long vengeance upon him by making him marry her and bringing him to this deplorable pass.

"Not that he would think it deplorable, poor little dear !"
Cyrilla thought, compassionately. " A better fellow than little
Fred doesn't breathe, and he would share his last crust with
me, and let me henpeck him all his life, and look at me with
tears of entreaty in his blue eyes, and be utterly and speech-
lessly wretched. But I would be a brute to do it. No, I must
run away from Fred, and see him no more. If I did, he would
force me into marrying him, and that way madness lies ! "

It will be seen that Miss Hendrick was a young lady of wisdom beyond her years, and capable of projecting herself into
the future. With a sigh, she dismissed the thought of running
away with Freddy. It would be very nice—very nice, indeed,
to be Fred Carew's wife ; to be able to pet him and tyrannize
over him alternately all one's life—oh ! what fate so desirable ?
But it was not to be. Then what remained ?

In one moment she had answered that question—solved the
enigma. She would go on the stage. Next to being a *grande
dame*, a wealthy leader of fashion, it had always been her ambition to be an actress. And Cyrilla thought of the life not as
one without knowledge. Theatrical people had formed the
staple of her acquaintances—gentlemen with close-cropped
heads and purple chins, deep, bass voices and glaring eyes—
ladies, slangy as to conversation, loud as to dress, audacious
as to manners, and painted as to faces. All the drudgery, all
the heart-burnings, all the petty squabbles and jealousies, all the
dangers of the life she saw clearly. But her bold spirit quailed
not. She had performed repeatedly in private theatricals, she
had even the year before coming to Canada " gone on " in one
of the Strand houses in the very droll extravaganza of "Alad-
din ; or, The Wonderful Scamp." No wonder her performance
in these mild-drawn *pensionnat* dialogues was strong meat to
milk and water. Yes, Cyrilla decided she would go on the
stage. She would leave her aunt's house for New York, and
in that great city it would go hard with her if with her handsome
face, her fine figure, her clever brain, she could not carve out a
bright destiny for herself. Vain, she was not ; but she knew to

the uttermost iota the market value of her black eyes, her long, waving black hair, her dark, high-bred face, her tall, supple form, her thorough knowledge of French and German, her rich contralto voice. Each one was a stepping-stone to future fame and fortune. And, as she thought it, worn out by watching and her unusual vigil, her head fell forward on the window-sill, and she dropped asleep.

It was six by the little chimney clock when the harsh, dissonant ringing of a bell awoke simultaneously all the inmates of the *pensionnat.* It aroused Mademoiselle Stephanie among the rest. The morning had broken in true November dreariness, in dashing rain and whistling wind, in bleakness and chill.

With a yawn Mademoiselle Stephanie sat up in bed, shivering and blue, and the first object upon which her sleepy eyes rested was the drooping form of her prisoner by the window, in sleep so deep that even the clanging of the bell had failed to arouse her. She had evidently sat there all night, cried herself to sleep probably, and a pang of pity touched mademoiselle's kindly old French heart. But it would not do to show it. Miss Hendrick had sinned, and Miss Hendrick, by the inevitable laws of nature and grace, must suffer. She dressed herself shiveringly, went over, and laid her hand lightly on the sleeper's shoulder.

"My child," she said, "wake up. You'll get your death of cold sitting here."

Cyrilla lifted her head, looking in the dim gray morning light pallid and wretched, and took in the situation at a glance.

"My death of cold?" she repeated, bitterly. "No such luck, mademoiselle. It is almost a pity I do not; it would be infinitely better for me than what is to come."

She stood up as she spoke, twisting her profuse dishevelled black hair around her head, looking like the Tragic Muse, and fully prepared to do any amount of melodrama for ma'amselle's benefit. Ma'amselle looked at her in distrust and displeasure.

"Do you know what you are saying, Mees Hendrick? It would be better for you to be dead than dismissed this school, —is that what you mean?"

"Not exactly. If nothing worse than being dismissed this school were to befall me," answered Cyrilla, with an inflection of contempt she could not suppress, "I think I could survive it. No, ma'amselle, much worse than that will follow."

"I do not understand, Mees Hendrick," says ma'amselle, stiffly.

"It means ruin, then!" cries Cyrilla, her eyes flashing, her

tone one that would have been good for three rounds from pi'
and gallery—"utter, life-long ruin ! Listen, ma'amselle, and I
will tell you this morning what I would have died sooner than
tell last night in the presence of that spy and informer, Miss
Jones ! Oh, yes ! ma'amselle, I will call her so. What does it
matter what I say, since I shall be turned ignominiously out in a
day or two? Even the murderer can say his say out when he
stands on the gallows !"

Ma'amselle stood perfectly transfixed, while Cyrilla, with impassioned eloquence, poured into her ears the story of Miss
Dormer's hatred of all who bore the name of Carew. How she
had wished her to swear never to see him or speak to him while
she lived ; how good he had been to her and her father in the
days gone by, what a pure brotherly and sisterly affection there
was between them, how absolutely ignorant she had been of
his coming to Canada, how petrified with astonishment at sigh*
of him, how he had striven to tell her news of her father, how
Miss Jones had interfered and prevented it, how in desperation
he had implored her to grant him ten minutes' interview in the
grounds, and how, in very despair at being unable to meet him
in any other way, or even write to him, she had consented. In
the torrent of Cyrilla's eloquence mademoiselle was absolutely
bewildered and carried away. How was the little simple-minded
schoolmistress to estimate the dramatic capabilities of her very
clever pupil ? For the girl herself it was half acting, half earnest.
She felt reckless this morning—equal to either fate. After all,
who could tell ? The glittering, gas-lit life of the stage, with its
music, its plaudits, its flowers, its rows of eager, admiring faces,
might be hard to win, but, once won, would it not be infinitely
preferable to the deathly dulness of existence dragged out as
the wife of the rich and respectable Mr. Donald McKelpin?
And if her dark, bold .eyes and gypsy face really brought her
money and fame, why, then, she might send for Freddy and
marry him, and "live happy ever after."

Mademoiselle Stephanie stood listening to Miss Hendrick's
vehement outburst with knitted brows and pursed-up lips, utterly
perplexed and at a loss. A great offence had been done, un-
paralleled in the annals of the *pensionnat*, an offence for which
immediate expulsion, by every law of right and morality, should
be the penalty. But if that expulsion was to ruin this young
girl for life, and it was her first offence, why, then, one must
hesitate. She had ever been such a credit to them all, and
really her story sounded plausible, and—mademoiselle was

staggered, divided, between pity and duty—completely at a loss.

"You are quite sure your aunt will deal with you in this severe fashion," she asked, her brows bent. "You are not deceiving me, Miss Hendrick?"

"I am not in the habit of stating falsehoods, mademoiselle," Cyrilla answered, majestically.

"And she will send you in disgrace back to your father?"

"She will try, mademoiselle, but I will not go. No! papa is poor enough without an additional drag upon him. I will never go back to be that drag."

"What, then, will you do?"

"Pardon, mademoiselle! I decline to answer.   Once I am expelled this school your right to question me ends."

"But I have not expelled you yet, and I demand an answer, Mees Hendrick," cried mademoiselle, her little brown eyes flashing.

Cyrilla laughed after a reckless fashion.

"I might marry the gentleman I met in the grounds. After compromising me in the way he has done it is the least reparation he could make, and I am sure he would if I asked him." Here catching sight of mademoiselle's face of horror and incredulity, Cyrilla nearly broke down.   "But you need not fear ; I shall not ask him. I shall go to New York and go on the stage."

Mademoiselle Chateauroy's eyes had been gradually dilating as she listened.   At these last awful words a sort of shriek burst from her lips :

"Oh, *mon Dieu !* hear her ! go on the *stage !*" cried little mademoiselle in piercing accents, and precisely the same tone as though her abandoned pupil had said, 'I will go to perdition !' "Mees Hendrick, do I hear you aright ?   Did you say the stage ?"

"I said the stage, mademoiselle," Cyrilla repeated, imperturbably—" no other life is open to me, and for the stage alone am I qualified.   When my aunt turns me from her doors I will go direct to New York—to some theatre there—an obscure one, I fear, it must be at first—and in that great city, in the theatrical profession, make my living. I can dance, I can sing. I have perfect health, my share of good looks, and no end to what our cousins across the border call 'cheek.' I shall succeed—it is only a question of time.   And when I am a rich and popular actress, Mademoiselle Stephanie, I shall one day return here and thank you for having turned me out !"

For a moment mademoiselle stood speechless, rooted to the ground by the matchless audacity of this reply, and once more Cyrilla's gravity nearly gave way as she looked in her face. Then, without a word, with horror in her eyes, she hastily walked out of the room, locking the door after her, and stood panting on the other side.

"I must speak to Jeanne," she gasped. "Oh, *mon Dieu!* who would dream of the evil spirit that possesses that child?"

Breakfast was brought to Miss Hendrick in the solitude of her prison by Mademoiselle Jeanne herself, who also made a fire. Miss Hendrick partook of that meal with the excellent appetite of a hearty school-girl, Mademoiselle Jeanne eyeing her in terror and askance.

How the matter leaked out it seemed impossible to tell, but leak out it did; perhaps Miss Jones's exultaion over her enemy's downfall got the better of her discretion, but as the four and thirty boarders sat down to their matutinal coffee and "*pistolets*" it was darkly whispered about that some direful fate had befallen Cyrilla Hendrick. In the darkness of the night she had committed some fearful misdemeanor, some "deed without a name," and was under lock and key down in Mademoiselle Stephanie's chamber.

Saturday in the school was a half-holiday. In the forenoon the girls wrote German exercises and looked over Monday's lessons. All morning the shadow of mystery and suspicion hung over the class-room—girls whispered surreptitiously behind big books. What had Cy Hendrick done? What was to be her punishment? Four and thirty young ladies were on the *qui vive*, some secretly rejoicing, some simply curious, two or three slightly regretful—for Miss Hendrick was by no means popular—and one, one only, really sorry and anxious—Sydney Owenson.

"What on earth can Cy have done?" Sydney thought, perplexedly. "We parted all right last evening, and this morning we wake and find her imprisoned and disgraced for the first time in three years. I wish I understood. Miss Jones looks compendiums—*she* knows. I'll ask her after class."

Lessons and exercises ended. At twelve the welcome bell rang announcing that studies were over for the week, and the students free to rush out pellmell and make day hideous with their uproar. Sydney alone lingered, going up to Miss Jones, whose duty it was to remain behind, overlook desks, and put the class-room generally in order.

"Miss Jones," she asked, "what has Cyrilla Hendrick done?"

If Miss Jones had a friend in all the school, that friend was Miss Owenson. Miss Owenson, besides being an heiress, besides dressing better and giving away more presents than any other half-dozen pupils together, was so sweet of temper, so courteous of manner, so kindly of heart, so gentle of tongue, so gracefully and promptly obedient, that she won hearts as by magic. A certain innate nobility of character made her ever ready to take the side of the weaker and the oppressed. Miss Jones owed her deliverance from many a small tyranny to Sydney Owenson's pleading. Now Miss Jones pursed up her lips, and her eyes snapped maliciously.

"Who says Miss Hendrick has done anything?" she asked.

"Oh, nonsense! We all know she has, and that she is in punishment down in Mademoiselle Stephanie's room. 'Toinette says she wasn't in her bed all night. Now, Miss Jones, what is it all about?"

"I regret that it is impossible for me to inform you, Miss Owenson. Any confidence Mademoiselle Stephanie may repose in me I consider inviolable. My lips are sealed."

Sydney shrugged her shoulders and turned away.

"I shall find out for all that. It is very odd, I must say. How *could* Cy have got into any trouble after going to her room last night?"

She ran down stairs and straight to the *chambre à coucher* of Mlle. Stephanie. She would find the door locked, no doubt, but at least she could talk through the key-hole. She rapped softly.

"It is I, Cy— Sydney," she whispered; "come to the door and speak to me."

"Come in, Syd," the clear voice of Cyrilla answered. "The door is unlocked. Pull the bobbin and the latch will go up."

Sydney opened the door and entered. At the window Cyrilla sat alone, calmly perusing that exciting work of fiction, Le Brun's *Télémaque.*

"I thought you were locked in! I thought you were in punishment!" Sydney said, bewildered.

"So I am," Cyrilla answered, laughing; "but I so flustered poor little Mademoiselle Jeanne when she brought me my breakfast by my dreadful talk about being an actress, that she went out 'all of a tremble,' as the old ladies say, and forgot to lock the door. Mlle. Stephanie I haven't seen since she got up this

morning. I daresay she has improved the raining hours in com-
posing a letter to Aunt Phil, painting my guilt as blackly as the
best black ink will do it. She will have a fit if she finds you
here in my company—the whitest of all her lambs side by side
with her one black sheep."

"Nonsense, Cy. What on earth have you done ? "

"Has it leaked out, then ? 'Ill news flies apace.' Has Miss
Jones told ? "

"Ah, Miss Jones *is* at the bottom of the mischief. My prophetic soul told me so, she looked so quietly exultant. You
didn't try to murder her last night in her sleep I hope, Cyrilla."

"Not exactly. If ever I get a chance I will, though. I owe
Miss Jones a long debt of small spites, and if ever I get a
chance I'll pay it off. What did I do? Why, I stole out of
my room last night at midnight to meet Fred Carew."

"Cyrilla !" Cyrilla laughed.

"My dear Syd, if I *had* assassinated Miss Jones last night in
her vestal slumber you couldn't look more horror-stricken !
Is it such an awful crime, then ? My moral perceptions must be
blunt—for the life of me I can't see the enormity of it. Look
here, I'll tell you all about it."

And then Miss Hendrick, with the utmost *sang froid*, poured
into Miss Owenson's ear the tale of last night's misdoing.

"If the man had been any other man on earth than poor
Freddy," pursued Miss Hendrick, "the matter wouldn't amount
to much after all. Expulsion from school I don't mind a pin's
point. I leave at Christmas in any case, and a shrill scolding
once a day from Aunt Phil until the day I married her pet
Scotchman would be the sole penalty. But now it means ruin.
Aunt Phil will turn me out—oh, yes, she will, Syd, as surely as
we both sit here. No prospective fortune, no Mr. McKelpin'tc
make me the happiest of women, no leading the society of
Montreal, no flirtation with Freddy, nothing but go forth, like
Jack in the fairy tales, and seek my fortune. Jack always
found his fortune, however, and so shall I."

"But, Cyrilla, good gracious ! this is awful. Do you mean
to say your aunt will really turn you out ? "

"Really, Syd, really—really. And, after all, one can't much
blame her, poor old soul. Last night I rather dreaded my fate ;
to-day I don't seem greatly to mind. After all, if the worst
comes to the worst, I can always make my own living."

"As an actress? Never, Cy. If the worst does come, you
shall make your home with me, sooner than that. Not a word,

4*

Cyrilla, I insist upon it. Oh, darling, think how nice it will be, papa and mamma, and Bertie and you, all in the same house ! "

Cyrilla laughed.

"And Bertie wishing me at Jericho every hour of the day. And papa and mamma, pinks of propriety, both looking at me askance, a girl expelled her school and turned out doors by her aunt. Oh, no, Syd ; you're the best and dearest of friends, bu· your scheme won't work. I shall go on the stage, as I say The dream of my life has ever been to be a popular actress, and the first time you and Bertie visit New York you will come and see me play."

"And Freddy ? "

"When I am rich enough I shall marry Freddy. Poor fellow ! how sorry he will be when he hears this. It is all the fault of that detestable Mary Jane Jones. If she had not in-terfered at Mrs. Delamere's, he would have said all he had to say there, and no more about it. It is her hour of triumph now, but if mine ever comes——"

"Enough of this, young ladies ! " interrupted the shrill voice of Mademoiselle Stephanie, entering hastily. "I have over-heard every word. Mees Owenson, why do I find you here ? "

In her hand Mademoiselle Stephanie held a letter addressed in most legible writing to Miss Phillis Dormer, Montreal. It was Cyrilla's sentence of doom. Sydney started up, turning pale and clasping her hands.

"Oh, mademoiselle, pray—pray, don't send that letter. You don't know how her aunt hates Mr. Carew—how implacable she is when offended. You will ruin all Cyrilla's prospects for life. It is her first offence. She has always been so good— you have always been so proud of her. She has been such a credit to the school. And she will never, never, *never* do so again. Oh, ma'amselle—dear, kind Ma'amselle Stephanie ! don't send that letter."

Tears stood big and bright in Sydney's beseeching eyes, as she stood with clasped, pleading hands before the preceptress.

"Hush, Sydney ! " Cyrilla interposed, gently ; "it is of no use. Ma'amselle has heard all that before."

"I have pleaded for Mees Hendrick," ma'amselle said, look-ing troubled ; "I have begged the good aunt to forgive her this one time."

Cyrilla smiled—serenely reckless.

"You don't know Miss Dormer, ma'amselle. If an angel came down to plead for me, she would not forgive this. Send your letter—what does it signify? I will never give her the chance to turn me out. I will go straight from this school to New York."

"You hear that, ma'amselle?" Sydney cried. "You will drive her to desperation. Do not—do not send that letter! She is sorry—she will never offend again. Oh, ma'amselle! listen to me. I am going away—you always said you liked me. Grant me, then, this parting favor. It is the first—it will be the last I shall ever ask!"

She twined her pearl-white arms about little ma'amselle's saffron neck and kissed her. And wavering, as she had been since morning, ma'amselle's resolution wholly gave way before that caress. She kissed Sydney's sweet, tear-wet face, and then deliberately tore her letter through the middle.

"It shall be as you say, *petite*. Ah! *le bon Dieu* has given you so good a heart. For your sake, and if Mees Hendrick will bind herself to repeat the offence no more, her punishment shall end here."

Cyrilla drew a long breath of relief. There had been a hard fight for it, but the day was won.

"Thank you, mademoiselle," she said. "I promise indeed with all my heart. Sydney, I owe this to you. I cannot thank you, but I feel——"

Sydney closed her lips with a jubilant little kiss.

"All right, Cy—never mind how you feel. I knew ma'amselle was too good to do it. And oh! ma'amselle, please make Miss Jones hold her tongue. She hates Cyrilla, and will hurt her if she can."

"I will speak to Mees Jones. You may send her to me at once. Go now, young ladies, and let this be the very last time, Mees Hendrick, I shall ever have to reprimand you."

The girls bowed and departed. Cyrilla broke into a soft laugh.

"What a tragic scene! 'Go, sin no more!' *That* quicksand is tided over safely, thanks to you, Syd; but I have the strongest internal conviction that one day or other I shall get into some horrible scrape through Fred Carew."

CHAPTER X.

THE LAST NIGHT.

T is raining still, and raining heavily; a Novembet gale surging through the trees of the play-ground, sending the rain in wild white sheets before it. No out-door romp for the Chateauroy *pensionnaires* to-day. They are congregated in the barn, a large and lofty building, and " Fèrre l'Hermite " is tumultuously beginning as Sydney and Cyrilla appear. At the sight of the latter, a whoop of surprise goes up, and Miss Jones, standing absently looking out at the storm, turns round, and sees her enemy—free.

She stands and looks—mute with surprise. There is an audacious smile, as usual, on Miss Hendrick's dark face, an audacious laugh in her black eyes. She quits Sydney and goes straight up to Miss Jones.

"You are to go to Mademoiselle Stephanie's room at once, Miss Jones," she says, with a most exasperating smile ; " I think she has a word of warning for you."

Miss Jones makes no retort, for the excellent reason that she has none ready. There is a pause of three seconds, perhaps, and they look each other straight in the eyes. It is to be a duel *à la mort* between them henceforth—and both know it. Then, still in silence, Miss Jones turns, quits the play-ground, and reports herself at headquarters.

Cyrilla is surrounded, besieged with questions, but she shakes them off, and orders them imperiously about their business.

Since she first entered the school she has been queen-regnant —queen-regnant she will be to the end. She joins as noisily as the smallest girl there in the game, her piercingly sweet voice rising in the monotonous chant high above all the rest. So Miss Jones finds her upon her return. The interview with mademoiselle has left Miss Jones a trifle paler than her wont, with anger 't may be, but she says not a word as she returns to her former occupation of gazing out at the rain.

The long, wet afternoon passes, night comes, and all retire. Sunday morning breaks, still wet and windy ; there is to be no church-going, greatly to the disappointment of the young ladies. Instead, mademoiselle reads aloud for an hour some book of sermons. They dine at three instead of one, a high festival dinner of roast-beef and plum-pudding. Then the girls are left to themselves, to wander about corridors and passages, visit each other's rooms, gossip, write letters, or read, as they please.

It is Sydney Owenson's last day. To-morrow morning she goes, to be married in a month. Four and thirty girlish bosoms beat with envy at that thought! It it like a fairy tale to them ; nothing of the kind has ever transpired before, nothing else is thought of, or talked of, all day. Sydney moves about among them, in a pretty dress of silk, the famous chain and locket around her neck, her engagement ring sparkling on her finger, a glistening watch at her girdle, all her golden, feathery curls falling over her shoulders—a shining vision. One by one, she visits the girls, sobbing a little sob here and there, and realizing for the first time how fond she is of them all. Cyrilla goes with her ; and so the desolate, lead-colored Sabbath afternoon deepens into night, and it is quite dark when Mademoiselle Jeanne comes up and says Colonel and Mrs. Delamere have called, and are in the parlor waiting to see her.

And, "But no, mademoiselle," Mademoiselle Jeanne says, laying a restraining hand upon Cyrilla's arm, "Mees Hendrick is not to accompany you."

Sydney descends. Firelight and lamplight illumine the parlor and dazzle her for a moment coming out of the dusk. She looks and sees, not alone Colonel and Mrs. Delamere, but that most coolly audacious of young officers, Mr. Fred Carew. Opposite him, her hands folded in her lap, her face like a small chocolate mask, sits Mademoiselle Stephanie.

Sydney gives a little gasp, a little laugh, and a little blush, as she meets his eyes. Then arises Mrs. Delamere with effusion, and Miss Owenson is folded to her brown-silk bosom. She shakes hands with the Colonel and Mr. Carew, and sits demurely down, understanding why Mademoiselle Jeanne had put a summary stop to Cyrilla's accompanying her.

The interview is not long. Mrs. Delamere chats with her in her kind, motherly way. The Colonel booms in occasionally with his ponderous laugh, and Mr. Carew sits and smiles upon her, and looks handsome and well-dressed, and addresses the few pleasant little remarks he does make almost exclusively to mademoiselle. In strong suppressed displeasure mademoiselle responds, mono syllabic responses, and then the call is over, and they are stand- ing up, and Mrs. Delamere, with tears in her eyes, is kissing

Sydney good-bj. Again she shakes hands with the Colonel, then shyly with Mr. Carew, and as he holds her hand for a moment and bows over it, she feels a note suddenly and deftly slipped into it. Her fingers close over it, but she does not look at him ; then they are gone, and she is alone, her heart beating guiltily, with mademoiselle.

"That is the young man, Carew, whom Mees Hendrick met last night, is it not ?" she asks, her little eyes flashing. "Most insolent his coming here. He shall be admitted no more."

Sydney flies off to deliver her note, and finds Cyrilla lingering on the upper landing.

"For you, Cy—from Mr. Carew," she whispers. "Would you believe such effrontery?—he actually came with the Delameres. He slipped this into my hand as he said good-by."

"It would be difficult to say what piece of effrontery Fred Carew would not be capable of. Mademoiselle Stephanie's face must have been a study."

"It was," laughs Sydney ; "he is not to be allowed here again. She was proof against his sweetest smiles and tenderest glances."

Cyrilla reads her note, her face softening, her eyes lighting. It is not long—the pen is by no means mightier than the sword in Mr. Carew's grasp—but it brings an eloquent flush to the girl's dark cheek.

"Poor foolish Freddy," she says with a half laugh, a half sigh. "What nonsense he writes. He goes to Montreal for the winter, and he wants—he actually wants me to marry him as soor as I leave school. 'Something will turn up,' he says, in his absurd way ; 'something always turns up to help virtuous poverty. And if it doesn't, why seven-and-sixpence a day will buy daily bread and beefsteaks, and what more do we want ? Lord Dunraith will send us an odd fifty now and then, and Miss Dormer will come round when there's no help for it. Throw over the soap-and-candle man, Beauty, and let us be a comfoitable couple.' Did you ever hear such idiocy, Syd ? And the best of it is he means every word."

"Is it idiocy?" asks Sydney. "I don't know, but it seems to me that, liking him as you do, it will be something worse than idiocy to marry the soap-and-candle man. I can't understand your loving Mr. Carew and marrying Mr. McKelpin."

"No, I dare say not," Cyrilla answers, calmly ; "but then you see you've been brought up in the lap of luxury, a bloated aristocrat, Syd, while I am a pauper, and have been from birth. If

I married Freddy, I would go a pauper to my grave. There is
no choice. 'Needs must,' saith the proverb, 'when the devil
drives.' I wish—yes, Sydney—with all my heart, I wish I
might marry Fred Carew, but I can't, and there the matter
ends. Don't let us talk about it, it always makes me uncomfortable. Let us talk of *you.* To think that this time to-morrow night you will be hundreds of miles away !"

They are pacing up and down the long, deserted class-room.
The rain has ceased, a few frosty stars glimmer through rifts in
the cloudy sky. Far below, the merry tumult of girlish voices
and laughter comes, far below they can see the lighted passages
and rooms. Outside, the lonesome wind sighs up and down
the deserted Rue St. Dominique.

"Hundreds of miles away !" Sydney echoes, with a sigh.
"Yes."

"You are not sorry, Syd. Honestly now. You are not
sorry to quit this stupid, humdrum school, these noisy, romping girls, the drudgery of endless lessons, for home and freedom,
Bertie Vaughan and bridal blossoms ! Don't say you are, for it
is too much for human credulity to believe."

"Sorry, Cy ? Well, no. I am glad to go home, glad to be
with papa and mamma, and Bertie, of course, but still——"

" But still that good, tender heart of yours, my Sydney, has a
soft spot for 'Frère l'Hermite,' and the Demoiselles Chateauroy,
and even crusty Miss Jones. It speaks well for you, *chérie*, but
is not over-flattering to Mr. Vaughan. You preached of love a
moment ago, yet here you are going to marry a man you don't
care a straw for."

" Don't I ? That is your mistake, Cy. I care whole bundles
of straw for Bertie—haven't I told you so, again and again ? I
like him better than any man I know."

"And you know—how many ? The fat old colonel—one,"
said Miss Hendrick, checking them off on her fingers; " the
fussy old doctor—two ; little old Professor Chapsal—three ;
venerable Jean Baptiste Romain—four ; your papa—five.
That comprises the list, does it not ? And you like him better
than any man you know. Happy Mr. Vaughan !"

" I like him better than any man I ever *saw*, then," cries Sydney, defiantly, "your pretty little lover included. And papa
and mamma like him, and wish me to marry him ; that is sufficient, if there were no other reason. I don't believe in that
mad, selfish sort of passion we read of, where girls are ready
to sacrifice their fathers and mothers, and homes, and soul's

salvatioı for some man who takes their fancy. I hate you when
you are cynical and sarcastic and wordy, Cyrilla. I wish you
would drop it ; it doesn't become you. Leave it for poor,
disappointed, crossed-in-love Miss Dormer."

" Bravo, Syd ? Who'd have thought it ? I begin to have
hopes of you yet. I only trust your Bertie may be worthy of
his sweet little wife. For you *are* a little jewel, Sydney, and
better than you are pretty."

" Oh, nonsense, Cy l Drop that."

" I shall miss you horribly, *chère belle*," Cyrilla goes on, plaintively. "You were the leaven in this dull house that leavened
the whole mass. Still, it's only till Christmas, and then——'
her eyes sparkle in the dusk, she catches her breath, and her
color rises.

" You will go to Montreal, and Freddy will be there. You
will see him surreptitiously, and all the time you will be promising Mr. McKelpin and your aunt to marry him," supplements Miss Owenson, gravely. "Take care, Cyrilla ; that's a
dangerous sort of game, and may end in bringing you to grief."

" Little croaker l the danger of it will be the spice of life.
And, meantime, if your papa writes a nice diplomatic note to
Aunt Phil, and gets her consent, I shall 'haste to the wedding,'
see Master Bertie, and bestow my benediction on your nuptials.
I will never forgive Aunt Dormer if she doesn't let me go."

Arm in arm the two girls pace up and down the long, chill
room, talking eagerly in undertones. In another half hour the
bell for evening prayers rings, and their last *tête-à-tête*, where
they have held so many, is at an end.

" Good-by, old class-room," Sydney said, wistfully. " I have
spent some very jolly days here, after all."

Prayers and pious reading were long on Sunday night ; most
of the girls were yawning audibly, a few were nodding, and one
or two of the most reprobate fast asleep before the close. Then
to their rooms, and silence and darkness brooded over the mini-
ature world of the boarding-school, with its bread-and-butter
hopes and fears, heart-burnings and passions.

Monday morning came—a perfect day, sparkling with frosty
fall sunshine. A buzz of suppressed excitement ran through the
school. A "round-robin " for a half holiday was sent to Mademoiselle Stephanie, and was granted. Breakfast was eaten amid
a gabble of conversation, and as they arose from the table a thrill
ran through all as a hackney-coach drove up to the door. The
messenger for Sydney Owenson had come.

She was dressed in her travelling suit, a pretty "conserve" of gray and blue, with hat and gloves to match. Her trunk stood packed and strapped in the hall. -Mademoiselle Stephanie came herself tremulously to bear the message that Rebecca was waiting, and that Miss Owenson must say good-by at once. There was no time to lose—their train started in less than half an hour. The scene that ensued! who may tell? "Good-by! good-by! good-by!" tears, kisses, promises to write *ad infinitum*, and then Sydney, her handkerchief quite drenched with weeping, tears herself away, and springs into the carriage. The door is closed, she leans forward her lovely tear-wet face. They are all there on the steps, teachers, pupils, servants, and, foremost, the tall, erect figure and fine face of Cyrilla Hendrick.

"Good-by, Cy—dearest Cy," she sobs, and "Good-by, Sydney." Miss Hendrick answers, gravely, but without tears.

The coachman cracks his whip, and they are off, rattling down the silent Rue St. Dominique, and the *pensionnat,* and the throng of eager faces out of sight. She falls back, crying quietly, but before they are half way to the station her tears are dried and she is listening eagerly to Rebecca's account of all at home.

The station is reached—smiles have totally routed tears, the pretty gray eyes sparkle, the delicate cheeks flush. The old life is at an end. After all, Cy was right, it *was* dull—and the new one is begun. The old one ended in darkness and rain, the new one begins in sunshine and brightness. It is emblematic, the girl thinks, and she gives her engagement ring a shy little kiss, and thinks, with a happy blush and smile, that she is going to Bertie, to her bridegroom—and so forgets the *pensionnat.*

CHAPTER XI.

"A LAGGARD IN LOVE."

HARLOTTE, what time is it? If it isn't past four that confounded clock must be slow."

Captain Owenson—"Squire Owenson" as he is known to all men hereabouts—asks this question for the twentieth time within the hour, turning over with an impatient half sigh, half groan, in his big invalid chair. And Charlotte, otherwise Mrs. Owenson, looks up from her tatting, and answers placidly, as she has answered placidly also twenty times before :

" It wants twenty minutes of four, Reginald, and the clock is right to a second."

" Oh-h-h ! " says the Captain.   It is a half groan of pain, half grunt of anger, and impatiently the invalid flounces over on the other side, and shuts his eyes.   He has not seen his Sydney, the " sole daughter of his house and heart," his one best treasure in life, for close upon a year, and all that year scarcely seems as long to his intolerable impatience, as do the hours of this lagging day that is to bring her home.   At no period of his career has patience been the virtue upon which the friends of Reginald Algernon Owenson have placed their hopes of his canonization, and years of ill-health have by no means strengthened it, as his wife knows to her cost.   He is a tall, gaunt man, with a face still handsome in spite of its haggardness, bright, restless eyes, and that particularly livid look that organic heart disease gives.   The large, gray eyes, closed so wearily now, are the counterpart of Sydney's, and the abundant and un-silvered hair not many shades darker.

By the lace-draped bay window of this her husband's invalid sitting-room sits Mrs. Owenson, serenely doing tatting.   A tall, thin, faded lady, with pale blue eyes, pale, fairish complexion, and a general air of cheerful insipidity.   In early youth Mrs. Owenson was a beauty—in the maturity of seven and forty years, Mrs. Owenson fancies herself a beauty still.

There is silence in the room for a few minutes.   It is a very large and airy room, furnished with the taste and elegance of culture and wealth.   There are pictures on the walls, busts on brackets, statuettes in corners, bronzes on the chimney-piece, books and flowers on the table, and over all, more beautiful than all, the crisp golden sunshine of the November afternoon. From the window you saw a lovely view, spreading woodland all glowing with the rubies and orange of that most exquisite and poetic season the " Fall," emerald slopes of sward, and far away the great Atlantic Ocean, spreading until it melted into the dazzling blue sky.

The minutes drag like hours to the nervously irritable man, who bears suffering as most men bear it, in angry, vehement protest.   A brave man in his day he has been, but brave under ill-health, slow, cruel pain, he is not.   Placid Mrs. Owenson, who sits, seeing nothing of the gorgeous picture before her,

whose whole small soul is absorbed in her tatting, who jumps
on a chair, and shrieks at sight of a mouse, would have borne
it all with the pathetic, matter-of-course, infinite patience of
woman, had *she* been chosen for the martyrdom.

Presently the sick man opens his eyes, bright and restless
with impatience.

" Bertie is late, too," he growls; "he was to return by the
two o'clock train.   A pretty thing for Sydney, a fine compliment indeed, to get here and find him gallivanting away in New
York.   It seems to me he does nothing *but* gallivant since his
return from England—returning plucked too!   Young dunder-
head!   I don't like it !   I won't have it !   He shall stay quietly
at home or I will know the reason why ! "

" My dear," says Mrs. Owenson, calmly measuring off her
tatting, "you mustn't excite yourself, you know.   Doctors
Howard and Delaney both said particularly you were never, on
any account, to excite yourself."

" Hang Doctors Howard and Delaney!   Don't be a fool,
Mrs. Owenson !   I'm not talking of those two licensed quacks.
I'm talking of Bertie Vaughan's gallivanting, and I say it shall
end or I will know the reason why."

" Well, now," says Mrs. Owenson, more placid if possible
than ever, " I don't believe Bertie's gallivanting, whatever that
may be ; and as for his going to New York two days ago, you
know, Reginald, you gave him permission yourself.   Lord
Dearborn is stopping there at a hotel, before going to shoot
what-you-call-'ems—buffaloes—and Bertie and he were bosom
friends at college, and naturally Bertie wanted to see him before
he left.   And you told him yourself—now Reginald, love, you
know you told him yourself, to invite him to the wedding,
and——"

" Yes, yes, yes, yes !   O Lord ! *what* a thing a woman's
tongue is !   Men may come and men may go, but it goes on
forever.   Don't I know all that, and don't I know, too, that he
promised faithfully to be here by the two o'clock train, in time
to meet Sydney.   And now it's nearly four.   People who won't
keep their promises in little things won't keep them in great.
And this is no little thing, by George ! slighting Sydney.   Isn't
it time for those confounded drops yet, Char ? Lay down that
beastly rubbish you are wasting time over and attend to your
duties."

Still serene, still unruffled, Mrs. Owenson obeys.   To tell
the truth, her liege lord's ceaseless grumbling has little more

effect upon her well-balanced mind than the sighing of the fitful
wind out among the trees. A perfect digestion, an unshattered
nervous system, an unlimited capacity for sleep, raise Mrs.
Owenson superior to every trial of life.

She lays down the obnoxious rubbish, pours out the drops
carefully in a little crystal cup, and hands it to her husband.
As he takes it the shrill shriek of the locomotive, rushing into
the station two miles distant, rends the evening air.

"Thank God, there's the train," he says, with a sort of gasp
—"Sydney's train. In fifteen minutes my darling will be
here."

"And I will go and see about dinner, Reginald," remarks
Mrs. Owenson, settling her cap with a pleased simper at her·
self in the glass, "if you can spare me."

"Spare you! What the devil good are you to any one
I should like to know! sitting there with your eternal knit·
ting——"

"Not knitting, Reginald, love," remonstrates Mrs. Owenson,
"knitting's old-fashioned. Tatting."

A disgusted growl is the gentle invalid's answer. He closes
his eyes and falls back among his pillows once more. Always
a bit of a martinet, in his own household and neighborhood, as
erstwhile on the quarterdeck, years of suffering have rendered
him irritable and savage to an almost unbearable degree.
Death is near, he knows, hovering outside his threshold by day
and by night—may cry "come!" at any moment, and his passionate protest against the inexorable decree never ceases.
His longing for life is almost piteous in its intensity—he holds
his grasp upon it as by a hair, and each outbreak of anger or
excitement may snap that hair in twain.

The great house is very still—the sick-room is far removed
from all household tumult. It *is* a great house—"a house
upon a hill-top," a huge red brick structure, with acres of farm
and field, of orchard and kitchen garden, belts of lawn and
wooded slopes. It stands nearly half a mile from any other
dwelling—a whole mile from the town of Wyckcliffe. A broad
sweep of drive leads up to the portico entrance in front, slop·
ing away in the rear down to the sea-shore. There are many
great men in the smoky manufacturing town of Wyckcliffe—as
great as half a million dollars can make them, but ever and
always Squire Owenson, *the* great man *par excellence*. He is
the wealthiest, he lives in the finest house, he drives the finest
horses, he owns the finest farms, he keeps the largest staff of

servants, and above all he has the air of one born and bred to
command. Loftily gracious and condescending, he has walked
his uplifted way among these good people, and the rich, shrewd
manufacturers submit good-humoredly to being patronized and
smile in their sleeve over it. " A tip-top old swell," is the universal verdict, "in spite of his British airs, free with his money
as a lord, ready to help any one in distress, and a credit to the
town every way you take him." A haughty old sprig of gentility this Squire Owenson, setting a much greater value on birth
and blood than either of these useful things are entitled to, and
loving, with a love great and all absorbing, his slim, pretty, yel-
low-haired "little maid" and heiress. The one desire of his
heart, when first he settled here, had been to found a house
and a name, that would become a power in the land, to have
"The Place" descend from Owenson to Owenson, for all time.
But Mrs. Owenson, who disappointed him in everything, disappointed him in this. Six babies were born, and with the usual
perversity of her contrary sex, each of these babies was a girl.
To make matters worse, five died in infancy, and Sydney,
" last, brightest, and best," alone shot up and flourished. Shot
up, slender and pretty, an Owenson her father rejoiced to see
in face and nature. It was then his thoughts turned to Bertie
Vaughan. Since Providence deigned him no son, Bertie
should be his son, should marry Sydney, should change his
name to Vaughan Owenson, and so in spite of Mrs. Owenson
hand down "The Place" to fame and posterity. The thought
grew with every year. No exception could be taken to the
orphan lad on the score of birth, and for his poverty the captain
did not care—*he* had enough for both. Yes, yes ! the very hour
the boy and girl were old enough they should be married. It
was the one hope, the one dream of his life, growing stronger
as death came near. Of late he had been a little disappointed
in young Vaughan. He had returned from Cambridge
"plucked," his name never appeared in the "University
Eight ; " at nothing, either physical or mental, so far as the old
sailor could see, had he distinguished himself. He was without
ballast, without "backbone," and never had Captain Owenson
sighed so bitterly over the realization as on his last return.
Still, all things cannot be as we would have them here below.
He would love Sydney and be good to her, he could hardly fail
in *that*, and with that both she and her father must fain be content.

" We can't make statesmen, or orators, or great reformers to order," the captain thought. "The lad's a good lad. as the class go—has no vice in him that I can see; will make a respectable, easy-going gentleman farmer, quite willing to be tied to his wife's apron-strings all his life; and as that's the sort of men women like, why, I dare say, it will be all the better for the little one that he's not clever. Your clever man rarely makes a good husband."

He lay thinking this for the thousandth time, with knitted brows and that expression of repressed pain that never left his face, more strongly marked than ever.

Twenty minutes had ticked off on the clock, the yellow lines of the slanting afternoon sun were glimmering more and more faintly through the brown boles of the trees, when carriage wheels came rattling loudly up the drive. He started upright in his seat, a red flush lighting his haggard face, his heart throbbing like a sledge-hammer against his side. There was the sound of a sweet, clear girlish voice and laugh, then a footstep came flying up the stairs, the door was flung wide, and fresh, and fair and breezy, his darling was in the room, her arms about his neck, her kisses raining on his face.

"Papa! papa! dear, darling, blessed old papa! *how* glad I am to be with you again!"

He could not speak for a moment; he could only hold her to him hard; gasping with that convulsive beating of the heart. The heavy, labored pulsations frightened Sydney; she drew herself away and looked at him.

"Papa, how your heart beats! Oh, papa, don't say you are any worse!" she cried out, in a terrified voice.

"No—darling," he answered, a great pant between every word; "only—the joy—of your—coming—" he stopped and pressed his hand hard over the suffocating throbs. "Give me —that—medicine, Sydney."

"I'll do it. Sydney," her mother said, coming in. "I told you, Reginald, not to excite yourself. I'm sure you knew Syd ney was coming, and there was no need to get into a gale about it like this."

The squire's answer was a glare of impotent fury as he took the cordial from the exasperatingly calm partner of his bosom. Sydney's great compassionate eyes were fixed upon him as she nestled close to his shoulder, one arm about his neck.

"Lie back, papa," she said, "among the pillows. I am sorry —oh, darling papa! sorrier than sorry—to see you like this. Now let me fan you. Please don't excite yourself the least bit about me, or I shall be sorry I came."

Little kisses, light as thistle-down, sorrowfully tender as love could make them, punctuated this speech. The father's gaze dwelt on her, as men do gaze upon that which is the apple of their eye.

" I am better now, little one. Stand off, my baby, and let me look at you. Charlotte, look here—Sydney is as tall as yourself."

"Sydney takes after me in figure," says Mrs. Owenson, with a simper. " I was always considered a very fine figure when a girl. They used to call me and my two cousins, Elizabeth and Jane Bender, the Three Graces. It runs in our family." .

" Runs in your fiddlestick!" growled her husband, with ineffable disgust. " Sydney is an Owenson, figure and face, wonderfully grown and marvellously improved. Ah, Bertie's going to get a golden treasure, that I foresee. You don't ask after your sweetheart, little one," her father said, pinching her ear.

"My sweetheart? Oh, how droll," laughed Sydney. "Yes, to be sure, where *is* Bertie? I rather expected to have met him at the station."

"And you ought to have met him at the station," answered her father, his frown returning. " Whatever else a man may be, he shouldn't be laggard in love. The truth is he has gone to New York to see his college friend, young Lord Dearborn, and something must have detained him. However, he is pretty sure to be here at eight. He has altered as much as you, little one, and grown a fine, manly, handsome lad."

" Bertie was always nice-looking," said Sydney, in a patronizing, elder-sister sort of tone ; "only too fair—I don't admire very fair men. Mamma, is dinner ready? I'm famishing ; and please, mamma, tell Katy to have something particularly nice, for life has been supported on thin bread and butter and weak tea for the past three years."

She ran off to her own room to remove her hat, and mamma trotted dutifully away to see after the commissariat. Papa gazed after her with eyes of fond delight.

" My little one," he thought, "my pretty little one, sweet and innocent, an heart whole. No mawkish blushing or sentimentality there. Bertie was always nice-looking, but too fair. Ha ! ha ! I hope she will take your conceit down a peg or two, Master Bert."

The dining-room of Owenson Place was like all the rooms, nearly perfect in its way, hung with deep crimson and gold paper, carpeted with Axminster of deep crimson and wood tints, curtained with red satin brocatelle and lace. Handsome chromos of flowers and fruit, of startled deer, and forest streams cov ered the walls. A huge sideboard of old Spanish mahogany covered with dessert, occupied the space between two tall win dows. A little wood fire snapped in the wide steel grate; under the big glittering chandelier in the centre of the dinnertable was set a huge epergne of autumn flowers, gorgeous in the centre. And, best of all, there were raised pies, and cold ham, and broiled partridge, and chicken fricassee, and ruby and golden jellies, and fruits, and sweets. Sydney's eyes sparkled as she looked. It sounds unromantic, but at the age of seventeen it is a matter of history that Miss Owenson's heart was very easily reached through her palate.

"We don't have regular 'dinners—roasts, and *entrées* and that, since Bertie's been away," said Mrs. Owenson. " I ordered all the things you used to like best. Papa never comes down to dinner when we are alone."

" Oh, how nice," cried Sydney; "how good it seems to be home. What a delicious pie. Nobody makes game pies like our Katy, bless her ! I must go down to the kitchen directly and give her a hug. Won't you have something, mamma ? Oh, how I wish Cyrilla were here."

"Who's Cyrilla, my love?" asked Mrs. Owenson, helping herself to partridge.

Mrs. Owenson has dined, but Mrs. Owenson is one of those happy exceptional mortals who can eat with ease and comfort at all times and seasons.

"My chum at school, Cyrilla Hendrick. Don't you remember telling me in your letter that papa said I might invite her here, as bridemaid. I have, and papa must write to her aunt immediately—to-night or to-morrow. I wish Bertie were here," runs on Miss Owenson, going vigorously into the raised pie.

" I'm dying to see him. Is he really handsome, mamma, and elegant, and all that?"

" Really handsome, my dear," responded mamma, " and *most* elegant. His clothes fit him beautifully, and he's *so* particular about his finger-nails, and his teeth, and his studs, and his sleeve-buttons, and his neckties, and his perfumes. And he bows magnificently. And he parts his hair down the middle. And he is raising a small moustache. It is so light yet you can barely see it, but I daresay it will come out quite plain after you are married. And he is going to ask Lord Dearborn down for the wedding, which will give everything an aristocratic air, you know. And, oh, Sydney, my love! all your things have come, and you must go and see them as soon as you have dined. The bridal-dress, vail, wreath, and pearls are expected from Paris in the steamer next week. They have cost a little fortune, and will be really splendid. And papa has fitted up three rooms for you and Bertie, after you return from your wedding-trip, and they are splendid also. Your papa may be fractious, Sydney, but I must say he has spared no expense in this. There never was a wedding like it in Wyckcliffe, and I don't believe ever will be again. The papers will be full of it, you may depend."

"Dear, generous papa!" Sydney exclaimed. "Mamma, you don't think him worse, do you—not really worse? His heart beats frightfully, but——"

"That was the excitement, my dear. He *will* excite himself over trifles, do as you may," answers placid mamma.

"But he is not worse? The doctors don't say he is worse, do they?"

"By no means. He only fancies he is. They tell him to avoid excitement, to go on with the drops as before, to take gentle carriage exercise, light diet and wines, and he may linger ever so long. Now, have you finished, my dear? because I do want to show you the things."

Sydney had finished, and putting her arm around mamma's waist familiarly, went with her up-stairs. The bridal apartments were first shown—sitting-room, bedroom, dressing-room, all in different colors, all of different degrees of sumptuousness. Pretty pictures, gilded books, stands of music, a new piano and work-table, knick-knacks, pretty trifles, costing hundreds of dollars, and making an elegant whole. Everything was the best and rarest money could buy.

Sydney went into raptures—school-girl raptures; but her color came and went, for the first time. For the first time, she was beginning to realize that she was really going to be married. The trousseau was displayed next. Dresses of silk, black, brown, blue, pink, white, all the colors that blonde girls can wear; dresses of lace, black and white; dresses of materials thick and thin—all beautifully made and trimmed. Then heaps of linen, ruffled, laced, embroidered, marked with the letters "S. V. O." twisted in a monogram—Sydney Vaughan Owenson.

Gradually, as she examined and admired, silence fell upon her. She was beginning to feel overpowered; her life of the

5

past and present seemed closing forever, and another, of which
she knew nothing, about to begin.

A sensation, akin to dread of meeting Bertie Vaughan, was
inexplicably stealing over her.   She shook it off indignantly.
What nonsense !   Afraid to meet Bertie !   Bertie with whom
she had quarrelled and made up, whose ears she had boxed
scores of times, whom she had laughed at and made fun of for
his incipient young-mannish airs years ago—afraid of *him !*   It
was all very fine, and must have cost oceans of money, still she
was glad when the sight-seeing was over and she could nestle up
to her father's side and kiss him a little, silent, grateful kiss of
thanks.

"How do you like it all, Mrs. Vaughan Owenson ? " he
asked, patting the cheek, from which the eager flush had faded.

" It is all lovely—lovely.   Papa, how good you are to Bertie
and me ! "

"You are all I have to be good to, child," he answered, sadly.
"Let me make you happy—I ask no more.   You think you will
be happy with our boy, don't you, pettie ? "

"I like Bertie very much, papa."

"In a sisterly way—eh, my dear ?   Well, that is a very good
way—much the better way, in a little girl of seventeen.   This
time next year he will be something more than a brother to you.
He will be very good to you, that I know."

"It is not in Bertie to be bad to any one, papa.   He always
had a gentle heart."

"Yes, my dear, I think he had.   There may be nobler qualities than gentleness and softness, but we don't make ourselves,
and, as young fellows go, Bertie is a harmless lad, a very harmless lad.   Be a good wife, Sydney, and don't be too exacting—
men are mortal, my dear—the best of 'em *very* mortal.   Be
happy yourself, and make your husband happy—it is all I
ask on earth."

" I'll try, papa," Sydney sighs, in a weary way, leaning
against his chair, "but——"

"But I wish I need not be married at all.   I wish I might
just live on as I used, with you and mamma, and have Bertie
for my brother.   It is very tiresome and stupid being married,
whether one will or no, at seventeen."

That is what she would have liked to say, but an instinctive
conviction that it would displease her father held her silent.

" But what, little one ? " he asks.

" Nothing, papa."

There is silence for awhile. The gray, cold evening is falling over wood and ocean ; a star or two glitters in the sky. Both sit and look at the tremulous beauty of these frosty stars. Suddenly Sydney springs to her feet.

" Papa, I would like to go and see Hetty. May I ? "

Hetty was once Sydney's nurse, very much tyrannized over, and very dearly loved. Hetty was married now and living in the suburbs of the town.

Papa glances at the clock. It is close upon seven, drawing near the time when Master Bertie may be looked for, and it will do him no harm to find Miss Owenson has not thought it worth her while to wait for him. So he gives a cheerful and immediate assent.

" Certainly, my dear. Hetty is a good creature, a very good creature, and strongly attached to us all. Take Ellen or Katy, or drive over if you like, or Perkins, the coachman, will attend you, or——"

"Oh, dear, no, papa ! " laughs Sydney. " I don't want any of them. As if one needed an escort running over to the town ! Besides, I've been watched and looked after so long that a scamper for once on my own account will be delightful. May I ? "

" It will be dark in ten minutes, Syd.'

" I will be at Hetty's in ten minutes, and she will come back with me if I want her. P—please, papa, may I ? "

" Why do you say 'may I,' you witch ? You know you can do as you like with me. Run away. Wrap up, the evenings are chilly ; and don't stay more than an hour."

" Not a second. Good-by, papa ; *au revoir*."

She ran up to her room, tied her dainty travelling hat over her sunny curls, threw a new and brillant scarlet mantle over her shoulders, and in the steel-white, steel-cold set off for her walk.

CHAPTER XII.

"ALLAN-A-DALE TO HIS WOOING HAS COME."

HETTIE, otherwise Mrs. Simpson, lived, as has been said, on the outskirts of the straggling town of Wyck cliffe, about three-quarters of a mile from the gates of Owenson Place, supposing you took the high road. Supposing you took instead the short cut, skirting the sea-side, you shortened the distance by half. Both were perfectly familiar to Miss Owenson, both perfectly safe, and without deliberating about it, she at once struck into the "short-cut," running along the high rocky ledge skirting the sea.

It was a rough, rock-bound coast, the steep rocks beetling up in some places almost perpendicularly, from fifty to two hundred feet. The steep sides were overgrown with stunted spruce, reedy grasses, and wild, flame-colored blossoms waved in the salt wind. A wide belt of yellow sand was left bare at low tide ; at high tide the big booming waves washed the cliffs for yards up. In wild weather the thunder of these huge Atlantic billows could be heard like dull cannonading to the farthest end of the town. It was a lonesome path, but one that always had a fascination for Sydney, as far back as she could remember. To lean over the steep top of "Witch Rock," the highest point of all these high crags, and look sheer down, two hundred feet into the seething waters beneath, had ever been her dangerous delight. She walked along now, rather slowly and soberly at first, thinking in her childish way, how prosy and humdrum it was to be married in this manner, the very moment one left school. All the married ladies she had ever known were staid and grave "house-mothers," not a frisky matron among them all. Was she expected to be a solemn and steady-going house-mother too? It was a little too bad of papa she thought, with a reproachful sigh. If he had only let her have a good time first, for three years at least—twenty is old, but it is not too old, after all, to be married. She might have come out, had a winter in New York, another in Washington, a trip to Europe, and a couple of seasons at Saratoga and Newport. But of course poor sick papa must be obeyed ; so with another heavy sigh the little bride-elect put aside her grievance, and wondered where Bertie might be at that particular moment, and whether he really would be at home to-night at all. It was satisfactory—very satisfactory, Miss Owenson mused gravely, that he was so nice-looking, and was a "clothes-wearing man," and was fastidious, as mamma had said, about his nails, and teeth and sleeve-buttons. Limited as her knowledge of the nobler sex had been she had known gentlemen—Colonel Delamere and sundry officers of his staff notably among the number—who were *not*.

Miss Owenson, musing thus over the serious things of this very serious life, continued her way, as you have been told, at first slowly and soberly, but accelerating her pace gradually, and brightening up. It was so good to be at home, to be free from school discipline ; now and forever done with lessons and lectures. It was such an exhilarating night too. The stars sparkled brilliant and numberless. There was no moon, but a steely radiance shimmered over everything. Down below the pretty baby waves lapped the ribbed sand, and the great ocean melted blackly away into the sky. She paused, leaning over Witch Cliff, and gazing with fascinated eyes at that illimitable stretch of black water. She was still lingering there, when there came to her voices and footsteps on the high road beyond. She glanced carelessly over her shoulder—carelessly at first ; then she started swiftly upright, and looked at the two advancing, with keen, surprised interest. A man and a woman, both young, going toward the town, the woman an utter stranger, but the man—surely the man looked like Bertie Vaughan.

She caught her breath. Could it be Bertie. It was his height, his walk, his general air and look. His hat was pulled over his eyes, and in that light, and at that distance, she could not discern his face. His head was bent slightly forward, moodily as it seemed, and he traced figures in the dust with his cane as he walked. His companion, a small, stylish-looking young lady, with a ringing voice and laugh, was rallying him as she leaned upon his arm.

"That's all very fine," Sydney heard her say. "Very easy for you to tell me you only went to see a friend ; but how am I to be sure it's true ? I know you men—deceitful every one of you. How am I to tell you hadn't a flirtation on hand up there ? Only, if you have——"

The man raised his head and answered her, but in too subdued a tone for that answer to be audible. It was the refined, the educated tone of a gentleman, and markedly different from **hers.**

She laughed again at his reply, whatever it was, and began to sing, in a low, mellow voice :

"It is good to be merry and wise,
It is good to be loyal and true,
It is good to be off with the old love
Before you are on with the new."

The last words were faint in the distance. The pair—lovers, it would seem—passed out of view.

And Sydney roused herself, her heart beating in the most absurd manner. The man was so like Bertie. Could it be ?—— Then she broke off. What a ridiculous idea ! Bertie was doubtless on his way from New York, and she was idly loitering here after promising papa not to stay a moment longer than she could help. She hurried on, and in five minutes was in Mrs. Simpson's cottage and in Mrs. Simpson's arms.

"Bless the baby !" her nurse cried, a buxom woman of forty, with the pleasantest of faces ; "how she is grown ! As tall as her mamma, and as pretty as a picture ! "

A shower of kisses wound up the sentence.

"When did you come home ? " Mrs. Simpson asked, placing a chair for her young lady, and removing her hat.

"About two hours ago, and have run over to see you the first thing. No, thank you, Hetty, I won't take my things off. I promised papa not to stay but a minute."

"Which he's been that worriting about your coming, Miss Sydney, that I thought he would have gone after you himself, sick as he is. And now your home and going to be married to Master Bertie right away. Oh ! my dear, darling Miss Sydney, I hope it may be for the best."

The pleasant face clouded a little as she said it, the pleasant eyes looked with wistful affection into her nursling's face.

"Certainly it will be for the best, Hetty," Sydney responded, brightly, and yet with a certain reserve in her tone that told Mrs. Simpson the matter was not to be discussed ; "and you shall have a brand-new brown silk—you always sighed for a yellow-brown silk, I remember—to dance at my wedding. How is the baby, and how is Mr. Simpson, and how are you getting on ? "

Mrs. Simpson's face grew absolutely radiant. The baby was well—bless him ! Miss Sydney must see him at once ; and Simpson was well, thank you, and *that* busy, and making *that* money, all thanks to the start her papa had given him, and she was the happiest and thankfulest woman in America, with not a want in the world.

"Only the gold-brown silk," laughed Sydney; "that's a chronic want, isn't it? Let me see the baby, and then I must be off."

Mrs. Simpson left the room, returning in a moment with a six-months' old ball of fat, rosy and sleepy, in her arms, trying to rub two blinking blue eyes with two absurd little fists.

"Oh! the darling!" cries Miss Owenson, jumping up and snatching at it as a matter of course. "Oh, oo love! Oh, oo ittle pet-sy-wet-sy!" Here a shower of kisses. "Oh, oo 'ittle beauty! Hetty, he's splendid! What's its name?"

"Which we've took the liberty of naming him after your par, Miss Sydney," responded the blissful mother; "his name's Reginald Algernon Owenson Simpson, and at his christening your par presented him with a silver mug—a real silver mug—and your mar with a lovely coral and silver bells."

Sydney had all a true girl's maternal instincts, strong, though dormant. Baby was smothered with kisses, which naturally taking baby's breath away, Reginald Algernon Owenson Simpson opened his cherubic mouth, and set up a howl that made his mother spring to the rescue.

"Poor 'ittle pets, did I scare it then?" cooed Sydney, pecking daintily at one little paw; "Aunty Syd shall fetch it something pitty next time she tomes! Now then, Hetty, I really must not stay another minute. I ought to be on my way home now, but I lingered in my old fashion to look over the rocks,—*you* remember?"

"I remember, Miss Sydney, it was the terror of my life that you would break your neck over Witch Cliff. Ah! that path isn't as quiet now as it used to be; they've got to calling it Lover's Lane, of late. All them factory girls and their young men go a courting along that way Sunday nights, and the actors and actresses at other times. I suppose you know they started a theatre over in Wyckcliffe?"

"No, I didn't know it. Have they?"

"Yes; and the best actress of them all boards in Brown's, - next cottage to this—Miss Dolly De Courcy she calls herself, a fine, fat, black-eyed, dressy young woman, with more young men running after her than you could shake a stick at."

"Happy Miss De Courcy! Well, good-by, Hetty. I'll run over to-morrow, or maybe next day. Dood-by, baby—div Aunt Syd one more tiss."

"How fond you are of babies! Ah! wait until you've got 'em of your own," says Mrs. Simpson, prophetically, at which Sydney laughs and blushes, and runs out, and starts more briskly than she came on her homeward walk.

She encounters no one this time; it is the loneliest walk conceivable, but she does not feel lonely. She sings as she goes; she is singing as she enters the gates of The Place, singing, as it chances, the refrain of the ballad she had overheard, half an hour before:

> "It is good to be off with the old love
> Before you are on with the new."

The belated moon has arisen as she emerges from the shadowy drive, upon the broad belt of sward that encircles the house. On the portico steps stands a tall, dark figure, smoking a cigar. Her heart gives a quick beat, but she sings gayly on.

With the last words she runs up the steps and stands beside him.

He has not offered to move—he stands coolly waiting for her to come to him.

"Bertie!" she exclaims, her frank gladness at seeing him overcoming her new and disagreeable shyness, and she holds out both hands.

He removes his cigar—holds it carefully between his finger and thumb, takes the two proffered hands in one of his, bends forward and kisses her.

"Ah! Syd. I thought it must be you. How cruel of you to run away when you knew I was coming as fast as steam would bear me. Stand off and let me look at you. By Jove! how you have grown and how pretty!"

He says it in a tone of admiration, languid but real, and Sydney laughs, remembering it is the twentieth time within the last four hours she has been told the same. With that laugh every shade of embarrassment vanishes. After all it is only Bertie—the old Bertie—a trifle more manly-looking, but as affected and nonsensical as ever.

"Certainly after all *your* efforts to improve me, could I do less? And you—I don't see much change or improvement in you, Bertie, except that I think you also have grown!" Then she pauses and regards him doubtfully. "When did you come?" she asks.

"Ten minutes ago," responds Mr. Bertie Vaughan, "and

was crushed to the earth by the announcement that you hadn't
waited.   Only one thing could have enabled me to bear up
under the blow—a cigar.   May I go on with it?   It's a capital
cigar—cost fifty cents in New York, and you must own—you
really must, sis, it would be a pity to throw it away."

"A sad pity," says Sydney, gravely.   "Pray, don't do anything so madly extravagant, Mr. Vaughan.   You came ten
minutes ago, did you?   Hum-m! that's odd, too."

"What's odd?   My getting here ten minutes ago?   Explain."

"I fancied—I was sure, almost—that I met you about half
an hour ago with a young lady on your arm."

She looks keenly at him as she speaks.   It is a fortunate
thing, perhaps, for Mr. Bertie Vaughan that the newly-risen
moon does not shine on the spot where he stands.   He has the
blondest of blonde complexions, and it reddens like a girl's as
he stoops to knock the ash, with care, off his cherished and expensive cigar.

"It was very like you," pursues Sydney, slowly; "the hat,
the height, the walk, the gray overcoat—I could have sworn it
was you, Bert."

"Dangerous thing to swear rashly," says Bertie, with that affected drawl that always exasperated Sydney; "must have been
my wraith—have heard of such things.   May have been my
double, and I may be going to die."

"It wasn't you, Bertie?"

"It wasn't I, Sydney.   Your own common sense might tell
you a man can't be in two places at once; but then, common
sense, I am told, is not one of the sciences taught at a young
ladies' boarding-school."

"Let us go in," Sydney says, abruptly.

She feels disappointed, she doesn't know how, or in what.   It
begins to dawn upon her dimly that Bertie is shallow and affected, weak and unstable.   The idea has long been taking
shape in her mind; as she looks at him to-night, languid and
nonchalant, she is sure of it.

They go in.   Captain Owenson's room is brilliantly lit with
clusters of wax lights.   Gas may illuminate the other rooms—
old-fashioned tapers shall light his.   Mrs. Owenson has exchanged the tatting for a novel, and sits near a table, reading.
A small Broadwood piano that, ten years ago, came from England, stands open in a corner.   The invalid is in his great
chair, holding a paper, but listening for his daughter's footsteps

5*

instead of reading. As she enters, Bertie behind her, his whole face lights.

"Well, puss," he says, "you are back safely after all. Did you come and go alone?"

"All alone, papa. Who was it said: 'I am never less alone than when alone?' It was my case to-night. I have had a surfeit of surveillance during the past three years. Freedom is sweet."

"You hear, Bertie?" says the squire; "strong-minded notions, eh? She lets you see what's in store for you betimes."

"Strong-minded notions are very pretty from pretty lips," Mr. Vaughan answers, and he gives Sydney the most thoroughly admiring glance he has given her yet.

She looks brilliantly well. Her walk in the frosty air has flushed her cheeks and brightened her eyes. She stands upright and slim, her scarlet cloak falling back, her yellow-brown curls falling loosely over it, the coquettish hat, with its long plume setting off the fair, star-like face beneath. The old sailor's doting eyes linger on her.

"She has improved in her dull Canadian school—don't you think so, Bertie? And shot up like a bean stalk, little witch!"

"Improved is hardly the word," answers, languidly, Mr. Vaughan. "I wouldn't mind going there myself, for a year or two, if they would turn me out 'beautiful forever,' like Syd."

He lays himself out upon the nearest sofa, long and slender, and very handsome, in a fair, effeminate way. He has hair in hue and silkiness like the pale tassels of the corn, large, dreamy, light blue eyes, a faintly sprouting moustache, and a Dundreary-ish drawl. A "Beauty-Man," beyond dispute—a Narcissus, hopelessly in love—with himself.

"Play us something, Syd," he says. "I pine for a little music. And sing us a song."

She sits down and obeys. She plays fairly well, and sings very nicely, in a sweet and carefully-trained voice, and is duly praised and applauded.

"Ah! you should hear Cyrilla Hendrick sing, Bertie!" she exclaims, twirling round on her stool. There's a voice and a player if you like! By-the-by, papa, you're to write to her Aunt Dormer, and ask leave for Cy to come here and be brides——"

She stops suddenly short, meeting her father's knowing smile, and Bertie's glance, and blushes vividly. Bertie probably understood, and the blush was contagious, for he too reddened through his thin, fair skin.

"And be brides—oh! yes, we know what she's to be—eh, Bertie, my boy? What! you blushing too! Bless my soul, what a bashful pair. Char, shove that writing-case over this way—I'll do it now. Comes of a very good family, does your friend, Miss Hendrick, on the distaff side. Her mother was third daughter of Sir Humphrey Vernon—ran away—disinherited—hum-m. The aunt, Miss Dormer, very wealthy old lady, engaged once to nephew of the Earl of Dunraith—hum-m-m. 'My dear Miss Dormer.'"

The letter was speedily written, folded, and sealed. More music followed, more talk. Mr. Bertie Vaughan was rather silent through it all, rather tired-looking, rather bored, and, it might be, a trifle anxious. Certainly his face wore anything but the expression of a rapturous lover. He lay on his sofa, pulled the ears of Mrs. Owenson's favorite pug, Rixie, and watched Sydney askance.

Early hours were kept at Owenson Place. Sydney, accustomed to going to bed at nine, and fatigued with her journey, was struggling heroically with yawns before the clock struck ten. The striking of that hour was the signal for prayers. The servants filed in, the squire, in a sonorous bass voice led the exercises. Then good-nights were said, and leaning on his wife's arm, Sydney going before, the master of the house started for his room.

"And I will smoke a cigar for half an hour, outside," said Mr. Vaughan, rising leisurely. "Virtuous as I am, and always have been, the primitive hours of this establishment are a height I haven't attained. Good-night, governor; good-night, Aunt Char; good-night, Syd."

"Sydney must cure you of smoking cigars after ten o'clock," the squire answered, good humoredly. "Good-night to you, my lad."

"Good-night, Bertie," said placid Aunt Char; "put on your overcoat, my dear boy, and tie a scarf around your neck, or even your pocket handkerchief will do. Consider these fall nights are chilly, and you might catch a cold in your head."

"By-by, Bert!" laughed Sydney, flashing a mischievous glance over her shoulder. "For goodness sake don't forget to tie your handkerchief round your neck lest you should catch that cold in your poor, dear head. Tell him to put on over-

shoes, mamma—the ground my be damp—and hadn't Perkins
better hold an umbrella over him to keep off the dew?"

She ran off, her mocking laugh coming back to him, and
vanished into her own room.   And Mr. Vaughan *did* put on his
overcoat, and button it up carefully to the throat, before going
out for that last smoke.   It might be fun to Syd, but Aunt Char
was right—he would take proper precautions against a cold in
the head.

He lit up, and walked and smoked, a reflective frown on his
face, and saw the lights vanish from the upper windows.   Mr.
Vaughan was doing what he was constitutionally unfitted for
and unused to—thinking.

" She's very pretty—uncommonly pretty, some fellows might
think "—a pause and a puff—"and to think of her seeing me
to-night. By George ! "

He looked up again—Sydney's light winked and went out.

" Yes," Bertie mused, " she's pretty, and she's doosid good
style, and she's an heiress, and a very jolly girl so far as I can
see, but still——"

He seemed unable to get any farther.   He looked uneasily
up at the house once more.   All was dark and quiet.   He
pulled out his watch and looked at that.   It was twenty minutes
past ten.   The moon was shining brilliantly now, silvering woods,
and fields, and house.   His eyes went slowly over the silver-lit
prospect.

" It's all hers, every inch of it, and mine the day I marry her.
I don't see how I can help marrying her.   It's a confounded
muddle, look at it how you will.   Sometimes I wish—yes, by
George, I wish I had never seen——"

Once more he abruptly broke off.   This time he flung away
his smoked-out Havana and started rapidly for the gates.   They
were bolted, and a huge English mastiff stood on guard—very
unnecessary precautions in that peaceful place, but of a piece
with the squire's general fussiness.

"Here, Trumps—quiet, old boy," he said, and Trumps'
hoarse growl rumbled away into silence.   He slid the bolts,
opened the gate, closed it, and struck at once into the rocky
path by which Sydney had come and gone four hours before.
He met no one until he left it and took the first street leading
into the town.   Here all was quiet too, the stores closed, a few
bar-rooms alone sending their fatal light abroad.   He drew
near a large building, at whose entrance lamps burned, and
from which strains of music came.   Turning an angle of this

building, he came upon a young girl standing alone, her shawl wrapped about her, her back against a dead wall—evidently waiting.

"Am I late, Dolly?" demanded Mr. Vaughan, in a breathless tone. "Awfully sorry, upon my honor, but I couldn't help it. I couldn't, upon my word."

He drew her hand under his arm and led her off, bending down affectionately to catch a glimpse of her face. A piquant face, lit with bright restless eyes, and plump as an apple. There was rouge on cheeks and lips, and powder, thick everywhere rouge was not, but the face he looked at was pretty in spite of that, with a certain *chic* and dash.

"Are you angry, Dolly? Upon my soul, I'm sorry, but I couldn't help it. By Jove, Dolly, I couldn't."

"Angry? Oh, dear, no!" answered Miss Dolly, with a flash of her dark eyes—"not I, Mr. Vaughan! Only when a young gentleman tells a young lady he'll meet her a quarter after ten, and doesn't come until a quarter past eleven, it's time for that young lady to find another escort home. It isn't pleasant waiting three-quarters of an hour out in the cold, and I won't try it on again, I can tell you that!"

"Come, now, Dolly, you don't mean to quarrel with me, do you? I couldn't stand *that*. I told you I positively couldn't get away, and I couldn't. There was"—a momentary hesitation—"a visitor at the house, and I had to stay and do the civil."

"A young lady, Bertie?" asked Dolly, quickly, with a sudden, swift, jealous change of tone.

"Oh, yes, a young lady. In point of fact, my—my cousin—home from school."

"Your cousin! You never told me you had a cousin before, Bertie."

"Didn't I, Doll? Because I forget everything and everybody in the world but you, I suppose, when I am with you."

"That is all very fine," says Miss Dolly, whose strong point, evidently, is not retort. "Is she pretty—this cousin?"

"'Still harping on my daughter!'" laughs Bertie. "Not at all my dear. A skim-milk school-girl, pallid, delicate; no more to you than a penny candle to the moon."

"And then she's your cousin, besides," says Miss Dolly, in a musing tone; "and I suppose you wouldn't fall in love with your cousin, even if she was ever so pretty. I've heard English people are like that."

" Fall in love with my cousin ! ha, ha !" laughs Bertie again.
"That's a good joke. Oh, no, Doll ; one young woman's
enough to be in love with at a time."

"And that's *me*," says Dolly, giving his arm a tender little
squeeze, her anger totally gone, and the twain walk in delightful silence on for some yards. " I suppose that grumpy old
uncle of yours wouldn't consent to your marrying an actress,
though ? " the girl asks again, with an impatient sigh.

"Well, no, Dolly, I am afraid he wouldn't. My uncle is a man
of tolerably strong prejudice, and tolerably strong selfishness. I
hate selfish people ! " says Mr. Bertie Vaughan, savagely.

" He would cut you off with a shilling, I suppose, as the heavy
fathers do in the pieces ? " suggests Dolly.

"Precisely, cut me off without a shilling ; and, by Jupiter,
Doll, I haven't a penny, no, not a halfpenny, but what the old
duffer gives me."

"Well, you could go on the stage," says Dolly, reassuringly.
"With your face, and your figure, and your aristocratic air, and
your education, and everything, you'd make a tip-top walking
gent."

" Don't say 'tip-top,' Dolly, and don't say 'gent,'" corrects
Mr. Vaughan. " Yes, there's something in that. I could go on
the stage, and I always liked the life. Well, if the worse comes
to the worst, who knows?—I may don the sock or buskin.
Meantime, here we are at your lodgings."

"And oh ! by-the-by, Bertie, I nearly forgot !" cries Dolly,
keeping fast hold of his arm. " We're to have a sailing party
over to Star Island to-morrow afternoon, after rehearsal, a clam
chowder, a dance, and a good time generally. I've refused
everybody, because I wanted to go with you. You'll come ?—
half-past one, sharp."

" Really, Dolly, much as I would like to, I'm afraid——"

" What ! You won't come ? "

" I'm afraid——"

"You must stay home and make love to the boarding-school
cousin. Oh, I see it all !" cries Miss Dolly, in bitterness of
spirit.

" Nonsense, Dolly ! Make love—nothing of the sort ; only
my uncle——"

"Oh ! your uncle, of course," cries Dolly again, with ever-
increasing bitterness. "Very well, Mr. Vaughan ! do as you
please. I wouldn't think of coaxing you for the world. Only
I can tell Ben Ward I take back my refusal and will go with

him. I hope *you'll* have a good time with your uncle and cousin!". The sneering scorn with which the actress brings out these two family titles is not to be described. "A *real* good time. Good-night, Mr. Vaughan."

Ben Ward is the richest and best-looking young mil.-owner in Wyckcliffe, and Miss Dolly De Courcy's most obedient humble servant. As she says good-night she turns to go, leave ing him standing irresolute at the gate. She is half way to the door, when he lifts his head and calls :

"I say! Look here, Dolly. Don't ask Ward, confound him. It'll be all right. I'll be there."

CHAPTER XIII.

"ALLAN-A-DALE IS NO BARON OR LORD."

T is the morning after, half-past eight, and breakfast time. Out of doors, yellow, crisp, sparkling sunshine lies over land and sea ; the orange and scarlet maples and hemlock glow and burn like jewels. A few gorgeous dahlias yet lift their bold, bright heads, where all the summer flowers are dead and gone, and the scarlet clusters hang from the rowan-trees like bunches of vivid coral. In-doors, the breakfast-table is spread, and silver and china and crystal flash back the sunlight cheerily. A fire snaps on the hearth, and makes doubly cozy the whole room. Around the table all are assembled—no tardiness at meal-times will be tolerated in the household Squire Owenson rules. Bertie Vaughan looks a trifle fagged and sleepy, and struggles manfully not to gape in the face of the assembled company. Sydney, who has been up and doing since half-past six, sits down with eyes like stars and cheeks as rosy almost as the clusters of rowan berries in her lovely loose hair.

"Look at that child?" says the squire, his whole face aglow with the love and delight he cannot hide ; "she might sit for a portrait of the goddess Hygea. And we used to think her deli-cate! Upon my word, a Canadian boarding-school, long lessons, and short commons must be capital things for health. Bertie, my lad, what's the matter with you this morning?

Didn't your last cigar sit well last night, or had you the night-mare? You look rather white about the gills."

"Delicacy is my normal state," Mr. Vaughan answers, languidly. "Aunt Char, I'll trouble you for another steak and a second help of those very excellent fried potatoes. I am but a fragile blossom at best, that any rude wind may nip in the bud. A second cup of coffee, Aunt Char, if you please. Really, Katy is a *cordon-bleu ;* I never tasted better in my life."

He meets Sydney's laughing eyes with pensive gravity, and the squire booms out a great laugh in high good humor.

"I'll tell you what it is, my fragile blossom," he says, "we will try if change of air won't do you good. Sydney, I've a treat in store for you. One hour after breakfast let all be ready in their very best rigging—the carriage will be at the door and we will go and make a day of it over at the Sunderlands. We'll see if we can't blow the wilted roses back into the lily-like cheeks of our fair, fragile Mr. Vaughan."

"Oh, how nice of you, papa!" cries out Sydney, in her school-girl way; "how glad I shall be to see Mamie and Susie Sunderland again. And we can have a row in the afternoon across the bay to Star Island. You are the very best and kindest papa that ever lived."

"Of course, of course—best of men and fathers. Hey, Bertie what do you say? Confound the lad! he looks as glum as if he had heard his death sentence. Say, don't you want to go?"

The flash in Squire Owenson's lion-like eye might have intimidated a tolerably strong man. A strong man—mentally, morally, or physically—Bertie Vaughan was not. His tone was deprecating and subdued to a degree when he spoke.

"Really, sir, nothing would give me more pleasure, but——"

"Well!" cried the old martinet, in an ominous voice, "what? No stammering—speak out!"

"I have another engagement—that is all. I—I might break it, of course," says Mr. Vaughan, rather aghast.

"Oh-h! You might break it, of course! Then will you have the very great goodness, Mr. Albert Vaughan, to break it! When I propose a pleasure excursion in honor of my daughter's arrival, no one pleads a prior engagement in my house. At half-past nine, sharp, young man, you will be ready!"

An angry flush arose, hot and red, into the delicate face of Bertie Vaughan. He set his lips with rather a sullen air and went silently on with his breakfast.

But Sydney came bravely to the rescue. She was not a whit

in awe of her domineering, tempestuous father, and, naturally, ·
had twice the pluck of Master Bertie.

" But, papa, if Bertie really has an engagement, it isn't fair to
make him break it. When he made it, how was he to know
you would propose this? Let him keep his engagement whatever it is, and afterward let him join us. I am sure that will do
every bit as well."

" Humph !" growled the squire, "you are taking up the
cudgels for him, are you? Well, lad, let us hear what this wonderfully important engagement is all about, and if it really is
worth noticing we will let you off duty. Come—speak up !"

But "speak up" was the last thing Bertie could do on *that*
subject. Good Heaven ! he thought his blood absolutely
chilling, if this fiery old sailor really knew. A lie Mr.
Vaughan would not have stuck at a second, but he was not
quick-witted enough to invent a lie. So there was but one way
out of the dilemma.

" It is an engagement of no importance," he said, hurriedly,
that sensitive conscious color deepening again "only a trifle.
I'm sorry I mentioned it at all."

" So am I," said Captain Owenson, curtly, and then profound
and most uncomfortable silence fell.

" Bertie has no tact," Sydney thought, a provoked feeling
rising in her mind against her good-looking feeble *fiancé*. " If
his engagement really was an engagement, why didn't he keep
it through thick and thin—papa would have respected him for
it, even if it did cross his will. If it was only a trifle, as he
says, why did he mention it at all? Now he has spoiled every.
thing beforehand."

The meal ended with a sonorous grace, said with lowering
brow and suppressed, angry intonation by the master of the
house. Then he arose and glared defiance across at Bertie.

" Be off to your rooms and dress, every soul of you !" he
ordered, in what Sydney called his " quarter-deck voice," "and
woe betide that one who is two minutes later than half-past
nine !"

All dispersed—Sydney with fun in her eyes, lingering long
enough to give her irate father's grizzled mustache an audacious
little tweak ; Bertie looking pale and uneasy ; Mrs. Owenson,
slow, sedate, and serene under her fiery lord's wrath, as under
all sublunary things.

" What shall I do?" Bertie thought, biting his lip and getting himself hurriedly into all the purple and fine linen the law

allows his sovereign sex.   " Dolly will raise the devil !   Yes, by
Jove, she will, and Ben Ward—hang him !—will cut in and
have everything his own way.   The mill owning cad wants to
marry her, and will if only to spite me.   And if Sydney insists
on going over to Star Island in the afternoon, as she will be
sure to do, with the confounded contrariness of her kind—by
Jove, what an infernal muddle !   Ten to one if Dolly sees me
there, with all those girls, she will make a scene on the spot.
But I won't go to Star Island—no, by George ! wild horses won't
drag me to the. that beastly little twopenny-ha'-penny island !"

But what should he do ?   At half-past twelve precisely Dolly
would be awaiting him, and to wait for any human being sat
as illy upon the imperious little actress as though she had been
Grand Duchess of Gerolstein in her own right.   He had kept
her waiting last night, and with this added she would never forgive him—never.   She would go off in dire wrath, and breathing vengeance, with that clod-hopping mill-man, Ward, and the
odds were he would lose her forever.   To lose Dolly De Courcy
was to Mr. Vaughan's mind, this morning, about the bitterest
earthly loss that could befall him.   As far as a thoroughly weak,
thoroughly selfish, thoroughly shallow man can love any one,
he loved this black-eyed, loud-voiced, sharp-tongued, plump,
dashing, daring, sparkling actress.   She sang the most audacious songs, danced the most audacious dances, played the
French Spy and Mazeppa, and set all the men in the house
crowing and clapping over her most audacious *double entendres*
and the air of innocence with which she said them.   Three
weeks ago he had lost his head—on the first night indeed on
which he had seen her at the little Wyckcliffe theatre, in the
dashing *rôle* of Jack Sheppard.   For the matter of that a dozen
other young men had lost *their* heads on the same auspicious
occasion, but among them all the blue-eyed, fair-haired, aristo-
cratic-looking young English gentleman proved conquering
hero.   Pretty, plump Dolly had a romantic, if rather fickle fancy,
and he captivated it.   Any one exactly like him, with his slow
trainante voice, his soft, languid laugh, his gentle, obsequious
manner, the provincial actress had never met before, and all
the rich young mill-men had been nowhere in the race.   They
might sneer at " Miss Vaughan's " pretty white hands, curling
Hyperion locks, soft little mustache like the callow down upon
a gosling's back, his lavender and lemon kids, his scented and
embroidered handkerchiefs.   Miss De Courcy liked all these
elegant and patrician things, because she wasn't used to them.

He was a gentleman pure and simple, born and bred, and that is what they were not ; plebeian, uneducated, and ignorant to the core herself, Dolly had an intense admiration of these things in him. In point of fact, Bertie Vaughan was " a thing of beauty and a joy forever " in her eyes, and she would rather have married him, to use her own forcible, if not too delicate expression, " without a shirt to his back," than Ben Ward, or Sam Hecker, or any mill-millionnaire of them all " hung with diamonds." She took his bouquets, and his costlier presents, and smiled upon him, and loved him, and was passionately jealous of every look, or word, or smile given to the humblest and homeliest of her sisterhood. This Bertie knew. How, then, would it be when she found him breaking his promise, staying away from *her* picnic to attend another, and play *cavalier servante* to his cousin !

" There will be the very dickens to pay," groaned poor Bertie, " and sooner or later the whole thing will blow up and reach the governor's ears, and then——"

A cold thrill ran through him, he could not pursue the horrible subject.

" I'll write her a note and send it with Murphy," he thought, after a moment's profound cogitation. " It's the best I can do —the only thing I can do. Confound the governor ! It's the first time since I've known him such a frisky idea as this ever came into his head, and to think of his pitching upon this day of all days ! Hang it all ! "

Mr. Vaughan completed his toilet, in a greatly perturbed state of mind, " hanging" and " confounding" things and people generally, and occasionally using even stronger anathemas. His necktie was tied at last to his satisfaction, and seizing pen and paper he dashed off this note to the lady of his heart :

" DEAREST DOLLY —:I can't go to the picnic—don't expect me to-day. Got to stay on duty at home. I'm awfully sorry, but I can't get out of it. Now don't fire up, there's a dear girl. You know there is nowhere in the world I would as soon be as by your side ; but ' there is a destiny that shapes our ends, rough '—as some fellow says—' hew them how we will.' I'll be with you to-morrow after rehearsal, and tell you all about it. And, meantime, I am yours—yours only, BERTIE.

" P.S.—Don't flirt with Ward or Hecker, that's a dear girl, B."

Mr. Vaughan hastily folded and sealed this eloquent epistle, and went off in search of "Murphy." Murphy was a small boy of twelve, and errand-runner in general to the household. An understanding—strongly cemented by dimes and quarters—had been established between him and "Masther Bertie;" and Murphy alone, perhaps of the whole family, knew how his young master was running after the actress. It still wanted ten minutes of the appointed hour, and without loss of time Murphy was hunted up.

"I say, Murphy!" called Vaughan, softly, whistling him aside, "I want you."

"Yis, sur."

"I want you to deliver this note before twelve o'clock," said Bertie, slipping the note and the customary fee into the youngster's grimy hand.

Murphy's grin broadened. He could not read, and it was the first time he had ever been called upon as letter-carrier; but he understood perfectly.

"I will, sur. It's to *them ye know*, sur, isn't it?" cried Murphy, shutting one eye and cocking up the other.

"It's to Miss De Courcy, and must be delivered before twelve. You will wait for an answer; and mind, Murphy, not a word to a living soul."

"Not a sowl, sur, livin' or dead! I'll be there an' back in a pig's whisper, sur. Long life to ye, Mishter Bertie!"

"Hi! there—you, Murphy. 'Old the 'osses' 'eads, will yer?" cried out Perkins, the cockney coachman. "Beg parding, Mr. Bertie, didn't see you, sir, but the hoff 'oss is a bit restive and fresh this morning. I say, Murphy! look alive, will yer. 'Ere's the squire."

Murphy held the frisky off-wheeler, and Mr. Perkins mounted to his seat. Squire Owenson, leaning on Sydney's strong young arm, appeared, Mrs. Owenson following. Bertie sprang forward to assist him in; then Mrs. Owenson, then Sydney; then with one parting glance of intelligence at Murphy, sprang after. Perkins cracked his whip and away they went at a rattling pace down the avenue.

The gloom of Bertie's untoward remark still hung over the horizon of the squire. His Jove-like front lowered portentously. Bertie saw it and fidgetted rather uneasily, essayed small remarks, and looked in the intervals out of the window. But Sydney, radiant of face and toilet, set herself assiduously to restore sunshine and harmony. She talked nonsense and laughed at it, made small jokes and laughed at them, and the laughter was infectious if the humor was not. By the time they reached the Sunderlands', general geniality had been restored; the squire smiled, and peace reigned.

A lively welcome awaited them. Two tall daughters and two taller sons blessed this household—all were rejoiced to see Sydney and Bertie ; and in the midst of laughter, and talk, and good fellowship, young Vaughan's last trace of uneasiness vanished—like mist before the sun. He was one of those people to whom it is a sheer physical impossibility to be unhappy long ·—who shake off all thought of evil to come, and will eat, drink, and be merry to-day, come death and doom to-morrow.

The young men smoked cigars, and compared notes of their doings for the past year—the girls played the piano, and did likewise. Sydney's approaching marriage was discussed in all its bearings, and the Misses Sunderland were invited to make two of the five bridesmaids to officate upon the occasion. Bertie's good looks and Chesterfieldian manners were rapturously praised. Sydney's improved prettiness eloquently commented on. Then the privy council became general. They played croquet, they played billiards, and did both with such gay laughter and tumult that they penetrated even to the, drawing-room, where the elders sedately sat, raising a smile to their sober faces.

Star Island was proposed as a matter of course, but Bertie Vaughan protested against it. They were very well off as they were—he always believed it was a good maxim to let well enough alone. So the idea was given up, and that difficulty tided over.

"Let us take a walk on the beach, then," said Sydney, who loved the sea; "it is an hour now till dinner time, and the water does look so calm and lovely."

They all went down—Sydney and the Messrs. Sunderland leading the way, Bertie and the Misses Sunderland following. It *was* lovely; the soft salt waves came lapping to their very feet, a faint breeze rippled the steely surface of the Atlantic, boats floated over it like birds, and Star Island lay like a green gem in its blue bosom. The elder Mr. Sunderland had brought a telescope, by the aid of which the revellers could be seen making merry afar off.

"'They're the theatre people from Wyckcliffe," Mr. Sunderland said, adjusting the glass for Miss Owenson, "and a lot of young fellows of the town. That's Dolly De Courcy's scarlet shawl, for a ducat, and that's her black plume. It reminds one

of the man in the poem—Dolly's ostrich feather is sure to be in
the thickest of the fun.

> " And 'mid the thickest carnage blazed
> The helmet of Navarre. "

"Who's Dolly De Courcy?" asked Sydney; and Bertie
Vaughan's guilty heart gave a jump, and then stood still.

"Oh! a pretty black-eyed actress from New York. Very
jolly little girl—eh, Vaughan? *You* know," laughed Mr. Sunderland the elder.

In an instant—how Bertie did curse his fatal complexion in
his heart—the red tide of guilt had mounted to his eyes. Both
the Sunderlands laughed, a malicious laugh. Sydney looked
surprised, and the younger Miss Sunderland, who was only sixteen and didn't know much, said:

"Law! look how Bertie's blushing."

"I—I know Miss De Courcy—that is, slightly," said Bertie,
feeling that everybody was looking at him, and that he was expected to say something. At which answer the two Mr. Sunderlands laughed more than ever, and only stopped short at a
warning look from Miss Sunderland the elder, and a wondering
one from Sydney.

"See! they're going home; they're putting off in two boats,"
cried Miss Susie Sunderland, holding her hand over one eye,
and squinting through the glass with the other. "Oh, I can see
them just as plain! one, two, three, four, oh! a dozen of them.
There's the red shawl, and black feather, too, and there's Ben!
yes, it *is*, Ben Ward, Mamie, helping her in. They've—they've
sat down, and oh! goodness, he's put his arm around her waist;
he, he, he!" giggled Miss Susie.

"Perhaps you would like to look, Mamie?" said the wicked
elder brother, taking the glass from Susie and presenting it with
much politeness to his elder sister, whose turn it had been to
redden at Susie's words. For the perfidious Benjamin Ward,
Esquire, had been "paying attention" to Miss Mamie Sunderland, very markedly indeed, before that wicked little fisher of
men, Dolly De Courcy, had come along to demoralize him.

"No, thank you," Miss Sunderland responded, her eyes
slightly flashing, her tone slightly acidulated; "the goings on
of a crowd of actors and actresses don't interest *me*. Mr
Vaughan, just see those pretty sea-anemones; please get me
some."

Mr. Vaughan goes for the sea-anemones with her, and Miss Mamie becomes absorbed in them, suspiciously absorbed, indeed, but all the same she covertly watches that coming boat, with bitterness of heart. Alarm is mingled with Mr. Vaughan's bitterness, and as the boat draws nearer and nearer, he rather nervously proposes that they shall go back ; the wind is blowing chilly ; Miss Mamie may take cold.

"I never take cold," Miss Mamie answers, shortly ; "I prefer staying here."

So they stay, and the boat draws nearer and nearer. Sydney, with an interest she cannot define, watches it through the glass adjusted upon Harry Sunderland's shoulder. They have a glass, too ; the gentleman who sits beside the scarlet shawl and black feather fixes it for his companion, and she gazes steadfastly at the shore.

Still they draw nearer and nearer. Does Ben Ward do it (he is steering) with *malice prepense?* They come within five yards. No need of glasses now. Dolly De Courcy is sitting very close beside Ben Ward, laughing and flirting, and she looks straight at Bertie Vaughan, who takes off his hat, and never sees him. Mr. Ward elevates his chapeau politely to the Misses Sunderland, which salutation Miss Mamie, with freezing dignity, returns.

"Pretty Dolly gave you the cut direct, Vaughan," says the elder Sunderland, enjoying hugely his discomfiture. Harry Sunderland is a manly fellow himself, and has a thorough-going contempt for insipid dandy Bertie ; "or else she has suddenly grown short-sighted."

But Bertie is on guard now, and his face tells nothing as Sydney wonderingly looks at it. For she has recognized the handsome, dark girl in the scarlet shawl as the same she encountered walking late last evening with somebody that looked so suspiciously like Bertie.

The water party float away in the distance, Miss De Courcy singing one of her high, sweet stage songs as they go. As it dies out into the sunset distance they turn as by one accord, and go back to the house ; two of the group thoroughly out of sorts with themselves and all the world. Sydney, too, was rather silent. What did all this mean ? she wondered. Most obedient to her father, she was most willing to marry Bertie Vaughan to please him, without much love on either side. Yet that he cared for her as much as she did for him, was as loyal to her as she was to him, she had never for a second doubted.

But now, a vague, undefinable feeling of wounded pride and distrust has arisen within her. What was 'hat actress with the black, bold eyes to him that he should redden and pale at the very sound of her name ?

"It surely was Bertie I saw walking with her last night," she thought, more and more perturbed. "I will ask him ; he shall tell me the truth, and that before this time to-morrow !"

CHAPTER XIV.

"MEN WERE DECEIVERS EVER."

DINNER awaits them. It wants but three minutes to the hour as they straggle in, and Captain Owenson sits, watch in hand, stormy weather threatening in his eyes. The signs of the tempest clear away as they enter, and all sit down to the festal board. And still through all the cheery talk and laughter Bertie Vaughan and Mamie Sunderland remain silent and *distrait*, victims to the green-eyed monster in his most virulent form, the image of Dolly De Courcy, in her scarlet shawl and sable plume, upsetting the disgestion of both.

"And I really think, my love," says Mrs. Owenson, when they arise from the table, "that we ought not to linger. These fall nights are cold, and you know the doctors all warn you against exposing yourself to cold."

There is wisdom in the speech ; and though on principle Captain Owenson contradicts pretty much everything Mrs. Owenson may see fit to say, he cannot contradict this. So adieus are made, and the Owenson party enter their carriage and are driven home.

It is a perfect autumnal evening—blue, frosty, starlit, clear. The wind sighing fitfully through moaning pine woods, the surf thundering dully on the shore below, ring dreamily in Sydney's ears all the way. She leans forward out of the window, something in the solemn murmurous beauty of the night filling her heart with a thrill akin to pain ; and still that dark and dashing actress occupies her thoughts—and the more she thinks, the more convinced she is, that last night Bertie was her companion. If so, he has told her a deliberate lie, and the girl's heart contracts with a sudden sharp spasm of almost physical pain and terror. If he has been false here, will he be true in anything? All her life Sydney has been taught to look upon lying with horror and repulsion.

" It is the meanest and most sneaking of all cowardice," her blunt and fearless old father had said to her a hundred times ; 'don't ever lie, Sydney, if you die for it."

" It is the most heinous and despicable of all sins," her ghostly directors had taught the child, in later years. "*No* goodness can dwell in an untruthful soul."

And now—was Bertie false ? Bertie, whom she was to marry and spend all her life with.

" I will ask him," she kept repeating ; " his tongue may speak falsely, but his face, his eyes, will tell the truth. And if there is anything between this girl and him "—she stopped and caught her breath for a moment—" then I will never, never be his wife."

She looked at him wistfully, but, lying back in his corner, his hands clasped behind his golden head, his face was not to be seen.

" How silent you young people are," the squire said, at last , " anything wrong with you, puss? A penny for your thoughts, Bertie."

There was a momentary brightening, but too forced to last. Bertie Vaughan's thoughts would have been worth much more than a penny to his questioner—they were solely and absorbedly of Dolly. He must see her to-night; impossible to wait until to-morrow. Ben Ward had been at her side all day pouring nis seductive flatteries into her ears, offering, very likely, to make her mistress of the new red-brick mansion over in Wyckcliffe. And women are unstable, and gold, and offers of wedding rings, have their charm. He had nothing to offer her but his handsome blue eyes and Raphael face ; he had never even mentioned wedding rings in all his love-making. Yes, come what might, he must see the coquettish Dolly before he slept. It was half-past ten when they reached The Place, and the moon was beginning to silver the black trees around it The squire was growling uneasily about the cold, and it was a relief to all when they drew up on the front steps, and Bertie and Perkins gave each an arm to the stiff and chill old sailor, and helped him to his room.

" Are you going out again, Bertie ?" Sydney asked, looking at him in surprise as he replaced his hat, and turned to leave the house.   .   .   .   . . .

"For my usual nocturnal prowl and smoke. Couldn't sleep without it, I assure you. Run away to bed, sis, and good-night."

He left the house and made straight for the town at a swinging pace. It was almost eleven now—if he could only reach the theatre in time to see Dolly leave.

He was in time. Moonlight and lamplight flooded the little square in front of the play-house, and standing himself in the shadow, Bertie saw the lady of his love come forth in the famous red shawl and black feather, leaning confidingly on the arm of Ben Ward. She was in the highest of wild high spirits, too, her clear laugh and loud voice mingling with the deeper tones of his rival.

"Awfully late to-night, ain't I?" he heard her gayly say; "I expect you're about tired to death waiting, Ben."

"As if all time would be too long to wait for you, Dolly," responded, gallantly and affectionately, Mr. Ben; and the listener gnashed his teeth as he listened. It had come to this then—it was Ben and Dolly: and who was to tell him it was not to be Ben and Dolly all their lives.

He followed in their wake, keeping out of sight among the shadows. Keenly sensitive to ridicule, Bertie would not for worlds be seen in the ludicrous *rôle* of jealous lover by Ward. They sauntered very slowly, peals of laughter telling how they were enjoying their *tête-à-tête*. They reached Dolly's cottage-home and paused at the gate. In the shadow of some trees across the moonlit road Vaughan hid and glowered. Mr. Ward seemed disposed to prolong the dialogue even here, but Miss De Courcy, with a loud yawn which she made no pretence to hide, declared she was "dead beat," and must go to bed right away.

"So good-night, Ben," cried the actress, opening the gate and holding out her other hand; "and thanks, ever so much, for the flowers, and the ear-rings, once more."

"But not good-night like this, Dolly," exclaimed Mr. Ward, drawing her nearer, and stooping his head; "not good-night with a cold shake hands, surely?"

But the gate had opened and shut smartly, and Dolly, on the other side, had eluded the embrace.

"Not if I know it! There's only one man in the whole universe I ever mean to kiss, and he isn't *you*, Mr. Benjamin Ward, I can tell you! Good-night."

"Is it Bertie Vaughan, then, I wonder? Pretty Miss Vaughan—'The Fair One With The Golden Locks' we follows call him, who cut you to-day to court his cousin? If it's that milk-sop, Dolly, I'm surprised at your taste; upon my word and honor, I am."

"It's no business of yours, Mr. Ward, who it is," cries out Dolly, her black eyes snapping in the moonlight; "it isn't you, anyhow, be sure of that. And if you think your ear-rings are thrown away, I'll give 'em back to you. It shall never be said that Dolly De Courcy took any man's presents under false pretences."

"Oh! d—— the ear-rings?" said Mr. Ward. "I never thought of them, and you know it. But, seriously, Doll, I think heaps of you; never saw a girl in all my life I liked so well; and I'll marry you any day you like—so there! Can I say fairer than that? It's no use your thinking of Miss Vaughan; it isn't, Dolly, upon my soul. He's booked for his cousin—she isn't his cousin, by-the-by—and has been, ever since he left off petticoats. He hasn't got a red but what the old man will give him; and the wedding is fixed to come off in a month. He's spoony on you, I know, Dolly, but he can't marry you, because he hasn't a rap to live on. Now think over all this, and make up your mind to be Mrs. Ben Ward, because you'll never get a better offer, no, by George! while your name's Dolly."

"Have you got anything more to say?" demanded Miss De Courcy, standing "at gaze," and with anything but a melting expression, as Mr. Ward poured forth his tender wooing.

"Well, I guess not at present. What do you say, Dolly?"

"I say good-night, for the last time, and go home and go to bed!" snapped Dolly De Courcy, marching with a majestic Lady Macbeth sort of stride to her own front door.

"All right," retorted the imperturbable Ben. "Good-night, Dolly."

But Dolly was gone, and Mr. Ward laughed a little laugh to himself, struck a match, pulled out a stumpy, black meerschaum, lit it, and went on his homeward way.

"It's only a question of time," he said aloud, glancing up at the one lighted window of the cottage; "she's a bewitching little devil, and I'm bound to make her Mrs. W. She's soft on 'The Fair One,' at present, but she'll get over that. He must marry little Miss Sydney, and then Doll will have me, if only for spite.'

As he strode away, out from the dark shadows of the pines stalked Bertie, pallid and ferocious with jealousy. It was precisely like one of Miss De Courcy's own situations on the stage.

"Will she have you if only for spite?" repeated Mr. Vaughan between his teeth in most approved style ; "and she's soft on me at present, is she ! Confounded cad ! I wonder I didn't come out and knock him down there and then."

Seeing that sinewy Ben Ward could have taken Bertie by the waist-band, and laid him low in the kennel any moment he liked, perhaps after all it was *not* to be wondered at. He opened the garden gate, flung a handful of loose gravel up at the lighted panes, and waited. There was a momentary pause ; then the curtains moved about an inch aside, and in a tone of suppressed fury a voice demanded:

"Is that you, Ben Ward?"

"No, Dolly—it's I—Bertie."

Like a flash the muslin curtain was swept away, and Dolly's eager face, eager and glad, in spite of all her efforts, appeared.

"You, Mr. Vaughan ! and at this time of night ! May I ask what this insult means?"

"Oh, nonsense, Dolly ! You're not on the stage now. Come down—there's a darling girl—I've something to say to you."

"Mr. Vaughan, it is almost twelve o'clock—midnight ! And you ask me to come down ! What do you think I am ?"

"The dearest girl in creation. Come, Dolly, what's the use of that rubbish ?"

Miss De Courcy, without more ado, drops the curtain, goes deliberately down stairs, unlocks the door, and stands in the moonlight before her lover.

"My darling !" He makes an eager step forward, but with chilling dignity Miss De Courcy waves him off.

"That will do, Mr. Vaughan ! I know what you're 'my darlings' are worth. If I told you my opinion of you this moment, you would hardly feel flattered. I hope you enjoyed yourself with your charming cousin to-day."

The withering scorn of this speech could only have been done by an actress. Miss Dolly, in a fine stage attitude, stood and looked down upon Mr. Vaughan.

"No, Dolly, I didn't enjoy myself. Was it likely, with you on Star Island with Ben Ward? I had to go. I tried to get out of it—tried my best—and failed. I can't afford to offend my uncle—that is the truth—and at the bare mention of my having an engagement he flew into a passion ; and you ought to see the passions he can fly into. No, I did *not* enjoy myself, but I had to go."

" Oh-h !" said Miss De Courcy, coldly. " I always thought you were a grown man, not a little boy, to be ordered about and made do as you are bid. Since you are so afraid of this awful Captain Owenson, then, and so dependent upon him, of course the moment he tells you to marry his heiress you'll buy a white tie and go and do it. Have you anything more to say to me, Mr. Vaughan ? because even an actress may have a reputation to lose if seen standing here with you after midnight."

She turned as if to go—then lingered. For he stood silent leaning against a tree, and something in his face and attitude touched her.

"Have you anything more to say ?" she repeated, holding the door.

" No, Dolly, since you take that tone—nothing. What you say is true—it *is* pitiful in a fellow of twenty-one to be ordered about like a lad of twelve, and I ought to have held out and braved the old man's displeasure and gone with you. I have nothing to say in my own defence, and I have no right to do anything that will compromise you in the eyes of Ben Ward. He's rich and I'm poor, and I suppose you'll marry him, Dolly. I have no right to say anything, but it's rather hard."

He broke off. The next instant impulsive Dolly was down the steps and by his side, her whole heart (and it was as honest and true a heart as ever beat in its way) in her dark shining eyes.

" No right !" she cried out. " Oh, Bertie ! if you care for me, you have every right ! "

" If I care for you ! " the blue eyes look eloquently into the black ones ; " do you doubt that too ? "

"No !" exclaimed Dolly, doubt, anger, jealousy, all swept away in her love for this man. " You do like me, Bertie ! Oh, I know that ! You do like me better than her ? "

" Than her ? Than whom ? "

" Oh ! you know—I've no patience to talk about her, your cousin, the heiress, Miss Owenson. She's sweetly pretty, too —but, Bertie, do say it ; tell me the real truth, you do like me better than her ? "

He bends down his handsome face, and whispers his answer —an answer that brings the swift blood into the dusk cheeks of the actress, and a wonderful light into the glittering black eyes.

" But what is the use of it all ? " she breaks out, with an impatient sigh. " You are afraid of her father. You are dependent on him.   You will not dare offend him, and—you will marry her."

"No, by Jove!" exclaims Bertie.   "I'll marry nobody but you, Dolly—that I swear.   If I lost you, if you married Ward, I'd blow my brains out.   I couldn't live without you, I don't know how I come to be so awfully fond of you, but I couldn't. And I wish you wouldn't take things from Ward ; ear-rings, or flowers even, or from any of them.   You belong to me, and I don't like it."

"Very well, Bertie," assents Dolly, with a long-drawn, happy breath, " I won't.   I don't care for them or their presents, but I *was* mad to see you there on the shore ; and then Ben Ward told me all about your going to marry Miss Owenson, and the wedding things coming from Paris, and the wedding to be next month, until he had me half insane.   It has been the most miserable evening in my life."

"Indeed!   No one would have thought so to hear you and Ward laugh."

"If I hadn't laughed I would have cried, and actresses can act off the stage as well as on.   Oh, Bertie! don't deceive me about this.   I love you so well that——" her voice actually faltered, tears actually rose to her hard black eyes.

"I won't, Dolly, I swear it!   And you—you're very exacting with me, but how am I to know how many lovers you have behind in New York?—how am I to know you are not engaged even to some fellow there?"

It was a random shot, but it struck home.   In the moonlight he saw her start suddenly and turn pale.

"Ha!" he said, "it is true, then?   You are engaged?"

"Bertie," she faltered, " I don't care for a single man on all the earth but you!   You believe that?"

"But you are engaged in New York?"

"Ye-e-s—that is, I was.   But I'll write and break it off—I will to-morrow morning.   Bertie, don't look like that.   I never really cared for him, he was too fiery and tyrannical."

"What is his name?" Vaughan gloomily asked.

"What does it matter about his name?   I'll never see him again if I can help it.   I'll write and end it all to-morrow. Come, Bertie, don't look so cross; after all, it only makes us even."

"Yes, it only makes us even," he repeated, rather bitterly ; "even in duplicity and dishonor.   I'm a villain and a fool too, I dare say, in this business, but I'll see it to the end for all that."

"A villain and a fool for caring for me, no doubt,' the actress retorts, angrily.

"Yes, Doll; but I *do* care for you, you see, and I have
never refused myself anything I cared for, and don't mean to
begin now. So I shall marry you—how or when I don't quite
know yet, but I mean to marry you, and you only."

She nestles close to him, and there is silence. The pale blue
moonlight, the whispering wind, the rustling trees, nothing else
to see or hear.

"Why didn't you tell me all this sooner?" the girl asks at
length. "Why did you leave it to Ben Ward? Even last night
you deceived me—making me think she was a little ugly
school-girl."

"Why didn't you tell me about the man in New York?
Why hadn't you told him about me? It won't do for you and
me to throw stones at each other—we have both been living in
glass houses. Let us cry quits, Dolly, and bury the hatchet.
You know all now. You believe I love you, and mean to marry
you, and not Miss Owenson, and that, I take it, is the main
point."

"But, Bertie, this can't go on long. She expects you to
marry her next month."

"Her father does—she doesn't. She would very much rather
not marry me at all. And next month isn't this. Sufficient
unto the day the evil thereof."

Unconsciously to himself Bertie Vaughan was a profound
fatalist, letting his life drift on, a firm believer in the "Some-
thing-will-turn-up" doctrine.

"You see," he went on, "the governor's life hangs on a
thread—on a hair. At any moment it may end. His will is
made, and I am handsomely remembered in it. He may die
suddenly before the wedding-day—in which case a comfortable
competence will be mine for life. The moment he finds out
this he will destroy that will, turn me out, and disinherit me.
Have I not reason enough for silence? Just let things drift on,
Dolly—it will do no harm; and if, on the eve of the wedding-
day, he is still alive, then I will throw up the sponge to fate,
run away with you, turn actor or crossing-sweeper, and live
happy ever after. There is the programme."

He paused. Dolly De Dourcy stood silent, her keen black
eyes fixed thoughtfully upon him. How selfish, how craven,
how utterly without heart, generosity, honor, gratitude, this man
she loved was! this man who looked like a young Apollo here

in the moon rays. False to the core, how could she expect
him to be true to her? Unstable as water, would not the love
of wealth prove the stronger love in the end? Might he not
play her false, and marry Captain Owenson's fair young heiress
after all?

" No ! " Dolly cried, inwardly ; " that he shall not ! I have
his letters—I will go to Owenson Place, and show them to this
haughty Englishman and his daughter first. He shall never
play fast and loose with me."

"And now, darling, I must be off," Vaughan said, looking
at his watch. "Ye gods ! half-past one. Farewell, Dolly ;
remember ! no more flirtations with Ward. Give him his ear-
ringsand his *congé* to-morrow."

"I'll keep the ear-rings, but I'll give him his *congé*," replied
prudent Dolly. "Good-night, Bertie. Be as false as you like
to all the rest of the worle but be true to me."

"*Loyal je serai durant ma vie !*" laughs Bertie Vaughan,
and then he is through the little garden gate and away. Dolly
stands and watches the slender figure of her lover out of sight,
then turns.

"Faithful unto death," she says to herself. "Yes, you will
be that to me, for I shall make you."

The clocks of Wyckcliffe were striking two as Vaughan came
in sight of his home. To his surprise a light burned in Captain Owenson's chamber, and figures flitted to and fro. He
stopped; a sudden thought—shall it be said, hope ! sending the
blood to his face. Was the squire sick, was he—dead ? The
rest of the house was unlighted. Perhaps his absence had not
been discovered. He softly inserted his latch-key and opened
the door. All was darkness. He closed it and stepped in.
As he did so a light appeared on the upper landing, and some
one lightly and swiftly began descending the stairs.

" Perkins, is that you ? " the soft voice of Sydney asked.

There was no reply. She descended two or three more
stairs lamp in hand, wrapped in a white dressing-gown, her yellow hair streaming over her shoulders and came face to face
with Bertie Vaughan.

CHAPTER XV.

"TO ONE THING CONSTANT NEVER."

HERE was an instant's pause—both stood and looked each other full in the eyes. Then Sydney spoke. " You, Bertie ? " she said, in slow wonder. " I, sis," he answered, lightly. "I have been to Wychcliffe. The engagement I had to break this morning I kept to-night. But what is the matter ? Your father——"

" Has been taken suddenly ill—a sort of ague. He must have got thoroughly chilled on our way home. Oh I I wish we had not gone at all. Perkins is away for Dr. Howard. Ah! here he is now."

The doctor entered with the coachman, and went straight to his patient's room. Sydney and Bertie waited outside, both silent, both pale and anxious, though from very different causes. If the old man died, the young man thought, with his will un-altered, his course lay straight before him. He would marry Dolly out of hand, and go off with her to New York. There would be a nine days' scandal—Sydney would despise him—he winced at the thought—but otherwise she would not care. And in two or three years some lucky fellow would win her heart and become master of Owenson Place. A pang of jealousy and envy shot through him as he thought it. He was prepared to resign both himself, but all the same, the idea of that other who would profit by his folly was unbearable to him.

Presently the chamber door opened and Doctor Howard came out, looking jolly and at ease. Sydney sprang up and ran toward him.

"It's all right, my dear, it's all right," the old doctor said, patting the cold little hands she held out to him ; "papa won't leave us yet awhile. He thinks he will, but, bless you, *we* know better. If he keeps quiet, he's good for a dozen years yet. ·Now, just run in and kiss him good-night, and then away to bed. Those pretty eyes are too bright to be dimmed by late hours. Ah, Mr. Bertie, good-morning to you, sir."

Sydney shot off like an arrow, and Bertie went slowly, and with a disgusted feeling, to bed. " Good for a dozen years yet ! " Oh, no doubt, no doubt at all. It is in the nature of rich fathers, and uncles, and guardians to hang to the attenuated

6*

thread of life, when they and everybody connected with them would be much more comfortable if they went quietly to their graves.

"No fear of his going toes up before the wedding-day," thought Mr. Vaughan, bitterly. "He'll tough it out, as old Howard says, to dandle his grandsons, I've no doubt. And then there's nothing left for me but the ' all-for-love and the world-well-lost ' sort of thing. By Jove, Dolly will have to work for me as well as for herself when I make her Mrs. Vaughan."

Next day, by noon, Squire Owenson was able to descend to luncheon. A letter from Montreal, in a stiff, wiry hand, lay beside his plate. It was from Miss Phillis Dormer, and contained a gracious assent to the visit of her niece, Cyrilla. That same evening brought a note from Cyrilla herself to Sydney:

"PETITE ST. JACQUES, Nov. 8th.

"DEAREST SYD:—It is all arranged. Aunt Phil cheerfully consents, and has actually (who says the days of miracles are past?) sent me ten pounds to buy my bridesmaid's dress. Three days from this I will be with you on unlimited leave of absence. In haste (class-bell is ringing), but, as ever, devotedly yours, CYRILLA."

Two days before, Sydney would have danced with delight, but now she read this note, her color rising, a look of undefined trouble on her face. Everything seemed settled—her trousseau had come, the very bridal veil and wreath were up-stairs. Cyrilla was coming to be bridesmaid, and Bertie had never spoken one word. She glanced across the table—they were at dinner —to where he sat trifling with a chicken-wing and tasting, with epicurean relish, his glass of Sillery. Was she worth so little, then, that she was not even worth the asking? Less vanity a pretty girl could hardly have than Sydney, but a sharp, mortified pang of wounded feeling went through her now as she looked at him—cool, careless, unconcerned.

"Papa forces me upon him, and he takes me because he cannot well help himself," she thought. "He is in love with that dark-eyed actress, and he will marry me and be miserable all his life. Oh! if papa had only let us alone, and never attempted this match-making!"

" Bad news, puss?" her father asked. "You look forlorn.
What's the matter, little one ?   Let me see the letter."

She hesitated a moment—then passed it over to him reluctantly, and the squire, adjusting his double eye-glass, read it
sonorously aloud.   Sydney's eyes never left the plate, her
cheeks tingled ; Bertie sat, an indifferent auditor, his whole attention absorbed by his champagne.

Squire Owenson laid down the letter and looked at his
daughter through his glasses.

" Well, petite, that's all right, isn't it ?   She'll be here in
three days—two more ; and you and Bertie shall meet her at
the station.   What's that troubled look for, then ?   You're fond
of this young lady, are you not ?

" Yes, papa, very fond.   Dear old Cy!"

" Then what is it ?   It isn't that you're afraid she'll make
love to Bertie—hey ? and are jealous beforehand ?"

But Sydney had finished her dessert, and jumped up abruptly
and ran away.   It was little short of maddening to see Bertie
sit there, that languid smile of his just dawning, and feel all the
cool, self-assured, almost insolent indifference with which he
took her without the asking.

The two days passed.   Bertie spent a great deal of his time
away from The Place, doing home duty at stated intervals,
when it was impossible to shirk it without arousing the quick
suspicions of the "governor."   He drove Sydney and her
mother along the country roads together, he rode out twice
with Sydney alone, but that conversation had not taken place ;
the explanation Miss Owenson meant to have she had not had
as yet.   It was one thing to resolve to ask Bertie whether or
no he was in love with the actress, to tax him indirectly with
falsehood, and another thing to do it.   Bertie Vaughan, her old
comrade and playfellow, was a man—"a gentleman growed,"
as Pegotty says, and every instinct of her womanhood shrank
from broaching the subject.   It was for him to speak, for her to
refuse or accept, as she saw fit.   He never did speak—never
came within miles of the subject, avoided it, ignored it utterly,
as the girl could hardly fail to see.   And so the day and the
hour of Cyrilla's arrival came, and matters matrimonial were in
statu quo.

It was a gloomy November afternoon, " onding on snaw,'
sky and atmosphere steel gray alike, a wild, long blast rattled
the trees and sent the dead leaves in whirls before it.   A few
feathery flakes were drifting through the sullen air, giving

promise of the first snow-storm of the season before mid night.

The train came thundering into the lighted station as Sydney and Bertie took their places. Sydney in a velvet jacket, a velvet cap, crowned with an ostrich feather, on her bright, wind-blown hair, and in a state of eager expectation. For Mr. Vaughan, he had not deigned to take much interest in the new comer from the first ; judging, from Sydney's talk, he was predisposed to dislike her indeed, as a young person inclined to " chaff." People inclined to chaff, Bertie had found, from experience, generally chaffed *him*, and, like most weak men, he was acutely sensitive to ridicule.

The train stopped ; the passengers for Wychcliffe, half a dozen in number, came out. Among them a tall young lady, in a travelling suit of dark green serge, at sight of whom Sydney uttered a joyous cry and plunged forward straightway into her arms.

" Oh, of course," says Bertie cynically, eying the pair, "they must gush. A quarter of an hour of kissing and exclamation points, as though they had not seen each other for a century or so ! She's not bad looking either—got eyes like Dolly."

She might have eyes like Dolly, but there all resemblance ended. Miss Hendrick's tall, pliant figure bore no similarity to Miss De Courcy's "rounded and ripe." Miss Hendrick's patrician profile, and clear cut, colorless, olive face, was as unlike, as can well be conceived, Dolly's little saucy *retroussé* nose and highly-colored complexion.

" Cyrilla, this is Bertie ; Mr. Vaughan, Miss Hendrick."

Bertie flung away his cigar, doffed his hat, and bent before Miss Hendrick with his best bow. Miss Hendrick looked at him—looked through him—with those lustrous ebon eyes of hers, smiled, showed very brilliant teeth, and frankly extended one invisible-green kidded hand.

" I don't feel at all as though I were meeting a stranger in meeting you, Mr. Vaughan. I have been your most intimate friend for the past two years—haven't I, Sydney ? "

" Miss Hendrick's friendship does me proud," says Bertie. He would like to utter some very telling and sarcastic compliment ; he has an instinctive longing to " take her down " at sight, but the truth is, he can think of none. Her pronounced manner has taken him decidedly aback. He had expected to meet a school-girl, more or less *gauche* and bread-and-buttery, and instead he saw a regal-looking young lady, with the "stilly tranquil " manner and gracious civility of a *grande dame*. The aggressive feeling he had felt, before he saw her, deepened tenfold. He had intended to be *very* civil—crushingly civil indeed—to Sydney's little school friend ; to patronize her in the most oppressive manner, to get up a mild flirtation with her even, if she had any pretensions to good looks ; and behold, here she was absolutely patronizing him, and looking him through, to the very marrow of his bones, with those piercing, steadfast black eyes—like in color, but wonderfully unlike in every other respect, Dolly's.

" I expect you two to become fast friends at once ! " cries Sydney. " You know all about each other beforehand, and are compatriots besides."

> " ' None know me but to love me,
>   None name me but to praise,' "

says Bertie, helping them in. " I have heard Miss Hendrick's praises sung so assiduously for the past week, that——"

" The very sound of her name bores you—yes, I understand," interrupts Cyrilla. " Syd, what a bewitching little turn-out, and what handsome steppers ! You will let me drive you, won't you ? I'm a capital whip."

" I'll let you do anything you please. Oh! darling, how good it seems to have you with me again ! " Sydney said, cuddling close to Cyrilla's side. " How are they all in Petite St. Jacques ? How is Freddy ? "

" I have not seen Freddy since the night I risked a broken neck and a shattered reputation getting out of the window to meet him. I managed to answer his letter, and there thing' remain. For the rest—Miss Jones has left the school."

" What ! '

" Perfectly true. It was suddenly discovered that she had a passion for novel-reading (Mlle. Stephanie's pet abomination), and was a subscriber to the town circulating library—that one of the French girls was in the habit of smuggling in the forbidden fruit, and having all her lessons done by Miss Jones in return. The crime was proven beyond refutation and—Miss Jones suddenly and quietly left the school."

" Oh h ! "—a very prolonged "oh," indeed—"Mlle. Stephanie dismissed her ? "

" So I presume. The fact remains—she went."

"Cyrilla," Sydney said, a look of pain on her face, "did—did *you* do this?"

"And what if I did, Syd? There was little love lest be-tween us from the first, and it pleased Heaven to diminish it on further acquaintance. Yes—indirectly it was through me that Ma'amselle Stephanie made the discovery, I must own."

There was silence; unconsciously, involuntarily, Sydney shrunk a little from her friend.

"Well, Syd, did I do wrong? Were you so fond of Miss Jones that you put on that shocked face?"

"Fond of her?—no," Sydney answered, slowly; "but I am sorry you did this. Poor Miss Jones! life had gone hard with her, I am afraid, and soured her. She stood quite alone in the world, and it was all the home she had."

"My dearest Syd," Miss Hendrick said, laughing, "if you carry that tender heart of yours through life you'll find it bleed-ing at every turn. I owed Miss Jones a long debt, and I have paid it—that is all."

"And she will pay you if ever she has the chance, you may be sure of that, Cyrilla."

"I am sure of it, Sydney. But it is not my intention to let her have the chance. She does not know Aunt Phil's address, and most likely never will. People who have to work for the bread they eat have no time for vendetta. Why do we talk of so contemptible a subject at all? Let us talk of yourself, *chère belle*. So that is our Bertie. He is as handsome as Narcis-sus."

"And, like Narcissus, knows it only too well."

There was a touch, all unconscious, of bitterness in Sydney's answer that did not escape the quick ear of her friend.

"Everything is settled, I suppose, and the happy day fixed? When is it to be, darling, this month or next?"

"The happy day is *not* fixed," Sydney answered, trying to speak lightly, and feeling the color burning in her cheeks; "not this month, certainly. Next very likely, if—at all."

"My dear child," Cyrilla cried, really startled, "'if at all!' What an odd thing to say!"

"Is it? But who knows what may happen? Who can tell what a day may bring forth, much less a month? I have the strongest prophetic conviction there will be no wedding at all."

She spoke almost without volition of her own—something within her seemed to say the words. In the tragic time that

was to come, that was even then at hand, she recalled that
involuntary sentence with strange, sombre wonder. For Cyrilla
—she sat and looked at her, rendered utterly speechless for a
moment by this unexpected declaration.

" Don't stare so, Cy," Sydney laughed, recovering her customary good humor. " It's very rude. Why, I may be dead and
buried in a month !"

" Very true—or Bertie !"

" Or Bertie."

" Or one of you may prove false."

" Or one of us may prove false ; " but as Sydney repeated
the answer the color slowly died out of her face.

" Sydney !" Cyrilla exclaimed, "it isn't possible—no, it isn't,
that you have gone and fallen in love since you left school ? "

Sydney's clear laugh rang out so merrily that no other answer
was needed, and Bertie turning around, demanded to know the
joke.

" Nothing concerning you, Bertie—only something very witty
Miss Hendrick has said by accident. Here we are. Cy—welcome to my home, which I hope you will make yours very,
very often."

Miss Hendrick was received with profoundest deference by
Captain Owenson, with a smiling kiss by Aunt Char, and
shown to the pretty room prepared for her—the prettiest by far
that she had ever occupied ; and here Sydney left her, to change
her own dress before dinner. Cyrilla sat down for a moment
in the low easy-chair in front of the fire, burning cheerily in the
steel grate, and slowly and thoughtfully removed her wraps.

"So," she thought, "that's the way the land lies—already.
Master Bertie has placed his pretty face and impecunious hand
at another shrine, and Sydney has found it out. He doesn't
like me. I could see that. We are antagonistic at sight. All
your weak men are fickle and foolish. I wonder who his inamo-
rata can be ?

> " 'Sigh no more, ladies, sigh no more,
> Men were deceivers ever,
> One foot on sea and one on shore,
> To one thing constant never.
> Then sigh not so,
> But let them go ——.' "

Cyrilla hummed softly as she dressed. She wore the before
mentioned garnet merino, the gold and ruby set, a jet comb in
her black hair, a cluster of scarlet geranium blossoms and velvet

green leaf over one ear. And so, with the air of a grand-
duchess in her own right, Miss Hendrick swept down to the
drawing-room.

"Thoroughbred," was Captain Owenson's inward critique;
"a Bohemian by accident, a lady by birth and breeding to the
core. Ah! they may say what they like in this new land, but
blood will tell."

He gave his handsome guest his arm to the dining-room,
with stately Sir Charles Grandison courtesy. Bertie followed
after with Aunt Char, and Sydney came in the rear.

"I say, Bertie, can't you get up anything to amuse the
girls this first evening?" the captain inquired. "There's
a theatre of some sort over in the town they tell me. Is it
eligible?"

"All the best people of Wychcliffe attend, sir."

"Ha! do they? And what is the piece to-night? Anything
worth going to see?"

"The 'School for Scandal' and the 'Loan of a Lover,'"
answered Mr. Bertie Vaughan.

"Ambitious at least—capital things both. And the actors,
my boy—very fourth or fifth class, no doubt, as befits strolling
players?"

"A few of them, sir; a few also are very good indeed," answered Vaughan, rather resentfully.

"Then what do you say, young ladies? What do you say,
mamma? Shall Bertie take you to see the 'School for
Scandal'?"

"I should like it of all things, papa," responded Sydney.

"And so should I, I am sure," said Aunt Char. "There's
nothing I used to be so fond of when I was a girl as going to
the theatre."

"And you, Miss Hendrick?" inquired the deferential host.

"I shall be charmed, Captain Owenson; I delight in the
theatre."

"Then that is settled. There will be no trouble about seats,
or anything of that sort, Bertie?"

"I am not so sure of that, sir. It is a benefit to-night, you
see, and the season closes to-morrow. The beneficiary is a
prime favorite, and the house is likely to be crowded."

"Who is the beneficiary?" asked Sydney, flashing a sudden
intent look into his face.

That fatal trick of blushing! Up came the blood of conscious guilt into the ingenuous face of Mr. Vaughan.

"Miss De Courcy—you saw her the other night, you re member. She plays Lady Teazle."

"What's the boy blushing about?" cried the captain. "Miss De—what did you say, Bertie?"

"De Courcy, sir—a *nom de théâtre*, no doubt," answered Bertie, his natural complexion back once more. As he made the reply he looked involuntarily across at Miss Hendrick to find that young lady's dark searching eyes fixed full upon him —a look of amusement in their depths.

"She should be a tolerable actress to undertake Lady Teazle," Cyrilla said, suavely. "I know of no more difficult part."

"She *is* a good actress—a charming actress," retorted Bertie, a certain defiance in his tone. "I have seen many, but never one much better."

"Isn't she rather wasting her sweetness on desert air, then?" suggested the captain. "It seems a pity such transcendant talent should be thrown away on mill-men. Suppose you all start early and so make sure of good seats."

There was a universal uprising, a universal alacrity in hastening away to prepare. Squire Owenson's proposal met the views of all capitally. Bertie, who had looked forward to a long, dragging, dull evening listening to Sydney and her friend playing the piano or gossiping about the school, brightened up wonderfully. Sydney had an intense curiosity to see again the actress whose very name could bring hot guilty blushes to Bertie's boyish face, and Cyrilla was desirous of beholding Syd ney's rival. So a hasty toilet was made, and the three ladies piled into the carriage, with Bertie, submerged in drapery, between them, and were driven away through a whirling snow-storm to the Wychcliffe theatre.

Half an hour later, and as the last bars of the "Agnes Sorel Quadrille," with which the provincial orchestra was delighting the audience, died away, there entered a group that at once aroused the interest of the house. A flutter of surprise and admiration ran along the benches—a hundred pair of eyes turned to stare with right good will. The theatre was filled, as Vaughan had foretold—pretty, piquant Dolly was so great a favorite that they were giving her a bumper house. All eyes, and a few glasses, turned upon these late comers, who swept up to the third row of seats, taking the play house in splendid style.

Bertie Vaughan came first, with a young lady on his arm—

not Miss Owenson—a tall, dark, stately young lady, wearing an opera wrap, a jet comb, and scarlet-geranium blossoms in her hair. Miss Owenson came next, with her mamma, looking fair as a lily, her light flowing hair falling loose and unadorned. A few significant looks, a few significant smiles, were interchanged. It would be rather good fun to see the actress Vaughan was in love with, and the heiress he was to marry face to face.

The broad, universal stare sent the color fluttering tremulously in and out of Sydney's childlike face. Miss Hendrick bore it all with the profoundly unconscious air of a three-seasons' belle, hardened by long custom to open admiration. A little bell tinkled as they took their places, the curtain went up, and the "School for Scandal" began.

Cyrilla, lying gracefully back in her chair, slowly fluttering her fan, smiled with barely-repressed disdain as she watched that first scene. Ah! she had seen that most bewitching of comedies played three years ago, in London, in a theatre where all were good, and a few were nearly perfect. To Sydney it was simply entrancing. It was almost her first visit to a play, and she was neither prepared nor inclined to make invidious distinctions.

So absorbed did she become that she almost forgot her principal object in coming, until at last Lady Teazle appeared on the stage. A tumult of applause greeted her ; and Dolly, looking charmingly in the piquant costume of old Sir Peter's youthful wife, bowed, and dimpled, and smiled her thanks.

"Ah! pretty, decidedly !" was Miss Hendrick's thought. She glanced at Bertie Vaughan. Yes, the tell-tale face had lit up, the blue eyes were alight, a smile of eager welcome was on his lips, his kidded hands were applauding tumultuously. She glanced at Sydney. A sort of pallor had chased away the flush of absorption ; a sort of gravity her friends had never seen there before, set her soft-cut, childish mouth.

"Poor little Syd !" Cyrilla thought ; "it is rather hard your father should insist upon making you miserable for life whether or no. You don't love this handsome dandy, but he will break your heart all the same. I would like to see the actress, were she beautiful as Venus herself, that Fred Carew would throw *me* over for ! "

The play went on. Dolly did her best, and received applause enough, noisy and hearty, to satisfy a Rachel or a Ristori. The smile, a smile of quiet amusement, deepened on

Miss Hendrick's lips—a smile that nettled Bertie Vaughan.
The great screen-scene came, and at Miss De Courcy's *posé*,
and the acting that followed, Cyrilla absolutely laughed aloud.

"You seem well amused, Miss Hendrick," Bertie said, ag-
gressively, an angry light in his blue eyes.

"I *am* well amused, Mr. Vaughan. I may safely say this
performance is a treat. I may also safely say, I never saw a
comedy so thoroughly comical before.

"You don't like it, Cy?" asked Sydney. "Of course, after
the London theatres, it must seem very poor. What do you
think of—of Miss De Courcy?"

"Miss De Courcy is the most original Lady Teazle I ever
beheld in my life," Cyrilla replied, still laughing. "Mr.
Vaughan, I thought you said they had some tolerable perform-
ers in this company? What has become of them to-night?"

"Miss Hendrick is pleased to be fastidious. For my part, I
think Miss De Courcy plays remarkably well, and gives promise
of becoming in the future a very first-class artiste. Try to recollect this is not the Prince of Wales' Theatre."

"I am not likely to forget it," laughed Cyrilla, with wicked
enjoyment of the young man's evident chargin. "And you
really think, Mr. Vaughan, that Miss De Courcy plays well, and
gives promise of becoming a popular actress?"

"Do not you, Miss Hendrick?"

"Most decidedly—most emphatically not. If she lives for
fifty years, and spends every one of them on the stage, she will
not be a whit better at the end than she is now. She does not
possess the first elements of a good actress. Personally, she is too
short, too stout, too florid, too—may I say it?—vulgar. Mentally
—she has not an ounce of brains in her head, she does not know
the A B C of her art. But I see I bore you, I had better stop."

"By no means," cried Bertie, defiantly. "Go on."

"Well, then, did you not see how flat the screen-scene fell?—
that is the best situation in the play—she made nothing of it.
And she is making eyes at the house all the while—a fatal mistake. An actress should be the character she represents, and
utterly ignore her audience. And she minces in her walk; she
talks English with a Yankee accent; she is coarse in voice and
manner; she hasn't the faintest conception of a lady. A tolerable "singing chambermaid," with training, she might make
a tolerable comedienne, never!"

"A strident sentence. But it is so much easier always to
criticise than to do better."

"I beg your pardon, I could do very much better," re
sponded Cyrilla, coolly. "I lived among theatrical people all
my life before I came to Canada, and was pretty thoroughly
drilled in the rudiments of the profession. Once I looked forward to treading the boards myself before my aunt changed all
that. If I were in Miss De Courcy's place to-night, I assure
you I would play Lady Teazle much better. Don't look so
disgusted, Mr. Vaughan, it is perfectly true."

Again she laughed, more and more amused at Bertie's irritated face. The curtain had fallen, and Ben Ward had left his
seat and gone out. Bertie knew what that meant—a quiet
flirtation with Dolly behind the scenes. He fidgeted uneasily,
galled by Cyrilla's contemptuous criticism, yet unable to resent
it, jealous of Ward, and longing desperately to break away and
rush behind the scenes also. The two girls were discussing the
play; Cyrilla in an undertone burlesquing Miss De Courcy
for Sydney's benefit. That was the straw too much; he arose.

"If you'll excuse me, Sydney," he said, pointedly ignoring
Sydney's friend, "I'll leave you for a moment. There's a—er
—man down at the door I wish to speak to."

Without waiting for a reply, he turned and walked out, with
his usual negligent saunter. Two minutes more, and he made
his appearance in the green room, in time to behold his rival
presenting Miss De Courcy with a very handsome bouquet.

"Ah, Vaughan!" Ward said, with a cool nod, "how are
you? Deucedly pretty girls those you escort to night. Who's
the dark one?"

"No one you know, Mr. Ward, or are likely to know," retorted
Bertie, turning his back upon him. "Dolly, you're in capital
form this evening, never saw you look or play better in my life."

"It's a pity you can't make one of the young ladies you have
with you think so," cried Dolly, her eyes aflame. "Do you
suppose I don't see her laughing at me—at us all—since she
came in? Such sneering fine ladies as that ought to stay at
home—not come here to laugh at their betters."

"Gently, Dolly—gently," put in Ward, maliciously; "you'll
hurt Vaughan's feelings. One of those two is the girl he is to
marry this month or next. It wasn't she who was laughing at
you, was it? Admiring you as Vaughan does, I should think
he would have taught her better."

"It was the girl in the white opera cloak and red dress," said
wrathful Dolly; "she sat and sneered every time I opened my
lips—*I* could see her. You had better go back to them Mr.

Vaughan," cried Dolly, with a toss of Lady Teazle's tall head-dress. " You're only wasting your time here."

" I think I am, by ——" exclaimed Vaughan, with a furious oath. " I've wasted too much of it already. You're a fool, Dolly, and you'll live to repent it ! "

He dashed out, his blue eyes lurid with jealous rage.

" Bertie," Dolly called, faintly ; but if he heard he never looked back. He strode straight out, straight into the theatre, and resumed his seat beside his affianced.

" By jingo !" exclaimed Mr. Ward, his shrill whistle of as-tonishment cutting the air; " who'd have thought there was so much fire in a milk-sop ! Let me congratulate you, Dolly, on your pluck in getting rid of him."

" Keep your congratulations," retorted Miss De Courcy, the fine furious temper she naturally possessed all afire, "and let me get rid of *you*. Keep your flowers, too—I don't want them. I wish I had never seen them or you ! "

She flung them at his feet.

" Go on, Dolly," said somebody, hurriedly ; " stage is wait-ing," and Dolly went on. Went on, white as ashes where rouge was not, playing worse than ever, half maddened by the sight of Bertie Vaughan laughing and chatting with his two fair friends. For Mr. Ward, he had calmly picked up his disdained bouquet, and sauntered back to his place in front.

" I'll throw it to her at the end," thought this mill-owning young philosopher ; " and she'll take it too. I know what Dolly's tantrums amount to. ' All things are possible to the man who knows how to wait.' "

The end came, the bouquet was thrown and—accepted. Ber-tie saw her pick it up, press it to her lips, and bow and smile to the donor, unmoved. She *was* coarse (so had set in the current of this most unstable gentleman's thoughts) ; she was a poor actress ; he wondered how he could ever have been so blind as to think her otherwise. If he married her he would be ashamed of her all his life long. He was the sort of man to make a mad marriage, and be ashamed of his wife all the rest of his days, and revenge his folly on her head. She was uneducated—she was vulgar—she had horrible relatives, no doubt—she had nothing in the world to recommend her but two bold black eyes and a highly-colored complexion. Was the game worth the candle ? Was this actress worth the sacrifice of honor, wealth and caste—all that had ever made his life ? And if what Miss Hendrick said were true—that she did not possess the first elements of theatrical success—what then? As her husband he would be a beggar—a miserable, seedy, shabby beggar. To marry an actress in receipt of three or four hundred dollars a week would be a sacrifice for a man of his appearance, prospects and standing—to marry an actress earning a wretched pittance of ten or twenty dollars a week only—good Heaven!—a shudder ran through him; what an escape he had had! He detested Miss Hendrick, but he felt absolutely grateful to her for opening his eyes. What an idiot—what an utter drivelling idiot he had been! Let Ward take her—greater fool, Ward—he was rich, and could indulge in folly if he chose. For himself, he would keep his honor intact, he would marry Sydney, and become master of Owenson Place, and the captain's noble bank stock. He looked across at her, her cheeks flushed with excitement and warmth, her eyes sparkling, her fair hair falling to her waist. How pretty, how sweet, how refined the was. Hers was the sort of beauty years would but improve—at thirty she would be a radiantly beautiful woman. What a contrast to Dolly De Courcy—poor Dolly! singing, dancing, coquetting before the footlights in her peasant garb in the "Loan of a Lover," casting imploring, penitent glances at him, doing her best to attract his notice. He put up his glass and surveyed her, a feeling akin to repulsion within him. He did not know it, but it was the turning-point of his life, his last chance of earthly salvation.

It all ended. They called Dolly out, and she came, curtseying, and with that stereotyped smile on her lips, her imploring eyes still bent on Bertie. But he would not see her, he was tenderly and solicitously wrapping Miss Owenson's blue scarf about her shoulders, preparatory to going out.

Through the white, whirling night they drove home. Two or three inches of snow already covered the ground. Winter had come before its time. And Bertie in a corner "pondered in his heart and was still."

"I'll see Dolly once more, and make an end of it all," he mused. "I would be the most contemptible cad that ever lived if I disappointed the governor after all he has done for me. To jilt an heiress like Sydney for a penniless, commonplace actress like Dolly would be sheer madness—a girl with lovers in New York and Wychcliffe, and the deuce knows where besides. And I would tire of her in a month. She's as jealous and exacting as the very dickens. Yes, by Jove! I'll throw over the actress and marry the heiress!"

CHAPTER XVI.

"HIS HONOR, ROOTED IN DISHONOR, STOOD."

YDNEY sat very silent and thoughtful during the homeward drive, lying back in her cozy corner, and watching the white, whirling night outside. All un-conscious of Bertie's good resolutions, her thoughts were running in an entirely opposite groove. If anything had been wanting to open her eyes to the true state of Mr. Vaughan's affections, to-night at the theatre had opened them. She had seen him look at Miss De Courcy as he had certainly never looked at her. She understood the secret of his brief absence as well as he did himself; there no longer remained a doubt in her mind. He cared nothing for her, and he did care a very great deal for this dashing actress.

"Then I shall never marry him," Sydney thought—"never —never! This is why he has not spoken—why he is so often absent, why he stays out so late nights. He is running after Miss De Courcy. Oh! why cannot he be brave, and speak out, and tell me the truth? I don't want to marry him, I don't want to marry anybody, and he must know it. Papa would not be so very angry, and he might forgive him—perhaps."

But here Sydney stopped. Papa would be most tremen-dously angry; papa would never forgive him to the day of his death. She could never dare tell papa the truth ; if the mar-riage was broken off, it must be through her own unwillingness to keep to the compact, not his, else Bertie was ruined for life.

"I will speak to papa this very night, if I get a chance. I couldn't marry Bertie—oh, never ! never !—knowing he cared for another more than me ; that all the time he was standing by my side in the church he was wishing another girl in my place. No, I couldn't, not even to please papa. I don't care for Bertie now, but if I were married to him, it might be different ; and to grow fond of him, and feel sure he cared nothing for me— no, I could not bear that !"

The pretty, gentle face looked strangely troubled, as Bertie helped her out, and she ran up the steps and into the hall. How wintry and wild the night had grown—the trees standing up ink-black in the whirling whiteness.

Captain Owenson had sat up for the return of his harem. A

bright fire and a comfortable supper awaited them. Mrs Owenson, Cyrilla, and Bertie partook of cold chicken and champagne, with appetites whetted by the keen wind, but Dolly De Courcy had completely taken away Sydney's. Her father was the only one who noticed it—her father, whose doting eyes n ever left her face for long.

"Well, little one," he said, "what is it? Has Lady Teazle been supper enough for you? You eat nothing."

It was altogether the most random of shots, but it went straight home. Sydney started guiltily, and seized her knife and fork; Bertie set down his glass untasted; Miss Hendrick, delicately carving a wing, smiled in malicious triumph.

"I do most sincerely hope this supercilious dandy will lose Sydney," she thought, "even at the eleventh hour. A dandy one could forgive—Freddy is that, bless him!—but a fool, never!"

"How did you find this famous actress, of whom Bertie speaks so highly?" pursued the captain, whose evil genius evidently sat at his elbow prompting him. "Is she the star he makes her out, or was the 'School for Scandal' a disappointment?"

There was a pause. As a matter of course, Mr. Vaughan reddened violently. The question being addressed generally, no one felt called upon to answer, and it was Aunt Char who came to the rescue.

"I am sure I think it was very nice," that good lady said, "and Lady Teazle played remarkably well. I don't think it's a very moral play myself, because it was, of course, shocking of that wicked Mr. Joseph Surface to make love to a married lady. But really I could not help laughing when the screen fell, and there she was before her husband and the two Mr. Surfaces. One had to feel for her, too, she looked so ashamed of herself. I saw you laughing, Miss Hendrick—you thought that particularly good, I am sure."

"Particularly good, Mrs. Owenson," replied Cyrilla, that malicious smile deepening in her dark, derisive eyes; "so good that I laugh now in recollecting it. I think we all admire Miss De Courcy excessively—not so much as Mr. Vaughan, perhaps, who is an old friend, but very much indeed for a first acquaintance."

Bertie lifted his eyes, and looked across at her with a glance of absolute hatred.

"Malicious little devil!" he thought, "I would like to choke her."

"Well, puss, and what do you say?" continued Sydney's father.

"I think Miss De Courcy is very pretty and very popular; but of actors and actresses I am no judge. Mamma, did you see Harry Sunderland with Augusta Van Twiller? I wonder if they really are engaged?"

Then the talk drifted to the Sunderlands, and Bertie was safe ′ again. He drew a deep breath; his eyes had not been opened a second too soon. He was suspected even by Sydney. For this obnoxious Miss Hendrick, her keen black eyes saw everything; she was his enemy, and would do him harm if she could.

"But that she shall not," he thought, as he said good-night. "I'll prove an *alibi* to Sydney, though I should have to swear black is white."

He went to his room, and his example was followed by Cyrilla and Aunt Char. For Sydney, she lingered yet a little longer, seated on a hassock at her father's side, her yellow head lying on his knee, her blue dreamy eyes fixed on the fire. For a moment or two he watched the thoughtful, childish face in silence; then his hand fell lightly on the flaxen hair.

"What is it, *petite?*" he asked—so tender the harsh old voice was! "What troubles my little one? For you are in trouble—I can see that."

The way was opening of itself, and Sydney felt relieved. She had been thinking anxiously how to begin.

"Trouble, papa" she answered, taking the hand fondly in both her own. "No, not trouble; that is too strong a word. Trouble has never come near me yet."

"And pray Heaven it never may. What is it, then?"

"Well, papa, I am—what is the word?—worried. Just the least bit in the world worried."

"About what?" he asked, quickly. "Not Bertie?"

"Yes, papa, Bertie and—this marriage. Don't be angry, papa, please; but if you wouldn't mind, I would rather not."

"A somewhat incoherent speech! Rather not—what?"

"Rather not be married, please. I don't seem to care about being married, papa."

Papa laughed.

"I am so young—only a little girl after all, you know; and a married lady ought to be wise and sensible and old."

"Old? One's ideas of age differ. What may seem a ripe age in your eyes, Pussy?"

7

"Twenty-one or two—that is a good age to be married, if one must be married at all. But I don't see why one must, especially when one doesn't seem to care about it. I would rather stay home with you and mamma just as I am."

"Mamma and I intend you shall stay home with us just as you are."

"Oh, but it will be different. I mean as we are at present. Bertie and I like brother and sister, not man and wife. Put off this marriage, papa—say for three years to come. What difference can it make? and I will be twenty then, and beginning to grow old and wise. I should prefer it—oh, so much; and I am sure Bertie would too."

"Bertie would too!" Her father sat suddenly upright. "Has he told you so, Sydney?"

"Oh, dear, no!" Sydney answered, laughing; "he is much too polite. You need not put on your court-martial face, Captain Owenson; Bertie hasn't said the least word about it one way or other."

"One way or other! Do you mean, Sydney, he hasn't spoken to you at all since your return?"

"Was it necessary?" Sydney said, trying to speak lightly, but not succeeding in keeping down the flush that arose over her face. "*You* saved us all that trouble."

"Sydney!" Captain Owenson cried, in a voice that made Sydney jump, "there is something more here than I know of. You were willing enough all along, willing enough when you came home a fortnight ago. What does this talk of breaking off mean now, at the last moment? What have you discovered about Bertie Vaughan?"

"Nothing, papa," Sydney came near gasping in her alarm; but even in this extreme moment she checked herself. It would not be true, and the simple, white, absolute truth came ever from Sydney Owenson's lips.

"You were willing enough a week ago," her father repeated. "What have you discovered about Bertie now?"

"I was willing enough because I had not thought the matter over," Sydney answered, her voice tremulous. "Papa, I—I don't care for Bertie—in that way."

"In what way? Falling in love, do you mean? Oh, if that be all—pooh! A very good thing for you too; the love that will come after marriage will be all the safer to last. Are you sure, quite sure, there is no other reason than this?"

"I think it is reason enough," retorted Sydney, a trifle indignantly. "I may be romantic if you like, but I *should* like to—to love the man I am going to marry."

Captain Owenson lay back and laughed, the thunder-cloud quite gone. For a moment he had been startled (boys will be boys, you know), but after all it was only a school-girl's sentimental nonsense. He patted the fair flax-head as he might a child's.

"And this is all! Well, I'm very glad. I am afraid you have been reading romances in the Chateauroy *Pensionnat.* Love, indeed! Well, why not? he's a tall and proper fellow enough, a young gentleman of the period, with all the modern improvements; parts his hair in the middle, wears a nice little moustache, and an eye-glass, lemon kids, and a cane. He can sing, he can waltz, can dress with the taste of a Beau Brummell, and has a profile as straight as a Greek's. Now, what more can any young woman of the present day desire in a husband? What is to hinder your loving him to distraction if you wish, since that is a *sine qua non?* It ought not to be difficult."

"No, I daresay not," Sydney thought, her eyes filling suddenly. "Miss De Courcy finds it easy enough, very likely. Oh! how cruel papa is!"

"Well, my dear, you don't speak," her father went on, bending down to catch sight of her face; "are you listening to what I say? it ought not to be difficult."

"Perhaps not, but I don't, and—that is all."

"What! cheeks flushed, eyes full, and voice trembling. Sydney! *what* is this? Is the thought of marrying Bertie Vaughan so hateful to you? Have you let things go on only to throw him over at the eleventh hour? Is this only a girl's caprice, or is there some reason at the bottom of it all? Speak, and tell me the truth. If he is unworthy of you I would sooner see you dead than his wife. But—if he is, by—," a tremendous quarter-deck oath, "he shall repent it!"

There it was. If she told the truth she would ruin Bertie's life forever—if she did not tell it she ruined her own. Tell, she could not, no matter what the cost to herself.

"Oh, papa, how cross you are!" she said, in a petulant voice, that she knew would bring him down from his heroics; "and I wish you wouldn't swear. It's ill-bred, besides being wicked."

"I beg your pardon, Sydney," he said, suddenly; "so it is. I beg your pardon, my dear. I beg—His!"

He lifted his smoking-cap reverently, then sank back in his chair.

"Dearest, best old papa!" Sydney cried, touched with contrition, jumping up and flinging her arms around his neck. "I am a wretch for worrying you with my silly fidgets. You're a gentleman and a sailor—that you are, every inch. After all, what's the odds? Lord Dundreary says, one woman's as good as another, if not better—I don't see why the same rule shouldn't apply to men. If I must marry somebody, whether or no, then I may as well marry Bertie since it will please you. I know him, anyhow, that is one comfort. Cecilia Leonard eloped from school with a young lawyer of the town two weeks after she was first introduced to him, and she told me when she came back that she was three months married before she was properly acquainted with her husband. Now I am acquainted with Bertie, and won't have the trouble of cultivating him when I'm his wife."

"And he isn't a bad sort of young fellow, as young fellows go," her father added, thoughtfully; "not any more brains than the law allows—your sharp little head has found that out for itself, I suppose, my dear. He never would make his way in the world alone; but dropping into my shoes, he'll make you a good husband, I think, my dear—a kind one, a faithful one, and a very excellent country squire. As you say, we know him, and I like the lad. He has been brought up to consider you his wife, and The Place his home for life, and it would not be quite the thing to throw him over now. He has no profession, and it is a little late in the day to learn one; besides, he isn't clever, and I don't believe could earn his salt if he were a lawyer or a doctor to-morrow. And he is fond of you, little one —don't get any foolish sentimental notions into your head to the contrary; and, for pity's sake, Sydney, don't be an exacting wife, don't expect too much from your husband. He doesn't speak to you, perhaps, because he takes it all for granted. Very likely he takes to much for granted, but that is easily set aright."

"Papa!" Sydney cried out in alarm, at his smile and tone, "you won't speak to him about this! You won't tell him to— to speak to me? Oh! I should die of shame."

"Foolish child! As if I would ever cheapen my darling's value, or make her blush. Trust me, Sydney. For the rest, when I am gone, if you were not Vaughan's wife, you might fall a victim to some subtle-tongued fortune-hunter; for you know you will be very rich, my dear, and your poor mother has no more worldly wisdom than a babe. Bertie is not a brilliant match—not at all the sort of man I would have had him—but he is ours, and we like him. I think he will make you a tender husband, and the fortune-hunters, by-and-by, will have no chance. Believe me, it is better as it is."

"Yes, I suppose so," Sydney sighs, hopelessly—fate seems closing around her, and it is of no use to struggle. "Forgive me for troubling you, papa ; I won't do it again."

"There is only one thing in the world that can trouble me very greatly," her father answers, "and that is to see my little girl un-happy. Are the doubts all gone, and will you take Bertie, or——"

"I will do whatever you think best, papa," is her answer, and then he holds her for a moment in silence.

"Heaven bless my good girl !" he says, softly. "Now go to bed ; it is close upon one o'clock."

Sydney goes, a glow at her heart. After all, just doing one's duty and simply obeying brings its own reward. She is quite happy as she kneels by the bedside to whisper her innocent prayers. It must be all right, since she is sacrificing her own will to please her father—since she is pleasing her father on earth, she must be pleasing her Father in heaven. For Bertie, she will be to him a wife so devoted, she will give him a heart so tender and true, that she will surely make him happy, surely wean him from all passing fancies for other women. And so, with a smile on her lips, she falls asleep like a little child.

But Captain Owenson lies awake long that night, thinking. One result of his cogitations he gives them at breakfast next morning. Sydney shall welcome her friend with a party, and introduce her to the best Wychcliffe society. The stately old sailor has all an Arab's notion of hospitality. He likes quiet, but he is ready to throw his house out of the windows any day to please the guest who breaks his bread.

"Not a large gathering, you know ?" he says ; "just an off-hand affair—say Thursday next. You and mamma can make out your list this morning and have them delivered before night. That will give four days to prepare—quite enough in this primi-tive neighborhood, I should say."

"Papa, I do think you have the most beautiful inspiration !" cries Sydney, with a radiant face. "How did you know Cyrilla and I were pining for a party ?"

She goes to work delightedly the moment breakfast is over.

"Come and help me, Bertie," she calls, brightly ; and when Bertie comes makes place for him, with a depth of shining wel-come in her eyes he likes, but does not at all understand.

He never will understand her : her nature is as far above his as the sunlit sky above the snow-whitened earth out-doors. She thinks, as he sits beside her:

"He is the one man of all men I am ever to care for. I want—oh, I do want to make him happy."

The invitations are all written and all dispatched. Then she and Miss Hendrick go off and hold a pow-wow on the subject of feathers and wampum—of their dresses and adorning, that is to say. Aunt Char descends to consult with Katy, the cook ; and Captain Owenson waylays Bertie, his hat on his head, his cloak over his shoulders, his stick in his hand.

"The morning's fine, Bertie," he says. "I'll take your arm for a turn on the piazza."

So they go ; Bertie with much greater alacrity than he would have shown yesterday. He has shaken off Dolly's gyves of steel, or so he thinks, and is about to slip on his wrists those of Sydney. He is the son-in-law of Owenson Place, and is prepared to behave as such.

The ground is white with snow, beginning to melt and run in little rivulets in the heat of the noon sun. They walk slowly up and down, talking of many things, and it is *apropos* of nothing and rather suddenly that the elder man at last looks in the younger man's face and asks :

"Bertie, Sydney's been home over a week. Have you and she settled upon your wedding-day ?"

Bertie starts, colors, as usual, and shrinks from meeting those keen, steely eyes.

"Really," he laughs, "I don't believe we have. I didn't like to hurry her, but I—I must ask her this week."

"Because," pursues the Captain, setting his lips, "she has grown tired of the engagement and wants to break it off."

"Wants to "—Bertie paused aghast—"wants to break it off ! Sydney !"

The idea is so absolutely new that he cannot for a moment take it in. *He* may flirt, may play fast and loose with his fetters, may contemplate even running away with somebody else, but for Sydney to want to break with him—Sydney ! No, he gives it up ; he cannot realize it.

"She spoke to me last night," goes on her father ; "urged me in the strongest terms to make an end of the proposed marriage. She's not in love with you, it seems, and has some girlish notions of the desirability of that emotion in connection with the married state. Of course, I could never think of forcing her in-

clination," pursues this artful old seaman, carelessly ; "and it is
never too late to draw back before the ring is absolutely on.
She would prefer it—she even appeared to hint that she thought
you would prefer it too."

"She is mistaken," cries Bertie, thoroughly startled, thoroughly alarmed ; "greatly mistaken, altogether mistaken. Give
up your marrriage ? Good Heaven ! Captain Owenson, you
will not listen to such a thing as that ? "

It seemed to him like a new revelation now that it was
brought before him from the lips of another. Sydney wanting
to throw him over—his little Sydney ! And then Owenson
Place and all his hopes for life ! Bertie Vaughan actually turned
pale.

" You won't listen to what Sydney says," he pleads ; "she
doesn't know her own mind. Not love me ? Well, of course
not, she hasn't had a chance ; we have been separated for the
last five years. I was so sure it was all right that I didn't pes-
ter her with love-making. I was so sure——"

" Ah, yes ! I daresay, a little too sure, perhaps. It doesn't do
to take too much for granted where a woman is in the question,
be she seventeen or seven-and-thirty," says the cynical captain.

" But it isn't too late yet," goes on Mr. Vaughan, in hot haste.
I'll talk to Sydney ; I'll convince her of her mistake. *I* want
to break off the engagement ! By Jove, what could have put so
preposterous an idea into her head ! "

" Yes, what indeed ! That's for you to find out, my lad. She
seemed tolerably convinced of it too."

" It's Miss Hendrick's work," exclaimed Bertie, resentfully ;
"confound her ! I beg your pardon, sir," as the captain turned
savagely upon him. " I know she's your guest and Sydney's
friend, but a serpent on the hearth to you and a false friend to
Sydney if she tries to poison her mind against me. Of herself,
Sydney would never have thought of so absurd a thing. Miss
Hendrick dislikes me, and I must say it—I dislike her. She
knows it too, and this is her revenge."

" Be good enough to leave Miss Hendrick's name out of the
question, if you please," say the seigneur of Owenson Place
in his most ducal manner. " As you say, she is my guest,
and nothing disparaging shall be spoken of her in my presence."

" At least I will go at once and speak to Sydney," says
Bertie, excitedly—"at once ! It is intolerable to me, that she
should remain one moment with so false an idea in her mind."

But the captain holds in this impetuous wooer.

"Softly, my lad—softly," he says, and he laughs in his sleeve at the diplomatic manner in which he has attained his end; "there's no hurry. Sydney won't run away, and if you speak to her to-day, aye, or to-morrow either, she will suspect I have been speaking to you. Let me see. Suppose you wait until the night of the party, making yourself as agreeable as may be in the meantime. Then broach the subject of the approaching nuptials, get her to name the day, and convince her of your undying devotion if you can. H'm! What you say is very true, my lad; those maples do want thinning out."

A significant squeeze of the arm—Bertie looks around bewildered by this sudden change from matrimony to maples, and sees Sydney and Cyrilla approaching. The question of their respective toilettes has been settled; they are, in hats and jackets, *en route* to Wychcliffe, shopping.

May Bertie be their escort? He looks eagerly at Sydney, and Sydney glances suspiciously at her papa. Surely, papa, after his promise too, has not—— But no; papa looks innocent and unconscious as some playful lambkin.

No, he may not be their escort, Sydney answers; the subject of shades and textures is altogether too important to be interfered with by the talk of a frivolous young man. So he stays, nothing loath, for the truth is, he is mortally afraid of meeting Dolly face to face in the Wychcliffe streets. And then, as that face arises before him, rosy, laughing, charming, a face he must never see or dream of again, he strikes into a path among the maples, with a sort of groan. If he could only care for Sydney as he cares for Dolly—little wild outlaw that she is! Ben Ward will marry her no doubt one day—hang Ben Ward. And the odds are, she will make no end of a row, insist on seeing Sydney it may be, or the captain, telling her story, showing his letters—— Oh! gracious powers! not that! At any cost she must be kept quiet, and these fatal letters got back. What a hideous scrape he has got himself into; how is he to get out of it? One whisper of the truth, and he will be expelled Owenson Place—disgraced and ruined for life. To keep Dolly quiet will be no easy matter, for she is fond of him, not a doubt of that. He groans dismally again as he thinks of it. She will not resign her claim upon him without a struggle. After all, swerving from the straight path of honor and rectitude may be very fine fun for awhile, but it doesn't seem to pay in the end. If he had kept his faith with Sydney intact, what a deuce of a worry it would have saved him now.

He thought until his head ached, but he could think of no way out of his troubles. Then in weary disgust he gave it up, and lit a cigar. It was of no use turning his hair gray thinking; something would turn up—something always turned up when things were at their worst. He must get out of this morass somehow; there would be no end of lies to tell, but Mr. Vaughan did not stick at a lie or two in a difficulty. He must appease Dolly in some way—get her out of Wychcliffe until the wedding was over. After that he didn't care. Sydney and her fortune would be his. Dolly might say and do what she pleased. Between this and the night of the party he would do the dutiful to Miss Owenson, avoid the town and the theatre. After that—but after that had not come; time enough to think of it when it did.

* * * * * * *

Thursday night. Vehicles of all sorts and sizes rattling up under the frosty sky to Captain Owenson's hospitable front door. The house is all alight from basement to attic—wonders have been done in four days. A tolerably large company had been invited, the upper skimmings, of course, of country society; and a "good time" was confidently looked forward to. For though Captain Owenson did not do this sort of thing often, he did do it when he did do it.

* * * * * * *

"They hav'n't invited you, Dolly, have they? No, I suppose they hav'n't. No more have they me. Well, the loss is theirs, let that console us," remarked casually Mr. Benjamin Ward, escorting home Miss Dolly De Courcy that same eventful night.

"Invited me where? I don't know what you're talking about. Who ever invites me anywhere?" retorted Miss De Courcy.

Dolly is looking thin, and her bright bloom of color has faded. Her piquant face has taken an anxious, watchful look of late—that longing, waiting look which is one of the most pathetic on earth. Since the night of the "School for Scandal" she has seen nothing of Bertie Vaughan—absolutely nothing.

"Why, to Miss Owenson's 'small and early,' of course. Hav'n't you heard of it? All the upper crust of Wychcliffe are bidden to the feast; you and I, my Dolly, alone left out in the cold."

"Miss Owenson!" At sound of that dreaded and detested

7*

name Dolly looks quickly up. "Is Miss Owenson giving a party?" she asks. "When?"

"To-night. Nothing very extensive, you know. Wine and sweet cake, cards and music, dancing and tea. Miss Sunderland's going—saw her yesterday, and she told me about it. Deuced shabby of them to leave me out; but it's all the doing of the 'Fair One with the Golden Locks,'" says Mr. Ward with calm indifference.

Dolly says nothing, but Ward hears her breath come quick, The cold, piercing November moonlight falls on her face, and he sees that frown of jealous pain and anger that never used to be there.

"It's of no use, Dolly," he says, not unkindly, "of no use waiting for Vaughan any more. He won't come."

"Who says he won't?" Dolly cries, angrily. "What do you know about it? You only wish he may not. He *will* come."

"He never will. He is going to marry the captain's daughter, he won't marry you. He likes you best—maybe—it isn't in him to like anybody but his own lovely self very strongly, but all the same, he won't marry you. You needn't keep that look-out for him, Dolly, that 'light in the window,' any more. He—never—will—come," asseverates Mr. Ward, a solemn pause between each little word.

She does not speak. She sets her teeth hard together, and her hands clench under her shawl.

"Give him up, Doll," says the young mill-owner, good naturedly; "let him take his heiress and have done with him. He isn't worth one thought from so true-hearted a little woman as you. Give him up and marry me."

She looks up at him with haggard eyes, that have a sort of weary wonder in them.

"Would you marry me, Ben, knowing how—how fond I am of him?"

"Oh, that would come all right," responds Ben, with his usual cheerful philosophy. "I'd be good to you, and fond of you, and women are uncommon that way; married women, I mean; they always take to a man that is good to 'em. Men don't; but then husbands and wives are different somehow."

Mr. Ward pauses a moment to ruminate on this idea, but it is too complicated for him and he gives it up.

"Say, Dolly, stop thinking of Vaughan, he's a sneak anyhow, and leave the stage and marry me. Marry me the day he

marries Miss Owenson—there will be a triumph for you, if you
like !" cries Ben, in a glow of happy inspiration.

But her lips set, and her eyes keep their haggard look.

"Thank you, Ben," she says, huskily ; you're a good fellow,
a great deal too good for me, but I can't do it, I can't give him
up. I know he's what you say, only I'd rather you didn't say
it. I know I can't trust him, all the same I can't give him up.
And he sha'n't marry Miss Owenson. No !" her black eyes
blaze up with swift flame, "not if the wedding-day was to-morrow. Her father's an officer and a gentleman. I'll go to him,
I'll go to her, and I'll tell them both what will stop the wedding.
Don't look at me like that, Ben—I can't help it, I wish I could.
And don't trouble yourself to come home with me any more
during the few nights I play ; it isn't worth while. You can
never get any better than a 'thank you' and a shake-hands for
your pains.

"I'll take them then, and see you home all the same," is
Ben's answer ; "but I wish you would think again of this."

"If I thought till the day I die, it could make no difference.
If I can't be Bertie Vaughan's wife—and he has promised me I
shall—it doesn't much matter whether I am ever anybody's at
all or not."

"That for his promise !" cries Ward, contemptuously.
"Dolly, you're an awful little fool !"

"I know it, Ben," answers Dolly, quite humbly. "I can't
help it, though. Don't come any farther, please. I am at
home now."

"And you'll never marry me—never ? You're sure of it ?"

"I'll never marry you—never. I'm sure of it. Good-night."

"Good-night," says Mr. Ward, and he pulls his hat over his
eyes and turns and strides home, as if shod with seven-league
boots. It is all over, he will never ask her again, but, when
months and months after, he asks the same question of Mamie
Sunderland and receives a very different answer, that scene is
back before him, and the gas-lit drawing-room "curtained and
close and warm," wherein they cosily sit, fades for a second
away. The chill, steel-blue moonlight, the iron-bound road,
the frostily-winking stars, and Dolly's miserable face, as she
says "good-night," are before him. Ah ! well, it would never
do for men's wives to know everything.

She does not enter the house. A fire, a fever of impatience
of jealous, sickening terror has taken hold of her. They have
not invited her—true ; nevertheless she will be there.

She starts rapidly onward, she reaches the high white house, and meets no one on her way. She ascends the portico steps ; all is brilliance within, lights and music stream out. The drawing-room windows are open, chilly as is the night, curtains of lace and brocatelle alone separate her from the dancers. No one is near ; she stands motionless, looking in. She sees him almost at first glance—he is dancing with the daughter of the house. A fierce spasm of hot pain goes through the little jealous actress's heart. How pretty—how pretty she is ! with her fair, feathery hair, her blue, bright eyes, her softly tinged cheeks, her sweet, smiling lips. How prettily she is dressed in palest pink, not a jewel about her, not even a flower in her hair, only a rose ribbon tying all its brightness back. And he—but Dolly turns away with a despairing gesture, words are poor to describe *him !* Just at the moment the dance ends, and with his partner on his arm, he comes directly toward the window at which she stands. She draws back in terror. There is a great stone urn close by ; she crouches down behind this, very close to where they stand. Are they coming out ? No ; they remain in the shadow of the curtains, and look out at the white, cold loveliness of the night. She sees—as soon as she is able to see anything distinctly, for the mist that is before her eyes—Bertie wrapping a fleecy white scarf about his companion's shoulders, hears (as soon as her startled hearing returns) the tender tones of his voice. She cannot catch his words at first, so lowly and hurriedly he speaks ; but by her drooping face and averted eyes she can guess he is wooing his bride. And she crouches listening here. A more dramatic situation could hardly have been devised for the Wychcliffe Lyceum. Even the accessories are not wanting. She out in the cold under the midnight sky ; they in the rosy light and perfumed warmth, the dancers in the background, and the slow German waltz music over all. She does not catch his words for a while, though she strains her ears to listen. But he raises his voice presently, and she hears :

"Care for her. An actress ! Sydney, what folly to think of me. I tell you I care for no one in all the world but you. I hold your promise to be my wife, and by that promise I claim you. You will not retract your plighted word ?"

"You know that I will not," she answers ; "but, Bertie, on your honor, would you not rather marry that actress than me ?'

"You insult me by the question, Sydney. I decline to answer."

"Oh' nonsen'se, Bertie," Miss Owenson says, half laughing; "don't try heroics. It's a very natural question, I think. Young men don't blush at the sound of a lady's name, nor brighten at the sight of her face for nothing, and I have seen you do both, sir, for Miss De Courcy. Honestly, now, you do like her better than me?"

"Do you insist upon my saying yes, Sydney? I see how it is—you wish to break off our engagement, and a poor excuse is better than none. Very well—so be it; it shall never be said I forced your inclinations, no matter how deeply I suffer myself."

He folded his arms in a grand attitude, and stood drawn up, looking very tall and slender, and affronted and cross.

"Oh, dear!" sighed Sydney, half laughing, half vexed; "you *will* do private theatricals. No, I don't want to break off—it would vex papa; and of course everything is arranged, and there would be a dreadful deal of talk. Besides, I like you—— Oh, nonsense, Bertie!" impatiently; "no tender scenes, if you please. But if I thought you cared for the actress, or were pledged to her in any way, I wouldn't marry you—no, not if I died for it!"

"Pledged to her!" Bertie repeated, flushing guiltily. "What awful nonsense."

"Well, yes, I suppose it is nonsense. You wouldn't go that far even—— There's Harry Sunderland asking for me—I must go."

"Promise me first that the last Thursday in November will be our wedding-day," he says, barring her way.

Harry Sunderland has espied the rose-pink robe, and is making for it. In desperation she pushes past him and out.

"What does it matter?" she says, impatiently; "as well one day as another. Whenever you like—yes, the last Thursday, then. Don't come out just yet—I don't want Harry to know I was——"

"Spooning here with me," says Bertie, laughing.

"Yes," says Sydney, with a little look of disgust; "spooning here with you. Don't appear upon the festive scene for the next ten minutes."

She vanishes. Bertie remains, a satisfied, complacent smile on his face, and regards the heavenly bodies. For a moment —then—"private theatricals" indeed! Sydney ought to be here to see them. A dark, crouching figure starts up as if out of the ground, directly in front of him. The streaming lamplight falls full upon an awfully familiar face, and a voice that sends every drop of traitor blood in his body back to his heart says:

"Bertie!"

CHAPTER XVII.

"HE'S SWEETEST FRIEND OR HARDEST FOE."

T is Dolly. White, unlike herself, with wild eyes and excited face, but—Dolly! He stands for a moment petrified, utterly petrified by the greatness and suddenness of the surprise. For the time being carried away by the excitement of his new wooing, he had absolutely forgotten her very existence. And now, like a stage Nemesis, like an avenging spirit, she stands here—pale, menacing, terrible. But it is not a stage Nemesis. Dolly is not acting to-night—but little of the bitter, jealous wrath and pain that fills her shows in her quivering lips, her dark burning eyes, and the white misery of her face.

"Bertie," she says again. For, full of anger and vengeance as she is, something in his face as he stands there and looks at her, frightens her. He has started back, staring as a man who cannot believe his own eyes. Her voice breaks the spell.

"Wait there," he says.

He glances quickly backward, no one sees him, no one is in sight. He stoops, raises the window a little higher, and steps out upon the piazza, by her side.

The round November moon is at its zenith, its cold, spectral light glimmers in the ebony blackness of the trees on the hard, frozen ground, ringing like iron to every sound, upon the glaring brightness of the house, upon the pale, stern faces of the man and woman who stand and confront each other. Bertie Vaughan wears a look that few have ever seen him wear; that Dolly De Courcy most certainly never has before.

"Come with me," he commands, and she obeys without a word. A tumult of pain and misery is within her; she feels that she has right on her side; in all ways she is the stronger of the two, nevertheless she is afraid of him now.

He leads the way—she follows. Beyond his name she has said nothing as yet. Beyond that imperious "Come with me," he has said nothing. They leave the brightly-lighted house, its warmth, its merriment, behind them. The music dies softly away in the distance. With the first sensation of cold she has felt yet the girl draws her shawl closer about her as she follows

Bertie Vaughan across the wide, gladelike expanse of lawn and into the shadow of a belt of trees. No one from the house can see them here—the very moonlight comes sifted in fine lances through the black, rattling boughs, and here the young man stops and faces his companion.

"What has brought you here?" is what he says.

There is white, concentrated passion in his face, but his voice is barely raised above a whisper. She looks at him fiercely, her head flung back, her eyes afire. It is a capital stage attitude—if poor Dolly were dying she must still act.

"You ask that!" she retorts, passionately. "I write to you and you do not answer. For five whole days you never come near me—and you stand and ask what brings me here!"

"Yes, I ask; and be good enough to remember that this is not the stage of Wychcliffe theatre, and that you're not talking for the pit and the gallery. Be kind enough to lower your voice. I ask you again, Dolly, what brings you here?"

"And how dare you ask it?" she cries, goaded to fury. "How dare you stand there and speak to me as you are speak ing? What brings me here? Who has a better right to come where you are than I?"

He laughs shortly.

"The right I grant you, if you never want to see or speak to me again as long as you live. If that's what you're after, you couldn't have taken a better way."

She stands and looks at him, shivering, partly with the cold, partly with nervous excitement, her eyes dark with terror, her lips white.

"Did you think I would stay away?" she asks, "knowing you had deserted me? I waited five days, Bertie—I wrote to you—you never came—you never answered. They told me you were engaged to Miss Owenson—that the wedding-day was close at hand. I knew there was to be a party here to-night—that while I suffered misery and loneliness there in Wychcliffe, you were dancing and enjoying yourself with her. And I was your promised wife, Bertie, don't forget that. Where you were I had a right to be. I came—I couldn't stay away; I thought if I could only see you for one minute, ar.d hear you say you forgave me for what I said that night at the theatre—oh! Bertie, I was sorry—only hear you say you weren't tired of me, and hadn't forgotten me, I would go away again and leave you to enjoy yourself, and ask no more. I didn't mean any harm—I didn't mean any one to see me, I only wanted to speak to you one minute. I went up there by the window with no thought of listening; but you came—with her—and I—I overheard—every——"

She had been growing hysterical as she went on, her voice choking and breaking; now she stopped, literally gasping for breath. Violent hysterics were imminent. In horrible alarm Vaughan seized her wrist in a grasp that left a black bracelet on the quivering flesh for a week.

"If you make a noise—if you faint or have hysterics, Dolly," he cried, in a furious whisper, " I swear I'll never speak to you again as long as you live!"

The threat had its effect. A few gasping breaths, a few choking sobs, a moment's convulsive quivering of body, and the perilous moment was past. Then a brief interval of silence, during which Mr. Vaughan relaxed his hold, and mentally consigned Dolly to a region where the night-air is never chill!

Miss De Courcy leaned against a tree, her wretched face hidden in her handkerchief, her bosom still heaving with suppressed suffocating sobs.

"Now, Dolly, look here," begins Bertie, his blonde brows knit, his mouth, under its little flaxen mustache, set in a tight, unpleasant line, " this is all most awful nonsense. You have come near making the greatest blunder of your life in coming here to-night. In the first place how did you know there was to be a party here at all?"

"Ben Wa—ard told me," she answered, in a stifled voice.

His eyes flashed. In the midst of his anger, while wishing her in the deepest depths of the Inferno, he could still be jealous of Ward.

"So!" he said contemptuously, "that fool is after you yet. Sees you home every night of your life, I'll be bound."

"There is no one else, Bertie."

"All right—that is your affair. Mine, at present, is to come to an understanding with you about to-night's visit. Once and for all, Dolly, I'll have no following, no spying, no dogging my steps, no eavesdropping, no jealous scenes. I would no more marry a jealous woman than I would shoot myself. The sooner you realize that the better."

The handkerchief fell. She looked up at him, the miserable, quivering face lighting all at once with hope.

"Oh, Bertie! You do mean to marry me then after all?"

Mr. Vaughan's look of surprise—of injured inocence—was fine.

"After what 'all'? I am a man of honor, Dolly, and as suct I keep my word! Have I not acted honorably toward you from the first? Did I not propose marriage to you a fortnight after our first meeting? Have I not treated you in all respects as —as a lady?

"You have—you have," sobbed Dolly, her tears penitent tears now. "O Bertie, you have been kind, been generous, been noble toward me. I am not your equal, I know—in station or education, and you have treated me in every way as if I were.

"Very well then," pursued Mr. Vaughan, loftily. "You can imagine, perhaps, what a blow to me to-night's escapade is. When people are jealous of each other, spy upon each other, dog each other, it is time those people should part. When confidence ceases love should end.

"But, says Dolly piteously, and a trifle bewildered by these beautiful sentiments, "I overheard——"

"Ah l yes, you overheard. You overheard what I said to Miss Owenson, very likely. By-the-by, Dolly, I did *not* think you could stoop to eavesdropping. May I ask what reason you had to be surprised at what you heard?"

"What reason? You ask her to marry you—denying that you care for me or ever did ; make her name the wedding-day, and —what reason have I to be surprised!" says Dolly, putting her hand in her head, her brain in a hopeless muddle.

"I explained all that. Call to mind the night I told you fully how I stood in regard to this young lady, the obligations I was under to her father, how my whole future depends upon his bounty, what he expects, what she expects, the compact made when we were children, which I always meant to ratify, which I would have ratified had I not fallen in love with you. How, until the last moment, my intention was to keep them in the dark, hoping that the old gentleman might kindly die off before the wedding-day. Meantime, my full intention of acting my part, the better to blind them. That I may one day marry you, a rich man, I asked Miss Owenson to name the day, to-night."

Dolly stands speechless. She looks up at the moon, at the stars, at the tree-tops, at Mr. Vaughan's handsome, rebuking face, as he utters these sublimated sentences, but her dazed brain absolutely refuses to comprehend. The more Bertie reasons the more hopelessly her senses reel.

"Since that night at the theatre (when you so gratuitously insulted me, Miss De Courcy, in the presence of that cad, Ward) some inkling of the truth has come to Miss Owenson's ears. She is jealous, and to appease that jealousy I spare no effort. Let one whisper reach her father, and I am turned out adrift upon the world, without a home, a profession, a shilling. If he dies before the wedding-day I am provided for, can say good-by to Miss Owenson, and marry you. I hope you are satisfied *now !*"

He asks his last question in a tone of suppressed triumph; his concluding arguments have evidently been clinchers. But Dolly only looks at him with a piteously bewildered face. She must be hopelessly stupid indeed, but the force of all this forensic logic is thrown away upon her. She is not satisfied.

"May I ask, says Mr. Vaughan, changing his tone, while poor Dolly stands dazed, "what you came for? what you intended to do?"

She lights up suddenly, she can understand that question at least.

"Shall I tell you, Bertie?" she says, a flash of her old fire in eyes and voice.

" I ask for information, Dolly."

"Then I meant to have gone straight to Captain Owenson, to Miss Owenson, and told them my story, shown them my proofs, and broken off your marriage. I know it would break it off—no lady of honor would marry you after reading your letters to me."

There is an outbreak of triumph in her tone, but it changes quickly. All through the interview they have not been in very affectionate proximity, but he starts back two or three paces at these daring words, and looks at her with a glance that sends a bolt of cold terror through Dolly's heart.

"You did !" A pause, an awful one. "And may I inquire why you did not carry out your dramatic intentions, Miss De Courcy?"

" Oh, Bertie, please don't look at me like that, and don't call me Miss De Courcy ! I—I didn't do it !" she says, with a gasp.

" No, you didn't do it. I ask again, why?"

"Because—because I couldn't, I heard all you said, and it maddened me, and still I couldn't. I don't understand myself; I never used to be a coward. Other men have been fond of me, but I never cared a pin whether I lost them or not; but I am afraid of you."

The confession seems wrung from her against her will. A slight smile of complacent power glides over his set lips a second, then it disappears.

"Well, now, Dolly," he says, "for fear any such temptation should occur to you again, let us understand one another. There is the house—whenever expatiating you choose you can see Captain Owenson or his daughter ; you can tell them your story—I shall deny nothing ; you can show them my letters— I will not refuse to admit them. Captain Owenson will at once order me from his doors ; Miss Owenson will probably never see me again while she lives. All this you can do ; and the moment you do it—the moment a word of our engagement gets wind through you, and comes to their ears—that moment is the last you will ever set eyes on me. I will never see you again, never speak to you again, so long as I live ! "

Another pause. All white and speechless, shrinking, trembling, Dolly De Courcy listens to her doom. Calm and stern as a stone Rhadamanthus, this youthful autocrat goes on :

"If you care for me, if you ever want to be my wife, you must obey me in what I say to-night. I cannot write to you or receive letters from you without danger; I cannot visit you without instant discovery. Therefore I will neither write nor visit you. You will leave Wychcliffe with the rest of them, and wait for me in New York. When do the company go ?"

"In a week," Dolly answers, with a shiver.

"Very well, you will go with them ; I will remain here. Captain Owenson may die any day of heart disease—may die before the last Thursday in November. If he does, all is right ; if he does not, all will be right, too. On the day before the wedding I will quietly leave Wychcliffe, join you in New York, and marry you out of hand. I have no more to say. This is my final decision. You will abide by it or not, as you think best."

"I am to go with the company, and see you no more until——"

"Until the last Thursday in November—not quite two weeks. An eternity, certainly ! " he says, sarcastically.

"It will seem so to me, for all the time I shall be fearing— Bertie I " she cries out, "you shall *not* marry her I Don't think it. I will never give you up."

He turns to leave her.

"I have no more to say. All my explanations have been thrown away. Do as you please."

"Oh, Bertie, stay ! Forgive me ! I will do as you tell me. I will trust you. Only—only say one kind word to me I This

has been a wretched night, and, indeed, indeed, I am dreadfully
miserable."

Sultan Bertie relents.   His slave is in her proper place, at his
feet.   He can afford one relenting parting word.

"Don't be a simpleton, Dolly," he says, taking both her
hands in his.   "If I wasn't idiotically fond of you, would I risk
all my prospects in life for you ?   It would be a good deal bet-
'ter for me if I cared for Miss Owenson as I do for you ; but I
don't and can't"—and here Bertie told the truth—"and that's
an end of the matter.   You shall be my wife, and no one else,
that I promise, for the hundredth time.   And now go, like a
good child, and come here no more.   Leave with the rest, and
wait for me in New York.   I shall see you once again, by some
means, and we shall have a pleasanter good-by than this."

A moment more and he is alone under the trees.   Out in the
open, in the full shine of the moon, a figure is hurrying toward
the gate, a figure in whose breast a tumult is going on.   Anger
and passion are spent, and deep, sullen resolve has taken their
place.   He is deceiving her—with the quick clairvoyance of her
kind she knows it, and she means to be even with him.   He intends to send her away quietly and marry the heiress of all this
fine place.   As well as he knows it himself she knows it also,
and just as firmly as he is resolved to succeed just as firmly she
is resolved he shall not.

He stands and watches her out of sight.   Half-an-hour has
passed in the interview—he will be missed, he fears.   He starts
rapidly forward—no one is about.   He is congratulating himself on Dolly's safe and unseen exit, when he runs up the portico
steps and comes full upon Cyrilla Hendrick.

She is standing there alone, the moonlit expanse, cold and vividly bright before ; how long, who is to tell ?

He is so stunned that he stands before her mute.   Of all the
people, she !

"Ah, Mr. Vaughan," she says, that malicious smile he has
learned to detest on her lips, "I knew you could not be in the
house.   I said so, although Sydney insisted that you were."

"And you volunteered to come out here in the cold and look
for me ?   How kind," he responds, his blue eyes glittering with
hatred.

"Oh, dear, no ; don't flatter yourself," Cyrilla says, with the
airiest of laughs ; "the parlors were oppressive, and I never take
cold.   The moonlight looked so inviting that I have been here
fully ten minutes enjoying the prospect.   And I have enjoyed

it," says Miss Hendrick, with slow emphasis, smiling up in his
face. "I can only regret that Sydney was not to be coaxed to
come out with me and enjoy it too."

"But you can describe it to her," suggests Bertie, in a hissing
sort of whisper. "I can imagine you really must be good at that
sort of thing, and every end will be answered as well."

"No," Cyrilla laughs; "I differ. You flatter me—I am not
at all good at that sort of thing, you mean describing what I see,
don't you? I never look for other people; let every one use
her own eyes. Will you give me your arm back, Mr. Vaughan?
I find I have had enough of moonshine. I hope Sydney is not
inclined to be jealous—she may actually think we have been
flirting here on the steps."

"Sydney will never be jealous of me," says Sydney's affianced,
with elaborate carelessness, "if she is left to herself. There is
nothing small, or prying, or suspicious about *her*."

The personal pronoun is fiercely italicized, the gauntlet of defiance is openly flung at her feet. Miss Hendrick lifts her big
black eyes and laughs in his face, a laugh of most unaffected,
thorough appreciation, good humor and enjoyment. And Mr.
Vaughan looks down upon her hanging on his arm and thinks
what a pleasure it would be to meet her by moonlight alone, in
some nice, shady nook, and murder her in cold blood.

CHAPTER XVIII.

"THE FEAST IS SET."

ONE—two—three—four, on lightning wings the days go
by. In mad haste they scamper over each other's
heels, frantic to quit time for eternity. Like flashes
they come and go. This is what Sydney and Sydney's
mamma think at least, hurried and busy with their preparations
for the fast-coming nuptials, only seven days off now.

To the bridegroom they lag—lag horribly. While the same
town contains Dolly De Courcy and Sydney Owenson, what
peace can there be for him? She has promised to trust him,
and go quietly; but there is no putting confidence in a woman.
Every day takes Sydney and her obnoxious friend into Wychcliffe—every day takes Dolly there for rehearsal. Who is to

tell him what hour may bring them together. What hour Dolly may "up" and tell them the whole story. As strongly as he had set his shifting heart upon marrying Dolly a fortnight ago, just as strongly has he set it now upon marrying Sydney. There is no love in the question, not a jot; it is simply a matter of money; it is, as he tells himself, that his summer's madness is at an end; that he is "clothed and in his right mind" once more.

During those four dragging lagging days he raises Miss De Courcy to the pinnacle of bliss by two visits; he soothes her with sweet words and sugared promises. She is very quiet, dangerously quiet, if Bertie did but know it. She takes her sweetmeats from her master's hand, and says very little. And the fourth day comes, and by the morning train the whole company, leading lady of course included, leave Wychcliffe. Leave, positively leave. Bertie risks all things, gets out of bed at the unhallowed hour of seven, in the cold gray of the frosty November morning, and appears, blue and shivering, upon the platform to see them off. But even this proof of self-sacrificing devotion does not take Dolly in. She smiles sarcastically as she shakes hands with him, and sees through his little artifice in a moment. She is unaffectedly glad to see him too—her dark face lights up, and she looks at·him as Bertie Vaughan most certainly does not deserve to be looked at by any woman on earth. Then they are in their places. What a long breath of infinite relief it is that Mr. Vaughan draws; she waves her hand to him from the window, looks at him with two solemn black eyes, and says in her deepest Lady Macbeth voice:

"REMEMBER!"

It reminds Bertie of Charles the First on the scaffold, and he laughs.

"All right, Dolly," he says. "By-by," and the lovers' parting is over.

He goes home, and is in wild high spirits all the rest of the day. He holds forth at breakfast upon the beauty and expediency of the "healthy, wealthy and wise" principle of early rising. To get up by gaslight on a bitter fall morning, to crack the ice in your wash basin, and to plunge off for a three·mile walk, is the acme of earthly bliss. Breakfast over, he insists upon escorting his affianced and her friend into town to do their diurnal shopping; to wait upon them, Bertie avers—to sit on high stools and listen to hyacinthe dry-goods men expatiating on the beauty of lace and ribbons and artificial flowers,

will be to him the supreme pinnacle of earthly blessedness! It
is as usual the odious Miss Hendrick who topples him down off
the high horse he is rampantly riding.

"A change has come o'er the spirit of your dream, rather,
hasn't there?" she says. "Up to this morning you have
obstinately refused to have anything to do with us. Apropos
of early rising, the theatre people were to go to-day—didn't
Mr. Sunderland say so last evening, Syd? You must have
seen them this morning in Wychcliffe, Mr. Vaughan?"

Again blue eyes and black eyes meet—again Mr. Vaughan
asks himself could it, would it, be wrong to privately assassinate this girl if he gets the chance.

"I saw them, Miss Hendrick; I even shook hands with two
or three of them. Are there any further particulars of the
theatre people you would like to hear?"

"None at all, thank you," Cyrilla laughs; "I am quite satisfied. In half an hour, then, Mr. Vaughan, we will place ourselves under your fostering care for the morning."

All Sydney's artless efforts to make these two friends, fall flat.
It is one of the thorns in her bed of roses that Cyrilla will per-
sist in saying "Mr. Vaughan" to the bitter end.

"I think it is really unkind of you, Cy," she says, reproachfully now. "Calling Bertie Mr. Vaughan, just as if he wasn't
to marry me next week. I am sure, if our cases were
reversed, I would have been calling Mr. Carew Freddy long
before this."

"I am quite sure you would," answers Cyrilla, laughing; "no
one ever does call Freddy anything but Freddy, so far as I can
see. There is no comparing the cases. There is a dignity, an
unapproachableness (that is a good word) about Mr. Vaughan
that forbids flippant familiarities with his Christian name. If I
were wrecked on a desert island with your future spouse, Syd,
I couldn't call him Bertie—not under eighteen months.

Sydney looks at her friend, half puzzled, half indignant, half
inclined to laugh herself. Bertie dignified! Bertie unap-
proachable! But Miss Hendrick's quizzical face baffles her.

"Do you hear from Fred often, Cy?" she inquires.

"Twice a week, poor boy! Ah! what a penance it must be
to Fred Carew, who hates the sight of pen and ink with an honest
hatred he never attempts to conceal. Each letter contains precisely thirteen lines. That military heart of his may be full to
overflowing, and no doubt is, but to sit at a desk and put down
in cold ink the gushing warmth of his affection—no, that is be-

yond Freddy ; I don't expect it.   I take my thirteen lines, and
am thankful.   What a rage Aunt Dormer would be in if she only
knew ! "

That day's devotion on Bertie's part was but the *fac simile* of
the next and the next.   The third was Friday—the Friday preceding the wedding—and on that day Captain Owenson dispatched his son-in-law-elect to New York on an important mis-
sion—no less, indeed, than the inspection of the old sailor's wed-
ding-suit and his own.   For upon mature deliberation it had
been decided that the tailors of Wychcliffe, sufficiently skilled
artist at ordinary times, were not to be trusted upon the present
important occasion.   The sombre regulation costume must be
got in the metropolis, and Bertie must be upon the spot to see
that no mistake was made.   There were other commissions also
to fulfill for the ladies—he would probably be detained until
Monday night.

"And upon my return, sir," said Bertie, "with your permission
I will take up my quarters at the Wychcliffe Hotel until Thursday morning.   In the usual course of things, the bridegroom
doesn't generally exist and have his being under the same roof
with the bride.   It will be more strictly *en règle*, believe me, if
I hang out at the hotel."

" Oh !—pooh — nonsense— fiddle-dee-dee ! " said   Captain
Owenson.

" All right, sir—as you please.   I merely mentioned the fact.
I know it's the thing in England, but of course you know best.
It doesn't matter to me," upliftedly responded Mr. Vaughan.

The mention of England brought down the Captain, as Bertie
knew it would.

" Stay !   Look here !   Wait a minute !   It's so long since
I've had anything to do with weddings that I've forgotten.   Will
it really be more in accordance with well-bred British customs
if you go to the hotel ?   It looks like tom-foolery to me."

" It's the thing, depend upon it," answered Bertie, calmly.
" If I only consulted my own inclinations, I would stay here,
of course, near Sydney.   But I never heard of such a thing before, as bride and bridegroom starting for church out of the
same house.   If it be an American custom, however, and if you
wish it, I bow, of course," says Bertie, with a graceful inclination, " to your superior wisdom."

" That will do," growls the captain—he hated American customs.   " Let it be as you say.   Stop at the hotel when you
come back.   Will it be a solecism of English wedding good

manners. may I ask for you to favor us with an occasional
call during those intervening two days?" concludes the captain,
sarcastically.

"I shall spend my days and evenings here, sir," answered
Bertie, repressing a strong inclination to laugh, "returning to
the hotel to sleep."

So this nice point of bridal etiquette was settled, and Mr.
Vaughan started for New York. A haunting fear that Dolly
would turn up, those last two days, and seek him out at the
Place, had underlain the hotel project. If she did come—he
groaned mentally as he thought of it—and visited him there,
less harm would be done. In some way—in what way he did
not know, but in some way—he would quiet her, and keep her
out of harm's way until the ring was on Sydney's finger. Then
let her do her worst. And yet, poor little Dolly! how fond he
had been of her, too!

He reached the great city, spent three days and a great deal
of money very agreeably. A strong, almost irresistible desire
to hunt up Dolly possessed him. He was never happier than
when with Dolly,—she suited him, as novels put it, "to the finest
fibre of his being." But it would not do; if she once set eyes
on him in New York, an inward conviction told him she would
never let him go. Who was to tell that she might not get a
gang of East-side brigands to bear him off captive to the deepest dungeon in the Bowery, and, willy-nilly, make him her husband? Some vague thoughts like these actually went through
Bertie's brain. No; it would not do; he must not go to see
Dolly; he must never see Dolly while he lived again. In spite
of Sydney's real estate and bank stock, it was a dismal thought,
and he sighed profoundly. After all, it was a pity Dolly wasn't
rich, or a great actress. He was fond of her—there was no
getting over that.

Monday morning came. The week "big with fate" had
arrived. He took the cars, his business satisfactorily completed, and started for home. It was only a three hours' ride
to Wychcliffe. As he took his seat and unfolded the morning's
damp paper, he was thinking that the crisis in his life had come.
How would he feel this time next Monday morning? Would he
be sitting by Sydney's side somewhere on their bridal journey,
her lawful owner and possessor, or would Dolly turn up and
make a grand theatrical tableau in the church—and would
ruin, and poverty, and disgrace be his portion for life?

He could not read. Again and again he tried; again and

again he failed   He gave it up at last, and sat staring out at
the wintry picture flitting by.   It was like a day cut in steel—
clear, windless, sunless, cold.   The sky was pale gray, the
earth frozen hard, ringing like glass at every sound.   The trees
stood up, tracing their black, sharp outlines against the steely
air.   A snow-storm was pending— would it storm on the wedding-day ?

"Dolly ! Dolly ! "   She haunted him like an importunate
ghost.   Her face was before him, her voice in his ears.   "Remember !"—what had she meant by that ?   He had laughed
then ; it was no laughing matter now.   Oh ! it meant that he
was to be with her on Wednesday night.   He had said he
would, if the captain did not die.   Die ! he looked of late as
though he would never die, as if he had renewed his lease of
life.

Remember !   How ominous a gleam there had been in her
black eyes as she said it.   Black-eyed women are always edge
tools to play with.   Why had she ever come to Wychcliffe?
Why had he ever gone to that infernal little theatre ?   What
would she do on Wednesday night when he did not come?
Would she even wait as long as Wednesday night ?   It was
only three hours' ride to Wychcliffe, and trains were running
all the time.   She was not a girl to stick at a trifle, and she
had told him she would not give him up.   The wedding hour
was eleven.   If she took the cars Thursday morning in New
York, there would be ample time to get to church in season
to——

He broke off with a pang of absolute physical agony.   He
could see it all, that horrible, sickening scene.   Sydney fainting, the guests standing horror-stricken, the old captain, his
friend, his benefactor, livid with fear and rage, Dolly, a black-
eyed Nemesis, wild and dishevelled, in their midst, her back
hair down, displaying her proofs before them all, pointing the
finger of retribution at him, and reading his letters aloud.   Those
fatal letters !   Spoony beyond all ordinary depths of spoonyism,
and he—he standing pallid with guilt, his knees knocking together, paralyzed, stricken dumb, *sheepish*.

He set his teeth.   No ! if it came to that there should be a
tragic ending that would take the edge of the sheepishness at
least.   He would provide himself with a pistol, load it, carry it
in his breast pocket, and when the awful moment came he
would thrust in his hand, hurl it forth, cry : " Woman—fiend !
behold your work ! " and pull the trigger.   There would be a

flash, a report, the wild shrieks of many women, and he would fall headlong at his bride's feet—dead!

"Wychcliffe!" shouted the conductor, putting in his head.

From his tragical reverie Mr. Vaughan sprang to his legs, seized his baggage, and got out of the car. There were many he knew at the depot, but no one from The Place, of course.

He took a hack and drove to the hotel, made some change in his toilet, jumped into his hack once more, and was driven to Owenson Place in time for luncheon and to give an account of his stewardship.

Nothing had happened—bright looks and cordial greetings met him everywhere. The captain wrung his hand as though he had been away a year or so. Sydney actually blushed and looked shyly glad to see him. Aunt Char kissed his mustache, and Miss Hendrick gave him one slim, dusk hand, the old quizzical, satirical look in her ebon eyes.

"How I do hate that girl!" he said, petulantly, to Sydney, ten minutes later, when they were alone.

"Bertie!" Sydney cried, in a shocked tone; "hate Cyrilla! You don't mean that?"

"Yes, I do—hate her as I do the——"

"Bertie!"

"Well, I won't, then; but, I detested her from the first moment I set eyes on her. After you're married, Mrs. Vaughan, I promise you she shall not wear herself out visiting us. Now, don't put on that horrified face, sis. You've known well enough I didn't like her all along."

"But why?" persisted Miss Owenson. "I think she's lovely. Why don't you like her? She's never done anything to you."

"Oh, no, of course not, and wouldn't either if she got a chance!" says Bertie, sarcastically. "Why don't you like a toad or a snake when you meet one? A little green snake is pretty to look at and never did any one any harm. Why do we take antipathies to people at sight?

> "'I do not like you Doctor Fell;
> The reason why I cannot tell.'

"I feel Doctor Fell toward her. I could see her bow-strung and cast into the Bosphorus in a sack by two of my blackest Nubians, with all the pleasure in life!"

Then there is silence—horrified on Sydney's part, ruminative on Mr. Vaughan's.

"And so everything's lovely, Syd?" he says, after a moment. "Nothing's happened? 'The feast is set, the guests are met, all correct and duly?"

"What could happen?" asks Sydney, gayly. "Of course everything is correct. Except the weather," adds the bride-elect, glancing apprehensively out of the window ; "that's cold and miserable enough even for the last week of November. By-the-by, it's a dismal month to be married in, Bertie."

"Is it? But there will be so much sunshine in our hearts that we will never see the weather. You didn't think I was so poetical, sis, did you? Honestly, though, if we are married on Thursday morning, I'll do my best to behave myself and make you happy."

It is about the nearest approach to a tender speech this ardent bridegroom has ever got, and Sydney laughs at it, but with a little tremble in her voice.

"'If we are married!' What an odd thing to say, Bertie!"

"Oh! well, one never knows—one may die any day. 'In the midst of life we are in death,' and all that. One never is certain of anything in this most uncertain world."

She looks at him in wonder as he makes this cheerful and bridegroom-like speech. He is lying back in an easy-chair, his legs outstretched, a hand thrust in each trouser pocket, a dismal look on his face that suits his dismal words. He is thinking of Dolly.

"Would you care much, Syd," he goes on, looking out of the window at the dreary grayness of the dull day, not at her wondering face, "if you lost me? You're not in love with me, I know—no more am"—"I with you" is on his lips, and he barely catches it in time—"no more do I expect it just yet; but we've been jolly good friends and comrades all our lives— quite like brother and sister ; and—would you be sorry if anything happened, Syd?"

She comes close to him, laying a timid hand on his shoulder, and looking down at his moody face.

"I don't know what you mean, Bertie. If anything happened to stop our marriage, is it?"

"Yes. It's only a suppositious case, of course, but would you?"

"You know I would," she answers. "I—I am not in love with you, as you say, but indeed, Bertie, I do mean to be a loving wife, and make you happy. I would be dreadfully sorry if anything happened to break off our marriage now. I really believe papa would die of the disappointment."

" Always papa ! "

He sits erect hastily, for just at that moment, enter Miss Hendrick, and all the softer sentiments take unto themselves wings and fly at sight of her deriding black eyes.

All the minor details of the important event are mapped out by this time. Cyrilla, Mamie and Susie Sunderland are to support the bride through the ceremonial—she thinks she can survive with only three bridesmaids. Harry Sunderland is to be best man. Grooms and groomsman are to meet bride and bridesmaids at St. Philip's, at eleven A. M., sharp. The nuptial knot tied, they are to return to the paternal mansion—then breakfast, toasts, speeches, good wishes, etc. A very large company are bidden. Then the bridal tour, due south, and un alloyed bliss for the rest of their natural lives!

The snow-storm still threatens, but has not begun to fall, when at ten o'clock Bertie returns to his hotel. All Tuesday it darkens and lowers, and glooms, and the wind blows from a stormy quarter, but still the impending storm holds up. It will be a heavy fall when it comes, and the world will wear its chilliest nuptial robe to do honor to Sydney's bridal. One step for his own protection Bertie has taken. On Monday night he wrote a brief note to Dolly, informing her that the wedding had been postponed a week. That would throw her off the track he fondly hoped. If he could have seen the bitter unbelieving smile with which Miss De Courcy perused it, his confidence in his own diplomacy might have been shaken.

On Wednesday morning the long threatening storm began. The feathery snow came down in great, white, whirling flakes— down, down, softly, steadily, ceaselessly. No wind blew, the bitter cold had changed to softness, and in two hours all the world was wrapped in a soft, soundless, ghostly carpet of white.

" Oh ! " sighs Sydney, as she flutters from room to room and looks wistfully out, "how sorry I am. I did so want to-morrow fine."

" Superstitious child ! What's the odds ? " says Mr. Vaughan ; "though the snow were piled mountains high, though the 'awful avalanche' that destroyed that rash young man, Excelsior, threatened, still would your devoted Bertie be there."

" Well, I wish the sun would shine," persists the bride. " You may say what you please, but a stormy wedding-day is unlucky ! "

" My child, I am saying nothing. And I am perfectly con-

fident the sun will shine.   It will snow itself out before evening
at this rate.   They can't have such a stock on hand up there,"
says Bertie, consolingly.

Bertie is right.   All day long it falls, soundlessly and thickly,
then as evening approaches it lightens and ceases.   The air
turns crisp and cold, the stars come out, the wind veers round
into a propitious quarter, and the sun will shine upon Sydney's
wedding.

The Misses Sunderland are here, Bertie, Cyrilla, Sydney—
this last evening.   They have music, and waltzes in a small
way over the carpet.   Down in the dining-room the marriage
feast is set out, silver and glass making a brave show under the
lamps.   Cold white cakes glisten, cut flowers in frosty epergnes
are everywhere !   Up in one of the spare rooms the bridal
dress and vail, wreath, gloves, and slippers, lie pale and wraith-
like in the starry dusk.

At ten o'clock Mr. Vaughan arises, makes his adieus, dons
his overcoat, cap and gloves, and departs.   Sydney escorts him
to the door.   How white and still all the snowy world below,
how golden and blue all the shining world above !   How tranquil, how beautiful heaven and earth !

"I am so glad it will be fine," she says, with a little fluttering breath.

He bends above her a smile, almost fond on his face.

"Good-by, sis," he says.   "After to-morrow there will be no
more good-bys."

Then he is gone.   She watches him in the starlight along the
snowy path.   Once he turns and waves his hand to her, that
smile still lingering on his lips.   So in her dreams, for many an
after year, Bertie Vaughan comes back to her.

He has disappeared, and Sydney, silent and thoughtful, goes
back.   Bertie tramps on his road, with only one thought in his
mind.   Dolly has not come—will she come to-morrow ?   He
takes the short-cut to the town—the path that Sydney affects,
which "gives" along the high cliffs above the sea.   All black
and mysterious that great sea lies down yonder under the stars
its soft-ceaseless whispering was sounding on the sands.   He
has reached Wychcliffe, the highest point, without meeting a
creature, and it is just here from behind the rock that a dark
figure starts up in his path, and a stern voice cries.

"Stay !"

CHAPTER XIX.

" THE GUESTS ARE MET."

YRILLA is finishing "Come Haste to the Wedding," in ten pages of wild variations, driving the old-fashioned tune distracted ; and she rises from the piano as Sydney enters. At sight of the bride's thoughtful little look, she laughs.

" My solemn Sydney ! what is it he has been saying to you so heart-breaking that you should wear that forlorn look ? "

" Do I look forlorn ? " returns Miss Owenson. " I don't feel so, I can tell you. Papa, do you know we are going to have a fine day to-morrow, after all, and I am so glad."

" And I am glad of anything that makes my little girl glad," says papa with loving eyes. "Now, young ladies all, which do you propose, to make a night of it here, and go to church to-morrow as yellow as lemons, or try the early-to-bed and early-to-rise principle, Bertie was advocating the other day ? "

" To bed ! to bed !" exclaims Miss Hendrick. "I for one don't expect to sleep a wink ; it is the first time I ever was bridesmaid in my life. Shall you, Syd ? "

" I hope so, at least," laughs Sydney. "*I* don't want to look as yellow as a lemon, to-morrow. Mamie, dear, it is your turn to look solemn—what is it about ? "

For the elder Miss Sunderland is staring in rather a dreary way at the fire, and saying nothing.

" I know !" cries that malicious elf, her younger sister, triumphantly.

" Miss Hendrick's last remark has upset her. This is the third time she has been a bridesmaid ; and three times a bridesmaid never a bride, you know. She is thinking how the celebrated and fascinating Miss Dolly De Courcy had stolen from her the fickle affections of Ben——"

" Susie !" cries Miss Mamie in an awful voice, and Susie, the irrepressible, shouts with laughter, and stops. Miss Hendrick laughs a quiet laugh to herself, too. Truly Wychcliffe is well rid, she thinks, of that small destroying angel Dolly De Courcy.

" Good-night, Syd—dear old Syd—*our* Syd, no more !" exclaims Susie Sunderland, flinging her arms around the neck of

the bride—in that sort of hug known to bears and school-girls.
"This time to-morrow—oh! dismal to think of—it will be Mrs.
Bertie Vaughan."

"Good-night, Syd—good-night, Sydney, repeat Cyrilla and
Mamie, each with a less vehement embrace.

"Good-night, Sydney, love," says mamma, coming last of all.
"Try and sleep well—it's very trying to the eyesight not to
sleep well. I recollect I didn't sleep a wink the night before *I*
was married—you remember, Reginald?"

"How should I remember?" growls Reginald. "I am sure
I wasn't there?" Whereat the girls all laugh.

"Well, I didn't," says Aunt Char, "and my eyes were as
red as a ferret's next day."

"And lest yours should be as red as a ferret's to-morrow,
suppose you be off to bed at once. Good night, young
ladies," says the old sailor with his grandest bow, "I wish
you all pleasant dreams, and a speedy coming of your bridal
eve."

They are all gone, and Sydney stands alone by her father's
side. He puts his arm about her and looks anxiously down in
her face.

"You are happy, Sydney?" he asks—"really and truly
happy?"

She lifts her smiling face and fair, serene eyes.

"Really and truly, papa—quite, quite happy."

"God bless my little daughter."

He holds her to him a moment, and lets her go. And Sydney runs to her room, that smile still on her lips and in her eyes.

The red glow of firelight fills the room. She turns low her
light and goes to the window, to make sure of the weather.
Yes, there are the stars, a countless host, studding that illimitable, blue dome. Something in their glittering, tremulous loveliness holds her there, and she stands and gazes. And then
Bertie's words come strangely back to her as if some soundless
voice had spoken: "One never knows—we may die any day.
In the midst of life we are in death."

She has heard many times the grand, solemn words, spoken
nine hundred years ago, by the saintly lips of the Monk of St.
Gall's—on the lips of all mankind since; but they have never
held the meaning to her they hold now. Yes, life with all its
hopes and plans, its births and bridals, is like a half-told tale at
best. Suddenly, when the story is at its brightest and fullest,
the frail thread snaps, and Time is at an end and Eternity begins

"What is this passing scene?
  A peevish April day!
  A little sun a little rain,
  And then night sweeps across the plain,
  And all things pass away."

All things but the good works humbly done, the duties cheerfully fulfilled, the crosses patiently borne—everything else life has held, lost—these alone to plead for us in that awful *dies iræ*.

She draws the curtain and turns away, her thoughts sweet and solemn, but not sad. Half an hour later, her fair hair fall ing loose over her pillow, a wondrously fair sight, in the rose shine of the fire she is sleeping like a tired child.

The sun is shining, filling her room with its early morning glory, when she awakes, and some one is standing by her bed-side smiling down upon her. It is Cyrilla.

"Laziest of brides," is Miss Hendrick's greeting, "get up. Look at that clock and blush for yourself."

Sydney looks—it is nearly eight.

"Well," she says, with a stifled gape, "that is a very good hour, isn't it?"

Then she is silent, and as it flashes back upon her that this is her wedding-day, her heart for a moment seems to stand still. She sits up in bed, throws her arms around her friend's neck, draws down her face and kisses it.

"Dear old Cy!" she says, "what good friends we have always been. I hope—oh! I hope to-day may never make any difference between us."

"It will make a great deal of difference," responds matter-of-fact Miss Hendrick. "Mr. Vaughan detests me with a cordial-ity worthy a better cause. Well, perhaps he has had some rea-son," and Cyrilla laughs.

"Reason?" Sydney looks puzzled. "What reason?"

"Never mind—you dear little innocent, it isn't well for you to know too much. But, be assured of this—however friendly Miss Owenson may have been to her vagabond friend, Mrs. Vaughan will keep her civilly at arms' length."

"Cy! as if I could ever change to you."

"Ah! wait," hints Cyrilla darkly; "wives and maidens are two different orders of beings. You will see with Bertie Vaughan's eyes, and think with his thoughts, before you are his wife three months. It is one of the fixed laws of nature, as immutable as the stars!"

"If I were three years—three centuries his wife," cried Miss

8*

Owenson, with heightened color, "I would still be your friend, as strongly and as firmly as I am to-day."

"Well," Miss Hendrick responds, heaving a profound sigh, "I hope so, I'm sure. I told you at school I had a firm conviction I would one day make strong claims upon that friendship, and I have it yet. If I am ever in trouble, friendless and cast out, I shall remind you of this promise. Now get up, do. and dress yourself, and come and have some coffee and a roll to nerve you for the trying ordeal. I should not be surprised if Mr. Vaughan were bracing his trembling nerves with a *petite verre* of the strongest fire-water in Wychcliffe at this moment."

Sydney has her bath, knots up her hair, throws on a dressing-gown, thrusts her feet into slippers, and runs down-stairs. It is nine o'clock now. In two hours precisely she will be standing at the altar.

From this moment all is fuss and haste, bustle and confusion, A hasty cup of strong coffee is swallowed all around ; eating is but a pretext with these excited maidens, then they scurry off to their rooms. In his, Captain Owenson is making the most elaborate toilet man ever made ; he began at eight and will probably not get through until eleven. For the first time in two years he is going to church. Sydney finds the hair-dresser awaiting her, and places herself under his hands. It is a lengthy operation. When it is over the maid who is to robe her for the sacrifice, approaches and leads her off. One by one they are on, dress, slippers, vail, wreath, necklace, gloves. As in a dream she sits or stands, wondering "if I be I." She can fancy the pains Bertie is taking over his wedding toilet, so fastidious and difficult as he is at all times, and she smiles to herself. Then she glances at the clock—twenty minutes of eleven.

" Look at yourself, miss," says the girl with a pleased simper. " I don't believe you have looked yet."

She scarcely has, but she does now. She almost starts ; she utters a faint, delighted exclamation. Can this be Sydney Owenson ? this radiant vision in silvery white, with all that gold hair *coiffed* so elaborately in this trailing splendor of shimmering silk, and pearls, and lace, and orange blossoms ? Then the door opens and the three bridesmaids come in.

" Oh ! "

It is a long-drawn, breathless aspiration from all three at once. They stand and survey the bride from head to foot.

" Oh, *don't* you look scrumptious ! " cries Susie Sunderland, dancing a little ecstatic jig around the bride ; "shouldn't I love to be a bride and look like that?"

They are all three in palest pink ! rose is Cyrilla's color, and fortunately suits the Sunderland sisters. In palest pink, with golden lockets, the bridegroom's gift, on their necks and blush roses in their hair.

"You really look lovely, Syd," says Minnie Sunderland, with a small, envious sigh. "I always knew being married was becoming to almost everybody, but it becomes you better than any one I ever saw. Your dress is exquisite."

"And don't she wish Ben Ward would ask her to put on such a one and come to church with him !" says Susie, in a stage "aside."

The door opens again ; this time it is mamma, brave in pearl satin, a diamond breast-pin and point-lace cap.

"Will I do, mamma?" the bride asks, holding up her face to be kissed.

"Yes, you look very well," says mamma, critically. "White silk is a trying thing to most complexions, but then fair people with a color can wear almost anything. I could myself when I was a girl. Everybody said I looked remarkably well the night I was married. I prefer a gaslight marriage myself—it's more imposing, but your papa would have the morning and the church. It's more English, I suppose."

Again a tap at the door—this time papa, looking stately and grand, an "officer and a gentleman" every inch.

"Ready, young ladies?—ready, Sydney?" he asks, his watch in his hand, "the carriage is at the door, and it is only five minutes to eleven. We shall be precisely ten minutes late."

"Oh, where are the wraps !" cry all, and a universal rush is made. Dazzling sunshine streams over everything, but it is the last week of November, and the air is iced accordingly. Wraps are found and thrown on, and all troop down-stairs with a joyous tumult of laughter and talk, and pile into the two carriages waiting there. Captain Owenson, Sydney and Cyrilla Hendrick in the first, mamma and the Misses Sunderland in the other.

"What a perfect day !" Sydney exultantly cries ; "sunshine everywhere and the snow sparkling as if it had been painted and varnished. It is a good omen—this heavenly day."

"I wish it were not quite so trying to the eyes, though," said her father ; "mine have been blinking in its dazzle and raining tears—the only tears that are to be shed at your wedding, Sydney."

Sydney smiles and nestles her hand in his.   There is an inter
val of silence—then they are in Wychcliffe. -And now the little
bride's heart begins to beat fast.   There is the church—a flock
of the town street Arabs around the gateth—e hour has come.
They stop.   Can Bertie and Harry have walked?   Theirs
are the only carriages waiting.   The girls fling off their loose
wraps, the door is opened and the captain is handed out.   A
red carpet is laid to the church door—upon it the bride steps
and takes her father's arm.   The Misses Sunderland and Miss
Hendrick follow ; mamma sails along in their wake, and the
bridal *cortége* sweep into the church.

There is a mist before Sydney's eyes, a dull roaring in her
ears ; her heart beats as if it would suffocate her.   She is dimly
conscious that the church is very full of people, and that they
are all staring at her.   Then—she never afterward knows how
it is—but a *douche* of ice-water seems to go over her, all palpi-
tation passes away, all tremor, all shyness—she feels suddenly
cold and still, and the bridegroom is not here !

They, are standing alone at the altar rails, her father, her
bridesmaids, herself, and—no one else.   Bertie and Harry
Sunderland were to be here before them, but neither Bertie nor
Harry has come.

Her father—it is her first thought—her proud, sensitive, invalid old father.   He had turned livid in the first shock of realizing the affront put upon him—he has turned purple now, a fine
imperial purple.   Then, as the vestry door opens and the parson in his surplice appears, changes to ashen pale again.   The
Reverend Mr. Sylvester beckons him aside and says in a whisper :

"This is very awkward, captain—it is a quarter past eleven.
Something has detained the bridegroom."

Awkward !   A mild way of putting it, certainly.   There stands
the bride—there stand the bridesmaids in a blank group, there
sit all the gaping people, dead silent, breathless, a dawning
smile on two or three faces.

Here he is—here is the parson ; but was ever such a thing
heard of before in all the annals of bridals?—the bridegroom is
late !

To her dying day, it seems to Sydney as she stands there, she
will never recall this moment without turning sick and scarlet
with pain and shame.   She is as white as the dress she wears,
she stands looking straight before her and seeing nothing.   So
they remain a petrified group, while one, two, three, four, five

minutes tick off. No one seems to know what to do, they just stand and look blankly before them. Then the captain pulls out his watch, his hand shaking as though palsy-stricken; it is twenty minutes past eleven. As he puts it back there is a sudden sound and bustle at the door. All start, all eyes turn, all hearts beat quick. A man enters, one man, one only—*not* the bridegroom. It is Harry Sunderland.

He is pale, his eyes look excited, he strides up to where they stand, heedless of the staring congregation, and addresses himself to the father of the bride.

"Hasn't Vaughan come?" he asks, in a hoarse, breathless sort of voice.

"He is not here," the parson answers.

The power of speech it seems has left Captain Owenson.

"Then in Heaven's name, where can he be?" the young man cries. "He is not at the hotel—he never was there all night. No one knows anything of him. He left yesterday afternoon and has never been seen since."

In the same hoarse, breathless voice, he says all this, staring blankly in the clergyman's face.

"I waited and waited, hoping he would come," he goes on.

"I sent messengers in search of him. No one has seen him, no one——"

"Papa!" Sydney shrieks. She springs forward, not a second too soon, and reels as her father falls headlong into her extended arms. Harry Sunderland catches him before both fall.

Then a scene of direst confusion begins, the cries of women, the rushing of many feet, the sounds of wild weeping, the excited clamor of many tongues. In the midst of it all the rector speaks:

"Carry him into the vestry," he says, and young Sunderland obeys. Like a dead man the old sailor lies in his arms. Is he dead? His doom has been long ago pronounced—a sudden shock may kill him at any moment. Surely he has had shock enough now.

"Fly for a doctor!" says Mr. Sylvester.

Sunderland places his burden upon a bench and goes. Sydney, sinking on her knees by his side, receives her father's head in her arms. She does not speak, she makes no outcry, she is the color of death, and her eyes are wild and black with terror, but she is perfectly still. Her mother in the grasp of Cyrilla Hendrick is in violent hysterics; the Sunderland girls stand near, sobbing uncontrollably. Sydney alone looks down in her father's corpse-like face and is still.

It may be a moment, it may be an hour, she does not know when the doctor comes. She does not quit her post as he makes his examination; it seems to her she hardly lives or feels as he searches pulse and heart, and pronounces it not death, but a death-like faint. Then remedies of all kinds are tried. Sydney is told to arise, and mechanically obeys. She stands beside her father, heedless of everything else that goes on, forgetful of everything else that has happened, and watches the slow return to life. Slow, but he does return; there is a struggle, a quiver of all the limbs, a gasping breath or two, and he opens his eyes. He is bewildered at first—he looks wildly around.

"Sydney!"

"Papa, darling, here!" She falls on her knees beside him again, again takes his head in her arms, and kisses him softly.

"Something has happened?" he asks in the same vacant way. "What was it? Oh, I know!" A spasm of agony distorts his face. "Bertie."

"Harry is going to try and find him. Don't think of Bertie now, papa. Can you sit up? We are going to take you home."

"Yes, home—home!" he makes answer, brokenly. "There will be no marrying or giving in marriage to-day. Oh, my little daughter."

They raise him up, Harry Sunderland on one side, the doctor on the other, and bear him between them to the carriage. He came here this morning a fine, upright, grand old gentleman, he goes, marked for death, unable to stand alone. The doctor follows him in, and sits beside him; then Sydney, Henry Sunderland helps to hers, Mrs. Owenson still sobbing wildly, and finally Miss Hendrick.

"You had better get into my sleigh, girls," he has said to his sisters; "it is at the gate. They want no strangers at Owenson Place to-day. You can drive yourself and Sue, Mamie."

They assent and go. The young fellow returns to the first carriage and looks with compassionate eyes at Sydney.

"I am going in search of Bertie," he says. "I will find him if he is alive."

She bends her head and the carriage starts. They go slowly —it takes all the doctor's strength to uphold the stricken man. The other carriage is at the house before them, and Mrs. Owenson and Cyrilla stand at the door.

"Oh, Reginald," Mrs. Owenson cries, with a wild flood of tears.

He neither seems to see nor hear her. Perkins and the doctor carry him up-stairs to his bedroom, take off all those brave
wedding-garments, which will serve for his shroud, and lay him
on the bed from which he will never rise.

In her chamber the unwedded bride is removing with rapid
hands vail, wreath, pearls, robe. There are no tears in her
eyes; she has shed none, she keeps that pale cold calm through
all. The clock strikes one as she throws on her dressing-gown
and hurries to her father's bedside. And where in the world of
the living or the world of the dead is Bertie Vaughan?

CHAPTER XX.

"DEATH IS KING—AND VIVAT REX."

HER father is calling for her as she goes in. She comes
forward and twines her arms around him as he lies.
Infinite pity, infinite love look at her out of those
haggard eyes.

"My little one," he says, "my little one, it is hard on *you*."

He cannot talk much. He has had spasms of the heart
since they brought him home, and he is greatly exhausted. He
lies with his daughter's hand clasped in his, and falls, almost as
he speaks, into a sort of stupor in which he remains for hours.
The doctor, Mrs. Owenson, Cyrilla, flit in and out, and offer to
relieve Sydney, but she shakes her head, and her pale tired face
never loses its patient, suffering look. Her mother is weeping
ceaselessly—Sydney sheds no tears. "How dreadful of you,
Sydney," Mrs. Owenson says with a suppressed outbreak of sobbing, "to sit there like that, and your poor papa as bad as he
can be—not to speak of Bertie. I am sure if I were in your
place I would die. I never thought you could be heartless before."

Heartless! is she? She puts her hand to her head with a
dreary gesture. A dull, dumb sense of misery oppresses her,
but she cannot cry—her eyes are dry and hot. Usually tears
come as readily to her as to most girls, even for trifles, although
she has never wept much in her short happy life; but if that life
depended on it she could not shed a tear now.

"Please, mamma, not so loud. You will wake papa," she

says, pleadingly, and mamma with another burst of stifled hysterics goes out and confides to Miss Hendrick how dry-eyed and
unfeeling Sydney sits.

Hours pass. The yellow afternoon sun is slanting farther
and farther westward; in the sick-room pale twilight is falling
already, when there is a loud ring at the door-bell. Sydney's
heart jumps wildly. Her father's dulled ears hear it, her father's
dulled eyes open.

"Who is this?" he asks.

"I don't know. Are you better papa, dear?"

"Have you been here ever since?" he inquires.

"Yes, papa; you know I would rather be beside you than
anywhere else in the world."

"My Sydney!" He presses her hand gently, and tears force
their way into his eyes; "there is—no—news?"

"None, papa—yet."

"They are searching?"

"Yes, papa. Mamma says Harry and the constable are
searching everywhere."

"How long have I slept?"

"Nearly three hours, papa."

"And you have been here all that time. Your mother must
relieve you. Ha! who is that?"

There is a tap at the door—it opens, and Mrs. Owenson
comes hastily in.

"Sydney!" she says, in an excited whisper, "there is a man
here, and he says he has news. He wants to see your father—
what shall we do?"

"Send him in!" exclaims her husband's voice, and Aunt Char
jumps and shrieks; "send him in, Char. Do you hear? At
once."

Mrs. Owenson vanishes. Sydney feels the hand her father
holds convulsively grasped, hears his quick panting breath, sees
the excited flash of his eyes.

"Oh, papa, be careful!" she pleads; "don't excite yourself.
You don't know the harm it may do."

He knows well enough, but he never thinks of himself in this
moment. The man is ushered in by the mistress of the house,
and stands, hat in hand, bowing awkwardly and looking embarrassed—a decent, intelligent working man.

"Well," the captain gasps, "quick! what is your news?"

The man advances toward the bed, and holds out something
to Sydney.

"Would you please to look at this, miss, and tell me if you know it?"

She takes it and utters a cry. It is a locket attached to a fragment of broken chain.

"It is Bertie's," she says; "his locket, papa—with his mother's picture, the one he always wore on his watch-chain. Look!"

She places it in her father's hand. He recognizes it, as she does, the instant his eyes fall upon it.

"It's the missing young gentleman's, then?" asks the man. "I thought so. Could you tell me, miss, what sort of a necktie he wore the evening you see him last?"

"A blue necktie," Sydney answers, without a second's hesitation. "A dark-blue necktie no broader than a strip of narrow ribbon."

"Is this it?" says the man. He takes out of his vest pocket a tiny paper parcel, opens it, and displays what looks like a strip of narrow dark blue ribbon torn in two.

"It is," Sydney exclaims; "I am sure of it! The ends are peculiarly stitched with white; Mr. Vaughan had this on his neck last night when he left this house. Oh, papa! what does this mean?"

"What I suspected from the first," her father answered, in a husky voice—"that Bertie has been waylaid and murdered."

Mrs. Owenson gave a faint shriek of horror, although she had been asserting as much ever since her return from church Sydney turns cold and trembles. But the old fire is in the sailor's eye, the old authoritative ring in his voice as he speaks:

"Where did you find these things, my man? Speak at once."

"I found them early this morning, the locket hanging from a cedar bush, half way down Witch Cliff, the necktie torn in two pieces as you see it, and tramped down in the snow on the ground above. It was about nine in the morning, and I was on my way to Bensonbridge, five miles as you know, 'tother side of this house, sir, and I had took the cliff path as a short cut. When I got to that high place, Witch Cliff, I could see the snow all tramped and trod down, as if a couple of men had been scuffling and wrestling along the very edge of that dangerous place. A piece away I spied these bits of blue ribbon, torn in two and tramped into the snow with their boots. I picked them up and looked over the edge, kind o' skairt like. I don't suppose I would have seen this 'ere gold thing, but the sun was a shinin' and a glistenin' right onto it. I went back to where there's a path, and reached it. It was hanging from a cedar

bush, as if whoever wore it had fell down and it caught there
and snapped off. The bush was a strong one, but it was rooted
nearly up, like's if it had been caught holt of sudden, and nearly
torn from the roots. I was skairt square, as I say, but I had
no time to spare. I put the things in my pocket and tramped
on to Bensonbridge. The first thing I hear when I come back
was this 'ere story about the missing young gentleman as was to
be married. I says nothin' to nobody, but I came right here.
And that's all about it."

There is dead silence ; Mrs. Owenson shrinks shivering into
the background ; the captain's eyes are full of fire, and Sydney stands rigid, her face like white stone in the gray dusk.
"There were the signs of a struggle ?" her father asks.
"Were there any traces of bloodshed on the snow ?"

"None at all, square—not a speck, jest the shufflin' and
t trugglin' and wrastlin' like, over the ground, and the edge of
the cliff broke and crumbled off as it might be if a man fell
over. And straight down from there I found the gold thing on
the bush. I'm afraid there ain't no two ways about it, but that
some poor fellow fell over there last night."

"And the height is——"

"Eighty-foot, square, if an inch, and as dangerous a place as
you'll find in the State. The sides as steep, pretty well, as the
wall of a house, and the rocks below stick up like spikes—the
devil's own to fall on, askin' the ladies' pardon."

"There was no sign——" the captain stops, a choking in his
throat.

"Not the fust sign, square," the man answered, understanding readily, "of a body on the rocks. The tide was at high-
water mark about eleven last night, and anything that fell down
there——"

He pauses and looks compassionately at Mrs. Owenson, who
has broken out into dreadful hysterical crying once more. A
horrid picture is before her—Bertie, her handsome, genial Bertie, hurled over that dreadful place, calling aloud in his agony
for help, where there were none to hear, lying all bleeding and
mangled on the black-spiked rocks below, until the long, cold,
cruel waves swept nearer and nearer, washing over his white
bruised face, and carrying him off on their black breasts out to
the awful sea. She shrieks aloud in her horror, and Sydney has
to go over and take her in her arms.

"Mamma, hush," she says, imploringly, "you will hurt papa.
You had better leave the room."

" Yes, leave the room," orders the captain, and poor, terrified Aunt Char goes, thinking how hard-hearted and utterly without feeling her husband and daughter are. In the passage she meets Miss Hendrick, and to her she wails forth all she has heard, all she has imagined. Cyrilla listens gravely and soothes her, administers red lavender, valerian and sympathy.

Miss Hendrick has her own version of Mr. Vaughan's disap-pearance, but she wisely keeps it to herself. Not for one second has she believed him dead. To her mind it has been a " put-up job " from first to last. He waited until the last moment that waiting was possible, and then quietly went off to Dolly De Courcy. He had never intended to marry Sydney, and has been too great a coward to say so. She recalls the night of the party, the meeting and parting under the trees, and Miss De Courcy scurrying home alone in the moonlight. He is not dead, Cyrilla feels sure, but somewhere in New York, comfortably under Dolly's protecting wing. She says nothing of what she knows and suspects. Better, she feels, a thousand times bet-ter, that they should think him dead than know him false.

She listens to Aunt Char's story now, and is not in the slight-est degree shaken in her belief. The torn necktie, and broken chain and locket, are but parts of his well-laid plan to throw them off the track. Very weak-minded men have some of the low cunning of idiots ; there is no end to the depth of duplicity she believes Vaughan to be capable of. She smiles scornfully to herself as Mrs. Owenson paints her vivid picture of Bertie bruised and broken on the merciless rocks. No, no ! Bertie's tender form is unbruised, his symmetrical limbs unbroken, his fair, blonde beauty unscarred. . Probably at this hour, while they sit lamenting him here, he is married to Dolly De Courcy.

The man who brought the token has left the sick-room and is speeding back to town. He is to send Mr. Wynch, the chief magistrate, to the Place. He comes as the short November day ends, and the lamps are lit, and is closeted with the sick man. The facts are laid before him, and when Mr. Wynch departs, it is with a promise to do everything human and magisterial power can do to bring the mystery of last night to light.

An hour later, Harry Sunderland, looking fagged and worn out, calls. He has discovered nothing, nothing at all, he says, spiritlessly. He is almost afraid to look at Sydney, but Sydney is very quiet, her head resting against the side of the bed, her face keeping its weary, tearless, patient look.

Mrs. Owenson sits up with her husband all night; Sydney is dispatched to bed. She goes and sleeps—there is no better anodyne, no surer anæsthetic, than heavy trouble. And next morning she takes her post by the bedside, and keeps it all day long.

It is a very sad and weary day. Her father has those dreadful spasms more than once. It seems at times as though he cannot live to see nightfall. But he does, and that nightfall brings no news. They are not one step nearer the development of the tragedy than at first.

They have sent to New York for a clever detective, and place the case in his hands. All seem to take it for granted that a murder has been done, but the *primâ facie* evidence of murder (the finding of the body), is wanting here. Had the missing man any enemies? the detective very naturally asks ; any one at all interested in his removal—a rival or anything of that sort ? And the answer is unanimously, no !

So far as all who were acquainted with him seem to know, he had neither rival nor foe, in the world.

No mention is made of Dolly De Courcy—no one except Cy rilla Hendrick and Ben Ward think of her in connection with the matter, and neither of them will speak. Still, by dint of inquiry, the detective finds out on the second day the little episode of the actress. This missing young gentleman paid her attentions, and deserted her for the young lady he was to marry. The actress was a young person of violent temper, and not the sort to stand by and be jilted quietly. The detective on this hint goes up to New York and ferrets out Dolly.

She is easily enough found. She occupies a suite of three rooms in a tenement house, with her mother. Dolly is short and snappish, not to say fierce, and knows nothing about it. She has read the account in the papers ; he was a villain, for whom any death was too good ; he treated her shamefully, and whatever has happened him, she is glad of it. And then Dolly does tragedy, and the fierceness turns to sobs. But she didn't kill him, does the detective suppose it ? She glances scornfully at him and laughs in his face. Would he like to know where she was that night? Well, she was at home ; he can ask her mother, if he doesn't believe her. Mrs. Snively—Snively is the name of Miss De Courcy's mother—being summoned, not only asseverates that her daughter was at home on the eventful night, but prays that she "may never stir" if she wasn't, and is ready to take her affadavy of the same. Dolly and Mrs. Snively are triumphantly prepared to prove an *alibi*, and the detective returns to Wychcliffe more puzzled than he came.

A week passes; no trace is to be found. If the sea holds him the sea keeps its secret well. Little by little people lose heart—the detective returns to New York, and a lull comes in the search.

At Owenson Place, its master lies dying—the wonder is that he has lingered so long. It has seemed to him at times that he *cannot* die until his boy is found, but death is here. He has never known how dearly he loved the son of his old friend until now.

It is the night of the fifth of December, a cold, white, frosty night. The light burns low in the sick man's room, the fire flickers, and on his bed Captain Owenson is drifting out to a wider, darker, lonelier sea than any over which he has ever sailed. In her old place Sydney sits beside him, silent, pallid, shadow-like, thin and worn. She has been the most faithful, the most tender, the most loving of nurses, but still that apathetic trance holds her; she hardly knows whether she is suffering or not. The sense that she must be here keeps her up, but she is not conscious of any acute sorrow. Her heart feels numb. Her mother has grown used to her dry eyes and heartlessness, now, but she never ceases to deplore it to her one sympathizer, Miss Hendrick. She has become a perfect Niobe herself, literally drowned in tears. She cries enough for both; her pale eyes look all faded and washed out with the constant briny rain.

"Sydney!"

Sydney starts up. She has been resting against the bed, in a dull torpor for the last hour—a torpor that is not sleep, but is almost as merciful.

"Yes, papa—here."

"Always 'here,' my darling." His voice is very faint; the merest whisper indeed—his face is all drawn. The awful seal and signet of Death is stamped upon it. "Sydney," he says in that faint whispering voice, "before I lose all power, I want to say a few words to you. There isn't much time left now. It's about—" a pause and a gasp—"Bertie."

"Yes, papa."

"They've about given up, haven't they? It doesn't take long to tire them; they don't care whether his body is ever found or not; whether his murderer is ever discovered. And I—oh! I cannot. But when I am gone, Sydney, dont give it up; search for his body, search for his murderer—search—search!"

"Yes, papa." She repeats the two words always in the same weary, worn-out way—the same look of mute misery on her face.

"Money will do everything, or almost everything, in this world, and you will have enough of that—more than you think. Keep detectives on the track, find Bertie's body and bury it beside me, find his murderer, and give him to the hangman!"

His eyes flamed up—a faint echo of the old fierce ring comes to his voice.

"Yes, papa," Sydney says again; she hardly knows what she is saying, poor child.

"Never give it up, Sydney," he pants, "never as long as you live. Sometimes, five, ten, twenty years pass before a murderer is found; but surely, sooner or later, the dead man's blood will cry out and the assassin will be found. And whether it be five, ten, or twenty years, if he ever crosses your path, hunt him down, bring him to justice, bring him to the gallows for the death he has done! Sydney, promise me this."

"I promise, papa."

"Don't forget! Don't let years blot Bertie from your mind. If ever you meet his slayer, hunt him down!"

"Yes, papa."

He has exhausted himself. He falls gasping back, the cold dew standing in beads on his face. In after years that scene came back to Sydney far more vividly than she saw it then. The dimly-lit, silent room, the December wind blowing outside, her father's burning eyes, and the straining, whispering voice—her own weary, half-conscious answers. It never left her to the day of her death.

She gave him a few drops of a reviving cordial, and then resumed her former place and attitude, her heavy eyelids closing, almost the last words she had heard Bertie speak sounding dully in her mind: "In the midst of life we are in death; of whom may we seek for succor but of Thee, O Lord, who for our sins are justly displeased."

What a weary dreadful time it all was; what sins had they done that this had fallen upon them?

Mrs. Owenson came in to relieve Sydney and watch for the night. The girl spiritlessly arose.

"Good night, papa—I do hope you may have a good-night."

"I will, Sydney—I am sure of it. My little one, good-night."

She kissed him and went. He turned to his wife.

"If I die in the night—now don't cry!" he said with some of
his old impatience—"don't disturb Sydney. Don't tell her
until she has had her breakfast in the morning."

Then there is silence. Mrs. Owenson stifles her sobs, and he
lies with his eyes closed. Presently he opens them and holds
out his hand, with the shadow of a smile.

"We have weathered fair weather and foul weather, for
twenty-odd years side by side," he says; "and you have been a
good wife. Good-night, Char."

She clasps his hand, and kisses and cries over it, and he does
not check her. Perhaps he is thinking he has been rather a
hard sailing-master to poor, foolish Char, in the trying voyage
of life. Then he drops into a heavy slumber with his face
turned from the light.

*　*　*　*　*　*　*　*　*

Cyrilla Hendrick is waiting at her friend's door next morning
when Sydney comes out. She passes her arms about her and
kisses her gently.

"How is papa?" Sydney asks.

"Better," Cyrilla answers very gravely. "He is at rest this
morning."

She leads Sydney down, sees her drink a cup of coffee and
eat a roll, then watches her toil slowly up the stairs to her father's
room.

Her mother meets her as she opens the door, and takes her
in her arms.

"Oh! Sydney, Sydney!" she sobs. She has cried all night,
cried until she thinks she has no more tears left, but she bursts
out afresh at sight of her orphaned child.

Sydney breaks from her and goes over to the bed. How
white he is—how still he lies—how peaceful he looks. It must
be an easy and pleasant thing to die after all!

She slips down on her knees by the bed, and lays her face on
the dead hand.

"In the midst of life we are in death; of whom may we seek
for succor, but of Thee, O Lord, who for our sins—"

There is a faint sobbing sigh, and she sinks from the bedside
to the floor. For the first time in her bright, happy, seventeen
years, Sydney has fainted wholly away.

CHAPTER XXI.

"'TWAS ON THE EVENING OF A WINTER'S DAY."

HE last night of a short February day was dying out over the city of Montreal. It had been a day of bitter cold; the wind had swept in wild, long blasts around Place d'Armes and Champ de Mars, and up and down Nôtre Dame street, all the sunless day long. Now, with the fall of evening, the gale had fallen too, and the intense cold was slowly but surely abating.

At the window of a house in a solitary end of the city, a young girl stood looking thoughtfully out at this gloomy winter nightfall. It was a house detached from all others, shut in rather extensive grounds, a group of noble horse-chestnuts in front lifting themselves in the gloaming like ebony goblins against a sky of lead. It was a house of dull, ugly red brick, with small, old-fashioned windows, and a general air of neglect, and desolation, and decay about it. A high wooden wall inclosed the grounds, with a high wooden gate, generally closed, but open now, showing the snowy path that led to the inhospitable-looking front door, and the two lighted windows, at one of which the watcher stood. Properly she was not a watcher, for she was looking for no one; she was only gazing aimlessly out at the dismal prospect of snow-covered ground and starless sky. It was Cyrilla Hendrick, and the house was Miss Dormer's mansion, in the good French city of Montreal.

Within, the house was silent as a tomb—without, few and faint the muffled noises reached her. Montreal is *not* a deafening city after nightfall. The only light in the room is the light of a large coal fire, and by its glow the apartment is discovered to be dingily comfortable—the red hue of the well-worn carpet, curtains, chairs, and sofas having something to do with the look of warmth and comfort. There is a small, upright English piano, a few dark oil paintings in fly-blown gilded frames. Everything looked the worse for wear and lack of cleanliness, and so did the small old lady dozing in the big arm-chair in front of the fire—Miss Phillis Dormer herself.

It is seven weeks since Miss Hendrick returned home.

Home! She never calls this gruesome, dull-as-death house that without a shudder. But her home it is, and the only one she is likely to know until she marries Donald McKelpin, Esquire, which will be a change from Scylla to Charybdis, from the frying-pan to the fire. All the same, Miss Hendrick has quite made up her mind to make it.

As she stands here waiting for Joanna, their one servant, to come in with the tea-tray, and draw the curtains, and Miss Dormer to arouse from her forty winks, she goes over in a dreary way all that has happened since she left school—her visit to Sydney Owenson, that brief glimpse of a brighter world that was not the world of Bohemia, and Bertie Vaughan's mysterious disappearance. Mysterious, not tragical—hardly even mysterious to Cyrilla's mind. No light whatever had as yet been thrown on the darkness of that extraordinary bridal eve, no news at all of the missing bridegroom; but Cyrilla still clung to her first firm conviction, that Vaughan had plotted the whole thing, and was now comfortably married to his actress. She thought of Captain Owenson's death—of that long exhausted swoon of Sydney's, from which it had taken an hour to arouse her—of the slow miserable fever that followed, turning her head and hands to fire, and her body to ice—of the hopeless apathy from which nothing could arouse her, the weary death-in-life torpor into which the poor, over-worn child sank. Then came Miss Dormer's imperious letter: Was she ever coming back? Had she engaged herself as hired companion to Mrs. Owenson, or as sick-nurse to her daughter? Would she kindly remember that she, her aunt, was ailing and alone, and return at once to Montreal? It was so nearly Christmas now, there was no use going back to school. Inclosed her niece would find a return ticket, " Good for Tuesday, December 12th, only."

Cyrilla packed her trunk, and went back, not altogether sorry. Owenson Place was a house of mourning now ; the fountain of Mrs. Owenson's tears as inexhaustible as ever, and Sydney did not seem to care whether she stayed or went. It was inexpressibly dreary. Even Dormer House—so Miss Dormer styled her red brick building at the top of her letters—might prove agreeable as a change, and there at least she would have Mr. McKelpin's wooing for a mild amatory stimulant.

In the middle of a whirling December snow-storm, Miss Hendrick's cab drove up to the wooden gate. The cabman carried in her trunk, bag and shawl, and Cyrilla, looking tall and handsome, and not in the least like the beggarly daughter of Vaga-

9

bondia she was, went up to the stiff-backed arm-chair, and stooped her high-bred olive face over the withered countenance of Miss Dormer.

"Dear aunt! how glad I am to see you looking so well. How good it seems to be at home again," she said, kissing her.

Miss Dormer laughed—the shrill, scornful cackle Cyrilla remembered so well.

"Ha!" the cynical old voice said. "You do well to begin in time, Niece Cyrilla. 'How glad you are to see me looking so well,' indeed! Much you care whether I am well or ill, so that I leave you my money when I die. 'How good it seems to be at home again!' I wonder when you would have left your fine friends and come home, if I hadn't made you? Don't try it on with me, Niece Cyrilla; I'm too elderly a bird to be caught with chaff."

This was Cyrilla's welcome to the only home she had on earth. She moved away from her aunt's chair, with a bitter smile.

"Thank you for reminding me, Aunt Phil. I won't try it again. I suppose I may go to my room?"

"Yes, go, and make yourself as good-looking as you like. You ought to be good-looking, with all the fine clothes I had to pay for, for the wedding—the wedding that never came off, ha! ha! Make haste, and come back and tell me all about it."

Cyrilla reappeared in one of the wedding-dresses, a soft, rich blue merino, trimmed with black lace, Bertie Vaughan's handsome locket and chain on her neck, and sweeping into the dim dingy room like some slender young duchess.

Mr. McKelpin was coming to tea, and to inspect his future wife, and preparations were on a scale of magnitude accordingly. The old silver, and cut glass, and fine Irish linen napery, were got out; there were cold meat, and sliced tongue, and mashed potatoes, and hot rolls for supper.

"If that estimable man, Mr. McKelpin, had a weakness," said Miss Dormer, grimly, to her niece, "it was his stomach. It was well to inform her in time since it was to be her life's destiny to cater to that organ."

Meantime she devoured Cyrilla with questions concerning the wedding that "was to have been and never was." She showed a horrible, a greedily repulsive delight in every detail. How did the bride bear it? Was she overwhelmed with pain and shame, with mortification and disappointment?

"Not at all, Aunt Phil," Cyrilla responded, coolly. "She didn't care for the man. From first to last she thought only of her father. You must remember she wasn't in love—that makes a difference."

"Ah, yes, that makes a difference," said Phillis Dormer, setting her false teeth, the old fierce light flaming up in her dull eyes.

Was she thinking of that old pain and shame, forgotten by all the world now save herself? Was the wound so long ago given not healed yet? Was it possible even a scar remained after five-and-twenty years?

"Do you hear from England often?" was her next question.

"I never hear," Cyrilla responded with a sigh. "Poor papa may be dead and buried, for what I know."

"And a very good thing, too, if he is," said Jack Hendrick's affectionate half-sister. "When men are of no use in the world the best thing they can do is to leave it. Did I tell you, Niece Cyrilla, that Mr. McKelpin was coming to tea?"

"You mentioned that fact, Aunt Dormer."

"He's coming to look at *you*," pursued the old lady, grimly. "If he likes your looks he'll ask you to marry him."

"What bliss!" murmurs Miss Hendrick. "To-night, aunt?"

"Don't be impertinent, miss. No, not to-night; whenever it suits him. That's if he likes your looks; if he doesn't——"

"Ah; don't mention the dreadful contingency!" interrupts Cyrilla, with a shudder; "let me at least live in hope until the fatal hour comes. Surely the lowliest of his handmaidens will find favor in my lord's sight!"

"Don't be sarcastic, Niece Cyrilla. If there is one thing men hate—and naturally—above another, it is a sarcastic woman. And don't interrupt me again. If you marry Mr. McKelpin I mean to make you my heiress, feeling sure that my money will never be idly squandered in his possession. If he doesn't care to marry you, I will leave you five thousand dollars. Meantime you are to read to me, nurse me when I am sick, play and sing for me, and make yourself useful and agreeable generally. I receive no company—none whatever. Mr. McKelpin and the doctor are the only men who ever cross my front door. And I shall countenance no gadding on your part—quiet and decorous, willing to resign your own pleasure to mine, I expect you to be. There is Mr. McKelpin's knock. Joanna will answer it to-night—after to-night it will be one of

your duties to go to the door. The kitchen is distant, and
Joanna is slow."

"Good evening, Mr. McKelpin—this is my niece, Cyrilla."

A short, stout man, in a heavy overcoat, had entered, a man
with a white, flabby, solemn face, scanty red hair, and bushy
red whiskers ; a man who shook hands with Miss Dormer and
who nodded coldly and severely to Miss Dormer's niece. For
Cyrilla, she just inclined that dark, imperial head of hers about
the sixteenth of an inch.

"I am verra glad, ma'am," said Mr. McKelpin, addressing
himself to the lady of the house in a deep, husky voice and a
Scotch accent, "that your niece is back with you again.
Running about does no young woman good, depend upon it,
ma'am."

"But I haven't been running about, Mr. McKelpin," put in
Miss Hendrick, opening her eyes. "I *never* run. Indeed, I
have been severely reproved more than once at school for the
slow manner in which I walk."

Mr. McKelpin gazed at her gravely for a moment in reprov-
ing silence. It is said it requires a surgical operation ever to
get a joke into a Scotchman's head. If you had split Mi
McKelpin's open like a cocoa-nut you couldn't have got in the
broadest piece of sarcasm.

"I did na refer," said Mr. McKelpin, with a magisterial
wave of the hand, " to actual running in the sense you mean.
Home is the spot for every young woman, where she may
lairn the science and duties of the household, and the state
in which it has pleased Providence to place her."

"H'm! let us go to tea," said Miss Dormer. She detected,
if her solemn friend did not, the irrepressible twinkle of mischief in Cyrilla's black eyes, and the fresh impertinence ready
on her lips. "Niece Cyrilla, wheel me to the head of the table."

And then profound silence ensued.

"For what we air to receive, gude Lord make us thenktul,"
said Mr. McKelpin, running his eyes approvingly over the cold
meats and hot cakes.

No more was said for ten minutes, but actions sometimes
speak louder than words, and Cyrilla's serious suitor was beyond mistake enjoying himself. The first pangs of hunger
assuaged, Miss Dormer and her guest appropriated the conversation ; or had, in the native dialect of the gentleman, " a twa-
handed crack " over the weather, the times, the rise and fall of
sundry stocks, in which both were interested ; and gradually, Cy-

rilla's thoughts drifted away hundreds of miles, and she forgot both.

What was Fred Carew about? When would she hear from him again? His regiment was not coming to Montreal until February—what a dreary time away February seemed.

After tea, by order of the chatelaine, Miss Hendrick aired her accomplishments for the benefit of her prospective husband, she played, she sang, she showed her drawings, she recited a poem in French and another in German, of which languages Mr. McKelpin knew as much as he did of Coptic and Runic. But he deigned to listen soberly to all, his ten fingers clasped before him as though in prayer—his chalky sodden face never losing its owl-like solemnity.

" Verra good, ver-r-a good, indeed," he said, when the performance ended. " You've improved your opportunities I make no doubt. But these things are but vanities and frivolity at best. Housekeeping in a' its brenches and ramifications is the great accomplishment the young miss o' the praisent day should lairn."

" My niece Cyrilla will begin to-morrow," put in the piping voice of Miss Dormer. " It is my intention she shall spend three hours of each day in the kitchen under the instructions of Joanna."

And so life began for Cyrilla. Three hours a day in a calico dress, in a hot kitchen, under the tuition of a deaf old cook, learning the mysteries of puddings and pies, roasts and broils, for the future delectation of Donald McKelpin. Four hours of reading and playing for Aunt Dormer ; no visitors, no going out, except at stated times with a market basket. Cyrilla's soul loathed it all. She hated household duties ; she abhorred cooking : she nearly stifled herself with yawns, reading aloud. Oh ! the deadly—deadly dullness of it ! Then Mr. McKelpin's evenings, three in a week, to play long whist at a penny a game with Miss Dormer, each greedily eager to win, and taking no notice of her yawning drearily in the background. What a Christmas that was—what a New Year—what a January ! Would Cyrilla ever, ever forget it !

But the stagnant calm was near its end, and Mr. McKelpin, of all men, the man to break it.

Stolid, dull, lumbering as the man was, he yet was a man, and as such had from the first cast an eye of approval upon the tall symmetrical figure, and haughtily handsome face of Miss Dormer's youthful relative.

"Your niece is a verra well-favored young woman, Miss Dor-mer," was all he had ever said about it; but the admiration was there, and in due course of time worked itself out of his slow soul to the surface. One evening early in February, at half-past eight to a minute (he religiously left at nine), Mr McKelpin opened his mouth, and in words grave, sedate and few, in the presence of the two ladies, asked the younger to do him the favor of becoming his wife.

"There's a disparity o' years, I am well aware," slowly and austerely said Donald McKelpin, "but the disparity is on the right side. For my own pairt, I think it's always best for a frivo-lous young pairson of the female sex to be united in wedlock wi' a man considerably her senior. You have given me to un-derstand, Miss Dormer, that you'll look wi' the eye o' favor on the match, and so, if Miss Cyrilla's willing, in the name o' Providence, we'll consider the thing settled."

And the thing was settled. What she said to this impas-sioned declaration Cyrilla never knew; she was only conscious at the time of a hysterical desire to burst out laughing. But Aunt Phil's fierce old eye was upon her, so she controlled the insane desire, and there and then became the affianced of Mr. Donald McKelpin. The next time he came he brought with him an engagement ring of plain gold, his mother's wedding ring, in fact, and worn rather thin, and with elephantine playful-ness pressed it upon his bride's acceptance.

Miss Hendrick took it with an unmoved countenance, and put it on the finger that wore poor Freddy Carew's. Poor Freddy Carew, indeed! He wrote to Miss Hendrick regularly, and as Miss Hendrick always answered the door she received his letters without the slightest trouble or danger, and most regu-larly responded. Mr. Carew, therefore, was not left to pine in ignorance of Miss Hendrick's matrimonial good fortune. This cold February day on which she stands, idly gazing out of the window, has been a day more than usually eventful among the eventless days of her life. The early morning mail brought a letter from Mrs. Owenson announcing her departure with Sydney for New York, to spend March and April.

"My dear girl is still in miserably poor health and low spirits," wrote Mrs. Owenson, "and I am taking her to my cousin's, Mrs. Macgregor, of Madison Avenue. Change of scene and the cheerful companionship of her cousins will no doubt cheer her up. In May we go to Europe, to remain two years at least. Sydney will write further particulars by next mail."

Happy Sydney Owenson! Cyrilla enviously sighs. Yes
happy, thrice happy in spite of her bereavement. To Miss Hendrick it looks no such great bereavement after all. She didn't
care for Bertie Vaughan, empty-headed, conceited noodle that he
was ! and for her father—well, of course, a doting, respectable
and *rich* father is a person to be grieved for—still, to Miss
Hendrick's philosophic mind, it wasn't a grief to embitter the
life of an heiress. A winter in New York—ah ! lucky
Sydney—two years in Europe—thrice-blessed orphan heiress !
Beauty and wealth unlimited. Yes! Sydney Owenson was
one of the elect of the earth, one of the darlings of the
gods.

The second event was the news that morning's paper had
given her. The ——th had arrived in Montreal, and were
quartered here for the winter. So ! Freddy was come, and she
would see a sympathetic human face at last.

The third event was the departure of Mr. McKelpin for Scot-
land on the morrow, to be absent until the first week in June.
The wedding is fixed for the close. This will be the last night
for over three months the devoted Donald will spend in the
company of his betrothed. But as she stands here and looks
dreamily out, it is not of her betrothed, I regret to say, Miss
Hendrick is thinking. Where—when—how—will she see Fred
Carew? Poor Freddy! he has not said much in his letters
about her faithlessness, but the news of her betrothal has been
as gall and wormwood to him, she knows.

" Shut the shutters, Niece Cyrilla, and don't stand mooning
there all night. I suppose you have been crying quietly over
the departure of Mr. McKelpin ? "

Thus sharply and sneeringly aroused from her nap by Miss
Dormer, Cyrilla obeys.

" I never cry, Aunt Phil ; it is one of the principles of my
life, and not even for Mr. McKelpin's sweet sake can I break
through it. Shall I tell Joanna to fetch in tea ? "

" You'll get something to cry for yet, mark my words, hard
as you are," croaks Miss Dormer.

"As Mr. McKelpin's wife ? I think it extremely likely,"
cheerfully assents Cyrilla. " Still I shall put off the evil day
until the evil day comes. Shall I call Joanna ? "

" Yes, call," says Aunt Phil, snappishly. Their encounters
are sharp and frequent, and she generally finds herself worsted.
Cyrilla is her dependent, certainly, but Cyrilla does not hold
her pauper head in that haughty way for nothing. She keeps

her own well with Miss Dormer, and Miss Dormer likes her none the less for it.

Joanna comes with their daily bread and butter and cold meat. It is a silent meal. The old maid is thinking how she will miss long whist and Mr. McKelpin, in the empty, endless, March evenings so near. The young maid is thinking how much brighter a look life has taken on since Fred Carew is in Montreal.

Half-past seven brings Mr. McKelpin. He shakes hands in a stiff way with his affianced, and hands her that evening's paper, and sits down to his last game with Miss Dormer. There is silence ; a paraffin lamp burns between them, the fire looks red and cheerful, the room cozy and comfortable, contrasted with the bleak coldness of the winter night outside. Miss Hendrick is reading the paper, searching for further news of the ——th, when loud and long there comes a knock at the door.

"The postman !" cries Cyrilla, starting up; "a letter from Sydney."

She rushes from the room, down the stairs, and throws open the door. A man stands there, but it is not the postman. He is not so tall as the postman, and he looks military. He wears a sealskin jacket and cap, the visor of the cap pulled over his eyes—he wears sealskin gloves and carries a cane.

"Ah-h !" says this gentleman ; "can you tell me if Mrs. Brown lives here?"

Cyrilla stands petrified. Surely she knows that voice Her heart beats as it has not beaten for four months. Can it—can it be——

"*Does* Mrs. Brown live here, Beauty?" asks again that familiar voice.

He raises his cap; the wan glimmer of the hall lamp falls full on his face, the serene, smiling face of Fred Carew.

Miss Hendrick gives one gasp.

"Oh, Freddy !" is what she says.

"How do you do, Beauty?" says Mr. Carew, pleasantly. "Shake hands, won't you, or is it permitted the future Mrs. McKelpin to go that far? You see I got to Montreal this morning, and naturally the first thing I did was to look you up."

"But to come here—to Aunt Dormer's house ! Oh, Fred !" Cyrilla gasps again.

"To the dragon's den. But then, really you know, I possess an overwhelming amount of courage. And I knew from your letters that no one ever came to the door but yourself. You told me, you remember?"

"But I dare not stay. Aunt Dormer will miss me; she and Mr. McKelpin are playing cards now."

"But you can go back and steal out again, can't you, Beauty? Say you have a headache and want to go to your room. I'll wait yonder under the trees. Only don't keep me long. Even friendship so glowing and ardent as mine may get chilled if kept too long in a Montreal February night."

"I'll try! I'll come! " Cyrilla exclaims. "Wait, Freddy; I'll be with you in ten minutes!"

She shuts the door and flies back. The glad, excited gleam of her eyes might tell its story, but the card-players are too much engrossed with their game to take heed.

"Well, who was it?" Miss Dormer querulously asks. She has lost ninepence and feels badly accordingly. "More letters?"

"No; a man; he asked if Mrs. Brown lived here," demurely answered Miss Hendrick.

"Mrs. Brown, indeed. Your deal, Mr. McKelpin; luck will surely turn this time. Did you bolt the door after him, Cyrilla?"

"Certainly. Aunt Dormer!"

"Well?"

"While you're finishing this game I'll run up to my room—my head rather aches, and I'll bathe it with camphor."

Miss Dormer is too deeply absorbed in the new deal to reply. Cyrilla departs. Five seconds later and she is under the stripped chestnuts, both hands clasped fast in Fred Carew's.

"Oh, Fred, I am glad to see you. How good of you to come."

"Goodness is my normal state, Beauty." The first greetings are over by this time. "And so I really behold before me the affianced of Mr. Donald McKelpin?"

"You really do, and as such please relinquish my hands; my shawl is as warm as as your fur gloves. Mr. McKelpin doesn't approve of indecorous familiarities."

"Doesn't he? Excepting himself, of course. He is privileged, lucky beggar!" says Mr. Carew, with a sigh.

"Not even excepting himself. He comes three evenings a week, says 'How d'ye do, Miss Cyrilla?' and gives me a hand like a dead, damp fish. I never know what to do with it, so I give it back to him again."

"And when is the wedding to come off, may I ask, Miss Hendrick?"

9*

"You may ask, Mr. Carew. To come off, *Deo volente*, the last week of June."

"Beauty," Mr. Carew says, gravely, "how is this to end?"

"In a cold in the head for me most likely," laughs Cyrilla, wilfully misunderstanding. "Don't look so doleful, Fred—it doesn't become you. June is June—this is February, and I am Cyrilla Hendrick still. He goes off to-morrow—*Dieu merci*—to be gone three months. Oh, if some kind Christian would invite me out to spend an evening, we might meet and have a chat now and then."

"That is easily enough managed, if your dragon will let you go. Mrs. Delamere is here, and she shall call upon you and invite you. The Colonel is about to retire from the army, and they sail for England in April. If she calls, do you think Miss Dormer will let you go?"

"I think so, so long as she does not suspect you are here. Warn Mrs. Delamere. If my aunt knew you were in Montreal, I believe she would never let me out of her sight. And now, Freddy, I positively must go."

He does not detain her. It is very cold, and cold Mr. Carew does not like.

"Mrs. Delamere shall call to-morrow; you will come to her house, and we can talk things over where the thermometer is not a hundred or so below zero. Don't make your farewells to the Scotchman too affectionate, Beauty, please, because my prophetic soul tells me you'll never write your name Cyrilla McKelpin."

The game of whist is finished as she enters, and the clock is striking nine. Miss Dormer has won her ninepence back, and is in high good spirits once more. Colorless and smileless, Mr. McKelpin stands up and buttons his coat to go.

"Good-by, Miss Dormer." He shakes hands. "Good-by, Miss Cyrilla." The dead damp fish is extended to her. "You'll write to me occasionally, I hope, while I am gone?"

"Oh, of course," Cyrilla answers, with cheerful alacrity. "I wish you a pleasant voyage, Mr. McKelpin."

He is gone. Miss Dormer retires to her room. Joanna bolts and bars the house. Cyrilla makes her aunt's night toilet and sees her safely in bed. Then she goes to her own room, lets down her hair, and looks at her own face in the glass—a face that has not looked back at her with so happy, so bright a glance, for three weary months. As she looks and smiles, Fred Carew's question returns to her—"Beauty, how is this to end?"

"How, indeed!" she thinks, "in disaster for me, I haven't the slightest doubt. But meantime Donald has gone and Freddy has come, and let it end how it may, I shall be happy until the close of June, at least."

CHAPTER XXII.

"OH, WHISTLE, AND I'LL COME TO YE, MY LAD."

MR. McKELPIN departed next morning from Montreal, and that evening there was no long whist, a penny a game, at Dormer House. Instead, Cyrilla read aloud a drearily-dull novel, over which she yawned surreptitiously, and Miss Dormer yawned aloud. And this was but the beginning of the end, the elder lady thought bitterly, but the beginning of a long series of such dull-as-death days and nights. True, when Mr. McKelpin was Cyrilla's husband the card-playing would be resumed, but meantime——

There can be no doubt at this point of her career but that old Miss Dormer would have married Donald McKelpin herself for the sake of his society, in spite of her fifty-odd years and crooked back, if a hopeless infirmity had not stood in her way. There can also be no doubt but that McKelpin would have married her if she had made it a *sine qua non.* No one in Montreal knew exactly how much Miss Dormer was worth as accurately as he did. In his secret soul (if he possessed such a sanctuary) he may have preferred the slim, dusk, handsome niece, but if he had had to choose between the niece of nineteen, penniless, and the aunt of five-and-fifty, with half a million, Donald would not have hesitated. He was hard-headed by nature and by nationality, but he was not destined to be put to the test. Miss Dormer dying slowly in her chair of an incurable distemper, could not dream of marriage for herself, and so, as the next best thing, passed him on to Cyrilla. In any case she meant him to have her money, and he could hardly do less than take her destitute niece with it.

Another heavy day, another dragging evening, both ladies gaping over their insipid novel until the *Finis* was reached

Outside, the February winds rattled the trees and sent the sleet drifting against the windows. Inside, firelight and lamplight did their best to dispel the vapors, and did their best in vain. Phil-lis Dormer's old eyes went drearily to the card-table; Cyrilla Hendrick's looked restlessly into the ruby heart of the fire, and both could have wailed with Tennyson :

> "Oh, for the touch of a vanished hand,
> And the sound of a voice that is still !"

Only, naturally, each was thinking of a different hand and voice.

The afternoon of the third day brought Mrs. Delamere. Cyrilla, as usual, answered the door, and after ten minutes' private chat, came back to her aunt's room, a flush of hope and expectation in her eyes.

" Who is it ? " Miss Dormer fretfully asked.

" Mrs. Colonel Delamere, aunt. You have heard me tell how kind she was to me at Petite St. Jacques. The Colonel is about to retire from the army, and they sail for England, where he has a large estate, in April. Meantime they are staying in Montreal. She wishes very much to make your acquaintance, Aunt Dormer. May I ask her up ? "

Miss Dormer looked keenly and suspiciously at her niece.

" What does she want to make my acquaintance for, a crip-pled, miserable old creature like me ? What does she want of me ? "

" She wants nothing but the pleasure of knowing you. I told her you never saw any one, but she begged you would kindly make an exception in her favor. Shall I tell her you will not see her ? "

" And insult a stranger in my own house ? No, Niece Cyrilla. I *will* see her. Show her up."

Mrs. Colonel Delamere, imposing in brown silk and velvets, was shown up accordingly; and quite awed for a moment, by her size and splendor, even grim Aunt Phil. But she was so cordial, so chatty, so friendly, that the awe speedily vanished and a pleasant excitement took its place.

She stayed for over an hour, retailed all the news of the day, discussed Canada and England, and Miss Dormer actually experienced a feeling of regret when at last she arose to go.

" I have overstayed my time," she said, with her soft, mel-low laugh; " but really, it is so pleasant to meet a kindred spirit, and countrywoman, with whom to abuse Canada, its dreadful climate and dreadful customs. Dear Miss Dormer, you really shouldn't lead the life of a recluse, as you do; it is positively unkind to your friends. At least you must make me the exception to your rule. And, meantime, as a great favor, I must beg of you to let this child come to see me. She was one of my especial pets at Petite St. Jacques, and, remember, I leave in 'April, and may never see her again."

Miss Dormer's face darkened.

"She never goes out," she said, querulously; "I can't spare her."

"Ah! but, dear Miss Dormer, as a great favor to *me*. She and Miss Owenson were quite like my own daughters. And as she tells me she is to be married so soon to a most estimable man—June, is it not, Cyrilla, love?—you should allow her a little more liberty. She must know somebody as Mr. McKelpin's wife. I am sure he would wish it himself, and I promise you she shall know none but the very nicest people."

"Well," Miss Dormer said, slowly and reluctantly; "but, mind, if she does, no gadding, no flirting with young men—I won't have it."

"Flirting!" Mrs. Delamere repeated, in a voice of horror. "Really, Miss Dormer, how can you think such a thing of me? No, no! even if our dear girl were inclined—and I am sure she is much too sensible—I would never countenance such levity in an engaged young lady. I receive, next Tuesday, Cyrilla, love. The carriage shall call for you very early. Only a few friends, Miss Dormer—not three unmarried men among them. Good afternoon, my dear lady, and a thousand thanks for your kind permission."

"Humph!" grunted Miss Dormer, distrustfully. "You're a deal too sweet, ma'am, for my taste—too sweet by half to be wholesome!"

Cyrilla laughed noiselessly as she escorted her fat friend to the front door.

"How well you did it!" she exclaimed. "What an undeveloped talent for intrigue you must possess, Mrs. Delamere! I believe I should have gone melancholy mad before spring if you had not come."

Tuesday night was five days off, and during these five days Miss Hendrick saw nothing of Mr. Carew. She received several notes from him, however, in his usual brief and trenchant style; and brightened up so, under their influence, and the thought of Tuesday night, that she looked quite a new being

Miss Dormer saw it, with a great many sneers and croaks, but Cyrilla bore all with angelic patience. Aunt Phil would not retract her plighted word, and she asked no more.

Very early—before eight o'clock, in fact—the Delamere sleigh was at the door, and Cyrilla, looking very eager and handsome, threw on her wraps, and was driven off.

"Mind, be back early—by midnight at the latest!" croaked Miss Dormer after her. "Joanna shall sit up for you."

The drive was not ten minutes long. Mrs. Delamere's "furnished apartments" were brilliant with gaslight; and, early as she was, Cyrilla found one guest before her—a very tall, elderly young lady, wearing diamonds and cerise silk, and to whom she was introduced as "Mrs. Fogarty."

"I had no idea she would have come at this absurd hour," whispered Mrs. Delamere to her *protégée*. "She's a widow, out of weeds, as you see, immensely rich, and very much sought after on that account. Leaving her money out of the question, she has that kittenish, coquettish style that takes—Heaven knows why—with men, and is sure to make a heavy evening go off. The late lamented (his name makes patent his nationality) was forty years her senior, a pork man, and, as I have said, immensely rich. After the two years of nuptial bliss he departed—to a better world, let us trust, since he was frightfully henpecked in this."

Miss Hendrick laughed as she threw off her cloak, and smoothed her shining coiled hair.

"I haven't seen much of Mrs. Fogarty as yet," she said, "but from the little I have, I should think any change the pork man could make would be for the better. Two years of her unalloyed society I should say would be enough to kill any man."

"The droll thing about it is," pursued Mrs. Delamere, with an odd little sidelong glance at her young friend, "is that she has come here at this unheard-of hour, and overdressed, as you perceive—all for the sake of Fred Carew."

"*What!*" exclaimed Cyrilla, knitting her brows.

"Perfectly true, I assure you. She met him three days ago for the first time, and conceived a *tendresse* for him at sight. She always has a *tendresse* for some one. This morning she encountered Carew and the Colonel in St. James Street, and the Colonel, in his usual ridiculous way, told her Freddy was coming early—very early, to smoke a cigar with him, and he hoped she would come early also and help entertain him! The result—there she is!"

"Is the woman an idiot?" Cyrilla scornfully asked.

"Oh, dear no! Freddy generally does make an impression on elderly young women at sight. Witness Miss Jones of the *Pensionnat.* Only it is not every elderly young lady who wears her heart on her sleeve as frankly as does Mrs. Fogarty."

"For the sake of common decency I should hope not," retorts Miss Hendrick with cold scorn.

"Hush, dear! here we are," says Mrs. Delamere. She opens the door of the drawing-room and sails majestically in. Miss Hendrick follows and sees—Fred Carew, faultless and elegant to behold, a camellia in his button-hole, sitting on a sofa by Mrs. Fogarty's side, submitting to being made love to, with his customary serene and courteous face.

"Mr. Carew, Miss Hendrick. You may remember meeting Mr. Carew once before, Cyrilla, love," says Mrs. Delamere, blandly. And Mr. Carew arises, and bows pleasantly and makes a smiling, foolish little speech about "the pleasure—er—of renewing Miss Hendrick's—um—acquaintance," etc.; and Miss Hendrick bends her rather haughty-looking head, and moves disdainfully away.

A batch of arrivals enter; the hostess sweeps forward to meet them. Mr. Carew makes an effort to get up and follow Miss Hendrick to where she has seated herself at a distant table, and opened that refuge of the destitute, a photographic album. But Mrs. Fogarty is a veteran of four-and-thirty, although she does not look it, and is equal to the occasion. For the sake of Mr. Carew she has put on her diamonds, her Point d'Alençon, and her cerise silk, and come to Mrs. Delamere's "Tuesday;" is it likely then she will allow Mr. Carew to fly off at a tangent? In her practised hands, Freddy is as an artless mouse in the grasp of a skillful, elderly mouser. By her side he is, by her side he shall remain!

And he does. He cannot break away—he cannot tell how—he makes half-a-dozen attempts—she skilfully meets and baffles them all. Without positive rudeness he cannot quit her side; and positive rudeness, even to a Mrs. Fogarty, is something Fred is quite incapable of. He sees Cyrilla monopolized by half-a-dozen of his brother officers, looking handsome and brilliant—her clear, sarcastic laugh comes to him where he sits, and he groans in anguish of spirit. At last—he never knows how—he rises—he says something—Mrs. Fogarty may know what; he never does—makes a bow, and finds himself by Cyrilla's side. She is alone, the last of the warriors for the moment has deserted her, and she looks upon Mr. Carew with no frien lly eye.

"'Man's inhumanity to man,'" murmurs poor Freddy, in a plaintive tone, "'makes countless thousands mourn.' But what is it—oh! what is it—compared with the inhumanity of woman?"

"I don't know what you are talking about," says Miss Hendrick, scornfully.

"I tried to get away," continues Mr. Carew in the same piteous voice, "give you my honor I did, Beauty, more than once, and she wouldn't let me. What did she do it for? What grudge does she bear me? I never did anything to *her!*"

"Can't you see,—imbecile," says Miss Hendrick, still more scornfully, but inclined to laugh; the woman's in love with you—painted, simpering ninny! I sat here and watched you, and thought I never in all my life saw a more idiotic-looking pair!"

"In love with me! Oh, good heaven!" exclaims Mr. Carew, so much genuine, unaffected horror in his tone that Cyrilla laughs outright. "You never mean to tell me that!"

"My dear Mr. Carew," replies Miss Hendrick, "a woman who will paint and powder to the extent that woman is painted and powdered, is simpleton enough for anything—even to falling in love with you. She's seven-and-thirty if she's a day, and she's made up to look seventeen. Observe those shoulder-blades and those cheek-bones—women never get *that* look this side of thirty. She's worth no end of money made in Pork—with a large P—and she has cast the eye of favor upon your manifold charms, Freddy. Let me be the first to congratulate you!"

"Beauty," says Mr. Carew, in a depressed tone, "let us change the subject. There isn't anything that woman took into her head she couldn't make me do. So the dragon let you off duty, did she?"

"As you see, Fred, else I wouldn't be here."

"Are you aware I have been on the look-out for you ever since that night at your aunt's gate? I have patrolled your street like a sentry on guard, early and late. Do you never go out?"

"Hardly ever. Once a week I do the marketing—give the orders, that is. Sometimes I have my 'Sunday out.' I express a wish to go to church and am allowed to go. Aunt Dormer is a professed heathen herself—another good turn she owes that false and faithless papa of yours, my Fred."

" What church do you patronize Sundays, pray ? "

" Nôtre Dame principally, for the sake of the music."

" Shall you be there next Sunday ? "

" If next Sunday is fine, and Aunt Phil's temper doesn't turn to gall and bitterness."

" When do you go—morning or evening ? "

" Morning."

" I shall attend Nôtre Dame next Sunday morning," says Mr. Carew, gravely. " Pending next Sunday, cannot you manage to meet me somewhere, Beauty. I have a million things to say to you. I proposed to relieve myself of a few to-night, but Mrs. Fogarty—bless her !—has frustrated all that. By-the-by, one of them was—what sort of a parting did you and Sandy have ? Not too affectionate, I hope ? "

" Mr. McKelpin's highly respectable name is Donald, as I think I have informed you before. For our parting—that is no concern of yours. The last farewells of those who love is much too sacred a subject to be exposed to the profane levity of out siders."

" Ah ! " says Freddy, in a quenched tone, and the depressed look returns. Miss Hendrick compassionately comes to the rescue.

" You said there were a million things you had to say to me —this is only one. Proceed with the rest, and quickly; for in the distance Mrs. Fogarty is eying you as a vulture its prey, and will swoop down upon you in three minutes."

" I want to see you, Cyrilla—I want to talk to you seriously —*seriously*, mind ! " says Mr. Carew, " about this engagement with McKelpin. At what hour, daily, does Miss Dormer take her after-dinner nap ? Old ladies always do take after-dinner naps, don't they ? "

" My experience of old ladies is extremely limited, I am happy to say. Miss Dormer goes to sleep at three o'clock every afternoon with the regularity of clockwork——"

" Then what is to hinder your stealing out every afternoon at three o'clock ? " cries Freddy, eagerly.

" —— and wakes," pursues Cyrilla, " as I was about to say when you interrupted me, on an average every five minutes. She looks about the room, and if I am not visible she calls for me. The instant I stole out to meet you, that instant the dear old lady would awake."

" Still let us try it," goes on Freddy, undaunted, " for see you I must. Look here, Beauty—every afternoon I will go to

your house—wind and weather permitting—and I'll give you
some signal to apprise you. Let me see—ah ! I'll whistle a
tune—' *La Ci darem,'* for instance. And you shall come to
the window and wave your handkerchief if there is a chance of
your getting off. If to-morrow is fine——"

" Oh, Mr. Carew !" exclaims the vivacious tones of the Pork
gentleman's widow, " we are making up a card table, and we
just want one. *Do* come and be my partner—*you* will be fortunate, I am sure, and I am *so* unlucky at cards. Miss Hendrick will excuse you, I am sure."

Miss Hendrick bows frigidly and turns away. And before he
quite realizes it, Mr. Carew is captured and carried off.

" I am *so* unlucky at cards," gushes the widow, " and I *do*
want a good partner *so* much."

The last thing that reaches Miss Hendrick's disgusted ears is
the imbecility Fred is murmuring : " unlucky at cards—lucky
in love—the inexpressible pleasure of being Mrs. Fogarty's
partner even for an hour, etc., etc." Then a brother officer of
Carew's approaches, and asks her to waltz. She goes, and as
the gentleman knows what he is about, enjoys the dance thoroughly.

She sees no more of Mr. Carew that evening, but she does
not allow it to spoil her pleasure. She frowns a little, to observe
how closely Mrs. Fogarty keeps him pinned to her side ; but
all the same, she thoroughly enjoys this small reception of Mrs.
Delamere's. The last thing she notices as she flits away to put
on her things and go home, is Fred Carew meandering languidly
through a square dance with his widow.

Next day Fred is faithfully at his post, and the first bar of
" La Ci Darem la Mano" reaches Cyrilla's ears at a quarter
past three. Miss Dormer is asleep, and she goes silently
out and disappears with her lover around an angle of the
house.

This meeting is but the beginning of many. At each interview Mr. Carew uses all his eloquence, employs every argument
he can bring to bear to induce Cyrilla to end the farce she is
playing, to throw over the Scotchman and engage herself to him.
Cyrilla listens, and laughs in his face.

" And starve with you in a garret, like a pair of modern Babes
in the Wood? No, thank you, Freddy—I like you very well,
but I don't wish to commit suicide for your sake. It's pleasant
to meet you in this way—forbidden fruit is always sweetest, and
it is good to see a face I knew in the old blissful, beggarly vaga-

ɔond days; but marry you—poor as you are now! No! not while I keep my senses."

About the middle of March, Mrs. Fogarty gave a ball at the Fogarty mansion in Shelbourne Street, which, for barbaric splendor and costliness, was long the talk of the town. Half Montreal seemed to be invited—among them the rich Miss Dormer's heiress and niece—the rich Donald McKelpin's affianced wife.

Miss Dormer's niece obtained permission to go. To despise your hostess and yet enjoy her parties is no uncommon phase of society. Miss Hendrick put on the " strawberry-ice " silk, presented her as bridemaid's dress by Sydney Owenson—a rich and beautiful garment, stylishly made and trimmed. She wore a cluster of pink roses (sent by Freddy) in her glossy black braids, and a set of pearls loaned her by Aunt Phil for this occasion only. Her bouquet (sent also by Freddy) was of pink and white roses. And as she came into Mrs. Fogarty's rooms, her dark head held high, her manner so eminently distinguished and self-possessed, she looked the handsomest and most thoroughbred woman in the rooms.

Mr. Carew was there, and on this night Mrs. Fogarty's attentions to him were painfully marked. To tell the truth, Mrs. Fogarty had made up her mind to marry him. She had married the pork man for money; she would marry Mr. Carew for love! Also for his handsome face, his elegant manners, his scarlet coat, and his connection with the British peerage. His grand-uncle was an earl; more than one life, as good as his own, stood between him and the succession; but these lives might be removed, and she might write her name Countess of Dunraith! She was still young—she owned to four-and-twenty, and the record of the family Bible no one knew but herself. She· was very rich, and half-a-dozen men this very winter had asked her to marry them. Mr. Carew was poor; his admiration of her was quite patent to—herself; before May he must propose. She would accept him, marry him, and take him for a honeymoon tour around the world, calling, *en route*, at Dunraith Park!

With all these good resolutions in her mind, she steadfastly held Fred at her side the whole night long. Men laughed and congratulated him; the havoc he had made in the fair Fogarty's affections she took no pains to conceal; the women, as a rule, expressed themselves disgusted. For Miss Hendrick, with her handsome face, betokening only tranquil enjoyment, she danced the long night through, without exchanging a dozen words with him.

Once, indeed he broke his fetters, and rushed to her side, and implored her to dance with him ; but Miss Hendrick, in a voice thoroughly iced, told him she was engaged for every dance she meant to dance until she left, and turned her white shoulder pointedly upon him, and resumed her animated flirtation with Major Riddell.

But once at home a few hours later, she tore off her pink silk, her pearls and roses, and flung them, a lustrous heap, in a fine fury, across the room. She was by nature intensely jealous ; Mrs. Fogarty's quiet monopoly of Fred Carew all night had half-maddened her. She did not mean to marry him herself ; but to give him up to that woman—that odious, brainless, giggling woman ! No ! She would ruin her every prospect in life, re-nounce Mr. McKelpin and her aunt's fortune, sooner ! Then an outbreak of vindictive tears, and the belle of Mrs. Fogarty's ball cried herself in a jealous rage to sleep.

Mrs. Delamere, still Miss Dormer's only visitor, came quite often, and helped on the ending of the drama.

" Really, Cyrilla, my love," she said, laughingly, more than once, " I think we will have fellow-passengers by the *Austrian*, in April. I am as sure as that I stand here Nelly Fogarty will be our traveling-companion."

" Alone ? " Miss Hendrick asks.

" Alone ? " laughs Mrs. Delamere. " Simple child ! have you no eyes ? She means to marry Fred Carew, and take him with her. Poor Freddy—it is a case of ' greatness thrust,' and so on. He doesn't like it, but when the proper time comes he will face his doom like a man and a soldier."

About this time too, the short letters, the signal whistle under the windows, were given up. Mr. Carew was evidently getting tired of wooing another man's future wife. Rumors on all sides reached the girl's ears of his perpetual presence at the Hotel Fogarty. The blooming widow took him shopping in her cunning little blue velvet sleigh, gave dinner parties, none of which he ever missed, went to church with him Sundays, and let him carry her ruby velvet and gold prayer-book into the pew. Widows have been dangerous from time immemorial—what was a poor little fellow like Fred Carew, totally unprotected, to do when laid siege to like this ? " Samivel, bevare of the vidders," said Mr. Weller, and Mr. Weller understood human nature.

The first week of April Mrs. Delamere gave a farewell re-union ; Miss Hendrick was bidden and had obtained leave to go,

" But mind," said Miss Dormer, grimly, " it is the last time

'This makes three in two months. You go to no more fandan-
goes, Niece Cyrilla."

"I am sure I don't want to," responded Cyrilla, wretchedly ;
"they don't afford me so much pleasure. I wish Mr. McKelpin was back, and my wedding comfortably over."

Once again, as a matter of course, Mr. Carew and Mrs.
Fogarty were present, and once again, also, as a matter of
course, in close juxtaposition. But presently Mr. Carew's
order of release came, and armed with a white satin fan he
sauntered over and took a seat beside her.

"Well, Beauty," he begins, in his pleasant, lazy voice, "I
have been waiting to come over for the last half hour and tell
you how uncommonly well you are looking to-night."

"And your keeper, Mrs. Fogarty, wouldn't let you, I suppose," says Miss Hendrick, scornfully. She's looking uncommonly well, too, isn't she ? Have you told her so ?"

"There is no need, Beauty—to look uncommonly well is
Mrs. Fogarty's normal state."

"Yes," says Miss Hendrick, her handsome short upper lip
curling, "there's nothing common about her, I admit, not even
common sense ! Might one inquire whose very bridal-like fan
that is you wield so gracefully, Mr. Carew ?"

"This ? Nelly's, of course. The rooms are warm, and she
kindly lent it to me. I must go back and return it, by-the-by."

It is the last straw, we are told, that breaks the camel's back.
Cyrilla Hendrick's eyes flashed and her lips quivered.

"Nelly ! It has come to that, then !"

Mr. Carew raises his eyebrows.

"It is not improper, is it ? We are excellent friends, and
she gives me the privilege. It's a pretty name and easy to
say. I don't cotton to Fogarty, strange to relate—no more
does she."

"Let us hope she will like her new name better. Has she
proposed to you yet, Mr. Carew ?"

"My dear Cyrilla, did I ever ask these embarrassing questions about McKelpin ? *Apropos*, he is coming back in a few
weeks, Nelly tells me, and the wedding is to come off—when,
Beauty ?"

This is too much. She turns upon him, passionate tears
in her black eyes, passionate anger in her voice, and exclaims :

"Fred Carew, how is this to end?"

CHAPTER XXIII.

FAIRY GOLD.

E raises his eyebrows and looks at her, placid surprise only in his face.

"How is this to end?" she repeats, in that passionately angry whisper.

"The very question I put to you, if you remember, that night under your aunt's chestnuts. I forget what you answered. By the way things are going on at present, I think it will end in your leading to the altar the manly McKelpin and I the lovely Fogarty."

"Freddy, do you mean to marry that odious woman?"

"Cyrilla, do you mean to marry that odious man?"

"There is no comparison," she vehemently cries. "I cannot help selling myself—you can. If she were nice, and not a widow, and not vulgar, and not——"

Miss Hendrick is absolutely growing hysterical, and Mr. Carew looks about him in alarm.

"My dear child, don't let us talk here," he says, hurriedly. "The Fogarty, confound her, is watching us with the eyes of Argus. Come into the next room; there is hardly any one there."

He leads her away—for once in his life with Cyrilla, he is master of the situation, and for once in his life means to remain so.

The room adjoining is the back drawing-room, where the piano stands, forsaken now. One or two card-tables, also forsaken, stand in one or two recesses.

They are more fortunate than even Fred has hoped. The back drawing-room is deserted.

He takes his stand before his fair friend, leans his elbow in an easy position upon the piano, and prepares to have it out.

"Now, then, Beauty," he begins, in a tone Fred Carew does not often use, "let us understand one another once and for all. This sort of fooling has gone on between you and me long enough—it shall end to-night. *How* is it to end? In your selling yourself to McKelpin and I to the Widow Fogarty? It is for you to decide."

"Fred, tell me, could you, would you, under any circumstances, marry that underbred, over-dressed, loud-voiced woman?"

"She's a very pretty woman, or was fifteen years ago," responds Mr. Carew, "and worth a hundred thousand dollars. Her taste in dress and laughter, I could tone down. Now, McKelpin at no period of his career could have laid claim to prettiness, and I don't think he is worth a farthing more. Of course, there is also your aunt's fortune in the scale. Still money is not everything in this world; almost everything, I admit, but not quite. If you set me the example, 'Rilla, you must not be surprised at anything I may do."

"You have not answered my question," she angrily says. "Do you mean to marry Mrs. Fogarty?"

"What difference can it make to you when you are Mrs. McKelpin whether I marry her or not?"

What, indeed! And yet Cyrilla feels that it *does*. She could marry her Scotchman and support life apart from Fred, if she could only feel sure Fred would live and die single for her sake. But to give him up to another woman; that woman a widow, and *such* a widow—no, that way madness lay.

"'Rilla," he says, and he leans forward and takes both her hands in his, "you know you can never marry any man in the world but me—I who was in love with you in pinafores! Make an end of this nonsense, and marry me at once. We won't starve; there's a special providence that watches over——"

"Fools!" interrupts Miss Hendrick, bitterly. "Yes, I know."

"Lovers, I was about to say," pursues Fred, in his pleasant way. "We'll be happy—you know *that*, Beauty. We suit each other as no two ever did before. Say you'll marry me on the quiet next week, and I give you my word of honor I'll cut Nelly dead from thenceforth forever."

She turns upon him, a blaze of fury in her black eyes——

"Nelly!" she cries. "If you ever call her Nelly again——"

"Very well, I won't," responds Mr. Carew, soothingly; "I'll call her nothing at all; oh, no, we never mention her, from the hour you promise. If you refuse——" he darkly pauses.

"Well?" petulantly, but not meeting the pleading eyes, "if I refuse?"

"I shall ask Mrs. Fogarty to-morrow morning, I swear it, 'Rilla; and the wedding shall come off a week before yours."

"Fred!" with a gasp, "you—you don't mean that?"

"I never meant anything so much in my life, Beauty."

"But to marry you in secret—to ruin all my prospects for life—that I have worked so hard for, too! Oh, I *cannot!*" she cries, distractedly.

"There will be no ruin in the case. At present I have my pay, and that will suffice for us in a quiet way——"

"Ah, very quiet!" interpolates Miss Hendrick, with scorn.

"In a quiet way," proceeds Fred. "Then I shall write to my Uncle Dunraith, he's an uncommonly game old bird in money matters; and if Miss Dormer finds us out before she dies, why she'll come around. Its a rule of nature, that parents and guardians always *do* come round. But my own conviction is, that Aunt Dormer will die comfortably before finding us out, and leave you her money, and virtue will be its own reward in the end."

She stands before him, a struggle going on, he can see, her chest heaving. His eloquence is not the cause, she is not listening to a word of it all; she is simply thinking, "If I do not marry him Mrs. Fogarty will."

"Mrs. Delamere will be our aider and abettor," goes on the voice of the tempter, "so will the colonel. The chaplain of the regiment will marry us, and after that——Ah! well, 'Rilla, love, after that there will be no more Nellys nor Donalds to trouble our peace. We will belong to each other—as we do, for the matter of that, now—to the end of our lives. Beauty, say yes!"

But she cannot—not even with Fred's flushed, handsome pleading face so close to her own.

"I cannot!" she cries out in desperation; "at least not now. Give me until to-morrow, and I will decide."

"You are sure—to-morrow?" he asks.

"I am sure—to-morrow. Come at the usual hour, give the usual signal, and if it be possible I will steal out and meet you. But mind, don't hope too much—the answer may not be yes."

He smiles.

"Would you really throw me into the arms of Nelly Fogarty?" he asks, and as he utters the name a sound startles them. Both look up, and see Mrs. Fogarty's white, angry face looking at them through the half-closed folding doors.

He drops her hands and they start apart.

"The devil!" exclaims Fred Carew.

The next moment he is alone—Cyrilla has walked straight over to the folding doors, but Mrs. Fogarty has fled. She is talking to Colonel Delamere when Miss Hendrick passes through the other room, and keeps her back turned toward her.

Can she have heard ? the girl wonders. No, that is impossible. She has not heard, but she has seen quite enough to know that Fred Carew will never be her husband.

For Fred himself, he lingers a moment, that well-satisfied smile still on his lips.

"The woman who hesitates is lost," he murmurs. "I think I may look out for a special license the day after to-morrow."

    *   *   *   *   *   *   *

The fifteenth of April was the day appointed for the departure of the Delameres from Canada. Very early on the morning of the fourteenth a little party assembled in Mrs. Delamere's drawing-room, on matrimonial business intent—the chaplain of the ——th, Frederic Carew, Cyrilla Hendrick, the Colonel and his wife. With locked doors and closed blinds, a ceremony was performed that required but a very short time. At its close the chaplain and Mr. Carew stayed to breakfast, and Cyrilla returned to Miss Dormer's house on foot—Fred Carew's wife.

It would have been a curious and rather cynical study to have analyzed the different feelings actuating the different people in the little bridal group. Fat Mrs. Delamere, with her head a little on one side, and a pensive simper on her fair and forty face, felt she was living a page out of one of her favorite romances. She had plaintive, sentimental theories about "two souls with but a single thought, two hearts," etc. The Colonel, with a jolly smile on his jovial face, gives away the bride, feeling that she is an uncommonly pretty girl, that he would not mind being in Carew's place himself, and that it is a capital joke to help outwit the two skinflints, McKelpin and Phillis Dormer. The chaplain is a dark and saturnine gentleman, of a bilious habit, about as social and conversable as an oyster, who keeps secrets so well that he mostly forgets them himself. Cyrilla's principal emotion as Fred slips the wedding ring on her finger is, that he can never, *never* flirt with that detestable Nelly Fogarty again. For the bridegroom, his are the best and honestest, and simplest feelings of all. True love shines in his blue eyes as they look in his bride's face, and he is recording a vow in his inmost heart that Cyrilla shall never repent this step she has taken for his sake.

    *   *   *   *   *   *   *   *

"Aunt Dormer," says Cyrilla, coming into her aunt's room

10

with an open letter in her hand, "here is a letter from Sidney Owenson. See what she incloses—a through ticket for next week to take me to New York. She and her mother sail for Europe on the tenth of May, and she begs I will spend a week with her before she sails. We may never meet again, she says, and we have been such good friends, aunt. May I go ?"

It is the afternoon of the last day of April ; but Miss Dormer, in her stuffy room, sits huddled and shivering over a glowing coal fire. She lifts up her fretful, sour old face, all pinched and drawn, with its customary growl.

"Always gadding, gadding I never done ! I thought when that Delamere woman went, a fortnight ago, there would be an end of it, and here you want to begin again."

" Have I been anywhere since Mrs. Delamere did go, aunt ? "

" And now you want to be off to New York, the wickedest city in the world, and gad about there. What do you suppose Mr. McKelpin will say when he returns in June ? "

There was a dangerous answer on the tip of Cyrilla's tongue, a dangerous flash in her eye at the question, but there was too much at stake for her to let temper get the better of her now.

" I'm not Mrs. McKelpin yet, Aunt Phil. I belong to you, not to him. And it is the last, the very last favor I will ask. If Sydney had not sent the ticket too ——"

"I suppose ,she thought I was too poor to pay for you," snarled Miss Dormer. " Well, I am too poor. I have no money to throw away, and never shall. To leave me, too, in my present wretched state, it is like your gratitude, after all I have done for you, Niece Cyrilla ! "

" Then I am to write to Miss Owenson, return her ticket, and tell her you will not let me go ? "

" And have her set me down as a monster, a tyrant, and your self a victim ! You would like that, would you not ? No, you shall go to New York, and you shall see Dr. S—— for me, ex-plain my case to him, and bring me back his medicines. I suppose your rich friend will give you a return ticket, since she seems to have more money than she knows what to do with."

" I am quite sure she will, aunt. As you say, it will be an excellent opportunity to lay your case before the famous Dr. S——. I have no doubt his prescriptions will add twenty years to your life. Let me see. To-morrow is the first of May. This ticket is for the fourth. Of course I can easily be ready to go on the fourth."

So it was arranged. That there was any duplicity about the

letter or the t'cket, that Fred Carew had obtained a fortnight's
leave—sick leave !—how was Miss Dormer in her stifling prison
to know ?

Cyrilla made her preparations—not many—with so radiant a
face that old Joanna lifted her deaf head from the work, and declared it did her old eyes good only to look at her.   There was
new light, new life in her dark face that turned the grave beauty
to absolute loveliness.   She sang to herself as she moved
through the gruesome rooms, quite a new sound in Miss Dormer's dreary home.   " Let us crown ourselves with roses before
they fade," says a Sybaritish old French proverb ; her roses had
bloomed, and she would gather them at their brightest.   She
was happy to-day.   She would not look forward to to-morrow ;
her day would last until the tenth of the month.   If the night
and the darkness came after, so much the more need to enjoy
the sunshine of the present.

Early on the morning of the fourth, Cyrilla started on her
journey for New York.   It was a veritable May day, even in
Canada, of soft winds and melting sunlight.   She lay back in her
seat, and looked with radiantly dark eyes at the flying prospect.
How good a holiday was !   She had been on the treadmill so
long—*such* a treadmill! that liberty alone seemed a foretaste of
heaven.   The girl was a gypsy by nature.   In the Cedar wood
palaces of her soul's desire she would have had backward yearn-
ings for the canvas tents and fetterless freedom of the nomad
tribes.   She was free now—one, two, three—nine whole days
she was to be happy.   Nine whole days only.   Ah, well I people
have gone through life without even nine hours of perfect bliss.

The day wore on—noon—afternoon—evening—night.   She
did not feel even a touch of weariness, her vitality was perfect.
Other people around her slept ; her eyes were like dusk stars.
Nine o'clock, ten o'clock, eleven o'clock, and " *Boston*" shouts
the conductor, putting in his head.   Her journey for the pres
ent is at an end.

There were not many people nor many hacks at the depôt at
that hour, but one of the few persons in waiting made his way
instantly in.   While Cyrilla was gathering her belongings together, some one came hastily to her side, stooped down and
kissed her.

" My wife I "

Her answer is a smile that repays Fred Carew for tiresome
hours of waiting.   He gathers up shawl, bag and book, draws
her hand through his arm, and leads her away tc a hack.

"Tremont," he calls, and they go rattling over the stony streets of Boston.

"And this is the Hub of the Universe," says Cyrilla, laughing "It has an English look. We must stay here to-morrow and explore it, Freddy."

"Certainly, Cyrilla. Ah! if Aunt Dormer could only see you now!"

. But Aunt Dormer, uneasily asleep at home, dreams not of such horrors. That she has been outwitted, defied; that her niece has secretly married the son of her arch-enemy—that the trip to New York is her honeymoon trip—it would be difficult indeed to convince Aunt Dormer of this.

They spend the next day in Boston very agreeably—take the evening boat for New York, and wake up next morning in the Empire City. They drive to an up-town hotel, breakfast, and then start out for their first day's sight-seeing.

"I shall put off going to see Sydney until the very last day," says Mrs. Carew to Mr. Carew. "She will ask questions, and I cannot tell Sydney lies. With those innocent, crystal-clear eyes of hers on one's face, one hates oneself for being false. It is odious enough to be obliged to tell them to Aunt Dormer.

"Still, for a novice, my love, I am quite sure you do it remarkably well," murmurs the adoring husband, "as you do everything."

All her after-life Cyrilla looked back with a sigh of envious regret to that week. She was so free, so happy, and with Fred. Everything was new and delightful—the streets, the stores, the parks, the people, the theatres—everything. Other days of delight the future might bring, but never again any like these. The bloom would be brushed off life's peach, the first freshness and zest gone, she could never enjoy again as she enjoyed now. Ruin and disaster might be in store for her when Donald Mc Kelpin came home—she could not tell—her gold might be fairy gold, after all, that would turn to slate stones in her grasp, but oh!-how brightly it shone. What a good and satisfying thing life could be made to two people who were fond of each other and—had plenty of money!

The tenth of May, as has been said, was the day appointed for Mrs. and Miss Owenson's departure. On the afternoon of the day preceding, Cyrilla presented herself at the door of a stately brown front on Madison Avenue, with the legend "MAC-GREGOR" on a silver plate.

"You will wait for me in Madison Square, Freddy," had said

Freddy's wife. " It will never do to shock little Syd by telling her the horrid truth, so you must not be seen."

Mr. Carew, in the present stage of his existence, lived but to obey.

Cyrilla rang, and the ring was answered by an ebony young man in livery.

" Was Miss Owenson at home ? "

" Yes, Miss Owenson was at home," made answer the ebony young man, throwing open a door and ushering the visitor into a perfumed and elegant reception room. " What name shall he say ? "

" I will not send my card," the lady answers ; " tell her an old friend."

" These Macgregors must be very rich people," thought Cyrilla, running her eyes critically over the costly furnishing and ornaments of the room ; " people of refinement and thorough good taste as well. Ah ! Sydney's lines seem to fall in pleasant places."

The door opened as she thought it, and Sydney came in. Cyrilla arose. Was it Sydney—rose cheeked, laughing Sydney, this pale, frail girl in deepest crapes and sables, with that sadly thoughtful face ?

" Sydney ! "

" Cyrilla ! "

It is a cry of very delight, and Sydney Owenson clasps the friend she loves in her arms, and kisses her in a rapture again and again.

" My darling ! what a surprise ! " she exclaims. " I never thought of seeing you. Johnson said an old friend, and described you in glowing terms, but still I never thought of you. Dear old Cy ! how good of you to come before I left ! When did you come ?—to-day ? "

" No—not to-day," Cyrilla answers, with a smile. " Sidney, child, how thin and pale you have grown. Have you been ill ? "

" No, not ill exactly, and yet not well. I suppose I got too great a shock—it was all so dreadful, and I was so little used to trouble. I do not think that I can ever feel again as I used —oh ! how long ago it seems."

" But you will, dear ; we all think like that in trouble. And Bertie—no news of him has ever transpired ? "

" None—none—none ! Oh ! Cyrilla, it breaks my heart ! To think of him hurried into eternity without a moment's warning, full of life and hope, unprepared for death. If we could even have found his body, if we could have given him Christian burial! But all is mystery; not even a trace of his body can be found."

Her voice breaks and she turns away; Cyrilla sits silent. With this last sorrow she cannot sympathize. The body is not found, of course, because there is no body to be found. Bertie Vaughan carries that about with him, and cares for it as tenderly as ever, no doubt.

"But you don't tell me how you came to be in New York," Sydney says, turning brightly around. "Is it not something wonderful for Miss Dormer to let you out of her sight?"

"Wonderful indeed; but you know, Syd, wonders never cease. Here I am; and, my dear child, I want to beg as a favor that you will ask me nothing about how or why I came. Aunt Dormer knows I am here; the rest is a secret. I am stopping at a hotel, and leave for Montreal to-morrow. Oh! how I hate, how I abhor, how I detest and dread the very thought of going back!"

Sydney sat gazing at her, silent, wondering, but unsuspecting. Cyrilla always was a girl of mysteries and secrets; that she was so still did not much surprise Miss Owenson.

"But now that you are here you will stay and dine with me of course," she says. "Aunt Macgregor and my cousin Katy will be charmed to meet you. They have heard of you so much from mamma and me. Poor mamma is never done singing your praises; how good, how tender, how sympathetic you are. She is out just now shopping, but will be back in an hour. Come up to my room and take off your things."

"No, Sydney. I can't stay. Don't be hurt, dear, but my time is limited. I will remain half an hour longer, and I want you to tell me all about your winter here and your plans for over the ocean."

They sit and chat, and the moments fly. Cyrilla half wishes she could stay to dinner, so interested does she become in it all, but she thinks mercifully of Fred, wandering aimlessly through the verdant groves of Madison Square, among the nurse-maids and perambulators, and arises at last and goes.

"You will not forget me, Sydney. You will write often and tell me all about your wanderings?" is her last injunction.

Sydney promises; there is a last embrace and they part, to meet again neither knows when.

Cyrilla rejoins her husband. They hail a passing omnibus to

return to the hotel. Four people in the stage, three gentlemen and a lady, when they enter. This Cyrilla carelessly sees, but she does not glance at any of them specially. She generally finds men's eyes fixed upon her with a stare of broad admiration which, though it does not disconcert her at all, she does not care to meet. A handsome girl in a Broadway stage is no such *rara avis;* still Mrs. Frederick Carew comes in for even more than the customary amount of staring. She sits supremely unconscious of it now, gazing out of the window, while Freddy passes up their fare and resumes his seat by her side.

"Look—not for an instant yet—at the woman sitting opposite," he says in French, in a guarded tone.

She is surprised, but she waits the moment and then glances across. The woman, a thin, faded, youngish woman, sits directly opposite, her eyes fixed full upon Cyrilla, a glare of deadly hatred in their pale depths. It is—Mary Jane Jones !

For a moment they transfix each other, mutual recognition in their eyes. It is a fortunate thing for Cyrilla that her creamy complexion never changes color. Then she looks straight over Miss Jones' head out at the crowds pouring up and down Broadway.

The ride to the hotel is a short one. Mr. Carew pulls the check string, and they get out. Miss Jones waits until another block is passed, evidently thinking deeply ; then she, too, alights, and walks back to the hotel. At the door of the reading-room she passes Fred Carew. She takes no notice, she goes on into the office and up to the desk, and accosts the official enthroned there.

"Are there a Mr. and Mrs. Carew stopping here ?" she inquires.

"Yes, ma'am. Mr. Carew's at the door there," answers the official, with a nod, and the admirable brevity of his class.

"They are from Montreal?"

"From Montreal."

"How long have they been here ?"

Official refers to big book, looking bored.

"Five days."

"Thank you."

With a smile on her lips, Miss Jones quits the office. Fred Carew is still standing where he stood when she entered, as she passes out. She pauses before him, with that smile—as unpleasant a smile as can well be imagined—and looks up in his face.

"How do you do, Mr. Carew?" she says.

Mr. Carew puts up his eye-glass, and looks at her in a bewildered way.

"Eh? I beg your pardon, you know," drawls Freddy; "but *have* I ever had the pleasure of—er—seeing you before, madam?"

Miss Jones laughs.

"You do it very well," she answers; "almost as well as she could herself. Give my best respects to Mrs. Carew—I don't think she knew me in the stage. I hope her aunt is in good health, and is quite reconciled to the match. Good-day to you, Mr. Carew."

CHAPTER XXIV.

VENDETTA!

"DRAW that curtain, Niece Cyrilla, and don't sit mooning there, out of nothing. You might know all that glare of light would hurt my eyes, if you ever thought of anybody but yourself."

The croaking, rasping old voice stops. With a tired sigh, Cyrilla rises and does as she is told.

"Will that do, Aunt Phil?"

There is no reply for a moment, then a dull, prolonged groan of misery from the old woman on the bed.

"Oh! my back. Oh! my side. Oh! this dreadful, racking pain. Niece Cyrilla, what are you sitting there like a stone for? You have no more feeling than a stone. Get up and do something for me."

The girl comes to the bedside, and looks pitifully down at the drawn, distorted face and writhing form.

"Aunt Dormer, what shall I do for you? I do feel for you, indeed. Shall I fetch your hot plates?"

Once again there is no reply. In the midst of her querulous cry, Miss Dormer has fallen into a fitful doze. Cyrilla goes softly back to her place; but she has hardly resumed her seat, when the harsh, complaining voice breaks out again——

"Isn't it time for my spoonful of morphine yet? You never

know or care whether it is time for me to get my medicine or
not. I wish *you* had this pain in your side and back, and all
over your body, as I have ; perhaps you would be as glad as I
am to get morphine Look at the clock, Niece Cyrilla, and
don't sit gaping out of that window like a fool."

For the third time the girl arises, almost like an automaton ;
it is only a specimen of what goes on all day now. Passing
her hand wearily across her forehead, she looks at the clock ; ‑
the morphine hour has not arrived, but she administers the drug
in a tiny crystal cup—this, at least, will quiet her tyrant for the
next hour.

The scene is still Miss Dormer's room, but the arm-chair has
been exchanged for a bed—Miss Phillis Dormer will never sit
in arm-chair or other chair again. It is almost the close of
May—a soft opal-tinted, exquisite May evening, but still a coal
fire burns on the hearth, the windows are sealed, the doors are
tightly closed by order of the invalid, the foul mephitic air is in
itself sufficient to kill any one. Cyrilla has been breathing it
since seven o'clock this morning ; she has been breathing it for
many weary days past. A fortnight ago Miss Dormer's incurable disease made one rapid stride forward, and brought Miss
Dormer to the door of death. At death's door she lies now.
The dread and gloomy portal that will open for all flesh one day
may open for her any moment, now. She knows it too, only
even to her own soul, she refuses vehemently, fiercely, to
believe. It is but a temporary illness—she will recover—she
must recover—her affairs are not arranged, her will is not made,
she cannot make it in all this pain and misery—she has not time
to die. When she is better she will make it, she will send for a
clergyman, she will read her Bible, she—she will try and prepare for death. She is not so very old, only fifty-five ; why,
many men and women, not as strong as she is, live to seventy,
eighty, ninety ! This is not death, she is only a little worse ; next
week, or week after, she will be better, and then—then she
will amend her life and get ready to die.

So she puts the thought fiercely from her, and no one dares
tell her the truth. She has lived a most godless and unholy life,
at wrath with all the world, for the wrong of one man ; she will
die an impenitent and most despairing death. Oh, *vanitas vani-
tatem !* What preacher that ever preached can speak to the
heart as does the death-bed of a hoary sinner.

She takes her anodyne, falls back upon her pillow and sinks
at once into dull stupor. Then, still with that jaded, worn face,

10*

Cyrilla gets up, leaves the room, descends the stairs and stands
out in the lovely freshness of the sweet spring night.

The air is full of balm, of perfume, of balsamic odors; it is
warm and windless as June—the June that will be here next week,
that is to bring Donald McKelpin to claim his bride. Up in the
blue sky shining stars look down; a faint, silver baby moon is
away yonder over her left shoulder, half-lost in the primrose lustre of the sky. Away in Montreal half-a-dozen bells clash mu-
sically out, calling the good French Canadians to the devotion
of " The Month of May." It is all sweetness, and peace, and
beauty, and the white, fagged look gradually leaves the girl's
face, and her dark melancholy eyes lose a little of their sombre
expression. But still she is very grave, and—where has her
youth gone to? she looks ten years older than three weeks
ago.

Will Aunt Dormer die without making her will? That is the
thought that haunts her by night and by day, that robs her of
appetite and sleep, that makes her bear imprisonment in that
most miserable sick-room, that makes her endure the fierce
impatience, the ceaseless complainings, of the sick woman, with
a patience that never fails. If Phillis Dormer dies without making her will, she and her father are heirs-at-law, and her father,
even if alive, will never disturb her in her possession. All will
be hers and her husband's. If she only dies without making
a will! if she only dies before Donald McKelpin comes
home.

Even to her own heart—selfish, mercenary, irreligious as
Cyrilla is, she will not own that she wishes this sudden death.
But she does; and the shadow of murder—the murder of desire—
rests upon her as she stands here.

With a horror none but those who fear death can know, Miss
Dormer shrinks from the thought of making her will. She loves
her money; all her dreary life long it has been to her husband,
children, friends, religion. To will it deliberately away to her
niece, or even to Donald McKelpin, is bitterer than the bitterness of death itself. This the girl knows; no will has been
made, none is likely to be made; on that now all Cyrilla's life
hangs. If Miss Dormer dies intestate, riches, happiness, this
world and the glory thereof, will be hers, with the husband she
passionately loves; if she does not——

" My solemn Cyrilla !" says a voice drawing near, " how wan
and unearthly you look standing here in the gloaming, gazing
at the stars. If you had on a white dress, you might have been

taken for the ghost of Dormer House. And Dormer House is just the sort of gruesome place to have a ghost."

"Freddy!" she exclaims, waking from her gloomy reverie and holding out her hand, "I must have been far away, indeed, since I never heard you come."

"And what were you thinking of, Beauty? The husband who adores you, I trust?"

"No, sir; of a much less tender subject—Aunt Dormer's will." There is a pause. She takes his arm and walks with him up and down the grassy path. The high wooden wall shuts them from the view of outsiders; Miss Dormer's drugged sleep will last for another half-hour. Old Joanna, deaf and stupid, never was guilty of looking out of a window in her life. So Mr. Carew can come to see his wife this time every evening without fear of detection.

"Beauty," he begins, gravely, at the expiration of that pause, "you think too much of Miss Dormer's will. Don't be offended at my saying so, but one may buy even gold too dear. I'm not a preaching sort of fellow as a rule," Mr. carew goes on apologetically, "and I never interfere with any of your projects, because I know you've got twice the brains I have, and in a general way know what you're about. But, my dear child, there is something absolutely revolting in the way you look forward to that poor old lady's death."

Cyrilla looks at him for a moment in whimsical surprise, then she laughs.

"My dear Fred, what a precocious little boy you are getting to be! Your sentiments do you honor of course, all the same; please tell me what we are to do if Aunt Dormer cuts me off with a shilling."

"Trust in Providence and my Uncle Dunraith, and live on my pay meantime," responds Freddy, promptly.

"Where, Fred? In the back bed-room of a third-rate boarding-house? And if Uncle Dunraith turns a deaf ear to the penniless cry of his starving nephew and niece, what then?"

"I'll sell out and start a grocery, set up a boarding-house, teach a school, sweep a crossing; anything, anything," says Fred, with a vague wave of his hands, "except wish poor Miss Dormer dead before her time."

"I don't wish her dead," answers Cyrilla, with asperity, "but die she must, and that speedily; is there any harm, then, in my hoping she may die without a will? If she does, all is well for you and me, Freddy; we will go back to England, dear, old

England, and when we tire of that we will run about the world together—that modern marvel, as the poet says :

> "'Two souls with but a single thought,
> That never disagree !'

"Ah ! Fred, we can be very happy together, with Aunt Dormer's money."

"We can be very happy together without," Mr. Carew answers. "If I lived in a garret and starved on a crust *I* could be happy, 'Rilla, love, so that you were near. Don't hope too much ; the disappointment when it comes will be all the harder to bear."

"Don't talk of disappointment," cries Cyrilla, angrily ; "I will not listen. There shall be no disappointment. She has no thought of making a will I know, no thought of dying ; and Dr. Foster told me only this morning, she would hardly live the week out."

Again there is silence. They walk slowly up and down under the scented, budding trees, with the pale, sweet shine of the little yellow moon sifting down on their grave faces. Presently Fred speaks.

"You have heard nothing yet from Miss Jones ? "

"Nothing ; she has not written. Every letter that enters the house passes through my hands. No one has been here except Dr. Foster. Mrs. Fogarty, as I told you, called twice, and each time I refused to let her in. She looked as if she meant mischief, too."

"And Miss Jones meant mischief, if ever I saw it in a woman's face. It is odd she has not written, but I have a conviction she will yet. I never saw such hatred before in human eyes."

"Miss Jones has eyes exactly like a cat," says Cyrilla. "Well, so that Aunt Dormer is comfortably in her grave, they may do their worst. Oh! Fred ; how can one help wishing she would die and have done with it, when so much is at stake !"

"All the money in the world is not worth one such wish, 'Rilla. What I want to say to you is this : if, through Miss Jones, it should come to your aunt's knowledge that we were together in New York, don't deny our marriage. Mind, Cyrilla, don't ! Neither Miss Jones, nor your aunt, nor any one else, shall ever think you were with me there, except as my wife."

"Nonsense, Fred ! Even if Aunt Dormer does hear it—and I will take care she does not—she still thinks I was visiting Sydney ; and I can prove our meeting was accidental."

"Miss Jones knows better ; she knows we were at that hotel

as husband and wife. For Heaven's sake, Cyrilla, don't tell that dying woman lies, it is *too* contemptible. Let us tell the truth if we must, and take the consequences. Nothing they can do can ever separate us, and our separation is the only thing I fear."

" The only thing." Cyrilla laughs, and all in a moment her face grows old and hard: "you don't fear beggary, then, or squalor, or misery, either for yourself or for me? That is not love as I understand it. Freddy, let me tell you, once and for all, if Aunt Dormer disinherits me, I shall hate you for having made me your wife !"

Again there is silence; again it is broken by Fred Carew in a troubled voice.

"When does McKelpin come home, Cyrilla?"

"Week after next; and if Miss Dormer is still alive, she proposes that the wedding shall be the day after his arrival. Her illness is a sufficient excuse for no preparation, no expense. It is a tangled web, Freddy, out of which I cannot see my way."

She passes her hand across her forehead with the same weary gesture as in the sick-room, and sighs heavily.

" I cannot advise you, Beauty ; I'm not a good one at plotting and duplicity. Tell the truth ; that is the only way out of it, that I can see. And you need not be so greatly afraid, things are not as black as you paint them. If the worst comes to the worst, tell the truth and trust in me."

" I must go in," Cyrilla answers, coldly. "Aunt Dormer will awake, and be furious if she misses me. I have watched with her two nights ; I feel hardly able to stand."

" You are wearing yourself out, my darling," her husband says, looking at her with wistful tenderness. Ah ! Cyrilla, I never much wished for fortune before. I always seemed to have enough ; but I wish I were rich for your sake. Good-by, then, since you must go."

"Good-by," she repeats, mechanically. She turns to go in. He has gone a few steps, when he wheels suddenly and comes back.

" Beauty," he says, " I want to warn you again. If our being together in New York comes to Miss Dormer's ears confess our marriage. It would take a good deal to make me angry with you—you know that ; but if you let any one—any one—think you were with me there other than as my wife, I couldn't forgive you. Promise me this."

" I will promise you nothing. Good-night," she says, shortly, and disappears into the dark and dreary dwelling.

Fred Carew goes back to his quarters, his handsome, genial face looking strangely anxious and troubled. And Fred Carew's wilful wife drags herself spiritlessly up to her aunt's room.

You may buy gold too dear, had said Fred. Surely she thought if every penny came to her, she was buying her gold at a fearful price.

It was Joanna's night to watch, and Joanna was already ir the sick-room. The dim lamp was lit ; the close atmosphere seemed stifling to Cyrilla, coming in out of the fresh, cool air. Miss Dormer opened her eyes at the moment and peevishly cried out for her wine and water.

"Here, aunt."

Cyrilla raised the feeble old head, gave her the drink, shook and adjusted the pillows and replaced her among them.

"I am very tired, aunt, I am going to my room, now. Joanna is here. Is there anything more I can do for you before I go ?"

"No. Go—you are only too glad to go. You hate to sit an hour with me after all I've done for you. Ah ! the Hendricks were a bad lot, a bad lot—how could you be anything but bad, too ? "

"Good-night, Aunt Dormer."

Aunt Dormer disdains reply. Cyrilla goes. She is so dead tired, so utterly exhausted, that she flings herself on her bed, dressed as she is, and in five minutes is soundly and dreamlessly asleep.

So soundly, so deeply, that when an hour later Dr. Foster comes, she never hears his loud knock. Two ladies are with him : two ladies who take seats in the chill, vault-like parlor, while he goes up to the sick-room. He feels his patient's pulse, says there is less fever ; she is sinking rapidly, but he does not tell her that.

"Miss Dormer," he says, "two ladies have accompanied me here on what one of them says is a matter of life and death. Her name is Miss Jones. The other is Mrs. Fogarty, one of my patients and the wealthiest lady in Montreal.· They are downstairs and beg most earnestly to be admitted to see you."

"I never see ladies," cries Miss Dormer, shrilly ; "you know that. What did you bring them here for ? You ought to be ashamed of yourself, Foster."

Doctor Foster knows her. He expects to send in a bill to her executors presently that will make them open their eyes. He bears this, therefore, like the urbane gentleman he is.

Furthermore, Mrs. Fogarty, one of his very best paying patients, has given him to understand that if he does not procure her this interview, she will be under the painful necessity of taking herself and her ailments elsewhere.

"My dear lady," he blandly says, "did you observe when I told you it was a matter of almost life or death? I really think you had better break through your excellent rule in this instance. They are ladies of the utmost respectability, and one of them of great wealth. They have no sinister motive, I assure you. It is concerning some extraordinary deception that is being practised upon you by your very charming niece, Miss Hendrick."

Miss Dormer has been lying back on her pillows glaring at him, an awful object. At these last words she utters a shrill cry.

"I knew it! I knew it! I always said so! She comes of a bad race, and she's the worst of them all. Fetch them up here at once! do you go, Joanna! fetch them up, I say at once."

A moment more, and with a rustle of silk, and a waft of perfume, Mrs. Fogarty sweeps smilingly into the chamber. Upright, stiff, angular, solemn Miss Jones comes after.

"My dear Miss Dormer, at last I have the pleasure of making your acquaintance. I have long desired it, and even under the present melancholy circumstances——"

Mrs. Fogarty has fluently and smilingly got thus far when Miss Dormer, with a harsh cry, cuts her short.

"I don't want any of your fine talk, ma'am. I know what fine talk is worth. Old Foster and my niece, Cyrilla, give me enough of that. It's about my niece, Cyrilla, you've come. Now what have you got to say?"

"First, I must really apologize for the hour of our coming," says Mrs. Fogarty; "but this, also, is the fault of your niece. I have been here twice this week, and she refused me admission. I don't call her Miss Hendrick, because Miss Hendrick has ceased to be her name!"

A second harsh cry from Miss Dormer, her sunken eyes are glaring in a ghastly way up at the speaker.

"Not her name? Woman, what do you mean? Why is Cyrilla Hendrick not her name?"

"Because," answers Mrs. Fogarty, snapping her white teeth together like an angry little dog, "it is Mrs. Frederic Carew!"

"Or ought to be!" in a solemn voice, puts in Miss Jones.

At the sound of that name, that name unheard so long, never forgotten, Phillis Dormer gives a gasp and lies speechless.

Frederic Carew! Frederic Carew! It is the father she is
thinking of, not the son.

"We have taken you by surprise," Mrs. Fogarty goes on.
"You did not know, I presume, he was in Canada at all. Such is
the fact, nevertheless. He came last October, and your niece
has been holding continual intercourse with him ever since."

She knows now, the first shock over. It is the son of Frederic Carew, whom Cyrilla knew years ago in England, they mean.
A savage light comes into her eyes, a horrid, hungry eagerness
comes into her face.

"Go on! go on!" she pants.

"It is Miss Jones who has the story to tell," says Mrs. Fogarty. "We have the strongest reason to believe your niece,
Cyrilla, is Lieutenant Frederic Carew's wife."

"Or ought to be!" croaks again Miss Jones.

"Or ought to be, exactly. Still I think she *is*. Three weeks
ago your niece was in New York and living with Mr. Carew
at a hotel as his wife. Tell her about it, Miss Jones."

And then Miss Jones begins at the beginning and tells her all.
All—all that occurred in Petite St. Jacques when Miss Hendrick was so nearly expelled the school, Cyrilla's revenge upon
herself, and their accidental meeting three weeks ago in the
streets of New York.

In stony, rigid silence the sick woman lies and listens, fury
and rage in her eyes.

"It may seem wicked to you," says Miss Jones, with grim
truth; "but I will own I have taken the trouble and expense
of this journey here, all the way from New York, to tell you
this, because I owe your niece a grudge. I know from Mademoiselle Stephanie Chateauroy, as I say, that you disliked this
young man; I felt certain when I saw them together that you
were being cheated and wronged. Still, it is for my own sake
I have come. One good turn deserves another. By the merest
accident I fell in with this lady upon my arrival in Montreal,
through her I have found my way to you. Your niece, Cyrilla,
and whether she is this man's wife or not, lived with him as such
for a week in the Clarendon Hotel."

"I have known this long time that they were lovers," interrupts Mrs. Fogarty. "I once witnessed a disgusting love
scene between them myself."

Still that stony, rigid silence, still the stricken woman glares
up at them awfully from her bed.

"This is all?" she hoarsely asks, at length.

"This is all; enough, I think," responds Mrs. Fogarty, with a shor. laugh.

The burning, eager eyes glance away from one cruel face to the other.

"You are prepared to repeat all this in my niece's presence, I suppose?"

"Whenever and wherever called upon," replies Miss Jones.

"Then you may go now; I'll send for you both to-morrow. I'll pay *you*, ma'am, for your news. I'm a poor woman, but I'm able and willing to pay for that. Ring that bell for Joanna, and go."

Her hands clench in a fierce grasp on the bed-clothes, her eyes stare, blind with pain and rage, up at the ceiling. The bitterness, the fury of this hour is like nothing the wretched woman can ever remember before. Long ago she loved and trusted, and was betrayed; now she has neither loved nor trusted, and she has been betrayed, once again, by the girl she has cherished and cared for, the only creature in whom her blood runs, and by the son of the man who wrecked her life.

Cyrilla Hendrick is the wife, or light of love, of Frederic Carew's son—to Frederic Carew's son will all her loved and hoarded wealth go, if she dies without a will. She shrieks out like a madwoman at that, and beats the bed-clothes with frantic hands.

"Go to Shelburne Street—go to Lawyer Pomfret's house. Joanna, do you hear? Go—go at once. Go, I tell you, quick!"

Old Joanna, returning from bolting her visitors out, stares blankly at her mistress.

"Idiot! fool! what do you stand gaping there for? Don't you hear what I say?—deaf old addle-head! Go to Lawyer Pomfret's house, and fetch him here. Tell him it's the rich Miss Dormer who wants him, and that it is a matter of life or death! Go!"

Joanna never disputes her mistress's will. She looks at the clock—only ten. Without a word she puts on her shawl and bonnet, locks the door after her, and starts at a jog-trot for the lawyer who is to make Miss Dormer's will.

In the lonely sick-room the dim lamp glimmers, shadows thick in the corners of the large room. On her death-bed the stricken old sinner lies, body and soul full of pain and torture, hatred and revenge. And up-stairs, in her bare, comfortless chamber, Cyrilla sleeps deeply, while the retribution her own hand has wrought gathers above her head.

*

CHAPTER XXV.

"GOOD-BYE, SWEETHEART."

YRILLA, as a rule, was inclined to sleep late of morn ings ; Miss Dormer, as a rule, was inclined not to let her. At seven, precisely, winter and summer, Joanna stood at her bedside, to summon her down stairs. At seven on the morning after her interview with Fred, Cyrilla expected to be routed out as usual. But when she opened her eyes, after the long unbroken sleep, it was to find the sunshine filling her scantily-furnished little upper chamber, and the clock of a neighboring church tolling the hour of nine.

Nine ! She sprang from her bed in dismay. What was Aunt Dormer, what was Joanna about, to let her sleep like this ? Had anything happened in the night? Was Aunt Dormer——, she would not finish the question even to herself, but her heart gave a great bound. The next moment she knew better; if anything *like that* had occurred, she would have been instantly summoned by the deaf old domestic, she felt sure. She hurriedly arranged her clothes, made her hasty ablutions, smoothed her dark rippling hair and ran down to her aunt's room. She softly opened the door and entered. The close, fetid atmosphere seemed to sicken her,—ill or well, Miss Dormer had an insuperable aversion to fresh air. She advanced to the bedside ; in the dim light, the skinny bloodless face lay still upon its pillows ; the eyes, glitteringly bright, looked up at her with a weird stare.

" Dear aunt, I am sorry I overslept myself. How was it Joanna did not call me as usual ? "

" You have watched with me two nights in succession, Niece Cyrilla. Young people need rest."

" How are you this morning, Aunt Phil ? Easier, I trust ? Have you had a good night ? "

At that question the old woman broke into the strangest, wildest laugh ; a laugh most dreadful to hear, most ghastly to see.

" A good night, Niece Cyrilla ? Yes, a good night, a good night, the like of which I've never had but once before, and that five-and-twenty years ago ! And I'm strong and well to-day ; you'll be glad to hear, for I've a great deal to do before night. Niece Cyrilla, do you believe in ghosts ? "

" Dear aunt."

"Yes. I am dear to you, am I not? You wouldn't deceive or trouble me in any way, would you? I'm going to see a ghost to-day. Niece Cyrilla—ghosts don't generally appear in daylight either, do they ?—the ghost of a man dead and buried five-and-twenty years. Five-and-twenty years! Oh, me, what a while ago it seems !"

Was the old woman going insane? Was this the delirium that precedes death? Cyrilla stood looking at her, and yet there was no fever in her face, no wildness in her eyes, and crazy as her talk was it did not sound like delirium. The golden rays of the jubilant morning sunshine tried to force a passage in, and here and there succeeded, making lines of amber glitter across the dull red carpet. All things were in their places, no voice spoke to tell her that in this room her ruin last night had been wrought.

" Go down-stairs, Niece Cyrilla, and get your breakfast. Fetch me up mine when you come. I have something to say to you when it is over."

Something to say to her ! Wondering, uneasily, the girl descended to the kitchen, the only clean and cozy apartment in the house, where Joanna, on a little, white-draped stand, had her tea and toast set out.

" Joanna !" shouted Cyrilla, sitting down to her morning meal, "did anything more than customary happen here last night ?"

The old woman nodded her deaf head.

" Aye, miss, that there did. She had visitors. Ladies," (Joanna spoke invariably in short jerks), "fine ladies. Silks and scents on one. Come with the doctor."

Ladies ! Instantly Cyrilla's mind flew to Miss Jones. But "silks and scents"—that did not apply.

" Was one of them tall and thin, with a sharp, pale face, a long nose, a tight, wide mouth, pursed up like this—and a way of folding her hands in front of her—so ? "

" Aye, miss—that's her. Tall and thin. With a long nose. *And* a wide mouth. And her hands in front of her. That's her, miss—to the life."

Miss Jones then, at last. " Hast thou found me, O mine enemy ? " While she slept, off guard, her foe had forced her way in and all her secret was told. She turned for a moment sick and faint—she turned away from her untasted breakfast and buried her face in her hands. This, then, was what Miss Dormer meant.

"'T'other one," began old Joanna, still in jerks. "Tall, too, White teeth. Silks and scents. Roses in her bonnet. Red spots on her cheeks. Paint, *I* think."

Mrs. Fogarty! There was no mistaking the description—the only two who hated her on earth. All was over—nothing remained but to "cover her face and die with dignity."

And then, in Joanna's little kitchen, all aglitter with its floods of May sunshine, a struggle began—a struggle for a soul.

"Tell the truth. All the money in the world is not worth one such lie as this. It is *too* contemptible to deceive that poor old dying lady," whispered her good angel in the voice of Fred Carew. "Come with me ; I will care for you. Things will not be so bad as you fear. Trust in Providence and my uncle Dunraith. Meantime we can live on my pay." Fred's honest blue eyes shine upon her, Fred's tender, manly voice is in her ears. "If this does come to your aunt's knowledge, don't deny our marriage. Mind! I warn you. It would take a great deal to make me angry with you, but I could not forgive that." The tender voice grows stern, the pleasant face grave and set as he says it. "Oh! tell the truth," her own heart pleads ; "it is a revolting thing to tell deliberate lies to the dying."

"And lose all for which you have labored so hard—suffered so much—borne so many insults—endured months and months of imprisonment worse than death! Leave this house and go out to beggary, to humiliation, to pinching and poverty, scant dinners, and scantier dress! Let your arch enemies, Fogarty and Jones, triumph over you, throw up the sponge to Fate at the first defeat, and resign the fortune justly yours—yours by every claim of blood and law—to Donald McKelpin! Never!"

She looks up, her eyes flash, her teeth set, her hands clench. Never! She will fight to the last against them all—against Destiny itself. She will die sooner than yield.

The battle is over, the victory won, and the tempter, whispering in her ear, in the archives below, "records one lost soul more."

"Joanna," she says, rising, "is Aunt Dormer's breakfast ready? I want to bring it up."

"But you've eat none yourself? Tea ain't drunk—toast ain't eat. Sick, are you?" says old Joanna, peering in her face. "You're white as a sheet."

"Am I?" Cyrilla answers, with a laugh. "I am never very red, you know."

She seizes a coarse crash towel and rubs her cheeks and lips until a semblance of color returns.

"Now, quick, Joanna," she says, with another reckless laugh. "I go to 'put it to the touch, to win or lose it all.'"

She takes the tray and ascends to the upper room. She places it before Miss Dormer, and assists her to sit up among her pillows.

"I hope you have an appetite this morning, Aunt Phil?" she says, pleasantly. "Everything is fresh and nice, and perfectly cooked."

Surely nature intended this girl for an actress. Every nerve is braced for the coming struggle—for lie upon lie—yet even the hawk eye of Aunt Dormer can trace no change in voice or face.

"Has Joanna been telling you I had visitors last night—ladies?" she asks, watching her keenly.

"Yes, aunt, and I have been wondering who they could be. Joanna doesn't seem to know."

"Don't you know, Niece Cyrilla?"

"I?" Cyrilla elevates her eyebrows. "I am not a clairvoyant, Aunt Phil."

Aunt Phil laughs, her elfish, uncanny, most disagreeable laugh.

"You're a clever girl, Niece Cyrilla—oh! an uncommonly clever girl. But the Hendricks were all clever—all clever and all bad—bad! bad! bad!—bad to the core!"

"You have told me that so often, Aunt Dormer," says Cyrilla, in an offended tone, "don't you think you might stop now? Seeing two of the bad Hendricks are your nearest of kin, bad as they are, you might spare them, I think."

"You think so, do you? Well, I mean to spare one of them to-day if she gives me the chance. Take away this tray, Niece Cyrilla. Now put up that blind and let in the light—plenty of light. Now sit here on the side of the bed, and look me in the eyes—straight in the eyes. I want to see if I can read the lies you will tell, in that nineteen-year-old face of yours."

"I am not in the habit of telling lies, Aunt Dormer," says Cyrilla, in the same offended tone, obeying all the grim orders as given.

"Are you not? Then you differ from all the Hendricks *I* ever knew. Your father never told the truth in his life, and we don't gather grapes of thorns, or figs of thistles, we are told. Your mother was a weak little fool—perhaps you take your

truth-telling proclivities from her. Let me see, where I want
to begin ! Niece Cyrilla, is Frederick Carew's son in Canada ?"

" Ah ! you have found that out ! How cruel to tell you—
you who hate the very sound of the name."

" You own it then ? He is here. You have met him ; have
been meeting him constantly since last October ? "

Cyrilla looks up—a flash of indignation in her eyes.

" No, Aunt Dormer, I deny it ! Whoever tells you that, tells
you a falsehood. I have seen him—only a few times—and I
did not speak of it to you. Why should I ? I knew it would
vex you to know he was here at all, and his presence made no
difference to me, one way or other."

" None ! Take care ! Is he not your lover, Niece Cyrilla ? "

" Aunt. I was a little girl when I knew him in England. I
never thought of such a thing as lovers. Here I have met him,
but a few times as I say, and always in the presence of others.
We have had no opportunity, if we had the desire to be lovers.

"Always in the presence of others," Miss Dormer repeats,
her basilisk gaze never leaving her niece's unflinching face.
" Who were the ' others ' the night you stole out of your bed-
room window at school, to meet him in darkness, and by stealth,
in the grounds of your school ? "

" They have told you that, then !" exclaims Cyrilla, in confusion. " Aunt, dear aunt ! do not be angry. I *did* do that—
a rash act, I allow, and one for which I nearly suffered severely,
but I did it only to hear news of papa. You do not believe me,
perhaps."—Oh ! the infinite scorn and unbelieving of Miss
Dormer's face—but I love my father, and am always glad and
eager to hear news of him. Fred Carew was just from England,
he had seen him shortly before, and brought from him a message
for me. He tried to deliver it at Mrs. Delamere's—where by
purest accident we met—but an odious woman, one of the
teachers, gave him no chance. I was dying to hear it—I know
and regret my folly, aunt—I did steal out and spend ten minutes
with him in the garden ; not more. The woman—a detestable
spy—found me out, and Mlle. Chateauroy threatened to expel
me. Aunt, I assure you that was the first and only time—oh,
well ! with one exception."

" And that exception, my dear Niece Cyrilla?"

" Was in New York. Leaving Miss Owenson's house one
day, I encountered him in Madison Square. He rode down
town with me in the omnibus, and in that omnibus we met by

chance, Miss Jones, the spying teacher. It is from her all this
has come. I know how spiteful, and contemptible, and false a
wretch she is."

" And that is all, Niece Cyrilla—all ? You never met him
at Mrs. Delamere's here in Montreal, or at that other woman's
—what is her Irish name—Fogarty ? "

" Aunt Phil, I told you I had met him a few times, but always
in the presence of others. I did not mention it to you at the
time. I was afraid you would forbid my accepting any more
invitations, and these parties were all the pleasure I had. Was
it any such great crime to meet him by accident there ? "

" No crime at all, only—what a pity you did not tell me. It
would be so much easier to believe you now, if you had not deceived me then. And this is all, absolutely all ? "

" All, Aunt Dormer ! " Unflinchingly still, the black steadfast eyes above met the fiercely questioning eyes below.

" He is not your lover ? "

" My lover ! Nonsense ! This is Miss Jones' or Mrs. Fogarty's doing. They were both in love with him themselves."

" What a fascinating young Lovelace he must be ! I should
like to see him. He is not your husband then, Niece Cyrilla ? "

" My——" But this joke is so stupendous that Cyrilla laughs
aloud.

" You did not live with him as his wife for a week in New
York ? " pursues Miss Dormer. Her eyes never seem to wink,
never seem to go for a second from her niece's face. Cyrilla
starts up indignantly, as if this were past bearing.

" Aunt Dormer ! " she exclaims haughtily, " this is beyond
a jest. Even you have no right to say to me such things as
these. If you choose to believe my enemies, women who hate
and are jealous of me—who will stop at no lie to ruin me—then
I have no more to say ! "

She stands before her, her dark eyes flashing, her dark face
eloquent with outraged pride. As a piece of acting, the *posé*,
the look, were admirable. When she said she would have
played Lady Teazle better than poor Dolly De Courcy, there
can be no doubt she spoke the truth.

" 'Then it is all false—all ? You own to having gone out of
the window to meet this young man ? " says Miss Dormer, checking off the indictments on her skinny fingers, " to having met
him at the Delamere's and at the Fogarty woman's. You own
to having come upon him by accident in New York, and ridden
with him in an omnibus. But he never was your lover, and he

is not your husband. You never lived with him for a week in
a New York hotel. That is how the case stands?"

Cyrilla bows; her face pale, her eyes black, her form erect,
her look indignant.

"You see I want to make things clear," continues Miss
Dormer, almost apologetically; "my time may be short," a
spasm convulses her face; "and a good deal depends on it.
Mr. McKelpin will be here next week, and your innocence
must be proven before he returns. I would rather believe these
women false than you. You will not mind denying all this in
their presence, I suppose, Niece Cyrilla?"

"Certainly not, Aunt Dormer."

"Then I think that will do. I am tired with all this talking.
Sit down there, and take that book, and read me to sleep."

Cyrilla obeys. Her heart is beating in loud, muffled throbs,
she feels sick and cold, a loathing of herself fills her. But she
will not go back—on the dark road she is treading there seems
no going back.

At noon the doctor comes, and Cyrilla quits the sick-room
for a breathing-spell. In that interval the doctor receives from
his patient a message for "the Fogarty woman." She is to
wait upon Miss Dormer with her friend Miss Jones at five
o'clock. She also dictates a note to a third person, which the
obliging physician undertakes to deliver.

Miss Dormer keeps her niece under her eye until about half-
past four in the afternoon. Then she despatches her to the
druggist's, with orders to be back precisely at five. Cyrilla is
glad to go out, glad to breathe the fresh, clear air. The
walk is long, she hurries fast, gets what she wants and hurries
back. But, in spite of her haste, it is ten minutes past five when
she lets herself in, and runs up to her aunt's chamber. She
flings open the door and enters hastily.

"The druggist kept me some time waiting while he——"

She has got this far when she breaks off, and the sentence is
never finished. Her eyes have grown accustomed to the dusk
of the room, and she sees sitting there, side by side, her two
mutual foes—Mrs. Fogarty and Miss Jones.

"You know these two ladies, Niece Cyrilla?" says the shrill,
piping voice of Miss Dormer.

Cyrilla stands before them, her black eyes flashing—yes, literally and actually seeming to flash fire. Mrs. Fogarty's gaze
sinks; but Miss Jones, the better hater of the two, meets, with
her light, sinister orbs, that look of black fury.

"It is my misfortune, Aunt Dormer," says Cyrilla in a ringing voice, "to have known them once. I know them no more, except as slanderers and traducers!"

The strong English words flash out like bullets. For a moment, they, with truth on their side, flinch and quail. It is a pugilistic encounter à *la mort*, and the first blood is for Cyrilla.

"Ha! well put," says Miss Dormer, a gleam of something like admiration in the looks she gives her niece. Whatever else the Hendricks lacked, they never lacked pluck, right or wrong. Open the shutters, my dear, and let in the light on this business."

It is the first time in all her life that Miss Dormer has called the girl "my dear." Cyrilla stoops over her, and for the third time in her life, kisses her.

"Do not believe their falsehoods, Aunt Phil," she cries passionately. "I am your niece; your own flesh and blood. They hate me, both of them. They have laid this plot to ruin me. Do not let them do it."

"Prove them false, and they shall not," Miss Dormer answers, her old eyes kindling with almost a kindly gleam. "You are my own flesh and blood, as you say, and blood is thicker than water. Open the shutters and raise me up."

She is obeyed. It is to be a duel to the death. Every nerve in the girl's body is braced, she will stop at nothing—at *nothing*, to defeat these two. A rain of amber sunset comes in ; over the thousand metal roofs and shining crosses of Montreal the May sun is setting. Miss Dormer is propped up, and looks for a moment wistfully out at that lovely light in the sky—last sunset she will ever see.

It is a highly dramatic scene. The death-room, the two accusers sitting side-by-side, the culprit standing erect, her haughty head thrown back, her eyes afire, her red lips one rigid line, her hands unconsciously clenched.

"Niece Cyrilla, there is a Bible yonder on the table. Hand it here."

It is given. Miss Dormer opens it, and takes out a folded paper.

"Niece Cyrilla, look!" she says, and holds it up; "it is my will! Last night while you slept I sent for my lawyer and made it. It bequeaths everything—everything—to Donald McKelpin--it does not leave you a penny. If I die without a will, all is yours, as you know. Prove these two ladies wrong in what they have come here to accuse you of, and I will give you this paper to burn or destroy as you see fit, and my solemn promise to make no other."

A gleam like dark lightning leaps from Cyrilla's eyes. Prove them wrong! What is there that she will stop at to prove them wrong?

"My Niece Cyrilla," goes on the sick woman, turning to Miss Jones, "admits that she stole out of her room to meet this young officer one night in the school garden. She admits," looking at Mrs. Fogarty, "having met him at your house and at Mrs. Delamere's. She admits," glancing again at Miss Jones, "having encountered him by accident in New York, and riding with him a short distance in the omnibus. But all else she denies, positively and totally denies. Mr. Carew is not her lover, is not and never will be her husband. She is to marry Mr. Donald McKelpin next week. Now, which am I to believe—my niece, ladies, or you?"

"Your niece is a most accomplished actress, madam," says the saw-like voice of Miss Jones; "she can tell a deliberate falsehood and look you straight in the face while telling it. She may not be Mr. Carew's wife—all the worse for Mr. McKelpin if she is not; for she certainly lived with Mr. Carew as *Mrs.* Carew in New York for a whole week. I saw them enter the hotel together, I inquired of the clerk, and he told me they had been there together five days as man and wife."

"Niece Cyrilla," says Miss Dormer, "what have you to say to this?"

"Nothing to her," replied Cyrilla; "to you I say it is false! totally false; a fabrication from beginning to end."

"Let us call another witness," says Miss Dormer, "since we don't seem able to agree. Open that door, Mrs. Fogarty, and ask the gentleman to walk in."

The widow arises and does as she is told, and for the first time Cyrilla starts and blanches. For there enters Fred Carew! She turns blind for an instant—blind, faint, sick. All her strength seems to go. She gives an involuntary gasp, her eyes dilate, she grasps a chair-back for support; then she sees the exultant faces of her enemies, and she rallies to the strife again. No, no, no! they shall not exult in her fall.

Fred Carew advances to the side of the bed, nearest the door. Cyrilla stands directly opposite. He looks at her, but her eyes are upon her aunt. He nods coldly to Mrs. Fogarty, and addresses himself to the mistress of the house;

"You sent for me, madam?" he briefly says.

She looks at him—a strange expression on her face. "I am going to see a ghost," she had said to her niece. Surely it is like seeing a ghost to see another Frederick Carew, with the same blood in his veins, the same look in his eyes, at her bedside after five-and-twenty years.

The old smoldering wrong seems to blaze up afresh from its white ashes! As in that distant time she hated and cursed the father, so now she has it in her heart to hate and curse the son.

"I sent for you, sir," she answers, "to settle a very vexed question. A simple yes or no will do it, for you are an officer and a gentleman, with noble blood in your veins—the blood of the Carews—incapable of deceiving a poor, weak woman." Oh! the sneer of almost diabolical malice in eyes and voice as she says it! Fred's face flushes. "It is only this—is my niece, Cyrilla Hendrick, your wife, or not?"

He looks across the bed and their eyes meet.

"For heaven's sake, Fred, say no!" her eager, imploring glance says. "Tell the truth, Cyrilla!" his command, imperiously. "For my sake!" their softening look adds.

"Speak!" Miss Dormer cries fiercely; "don't look at her. Speak for yourself! is she your wife or not?"

"I decline to answer so extraordinary a question," Fred says, coolly. "If I had known your object in sending for me, Miss Dormer, I would not have come."

"Do you deny that she is?"

"I deny nothing—I affirm nothing. Whatever Miss Hendrick says, that I admit."

"She is Miss Hendrick, then—you own that?"

"I have never heard her called anything else, madam."

"Will you speak, or will you not!" cries Miss Dormer, in a fury. "Are you my niece's husband? Did she live with you in New York as your wife?"

He folds his arms and stands silent.

"And silence gives assent," says the spiteful voice of Miss Jones.

"Speak, sir!" goes on Miss Dormer. "I am a dying woman, and I demand to know the truth. What is my niece to you?"

"My very dear friend. More, I positively refuse to say."

"Cyrilla!" the old woman almost shrieks, "he will not speak—you shall. Come nearer and repeat what you have already said. Is that man your husband or not!"   .

The agony of that moment! There are drops on Cyrilla's face—cold, clammy drops. A rope seems to be tightening around her neck and strangling her. Across the bed, Fred Carew's eyes are sternly fixed on her changing face.

"Speak!" her aunt screams, mad and furious.

"He—is not!"

"You never lived with him in New York as his wife?"

"I did not."

"You are not married to him, and never will be."

"I am not, and never will be."

"Swear it!" cries the sick woman, frenzied with excitement. "Your word will not suffice. I must have your oath." She flings open the Bible at the Gospels. "Lay your hand on this book and say after me! I swear that Frederic Carew is not my husband, and never will be, so help me God!"

She lays her hand on the book—blindly, for she cannot see. A red mist fills the room and blots out every face except one—the one across the bed, that looks like the face of an avenging angel—the face of the husband she loves and is forswearing.

"Speak the words," cried Miss Dormer: "'I swear that Frederic Carew is not my husband'—begin!"

Oh! the terrific, ghastly silence. The two women have arisen, and stand pale and breathless.

"I swear—that Frederic Carew—is——"

Her face, the livid hue of death a second before, turns of a deep dull red, the cord around her throat, strangling her, all at once loosens, and she falls headlong across her aunt's bed.

"She has been saved from perjury," says the sombre voice of Miss Jones.

Fred Carew is by her side as she falls. He lifts her in his arms and carries her out of the room. Old Joanna is without in the passage, and recoils at the sight of the young man's stony face and the burden he bears.

"Take her up to her room," she says, and leads the way. "Poor dear, has she fainted?"

Cyrilla has not fainted—vertigo, congestion, whatever it may be. She is conscious of who carries her; knows when she is laid upon her bed, in a dull, painless, far-off way. She tries to open her eyes; the eyelids only flutter, but he sees it. His face touches hers for a second.

"Good-bye—good-bye!" he says.

Then, still in that dulled, far-off way, she knows that he has left her; she hears the house door open and shut, and feels, through all her torpor, that for the first and last time in his life, Fred Carew has crossed Miss Dormer's threshold.

CHAPTER XXVI.

"OH! THE LEES ARE BITTER, BITTER."

HE lies there for the remainder of the day, while the rose light of the sunset fades out, and the pale primrose afterglow comes. The moon rises, and her pearly lustre mingles in the sky with the pink flush of that May sunset. The house door has opened and shut again and again, while she lies mutely there, and she knows that her triumphant enemies have gone, that Dr. Foster has come, for it is his heavy step that ascends the stairs now.

A torpor, that is without pain or tears, or sorrow or remorse fills her, and holds her spell-bound in her bed. Her large, black, melancholy eyes are wide open, and stare blankly out of the curtainless windows, as she lies, her hands clasped over her head. She can see the myriad city roofs, sparkling in the crystal light of moonrise and sunset, a dozen shining crosses piercing the blue heaven, which she feels she will never see. As she gazes at them dreamily, the bell of a large building near clashes out in the quivering opal air. It is a convent, and the bell is the bell of the evening Angelus. How odd to think that there are people about her, scores and scores of people who can kneel before consecrated altars, with no black and deadly sins to stand between them and the holy and awful face of God.

And now it is night. All the little pink clouds have faded in pallid gray, and the clustering stars shine down upon Montreal. How still the house is. Are they both dead—her aunt and Joanna? No! While she thinks it, Joanna comes in with a cup of tea and a slice of toast.

"Better, miss?" says the old servant, interrogatively. "Would have come sooner. Could not get away. Waiting on *her*. Very low to-night. Eat something, miss."

Cyrilla drinks her tea thirstily, and makes an effort to get up. It is a failure—there is something the matter with her head; she falls heavily back.

"Lie still, miss. You look gashly. I'll stay with her to-night. Have a sleep, miss." And old Joanna takes her tray and untouched toast, and goes.

So she lies. Presently the high bright stars and the twinkling city lights fade away in darkness. There is a long blank—then all at once, without sound of any kind, she awakes and sits up in bed, her heart beating fast. Some one is in her room, and a light is burning. It is old Joanna, standing at her bedside, shading a lamp with her hand.

"She's gone, miss," says Joanna.

"Gone!" Cyrilla repeats vaguely; "who? Gone where?"

"Yes—where?—I'd like to know," says Joanna, staring blankly for information at the papered wall. "The Lord knows, *I* don't. But she's gone. Went half-an-hour ago. Four o'clock to a minute. The cocks begun to crow, and she riz right up with a screech, and went."

The girl sits staring at her—her great black eyes looking wild and spectral in her white face.

"All night long she talked," pursued Joanna; "talked—talked stiddy. It was wearin' to listen. About England and the time when she was young, I reckon, and Frederic Carew and Donald McKelpin, and her wild brother Jack. That's what she called him. And she talked it out crazy and loud like, else I wouldn't a-heerd her. It was awful wearin'. Then she was quiet. Kind o' dozin'. I was dozin' myself. For it was *very* wearin'. Then the cocks crowed for mornin'. Then she riz right up with that screech, and went. Will you come, miss? It's wearin' there alone."

Cyrilla rises and goes. The house is so still—so deathly still that their footsteps echo loudly as they walk. The shaded lamp still burns in Miss Dormer's room, and on the bed, stark and rigid, with wide-open, glassy eyes and ghastly fallen jaw, Miss Dormer lies—the "rich Miss Dormer." Lonely, loveless and unholy has been her life—lonely, loveless and unholy has been her death. Even old Joanna, not easily moved, turns away with a creeping feeling of repulsion from this grisly sight.

"She won't make a handsome corpse, poor thing," remarks Joanna, holding up the lamp, and eyeing her critically, as if she had been waxwork; "but I suppose we must lay her out. We must shut her eyes and put pennies on 'em. And wash her. And make a shroud, and straight her out. And——"

"I cannot!" the girl cries out, turning away, deathly sick, "it would kill me to touch her. You must go for some one or else wait until some one comes."

But Joanna does neither. Dead or alive, she is not afraid of Miss Dormer. She goes phlegmatically to work and does all herself, while Cyrilla sits or rather crouches in a corner, her folded arms resting on the window-sill, her face lying upon them. She has stood face to face with death before, calmly and unmoved, but never—oh! never with death like this. So—when morning, lovely, sunlit, Heaven-sent, shines down upon the world again, it finds them. The sun floods the chamber with its glad light, until old Joanna impatiently jerks down the blinds in its face. On her bed Miss Dormer lies, her ghastly eyeballs crowned with coin of the realm, her skeleton arms stretched stiffly out by her sides, but the mouth is still open, the jaw still fallen, in spite of the white bandage.

"I knowed it," Joannna observes, with a depressed shake of her ancient head, stepping back to eye her work. "You *can't* make a handsome corpse of her, let you do ever so."

Then her eye wanders from the dead aunt to the living niece. "You ain't no use here, miss," she says, with asperity. "You'd better come down with me to the kitchen, and I'll make you a cup 'o strong tea. It's been a wearin' night."

They descend, and the strong tea is made and drank, and does Cyrilla good. Joanna bustles about her morning duties. At nine o'clock Doctor Foster knocks, is admitted, hears what he expects to hear, that his work is finished, and his patient has taken a journey, in the darkness of the early dawn, from this world to the next.

After that, many people, it seems to Cyrilla, come and go—come to look at the rich Miss Dormer in death, who would never have crossed that doorway in her life. Mrs. Fogarty and Miss Jones come with the rest. She sees them from her bedroom window, but she is conscious of no feeling of anger or resentment at the sight. All that is dead and gone—gone forever—with hope, and love, and ambition, and daring, and all the plans of her life. Only a day or two ago—a day or two! it seems a lifetime! She keeps her room through it all, stealing down to the kitchen now and then, through the startling stillness of the house, for the strong tea or coffee on which she lives. No one sees her, though dozens come with no other object. For the story—her story—is over the city. Mysterious hints of it are thrown out in the morning papers; it is the chit-

chat of barrack and boudoir, mess-table and drawing-room
Nothing quite so romantic and exciting has ever before happened in their midst, and Mrs. Fogarty and Miss Jones awake
and find themselves famous.   The heroine keeps herself shut
up, ashamed of herself, very properly; the hero is invisible,
too.   And how has Miss Dormer left her money !   That is the
question that most of all exercises their exercised minds.

The day of the funeral comes, and Miss Dormer, in her cof-
lin, goes out, for the first time in years, through her own front
gates.   It is quite a lengthy and eminently respectable array of
carriages that follow the wealthy lady to her grave.

"I am the Resurrection and the Life.   He that believeth in
Me, although he be dead, shall live ; and every one that liveth
and believeth in Me, shall not die forever !" says the reverend
gentleman in the white bands who officiates, and they lower
Miss Dormer into her last narrow home, and the clay goes rattling down on the coffin lid.   It is a wet and windy day ; the
cemetery looks desolation itself—a damp and uncomfortable
place in which to take up one's abode.   The sexton flings
in the clods, and no tears are shed and no sorrow is felt.
They are glad to get back to the shelter of their carriages, and
men laugh and crack jokes about Fred Carew and the dead
woman's niece all the way home.

The dead woman's niece has not gone to the funeral.   Old
Joanna alone represents the household.   The doctor is there,
and the lawyer is there, for they expect ample fees for their
pains presently ; but the dead woman's niece expects nothing.
She sits in her lonely room ; a lost feeling that something has
gone wrong with her head ever since that cord snapped around
her throat and she fell across her aunt's bed—her principal
feeling.   She puts her hand to it in a forlorn, weary way, wondering why it feels so oddly *hollow*, as if the thinking machine
inside had run down, and the key was lost.   She suffers no
acute pain, either mental or physical, only she seems to have
lost the power both to sleep or eat, and does not feel the need
of either. ￼ There is a tiresome, ceaseless sense of aching at
her heart, too; a blunted sense of misery and loss, that never
for a moment leaves her.   She plucks at it sometimes, as if to
pluck away the intolerable gnawing ; but it goes on and on,
like the endless torture of a lost soul.

Mr. Pompet, the lawyer, has come to look after bonds and
mortgages, receipts, bank accounts and papers of value, to remove them to his own safe, until the arrival of Mr. McKelpin.

He is engaged in this work when the door of the room opens, and a figure comes gliding toward him—a figure with a face so white, ·eyes so black, and weird, and large ; that, albeit not a nervous man, Mr. Pompet drops the deed he holds and starts. up with a stifled ejaculation. It is the dead woman's niece.

" Don't let me disturb you." The weird, dark eyes look at him—the faint, tired voice speaks. " I will only remain a moment. You are the lawyer who made Miss Dormer's will ?"

"Yes, miss—I mean Mrs.——" Here Mr. Pompet comes to a dead lock. He has heard so much about Miss Hendrick being Mrs. Carew, that he is at a loss how to address her.

" I am Miss Dormer's niece. Will you tell me how she has left her money?" He looked at her compassionately—how wretchedly ill the poor girl is looking, he thinks. A handsome girl, too, in spite of her pallor and wild-looking eyes—Lieutenant Carew has had taste. " Has Mr. McKelpin got it all? Don't be afraid to tell me, or—am I remembered?"

" Except a small bequest of one hundred dollars to her servant Joanna, Mr. McKelpin has it all," answers the lawyer.

"I am not even mentioned in her will?"

Again Mr. Pompet is silent—again he looks embarrassed and compassionate.

" Please answer," she says, wearily. " I would rather know."

" You are mentioned then, but only to say she has disinherited you for your falsehood and deceit, and to warn Mr. McKelpin in no case to aid or help you."

She bends her head with the old graceful motion.

" Thank you," she says, and goes.

So it is over, and she knows the worst—it is only what she has known all along. the lawyer has but made assurance doubly sure. In striving to keep love and fortune she has lost both. She has lost all, good name, lover, home, wealth, everything she has held most dear. And her own falsehood has done it all. If she had been honest and dealt fairly by her aunt, she would at least, as Donald McKelpin's wife, have been a rich woman. If she had been honest and dealt fairly by Fred Carew, she would have had his love and presence to comfort her. But she has lost both. Truly, even for the children of this world, honesty is the best policy—truly, also, the way of the transgressor is hard, and the wages of sin is death.

Another night falls upon the lonesome, dark old house, another ghostly, hushed sleepless night. She lies through the long, black, dragging hours, and listens to the rain pattering

11*

on the glass, and the wind blowing about the gables. " Blessed is the corpse that the rain rains on," says the children's rhyme. The rain is beating on Aunt Dormer's grave—is Aunt Dormer blessed ? she wonders.

Again it is morning—another gray, wet morning. In the early dawn, sleep reluctantly comes to her, and with sleep dreams. The sleeping is more cruel than the waking, for she dreams of her husband. She is back with him in New York, living over again that one bright honeymoon week—that week that will stand out from all the other weeks of her life. With a a smile on her lips she awakens, and then a moment after there is a desolate cry. For the truth has come back to her with a pain sharper than the pain of death. She has heard nothing of him or from him since their parting—she never will again—that she knows. That whispered ' good-bye' was for all time. Why should she expect otherwise ? In the face of all she denied him—forswore him. What could he have left but scorn and contempt for her. It never occurs to her to think of see-ing or hearing from him again. Her sentence is passed—its justice she does not dispute.

That forenoon brings a telegram from Mr. McKelpin. He has landed at Quebec—by to-morrow he will be in Montreal. Her brief respite is at an end—she must be up and doing now. She has no right in Donald McKelpin's house. He is an honest man, and she has betrayed him. She has no intention of allowing him to find her here—by to-morrow morning's early train she will go.

She will go—but where ? In all the world she has neither home nor friends. She thinks of Sydney, good little, loyal Sydney—but Sydney is far away. Still she has her plans. In the long watches of the night she has made up her mind to go to New York. Why, she does not know ; only in a great city it is so easy to lose one's self, to die to all one has ever known. Perhaps there she will get rid of this gnawing, miserable pain at her heart ; perhaps there, her wandering brain may feel as it used. And she has been so happy there—so happy. She will go back, and walk in the places where they used to walk together, as Eve may have come back and looked over the closed gates of Eden. And then—well, then, perhaps, there may be mercy for her, and she may die. She is of no use in the world, of no use to any one—she is a wicked wretch, of whom the earth will be well rid—"a sinner viler than them all." People die every day, every hour ; why should not she?

To-morrow morning comes. She has packed her trunk and her little hand-bag. Old Joanna fetches her a hack, and she puts on her hat, and holds out her hand and says good-bye to the old creature mechanically, and tells her (when asked) that she is going to New York. She never once lifts her heavy eyes to take a last look at the gloomy red brick house as the hack bears her away.

She has some money—not much, but enough. Since their marriage Fred has made her his banker. It will take her to New York—after that, it doesn't matter what happens.

She is in the cars. She lays her head with a tired-out feeling against the window, and closes her eyes. They are flying along in the warm June morning, and thoughts of the last time she made this journey, not yet a month ago, drift vaguely through her mind. She never looks up or out. Her forehead is resting against the cool glass—it feels to her like a friendly hand; and so, dead to all about her, dead to herself, to everything that makes life dear, Cyrilla drifts out of the old life—whither, she neither knows nor cares.

PART SECOND.

CHAPTER I.

SYDNEY.

"Yet, is this girl I sing in naught uncommon,
And very far from angel, yet I trow
Her faults, her sweetnesses are purely human,
And she's more lovable as simple woman
Than any one diviner that I know."

TWO o'clock of a cold November afternoon, a shrill rising wind, whistling up and down the city streets, stripping the gaunt brown trees of their last sere and yellow leaf, and making little ripples all along the steely pools of water, which the morning's rain has left. The rain has ceased now, but a gray, fast-drifting sky yet lowers over New York, ominously suggestive of the first wintry fall of snow. Omnibuses rattle up and omnibuses rattle down, private carriages, all aglitter of black varnish, prancing horses and liveried coachmen whirl up park-ward. A few ladies trip past in the direction of Broadway, a few beggar children creep around the areas. That is the street scene, the tall young lady with the fair hair, mourning dress, sits and looks at rather listlessly, considering that more than four years have elapsed since these blue-gray eyes looked upon it before. The young lady is Miss Sydney Owenson, newly returned from a five years' sojourn abroad, and domiciled with her late mother's cousin, Mrs. Macgregor, of Madison Avenue.

Her mother, Mrs. Owenson, is dead. Except these cousins, Sydney Owenson, orphan and heiress, stands quite alone in the world. Four years ago, one sunny May day, Captain Owenson's widow and only child left New York for Havre. Four quiet pleasant years followed for poor badgered Aunt Char; more quiet and pleasant than Aunt Char would ever have owned even to herself, with no terrible marital voice to thunder at her for the thousand and one foolish little deeds and speeches of every day. There was one long balmy winter in Florence, another in Rome, where the churches and picture galleries, the delights of her daughter's heart, made her head ache, and where St. Peter's with its splendors and its vastness, and its majestic music and wondrously beautiful ceremonies, nearly tired her to death. Physically, mentally and morally, Aunt Char was weak, and growing weaker every day. For Sydney, that Roman winter was one long dream of delight ; it seemed to her mother she literally lived in the churches and picture galleries. The summers were spent rambling in a vagabond sort of way through Switzerland, Germany and Bavaria. The fourth winter was spent in Paris, and in that city Aunt Char's feeble hold on life grew weaker and weaker ; and one bleak spring morning ·Sydney awoke, to find herself an orphan indeed, and that weak and gentle mother, lying with folded hands and placid face and life's labor done.

Four years before, on that December morning when she knelt down by her dead father's bed, the girl had been a child, a very child in heart and knowledge, in thought and feeling. But with that day her childhood seemed to cease, and womanhood to dawn. She had loved her feeble little mother very dearly, but never—no never—as she had loved her father. In those years of aimless wandering hers had been the guiding spirit, hers the ruling voice. To rule was not in Mrs. Owenson's nature— all her life she had been meekly under orders until its very last day. Strong, self-reliant, fearless, she looked upon her slim, stately young daughter with wonder and admiration, and leaned upon her from the first day of her husband's death. That by-gone tragedy had left its impress upon the girl for life. Grave beyond her years, with a gravity most people found very charming, thoughtful, but very gentle and sweet, her seriousness was an added witchery. She had shot up in these years, supple and tall, healthful and handsome, with eyes as bright as these southern skies, at which they gazed, a complexion not pale, and yet colorless, and a fearless frankness of manner, that her unfettered, wandering life could not fail to give. In her heart, her whole life long, she would mourn for the father she had so dearly loved, the brother who was to have been her husband ; but her face was bright as the sunshine itself, and the handsome American heiress did not reach her twenty-first birthday, be very sure, without more than one manly heart and hand (more or less short of ready money) being laid at her shrine, and just at present it was the business of the Macgregor family to discover whether their fair and rich relative had brought her heart home with her, or had left that useful organ behind in foreign parts. She had been with them three weeks now, and the discovery had not been satisfactorily made yet, and Dick Macgregor, son of the house and graduate of West Point, was growing seriously anxious on the subject.

Miss Owenson had remained a full year abroad after her mother's death with some English friends, whose acquaintance she had made in Paris. These friends were Sir Harry Leonard and his sister, a maiden lady of forty. With the sister, Miss Owenson frankly owned to having fallen in love at sight—the brother, Mrs. Owenson had more than hinted in her letters, had done precisely the same with Sydney. Sir Harry was a man of thirty, not bad-looking, and rich enough in Cornish tin mines to put the possibility of mercenary motives entirely out of the question. Miss Owenson had spent many months following her mother's death with Miss Leonard, and now the question arose, was Sydney the *fiancé* of Sir Harry Leonard? Dick Macgregor, his mother, and sister revolved this question in all its bearings and revolved in vain. Sydney was serenely silent on all these tender matters, and there was a quiet dignity about her that forbade questions. Dick's attentions she took with a cousinly indifference and good nature that was exasperating to a degree.

"It seems a pity to let the fortune—a million, if a dollar—go out of the family," says Mrs. Macgregor, knitting her brows, until they made a black archway over her lofty Roman nose.

"If she were to marry Dick, I needn't sell myself to that fat beast, old Vanderdonck," says Miss Macgregor, with considerable asperity. "One of us must marry money or starve. Of course I will be the sacrifice, though. Old Vanderdonck is as fond of me as it is possible for him to be of anything, except his bank account, and Sydney is about as much in love with Dick as she is with your new black coachman, mamma. Who can wonder, though, after the men she has associated with abroad, and it's not your fault, I suppose, my poor Dick, that you've neither brains nor beauty."

"She's engaged to the baronet—that's where the trouble is," responds Dick, with a gloomy glance at his sister, "or that other fellow—what's his name, the German that wanted to marry her? American girls are all tarred with the same stick—

they'd marry the deuce himself, horns and hoof, if he only had a title."

Of this family conclave, of the plots and plans in regard to her, Miss Owenson was most supremely unconscious. Those bright gray eyes of hers would have opened very wide indeed if any one had told her Dick Macgregor wanted to marry her— not only wanted to marry her, but had fallen in love with her. She would stay with them for this winter, she thought, and after that—but the "after that" was not quite clear in Sydney's mind. Youth, beauty, many friends, two or three lovers, and great wealth are hers; but as she sits here to day and looks out at the bleak, wind-blown street, she feels lonely and sad enough. The Macgregors are relatives, and are very good to her after their light, but their house is not home, nor even like the Cornish home that was hers so lately, and oh! so unutterably unlike the dear old home at Wychcliffe forever lost now. This day is an anniversary—this day five years ago was the day before her wedding—this day five years ago, and just at this hour, she and Bertie Vaughan stood looking out at the whirling snow. Again she sees him lying back in his chair, that moody look on his blonde, boyish face; again she hears him speak, "Who knows what may happen? In the midst of life we are in death, and all that, you know." His words had been prophetic. Ah! poor Bertie. Looking back now, with the knowledge and experience of five years added upon her, Sydney knows that as Bertie's wife she would have been a supremely wretched woman. Looking back now, she knows he was weak and unstable as water—that she would have outgrown him, and that they would have wearied to death of the tie that bound them. She knows that for herself and her own happiness it is infinitely better as it is. Yet none the less does she regret him, none the less does she mourn his tragic end. The mystery of that night's disappearance is as dense a mystery as ever; nothing has ever come to light—nothing, it is probable now, ever will. Whether a murder was done, whether an accident befell him, may never be discovered. Of late years Sydney has inclined to the latter belief. Bertie had no enemies—not one—and just there an accident might very easily befall. A slip, a false step, and the rising tide would speedily bear away all traces.

She rises from her reverie with a sigh to the memory of those pleasant by-gone days, and goes in search of a book. The room she is in is called a library, although one small bookcase holds all its literature—the Macgregors are not a reading family. Pictures there are in profusion—chromos and engravings mostly; the carpet is soft and rich, the curtains are elegant and costly, the furniture is blue silk rep, and there are half-a-dozen lounging chairs. How Mrs. Macgregor furnishes her house, dresses her daughter, keeps her carriage, gives her quantum of parties in the season, and goes everywhere, is a conundrum several families on the avenue are interested in solving, and cannot. All this she does and more. Newport and Saratoga know them in the summer solstice; their seat at the opera and at Wallack's is always filled; they have an open account at Stewart's and another at Tiffany's. "And how on earth *does* Mrs. Macgregor do it," ask the avenue families, "when we all know how John Macgregor left her nothing but the house he lives in and a beggarly two thousand a year."

Miss Owenson takes down a book at random, and returns to her chair. The book turns out to be "Sintram," a very old friend, and a very great favorite—one that will bear reading many times, and the closing page of which Sydney has never yet reached with dry eyes. She opens near the middle and begins to read, and soon all things, all cares of her own, the very memory of her own life-sorrows, are lost in the ideal sorrows of "Sintram." Brave, tempted, noble, forsaken, her heart is with him through all, far more than with Sir Folko, stainless knight and happy husband. Her eyes are dewy as she reads lines that tell poor, tempted, sorrowing Sintram that his trials are almost done.

> "Death comes to set thee free;
> Oh! meet him cheerily,
> As thy true friend;
> Then all thy fears shall cease,
> And in eternal peace
> Thy penance end!"

"Sydney," calls a voice, the clear, fresh voice of Katherine Macgregor. Then the library door is thrown open by an impetuous gloved hand, and Katherine Macgregor, in stylish carriage costume, stately as her name, tall and elegant, rustles in.

"What! reading," she exclaims, and not dressed—and it is half-past three, and we promised to be ready at three, and poor Uncle Grif pottering about the drawing-room waiting for the last hour? Oh! this is too much! even my patience has its limits. What is that you have got hold of now?"

Without ceremony Miss Macgregor snatches the book, and her little, piquant *nez retroussé* curls scornfully as she glances at the title.

"Sintram and His Companions! That you should live to be two-and-twenty, and still addicted to fairy tales!"

" It isn't a fairy tale," says Miss Owenson, laughing.

" It is all the same—goblins and demons, and skeletons, and death's heads. Ugh! I began it once and had the nightmare after it. How any one can read such rubbish, with dozens of delicious new novels out every day, I cannot imagine."

" Your new novels are the rubbish, judging by the criticisms I read of them. One Sintram, wild, pathetic, old legend that it is, is worth the whole boiling——"

" I don't care for pathetic things," says Miss Katherine Macgregor, shrugging her shoulders ; " one's daily life and its worries are as pathetic a legend as *I* want to know anything about."

Sydney lifts her eyes and looks at her. A tall brunette, not really handsome, but making the most of herself, of a fine erect figure, a pair of sparkling black eyes, and set of very white teeth. Vivacity is becoming to Miss Macgregor's peculiar style, consequently Miss Macgregor is charmingly vivacious and high-spirited everywhere except—at home. Dull parties " go off " with Katie Macgregor to the fore ; heavy dinners are lightened ; very young men fall in love with her at sight ; married men are invariably smitten when they sit near her. She plays the piano well, waltzes well, dresses in excellent taste, sings a little, and can " take " Broadway of a sunny afternoon, with a dash and *élan* that makes every masculine head turn involuntarily to look again. And it must be added that Miss Macgregor's face is very well known on Broadway, indeed, better and longer than she likes to think, herself. She is three years Sydney's senior, and as she came out at sixteen, the ways of the wicked world are as a twice told tale to Katherine Macgregor, and Money and Matrimony—" the two capital M's," as her brother Dick calls them—long ago became the leading aims of her life. As indeed of what well regulated young women are they not ?

" *You* worried, Katie?" Sydney says, still laughing; " do my ears deceive me? Who would think Katie Macgregor, the 'Sunbeam of New York,' as I heard poor young Van Cuyler call you last night, had a care."

" The laughing hyena of New York is brother Dick's name for it, and the more suitable of the two," responds Miss Macgregor, rather bitterly. " To eat, drink, and be merry, mamma

told me when I was sixteen, was to be my *rôle* through life—
laughter is becoming, you know, to people with white teeth
and black eyes, so I began at her command, and have gone on
ever since. It has become second nature by this time, but to
laugh is one thing, to be happy another."

"What is the trouble, dear?" Sydney asks; "is it anything
in which I can help you? If so——"

"Thanks, Syd—no, you cannot help me, unless you can induce somebody to leave me fifty or sixty thousand dollars.
Dollars, the great want of the world, are *my* want. With them
I need not become Mrs. Cornelius Vanderdonck—without
them I must."

"Katie! Old Mr. Vanderdonck! Ill-tempered, rheumatic,
sixty years! You surely do not dream of marrying him?"

"I surely do—only too happy and thankful to have him ask
me. I am tired, tired and sick, Sydney, of the life we lead,
hand to mouth, pinching here, and saving there; servants un-
paid, bills, duns, mamma nearly at her wits' end. Oh! you
don't know! In my place you would be as mercenary and heartless as I am."

"But I thought," Sydney says, with a puzzled look, "that
Aunt Helen was rich?" (Aunt Helen is a convenient term for
her mother's cousin.) "If money matters are your only trouble,
Katie, why do you not draw on me? I have more than I can
possibly use, and you must know, Aunt Helen must know, that
I would be only too glad——"

"We know you are generosity itself, Sydney, dear," responds
Miss Macgregor, still with that touch of cynicism in her voice
that she keeps strictly for family use, "but even you might grow
weary after a time of supporting a large family of third cousins.
And of the two evils—marrying sixty years, ill-temper, and
ugliness, or swindling you to your face, I really think I prefer the
former. But this is all a waste of time." Miss Macgregor
pulls at her watch. "Twenty minutes to four and the daylight
waning already, and Von Etté's studio closes invariably at five.
I give you just ten minutes to dress, Miss Owenson. The carriage is already at the door."

"The new picture! I had forgotten all about it!" cries
Miss Owenson starting up. "Ten minutes is it, Katie? Very
well—in ten minutes I will be ready."

Strange to say, Miss Owenson keeps her word. In ten
minutes she descends, a seal jacket over her black silk dress, a
black hat with a long black plume on her head, and her fair

face and golden hair, very fair by contrast. Deep mourning Sydney has left off, colors she has not yet assumed.

"Uncle Grif grew tired of waiting," says Miss Macgregor, as they enter the carriage, "and toddled off by himself to meet us at Philippi—I mean at Von Etté's."

"Who is this Monsieur Von Etté?" Sydney asks. "His name is new to me."

"The name is new to us all. A year ago Carl Von Etté was a beggar—literally a beggar in the streets of New York, hawking his own pictures from door to door, and earning a crust and a garret. One day he fell down in a fainting fit in he street, from sheer starvation, and a man nearly as poor as himself, took him home, nursed him, encouraged him, and the result—Von Etté has painted a picture that the town talks of, and is on the high road to fame and fortune."

"And his friend—the good Samaritan—what of him?"

Sydney's eyes glisten as she asks the question. Her sympathetics are very quick—it is things like these that go home to her heart. For Miss Macgregor, her cynical look comes back.

"The good Samaritan is precisely where he was—the usual fate of good Samaritans, is it not?—plodding along in a lawyer's office. Lewis Nolan may be the cause of greatness to others, but I have a presentiment he will never be great himself. He has exploded theories about honor and honesty, that keep men back. Here we are. Raise your dress, Sydney. These stairs may have been swept during the last ten years, but I doubt it. Your true artist is a dirty creature, or nothing."

She lifts her glistening silk train and runs lightly up the stairs, her vivacious society face in its best working order. Miss Owenson, with an expression of extreme distaste for the dirty, unswept stairs, gathers up her skirts and follows.

"Shall we see the artist, Katie?" she asks.

"No, decidedly. Von Etté is a perfect miracle of ugliness—is next door to a dwarf, and has a hump. No one ever enters his studio when he is there but Uncle Grif and Lewis Nolan."

"The good Samaritian! Shall we see *him?*"

They have reached the landing. Miss Macgregor gives herself one small shake, and shakes every ribbon, every silken fold into its place in a second. She pauses at her cousin's question, and looks at her for a moment.

"Perhaps!" she answers, slowly; "and if we do, I want you to look at him well and tell me what you think of him. Lewis

Nolan has been my puzzle for the past ten years, and is more
my puzzle to-day than ever.   Let us see if *you* can solve it."
   She taps at the door, opens it, and the two young ladies are
in the studio.

CHAPTER II.

" SINTRAM."

T was a large and well-lighted room, the floor covered
with dark-red wool carpet, the walls colored of some
dull, neutral tint and, containing by way of furniture
three queer spindle-legged, old-fashioned chairs.
Three or four ladies and as many men stood clustered around
a picture—*the* picture, the only picture upon the wall.   At the
extreme end of the room two or three others hung—excepting
these the plastered walls were quite bare.
   "Von Ette's studio is as grim and ugly as himself," remarked
Miss Macgregor, taking in the place and the people with an
American girl's cool, broad stare.   "There is Uncle Grif gazing through his venerable old specs, lost in a trance of admiration, just as if he had never seen it before.   The dear old soul
has no more idea of art than a benevolent tom cat, but a sign-
board painted by little Von Etté would be in his eyes as a
Murillo or a Rubens in those of other people."
   M. Von Ette is then a *protégé* of Uncle Grif's?" asks Miss
Owenson.   "Let us take a seat until these good people disperse.   I detest looking at a picture over other's shoulders."
   "Carl Von Etté is a *protégé* of Lewis Nolan.   Lewis Nolan,
since he was twelve years old, has been a *protégé* of Uncle
Grif's ; while Uncle Grif, ever since I can remember, has been
mamma's abject slave.   I never knew him to rebel except on
one point, and that point this same Lewis Nolan.   ' The money
you spend upon that Irish boy, Brother Grif,' says mamma,
looking at him with *her* glance, beneath which the stoutest
heart may well blench, ' would be much more suitably employed
in educating your only sister's orphan children.   Charity begins
at home, sir.'   And Uncle Grif, bless him ! quails and trembles, and makes answer, in quivering falsetto, ' Little Lewis is

like a son to me, Sister Helen. It is but little that I can do
for him; that little I mean to do; whatever is left, you and the
children are welcome to, I'm sure.' "

Miss Macgregor, in her most vivacious tone, parodies her
mother and uncle without the smallest compunction, and the
mimicry is so good that Sydney has to laugh.

" Mr. Nolan is Irish, then, and poor ? "

" Of Irish extraction, and poor as a rat. His mother and
sister are seamstresses. He is a lawyer now, admitted to the
bar, thanks to uncle. He began life selling papers, was elevated to office-sweeping, was one of those boys you read of in
Sunday-school books, and goody literature generally, who are
athirst after knowledge, spend their leisure hours in hard study,
rise to be prime ministers, and marry a duke's daughter. Mr.
Nolan has not had greatness of any kind thrust upon him yet,
but, after all, I shouldn't be in the least surprised to see him a
ruler in the land before his hair is gray—one of those self-made
men, who are so dreadfully priggish and pompous, and who
never tell a lie in their lives. There! an opening at last. Now
let us go and look at the pictures."

Kate Macgregor's cynicisms and worldly knowledge, her sarcastic strictures, on every subject under the sun, were a never-
failing source of wonder and amusement to Sydney. A very
good type of the girl of the period was Miss Macgregor,
devouring with relish the newspaper literature of the day, mur-
ders, divorces, scandals the most atrocious, and ready to discuss and analyze the most revolting cases with perfect *sang
froid*—a girl to whom love had meant nothing since her seven-
teenth birth-day, and marriage and an establishment everything—a girl who flirted, waltzed, took presents, went to watering-places every summer, went to parties every winter, and in
the midst of all kept a bright look-out for the main chance—
a girl who looked calmly in the face of every man to whom she
was introduced, with these two questions uppermost in her
mind: "Is he rich?" and "Can I induce him to marry me ? "
Not an evil-minded or bad-hearted young woman by any
means; simply a latter-day young lady, true to the teachings
of her life, and of the world, worldly, to her inmost soul.

The little group before the painting had dispersed, and the
cousins were free to look at their leisure. Miss Macgregor
doubled up her gray gloved hands, pursed her lips, and set herself to find out its faults.

" H'm ! a very pretty picture—subject somewhat *triste—*

'The Little Sister.' Nuns are rather a hackneyed subject, but always effective. The gas-light falling on that girl's face is very good—very good, indeed—a fallen woman in more senses than one. The Sister's dress is painted with pre-Raphaelite fidelity, and the face—I should say, now, the face was painted from memory—not exactly pretty, but very sweet. I have seen Sisters of Charity with just that expression. Do you like it, Sydney—you, who have lived in an atmosphere of pictures, so to speak, for the last five years?"

"Like it?—yes." Sydney answers dreamily, and that eloquent face of hers—truly an eloquent face, where all feelings of the heart are concerned—says far more than the quiet words. The picture pleases her artistic sense, but it has done more—it has touched her heart, and she stands very silent and looks at it long. It is a city scene—a twilight scene. A primrose light yet lingers coldly in the wintry sky—the haze of early evening fills the air, and the street lamps blink dimly through it. One or two bright frosty stars pierce the chill opaline lustre, but day has not yet departed. In the archway of a large building a woman—a mere girl—seems to have fallen, huddling her rags about her in a strange, distorted attitude of pain. Her face is upturned, the gas flares upon it, and the haggard eyes stare fiercely in their infinite misery, their reckless, crazed despair. Above her, bending over her, her basket on her arm, stands a little Sister of the Poor, in her black nun's dress. Infinite compassion, angelic pity, heavenly sweetness, are in the nun's wistful face, its peace, its purity, its tender gentleness, in striking contrast with the fierce despair, the haggard pain, the reckless wretchedness of her sinning sister.

"Oh!" Sydney says, half under her breath, "how beautiful it is, how pathetic a story it tells! Katie, your Von Etté is a genius."

"Very likely," says Miss Macgregor, with one of her shrugs; "he is hideous enough, I am sure. The contrast between those two faces is very good. By-the-by, there is Mrs. Grierson—odious creature—and, as usual, disgustingly overdressed. I must go and speak to her. The idea of that woman coming to see a picture! the only painting she has soul enough to appreciate is the drop scene of a theatre, when Grierson isn't there, and she has a new flirtation in hand."

And then Miss Katherine sweeps gracefully and graciously over, and kisses her friend with effusion, and in a moment they are in the midst of a most animated conversation, abusing their

absent and mutual friends, no doubt, Miss Owenson thinks
with disdain. She presently leaves the picture she has come
to see and saunters down the room to view the others. They
are not of equal merit, rather poor in fact, with the exception
of one which rivets her attention from the first. For it is called
"Sintram," and is oddly enough a scene from the story she
was reading an hour ago.

It is a very small picture, but, in a different way, quite as
striking as "The Little Sister." A dead white expanse of
frozen snow, paling away into the gray and low-lying sky.
Black and spectral against this ghostly whiteness stands out the
tall, powerful figure of Sintram, his dark face, full of passion,
remorse, and horror. Behind him, leering and evil, tempting
him to the murder of his friend for the sake of that friend's wife,
crouches "The Little Master." Away in the distance, at the
foot of an icy precipice, lies prostrate and helpless the gallant
Sir Folko. But the interest of the picture centres in Sintram.
You can *see* the fierce battle between temptation and honor,
between the inherent ferocity and nobility of his nature, and
you wonder almost painfully how the struggle will end.

Sydney lingers, fascinated, and while she stands, Katherine
deserts her friend and returns to her. An exclamation from
Miss Macgregor makes her glance round; that young lady
pauses and gazes at "Sintram" with an inexplicable expression
of face.

"Is it not exquisite?" Sydney asks; "even better in its way
than the other? You can see the torture poor, tempted, loyal
Sintram is suffering in his very face."

"I don't know how it may depict Sintram," says Katie, in
her most caustic voice. "I know it is a very good portrait of
Lewis Nolan, although I never saw him wear any such gruesome
expression as that."

She stands and regards it with a look in her eyes that Syd
ney does not understand, but which is something deeper than
mere criticism.

"I wonder if it is for sale?" Sydney eagerly asks. "I should
like to buy it. It is my ideal Sintram exactly."

"You can very easily ascertain. Uncle Grif will negotiate
the transaction for you with Von Etté. I will call him now."

She breaks abruptly off. Uncle Grif still remains where she
has left him, but no longer meekly alone. A man has entered
and stands talking to him, his tall head slightly bent, a grave
smile on his face, Mr. Nolan, Sydney knows in a moment, partly

by the expression of her cousin's face, partly by his vivid resemblance to the "Sintram." Miss Macgregor is right, the
likeness is a very good one, lacking of course, the agony of
despair. A very tall man is Mr. Nolan. Sydney glances approvingly at the active figure and broad shoulders, with a black, close-
cropped head, and a dark, rather sallow face, a face whose
habitual expression will be that of profound gravity, but which
is lighted just now by a very genial smile. By no means a handsome face, but a very good one, a thinking face, a strong face,
the face, it might be, of a man of powerful passions, held well
in hand by a still more powerful will.

"Here they come," says Katherine Macgregor, half under her
breath. "Now, then, Sydney, solve my riddle if you can. Tell
me what manner of man Lewis Nolan is?"

"He is a man who carries himself well, at least," says Miss
Owenson, with a second calmly approving glance. "Your very
tall man slouches, as a rule ; Mr. Nolan does not."

"Lewis," says Uncle Grif, shambling up to his niece and
looking at her in meek deprecation, for the old man stands in
mortal awe of his dashing young relative, "this is Katherine,
my niece, Katherine. You remember Katherine, don't you?"

"It is much easier to remember Miss Katherine than to
forget her," says Mr. Nolan, with an amused glance into Miss
Katherine's laughing eyes. "My memory in some cases is
fatally good."

"Uncle Grif himself never remembers my existence five seconds after I am out of his sight, and naturally takes it for granted
the rest of mankind are equally criminal," says Katherine.

"We have come to see the picture, you perceive, Mr. Nolan.
It is charming. I have fallen quite in love with Mr. Von Etté
since I saw it. I always do fall in love with genius."

"Happy Von Etté—happy genius? Would that I—but of
what avail are wishes? I shall transport Carl to the seventh
heaven this evening by letting him know."

"As for this," says Miss Macgregor, with a graceful motion
toward the "Sintram," "my cousin is enchanted with it. Oh !—
excuse me—my cousin, Miss Owenson, Mr. Nolan. Quite a
foreigner, I assure you, and a judge of pictures ; has spent the
last five years of her existence running from one picture gallery
of Europe to another."

"Poor Van Etté ! How wretched the knowledge will make
him, that so formidable a connoisseur has been criticising his
poor attempts."

"I am afraid that speech is more sarcastic than sincere," answers Miss Owenson, coolly. "I am not in the least a critic. I know when a picture pleases me, and very often the picture that pleases me is one connoisseurs pass over in contempt."

"And 'The Little Sister,'" Mr. Nolan asks, "you really like it, I hope?"

"I really do. It is a charming subject, charmingly executed. But it may surprise you to hear, I like this better."

"That! 'Sintram?' Why, Von Etté put that in a corner out of the way. I am nothing of a judge myself; I fancied it rather good. I am not unprejudiced, though, for Sintram, on canvas or off it, is a very old friend of mine."

"Is he?" Miss Owenson, relaxes into an approving smile. "You have sat—stood rather—for this Sintram evidently." Mr. Nolan laughs.

"Yes—Von Etté read the book in one of his lazy evenings, and conceived the happy idea that I resembled the hero. Sintram had a black complexion, if you remember, and a corresponding ferocity of disposition; so the happy idea was not personally flattering. I posed with a tragic expression accordingly, and you see the result."

"A very satisfactory result," interposes Katie; "you have rather the look of a first murderer in a melodrama. Did you really hurl the gentleman yonder over the precipice in a transport of madness, or how? My recollections of Sintram are hazy."

Both young ladies, as it chances, are looking into Mr. Nolan's face and both see a most remarkable change pass over it as Katie Macgregor speaks. The dark, colorless complexion fades slowly to a gray white. But he neither starts, nor turns away; only Sydney notices that his hands tighten over the felt hat he holds.

"My favorite Sintram does no such dastardly deed," she says, coming intuitively to the rescue, and glancing away from Mr. Nolan's altered face, "Sir Folko falls over, and Sintram flies to the rescue like the gallant knight he is. Is the picture for sale, Mr. Nolan? I should like to have the pleasure of possessing it."

"It is for sale," he answers. "Von Etté will only be too glad to dispose of it."

He speaks quite calmly, but the traitor blood does not return. He is deadly pale still, and his eyes—very handsome

12

dark gray eyes Sydney notices, are fixed in a curious way on the
picture.

"Then, Uncle Grif, may I commission you to purchase it for
me," says Miss Owenson. "I really have seen nothing in a
long time which has so completely taken my fancy."

Uncle Griff is no kin of Miss Owenson's, but he is Uncle
Grif to all who have ever known him. Indeed, his sprightly
niece goes so far as to affirm that in his tender years he was
"Uncle Grif" to the other boys of the school. A thin,
patient-looking old man, whom you intuitively know for an old
bachelor at sight, badgered by his strong-minded sister, patronized by his nephew and niece, and imposed upon in a general
way by all the world. One of those men who battle weakly all
their lives with Mammon, and end as they began, hopelessly
poor—one of the great brigade of the Unsuccessful.

"Uncle Grif tells us you are engaged in the great Harland
case, Mr. Nolan,"- remarks Katherine Macgregor.

"As junior counsel—yes."

He answers rather dreamily, his eyes still fixed with that curiously intent look upon the "Sintram."

"It is a great opening, is it not? You will have a chance—
and you only need a chance, I am sure, to distinguish yourself."

"Mr. Graham will have chance enough ; there is very little
for me."

He takes no notice of her smooth compliment ; he appears to
answer mechanically, his thoughts with the picture, or something
it suggests.

"You are for the defence," persists his fair inquisitor—"for
Mrs. Harland, are you not ? "

"Yes."

"Poor thing ! "—Katherine heaves a sympathetic sigh—"how
dreadfully she must feel, to be tried in a week for her life."

"There is no question of her life," says Mr. Nolan, still in that
absent tone ; "they cannot bring it in wilful murder, do their
worst. It will be outrageous to bring it in even manslaughter.
Our hope is that we will get a verdict of 'not guilty.' "

"But she *is* guilty," says Miss Owenson, opening her eyes ;
"she killed her husband. Killing is murder, is it not ? "

"God forbid ! " cries Lewis Nolan, so suddenly, so energetically, that Katie absolutely recoiled.

"What then do you call it ? " asks Sydney, looking at him
with wondering blue eyes.

"Not murder, certainly, else Heaven help the world   To

hate a man, to lie in wait for him, to assassinate him, coolly and deliberately, and with *malice prepense*—that is murder, if you like, and worthy of the gallows."

" Ah, yes !" says Katherine, with a second sympathetic sigh.

" I don't see that it makes much difference to the victim, though," says Sydney ; " the result is the same so far as he is concerned, whether he is murdered in hot blood or cold. Mr. Harland was sent into eternity by the hand of his wife just ·as surely as though she had lain in wait there for hours, pistol in hand.

" He was a brute," exclaimed Miss Macgregor, " for whom shooting was too good."

" A brute I grant, if what the papers say of him be true, who most shamefully insulted and ill-treated his wife. All the same, he has died by her hand, and his blood is upon her."

" She did not mean to kill him."

" Can that avail the soul sent before its Maker in a moment of time, with all its transgressions upon it ? " cries Sydney, her eyes kindling. She did kill him, and she is his murderess."

" Miss Owenson, she is guiltless," exclaims Lewis Nolan, an answering fire kindling in *his* eyes—" guiltless before Heaven, as we shall try to prove her before man."

" And I hold her guilty, with blood to answer and atone for, in this world and in the next."

" You have not read the papers—you cannot have read the case," says Mr. Nolan in suppressed strong excitement. " The man was, as Miss Macgregor says, a brute, a devil incarnate. He maddened his wife in every way that a man can madden a wo-man—he starved her, he beat her, he slandered her, he insulted her ; her very life was not safe. In a moment of madness, goaded beyond human power of endurance, she snatches his revolver from the table, where he has just laid it, fires, and kills him— by sheer chance, for she never fired a pistol before in her life. I tell you the man is guilty of his own death, not she. It was rightful retribution.

" Retribution, perhaps," Miss Owenson responds, in a tone whose clear coldness contrasts strikingly with the repressed, almost passionate earnestness of his " still a murderess." Her hand sends a human soul unprepared before its Judge. I hold it, palliate the circumstances as you will, the most horrible of earthly crimes. She may live, repent, be forgiven—so might he in time, had she not taken his life. It seems to me that no earthly remorse or repentance can ever atone for blood-guiltiness.

It seems incredible to me that any conscientious lawyer can plead for the man or the woman who has taken a life."

" Not even if taken in a moment of madness, unpremeditated, regretted as soon as done ? "

" No ; for once done it can never be undone. No remorse, no repentance can give back life. I hold that no provocation—none—none—can pardon or condone the crime of taking life."

" Miss Owenson, you are merciless. Those are very cruel words from a woman's gentle lips."

" I think of the victim, Mr. Nolan, as well as the slayer. And justice is a virtue as well as mercy."

She is nearly as pale as Mr. Nolan herself, and both are paler than Miss Macgregor has ever seen them. Sydney is thinking of Bertie Vaughan as she speaks. If *he* were murdered, what would all the remorse and repentance of a lifetime avail to atone for that death ? Heaven's forgiveness it might obtain, since supreme mercy reigns there ; but her forgiveness—could she ever give that ?

" Dear me ! dear me ! " says Uncle Grif, looking beseechingly from one to the other, " don't excite yourselves—now, don't. What's this Mrs. Harland to you, Lewis, my boy, that you should fight her battles ? Miss Owenson, don't mind him ; he doesn't mean a word he says, I'm sure. He wouldn't commit murder for the world."

" Bless you, Uncle Grif ! " says Katie, patting the seedy brown coat affectionately, " what a counsel for the defence you would make ! "

" I beg your pardon, Miss Owenson," Mr. Nolan says, but he says it with unconscious coldness ; " I have let my professional feelings carry me too far. I look at this case from a man's point of view—Miss Owenson from a young lady's."

" It is I who should apologize," retorts Miss Owenson in her stateliest manner, while Katie turns aside to hide a satirical smile. " I should not have expressed an opinion at all."

" All the same, though, you adhere like wax to the opinion you have expressed," says the sarcastic voice of Cousin Katie.

" Decidedly," still coldly, and turning for a last look at the picture.

Mr. Nolan follows her glance gloomily and is silent.

Once again Katherine Macgregor throws herself manfully into the breach.

" Nearly five, Sydney, and nearly dark. We will barely have time to reach home before dinner. Lewis "—she turns to the young lawyei with her most winning smile—"shall we **see** you at Mrs. Graham's conversazione to-night? Mrs. Graham's I know to be one of the few houses you frequent."

"Yes—that is, no—I think not. I half-promised, but we are busy at the office, and I am not sure I can get off."

"Preparing for the great case, I understand. Still, come if you can. All work and no play—you know the rest. Over work is worse than over-idleness."

"My brain will stand the pressure," he answers, somewhat grimly. "Thanks, all the same, for your friendly interest, Miss Macgregor."

"She calls him Lewis," Sydney thinks. "They are older friends than I fancied. I don't think that I like Mr. Nolan."

Mr. Nolan escorts them to their carriage, and stands, hat in hand, at the door until they drive off. Miss Macgregor is warmth and cordiality itself. Miss Owenson's final bow is slightly iced.

"Well, dear, and how do you like him?" sweetly inquires Katie.

"Not at all," Sydney responds. "Pleading the case of a woman who shoots her husband in a fit* of ill-temper, and then patronizing *me!* 'I look at it from a man's point of view— Miss Owenson from a lady's.' Impertinent! I wish my 'Sintram' did not resemble him. It will half spoil my pleasure in its possession."

"I foresee," says Miss Macgregor, calmly, "that when you have met Lewis Nolan a few times more, it will be a case of mutual and reciprocal adoration. He was white with anger, Sydney, when talking to you. And what did he turn so ghastly for, in the first instance, when I asked my innocent question if Sintram threw the other man over the cliff?"

"I don't presume to understand the various moods and changes of Mr. Nolan's ingenious countenance," replies cousin Sydney, impatiently. "Do drop the subject, Katie."

"I sincerely hope he may put in an appearance at Mrs. Graham's to night," is Cousin Katie's answer. "An acquaintanceso auspiciously begun cannot fail to end happily. Here we are at home."

Miss Owenson, disdaining all reply, goes up to her own room. On the table a big English letter lies, and with an exclamation of pleasure she pounces upon it. It is from Cornwall. From the baronet's sister; and in Alicia Leonard's copious pages, she forgets her late annoyance, forgets there is such a being in the scheme of the universe as Mr. Lewis Nolan.

CHAPTER III.

TALK AND TEA—AND A LETTER.

"HARRY has refused to go, at the last moment, with the Arctic expedition, although to go with that expedition has been the dream of his life for the past two years. Need I tell you the reason why, little friend? The word 'Come' may be in one of her letters, sooner or later, Alicia,' he said to me the other day. 'What are all my adventures and ambitious dreams compared to that one word from her.' Poor fellow! you should see with what wistful eyes he watches your letters, and my face as I read them, for one sign of hope. And, my darling, he hardly longs for your return more than I do. All the sunshine seems to have gone with your sweet face, from our old home."

That was one of the concluding paragraphs in Miss Alicia Leonard's letter, and very thoughtfully, a little sadly, Sydney folded it up, and sat musing long and deeply. Why should she not say that word "Come" after all, and bring Sir Harry Leonard across the ocean, to claim her as his wife. No one would ever love her better, no one would ever be more worthy of her love. And home, and two loyal hearts would be hers. Here she had no home ; these relatives of hers could never be tried and trusty friends. Mrs. Macgregor, cold, hard, calculating, repelled her ; Katherine, cynical, mercenary, old at five-and-twenty, at times she revolted from. Her heart was as untouched to-day as it had been five years ago when she was Bertie Vaughan's plighted bride—no man of all the men she had ever seen, had ever awakened any stronger, deeper feeling than cordial, sincere friendship. Frank, and heart-whole, she had gone through life—it seemed to her must ever go. She had her idea of the man she would like to marry, if she ever married, which she was not at all certain of, but certainly none of the men she had yet met approached that ideal. No doubt she expected too much ; more than she would ever find. Why, then, not write "Come," and go back with Harry Leonard to that bright English home where Alicia awaited her, and where she had spent nine such happy months? She did not love him—no ; but she liked him well, and love might follow. Why not write "Come" to Sir Harry Leonard?

"Now, Sydney, my dear child," says Katherine, putting in her head, and looking imploringly, "don't sit mooning there by yourself, and forget all about the conversazione, I beg. What! the Cornish post-mark again? From the baronet, I bet.'

For Miss Macgregor said " I bet," and " I guess," was well up in the expressive slang of the day, and could use it with killing effect at proper seasons, on her victims.

"My letter is from Miss Leonard," said Sydney, folding it up.

" Ah ! Miss Leonard—with an inclosure from *mon frère.* Sydney, own up—don't be so dreadfully secretive. I am sure I tell you everything. You are engaged to Sir Harry Leonard ? "

" Am I ? "

" I am sure you are. Young, good-looking, rich, a baronet— how could you refuse him ? "

" How indeed ! I never said I refused him. I never said he asked me. Miss Leonard and her brother are two of my very dearest friends. Has the dinner bell rung ? I never heard it. Tell Aunt Helen I will be down in three minutes. "

Thus civilly dismissed, Miss Macgregor goes—more and more at a loss to understand Miss Owenson.

" Her very dearest friend ! Ah ! but I don't believe in the very dearest masculine friends of handsome young heiresses. But whether engaged to the baronet or not, Dick has'nt a chance, not the ghost of a chance—of that I am certain. ,Not that his poverty would stand in his way—she is just one of those foolish virgins who will fall in love with a beggar, and raise him to the dignity of prince consort, and consider herself and her money honored by his lordly acceptance. Such a man as Lewis Nolan, for instance."

Katherine Macgregor's face darkened suddenly—perhaps as heiress of a million it was a folly even she might have been capable of.

Dinner over, the young ladies dressed for Mrs. Graham's reception. Miss Owenson, as has been said, did not yet wear colors, but black velvet and point lace can be made a very effective toilet when crowned by a pearl pale face, and feathery blonde hair. " Too matronly," Katherine Macgregor pronoun- ces the velvet ; but the rich sable folds falling about the tall, slight figure, the square, classic corsage, the white tuberoses and stephanotis, would have delighted the eye of an artist. Miss Macgregor herself shines in the azure resplendence of her silver blue silk and pearls ; brunette as she is, some shades of blue, by gas light, she finds extremely becoming.

" A daughter of the gods, divinely tall,
And most divinely fair."

quotes Dick Macgregor, as Miss Owenson comes forward, her
black velvet sweeping behind her.   "By George, Sydney, you
look like a princess royal or something of that sort.   Only
black and white too!   How do you do it?   The other girls pile
on the colors of the rainbow—Katie among 'em ; but you have
a look somehow, a general get-up—Dick waves his hands,
vaguely hopeless of expressing his meaning in words.   Sydney
laughs, and takes his arm—his sister cries out in indignant
protest.

" Only black and white indeed.   Only black velvet and point
lace—a costume fit for a young duchess.   That is how men are
deceived.   Every one of them at the conversazione will echo
Dick's cry—' only black and white—modest simplicity itself—
how economically and tastefully the heiress dresses, what an
example for these gaudy, extravagant butterflies around her.'
And all the time Miss Owenson's costume will be far and away
the richest and most costly in the room.   There will be nothing
like that point," says Katherine, with a sigh of bitterest envy,
" at Mrs. Graham's conversazione to night."

" Hang Mrs. Graham's conversazione," growls brother Dick ;
"hang all such shams with their fine French names.   It is a
cheap and nasty substitute for a decent party ; instead of a
German band, and a sit-down supper, scandal and weak tea."

" The tea need not be weak unless you wish it—the scandal
I acknowledge," interposes his sister.

" Sitting ranged around the walls, a crowd of guys," proceeds
Dick, in a disgusted tone, " tea handed round in Liliputian cups,
and all the guys jawing in pairs, as a matter of duty.   Talk and
tea—that's what Mrs. Graham's conversazione comes to in
plain English ; and hang all such shams, I say again."

" Then why come, my dear boy?" inquires Miss Owenson ;
" why make a martyr of yourself, why immolate yourself in the
flower of your youth and loveliness, a victim to brotherly duty?
Why not express those natural sentiments of your manly heart
at dinner, and Aunt Helen would have matronized us, or even
poor, dear Uncle Grif might have been reluctantly forced into
the breach.   Anything to have spared you."

" The cousin with whom I go will make even Mrs. Graham's
talk and tea go down with relish," says Dick, gallantly ; "and
if Nolan's there—as he is pretty sure to be—we will have some

decent music, at least. I'd rather hear that fellow sing than Brignoli."

"Mr. Nolan is musical, then ?" says Sydney. "He has the face of a man who can sing."

"And men who sing at evening tea parties, like Tom Moore, are flukes as a general thing," answers Dick. Nolan's an exception, however. He never does sing, except at Mrs. Graham's, and whether he sings or is silent, he is as good a fellow as ever breathed. He was out with us the first year, and fought like a brick. He has just Irish blood enough in him to make fighting come naturally, I suppose."

For be it known that Dick Macgregor—Captain Macgregor, to the world at large—is only in the bosom of his family for a two months' furlough, and his regiment awaits him down in Virginia. It is the second year of the "Unpleasantness," and Dick Macgregor went out with the first.

"Mr. Nolan's one talent, leaving his forensic abilities out of the question," says Katherine, "is a passion for music. As a boy, I remember, he would come in and sit down at the piano, play harmonious chords intuitively, and rattle off street tunes by ear. As he grew older, Uncle Grif, exceedingly vain of his boy's abilities, had him taught. Did I tell you that Uncle Grif adopted him, in a measure, when ten years old, and that to him Lewis Nolan owes it that he is a promising young lawyer to-day ? He is also organist of St. Ignatius', where you and I must go some Sunday, Syd, and hear one of the finest choirs in the city." •

They have reached Mrs. Graham's, and enter with a flock of other guests. Most of them Miss Macgregor knew. Friendly greetings are exchanged, and introductions performed on the way up-stairs. •

"I hope the evening won't drag," Katherine remarks, as she adjusts her ribbons and laces. "Dick is right ; as a rule this sort of thing is slow. Talk and tea are not the most stimulating amusements on earth. If you feel bored, Sydney, be sure you let me know, and we will leave early."

The guests had nearly all arrived, when they descend and make their way to their hostess' side. Mrs. Graham is a large, and cheerful looking lady, in mauve silk—that "refuge of the destitute"—addicted to *embonpoint*, good nature, and colors that "swear," as the French phrase it. Katherine Macgregor's face is known to every man and woman in the room ; but who is the tall, regal-looking blonde, so lovely of face, so distin-

12*

guished of manner. And when the whisper goes round that she is *the* Miss Owenson, the rich Miss Owenson just returned from Europe, Miss Owenson becomes *the* star of the assembly, and Miss Macgregor and Mrs. Graham are besieged with pressing aspirants for introductions. It grows a bore in time, but Sydney shows no sign of boredom in her gracious face. Still it is something of a relief when she finds herself in a quiet corner, with Dick devotedly beside her, and free for a moment from her court.

"Oh, Solitude, where are thy charms?" says Dick. "'Oh for a lodge in some vast wilderness,' where talk and tea are unknown. Let's sit down here, Sydney, and be a comfortable couple. Here is a book of engravings, they always turn over books of engravings in novels, if you notice. Let us live a chapter out of a novel, and turn over the engravings."

He thinks, as he says it, that there is not a picture of them all as fair and sweet as Sydney herself—a slight flush on her clear, pale cheek, the golden hair flashing against the rich blackness of her robe.

"Your friend Mr. Nolan is not here," she says, as Dick spread out his big portfolio, preparatory to examining the engravings.

"Isn't he? Very likely not. You see he is a young man of uncommonly high-toned notions—poor and proud, as they phrase it. As Katie says, he owes all he has to Uncle Grif. His mother and sister are dressmakers, I believe, and as yet Nolan hasn't achieved any distinction worth speaking of. He never goes anywhere; his voice would open no end of doors, but he won't be asked for his voice. He makes an exception, somehow, in Mrs. Graham's favor. Ah! there he is now."

The piano in the back drawing-room had been going industriously since their entrance; but now a new hand, the hand of a master, touched the keys, and the grand, grateful notes were wondrously different from the young lady-like jingle that had gone before. This was the touch of a musician, and the instrument seemed to know and respond. *"La ci Darem"* was what Mr. Nolan sang and played; and the pictures were untouched, and Dick and Sydney sat absorbedly listening. It was a powerful tenor, with that veiled sympathetic vibration, that undertone of pathos in its sweetness, that reaches the heart.

"I don't care for Italian opera," says Captain Macgregor; "it's a deuce of a bore, as a rule; but I like that. *La ci Darem la mano*, he is singing now. Niceish voice, isn't it."

" Niceish is a new adjective to me," responds Sydney, laughing, " and one that hardly applies. Mr. Nolan is the fortunate
possessor of one of the finest tenors I ever heard, and I have
heard some good tenors—Sims Reeves was one. There, he has
finished ; how sweet, how tender those lower notes were.
Surely they will not let him stop."

"Oh, he is not stingy—when he does sing he does sing ;
nothing niggardly about him. I have heard him rattle through
a whole opera bouffe—shriek like the soprano, growl like the
bass father, shout like the chorus—take 'em all off capitally, I
assure you. There, he is singing again : let's follow the crowd,
and see him."

They leave the table and make their way to the other room,
where Mr. Nolan, in regulation evening dress, sits at the piano,
and where Katherine Macgregor leans gracefully against the
instrument, fluttering her fan and listening with downcast
eyes.

"As a rule," observes Dick, in a profound tone, " it's a painful spectacle—a very painful spectacle—to watch a music man.
The contortions of his facial muscles, the hideous extent to which
he opens his mouth, the dislocating way in which he flings back
his head, the inspired idiot style in which he rolls his eyeballs up
to the chandelier, the frenzied manner in which elbows and fingers
fly, are trying didoes to witness without a still small feeling of disgust. But Nolan doesn't contort, doesn't roll his eyeballs, doesn't
look like a moonstruck lunatic, and doesn't open his mouth
even to any very disgusting extent. Brava !" Mr. Macgregor
gently pats his kidded paws. " Very good—very good indeed !
We will take your whole stock at the same price."

Mr. Nolan concludes his second song and makes an attempt
to get away, but he is besieged by soft pleadings, and Katherine Macgregor gives him one of those long, tender glances
from beneath her sable lashes that have done such telling execution in her time.

" Just one other—in English this time—a ballad for me."

" For you ? " repeats Mr. Nolan, a laugh in his dark eyes,
but his lips grave. " If I were hoarse as a raven, put in that
way, refusal would be an impossibility. Something in English,
something pathetic, of course. Will this do ? "

He plays a jaunty, tripping, waltz-like symphony, into
which his voice blends in an air that exactly suits the words,
a mischievous light in the eyes he keeps on her eager
face :

" My eye ! how I love you,
   You sweet little dove, you !
   There's no one above you,
                     Most beautiful Kitty.

" So glossy your hair is,
   Like a sylph or a fairy's,
   And your neck, I declare, is
                     Exquisitely pretty.

" Quite Grecian your nose is,
   And your cheeks are like roses,
   So delicious—oh, Moses !
                     Surpassingly sweet !

" Not the beauty of tulips,
   Nor the taste or mint-juleps,
   Can compare with your two lips,
                     Most beautiful Kate.

" And now, dearest Kitty,
   It's not very pretty,
   Indeed it's a pity
                     To keep me in sorrow :

" So, if you'll but chime in,
   We'll have done with our rhymin',
   Swap Cupid for Hymen,
                     And be married to-morrow."

A low murmur of laughter and applause follows, and Katherine Macgregor actually flushes under his eyes.

"And if he really asked her it might go hard with the chances of Vanderdonck," muttered Dick ; "but no, our artless Katherine's heart will never run away with her head."

"Mr. Nolan has an old *tendresse*, then, for Kate ?" Sydney asks, carelessly. "I half thought so this afternoon.

"By no means. He certainly has an old *tendresse*, something more than a *tendresse*, and I doubt if he is quite over it yet, for——"

Dick does not finish his sentence, for the subject of it arises from his seat, sees them, and approaches. As he looks now, warmth in his dark face, animation in the large gray eyes, a smile on the grave lips, Sydney wonders to see that he is handsome.

"That was all very delightful indeed, old boy," is Dick's greeting. "Why weren't we all born with black eyelashes or tenor voices, or both, and be the centre of such a group of adoring angels as you are wherever you go? Miss Owenson and I have been listening entranced in the background—you know my cousin, by the way, I think."

" I had the pleasure of meeting Miss Owenson this afternoon," says Mr. Nolan, with that very genial smile of his. " Apropos, Miss Owenson, you have been the means of making very happy one poor fellow who has not been used to over-much happiness—Von Etté—the most excitable of living beings ; he nearly expired with ecstasy when I told him of your admiration of ' Sintram,' and your intention of purchasing it. He flew to the studio on the instant, had it packed, and sent, and you will find it at home before you upon your return."

" Then I have been fortunate, indeed," Sydney responds, "if in giving pleasure to myself I have given pleasure to another. Mr. Von Etté is destined to win far higher praise than any poor appreciation of mine."

" I doubt if he will ever value any more highly. Miss Owenson," he says, abruptly, " I am afraid my manner, my words, must have offended you. The thought that it may be so has troubled me more than I can tell. It is a subject upon which I feel deeply, and one which is likely·to·carry me away. Pray, forgive me."

" Is he in love with this Mrs. Harland, I wonder?" thinks Miss Owenson. " Was that what Dick meant?"

"The apology is needless," she says, cordially. " There was no offence—how could there be? I never thought of it after."

The dark gravity of the afternoon overspread· his face again —the smile vanished. What a strong, thoughtful, intellectual face it was, the girl thought. What a good face, if she were any judge of physiognomy.

This clever Mr. Nolan, with his charming voice, a thing that will make its way to a woman's foolish fancy sooner than more solid qualities, and his profound convictions, was beginning to interest her. Dick had been summoned by some fair enslaver, and had reluctantly obeyed. Mr. Nolan and Miss Owenson had slowly been making their way to the front drawing-room while they talked, and Sydney resumed her seat by the table and the engravings. Mr. Nolan took the vacant seat by her side, still wearing that earnest look.

" I am glad that my words did not trouble you. Yours most certainly have troubled me." Sydney looks at him in surprise. " Yes, Miss Owenson, troubled me : for if my convictions were not with Mrs. Harland, most assuredly I would not plead her case. I have conscientious notions about this sort of thing that are exceedingly unprofessional, I know—notions I will never outlive. But that Mrs. Harland is a murderess, I will not, cannot believe."

"Not with intent, perhaps——"

"Not at all, Miss Owenson. See! for years her life with this man was a daily and hourly martyrdom. He starved her, he insulted her—he was all the worst husband can be to the most helpless wife. She bore it patiently, submissively; she was friendless, poor, and alone—for years she endured it. One day he comes home half drunk, lays his revolver on the table, is more brutal than usual, offers her an insult, devilish in its atrocity. It maddens her. Hardly conscious of what she is doing—goaded beyond endurance—she lifts the pistol, fires, and he falls*dead. She had not meant to kill; without thought, hardly knowing what she does do, she kills him. Is this murder?"

Sydney is silent; his suppressed vehemence almost frightens her. How interested he is in this Mrs. Harland! Does he mean to free her, and marry her after?

"She is filled with a remorse, a despair, an anguish I never saw equalled," he goes on. "How she lives or keeps her reason is more than I can understand. If she could give her life to restore his she would give it thankfully, joyfully. Is this woman then guilty? Does the crime of murder lie at her door?"

"Oh! I don't know," Sydney says, with a look of distress. "No, surely not. And yet it is an awful thing—whether by accident, by passion, or by intention—to take a human life.

"Awful! Great Heaven! yes," he says, in a voice so thrilling that Sydney looks at him in ever-increasing wonder!

Surely he must love this Mrs. Harland, else why the passionate agony of that whisper?

"Poor fellow!" she thinks; "it is hard on him. He deserves something better than to care for a woman whose hands are red with her husband's blood."

There is a pause. Sydney turns over the pictures without seeing them, conscious of a dawning and strong interest in this man. He rests his forehead on his hand, so dark a look in his face that she absolutely wonders if this be the same man who a few minutes ago sang laughingly a comic song. That he should keep his levity for them, his earnestness for her is a subtle flattery that conquers her as no other flattery could.

" Surely my foolish opinions can have no weight with you,
Mr. Nolan, no power to pain you," she says, very gently. " If
so I am indeed sorry. It shall teach me to be less hasty and
presumptuous in proffering opinions for the future. In the
sight of Heaven I cannot believe your friend is guilty of this
dreadful crime, and I sincerely hope you may get a verdict."

" My friend," he says, and he lifts his head, and a smile breaks
up the dark thoughtfulness of his face, " I have not seen Mrs.
Harland three times in my life : after the trial I shall probably
never see her again while I live. I am interested in her as a
woman who has suffered greatly ; but it is whether or no the
guilt of murder is upon her that centres my interest. This is
what I would give worlds, if I possessed them, yes, worlds, to
know."

"He is not in love with this unhappy Mrs. Harland," Sydney
thinks. " I am glad of that. I like him. He deserves something better. He looks like a man

> " 'To bear without rebuke
> The grand old name of gentleman.' "

" I am afraid I have bored you mercilessly with this tragic
affair," he goes on, his face and tone changing ; " it is uppermost in my thoughts ; I feel it so deeply ; but hold—I am sinning again while I apologize. Let us look at the pictures ;
Mrs. Graham never affronts her guests' intellect by offering
poor ones."

They look at the pictures accordingly, and talk of the pictures. Miss Owenson has seen many of the fine old paintings
from which these engravings are taken, and Mr. Nolan has a
cultivated eye and taste, and a keen love of art. They talk of
Italy and Germany, and those classic foreign lands which she
has seen and loved, which he longs but never expects to see.
And minutes fly, and hours, and to Sydney's horror—for she
hates anything like a pronounced *tête-à-tête*—their conversation
does not end until Katherine seeks her side, and the company
rise to disperse.

" Really," Miss Macgregor says, and if there is a fine shade of
irony in her tone Sydney does not take the trouble to detect it,
" for two people quarrelling fiercely at their first meeting, you
seem to have got on well with Mr. Nolan. Were you quarrelling
again, my dear, or making up, and was I not a true prophetess ? "

" A true prophetess ! What did you predict ? " asks Sydney,

with equal carelessness. "Mr. Nolan and I neither quarrelled
nor made up, and I have to thank him for spending a very pleasant evening. If I have a weakness it is for men of intellect."

"And you don't meet them every day. Poor Dick !" laughs
Dick's sister. So talk and tea are not so utterly flavorless after
all, *belle cousine.*"

"If the talking is done by Mr. Nolan—no," retorts Sydney,
with spirit.

"Don't excite yourself," says Miss Macgregor. "I have
heard before that Lewis Nolan improves on acquaintance.
Does he not sing divinely? Has he not a thoroughbred look
for one with so few opportunities? Ah !. what a pity he is so
poor."

> "'Lord of himself, though not of lands,
> And having nothing yet hath all,' "

quotes Sydney. "What would you? Men cannot expect to
have money, and brains, and divine voices. For my own part,
all the men I ever found worth talking to, ever was interested in,
were men without a sou."

"Ah ! you are interested in Mr. Nolan ? "

"Yes," says Sydney, flinging back her head, and accepting
the challenge.

"And only in poor men ! Sir Harry, I have heard, is worth.
twenty thousand pounds a year. I am afraid I shall not have a
baronet for a cousin-in-law, after all. Now, now! don't freeze
into stateliness, Syd. I don't mean anything—I never do mean
anything. Come."

Dick, at the foot of the stairs, looking depressed and unhappy,
offers Sydney his arm. Mr. Nolan, who stands talking cheerfully
to him, does duty for his sister.

"You never come to see us now," the couple in front heard
Katherine say, in a plaintive voice. "Have you vowed a vow
to honor Mrs. Graham alone with your friendship ? "

"I am not sure that Mrs. Graham looks upon my friendship
in the light of an honor. It is a new idea, however, and I shall
inquire."

"That is not an answer to my question. Why do you not
come to see us as—as you used ? "

"As I used ? " Mr. Nolan lifts his eyebrows. "Used I ever ?
I have no time for dangerous delights. I have to work ' from
early morn 'til dewy eve ' for my daily bread and butter."

"Dangerous delights ? " says Miss Macgregor with an artless
upward glance. " What do you mean by that ? "

" Do I really need to explain, Miss Macgregor?" retorts Mr. Nolan, looking down into the upturned dark eyes.

" Miss Macgregor?—it used to be Katie," says Katie, and in the low voice there is a tremor, either real or well assumed.

" Oh, by George ! let us get on," says Dick, with a face of such utter disgust that Sydney laughs. She has been trying to get on herself, for the last two minutes, out of earshot of this conversation, and succeeds so well that Mr. Nolan's response to Katie's last is inaudible. Katie's cheeks are slightly flushed though, as she reaches the carriage, and the smile on her lips shows it has been to order.

" I wish to Heaven, Katie," growls Dick, " when you make love to fellows, you wouldn't do it quite so loudly. Old Van- derdonck himself—deaf as an adder—might have heard you spooning to Lewis Nolan, if he had been there."

" Old Vanderdonck might have heard, and welcome, my gen- tle brother."

" And if you think Nolan's to be taken in by your soft sawder, you're a trifle out of your reckoning, let me tell you. He isn't an old bird, Nolan isn't, but he's not going to be caught with chaff."

" Dick," says Miss Macgregor, " it is patent to the dullest observer that the attentions of Miss Emma Winton have been painfully marked ; also, that five cups of gunpowder tea do *not* agree with your digestive organs. Therefore we excuse the rudeness of your remarks, and prescribe total silence for the rest of the drive home."

Dick growls, but obeys—Katherine is the ruling spirit of the household.

The city clocks are striking two when Sydney reaches her room. On the wall hangs " Sintram." She greets it with a smile of welcome, and the likeness to Mr. Nolan does not spoil her pleasure in looking at it, as she has feared. On the table lies a letter with a Canadian postmark, and in a stiff, mercantile hand. She turns up the gas, and tears it open eagerly, without waiting to remove her wraps. It is from Mr. McKelpin, in answer to one she had written him for news of her lost friend Cyrilla Hendrick.

MONTREAL, *Nov.* 23*d*, 18—.

" RESPECTED MISS : "

Here Sydney smiles ; the " Respected Miss" is so like what poor Cyrilla used to tell her of her middle-aged Scottish suitor

"Yours of the 17th inst. came to hand yesterday, and con-
tents duly noted.   In reply, I have to say I know nothing of
the present whereabouts of the late lamented Miss Dormer's
niece.   On the day before my return to this city, four years ago
last May, she left by train direct for Boston.   I made inquiries
concerning her—advertised for her in the Boston papers, and
placed a certain sum of money at her disposal.   In the course
of the following week I received, in reply to my advertisement,
a letter from the head physician of one of the public hospitals of
Boston.   A young lady answering the description, from Montreal,
was lying very ill under his charge ; some mental strain, apparently, and physical exhaustion, had prostrated her to such an
extent that it was doubtful if she would ever recover.   I went
to Boston ; I saw and identified her (herself unconscious), and
ordered every care and attention.   She recovered eventually,
wrote me a brief note of acknowledgment, and at the earliest
possible moment quitted the hospital.   Since then I have neither
seen nor heard from the late lamented Miss Dormer's niece.
This is all I have to communicate, and I remain, Respected Miss,
yours to command,   DONALD MCKELPIN."

CHAPTER IV.

A BASKET OF FLOWERS AND A DINNER.

"**K**ATHERINE," says Mrs. Macgregor, "do lay down
that book, get off that sofa, dress, and go down town,
match this fringe, go to Fratoni's for ices, and to
Greenstalk's for the cut-flowers.   Do you hear ? "   .
    "I hear.   Anything else ? "
    "And make haste.   Where your own personal gratification is
not concerned, Katherine, I must say you are unbearably lazy.
Here, the whole forenoon was spent in bed——"
    "Did you really expect me to get up, and go to matins at
St. Albans after dissipating at Mrs. Graham's until two this
morning ? "
    "I expect very little of you, my daughter, that will put you
to the least inconvenience.   I know of old how useless it would

b. ... expect it. Those commissions I mentioned must be done this afternoon. My dressmaker is at a dead-lock for the fringe. Perhaps you expect me—worn out as I am, to go after it myself—"

"Blessed are they who expect nothing—of which number am I," retorts Miss Katherine.

She has been lying on a sofa in the family sitting-room during this discussion, a provoking drawl in her voice—her eye never once leaving her book. In an arm-chair by the window, also reading, and in a dress whose faultless neatness is a striking contrast to her cousin's, sits Miss Owenson. Mrs. Macgregor, a portly matron, with a frisette of glossy darkness, coldly glimmering blue eye, an austere Roman nose, a thin, severe mouth, and a worried and anxious air generally, looks up from her sewing to regard her undutiful daughter with an angry glance.

"Katherine, will you or will you not get up and go down town?"

"Best of mothers, I would much rather not. The day is cold and disagreeable ; I feel dreadfully sleepy yet, and this novel—Mr. Van Cyler's, mamma—is thrillingly interesting. Send Susan."

"Aunt Helen," cries Sydney, starting up, "let me go. I will match your fringe, and deliver your other messages with pleasure."

Miss Katherine shrugs her shoulders, and smiles sarcastically behind her book.

"Thank you, my love, I cannot think of troubling you——"

"It will be no trouble ; I was just meditating a walk on my own account—my daily constitutional, you know. It will give me pleasure to be of service to you."

"Very well, my dear ; but if my daughter thinks she can set me at defiance after this fashion, she is mistaken. "Katherine," and the cold blue eyes light and flash, "put down that book this instant, and do as I command you."

"When my mammy takes that tone," says Katherine, with imperturbable good temper, and addressing her remark placidly to Sydney, "I know better than to disobey. Let us see—match the fringe—order the ices—see to the flowers. But the confectioner's and the fringe stores are at opposite ends of the town—can't do both in one short, dark November afternoon. One of them must go, dearest mother."

"You and Sydney can go to Greenstalk's from here, then she can walk over to Sixth Avenue and match the fringe while you take a car and visit Fretoni's," rapidly and concisely, says Mrs Macgregor.

"What a business-like head this *mater* of ours has, Sydney! Pause, wonder, and admire. Very well, Mrs. Macgregor—you shall be obeyed to the letter; but what a pang it costs me to give up Van Cyler's novel! There are times when even filial duty is a painful thing."

Mrs. Macgregor's brow cleared. Sydney laughed. Katherine's habitual manner of cheerful impertinence to her mother at times startled, at times amused her. Real impertinence the girl did not mean, but this vapid surface manner had become second nature. The young girls started forth together. Sydney with her seal jacket buttoned across her chest, and a tall black hat and plume. The day was cold, gray, and overcast—windy, dusty, and supremely unpleasant.

"I feel like the little boy who thought it was such a delightful thing to be an orphan, and do as he liked," says Katherine, bending before a windy gust. "Poor mamma, she works and worries, toils and troubles, year in, year out, for Dick, and me, too."

"When you are Mrs. Vanderdonck, the wife of the millionaire, you will be able to do as you please, with a whole regiment of lackeys to fly at their lady's bidding."

"I am not so sure of that. A millionaire old Vanderdonck is, that is historical : and that he intends to ask me to marry him, I am also quite certain ; but about the lackeys and the liberty I have my doubts. He is stingy as a miser, jealous as a Turk, relentless as a Nero, his inward man as hideous as his outward. What a happy destiny will be mine as Mrs. Vanderdonck ! "

" Don't marry him, Katherine."

" And go to the dogs with mamma and Dick ? We are over head and ears in debt, Sydney, and nothing short of this marriage can save us. I actually wonder that mamma's frisette does not turn gray with all the struggling she has to keep up appearances. I owe it to her to tide her over these troubled waters. Vanderdonck, miser as he is, shall pay my price to the last farthing before he puts the ring on my finger. It shall be a clear matter of money from first to last. He shall give his written bond to pay mamma's debts, and settle five or six thousand a year on me, or he shall never call me wife. If I must be sold, I shall fetch as good a price as I can."

Sydney shuddered.

"It is horrible. It seems to me I would go out as a shop girl, as a servant, sweep a crossing, starve, sooner than that." "Yes, I daresay," Miss Macgregor retorts, coolly; "rich people always say that. They would work their fingers to the bone, starve, die, sooner than degrade themselves. Unhappily I have no talent for work. I can't go on the stage and become a Ristori in a night, or write a novel and become famous, as they do in books. Starvation would not agree with me. I am something of an epicure, as you may have noticed, and dying —ah! dying is something I never want to think of. In my place, *belle cousine*, you would be as heartless, as mercenary, as calculating as I am. In my place you would marry old Vanderdonck."

"Never!"

"Love is all very well," pursues Katie, a hard, cold look, curiously like her mother's, crossing her face and ageing it; "it is one of the luxuries of life—life's very sweetest luxury perhaps; but for me it is not to be thought of. You can afford it, can fall in love with a beggar if you choose, and turn him into a prince. Oh! Sydney! cousin mine, what a lucky young woman you are. This is Mr. Greenstalk's."

Baskets and bouquets littered the counters and perfumed the warm air; wreaths festooned the walls, shrubs stood around in pots. A damsel in attendance behind the counter, waiting on the one customer the shop contained, a gentleman bending over some curious foreign plant, his back towards them.

"What a lovely basket!" says Katherine. "Look, Sydney."

It was a small flat basket, such as florists use, of purest white flowers, camellias, white roses, Japonicas, stephanotis. On top lay a card, having this legend in pencil, and in a man's writing: "WITH LOVE. L." And whether the hand struck her as familiar, or something in the back view of the man, Miss MacGregor turned, and looked curiously at him.

"You will send the basket the first thing," says a voice she recognizes. "Here is the address; and you will fasten the card I have laid on it among the flowers. Don't fail."

"All right, sir; it shall go the first thing to-morrow," cheerfully responds the lady in waiting.

"Look, Sydney!" says Katherine; and Sydney looks, and sees the tall form and dark face of Lewis Nolan. He pushes a five-dollar bill to the shopwoman, buttons up his overcoat, and with an absorbed look on his face hurries out without casting a last look at his purchase, or a first look at the two ladies beside it. " Lewis Nolan, poor as a church mouse, spending five dollars for flowers ! " exclaims Katherine, aghast. " Now what does this mean ? "

" You need not look at me. I am sure I don't know," answers Sydney, laughing. " Mr. Nolan shows very good taste in his selection—that is the only opinion I have on the subject."

" With love," pursues Katherine, "and the first thing tomorrow morning. Whom can they be for ? Sydney, I shall ask."

" Katie ! " cries Sydney, indignantly.

" No, I shall not. But whom *can* they be for ! Is he really in love with that horrid Mrs. Harland ? "

" Are you concerned in knowing, dear ? Mr. Nolan would feel flattered if he were aware how deep is your interest in him."

" Mr. Nolan would not feel in the slightest degree flattered. Vanity, the predominant weakness of his sex, is not *his* weakness. But he cannot be as poor as I imagined if he can afford to spend five dollars in flowers."

" Under the influence of the tender passion a man may be extravagant to the extent of five dollars, and still be pardoned," says Miss Owenson.

The flower woman approaches, Miss Macgregor gives her various orders for the day after to-morrow, which are duly transcribed in black and white, and the two girls depart.

" I *wonder* who the flowers are for ! " is Miss Macgregor's thoughtful remark as they reach the street. " Sydney, your fastidious notions are decidedly in the way. I've a good mind to go back and ask."

Sydney laughs outright, then stops, and blushes, for a gentleman, approaching rapidly, lifts his hat, with a smile. It is Mr. Nolan.

" Quand on parle du diable——" begins Miss Macgregor, in execrable French, and with unruffled coolness. " We were just talking of you. We saw you in Greenstalk's, ordering flowers, but you never deigned to notice us."

" What unpardonable blindness ! " answers the gentleman. " I am on my way back to Greenstalk's ; I forgot one of my gloves."

" Your floral taste is excellent, Mr. Nolan," says Katherine, mischievously. " Your big bouquet is beautiful."

" Do you think so ? Yes, it is pretty. She prefers white flowers. Cold, is it not," says Mr. Nolan, "for November ? "

" You dine with us, do you not, on Friday evening ? " inquires

Katherine. "Mamma sent you a card, I know, but I want to add a verbal invitation."

"Thanks, very much; but I am afraid I cannot have the pleasure. I am very busy, Miss Katie."

"You are never too busy to go to Mrs. Graham's, it seems," says Miss Macgregor, with her most effective and best-practised pout. "I insist upon your coming. That stupid trial will surely take no harm for being laid aside one evening."

"You are most kind, and I am most grateful; all the same——"

He pauses, and involuntarily, unconsciously, glances at Miss Owenson. She meets that glance with a bewitching smile.

"I think I must add my entreaties to Katherine's," she says. "I should very much like to hear Körner's Sword Song once more."

"You will come?" asks Katherine.

"You do me too much honor," replies Mr. Nolan, flushing slightly. "Yes, I will come."

Then he was gone, and the cousins go on their way, in silence for a moment, silence broken first by Sydney.

"What a great deal of coaxing your Mr. Nolan takes. Evidently the honor of his presence is not to be lightly bestowed."

"But he yields at your request, dear, not mine," says Katie, with a sudden sharp ring in her voice. And for a moment there is silence again.

"What does Katherine Macgregor mean by her new cordiality?" thinks Mr. Nolan, rather ungraciously. "An invitation, and pressing one to the Macgregor's mansion is altogether a new distinction. I suppose singing to amuse the company is at the bottom of it. What a noble and loving face that is!" But he did not mean Miss Macgregor.

The cousins parted at the junction of Broadway and Grand Street, Katherine to go across town, Sydney to seek Sixth Avenue, and match the fringe. This was a tedious process, and the street lamps were twinkling in the gray November dusk before it was concluded. Fearless in most things, Sydney yet had a nervous dread of being out alone in the streets of a city after night-fall, and hailed a passing car, which she knew would convey her to within a couple of blocks of home.

The car was filled, not a vacant seat, but a very youthful gentleman sprang up as if galvanized at sight of a beautiful young lady, and with a smile and a little bow Sydney thankfully took his place. At the next corner the car again stopped, and an elderly woman, with a large and heavy market basket on her arm, got in. She looked tired, and proceeded to hang her-self up by the strap. The double row of men glanced over the tops of their papers, saw only an old woman, rather shabby of aspect, and dived back again. Evidently she was to be allowed to stand, and Sydney realizing it, arose and proffered her place.

"Oh, no, thank you—no," the woman said. "I could not think of it, my dear young lady. Keep your seat."

"You are tired and I am not; I don't mind standing. Oblige me by sitting down."

"Thank you, I am tired," the woman said, with a sigh of re-lief, sinking down ; but it's too bad to make you stand."

"I have not far to go ; that is, I think not. How far is it to ——th street ? "

"Fully fifteen blocks ; too long for you to stand, I ought not to have taken your seat."

"I won't have to stand ; just wait and see," whispered Syd-ney, with an arch smile ; and as she said it the man beside the old lady got up, with a bashful " Here, miss," and suspended himself in mid-air.

"Did I not tell you ? " says Sydney, with a subdued laugh. "Virtue is its own reward."

"An, it is a fine thing to be young and handsome," answers her new acquaintance.

Miss Owenson glanced at her and made up her mind that she must have been handsome in her day, also. It was a kindly and matronly face, with dark, gentle eyes, and snow-white hair.

"Tell me, please, when we get to ——th street," Sydney said. "I am almost a stranger in New York, and don't want to get belated. What uncomfortable conveyances these street cars are."

She chatted with her chance acquaintance until her street was reached, then with a smiling "good-bye," got out and walked rapidly into Madison Avenue, and her aunt's house.

On Friday night Mrs. Macgregor gave a dinner party for the special delectation of Mr. Vanderdonck. There were but seven or eight guests in all, and Mr. Nolan made one of the number.

"Although, really, what you want to ask that young man for,

I cannot understand. It is all nonsense having him here. These sort of people should keep their place. I can't see what you want him for, Katherine."

"Can't you, mamma? 'There are more things in heaven and earth, Horatio, than are dreamed of in your philosophy.'— Perhaps I want to flirt with this poor young man and make Mr. Vanderdonck jealous. Is not that a laudable object?"

"Mr. Vanderdonck knows you well enough not to be jealous of a pauper, my daughter. And I do hope, Katherine, you will manage to make him speak soon, for these entertainments I can *not* afford."

"Poor, dear mamma! Well, never mind: when the five thousand a year are settled on me you shall have half for life."

Miss Macgregor certainly did flirt with Mr. Nolan, and as certainly succeeded in causing Mr. Vanderdonck to scowl with malignant blackness, as they reversed the usual rule, the gentleman singing and the lady bending devotedly by his side and turning his music.

But at last Miss Macgregor deserted him for her Auld Robin Grey, and Mr. Nolan sought out the owner of the "noble and lovely" face, and lingered in its vicinity until the hour of departure. They seemed to find endless subjects in common, those two—literature, art, music, travels; their conversation never seemed to flag.

"Decidedly, Mr. Nolan improves on acquaintance," thought Miss Owenson, *en route* to bed; "it is a positive pleasure to hear him."

"'To know her is a liberal education,'" quotes Mr. Nolan, wending his homeward way. "What a very excellent thinking-machine there is behind that Madonna face. How poor Von Etté would rave of its beauty; how he would delight to paint it.

> "And if any painter drew her
> He would paint her unaware,
> With a halo round her hair."

"What a contrast she is to that dark daughter of the earth, Katherine Macgregor."

13

CHAPTER V.

A LONG TALK AND A LITTLE WALK,

HE dinner was a pleasant affair, and my chat with Mr. Nolan most agreeable, but, after all, I doubt whether the game was worth the candle."

"Miss Owenson makes the remark, and makes it to herself alone. She holds up to view at the same time, a mass of rich Chantilly lace, woefully torn and rent. On Friday night last it was the costly appendage of a silken robe, upon which a masculine boot heel has accidentally trodden, with the aforesaid result.

It is the afternoon of Monday, and with the exception of Uncle Grif, Miss Owenson is quite alone in that coziest apartment of the Macgregor house, the family sitting-room. Her aunt and cousin are out making calls, in which social martyrdom she has declined participating.

"I must have it mended," thinks Miss Owenson ; "but who is to do it? Experts in lace work are rare, I fancy, in New York. I must ask Katie."

"Is anything the matter, my dear Miss Sydney?" inquires Uncle Grif, in his timid way, coming forward.

"Do I look so woe-begone over my torn flounce, then?" says Sydney, laughing. "This is the matter," she holds up the large rent, "not a matter of life or death, you see."

"Ah! torn," says Uncle Grif, in profound sympathy. "What —what is it?"

"It *was* a flounce, and will be again if I can get it mended."

"Are you going to do it yourself, Miss Sydney?" asks Uncle Grif, and his dull eyes light suddenly.

"Not I!" replies Miss Owenson. "I never did anything half so useful in my life. This lace belonged to poor mamma —she wore it when a girl, and it is a souvenir, so of more value than its intrinsic worth."

The sparkle in Uncle Grif's dull eyes grows brighter, and more eager.

"Miss Sydney," he says, "*I* know a person—a lady who will mend that for you. She makes lace—and embroidery, and all that. She was educated in a convent, and does the loveliest needlework you ever saw. If you'll come with me I'll take you to her, and you can ascertain for yourself."

"Uncle Grif, you are a household treasure!" exclaims Sydney, rolling up her lace, and rising. "Wait ten minutes, and I will be with you."

She makes a parcel of her torn Chantilly, hastily arrays herself for the street, and sallies forth under the protecting wing of Uncle Grif. That amiable old gentleman's face beams with delight.

"We will take a Seventh Avenue car. You don't mind taking a car, do you, Miss Sydney?"

"Decidedly not, Uncle Grif. Why on earth should I?"

"Katie does; that is all. One has to ride with such a motley assembly of the Great Unwashed—that is what *she* says."

"Katie says more than she means; you must not take her literally. There is nothing I enjoy more than riding in those city street cars, and watching the different phases of the human face divine. It is quite a new experience to me. Who is the —the lady who does the lace work?"

"A most respectable person, Miss Sydney. Oh, a *most* respectable person," cries Uncle Griff, eagerly.

"Of course," Sydney answers; "that goes without saying, since you are taking me to her. But what is she, maid or matron, wife or widow?"

"A widow lady and her daughter; there are two. Once she was well off, and she is a person of culture and refinement. They are poor now, and she ekes out her income by doing fine needlework for ladies, and for fancy stores."

They are riding up town now, and as Miss Owenson does not fancy conversation at the pitch at which it must be carried on in a street-car, she relapses into silence, and watches with never-flagging interest and amusement the people who perpetually get in and out.

Presently their own turn comes, and they walk three or four blocks westward, and stop at last before a two-story wooden house, sadly in want of paint. A tiny plot of grass is in front; there are flowers in all the windows, Miss Owenson notices, and augurs well therefrom. Uncle Grif knocks with his knuckles, and this primitive summons is answered immediately. An elderly woman opens the door, smiles upon Uncle Grif, and glances at his companion. Then there is a simultaneous exclamation.

"My dear young lady!"

"My dear old lady!" Sydney was on the point of saying, but substituted "madam;" and Uncle Grif gazes agape from one to the other.

"Why, you're not acquainted already, are you?" he asks.

"We met; 'twas in a crowd," laughs Sydney; "we met by chance the usual way, last week, Uncle Grif, in a car. Really it is quite a coincidence."

"Come in," says the mistress of the house, and ushers them into the tiniest, the trimmest little parlor Miss Owenson has ever seen out of a doll's house. A flower-stand filled with pots is in each window; muslin curtains, delicately embroidered, draped them; a little upright piano, its keys yellowed by time, covered with music, stands in a corner; one or two oil chromos and steel engravings, in home-made rustic frames, hung on the papered walls; books in profusion litter the centre-table. The chairs are cane, the carpet old and faded, but the little room is so sunny, so sweet, so dainty, that it is a positive pleasure to be in it.

"People who have seen better days, decidedly," Miss Owenson infers, taking all this in with one comprehensive feminine glance. "What a *very* nice face the old lady has."

"Will you not introduce this young lady, Mr. Glenn?" says the mistress of the house, as she places chairs. "We have met before, and the young lady did me a favor, but I have not the pleasure of knowing her name."

"I beg your pardon, I—I forgot to introduce you," Uncle Grif responds in his flurried, nervous way. "This is Miss Owenson, Mrs. Nolan—Miss Sydney Owenson. And this is my old friend, Mrs. Nolan, Miss Sydney."

"Nolan," thinks Sydney, a little startled.

"You—you know Lewis, you know?" continues Uncle Grif, apologetically to Sydney. "This is his mother. She—she is acquainted with your son, Mrs. Nolan, and—and her lace is torn, and I made her bring it here to have it mended."

Uncle Grif pulls out his handkerchief and wipes his forehead, very much upset at finding himself master of the ceremonies, even on this small scale. Mrs. Nolan looks at her fair visitor with a pleased smile.

"You have met my son, Miss Owenson?"

"More than once, madame. But I had not the slightest idea, I assure you," says Miss Owenson, blushing suddenly, "that in coming here——"

" Didn't I tell you it was Lewis' mother?" says Uncle Grif, looking surprised. "No, by-the-by, I believe I didn't. She tore her—what was it, Miss Sydney? Oh, her flounce, and I asked her to bring it here, and let you mend it. You can mend it, you know, Mrs. Nolan?"

"I will be able to tell better when I see it," Mrs. Nolan answers; and Sydney unwraps her parcel and hands it to her, feeling oddly nervous herself.

Lewis Nolan's mother—Lewis Nolan's home—she looked at both with new and strong interest. That was his piano, those his books—how refined everything was in its poverty. What was the sister like, the girl wondered. Mrs. Nolan took the torn lace to the window and examined it with the admiring and appreciative eye of a connoisseur in laces.

"What exquisite Chantilly—what a beautiful pattern—what a pity it should be torn. I never saw a lovelier piece of lace—it must be very valuable."

" It is," Sydney answered; "but its chief value, in my eyes, is that it belonged to my dear mother. Can you mend it, Mrs. Nolan?" Uncle Grif assures me you work miracles with your needle."

" My eyes are very bad for fine work, particularly black; but Lucy can, I am positive. Lucy is my daughter, Miss Owenson, and very proficient in lace work. She is an invalid, and cannot come down-stairs, but I will bring it up, and show it to her, if you like."

"Cannot Miss Sydney go up too?" cries Uncle Grif, in his eager way. "I—I should be glad to have her know Lucy."

" And Lucy will be very glad to know her," says Mrs. Nolan gently, "if you will come up, my dear Miss Owenson——"

Sydney rises at once; that strong feeling of profound interest still upon her, and follows Mrs. Nolan up a little flight of steep stairs to an upper landing off which three small rooms open. The door of each stands open; they are all bed-chambers, all spotless and tasteful, one the mother's, one the son's, the young lady decides, and this front one the invalid daughter's. Sydney pauses a moment on the threshold and takes in the picture. The green carpet on the floor, the small white bed in the corner, the two pictures that hang near it—"Ecce Homo," and "Mater Dolorosa,"—a trailing Irish ivy filling one window, roses and geraniums the other. The same muslin draperies as downs-tairs, a large photograph of Lewis Nolan's strong face and thoughtful forehead over the mantel; a table

with a family Bible and one or two other books of a grave nature, judging by their binding, and—a little thrill goes through
Sydney as she sees it—a basket of pure white flowers that a
few days ago graced the counter of Greenstalks. This, then,
is the lady-love for whom the young lawyer spends his money.
Mr. Nolan rises in one second to a place in Miss Owenson's
regard, which it might else have taken him months to attain.

She looks from the room to its occupant with ever-growing
interest.   In a great invalid chair she sits, no girl—a woman of
thirty evidently, so slight, so fragile, so bloodless, that the thin
face and hands seem almost transparent.   But it is the sweetest face, Sydney thinks, her eyes have ever looked on, with an
expression so gentle, so patient, so womanly, that her heart is
taken captive at a glance.   There is a subtle likeness to the
brother in the sister, the same dark, deep eyes, the same
thoughtful brow, the same cast of feature.   Only the somewhat stern mouth of the young man is soft and tender in the
woman, and the likeness makes the contrast between them
more marked and pathetic—he, the very type and embodiment
of perfect health, strong and manly vigor—she, with death, it
seems to Sydney, already imprinted on her face.

"Lucy," Mrs. Nolan says, "this is Miss Owenson.   She has
brought some lace to be repaired, and Mr. Glenn, with his customary kindness, recommended us."

"Miss Owenson?" Lucy Nolan's face lights up.   "The
Miss Owenson who resides with Mrs. Macgregor?"

"Mrs. Macgregor is my relative—yes."

How much the sister resembles her brother, Sydney thinks,
when she smiles, and where—where has she seen Lucy Nolan
before?   In a moment it flashes upon her.   Idealized, and as
this sick woman may have looked ten years ago, her face is the
pictured face of "The little Sister."

"Evidently Monsieur von Etté derives his inspiration from
this family," thinks Miss Owenson, amused.   "That is a very
good likeness of Mr. Lewis, over the mantel.   That strong,
dark face, and those piercing eyes of his photograph well."

"You can do this, can't you, Lucy?" says her mother, ex-
hibiting the rent; and Lucy examines it in her turn through a
pair of glasses with a practical eye.

"I have to wear glasses at my work," she informs Sydney.
"What lovely lace!   Yes, I can do this easily, and so that the
mending will never be known from the original pattern; but
not this week.   Are you in a hurry, Miss Owenson?"

" Not at all—next week, next month, will do if you like."

" Ah ! but we don't like," responds Lucy Nolan; "we do not want to keep a flounce worth a thousand dollars in our possession any longer than we can help. I shall do it early next week."

" I must go and see after Uncle Grif," says Mrs. Nolan, leaving the room. " He is languishing in solitude down-stairs."

" What very lovely flowers," remarks Miss Owenson. " Your windows are perfect floral bowers, Miss Nolan."

" Yes, plants flourish with me. Is not that calla beautiful ? My brother takes the trouble of banishing them every night. He has hygienic notions about their absorbing all the oxygen that my poor lungs need."

" Your brother is right. Yes, your calla lily is a gem. And what a superb ivy. This," Sydney points to the basket, " is an old acquaintance."

" Yes, Lewis sent me that on my birthday. I was one-and-thirty last Thursday ; and he told me he met you and Miss Macgregor at the florist's. I am glad I have met you, Miss Owenson," Lucy says, with a smile.

" I have heard of you until my curiosity has been strongly aroused."

" Heard of me ? " Sydney repeats, her blue eyes opening.

" I never go out ; it is months since I left this room, and Lewis tries to amuse me by telling me every evening what goes on in the outer world, the people he meets, and the sights he sees. And he has told me a great deal about you."

" Indeed," says Miss Owenson, coloring.

" I wish I might tell you what he has said. I wonder if you would be offended," laughs Lucy.

" Well, so that it be not very uncomplimentary I think I might stand it. It is well sometimes to see ourselves as others see us."

" Then ! you're not to be offended, mind ! He told von Etté he had seen many beautiful faces in his time, but never one of such ideal purity and nobility, half womanly, half angelic."

" Oh ! " Sydney cries, " hush ! " The rose-pink blush is scarlet now. " If Mr. Nolan had the bad taste to say that, you should not have repeated it."

" I apologized beforehand, remember. He would be as in-dignant as yourself if he knew I had told. Von Etté says you have bought ' Sintram.' What do you think of the likeness ? "

" It is a very good one, if one could imagine your brother

in so tragic a frame of mind. So you never go out · how sad
that must be. You look very ill—too ill to work. Have you
been an invalid long ? "

" For ten years," said Lucy Nolan.

" Oh ! "

" I have consumption, as you may see," pursued Miss Nolan,
with perfect cheerfulness, "and complaint of the spine, that
chains me to this chair. But I am quite able to work. Oh, I
assure you, yes ; and my work and my books are the two chief
pleasures of my life. You don't know how thankful I am to
be able to work and help mother and Lewis, who work so hard.
My needle passes the days, and then there are the evenings.
My sun rises, Miss Owenson, when other people's set, for the
evening brings Lewis and Carl von Etté, and we have music and
the magazines, and the news of the world outside. And I am
happy, I assure you. Oh, just as happy as the days are long."

There are tears in Sydney's eyes as she listens to the bright
voice, and looks in the wan face, all drawn and pallid with
pain.

" But you must suffer, surely—your face shows that."

" Yes," Lucy says, and says it still cheerfully, "a little sometimes. My back "—a spasm twitches the pale lips—" I suffer
at times with my back. The worst of it is, I have a nasty,
hacking cough that worries mother and Lewis, and keeps them
awake nights."

" It keeps you awake too, does it not ? "

" Yes, but it doesn't matter so much about me. They have
to work so hard all day, that it is too bad their rest should be
broken by my wretched cough."

Lucy Nolan says this with such genuine sympathy for them,
such genuine indignation at herself, that Sydney smiles, although tears still stand in her eyes.

" Are you ever confined to bed, Miss Nolan ? "

" Miss Nolan !—how comical that sounds," says the invalid,
laughing. " Call me Lucy, please—I don't know myself by
any other name. Yes, I am sometimes, when my back is very
bad, and then poor mother is nearly worn to death waiting on
me, and Lewis *will* have a doctor and expensive medicines, say
what I will. I am a dreadful drag on them both—all Lewis
earns he is obliged to spend on me. Ah ! you don't know how
good he is, Miss Owenson. Night after night he has had tc
watch with me, and toil all day long at he office after. He
would insist upon mother's going to bed, and letting him take

her place. The trouble of my life is the trouble I give them."

" ' Honor thy father and thy mother, that thou mayest be long-lived upon the land,' " thinks Sydney. "A good son and a good brother. Mr. Lewis is a gentleman and a Christian, and I like him."

So they sit and talk, and the minutes fly. Sydney is so vividly interested that the afternoon wanes and she does not see it. The charm of manner that makes the brother so agreeable a companion is possessed also by the invalid sister. Her needle flies as she talks, her eyes laugh behind her glasses, she is free from pain to-day and quite happy. It is only when Lucy lays down her work that Sydney sees the shadows of coming night filling the room.

"Oh !" she exclaims, starting up in consternation, "how I have lingered. It is nearly dark. What *will* Uncle Grif say ? "

" Uncle Grif went away half an hour ago," says Mrs. Nolan, entering. "I left him to do something in the kitchen, and when I looked in again he was gone."

" Highly characteristic of Uncle Grif," says Lucy, laughing. Don't feel mortified, Miss Owenson, but he forgot all about you five minutes after you were out of his sight."

" What *shall* I do ? " cried Sydney, in despair.

" Here is Lewis—you must let him take you home," says Mrs. Nolan. "It is altogether too late for you to venture alone."

The house door opened and closed, a man's step came two or three at a time up the stairs, and Lewis Nolan, " booted and spurred "—that is, in great coat and hat—stood in the doorway amazedly contemplating the group.

" Miss Owenson ! "

The color flashed vividly into Sydney's cheeks, but she held out her hand with a nervous laugh.

" You see before you a damsel in distress, Mr. Nolan. Uncle Grif—perfidious, like all of his kind—inveigled me here and then basely deserted me."

In a few words Mrs. Nolan explained the situation, while Sydney hastily drew on her gloves.

" You must permit me to take Uncle Grif's place, of course," said Lewis Nolan. " His loss is my gain. Uncle Grif is to be trusted no further than you can see him. If he were a genius he could not be more absent minded."

" Stay for tea," said Mrs. Nolan, hospitably. " The evening is cold, and a cup will warm you."

" Tea is my mother's panacea for all the ills of life," said Mr. Nolan.

But Sydney would not listen to this—she was nervously anxious to reach home before Aunt Helen and Katherine, and avoid questioning. So taking the arm of Mr. Nolan, Miss Owenson went forth into the gaslit highways of New York.

" Come again soon—do," pleaded Lucy, at parting; " you don't know what a pleasure it will be to me."

And Sydney had kissed the patient, gentle face, and promised.

" Your sister is charming, Mr. Nolan," she said; she " bewitched the hours, I believe. How patient she is, how sweet, how good."

" Poor Lucy !—yes. I hope, among your multiplicity of engagements you will sometimes steal an hour for her. Her pleasures arc so few, her sufferings so great."

" She does suffer then ? She would not say so to me."

" Miss Owenson, her life for the past ten years has been one long martyrdom, and she has borne it all with patience angelic. She does not seem to think of her own suffering, only of the pain and trouble she gives us. Her happiness is in days like this, when she can sit up and work, or talk to a friend. So it will be a work of charity if sometimes——"

" I shall come often—very often," says Miss Owenson. " The visits will be a greater pleasure to me than they can possibly be to her. I owe Uncle Grif a debt of gratitude for having brought me."

" In spite of his heartless desertion ? " asks Lewis Nolan. " Miss Owenson, shall we ride or walk ? The cars are sure to be crowded at this hour, and it is doubtful if you will be able to get a seat. Besides, their progress is so slow, with continual stoppage——"

" I will walk then," Miss Owenson answers. " I have no fancy for bad atmosphere and hanging suspended in mid-air. Besides, I am an excellent walker; I have had no end of practice among the Swiss mountains and over the Cornish moors."

" You have been in Cornwall, then ? "

" For nine months—and thought a six-mile walk between breakfast and luncheon a mere bagatelle."

She pauses suddenly with a keen sense of pain. There is Miss Leonard's letter to be answered, and it flashes upon her she can never say " come " to Sir Henry Leonard. She has never been sure before, but she is to-night.

The walk is nearly an hour long, and the frosty stars are all a-twinkle in the November sky when they reach the palatial brown-stone front, and lights flash from dining-room and hall.

"You will come in?" Miss Owenson says.

"If you will excuse me, no. I shall be busy writing until midnight. Good-night, Miss Owenson."

He rings the bell, and waits to see her admitted; then, with another good-night, Lewis strides away.

"What a long walk I have given him, and no doubt he is tired enough already," Sydney thinks.

"Susan, have Mrs. Macgregor and Miss Katherine returned?"

"No, Miss Sydney, not yet."

"Dieu merci!" thinks Sydney, running up to her own room. Strangely enough, when they do come, and all meet at dinner, she says not a word of where she has spent the afternoon.

At ten o'clock she goes up to her chamber, but before she goes to bed she writes her letter. It is rather a difficult letter to write; but since it must be written, why, the sooner the better. Near the close she says this:

"I hardly know whether to be glad or sorry Sir Harry has not sailed with the expedition. I am glad for your sake, certainly. But, dear friend, I can never say to him the word he wants—I can never say 'come.' If I ever doubted, I doubt no longer. I do not love him, worthy of all love as he is; and I shall love my husband, or go to my grave unwedded. Tell him this as gently as you can, and forgive me all the pain I cause you both."

CHAPTER VI.

"ONE YELLOW NEW YEAR NIGHT."

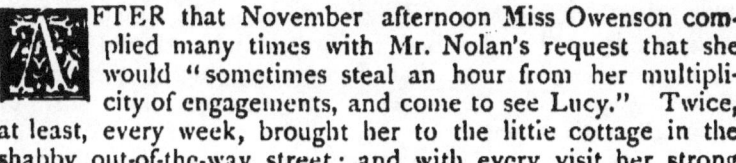 FTER that November afternoon Miss Owenson complied many times with Mr. Nolan's request that she would "sometimes steal an hour from her multiplicity of engagements, and come to see Lucy." Twice, at least, every week, brought her to the little cottage in the shabby, out-of-the-way street; and with every visit her strong

first liking for m.other and daughter grew stronger. Bouquets, luxuriant and rare house-plants, baskets of luscious white grapes, new books, and beautiful engravings, new music, all the refined and delicate things the invalid best loved, began to find their way to the cottage. It was easy for Sydney to imagine her tastes, for they were her own. It was understood, also, that these things were not to be mentioned at the donor's next visit; the thanks and gratitude were to be understood, not expressed. Best of all, work never flagged now; all the time the widow and her daughter could spare from their regular customers, Miss Owenson filled up.

During these weekly visits the son of the house was but rarely met. A shyness altogether new in Miss Owenson's experience of herself, made her shrink from meeting him when she came to see his sister, although always very frankly and cordially glad to meet him elsewhere. They did meet tolerably often in this way—most often of all at his friend Mrs. Graham's, rarely at the Macgregors', and occasionally at concerts or opera. Mrs. Graham, like most happy little wives and women, was a match-maker by instinct, and conceived the happy idea from the very first night, of marrying Miss Owenson to her favorite Lewis.

"It arranges itself as naturally as life, John," says Mrs. Graham to Mr. Graham, in connubial confidence. "Both are young—he clever, she handsome—he struggling for fame and a start in life, she with more money than she knows what to do with. She is the sweetest girl I have met for many a day—sim-ple, unaffected, intelligent and lovely. She is worthy even of *him*. All is said in that."

"I feel," observes Mr. Graham, calmly, "that if this sort of thing goes on much longer I shall become a victim of the green eyed monster—ferociously jealous of Lewis Nolan."

"Nonsense, sir! You know you are as fond of him as I am, and just as anxious to see him marry well."

"Ah! but heiresses don't throw themselves away, as a general thing, on impecunious young attorneys. Money marries money. 'He that hath a goose shall get a goose.' This Miss Owenson was of English descent—lays claim on the father's side, so I understood, to birth and blood, and all that. And everybody knows that Lewis—my junior partner at present—began his career as my office boy. That sort of thing tells with women."

"It does not with Miss Owenson," cries Mrs. Graham, with

spirit. "Don't class her with the ordinary run of young persons—that fast Katie Macgregor, for instance."

"Fast, my dear?" remonstrates Mr. G.

"Certainly; she is audacious enough for anytning. Did you hear her discuss that odious divorce case lastnight with Mr. Van Cuyler?—Van Cuyler, of all men, with his high and mighty notions of womanly delicacy and dignity. And the way she angles for Mr. Vanderdonck—the way she has been angling for the past six years! It is a thousand pities so pure, so true, so thoroughly sweet and womanly a girl as this Sydney Owenson should be among them."

"She is one of the family, and they are going to marry her to Dick," says Mr. Graham.

"Ah! Dick? I hope your head won't ache until they do," darkly retorts Mrs. Graham. "She will no more marry Dick Macgregor than—than I would if I were single."

"Thank you, my love," says Mr. Graham, and falls asleep.

Mrs. Graham, acting on this philanthropic idea, took every opportunity of throwing these two young people together. She conceived a great and sudden passion for the orphan heiress, carried her about with her wherever she could induce her to come, had her at her house a great deal, and gave Mr. Nolan ample opportunity, if he so desired, to win his way to the heiress' favor. But favors are vainly thrust on some people. Mr. Nolan showed himself insensible, in a most exasperating degree, to all this loveliness and wealth. He and Miss Owenson got on remarkably well in a general way, danced together, talked together, even sang together, on very private evenings, but of love-making, the alphabet was not yet commenced,

"Perhaps Mr. Nolan's modesty stands in his way, my dear," is what Mr. Graham said, soothingly to Mrs. Graham, when that best of women bitterly complained of her favorite's defection. "Bashfulness *is* the bane of most young barristers' lives."

"Bashfulness!" cries Mrs. Graham, with ineffable scorn. "The remark, sir, is too contemptible to be answered. The worst of it is that I think——"

But here Mrs. Graham paused, too honorable to betray even to her husband the secret of a sister woman's heart.

"You think young Nolan *might* go in and win, my dear, if he liked?" insinuates Mr. Graham, which coarse remark his spouse disdains to answer.

Many new friends were being made in the December weeks, many invitations pouring in for the fair heiress, many engage-

ments for every day. A net of entanglement seemed to be
closing around Sydney, in spite of her rebellious protests and
chafings. Invitations could not be rejected without rudeness,
and although for general society Sydney did not much care, she
found herself being drawn into the maelstrom, whether she
would or no. It was most difficult, at times, to keep up her
visits to Lucy Nolan, and in these latter weeks Lucy was ailing
and in pain.

The wan, patient face saddened when Sydney went, and
lightened into temporary forgetfulness of suffering when she
came. Some of the December sunshine seemed to enter in her
face, the little sad house grew glad with her presence. "Sydney's days" were the sunniest days in the week to Lucy; and
Sydney, realizing it, resolved that no engagement should here
after interfere with those visits. The place that Cyrilla Hen·
drick had once held in her heart, vacant ever since, was rapidly
being filled by this wan, gentle Lucy.

"The great trial of "The State vs. Harland" was to com-
mence about the close of December, and Lewis Nolan became
so busy and absorbed that he no longer was visible even in the
drawing-room of Mrs. Graham. He came home very late, to
sleep, left early, and was seen no more until the following
night. Mrs. Graham poured her complaints into Miss Owenson's ear.

" He is working himself to death. I saw him last evening.
I went down to the office for Mr. G., and Lewis lifted such a
worn face from a pile of hideous law papers—those great eyes
of his, hollow, and with *bistre* circles beneath. I miss him so
much at my receptions, that tall black head of his towering
over the heads of his fellow men.

> "' He seemed the goodliest man
> That ever among ladies sat in hall,
> And noblest—when she lifted up her eyes,
> And loved him with a love that was her doom,'"

said Mrs. Graham, gushing out in the most unexpected manner
into blank verse. Sydney laughs—rather unsympathetically.

"Dear me! how very tragic. 'With a love that was her
doom!' You do not mean yourself, I hope, Mrs. Graham?
For the sake of morality, and my friendly regard for Mr.
Graham—"

"Ah ! you are like the rest," says Mrs. Graham, shaking her
head ; " the girls of the present day have no heart. When I was

you.ıg we would all have lost our heads for such a man as Lewis Nolan."

" What very ill-disciplined heads must have been in vogue. And how odd it seems to be talking sentiment at the fashiona·ble hour, and on the sunny side of Broadway," answers the heiress.

Mrs. Graham might have her own ideas, but Miss Owenson baffled even her.   Certainly the bright face of this stately young heiress betokened anything but love-sickness, and that frank, rather satirical laugh must come from a heart-whole maiden. The gentleman was immersed in a horrid murder case, the lady in running the round of a New York season—yes, it seemed a a hopeless affair.

Sydney's acquaintance had come long ago to the ears of her family.   And Katie Macgregor had looked up from a fashion-book and the latest style of coiffures, and given her blonde cousin a long, peculiar glance.

" So *that* is where you go ? " she said, slowly.   " Do you know it has rather puzzled me lately where so many of your afternoons were spent ? "

" Indeed ! " said Miss Owenson, going on with her knitting in unruffled calm.   " How very unnecessary for you to puzzle yourself.   Had you inquired I would have been most happy to have told you."

There was silence.   Miss Macgregor looked back at the heads of hair with compressed lips.

" You went first with Uncle Grif, to have your torn flounce repaired ? "

" Yes."

" I knew they were seamstresses of some sort—dressmakers or shirtmakers, I fancied. What kind of people are they ?   Vul-gar, or like Lewis ? "

" Vulgar is the last word I should think of applying to Mrs. or Miss Nolan.   If I ever saw ladies, they are ladies."

" Ah ! persons of education ? "

" That is understood."

" But it must be a very unpleasant neighborhood for you to visit—some low street, is it not, near the North River ? "

" It is a street of poor people, if that is· what you mean. Does poverty inevitably include lowness ?   I do not find it at all unpleasant."

" And then, of course, Lewis is always there to see you safely home," carelessly suggests Miss Macgregor.

Miss Owenson lifts her eyes from her work—a gray and crimson breakfast shawl for Aunt Helen—and looks across at her cousin.

"Mr. Lewis came home with me on the evening of my first visit, as Uncle Grif had forsaken me. Since that day I have not had the pleasure of meeting him once at his mother's house."

Was there a ring of defiance in Sydney's tone? Instantly Katie became cheerfully apologetic.

"Uncle Grif always said they were the nicest possible people, the Nolan family. I never met any of them but Lewis. He was a *protege* of uncle's, as I have told you, and it was uncle who first got him into Mr. Graham's office to open and close, sweep, go errands—not a very dignified beginning—and finally sent him to the same school with Dick. Dick used to bring him here at times, and we all romped in a friendly way together; but as we grew up, of course, our paths swerved. I have no doubt, however, that Lewis Nolan's will one day be a well known name throughout the land."

"One, two, three, four, five—seven—twelve loops of gray," is Miss Owenson's answer to this, as she bends over the breakfast shawl.

"The trial begins to-morrow," pursues Katie. "How I should like to go."

"Should you?" growls Dick, rising suddenly from his seat in a distant window and throwing down his paper. "I dare say : women are always fond of going where they're not wanted ; divorce trials, murder trials, everything new and nasty. They go to hangings, sometimes, and bring their babies. I don't suppose it would do *you* any harm ; but, for all that, you won't go."

"Don't attempt sarcasm, Dick, at least until you grow a little older. I want very much to see Mrs. Harland, and hear Mr. Nolan's speech. Mrs. Graham is going, Mrs. Greerson, and lots more. Why cannot you get Syd and me admission, like a man and a brother?"

"Would you go?" asks Dick, looking at Miss Owenson.

"No," says Sydney, quietly.

"Ah!" Captain Macgregor's manly brow clears ; "I thought not. You may go if you choose, Katie ; you're big enough and old enough to look out for yourself ; but I wouldn't if I were you. Fellows talk about that sort of thing, and it spoils your chances."

"Mr Vanderdonck wouldn't care," responds Katherine, with unruffled good temper.

" No, but Van Cuyler might. You've been making eyes at Van Cuyler lately, haven't you? Not that it's of any use, mind you," says Dick, darkly. " He has registered a vow, has Van Cuyler, like those fellows with the crosses on their legs—cross-legged, eh?—Crusaders, never to marry. He'll take all the love-making you can do—he's used to it, bless you—and never think once you're out of his sight."

" What a ' blessing in disguise ' is a brother," observes Katie as the door closes after Captain Dick's stalwart form. " He is right to a certain extent, after all ; I *should* like to go."

She did not, however ; but the papers and Dick brought daily reports of the trial. The opening speech for the prosecution was crushing—the learned counsel inveighed against the man or woman " who anticipates the great prerogative of the Almighty, and sends a soul from time to eternity." Great interest was felt on all sides, for Mrs. Harland had youth and good looks, and many friends. The trial lasted a week. Mr. Nolan came to the fore nobly, and displayed a forensic skill and acumen that would have done honor to twenty years' experience at the bar. That was what the papers said, and Dick and Mrs. Graham endorsed. He arose and spoke for his client in a way, the latter lady declared, that brought tears to every eye. He painted a long catalogue of wrongs she had endured, the nameless insults she had undergone, the outrages of every kind that a brutal husband can inflict. His speech, Mrs. Graham declared, was one outburst of impassionated eloquence—his whole heart and soul seemed to be in it. Sydney listened with profound sympathy. Mr. Nolan himself could hardly hope more ardently than did she now, that the unhappy prisoner might go forth free. But the hope was in vain, the trial ended, the sentence was a light one, most people thought—four years.

" She heard it with stony calm," narrated Mrs. Graham, with a half sob ; " but she grasped Lewis Nolan's hand as he held it out to her, and kissed it. ' I will never see you again,' she said ; ' I will never live to come out. My sentence is just ; but all my life I will thank and pray for you.' I cried, I assure you, as if my heart would break," said Mrs. Graham, who cried as if that organ would break on the smallest provocation. " Death was imprinted on her face, poor thing ; and for Lewis himself, he hardly looked better."

That evening a little note from Lucy reached Sydney.

" DEAR," it said, " come to-morrow. I am sick in body and

sick at heart. Let me see your bright face, and tell you my troubles.   Lucy."

It was so rare a thing for patient Lucy to complain that Sydney was troubled. She went to the opera in the evening, and the celebrated Mr. Van Cuyler, the pet this winter of the best metropolitan society, came into their box, and in a Sultan-like way made himself agreeable to her; but she was *distrait*, answered at random, heard the singing as in a dream, and had a restless and broken night, haunted now by the pale face of the sister, now by the dark face of the brother. It was a relief when, luncheon over, she could start for the cottage.

She invariably walked now; she liked walking for walking's sake, and reached the house with cheeks like pale pink roses. The house-door was only closed, not locked. She never waited to knock now. She opened it, and entered, opened the parlor door, and looked in. The blinds were closed, green dusk filled the room; but through the twilight she could discern a figure lying on the sofa. She went forward softly, and knelt down.

"Mrs. Nolan," she said, slightly touching the cheek with her hand, "are you asleep? It is I—Sydney."

The figure started upright, and she saw that it was Lewis, who had been lying motionless, his face upon his arm. Sydney sprang to her feet.

"Mr. Nolan!"

It was nearly a fortnight since they had met, and the change in him positively shocked her. Worn and haggard, hollow-eyed and thin, something more than Mrs. Harland's trial was at work there.

"You—you are not ill?" she said, with a gasp.

He passed his hand with an impatient sigh, a gesture of spiritless weariness across his forehead.

"Ill? Oh, no—I never was ill in my life—only a little used up after my labors."

"You are looking badly. I am sorry your cause has lost, Mr. Nolan," she said, gently.

"Thank you," he returned, in the same half apathetic way. "It was justice, I suppose, and justice must be done though the heavens fall. 'Burning for burning—an eye for an eye, a life for a life;' it holds as good to-day as in the old Levitical times. They have killed her as surely as if they had hanged her—it is only a question of time."

"I am very sorry."

"You are kind; but why should you be pained by such hor·
rors at all? Do not think of it. Lucy expects you, I fancy.
This miserable business has upset her too, on my account, as if
she had not enough to endure already."

Sydney ascended to the upper room. Lucy was not in bed;
she was in her large invalid chair, with the little book she so
dearly loved in her hand, the " Imitation."

"Reading poetry," Sydney said, kissing her. "Nobody can
equal A'Kempis. What is the trouble now, dear?—that weary
pain again?"

"No, no—if it were only that! Physical pain is not the
hardest thing in the world to bear."

"You have been crying," Sydney said, "you who never cry
Lucy, what is this?"

"Lewis is down-stairs; have you seen him?"

"Yes. Is it the loss of the trial? Dear Lucy——"

"No, no, no; that I expected. It is——"

" *What?*" Sydney almost sharply cried.

"That Lewis is going away."

A stifled sob broke from her, as she laid her head on her
friend's shoulder. There was silence—then :

"This is very sudden, is it not?" Miss Owenson asked,
quietly, almost, it might have been thought, coldly. "Has the
verdict affected him then so greatly?"

"It is not the verdict, although that has something to do
with it. He has been thinking of it for over a year."

"But he is Mr. Graham's partner, and his prospects seem
excellent. Is this not a rather foolish notion?"

"He thinks not, Mr. Graham himself thinks not. He
would have gone a year ago, but that I was so ill."

"You are not particularly well now."

"No; but if he feels he must go, dearly as I love him, inexpressibly as I shall miss him, I will not bid him stay."

"Where does he propose to go?"

"To California—to Sacramento. He has a friend in that
city, with more business by far than he can attend to, and he
has written again and again for Lewis to join him. It is just
the opening Lewis wants, with his talents and energy, for he is
talented, you know, Sydney."

"I know, dear," a little tremor in the clear voice. "And
he is going—when?"

"Early in March. He will write and tell his friend so this
week. Oh, Sydney! Sydney!"

She flung her arms around her friend's neck, and held her close, sobbing as that friend had never heard her sob before. Sydney held her without a word; but perhaps Lucy Nolan needed no words to know that her sorrow was keenly felt.

Miss Owenson remained later than usual this afternoon, her presence seemed such a comfort to Lucy in this new trouble. They ceased to talk of the coming bereavement, and Sydney animatedly gave Lucy an account of New Year's Day—the grand levee they had held, in robes of state, with darkened parlors and flaring gas, of the innumerable calls, the absurdities of the men as the day grew older and the champagne grew heady."

Lucy absolutely laughed aloud, and Lewis, busy among sundry documents, in spite of a bad headache, listened with a sense of absolute physical pain as Miss Owenson's soft musical peal reached him. He was too much occupied to put in an appearance until tea, served in Lucy's room; and as they met around the little table, they four, Sydney was more than ever struck by the worn pallor of the young man's dark face.

" It is nothing," he said indifferently; "I will be all right again directly. A few weeks hard cramming in my student days used to knock me up in the same way. We colored people grow haggard upon very little provocation, but we are toughest at bottom after all."

On this evening Mr. Nolan was of necessity Miss Owenson's escort to Madison Avenue, for the second time. It was a perfect night; a yellow, melting full moon flooded the sky with light and the earth with amber haze; it was mild as September, the streets were brilliant with gas-lit shops and busy people.

" It is a night like a topaz," said Miss Owenson—"a night to be remembered."

" It is a night I will remember when my life in New York is a dream of the past. I am going away, Miss Owenson—has Lucy told you?"

" Yes, she has told me," the young lady answers, in a curiously constrained voice.

" It is rather an effort to pull up stakes and go; rather a wrench to tear myself away from poor Lucy and my mother; but I feel that my chances are better there, and I have many reasons to urge me to go."

" Your friends will miss you very much—we will all miss you," Miss Owenson says.

" All ? " His dark eyes flash for a moment, and he looks at her. " Do you mean that, I wonder, or is it only the proper thing to say ? "

" I mean what I say, as a rule, Mr. Nolan. I certainly mean that. We will miss you—some of us—notably Mrs. Graham —will break our hearts."

A little tremor, with the soft laugh.

" Mrs. Graham has been my very good friend always ; I owe her and her husband more than I can say," Nolan answers in a tone of feeling.

There is silence, and they walk on, and Sydney seems to feel —to feel with a sharp, swift pang altogether new—that it is their last walk.

" When do you go ? " she inquires.

" The first of March, probably five weeks from now, if I can be ready ; and I think I can."

" Then this is good-night and not good-by ? " she says.

" Good-night certainly, and not good-by," he answers, smiling.

" Shall you be at Mrs. Graham's to-morrow evening ? "

There is an unconscious wistfulness in her tone, but he does not detect it.

" I think not. These evenings out unfit me for work, and I shall not have an hour to spare before I go."

" Good-night," she says, abruptly.

She runs up the steps, rings, is admitted, and goes at once to her own room. Her heart is full of bitterness, full of impatient pain, full of wounded pride and feeling, full of anger at herself. She sits down and lays her head miserably on the table, and knows fully for the first time that what Sir Harry Leonard has sought in vain Lewis Nolan has won, unsought.

CHAPTER VII.

" FAIR AS A STAR."

OVE troubles are like other troubles, they seldom come singly. Lewis Nolan might exasperate his best friends by his stoical indifference to beauty and fortune, but other gentlemen possessed more appreciative taste. Foremost among them was the son of the house, Captain Dick

Macgregor. Early in February Captain Macgregor was to go where glory awaited him ; his furlough would expire, and he must return to his duty and the banks of the Potomac. This was why, perhaps, so gloomy a change came o'er his warlike brow, why he fell into moody reveries, and sighed like a furnace, why he lost his appetite, and weighed five pounds less than his usual one hundred and sixty, why he sat like a death's head at the family banquet, why melancholy had marked him for her own. On the other hand, as Captain Dick liked his camp life, with all its hardships and skirmishes, much better than the switch-cane and kid-glove swelldom of Broadway, it is just as likely it was not. But spirits and small talk, appetite and " airy laughter," the young man had lost, beyond doubt ; and instead of awaking sympathy, his altered visage was made game of in the social circle.

> " ' And 'mid his mirth 'twas often strange,' "

quotes Miss Katie Macgregor, doubling up her hand and gazing at her brother as if he were a work of art,

> " ' How suddenly his cheer would change,
> His looks o'ercast and lower.'

" Where is your appetite gone to, dearest Richard ? It has struck me of late that ' green and yellow melancholy,' like ' the worm i' the bud,' is preying on your damask cheek. How does it strike you, Syd ? "

" It strikes me," says Miss Owenson, " that Dick is growing unpleasantly like the misanthropic skipper in the poem—

> " ' His arms across his breast,
> His stern brow firmly knitted, and his iron lip compressed.' "

" That sort of gentleman has heretofore been my ideal, but I begin to find ideals in real life are mistakes. If pouring your sorrows into our sympathetic ears, Dick, will relieve you, you are at liberty to pour."

Captain Macgregor looks gloomily toward Miss Owenson. The hour of his departure is here ; he may never return, and she can chaff.

" Knitted ? " pursues Katie, still regarding Dick with the eye of a connoisseur. " Well, yes, he does remind one a little of the industrious old lady who, when she had nothing else to knit, knit her brows."

"For Heaven's sake, Katie!" exclaims Dick, with a look of disgust, "spare us jokes of such ghastly antiquity as that. Perpetual silence is better than the threadbare facetiousness of an ancient almanac."

"Emmy Vinton can't have refused him," goes on Katie, meditatively; "her attentions of late to the heir of this house have been painfully *prononce*. Can it be that she only lured him on to make the final blow more bitter ? "

"Shows very bad taste on Miss Vinton's part if she has," laughed Sydney, rising from breakfast, at which matutinal repast this family conclave has taken place.

Although Miss Owenson could laugh at Captain Dick without the faintest, remotest idea that she was in any way the cause of his gentle melancholy, she was by no means in very high spirits just at present.

Her semi-weekly visits to the Nolan cottage continued as usual ; she was far too proud to stay away now, although she shrank from the thought of meeting there the son and brother. She never did meet him. Mr. Nolan knew her visiting days, and on these days lingered an extra hour in the office. Evidently he wished to avoid her. Did he suspect the truth ? Alone, as she was, when the thought flashed upon her, the scarlet blood leaped over her cheek and brow, dyeing both a burning, shameful, terrified crimson. It could hardly be, and yet—that he avoided meeting her at his mother's was palpable. The red tide slowly ebbed, leaving her as white as the white cashmere morning robe she wore.

"My going there must cease," she thought, "at least become infrequent, until he goes. After that I may surely visit Lucy as much as I please."

Her lip quivered slightly, with a sense of wounded pride, perhaps, but with a deeper feeling beside. And from that day, once a week was as often as Sydney could find time to visit her friend.

Lucy was poorly, these January days ; and the sea-gray eyes, wonderfully like her brother's, would gaze in silent reproach at Miss Owenson when she came.

"Forgive me, dear," Sydney said, kissing her. "I know I should have been here before, but indeed I am very busy. ' From sport to sport they hurry me,' etc. I am on a sort of treadmill, my Lucy, where once on, to stop is impossible."

"You go out too much, I am afraid," Lucy returned, clasping in both her fragile ones the warm jewelled hands of her friend.

"Dissipation does not agree with you. You never had much color, but you are growing white as a lily, and as thin."

"Are lilies thin?" laughed Sydney. "It is news to me that lilies lose flesh. Too much dancing and dressing, gaslight and glitter, are not conducive to rosy bloom. But I am wonderfully strong, I never even have a headache—that pet feminine disorder. My patient Lucy, I wish I could give you a little of my super-abundant vitality."

"You do when you come; if I saw you every day I believe I should grow well. Yet it is selfish to wish to bring you to this room, although your very presence is a tonic."

Sydney laid her fair rounded cheek tenderly, pitifully against the hollow, wasted one of the friend she loved.

"Wait a little, dear," she said, softly. "When Lent begins, dissipation must cease; and then even every day may not be too often for me to find my way here."

"And do penance," supplements Lucy, with a little laugh that ends in a little sigh. "Lewis will be gone then—how lonely we shall be."

Miss Owenson is silent, but her fair head still rests in sympathy on Lucy's pillow, and, perhaps, in the way women know these things, Lewis Nolan's sister knows that her trouble was felt.

Sydney was very busy—was on a sort of social treadmill as she said, from which there seemed no escape, even if escape she wished. But she did not wish very strongly—it was pleasant enough to meet kindly new faces, and be petted, and admired, and made much of, wherever she went. She was tolerably used to admiration, and so that it was not offensively paraded did not dislike it. Mrs. Graham regarded her with eyes of silent reproach. Was she a frivolous "butterfly of fashion," like the rest? Sydney understood the look, and smiled rather bitterly to herself.

"She thinks it is my fault he is going," Miss Owenson thought.

"I suppose you know Lewis Nolan is going away?" Mrs. Graham asks, looking the young lady full in the face.

"Mr. Nolan? Oh, yes, his sister told me—he mentioned it afterward to me himself. A very good thing, is it not, for him?" inquires Miss Owenson, calmly. "Although *you* will miss him," she laughingly adds, as an afterthought.

"Although *you* will miss him," and she smiles as she says it. Mr. Nolan may go, and deeply and keenly Miss Owenson may feel it; but the *rôle* of the "maiden all forlorn" is one she is not prepared to play for any man alive.

January goes out and February comes in, and in three days

Captain Macgregor departs upon the war-path. Deeper and deeper grows the gloom that mantles his manly brow. Fear, wild hope, dark despair alternately play upon his vitals. So many men are after her—Van Cuyler, the best match in the city among the rest—what chance has he, without beauty or brains, as his engagingly frank sister has told him, with nothing to offer but his captain's pay and the deepest devotion of an admiring heart, etc.? There are times when he resolves to rush away, and bury his secret in the deepest recesses of his soul, others when hope reigns paramount and he resolves to pour out his passion before her. Complicating feelings tear him, and he becomes a spectacle of pity to men and gods.

" If anything were preying on my mind," remarks his sister, one day, casting up her eyes to the ceiling and apparently addressing the observation to the chandelier, "I would speak out or perish! No secret sorrow should consume my heart—not if I knew my-self, and the object of that secret sorrow my own third cousin.

> " She is a woman—therefore may be wooed ;
> She is a woman—therefore may be won."

Miss Macgregor sailed out of the room as she concluded. Dick never looked up from the book he was *not* reading. In the back drawing-room Sydney sat playing softly to herself, dreamy Mozartian melodies. After a moment's deliberation he threw down his novel and went in to join her. The gas was turned low, so that his sudden paleness was the less observable, and the soft musical murmur drowned the dull heavy thumping of his heart.

She looked up with a smile of welcome. Of all the house-hold she liked Dick best, and was really sorry to see him go. But of the wild work she had made inside the blue and brass she never for a moment dreamed. A coquette in the very least, in the most innocent way, Sydney Owenson was not ; she was ignorant of the very rudiments of the profession. Dick and she were good friends and distant cousins, nothing more.

The melancholy "Moonlight Sonata" changed, and, with a mischievous upward look, "*Partant pour la Syrie*" began the young lady. Dick gave her no answering smile ; he leaned moodily against the piano with folded arms, and looked down at the slender white hand on which diamonds and opals shimmered in the soft light.

" Dick, how dismal you look," she says, half laughing. " If I did not know what a fire-eater you are, I should think war and

14

its glories were depressing your spirits. I must work a scarf for our young knight before he returns to the battle-field ; and Emma Vinton—little Emmy, who is dying for you, Dick—shall tie it round your arm, *à la* Millais' ' Huguenot Lovers ! ' "

" Is it necessary to give it to Emmy Vinton when it is worked ? " says Dick, in an agitated voice. " I should value it more if some one else tied it on."

" Should you ? " Sydney says, opening her eyes. " Poor little Emmy ! Who, Dick ? "

" You ! " says Dick Macgregor.

" I ? "

" You—you, Sydney—you ! " he replies, in a voice that trembles with the intensity of the passion he represses. " Oh, don't, *don't* say you never knew this ! "

" I—never—did," slowly and blankly Sydney answers.

" But now that you do know, you will not—Sydney, you will not send me away ! I am not worthy of you, I know that. I have been afraid to speak, but I had to tell you before I went. Give me just the least hope ; I will not ask too much. I love you so dearly——"

" Oh, Dick, hush ! " she cries out, shrinking away ; " don't, don't say another word. Oh, how stupid and blind I must have been ! How sorry I am for this ! "

" Sydney, are you going to send me away ? Is there no hope for me ? I know I am not worthy——"

" Worthy ! Hush ! hush ! " she interrupts ; " it gives me pain to hear you. You are most worthy, and I like you, but—not in that way."

" There is no hope for me, then ? " Dick says, hoarsely.

" None. I am sorry—sorrier than sorry ; but you must never speak to me of this again.

There is blank silence for a little. Dick stands and stares at a picture on the wall—a simpering young person, in a short red petticoat and white bodice, about to wade, barefoot, across a very blue brook. And months after, in misty moonlight nights, lying beside his bivouac fire, smoking his short, black pipe, and looking up at the shining Virginia stars, Captain Macgregor sees the simpering young person in the short petticoat, with a curious sensation that *she* is the cause of the sharp, hot pain that goes with the memory.

" Dick," Sydney falters at last, looking up, with tears in her eyes, and touching wistfully his arm—" dear Dick, you are not angry ? "

"Angry," he answers, in an odd, hushed sort of voice. "No. God bless you, Sydney!"

He goes abruptly, drawing a deep, hard breath, and presently the street-door bangs after him ; and Sister Katie, on the watch-tower, knows that he has gone out to cool off, and has put his fate to the touch, to win or lose it all—and has probably lost. For Dick's success his sharp-sighted sister has had no hope from the first.

Miss Owenson's sympathies have ever been quick, but just at present she is more than ordinarily capable of sympathy for Dick. "A fellow-feeling makes us wondrous kind." The surprise of this evening has been a most distressing one. The mystery of Captain Dick's gloom is solved, but Sydney would have greatly preferred it had ever remained a mystery.

"To-morrow night is *the* night," says Miss Macgregor, sauntering in—"a night big with fate for me ; for it is my intention to bring things to a focus with Mr. Vanderdonck. The old gentleman has been rather backsliding lately—rather inclined to shift his allegiance to the Widow Chester. I hate widows."

"Yes, they are dangerous; we never needed Mr. Weller to tell us that," laughs Sydney. "But pray remember poor Mr. Vanderdonck was fidelity itself until you set him the example by paying attentions to Mr. Van Cuyler."

"And Mr. Van Cuyler ignores me for you. Mr. Vanderdonck goes over to the enemy, and Lewis Nolan goes to foreign parts.

"Was there ever a maid in all this world
So crossed in love as I?"

sings Katherine, lugubriously, and with a piercing look at Sydney.

But Sydney's face baffles her ; it lies back, pale and rather spiritless against her blue cushioned chair.

"What is that you are reading? Oh! the *Phenix Monthly* and Van Cuyler's new novel. How do you like it?"

"As well as most novels. They are all alike—with a difference," Sydney responds, rather listlessly. "They all sing the same song of woman's peerless beauty, man's deathless devotion, or *vice versâ*, with a proper symphony of jealousy, heroism, total depravity, or superhuman self-abnegation."

"But they set the song to different tunes," says Katherine ; "and Van Cuyler's is like himself, stately and—slow. Do you know what I believe?"

"Your beliefs are so many, my dear Katie——"

"I believe that Van Cuyler has taken you for the heroine of his new story, 'Fair as a Star.'"

"Very complimentary to me—so complimentary that I am sorry I cannot agree with you."

"Why can you not? The description tallies exactly—tall, fair, golden hair, blue eyes, a complexion of pearl, a slender, graceful figure ; that is you, is it not?"

"It is extremely kind of you to say so. Pray, do not expect me to answer a question of that delicate nature."

"Oh, nonsense ! And the man is in love with you—that is as much as the consuming passion he cherishes for himself will allow him. It is patent to the dullest observer."

"I must be a very dull observer then, for it is by no means patent to me. Mr. Ernest Vandervelde Van Cuyler—that is his distinguished name in full, is it not?—has certainly stooped from those heights of high-and-mighty-dom whereon genius dwells, to honor me with his notice on several festive occasions. Overpow-ering as the honor is, I have survived it, as you see, and though it should be repeated to-morrow night, still hope to do so."

"Sydney," says Katie, with real solemnity, "answer me this : If Ernest Van Cuyler—rich, aristocratic, talented, famous, handsome—asks you to marry him, will you say no?"

"Katie," responds Sydney, taking an easier position in her easy-chair, "when Mr. Ernest Van Cuyler asks me, I will—an-swer Ernest Van Cuyler. Now please spare my blushes."

"I believe, after all, she is engaged to the baronet," rumi-nates Katie Macgregor; "she has refused Dick, and doesn't seem to care whether Lewis Nolan goes or stays. And unless she is engaged to Sir Harry, she never in her senses would re-ject Van Cuyler."

For Ernest Vandervelde Van Cuyler was a very great man in very many ways. The oldest of all old Knickerbocker families was his, and if Mr. V. V. C. had a fault, it was that he was rather too fond of "shinning up his genealogical tree." The family homestead was as ancient as the first Dutch settlement of Manhattan, and that is blue blood surely in New York. He was rich—held indeed, the purse of a Fortunatus. He was clever—his novel of "Hard Hit," two years before, had hit the public fancy ; the press called it an American "Pelham," and predicted great things for this rising genius, and the rest of the press chopped it in vinegar, and the more they chopped the better the book sold. In addition to all these virtues, he was most unnecessarily good-looking—a tall, blonde, melancholy Hamlet, with cold, colorless eyes, and the general air of an exiled prince. A trifle self-conscious maybe, no end conceited, and looking out of those cold blue eyes of his upon all the delicate loveliness of New York belledom perfectly unmoved. They sharpened their toy bows and arrows, did those fair daughters of Gotham, and took aim often and well ; but this gold-plumaged bird of paradise flew too high for their shooting. And it was Sydney Owenson who in her secret heart thought him a prig and a bore, at whose shrine Prince Charming seemed at last inclined to bow.

It was Carnival time : next week Lent would begin, and the last ball of the season was to be a very grand one. Miss Owenson in white lace—an imported dress fit for a lady-in-waiting, and pearls and creamy-white roses, looked like a vision, and so Mr. Van Cuyler seemed to think. In a dignified and uplifted way he paid court to her all night. He was harder hit than even sharp-sighted Katie suspected, and more than once—still uplifted—made an effort to obtain a private audience. But Sydney's intuitions were correct here, and she skilfully evaded it. Perhaps she thought one declaration in a week quite enough ! Dick's dreary face made her miserable whenever she looked at it. Not that it would give her the same pain to refuse Mr. Van Cuyler, but refusing was tiresome and profitless work to one not brought up to the business. So, although the "talented young author" did his best, made his attentions so pronounced that he who ran might read, Miss Owenson, with the calm generalship which comes naturally to women, out-manœuvered every move. Not once could Mr. Van Cuyler find himself alone with her.

But next day at luncheon, there lay beside her plate a letter —a square, determined-looking letter, in almost illegible chirography.

"Are you certain it is for me ? " says Sydney, eying it dubiously, and trying to decipher her own name. "If it were a doctor's dun, or a lawyer's bill, the writing could not be worse."

"Or an author's autograph," says Katie, maliciously. "Hand it here. To be sure—'Miss Sydney Owenson,' anybody might read it—after studying it ten minutes. Monogram in scarlet and gold, ' E. V. C.', all quips and quirls—pale gray wax, with a coat of arms, and a motto in one of the dead languages."

"Irish, maybe," suggests Dick.   It is his last day home, and no one smiles at the ghostly attempt.

Sydney put it quietly in her pocket.   Instinctively she felt what it contained, felt that it was a letter not to be read here. Luncheon ended, she went up-stairs and opened Mr. Van Cuv- ler's elegant epistle :

"CLARENDON HOTEL, *Feb. 6th*, 18—

"MY DEAR MISS OWENSON."

That much Sydney could make out without much difficulty, but the rest—— Fortunately it was not long ; authors, as a rule, whatever their sins, are seldom guilty of long letters. This was three small pages, no more. Conscientiously Sydney set herself to the task, half-an-hour to each page, and by dint of skipping a word here, guessing a word there, reached the end at last. If his writing was bad, his English was good ; in the most courtly and grandiose manner Mr. Van Cuyler told the tale of his love, and asked Miss Owenson to become his wife.

Sydney sighed a little as she laid it down.   After all, to win the affections of such men Sir Harry Leonard and Ernest Van Cuyler was an honor.   Why was it she could feel no answering affection for either?   Why was it that erratic heart of hers, un- touched all these years, had gone at last, unasked, to a man whom her world would have called beneath her?—a man far less handsome, and no more talented than Van Cuyler, with neither name nor fortune to offer her?   *Why* did she care for him ?   Why did his face haunt her so persistently, his voice sound ceaselessly in her ear, his most careless words linger in her memory?   Why could she not forget him ?   What was there in him or about him, beyond other men, that he and he alone should have power to disturb her peace ?

"Curious fool be still—
Is human love the growth of human will?"

Surely not, for Sydney Owenson had never willed to fall in love with Lewis Nolan.

That very same night Mr. Van Cuyler received his answer; next morning he departed from New York ; a week later, and on a Havre steamer he was half-way across the Atlantic.   Perhaps the author of "Hard Hit" and "Fair as a Star" was right— there can no more effectual remedy for love-sickness than sea sickness. It was a short answer, too, to send a man on so long a journey:

"DEAR MR. VAN CUYLER: Your letter has touched me deeply; believe me I feel all the honor your preference does me quite as much as if I accepted. But I cannot accept. I do not love you. I never can. Regretting that I should give you pain, I am,

"Very sincerely, your friend,
"SYDNEY OWENSON.

"*P.S.*—My decision is irrevocable. I trust you will not heedlessly pain us both by attempting to change it. S. O."

CHAPTER VIII.

TWILIGHT IN LUCY'S ROOM.

AND now Miss Owenson is rid of all her lovers, Dick departs for the fighting ground of the South, and Ernest Van Cuyler disappears all at once, and is in Paris before he has been properly missed. He is a young man not used to the word No; and wounded pride, and hurt self-love, and mortified vanity, have perhaps as much to do with his chagrined flight as the tender passion. In the mysterious way these things get wind, it is whispered about in awe-struck undertones that Miss Owenson has rejected him, *the parti* of the season.

"Is she insane, I wonder?" Mrs. Macgregor asks, rather bitterly, "to refuse Van Cuyler. For whom is she waiting—a prince of the blood royal?"

For Aunt Helen is fiercely angry and disappointed, not that she has rejected Van Cuyler, but that she has rejected Dick.

More than even Katie suspects her mother has counted on this match. To keep the Owenson shekels in the family, to pay her debts, to provide herself with a home for life free of cost and worry—that has been her dream.

The dream is at an end. Sydney has refused him, and the way out of her difficulties seems as far off as ever. Her daughter is disappointing her even more bitterly than her son; the winter campaign is ended, and Mr. Vonderdonck has left town,

his own lord and master still. In a few months another season
of expense and watering-places will begin.

Katherine was five-and-twenty last birthday, and is *not* growing younger with every passing year. She was one of the innumerable "Marthas" of the world, "troubled and anxious about
many things," and daily that austere Roman nose grew more and
more austere, the cold blue eyes harder and more haggard, the
crow's-feet ploughed in deeper ridges, and her manner to her
cousin's daughter as frigid as her great respect for that young
lady's fortune would allow.

Sunday in the Macgregor mansion was at all times rather a
dreary day—the Sunday following Dick's departure more than usually dreary.   In the first place it rained, not a hearty down-pour,
but a miserable, ceaseless, chilling February drizzle, that blotted
out heaven above and earth beneath, in a wet blank of fog and
mist.   Miss Owenson, who was somewhat of a devotee in the
eyes of the family, arose early and went to church. Katie slept until noon, and came down, yawning and slipshod, to luncheon.   It
was a dismal meal; Aunt Helen's face' looked cold, and gray,
and hard as stone.

"Poor Dick! I wonder if they are fighting down there in this
rain," says Katie.   "What a desolate day Sunday is, and only
last week they told us in the sermon, that heaven would be one
perpetual Sabbath! Sunday's rain is wetter, Sunday's cold
colder, Sunday's heat hotter, and Sunday's blues bluer, than any
other of the week."

"Your mental thermometer has fallen since last night," Sydney remarks.   "You were in wild, high spirits starting for Mrs.
Holland's *soiree musicale.*"

"Natural reaction, my dear. I am like a bottle of champagne,
all fizz and sparkle overnight, dead flat next morning.   And
my last state is worse than my first.   After all, I am half glad
the wear and tear of the season is over, and Lent at hand, to
give us a chance to recruit.   Even perpetual parties become a
bore, the theatre monotonous, the opera a dreary delusion.
Daily church-going will be a diversion, and I don't mind fasting
on rock-fish and oysters. *Apropos* of the opera, will you go to
hear 'Il Puritani' in the Academy to-morrow night?"

"Yes—no—I don't know, I will be better able to tell you
when to-morrow night comes," Sydney answers, wearily.

The weather, the change in Mrs. Macgregor, or something,
is producing its effect on Miss Owenson's splendid vitality
and spirits. To-day she looks pale and fagged, listless and

dreary, and the moment luncheon ends goes back to her own room.

"It's my opinion, *madre mio*," says Katie, taking up a novel and glancing carelessly at her parent, "that if that Spartan sever ity of manner of yours doesn't thaw out, Sydney Owenson will take wing one of these days and fly back to her English friends You see she is not used to that sort of thing ; she has lived in an atmosphere of petting all her life, and doesn't understand it. Mrs. Owenson was one of those weak characterless creatures who never scold and make everybody about them miserable for their good, and Sydney naturally doesn't take to it now. I merely throw out the suggestion, mamma ; you will continue to act of course as your superior wisdom may suggest."

Then, novel in hand, placidly ignoring her mother's irritated reply, Katherine saunters away to read until dinner.

Katherine was right ; Sydney was half meditating a flight. across the ocean. Low spirits rarely, almost never, attacked her ; her nature was thoroughly strong, sunny, and inclined to "serve the Lord with a cheerful heart ; " but she was miserably out of sorts to-day. How unkind of Aunt Helen to visit it upon her that she could not marry Dick. In spite of her riches how poor she was after all, fatherless, motherless, homeless—alone. She closed her eyes, and leaned her head, in a tired way, against the back of her chair. If she could only have said "Come" to Sir Harry Leonard, and sailed away with him to the dear, romantic old Cornish house, where cold looks and icy speeches would never have embittered her life. And yet how could she go back now ?

"If mamma had not sold Owenson Place I might return there, find some nice old lady to keep house for me, and have a home, a real home, a home of my own at last. Or if I could find Cyrilla Hendrick—dear old Cy—we might start off to Italy and be free and happy in the gypsy, rambling way poor mamma and I lived so long."

The rain beat and pattered against the glass all day as Sydney sat homesick and lonesome. She had felt from the first that this house could never be home, her relatives never friends. She was convinced of it now. To be in Lucy Nolan's little white chamber, with Lucy's gentle face to make her patient, Lucy's tender voice to soothe her sorrows, would have been comfort ; but Sunday was *his* day home, and on Sunday she never went.

Sunday ended, and Monday morning's sunshine and bustle

14*

dissipated the vapors. After all, what was she that life should not bring its dark days? She must take the bitter with the sweet, like the rest of the world, and make up her mind to life as she found it.

Monday morning brought a note from Lucy Nolan.

" To-morrow is Shrove Tuesday," Lucy wrote ; "and mother is famous for her Shrove Tuesday pancakes. Will you not come and try one? You have not been to see me in five days."

" Poor little Lucy! Yes, I will go." Sydney thought half remorsefully, " why should any foolish feelings of my own keep me away since my going gives her pleasure? She, poor child, who has so few."

She sent a brief word of acceptance with the messenger. In the afternoon she went with Katherine to return calls ; in the evening she went with her cousin's party to the Academy. It was a more than usually brilliant night—bows and smiles greeted them on every hand ; Miss Owenson was a universal favorite in society.

" I said yesterday, I had no friends," she thought, with a half smile. " It seems I was mistaken. I shall never lack friends while I remain an heiress."

" Evil communications," etc. Five months of Katherine Macgregor's society was making even Sydney cynical. She sat rather silent in the midst of her gay circle, lying listlessly back in her chair, her eyes fixed upon the stage and the singers, Presently Katie leaned forward, and spoke in a half whisper :

" Look, Sydney, there are the Graham family. That very stylish girl in the striped opera-cloak and with the scarlet camelias is Mrs. Graham's sister. And—positively, yes—Lewis Nolan is with them. I thought he had left this wicked world altogether of late."

Sydney glanced across, and saw her large friend, Mrs. Graham, as usual, in loudly swearing colors, and by her side an extremely graceful and rather fragile-looking girl, in an opera wrap of distinguished hues. Leaning across Mrs. Graham' chair was Lewis Nolan, his eyes upon the prima donna of the night, evidently absorbed in the music. The young lady leaned back in her chair, and addressed him with a coquettish smile. He bent his tall head to catch her remark with an amused expression.

" What ! " exclaimed a gentleman of Miss Macgregor's party, "is Nolan going in for Nellie Lincoln? I never thought

of it before, but the whole thing would arrange itself beautifully. She is Graham's sister-in-law ; her family have both money
and influence. With his talents all he wants is a push upward,
and if he does not get the push, even his talent will find it up-
hill work, heavily weighted as he is in the race of life."

" I understood Mr. Nolan was going to California to seek
his fortune," observed Katie.

˙ " But if he finds the fortune ready made to his hand at home ?
Why go to California for what hé can get in New York ? "

"Why, indeed, if he can get it, of which I am not at all
sure. He is a friend of the Grahams, and has a passion for
music, consequently Mrs. Graham makes him do escort duty
for her husband. I do not believe there is anything between
Miss Lincoln and—— Sydney, they are bowing."

Mrs. Graham, sweeping the house with her double-barrels,
espied the cousins, and bowed. Then she spoke to her escort,
and Mr. Nolan, glancing across, bowed in his turn.

"What a very lovely face !" said Mrs. Graham's sister.
"Your description has not done Miss Owenson justice. Does
she not make a picture, Mr. Nolan, as she sits there, with all
that golden hair and that scarlet drapery ? I never saw a
sweeter face."

"About Miss Owenson's beauty there can be no two opinions," is Mr. Nolan's answer.

"And as good as she is beautiful," says enthusiastic Mrs.
Graham :—" it is a heart of gold. There is a fascination about
her that won my heart at sight."

"Ah ! but Mrs. Graham's heart is so very easily won," says
Nolan.

"And so very often," says Mrs. Graham's sister. " I never
pay any attention to Bella's rhapsodies ; she is always infatuated about somebody ; but really, Miss Owenson justifies a
little raving. They say she even captured the invincible Ernest
Van Cuyler."

"So it is said," Nolan answers. " Mr. Van Cuyler's taste
is excellent."

" I wonder if there *is* anything in that, Sydney ?" Katie remarks, as they go home. " I wonder if Lewis Nolan is really
épris of Nellie Lincoln ? As Major Lloyd said, a little while
ago, it is just the start in life he wants. He could not do better."

" Let us hope it is so, then," Sydney responds, serenely
" Whatever good fortune befall him, I am quite sure it is deserved."

Katie looks at her earnestly ; she is shrewd, but she is baffled.

"No," she thinks, "she does not care. She never could look like that if she did."

An influx of callers next day detained Sydney in the drawing-room until quite late. It was half-past four before she could make her escape and change her dress to visit Lucy. She was feverishly eager to go—perhaps there she would hear whether there were any truth in this new rumor or no.

She rode to her destination, but it was nearly six before she reached the house. Lucy would be waiting, would think she did not mean to come, and she hurried in, opening the house door without knocking. She looked into the parlor—no one there. She turned and ran lightly up to Lucy's room. In the doorway she paused, struck by the picture before her. Coming darkness shadowed the little chamber, the fire in the grate had burned low and cast fitful gleams over everything. Lucy sat in her accustomed place, and leaning over the back of her chair was Lucy's brother. Neither saw her from their position, both were absorbed, and it was her own name, uttered by Lewis Nolan, that chained her to the spot.

"Sydney Owenson," he was saying, in an intense tone of concentrated feeling. "Yes, Lucy, you have guessed the truth It is because I dare not see her, that I avoid her, because I have no trust in my own strength, that I shun her presence. If I met her oftener than I do, I would have neither self-control nor power left. There are some temptations a man can face, defy, and trample under foot—there are others from which flight is the only salvation. This is one."

"I have suspected this," Lucy said. "Who could see her and not love her, so lovely, and so lovable, so true, and tender, and sweet?"

"And so far above us. She does not suspect my presumptuous folly?"

"I think not. I am sure not. But, Lewis, is it such presumptuous folly? I know she is very wealthy, and of a very proud family ; but is mere wealth, then, such an insuperable barrier? Why not tell her at least before you go? It is only fair she should have a voice in the matter, since you go on her account. She is so gentle, so good, she would not look upon it as presumptuous folly even if she refused you——"

"Even if she refused me," Lewis repeats with a short laugh "Your knowledge of the world is limited, Lucy, but even you can hardly doubt that. She is surrounded by suitors of a beauty and a fortune equal to her own, and Van Cuyler, surrounded by a glamor of fame, at their head. Nothing succeeds like success Van Cuyler will win her, and I—will carry the crowning mad-ness of my life with me to Sacramento, and in new scenes and hard work live it down."

The spell is broken. Sydney makes a step forward and stands still. Lewis Nolan starts around, Lucy utters a cry; Miss. Owenson, pale as ashes, trembling violently, comes forward.

"I—I beg your pardon," she says, in a gasping voice, "I did not mean to listen. But I caught my name and——"

She comes over to Lucy's side ; and Lucy takes the two hands, imploringly held out, in hers, and clasps them hard.

"You have heard," Mr. Nolan asks, quite white with the shock of his surprise.

"All. Oh! forgive me. Indeed I did not mean to listen——"

"Forgive *you* /" he repeats, mastering himself by an effort. "But you will do me the justice, I am sure, to believe I would not wilfully have pained you by this avowal."

She stands silent, but her color is coming and going, her breath quick, her eyes intent upon the carpet pattern.

Lewis Nolan, in spite of the poverty of his antecedents, is an adept in the polite art of self-repression. He holds himself well in hand now.

"My sister has been trying to overthrow my resolution of going away next month," he says, but the deadly pallor of his face belies the calmness of voice and words, "and in an uncon-trollable moment I have told her the truth. That I have learned to love you is at once my loss and my gain, but knowing its hopelessness I never meant to pain you by the knowledge. Now that by chance you have heard, if it does pain you, you will still forgive me, I am sure."

She stands silent. "Forgive him!" He only asks that. "Have I indeed offended you?" he says, coming nearer. "Shall we not part friends, then, after all ?"

Part? She cannot bear that. She sinks down on her knees, and lays her face against her friend.

"Tell him, Lucy,"—clinging to Lucy's hands—"*you* know."

And Lucy laughs softly at the little comedy of errors, and holds her close, and looks triumphantly at her brother.

"Miss Owenson!" he cries—"Sydney, what does this mean ?"

"Oh, stupid Lewis ! "Lucy laughs ; "how blind men are ! It means you are not to go to Sacramento—that is all."

CHAPTER IX.

"MY LIFE HAS FOUND WHAT SOME HAVE FOUND SO SWEET.'

T is half-an-hour later.

Twilight, pale and gray, has given place to night: outside the frost February stars sparkle, and a new moon glimmers like a broken silver ring. Inside, the red glow of the fire still fitfully lights the room, and lingers on the two figures standing at the ivy-wreathed window, and on Lucy Nolan lying back, her eyes upon them, her hands clasped, praying, perhaps, but with a face of infinite content. For the two persons most interested, they just stand here and say very little. They have said very little in the past half-hour, but Sydney knows that the desire of her heart is hers. And Lewis Nolan knows, that what in his wildest moments of hope he never dared hope for, what Ernest Van Cuyler has vainly sought, is his. And among all the elect of Mammon, whom the news will probably shock and amaze, not one will be more honestly surprised than is at this moment the happy man himself. He has spoken little either of love, or rapture, or gratitude, as they linger here. Long ago—he is thinking of it as he stands by Sydney Owenson's side and gazes out into the starry darkness— the strong passions nature has given him, slipped their leash, and the memory of that time has darkened his whole after-life. The power of self-repression, his life-study since, has become second nature now, and he stands beside the beautiful woman he has never hoped to win, and keeps those turbulent emotions of joy and love well reined in. But Sydney is content, the silence is eloquent, and his few broken words, his face, his eyes, have told her all she asks to know.

"Sydney," he says, and the name comes as naturally to his lips as though they had spoken it for years, "Mrs. Macgregor will never consent."

Sydney, leaning lightly against the window frame, her eyes fixed on that broken, little yellow moon, smiles dreamily, and glances shyly up in her tall lover's face.

"Will she not? Very likely. But it doesn't matter, does it? A second cousin is—well, a second cousin. I am not sure that her consent or approbation signifies."

He smiles at the easy air and tone of utter indifference.

" But I am afraid it does, my little princess. You are making a very shocking *mesalliance*, stooping very low in stooping
to me. Do you not know that ? "

" I did not before. You should know best, however. I bow
to your superior wisdom, Mr. Nolan."

" Ah ! it is no laughing matter. Mrs. Macgregor's house is
your home ; she can make it very unpleasant for you, Sydney."

Sydney knows that ; Mrs. Macgregor has made it excessively unpleasant for her already.

"And you have no other home. Do you know, my princess,
that, rich as you are, you are not as well off as other girls after
all."

" I am to-night," she answers, softly, and with a glance that
thrills his inmost heart.

" If I only had a home," he says, drawing a tense breath ;
"a home no matter how inferior to what you have been used,
to offer you, I would take you from them at once. But I have
not ; I can offer you nothing."

" Except yourself. Oh ! Lewis, I ask nothing in all the world
beside."

They clasp hands, and again there is silence ; one of those
long, delicious blanks that are better than words. But the
cloud still lingers on the young man's brow ; *her* face is
radiant.

" I suppose you know, Sydney, that you will be set down as
the prey of a fortune-hunter. And very naturally, too. When
a pauper aspires to a princess what other motives can actuate
the pauper than mercenary ones ? "

" Lewis," says Sydney, and the way in which she utters her
lover's name for the first time, is a caress in itself, "don't be
disagreeable, please. What does it matter to you or to me
what all the world says ? You are the only one who will have
the impertinence to repeat such a thing in my presence."

He laughs, then sighs.

" I am not so sure of that. Mrs. Macgregor will consider it
her duty and her privilege to put things before you very plainly
—oh, very plainly indeed. She will tell you—what is true—
that I am beneath you in every way. That while you were
born to the purple, I was born a newsboy ; that while you
walked in silk attire, and siller had to spare, I swept offices and
ran errands ; that while you reigned ' queen, lily, and rose in
one,' in a fashionable boarding-school, I was educated by the
bounty of her brother ; that while you are an heiress, and of

the salt of the earth, I am an out-at-elbows Bohemian, fighting
my way inch by inch, obscure, unknown to fame, with a mother
and sister who sew for a livelihood.   And all Madison Avenue
will be scandalized, and the best metropolitan society will cry
out that one of their Order has put them to shame.   Oh ! little
princess, think of it in time.   It is not yet too late to draw
back, to repent of your sin against society."

"That is a very eloquent outbust, Mr. Nolan," replies Miss
Owenson, coolly ; "but, as a rule, eloquent outbursts are
thrown away upon me. If you have been surprised into telling me you—you care for me a little, and want to get out of it,
please put it in plain words. If you tell me to give you up, I
will do it ; if not, the rest of the world, though it cried out to
me with one voice, is as nothing."

"My own ! how can I ever prove my gratitude for this ? "

"By never saying such hateful things more. All New York
can neither make nor mar my happiness, but you can with a
word.   All the wealth of the world, if I possessed it, would not
weigh a feather-weight against my—love."

She speaks that last word in a shy whisper, as one not yet
used to its sound.   For two-and-twenty years she has gone on
her way, her heart her own, to lay it down humbly here.   She is
sweetness, and nobleness, and generosity itself, but even yet this
difficult Mr. Nolan is not at rest, for he knows she speaks of
wealth and position with the grand disdain of one who has never
known the lack of either.

And now Mamma Nolan puts in her best black Sunday cap,
and calmly announces that the pancakes are ready, and will
they please come down to tea, and at this descent from sublimated sentiment to flap-jacks, all laugh.

"Dear me," says Mrs. Nolan, "what are you laughing at and
what are you all doing in the dark ?   Lewis, I should think you
might have lit the lamp. It can't be pleasant for Miss Owenson to sit in darkness like an owl."

"I don't mind being an owl for a little while, Mrs. Nolan,"
responds Sydney, demurely. "Mr. Nolan and I have been discussing society and its creeds, and forgot that it was lamplight
time."

"Well, come down to supper," says Mamma Nolan, innocently. " Lewis, be very careful in carrying Lucy on the stairs."

For it is one of Lucy's best days, and she is to go down-
stairs. The warning is not needed, no woman could be more
tender of touch than is Lewis with his frail sister. He carries

her down to the cozy parlor, where fire and lamp make warmest
light, and where china tea cups glisten, and an old silver tea-
pot, the one relic of affluent days, sparkles, and where there are
cakes, and coffee, and chickens, and ruby jellies and snowy
bread, cold ham and hot pancakes, all tempting and nice.   It
is a delightful meal, although Sydney finds to her surprise that
she has no appetite, and her effort in the eating way is only an
effort to please her hostess.   Lewis is rather silent, but he looks
wonderfully happy, even his mother notices, and her artless
remarks on the subject make Miss Owenson blush.   There is
a ring in one of these pancakes, Mrs. Nolan gravely informs
her company, whoever gets it is to be married before the year
ends ; and this blissful symbol, the propitious Fates will, shall
fall to Miss Owenson.   Thereupon everybody laughs, and the
bright hue of the young lady's cheek grows brighter, and altogether it is a feast to be remembered, a symposium of the gods.
All the while not a word is dropped that can enlighten the mind
of mamma.   After tea there is music, and Lewis is the musician, all his heart in the songs he sings, in the rich melody his
fingers awake.   Sydney sits in a trance, and listens, and knows
that if the deep happiness she feels were to end with this night,
it might still compensate for a lifetime of sorrow.   Presently it
is nine, and she starts up, and announces that it is time to go.
She kisses Lucy and Lucy's mother, with an ardor only one of
them understands ; and so, with Lewis following, flits away and
disappears.

It is a bright winter night, cold and clear, a night that photographs itself on the memory of both.   The streets are full of
people, but these two are in solitude — they drift on slowly, silent
again, and neither knowing they are silent.   But, presently, the
gentleman breaks the spell.

"Sydney," he says, and the troubled look that worries Sydney is back in his eyes, "after all, this is a leap in the dark for
you.   What do you know of me in reality ? "

> " 'A lightsome eye, a soldier's mien,
>   A feather of the blue,
> A doublet of the Lincoln green,
>   No more of me you knew
>   My love,
> No more of me you knew ! ' "

laughingly says Sydney, out of her radiantly happy heart.

But Nolan will not laugh, he looks down at her with those

gray, dark eyes of his, Miss Owenson thinks the most beautiful
in the world, and reiterates his remark.

"You know nothing of me or my life. I may be the greatest
villain on earth for all that you can tell."

"Excuse me, Mr. Nolan, that is your little mistake. Partly
from Lucy, partly from your doting mamma, partly from Mrs.
Graham, partly from Uncle Grif—all your devoted slaves—I
have heard the whole biography of Lewis Nolan since he was
an interesting cherub in long robes, 'and the best child,' as
Mamma Nolan emphatically tells me, 'that ever lay in a cradle.
Could the most exacting inquirer ask more?'"

Mr. Nolan sees fit to laugh at this, but to Sydney's disgust
grows grave again directly.

"I may have secrets in my life that even these good friends
do not know: Which of us are known to our nearest and dearest as we are. Sydney, there is something that I ought to tell
you, that you have a right to know, and—that may part us."

"No, no!" Sydney cries out, holding his arm tighter; "I
do not believe it. Oh! Lewis, you have not—you have
not——"

"A hidden wife?" supplements Lewis and laughs again.
"My dear child, no. No woman on earth has the faintest
claim upon me excepting yourself."

She draws a long breath of relief. For a moment the absurd
notion that he has put into words has actually flashed across her
brain.

"Nothing else can matter then; if you love me and no one
else will suffer. For I could not take even you, Lewis, from
one who had the slightest prior claim."

"No one has a prior claim, now. Once—years ago—I
cared for, or fancied I cared for, which amounts to the same
thing, a girl who threw me over. Think of that, Miss Owenson!
You honor with your preference a jilted man!"

"I owe her ten thousand thanks that she did jilt you. But
what atrocious taste she must have had! Is that your awful
secret, Lewis?"

"No, Sydney; I wish to heaven it were. In my past life
I——"

"Lewis, stop!" she cries out again, in affright. "I don't
want to know. I would rather not know. I *won't* know!
No matter what it is—even if a crime—it has been repented of
and atoned for, I am sure. With your past life I have nothing
to do; I take you as you are, asking no questions. Only be

faithful and true to me, loving me with your whole heart
always, for with less I will not be content, and I ask no more."·
"No more," he repeats, strong repressed passion in his tone,
fire in his eye. "Sydney! you mean that?"
"I mean that. I ask no more."
"And whatever comes—if in the future what I would tell you
now comes to your ears, you will hold me blameless?"
"I hold you blameless, so that you are still all mine."
"Thank Heaven!"
Did he say it, or did she only fancy it? He drew a deep
breath of great relief, and looked at the fair and noble face with
eyes of almost adoration.
"Sydney, you are an angel. No, you are what is infinitely
better for me—a perfect woman."
"Oh! no, no," she said, earnestly—"a very faulty and erring
woman, wanting a clear head and a loving heart to guide her;
wanting some one braver and wiser than herself to help her
through life."
"And you think me that better and wiser guide? My poor
little Sydney!"
There was an unutterable bitterness, unutterable remorse and
pain in his voice. Was he doing wrong in taking this trusting
girl at her word, in all the innocence of ignorance, and making
her his own, the secret of his life untold?
"I, too, have my confession to make," Sydney says, shyly.
"J, too, was once before engaged. Did you know it, Lewis?"
"No," he answers, "I did not know it."
And the knowledge now gives him a curious sort of jealous
pain.
"Yes, and was very nearly married, but he died, poor fellow;
was killed in fact. I did not care for him in—in this way. We
had grown up together, and I was fond of him as a sister. My
father desired me to be his wife; I was only seventeen, and
knew no other will than my dear father's. But he died."
Sydney's voice trembles even now, as she recalls that dreadful time.
"Do not say any more," Nolan says, tenderly. "I can see
it pains you to recall it. Let the dead past be buried, and from
this night, I swear my whole life, my every thought shall be
open to you. If perfect love, if perfect fidelity, all I have to
offer, can in any way repay the sacrifice you make for me, then
they are yours."
"I wish for no more," she says, and gives him both her hands.

They are at Mrs. Macgregor's door ; and, as she speaks the
words, and he clasps in his those two extended hands, that door
suddenly opens, a blaze of light falls upon them, and Mrs. Macgregor, awful as Macbeth, majestic and stern, in full evening
dress, stands before them.

Tableau !

Mr. Nolan takes off his hat, Sydney blushes vividly, Mrs Mac
,gregor stands and glares petrified, middle-aged gorgon.

" Good-evening, Mrs. Macgregor," says Mr. Nolan, politely,
and by no means crushed.

His voice breaks the chilling spell.

" Will you not come in, Lewis ?" says Miss Owenson, bravely
"No ? Well, then, good-night. Tell Lucy I shall see her to-
morrow."

"Good-night," he says, biting his lip to repress a smile, and
runs down the steps. .

She lingers a moment to watch him, and even Mrs. Macgregor cannot but read what is written so radiantly in Sydney's
lovely eyes.

" Will you come into the drawing-room, Miss Owenson?"
she says, in a sharp metallic voice. " I would like to speak to
you before you retire."

" Not to-night, Aunt Helen," Miss Owenson replies, smiling
gayly, at the same time turning to go up-stairs.

" It is half-past ten," says Aunt Helen, in an acrid tone, and
a glance of the darkest displeasure.

" Is it ?" retorts Sydney, carelessly. " All the more reason I
should go to my room at once. Good-night, Aunt Helen."

She runs up lightly, that smile still on her lips. There will be
a scene to-morrow, and the truth must come out. The scene
will be unpleasant, and Sydney wants nothing unpleasant to
mar the memory of this perfect night. She does what all young
women in love do, in books and out of them, sits at the window
and contemplates the moon.

Sunday was dreary, yesterday was dull, to-day had been
weary—to-night all that earth held of ecstasy was hers, because
a sallow young man with gray eyes and not a rap in his pocket
tells her he is in love with her. She looks up at her " Sintram "
—the moonlight is full on the dark, sad, remorseful face.

" I have seen Lewis to night with just that look," she thinks,
with a sort of tender trouble. "What can his secret be ? But it
is nothing that concerns me—he has told me that ; and I shall
make his life so happy that he will cease to resemble poor,

tempted, melancholy Sintram. I never rejoiced in my wealth before, but I do now for his sake. And to think—to think he would have gone away without telling me if I had not chanced to overhear.

> " My life has found
> What some have found so sweet ;
> Then let come what come may,
> No matter if I go mad,
> I shall have had my day." ·

CHAPTER X.

"I SHALL HAVE HAD MY DAY."

SYDNEY goes down to breakfast next morning with a face from which even the prospect of what is to come cannot dim the sunshine. Mrs. and Miss Macgregor are already seated, Katherine immersed in the morning paper, and Mrs. Macgregor majestic behind the coffee-pot, her Roman nose higher in the air, and more awfully Roman than Sydney ever remembers to have seen it. But Miss Owenson is the daughter of a fighting sailor, and not deficient in pluck. She encounters the stony stare of the mistress of the mansion with a frankly pleasant smile, although her heart beats a trifle faster than is its wont.

" Coffee or tea ? " says Mrs. Macgregor to her young relative, as who should say, " Pistols or poison—take your choice ! "

" Tea, please. Any news this morning, Katie ? "

" Nothing especial," answers Katie, rather coldly, and Sydney receives her tea-cup and stirs her tea.

" Sydney ! " begins Mrs. Macgregor, in a voice that makes every nerve in Sydney's body wince, " it is my duty, unpleasant though it may be, to speak seriously to you this morning. Your parents are dead, I am your nearest living relative, and you are a member of my family. All these considerations compel me to tell you that 1 was shocked—yes, Sydney, honestly shocked—by what I saw last night.

" Did you see anything very awful, Aunt Helen ? " inquired Miss Owenson, taking some dry toast.

"I saw what I did not expect to see—Reginald Owenson's daughter lowering herself——"

"Lowering herself? I do not think I quite understand, Mrs. Macgregor."

Sydney's voice is quite calm, her blue eyes look steadily across the table, but she is growing very pale.

"I repeat it—lowering herself," says Mrs. Macgregor. "Is it necessary for me to say that Lewis Nolan is no fit companion for Captain Owenson's daughter?"

"*Your* daughter first introduced me to Mr. Nolan. I take it for granted she would not introduce me to any one unfit to be my companion, and I met him next at the house of one of your most intimate friends. He is a gentleman, is he not, Aunt Helen; and, as such, a fitting companion for any lady in the land?"

"A gentleman! He is a pauper, a dependant on my brother's bounty; a young man very well in his way no doubt, but low—low both in bringing up and connections; at no time the proper associate of a young lady in your position, and notoriously unfit to be her solitary escort home at ten o'clock at night!"

Miss Owenson has thrown back her head, her face is pale, her eyes are shining as only blue eyes shine in intense, repressed anger.

"I have long intended," Mrs. Macgregor's metallic voice goes on, "to speak to you of the impropriety of your frequent visits to this young man's house; but, knowing you were very charitable to the poor, I forced myself to believe your visits there were as your ordinary visits to the homes of your pensioners. But last night I heard you—even now I can scarcely credit my ears—I heard you call that young man Lewis, saw you stand with both hands clasped in his! I know that Mrs. Graham, in her foolish way, has taken this young man up; that her equally foolish husband has taken him into partnership. All the same, he is none the less your inferior, and beneath your notice; and when you permit him the freedom I saw with my own eyes last night, you—it is a strong word, but I must use it—you degrade yourself, Sydney."

"Mother!" cries Katherine, throwing down her paper.

Miss Owenson rises to her feet, and stands tall, and stately, and pale as death.

"It is a word that has never been used to me before; it is one that shall never be used to me again in this house. All

Madison Avenue, all the friends you have, Mrs. Macgregor, might have been standing as you were last night, looking on, and I would have held Lewis Nolan's hand all the closer, and stood by his side, prouder of my right to stand there than of any one else on earth. For I have the right," Sydney says, a flush of exultant joy, triumph, and love lighting her face, "it is my great happiness this morning to tell you, the right to stand by his side my whole life long!"

"Sydney!" Mrs. Macgregor exclaims. She rises also, blanched with horror. "You do not mean—you cannot mean——"

"That I am to be Lewis Nolan's wife? Yes, Aunt Helen, whenever he sees fit to claim me."

Aunt Helen drops back into her seat with a thud. Katherine sits and gazes at Sydney with glittering cold black eyes.

"I am sorry if I in any way cause you annoyance, Aunt Helen," Sydney goes on in a gentler tone. She is so infinitely happy that she can afford charity to others. "You are my nearest relative, as you say, and I am at present under your care. It will afford me pleasure to please you in any way in my power, to yield to you in all proper matters, but here you must not interfere. I am Mr. Nolan's plighted wife; you are free to announce it to every acquaintance you have, and as soon as you please. Any affront offered to him I shall resent, as I would never think of resenting an affront offered to myself."

And then Miss Owenson, still stately and uplifted, bows her head and goes. Mrs. Macgregor sits up paralyzed; Miss Macgregor holds her *Herald* up before her face and stares at it, and never sees a word.

"Lewis Nolan!" the mother faintly gasps, at last. "Sydney Owenson to marry Lewis Nolan! Katherine, are you deaf, that you sit there and read? *Did* you hear what she said?"

"I heard, mother," Katherine answers, icily. "I am not surprised. She is worthy of him—I can praise Sydney no more highly than that."

"Katherine!"

"And, mother, as Miss Owenson is her own mistress, and you have not a shadow of right over her, and as she pays you trebly for her board, and is rather a lucrative-item in our household, I would strongly advise you to be civil. An heiress need never want friends; doors will be open to her if you make your house too hot to hold her. She may even marry Mr. Nolan out of hand, and have a home of her own. I would in her place!"

With which Katherine leaves the room, and her mother

is alone, to chew the cud of sweet and bitter fancies. Very bit
ter she finds them. To refuse Dick, to refuse Van Cuyler—
all for this Lewis Nolan. What does she see in him? Aunt
Helen thinks, helplessly. If he were a very handsome man she
could understand a romantic girl's fancy and folly ; but he is
not—he is dark and sallow, and thin, with prominent features,
and nothing attractive about him except a voice for singing,
a gift that rather detracts from a man's manliness, in Mrs. Macgregor's eyes. He may be clever in his way, but if Sydney
wanted cleverness, why did she not take Ernest Van Cuyler, a
gentleman and a scholar, and a man who wrote books, surrounded,
too, by the aroma of conquest and fame. Why had she fallen
in love with this young man, Nolan? What does she see in
him? The case is hopeless, the conundrum unsolvable. In a
stunned way she rises and gives it up at last.

Katharine runs up to Sydney's room and raps at the door.

"Let me in, Sydney, please," she says ; "it is only I."

Sydney obeys. She has been crying, Katherine can see—the
usual ending of feminine heroics ; and Katie takes her in her
arms impulsively and kisses her.

"Sydney, you are the best and pluckiest girl in the world,
and I wish you joy. I think I half expected this from the first."

Sydney leans her arm on the mantel and her face on her arm,
tears welling up in her eyes again.

"Don't mind mamma," goes on Katherine. "Your conduct
is sheer madness in her eyes, nothing less. And who can wonder? Refusing Ernest Van Cuyler last week, and accepting
Lewis Nolan this! How pleased Mrs. Graham will be ; she set
her heart on this long ago, and was nearly in despair when she
heard of his departure. Of course the Sacramento exile is at an
end now," says Katie, with a touch of her old satirical smile.

"I hope so. I don't know," Sydney answers, in a stifled
voice.

There is silence, and Katherine stands and looks at her, half
curiously, half admiringly.

"And so my beautiful Cousin Sydney, captor so long, is captive at last ! Shall you be married after Lent, Sydney?"

"I don't know."

"*I* would !" says Katherine, energetically. Why should you
wait? you will be ever so much happier in a home of your own,
and where is the object in waiting half-a-dozen years while he
struggles upward. One of you has money, and I know in your
primitive creed it doesn't matter which, though it would to most

people. But then most people would not throw themselves away—don't be angry, Syd—it *is* throwing yourself away in one sense."

"Be kind enough not to say so, Katie. If I were told a kingdom and a crown were awaiting me, they could not give me a tithe of the happiness the knowledge that he loves me does."

"It must be nice to be unworldly and fresh-hearted like that," says Katie, with a half sigh; "but then it is a luxury you can afford. In your place, even I might fall in love with and marry a poor man."

Ill news travels apace—perhaps that was how Mrs. Macgregor accounted for the rapidity with which the stunning fact of Miss Owenson's engagement extraordinary transpired. To Lewis Nolan! Who was this Lewis Nolan? cried out the uninitiated; and the answer came crushingly:

"A young fellow without a penny; his mother an Irishwoman who sews for a living—son educated for the bar through the charity of Mr. Griffith Glenn and John Graham, Esquire—man who plays the organ in a church for a salary, and sings at evening parties."

Can it be wondered at, that the best society of this democratic city held up its hands aghast, shocked, outraged, indignant? One of the richest heiresses in New York, the last of a fine old English family, a young lady who had refused Ernest Vander-velde Van Cuyler only a few weeks ago! There must be something intrinsically wrong, mentally or morally, with this handsome and high-spirited Miss Owenson—insanity latent probably in the family.

Of course very little of all this came to Miss Owenson's ears, but of course also, she could hardly fail to read the wonder, the pity, the curiosity in the faces she met; and, what was much worse, Aunt Helen, afraid of open warfare, had frozen into strong rigidity. Not Lot's wife had ever been stiffer, harder, colder, than was displeased Aunt Helen Macgregor. She had always disliked this fortune-hunter, this adventurer, this Bohemian young Nolan. As a boy, the money brother Grif should have spent on Dick had been wasted on this pauper lad. As a boy, at the same school, this audacious mendicant had carried off prize after prize over Dick's devoted head. And now this final and never-to-be-forgiven sin of winning Sydney Owenson by his artifices, and for her fortune only, had been committed. *He* had been taken—Dick left. No wonder Mrs. Macgregor's thoughts were gall and bitterness; no wonder that severe Ro-

15

man profile grew awful in Miss Owenson's sight ; no wonder every 'vord that fell from her lips were as so many icicles.

Mrs. Graham, on the contrary, was transported, and embraced Sydney over and again in an ecstasy of gushing, match-making joy.

"You were made for each other, my darling ! I saw that from the first. I should never have forgiven you, Sydney, if you had let him go."

Mrs. Graham was Sydney's one friend. At her house she and Lewis sometimes met, but not often, for Mr. Nolan was, as usual, very much occupied, and seemed to have received a new impetus to work. He had even for a brief time no intention of giving up his California project—he could attain the desired end so much more quickly there. Sydney had looked reproachfully and imploring, and Mrs. Graham had scolded him roundly for such "a tempting of Providence"; Lucy and his mother had pleaded, and finally, and not without some reluctance, it was abandoned. He was working hard, as has been said, with thoughts and hopes now that made the dry-as-dust office work sweet, and at infrequent intervals he and his affianced met chiefly at Mrs. Graham's. Mrs. Macgregor's doors were closed against him. On Sydney's visits to his home he was almost invariably absent, and his partner's house was the only one he visited. When they met in company here, it was good to see Sydney take her place at his side, as one having the right, jealous lest any should fancy for a moment that she was either afraid or ashamed of her choice. The reserve that would have been hers had her lover been what the world called her equal, and that would have forbidden any public pronounced attention, she resolutely banished. The world should respect, if she could make it, this man whom she delighted to honor.

But it was a false position, and the girl, delicate and sensitive, felt it.

As the spring wore on and Easter drew near, her life at the Macgregors' began to grow intolerable. Katie was kind, but unsympathetic. Katie's mother was simply unendurable. All her life Sydney had been the beloved and petted of the household—unkindness, coldness, covert sneers, icy glances, stabbed her like daggers. Without creating infinite gossip and scandal, she could not quit Mrs. Macgregor's house, and gossip and scandal were the nightmares of her life. Her wealth would have opened scores of doors, but not one home. She was happy, infinitely happy in her heart's choice, but that did not prevent very many bitter tears being shed in the solitude of her own room. She

grew pale and nervous, lost flesh and color rapidly in this
ordeal, and a troubled, startled look was growing habitual to
the lovely serene eyes. Mrs. Graham saw with ever-growing
indignation the change in her young friend, and at last her feelings grew too many for her, and she lifted up her voice and
spoke.

"I never thought, Lewis, whatever your faults—and their
name is legion, very likely—that you were altogether heartless!"
cries Mrs. Graham with compressed lips and flashing eyes.

"My dear madam," expostulates Mr. Nolan, looking up
laughingly from a pile of legal cap, for the lady had gone all the
way to the Wall street office to rate the delinquent, "what have
I done now?"

"What are you not doing, rather? Have you no eyes? Car-
not you see that she is growing thin as a shadow and white as a
spirit in that house, under the tyranny of that old gorgon? But,
of course, you cannot. Men are proverbially as blind as bats.
Other people can see how wretchedly the poor child is looking ;
but you, who ought to be the first, don't or won't see anything
at all. Go to!" cries Mrs. Graham, who laid down an Eliza-
bethan novel just before coming out. "I have no patience
with you."

"Do you mean Sydney?" Lewis says, in a troubled tone.
"My dear Mrs. Graham, what can I do? I have seen the
change in her ; I know they make her suffer for my sake, and I
—I am powerless to help her or take her from them."

His dark eyes glow, his lips set sternly. Never has he felt
the bitterness of being a poor man as he feels it now. He
would give his life to save her pain, and he must stand by and
see her suffer, powerless to help her.

"What can you do?" retorts Mrs. Graham, with a scornful
little snort. "You can marry her, I suppose. If *I* were a
man," cries this stout and excitable matron, "and a lovely girl
were ridiculous enough to love me, and that girl had money
enough for a dozen, do you think I would leave her to be made
miserable by a cantankerous old cat like Helen Macgregor?
No, sir, I would marry her out of hand, and give her a home of
her own, and a husband to take care of her, and never stop to
think of it twice."

"But as I am so utterly poor, what would the world say?
Would it be honorable——"

"A fig for the world—that for your honor. What is all the
world to you compared with Sydney's health and happiness?

Honorable—I like that. Is it more honorable for you to grub along in this office for the next ten years, making a competence while you let her life be tortured out of her, than to marry her and make her happy? I admire such honor! Good morning to you, Mr. Lewis Nolan. Unless I hear something more manly of you soon, you will kindly consider our acquaintance at an end."

In spite of himself, Nolan laughs—Mrs. Graham's excitement and indignation are so real. He escorts her to her carriage.

" ' Beggar that I am, I am poor even in thanks ; but I thank you,' " he says, "for your more than friendly interest in Sydney and me."

"Show your gratitude then by acting as you should. Home, Thomas," retorts Mrs. Graham, snappishly.

He returns to his work, but he cannot work. It has been his dream to make a name and a home for his bride, not such a home as she has been accustomed to just at first, but still one of his making. But what if Mrs. Graham is right? Is Sydney unhappy among the Macgregors, and for his sake? If so, is it not his duty to take her from them, to pocket his pride and ambition, defy the world's scoff, and make her his wife at once ?

He tries in vain to concentrate his mind on the brief before him. He throws it aside, puts on his hat and coat, and goes home. It is one of Sydney's days, he has a chance of finding her there yet. He has noticed, with keenest pain, how fragile and changed she has grown of late. He can infer pretty well what kind of enemy Mrs. Macgregor can be.

Sydney is still there ; is alone in the little parlor, playing for Lucy in the chamber above. She starts up, a flush of surprise and delight making her face bright at sight of him.

"You, Lewis, and before five ! How could you tear yourself away from that enchanting office and those fascinating big books bound in calf?"

"Don't be sarcastic, Sydney," says Mr. Nolan ; "sarcasm is *not* the strong point of your sex. I tore myself away because I fancied you might be still here, and I was hungry to see you."

The bright color stays in her face under his grave eyes and at his words, but in spite of it he can see the change in her. The hands that lie loosely in her lap are thin and transparent. He takes one and slips off without an effort the simple engage-ment ring he has given her.

"Three weeks ago, Sydney," he says, that troubled look in his eyes, "this ring fitted so tightly that it was an effort to get

it on. Now see it drop off. My princess, what is the
matter?"

The rosy light leaves her face ; she looks away from him, out
into the grimy street, upon which the red flush of an early April
sunset lies.

"You are suffering for me," he goes on ; "Mrs. Macgregor
is making your life miserable. You are not happy there, Sydney, I can see that. I have seen it from the first. And I—it
will be so many years before I have a fitting home to offer you."

She does not look at him, she watches those ruby gleams of
sunlight on the dusty street, her color coming and going. Her
heart is full of words, but she is a woman, and her lips may not
speak them. He has dropped her hand, and is walking up and
down, his brows bent. He stops abruptly before her in his
walk, takes both hands, and gazes down at her, a resolute look
in the shady darkness of his eyes.

"Sydney," he says, "without a home ; with neither fame nor
fortune to offer you, will you marry me—at once?"

She lays her face down on the hands that clasp hers, almost
with a sob.

"My only home can be where you are," she answers ; "*that*
is no home. I am—oh I so miserable there, Lewis ; I can
never have any home except as your wife."

So it is settled.

*　　*　　*　　*　　*　　*　　*

Now that the plunge is taken, Mr. Nolan shows himself a
man of energy and decision. The marriage shall take place
at once—this very month. Miss Owenson pleads for a little
longer respite.

"Not quite this month, Lewis—say next. I can never be
ready."

"Ready? What do you call being ready? You don't mean
to go in for an expensive trousseau, I hope. At our wedding
such a thing would be a mockery."

Sydney knows that, and hesitates. Then Mrs. Graham goes
over to the enemy, and her side kicks the beam.

"Married in May! Don't you know May is the unluckiest
month in the year for marriages? It is not to be thought of."

"They do nearly all their marrying and giving in marriage, in
May, in London," says Miss Owenson.

"They may do in London as they please ; you shall do in
New York as New Yorkers do."

"Does nobody marry in New York in May, Mrs. Graham?"

"Don't ask ridiculous questions, Miss Owenson. Be guided by the superior wisdom of your elders. May is an unlucky marrying month. Let us call it the last week of April and be happy."

Sydney laughs, blushes, glances shyly at Mr. Nolan, and yields the point ; but in her eyes no month will be unlucky that will make her Lewis's wife. As this is the close of the first week, there is very little time for preparation. Sydney screws her courage to the sticking place, and announces the fact at home, and Mrs. Macgregor turns yellow with passion.

"I cannot prevent this madness of yours, Sydney," she says, in a voice of concentrated rage ; "but in no way will I countenance it. No one from my house shall be present. Across this threshold that man shall never come."

"That is understood," said Sydney Owenson, very pale, but quite calm. "What I wish to know is, if I have your permission to remain here until my wedding day? I would prefer it myself. An open family feud is detestable. If not, I will go to Mrs. Graham's.

"And add insult to injury. That I could never forgive."

"Then I remain. For that, at least, Aunt Helen, I thank you."

But Aunt Helen's answer is a look of exceeding bitterness Katherine says little; but, two days after, she discovers she owes a long-standing visit to Philadelphia, and flits away to pay her debt.

And now the days fly : one by one they dawn, glide by, and are over, and all at once the wedding-day is here.

A lovely day—sunny, serene, cloudless. In Mrs. Graham's carriage, by Mrs. Graham's side, the bride goes to church. She wears a, pale gray travelling suit, with a trifle of white lace and blue ribbon at the throat, a gray hat and gray gloves. Not a flower, not a jewel ; a shop girl would have thought it plain. She is quite white with emotion, but in her heart there is not a doubt, not a tremor. That other wedding day, with all its bridal bells and bravery, its bright array of bridesmaids, comes back for a moment, but she banishes the uncanny resemblance. Indeed, Bertie Vaughan is but the palest shadow of memory now, and has been ever since she met Lewis. To-day there are neither bells nor bridesmaids, but in the church. the bridegroom stands looking as he always looks in Sydney's eyes "a man of men."

Uncle Grif awaits her at the door, and on his arm she goes up the aisle. Little Monseiur Von Etté is dancing about, wild with repressed excitement, and there, grave and gray, is Mr. Graham, and there tearful and trembling Mrs. Nolan. And now she kneels, and he is beside her, and the marriage is begun. Uncle Grif gives her away, blushing all over his bald head ; Mrs. Graham sniffs audibly behind her pocket-handkerchief, and in Mrs. Nolan's eyes there are quiet tears ; but Sydney lifts two eyes of heavenly radiance to the bridegroom's face as he slips the ring on her finger, and knows that the desire of her heart is hers.

They are married. For the last time the door of the Macgregor house has closed upon her as home ; it is to Mrs. Nolan's they go to breakfast. And there Lucy awaits them, and into Lucy's arms the bride goes, and cries for a moment hysterically.

"My own dear sister," Lucy says, "Heaven bless and keep you both."

So she has been married, and the outrage upon society consummated. With neither bridesmaids nor bridal gifts, nor reception, nor veil, nor wreath, nor trailing whiteness of wedding-robe, nor anything proper.

But it is doubtful if ever more blissful bride stood by her wedded lover's side than Sydney Nolan.

CHAPTER XI.

"HER HEART'S DESIRE."

THE nine days' wonder was at an end ; the Wonderful Wedding had become a thing of the past. Mr. and Mrs. Nolan had been wandering about for fully six weeks, and were shortly expected home.

Home! Where ultimately that was to be, Lewis Nolan had not the faintest idea. His intention was to take his wife to a hotel upon their return, and once he had asked her, if among them she had any preference, and Sydney had blushed in a guilty way and evaded an answer. The man's pride to a certain degree had been excoriated by his marriage, and he shrank with, perhaps, a morbid sensitiveness from renewing this subject. They had gone to Washington first, then westward ; it did not matter where just at present, you know ; they did not

tread the earth, but a sublimated, etherealized, rapturous world
of their own.   Mrs. Nolan had desired to go to Europe, and show
Mr. Nolan Italy and the Rhine, Paris, and Napoleon the Third ;
but Mr. Nolan had incisively declined.   A six weeks' holiday
he might afford ; a six months' scamper was not to be thought
of.   Did Mrs. Nolan expect to henpeck him at this early stage
of proceedings ?   He objected to being trotted about Europe
at present ; his wife might consider herself fortunate that he
had humored her by leaving Wall Street, even for a day.   And
Sydney had laughed, and given up the point.   It was delightful to
obey Lewis, to feel he had the right to command, that she belonged to him, to him alone, wholly and for all time !

But the six weeks ended, and they were coming back.
Coming back—where ?   Once more Nolan broached the
hotel question—once more Sydney slipped out of it with
a caressing : " Wait until we get to New York, Lewis ; I'll decide then."   All through the honeymoon a conspiracy had been
in progress ; mysterious letters passed between Mrs. Graham
and the bride, which the bridegroom was not permitted to see,
and which wreathed Mrs. Nolan's face with dimples.

One lovely June morning, a steamer floated up to her pier,
and the happy pair were back in the dear familiar din and dust
of Gotham.   A very elegant private carriage, with a pair of
handsome black horses and a coachman, blacker than the
horses, was drawn up to the pier.   Within sat Mrs. Graham
and Uncle Grif, and handshakings and kissing ensued, and inquiries all round, and the young wife was informed she was
looking uncommonly well, ano then the quartet were flashing
away up town.   Sydney sat, and talked, and looked nervous
and cast wistful sidelong glances at her husband.   Mr. Nolan,
uncomfortably unconscious of his destiny, but with a feeling
that all the rest knew, took out a damp morning paper, and
with a true " married-man manner" calmly began to read.
Presently they were very far up town in quiet and dignified
streets of brown-stone stateliness, and before one of these " palatial "· residences, semi-detached, with shrubbery in front and
an air of elegant rusticity, the carriage stopped.

" Lewis," Sydney said, in a tremulous whisper, laying her
hand on his arm, " this is—*home*."

His eyes answered her ; he said nothing, only sprang out and
assisted the ladies, Uncle Grif ambled after, and the carriage
was driven round to certain stables in the rear.

They entered an imposing hall, hung with paintings, rich in

bronzes and statuary, and into a dining-room, perfect in every
dark and handsome appointment, where a table stood with a
silver and china breakfast equipage, and where Mamma Nolan
came forward to meet and welcome her son and daughter.
And still in silence Lewis saw it all.

" How is Lucy ? " Sydney asked.

" Better than usual, and Sydney-sick, as perhaps her letters
have told you.   Will you go up-stairs and take off your things ?
You must be famished after your journey.   I will show you the
way."

"Come, Lewis," Sydney said, shyly, and Lewis followed up
the long easy stairway, to another hall both perfect in every
minute detail of costly upholstery.   Mamma Nolan threw
open a door and displayed a vista of three rooms *en suite*,
quite superb in coloring and appointment.

"I hope they will please you," said Mamma Nolan.   " Mrs.
Graham followed your instructions to the letter.   Now make
haste, like good children, and come down to breakfast."

She bustled away, and husband and wife were alone.   Sydney stood, that fluttering color of hers deepening and fading,
then she turned and threw herself into his arms.

" Oh, Lewis," she said again, "this is home."

He held her still in silence, gazing about the rich and beautiful rooms.

"You—you are not angry that I did not consult you ? " she
said, pleadingly.   " I wanted to surprise you.   It is so long
since I have had a home, a real home, that the thought of this
has been sweet to me.   You do not mind, Lewis ?   Why don't
you speak ?"

" What can I say, Sydney ?   I feel crushed.   Fortune seems
to shower fairy gifts upon me.   I receive all and give nothing.
There are no words that I can speak.   Some day—if ever—when
I am a successful man I will tell you what I feel ; just now I
cannot.   I can only say—I love my wife."

Perhaps Mr. Nolan could have said in his most eloquent
moments nothing his wife would have liked so well.   She laughed
as she threw off hat and jacket, and began to smooth her hair.

" It is a lovely house, is it not ?   Mr. Graham and Uncle
Grif, Mrs. Graham and your mother were all in the plot.   You
never can tell, Lewis," said Mrs. Nolan, plaintively, " what I
have suffered the past six weeks keeping this secret."

" I am quite sure of it, my love."

"And it is the last, the very last I ever mean to keep from
15*

you for a moment. Now let us go down to breakfast, for I am most excruciatingly hungry."

Sydney's new life was fairly begun—her unclouded new life. Lewis made his daily pilgrimage to Wall Street early in the morning, and madam generally drove down for him early in the evening. Lucy was well, that is, much better than usual. Katie Macgregor was back, had roped in the erratic old Vonderdonck at last, and was to lasso him for good at St. Alban's, in early autumn. Mrs. Macgregor, now that the evil was inevitable, smiled upon her fair, erring relative once more, even upon that fair relative's pauper husband. Finally, Mr. and Mrs. Nolan gave an "At Home," preparatory to Mrs. Nolan's flitting away before the July heats, and a large assembly were bidden and came. It was an affair to be remembered—the romantic interest attaching to the marriage ; the lovely, blissful face of the young wife, her exquisite toilet and diamonds ; the stately bearing and *air noble* of the young husband, carrying himself as one to the manner born ; the magnificence of the house itself—all combined to make this reception quite out of common—a brief glimpse of romance.

And so Sydney has her heart's desire, the husband she loves, and a home that is an ideal home in its beauty and perfectness ; and is that world's wonder, rare as the blossom of the century plant—a perfectly happy woman.

CHAPTER XII.

TEDDY.

HE first days of July send Mrs. Nolan to Newport for the blazing weeks, and Mrs. Graham and Katherine Macgregor go also. Mr. Nolan escorts them, stays a day, and returns to town. He has grown used to being stared at as the hero of a love match, a sort of modern Claude Melnotte, a lucky young barrister, who has successfully carried off, over the heads of all competitors, the beautiful heiress of fabulous thousands. Great things are predicted of this fortunate young man by the knowing ones.

"A young fellow of prodigious talent, sir, great oratorical powers, keen forensic abilities. With his own cleverness, indus-

try and ambition, combined with the great beauty and wealth
of his wife, and the social power she will wield, any career is
open to Nolan—ANY, sir—bar, bench, or senate. The young
man will be a judge at thirty, sir—a fellow of infinite capabilities, and amazingly shrewd for a youngster. Lovely creature,
the wife."

It seemed as if Nolan himself, who said very little about it,
had notions that coincided. Certainly he did not spare himself; he worked without stint or measure. Sydney entreated
him, when he made his flying visits, to remain a week ; he
kissed her, laughed at her, and returned inexorably. She was
growing jealous of those grimy big tomes, of his office and profession, that enchained him. How much stronger hold they
seemed to have upon him than she had. Ambitious he had always been, and his affection for his wife was but an added spur.
She must be proud as well as fond of the penniless husband she
had chosen, and he grudged every lost hour as one that kept
success an hour longer off.

Every Saturday evening he went to Newport and spent Sunday with his wife. As a matter of course, therefore, Sunday
became the one day of the week to this infatuated young
woman. Still the intervals, with their water parties, driving
parties, horseback rides, long walks, evening hops, surf bathing,
band, the well-dressed, well-mannered crowd of men and
women, all the light, *insouciant*, sunny, sensuous life of a fashionable watering-place, could hardly drag to any very weari-
some extent. Sydney grew plump and rosy as Hebe's self, and
seemed to have found a fairy fountain of perennial beauty and
youth. Mr. Nolan, on the other hand, as August blazed to a
close, began to look a trifle jaded and worn ; hot weather and
hard work were beginning to tell upon him, and Sydney, quick
to note the slightest shade on that one face of all faces, grew
alarmed, and despite the expostulations of friends and admirers, flitted back to the city to see that Lewis did not go off
with congestion of the brain from over-study.

" What could that beautiful creature have seen in that fellow ?"
queried the Newport gentlemen, pulling their pet mustaches
meditatively. " A clothes-wearing fellow, with nothing to say
for himself, nothing in the way of looks to speak of, besides a
tolerable figure and a pair of overgrown eyes. What's there
about *him* that she should have thrown away herself and her
ducats upon him, and after four months of matrimony, adore
.he ground he walks on ?"

Sydney was looking forward to a very gay winter. She knew that she could further her husband's views by her own gracious hospitality. In the case of almost every successful man there is always a woman who does for him what he cannot do for himself, a good genius in petticoats without whom success could never have been achieved. She may be his wife or she may not, the world may know of her or it may not, but she clings to him and loves him, and her slender hand either pulls or pushes him to heights he else would never attain. So Sydney purposed taking society by storm this winter, giving a series of brilliant entertainments, and making her husband's face as familiar to all influential New York as the statue in Union Square. But woman proposes—the Infinite Justice that disposes had decreed very differently from Mrs. Lewis Nolan.

September was here, and September in New York is a perfect month, a gem in the necklace of the year.

Coming home from a shopping expedition one afternoon, Mrs. Nolan was informed by the smart black boy in buttons who answered the bell, that a caller awaited her in the drawing-room.

"Been waitin' more'n half-an-hour, missis," says Jim; "said jest to tell you, please, as how a very old friend wished to see you. Didn't give me no name, nor card, nor nuffin, missis. Got a little boy wid her, missis."

Sydney descended to the drawing-room. A lady, dressed in black, sat on a sofa, her back to the door, turning a photograph book, and for some seconds did not turn. A child of four, a handsome little fellow, in velvet blouse and breeches, golden ringlets and a pair of shapely juvenile legs, looked up at her with a friendly smile.

Very much puzzled, Sydney drew near; the child was a stranger to her—who was the lady?

The lady arose at the moment, turned, and faced her. There was a gasp, a cry, a rush, and Sydney was clasping in her arms Cyrilla Hendrick!

"Cyrilla! Cyrilla! oh, darling Cy!"

"My dearest Sydney!"

Yes, it was Cyrilla's voice—Cyrilla's dear, familiar face upon which she was raining kisses. The old fascination of her school-girl days was not outgrown by later loves. As the world held but one perfect man, that man her husband, so it held but one Cyrilla Hendrick, friend dearest and best beloved.

"My pet, my pet!" cries Mrs. Nolan, in a rapture, "what a

surprise this is ! Oh ! Cy—darling—how I have longed for you, worried about you, all this time ! Where have you been ? Why did you not find me out before ? Let me look at you and make sure it is my very own Cyrilla."

She holds her off and gazes. Cyrilla smiles. She is changed, but not greatly. There is the creamy, colorless beauty, the youthful roundness, the perfect contour of other days, the old haughty poise of the head, the great dusk, sombre eyes, the high-bred, distinguished air Sydney remembers so well.

" Well ?" Cyrilla says, coolly.

"You have changed, dear, and yet, where the change is I cannot make out. Oh ! my Cy—my own dear friend, I cannot tell you, indeed I cannot tell you, how happy it makes me to see you again."

" I was sure of it," is Cyrilla's answer, " else be very certain, Sydney, I had never come. It is my turn to look at you. *You* have changed certainly. How handsome you have grown ! You were always pretty, but not like this."

" Happiness is an excellent cosmetic," laughs Mrs. Nolan, "and I am very happy, Cyrilla."

"You look it. And so you are ' wooed and married and a' —what a fortunate man is Mr. Nolan ! I hope he appreciates it."

" Fully, I assure you."

All this time they have been standing clasping each other's hands, gazing in each other's faces. Now the youthful personage in the velvet blouse, who has been standing unnoticed regarding this scene, pulls Cyrilla's dress and pipes in :

" Mamma—mamma, who is the pretty lady ? "

" Mamma !" Sydney starts as if she was shot, and looks from one to the other. She has absolutely forgotten the child in the sudden surprise of the meeting. Cyrilla's son, surely, for Cyrilla's black, solemn eyes shine in the baby face, although the small, fair features and flaxen curls are very unlike her friend's dark skin and jetty hair.

" This lady is Auntie Sydney—*you* know Auntie Sydney ?" The small head nods intelligently.

" Now go and tell Auntie Sydney who you are, my pet."

" The young gentleman advances, very much at his ease, looks up into Mrs. Nolan's face, and gives his biography.

" I is Teddy Croo."

" Oh, Cy !" Sydney says, and snatches Teddy Croo in her arms and takes away his breath with kisses, " I never dreamed of this."

She is paler than Cyrilla with emotion, as she bends over Cyrilla's son, all the maternal heart in a wife's bosom aroused.

" You knew that I was married, did you not ? " Cyrilla says, quietly. " You remember my visit to you at Mrs. Macgregor's five years ago last May ? That was my bridal tour, Sydney. I had been married two weeks then."

She stops a moment. She has great self-command, always had, but even *her* self-command is shaken a little as she thinks of then and now.

" I married Fred Carew at Mrs. Colonel Delamere's house, Sydney, and under pretext of visiting you, came to New York with him. It was all of a piece—duplicity on my part from first to last, duplicity that worked its own retribution. The very day I left you I met Miss Jones in a Broadway omnibus, and she went all the way to Montreal to tell my aunt. The deceit, the plotting, the falsehoods, from beginning to end, were mine— mine alone. Fred urged me to tell the truth—he only yielded to please me. I wanted him and I wanted Miss Dormer's money, and in trying to secure both, lost both. It was simple justice— I acknowledge that."

" I wrote to Mr. McKelpin," faltered Sydney. " There were such extraordinary rumors afloat. Some said you had been married to Mr. Carew ; others, that although you were with him in New York, you were not his——"

" His wife—go on, Sydney. That I should lose reputation as well as husband and fortune, I also richly deserved ; for across my aunt's dying bed, with Fred's eyes upon me, I denied our marriage."

" I never believed that story," says Sydney. " I mean, that you were not married. If you were with Lieutenant Carew in this city, I knew as surely as I lived, it was as his wife ! "

" My loyal Sydney ! Yes, I never feared your hearing, I never doubted your fidelity. Whatever has befallen me, I have fully merited. You know how poor Aunt Phil hated Fred—well, she was dying, and she asked me to swear that I was not his wife. I see that scene at this moment, Sydney, as vividly as I saw it then. I live it over in dreams. I awake with a start a dozen times a day, and come back from that dingy, stifling room, with Aunt Dormer, a ghastly sight in the bed, Mrs. Fogarty and Miss Jones watching with deadly hatred for my downfall, and Fred standing with folded arms waiting for me to speak. I have never seen him since, Sydney—no, not once—never even have heard of him from that dreadful day."

For a moment—only a moment—she falters and breaks
down, but she neither sobs nor sheds a tear. It is Sydney's eyes
that are full.

"I lost all, Sydney," Cyrilla goes on. "Aunt Dormer died
and left all she possessed, all I had slaved and sinned for, to
Donald McKelpin. I fell down in a fit of some kind on Miss
Dormer's bed. I remember that, and I know that it was Fred
who lifted and carried me to my room. I heard him whisper
'good-by,' and go. After that all is hazy—my head was not
clear, it had the queerest feeling, as if it were grown enor-
mously large and as light as a cork.

"The strain had been too much for me—the illness was coming on even then that nearly ended my life. I had but one
idea—to get away from that house, from Montreal, before Mc-
Kelpin came. I did it. I got on the train, found a seat somehow, and seemed to be going spinning through empty air. I can
recall no more for many weeks. I was in a Boston hospital
when life came back, so weak that I could neither lift my hand,
nor speak aloud, nor care whether I lived or died. They were
very kind to me. One of the physicians had taken a fancy to
me, it seemed, and gave me devoted care and skill. Gradually
I grew stronger, and from Dr. Digby I discovered where I was
and how I had come there.

"Some time in the evening, it appeared, the conductor going his rounds, had found me lying in my seat to all appearance
dead or dying. There was great excitement and alarm, and
the moment we reached Boston I was brought here. I had
been ill, very ill—so ill that at one time Dr. Digby had thought
death inevitable. My friends in Montreal had advertised for
me, he said. I stared at this—one of them, he went on, had even
come here to see me. His name was McKelpin, and he had
left a note for me, and the sum of five thousand dollars to my
credit in the bank. Donald McKelpin, whom I had always
even laughed at, whom I had shamefully led on and deceived,
was an honorable gentleman after all, it seemed. I cried over
his note, Sydney—I, who never cry, but I was weak and broken
down, and kindness so undeserved moved me. It was a cold
and civil note ; he made no allusion to my marriage or my
treachery ; he simply said that his late lamented friend, Miss
Phillis Dormer, having left him her whole property, he considered it his duty to see that the services I had rendered his es-
teemed friend in her last illness were not unrequited. It
was what I had no right to expect from him, of all men, but

I felt that it was no more than I had rightfully earned from her. Twice that amount would not have repaid me for the life I led at Miss Dormer's, so I answered Mr. McKelpin, accepted the money humbly and gratefully, and then turned my thoughts to the future. I was not to die, it seemed, and lonely and desolate as life would be, I clung to it as we all cling. I had five thousand dollars, and youth, and just then that seemed affluence. Long before Dr. Digby thought me fit to leave his care, I bade him good-bye and came here to New York, found a boarding-house, and grew strong at my leisure.

"I am not going to tell you, Sydney, how desolate and heart-sick, remorseful and despairing I was at times. If you had been here I would have come to you; you were just the only person in the world whose pity I could have borne. I had not one friend in the whole great city, and of all loneliness the loneliness of one utterly alone in a great city is the most utter. To see thousands pass you by and not one familiar face, to feel a lost, unknown creature among all who come and go, to know that you might drop down and die in their midst and not one to give you a second thought. Oh! *you* cannot realize this. It was the most absolutely wretched time of my life; but in spite of that I grew strong and hearty, and the old question rose up—what should I do? Five thousand dollars would not last forever. I must earn my own living.

"My first thought, one that I found hard to give up, was of the stage. If I had capabilities for anything, if I had a vocation in life, that was it. I was an excellent elocutionist already, thanks to long training and natural taste; I had a tall and good figure, a passable face, a head of good hair below my waist, and two black eyes. I took stock of myself as any manager might appraise me; I had a flexible voice; I could dance, sing, speak French, and would never know the meaning of stage fright. I had money enough to live upon until the initiative training was complete. I felt certain of success if I tried, and still—and still I hesitated. I had outraged my husband, driven him from me, and now that I had lost him, I did what I never had done before in my life—stopped to think whether or no he would have approved of my impulses. Easy as you may have thought him, free from prejudices, he yet had very strong pride and prejudices about certain things. One of these was the stage, for me. He had vetoed it ever since I had known him. 'It's no place for you, Beauty, he would say, 'with your gunpowder temper, and peppery pride, and overbearing little ways generally. You would come to grief in the green-room in a week. Besides, the theatre's well enough for those that must go in for that sort of thing; some of the women are trumps, take 'em anyhow you like; but it's not the place for you, Beauty; I never want to see your face behind the footlights."

"And I knew Freddy felt much more strongly and deeply on this subject than he could express. And I, who had never acknowledged any will but my own heretofore, now that he and I were parted forever, obeyed his wishes, gave up my one ambition, and resolved that my life for the future should be one of expiation for the past. I had found a quiet home about this time with a widow, 'poor but honest,' as they say, who took no other boarders; and here, one January day, my baby arrived. Life all at once grew bright again; I had something to love, live for, and work for. After all the tears and weeping, joyfulness had been poured in at last.

"Four months after baby's birth, I set myself resolutely to look for labor. I had lived so economically that I had nearly four thousand dollars still, but I was growing niggardly for baby's sake, and must keep that for him. I advertised in the daily papers, and answered advertisements without number, ladies wanted companions—families wanted governesses—there seemed no end of situations; but when one applied there was always something that rendered it impossible to accept. I advertised for pupils in music and French; but the market was drugged, it seemed, with French and music teachers. Four months had passed, and I seemed as far off a livelihood as ever, but baby thrived and grew, and I was happy, Sydney, as happy as I could be in this world again. At last, it was by the merest chance I saw an advertisement of a young ladies' seminary in Chicago that stood in need of a French, and music, and singing governess. With credentials from the clergyman who had baptized Ted, and the doctors, I went to Chicago, suited the vacancy, and got it. I had lost my husband, I told the gentlemanly principal and his wife, and they looked sympathetic, and did not press me with questions. Of course I could not keep my baby in the school, and the thought of parting with him almost made me resign the position. But this would have been folly, and I was worn out trying so long, so the sacrifice had to be made. After some trouble I found a young married woman, with a seven-months boy of her own, willing to take charge of Teddy on reasonable terms, and to her care I was obliged to resign him. One inducement was, that she kept a cow, and Teddy could have plenty of fresh milk. And she has been the best and most tendor of nurses to my boy; he has been with Mrs. Martin ever since."

Cyrilla paused, as if her story had come to an end, and looked with tender eyes at her little son.

" Who is he like, Sydney ? " she wistfully asked.

" Like Fred Carew, with Cyrilla Hendrick's black eyes. My own dear Cy, how lonely and miserable you must have been all these years—how much you have suffered since we met last."

" I have wrought my own destruction, Sydney—I deserve no pity. I can only think that I have wrecked *his* life, and hate myself for it."

" You have heard nothing from him all those years ? "

" Nothing of him or from him : I never expect to—I do not even wish it."

" Not wish it ? "

" No—we could never be happy together ; he could never trust me, he could have nothing but contempt for the wife who so basely denied him. If he took me back at all, it would be through pity, and I would rather be as I am than that."

" Ah ! Cy, the old pride is not dead yet. If it were my case, I think I would only be too glad to be taken back on any terms. It is strange to me that Mr. Carew has not sought you out. He was so fond of you, Cyrilla, I can't understand his resigning you wholly for one fault ; love forgives everything."

" Not such a sin as mine ; and Fred, slow to anger, is also slow to forgive. Don't let us talk about it. I am resigned, or try to be. But to go on—I have to think of the future, not the past."

" And all of these years you have been a governess in a school. What a destiny for you, my brilliant Cyrilla ! "

Cyrilla half laughed.

" Do you remember Aunt Phil's cheerful prediction, croaked out so often ? ' Mark my words, my niece Cyrilla will come to no good end.' She was a true prophetess, was she not ? And it does not lighten labor, or cheer the monotony, to feel that I owe it all to myself. Well, I ought to be thankful in the main, I suppose. I have Teddy, a respectable home and profession, they are all kind and friendly, and I save money for a rainy day. It is better fortune than I deserve."

" You are greatly changed, Cy ; this sad, resigned manner is not much like the bright, ambitious Cyrilla Hendrick of Petite St. Jacques. What shuttlecocks of fortune we all are ! "

" Life's battledore has hit you gently, Syd ; I never thought that you would grow half so lovely. Can you imagine why I have sought you out at last ? "

" Remorse of conscience at having neglected me so long, I should hope."

" I am afraid not. I have come to remind you of a promise —made first in school, afterward in your old home ; a promise that if ever I stood in need of a friend, do what I might, you would be that friend."

" I remember," Sydney answered, with emotion. " To see you and be your friend is all that has been wanting, since my marriage, to make my happiness complete. What is it, Cyrilla ? "

" That you will take my boy and keep him for me until I can claim him. Mrs. Martin and her husband are going to Galveston, and Teddy will lose his home. To give him to strangers I cannot endure ; but if you will take him, Sydney——"

Sydney's answer is the delighted hug she inflicts on Master Teddy.

" Oh, Cy ! how good you are to think of me. I love children ; do I need to tell you that I love yours above all ? My pet, kiss Auntie Sydney ! I am going to be your mamma, now. You will stay with me Teddy, won't you ? "

" Does you have Johnny-cake for tea ? " asked Teddy, cautiously, before committing himself to rash promises. " 'Cause if you hasn't I won't."

" Johnny-cake, pound-cake, jelly, oranges, candies, ice-cream —everything ! " says Auntie Sydney, magnificently.

" Sen I'll stay with you," says Teddy, manifesting no emotion of any kind. " I likes oranges, and candy, and ice-cream. Does you keep a cow ? "

" Not a cow, Teddy, but I think we might get one if you wish it very much. And a pony—can you ride a pony, Ted ? "

" I can wide a wockin' hoss," answers Teddy, rousing to enthusiasm at last. " I can make him gee up, bully, like everysing ! "

" Then consider yourself master of a wockin'-hoss and a cow, and oranges unlimited. Oh ! Cyrilla, why cannot you stay as well as Teddy, and make your home with me ? I would be so happy——"

" And Mr. Nolan also, no doubt," says Cyrilla, smiling ; " men are *so* fond of having their wives' bosom friends domiciled with them. No, thank you, Syd ; I have my life work to do, and will do it. You have made me unutterably grateful by taking Ted."

"You will miss him dreadfully, Cy."

"Naturally, but it must be done. I look forward to a time, a few years hence, when I will have a home of my own, however humble, where my pupils may come to me. And now tell me about yourself, dear; I have selfishly monopolized the time with my talking."

"What shall I tell?" Sydney answers with a radiant look. "In a happy wife's history there is no romance. It is only life's sorrows and sufferings that make interesting stories. No, there is nothing to tell. I am married and happy—all is said in that."

"I have never seen your husband. What is he like? Tall, short, dark, fair—which?"

"I will show you his photograph. I have a score, more or less, about the house. Oh, dark of course, but it is useless to ask me what he is like. *I* don't know. It is months since I ceased to see him—as he is."

She laughingly produces two or three large-sized photographs, taken in different attitudes. Cyrilla examines them thoughtfully.

"Is—is Mr. Nolan handsome?" she asks, hesitatingly. "These things are such caricatures sometimes."

"Handsome?" repeats Mr. Nolan's wife, still laughing; "is he not? I am sure I do not know. I see only an idealized Lewis, with a countenance like a king, whom nobody else, not the real Lewis himself perhaps, would recognize. I only saw him once as others see him, and then I recollect I fancied him rather plain. Need I say it would be rank heresy to call him plain in my presence now?"

Cyrilla laughs in answer, but she also sighs.

"Happy Sydney! It is a face one likes, strong and intellectual; better still, the face of a good man. Give me one, and one of your own; it will be pleasant to have them in my room."

"And so you will not stay?"

"Not another moment. No, Sydney, do not entreat, please; it was difficult to get off—a great favor, and I am bound by promise to make no delay in New York. I shall start again in an hour."

"But you will wait and see my husband?" Sydney cries, aghast.

"Not even that will tempt me. A promise given should be a

promise kept. I must go this very instant. Teddy, mamma is going; what have you got to say?"

"Dood-by," says this young philosopher, his two little paws in his two little pockets, and not moving a muscle. Cyrilla's lips quiver as she clasps him and kisses him.

"Teddy will be a good boy, and not make Auntie Sydney any trouble?"

"Yes, I'll be dood when I gets de wockin-hoss," Teddy replies, still careful not to commit himself. He accepts rather than returns his mother's caresses, and sees her depart without winking once. Of a phlegmatic and unemotional nature, evidently, is Frederic Carew, junior.

So Cyrilla goes, and Sydney leads Master Ted up to her own room, feeling as if in a dream, feeling also that the last drop of content has been added to her cup, and that one other will make it brim over with bliss.

CHAPTER XIII.

AT THE PLAY AND AFTER.

HE first week of October, there was brought out at a fashionable Broadway theatre, a new play by an old actor and dramatist. The new piece, like all the new pieces by this popular playwright, was stolen bodily from the French—so all the other players and playwrights said at least—the *mise en scene* changed from Paris to New York. The little three-act comedy, sparkling with epigrams, peppered with satire, rich with old jokes juicily done over, and as full of capital situations as a pudding of plums, was an immense success. Whatever carping critics might say, the good-natured public were disposed to forgive many sins to the dramatist because he charmed much. The great man himself, just over from Europe, was to play the principal part, a fascinating old serving-man; the scenery and effects were exceptionally fine, and the music— but everybody knows what the orchestra of *that* theatre is like.

The house was filled half an hour before the rising of the curtain, and packed at a quarter to eight. At eight, there was not standing room—people had secured their seats a fortnight ahead. A brilliant assemblage was there, the women beautiful, with that rare, delicate beauty of America, to be surpassed nowhere in the world, and the curtain arose before one of the most fashionable audiences the city could show.

In one of the stage boxes sat a lady who had attracted considerable attention before the rising of the curtain. This lady, tall, blonde, beautiful, very simply dressed, attracted, for a few moments, a steady fire of lorgnettes, and was Mrs. Lewis Nolan. Another lady, a dashing brunette, much more brightly arrayed, and wearing coral ornaments, was Miss Katie Macgregor. Behind his wife sat Mr. Nolan, partly screened by her chair, surveying the house with a look of amusement at the attention he and his party were receiving. The young ladies sat in full view, with that inimitable air of utter unconsciousness which comes so naturally to women.

Presently the orchestra burst forth in full blast with a grand march, and Mr. Nolan for whom music had charms, resigned himself to listening and waiting for the rise of the curtain. Just then Mrs. Nolan, perusing her bill, uttered a little exclamation.

"Well, Sydney," her husband said, "what now?"

She glanced back at him, a startled expression in her eyes.

"It is a name here in the play-bill—a name that I have seen before."

"Nothing very startling in that, I should say. The names on your play-bill, one and all, should be tolerably familiar by this time. Let me see."

She hands him the play-bill, and points to a name near the end of the list. He looks, and reads Dolly De Courcy."

It has startled Sydney. In one instant the scene changes, and it is a stormy November night, and she and mamma, Cyrilla and Bertie, are seated in the primitive play-house, waiting for Lady Teazle. Five years ago only, and what great and saddening changes. Papa and mamma dead, Bertie murdered, Cyrilla worse than widowed, she alone of them all happy, and here, and again to see Dolly De Courcy. She had been happy then in a different way. Yes, positively happy, although she had not known such a being as Lewis Nolan existed on earth. How impossible to conceive of any happiness now where he was not the central figure. She leans back and glances up at him, a smile in the lovely eyes, and holds out her hand for the paper.

"Are you committing it to memory, monseigneur? The curtain is rising—my bill, please."

The gravity that has left her face seems to have found its way into his.   He hands her back the paper with no answering smile.

"Where did *you* ever see this name before?' he inquires. "It is her first appearance here."

"I saw her over five years ago at a theatre in Wychcliffe."

"It is odd you should remember the name so well after so many years."

"It would be, under ordinary circumstances," Sydney says, in a low voice, "but I knew her under rather extraordinary ones. I lost a very dear friend, and she was at one time supposed to be associated with his death. I will tell you all about it another time—it is impossible here."

For Sydney, five months a wife, has not yet, in any outburst of connubial confidence, told her husband the story of Dolly De Courcy and Bertie Vaughan ; the name of either, in fact, has not passed her lips.   She has a vague theory, but men are averse to knowing that the woman they marry has had a former lover and actually been on the brink of matrimony with another man.   And the slightest thing that can annoy Lewis she avoids. It is an exceedingly painful subject even at this distant date, a black cloud of the past, that will only needlessly darken the sunlight of the present.   Besides, they make a compact before marriage to let the dead past stay dead on both sides.   She has told him she was once engaged : he that he was once before in love—disagreeable facts both, best forgotten.

The play goes on—it is very bright and witty, and Sydney laughs.   The music is fine, the scenery and costumes perfection.   It is a drawing-room comedy, one of the Charles Mathews' sort, in which people *seem* to behave themselves as they might in their own drawing-rooms at home—only such badinage, such re-partee, such smart epigrams, such flashes of wit and wisdom, unhappily one rarely hears in the conversations of every-day life.   Mrs. Nolan, lying back in her chair and enjoying it im-mensely, forgets all about Dolly De Courcy and the memories the name brings, and at every telling hit glances back at her husband to see how he takes it.   He takes it all rather absently, Sydney thinks, his very answering smiles are *distrait ;* thinking of his eternal (if she had been a man she would have thought *infernal*) law business, she thinks, half-impatiently.   But it is not of law business Nolan is musing, for when the curtain falls he leans over his wife and resumes the subject of the actress.

" You have made me rather curious, Sydney," he says, "by

your remark.   How was it possible for this actress to be in any
way associated with the death of any friend of yours ? "

"She was suspected at one time of—having killed him,"
Sydney answers, in a nervous tone.   "Don't let us talk of it,
Lewis, please—at least not here."

"One more question : What was your friend's name?"

There is something more than mere curiosity in the young
lawyer's face, as he puts this question, but that face, in which
Sydney's eyes can read all changes, she cannot see as she sits.

"Are you trying to get up a case at this late day ? His
name was——" she pauses a second, with the strangest feeling
of repugnance to uttering it—"Bertie Vaughan."

"Sydney," exclaims Katie, leaning forward, "here comes
Mr. Vanderdonck.   I thought he would run us down before
the evening ended."

Her venerable lover enters as she speaks, makes his bow to
the ladies, and accepts a seat beside his betrothed.

Another gentleman, a poet and journalist of half a century,
with a snowy beard and a dreamy brow, a professed admirer of
beautiful Mrs. Nolan, follows, and takes a seat for the remainder of the performance by her side.

Conversation becomes general; but Sydney notices that
although her husband drops a remark now and then, and so
avoids notice, he is singularly silent, and that a sort of grayish
pallor has come over his face.

"You're not looking well, Nolan ; upon my life, you're not,"
remarks Mr. Vanderdonck.   "Don't overwork yourself among
the big books, my boy.   Distinction will come soon enough.
It never pays to burn the candle of life at both ends."

The curtain rises again, and a coquettish chambermaid is
discovered dusting the furniture, and talking to herself, as is the
way of chambermaids—on the stage—singing between whiles
snatches of popular songs, in a very nice voice.   The chambermaid is Dolly De Courcy.   Sydney looks at her with interest.
So far as she can see, years have made no change in her.   She
wears her own abundant black hair under a natty cap ; and the
plump figure, she can recall, is as rounded and ripe as ever.
But to Sydney the face is repulsively bold, the high color coarse,
the manner brazen.

Presently, as she dusts and sings, and vivaciously says her
lines, she approaches their box, glances up, and stares full at
Sydney.   The recognition is mutual.   For the space of five
seconds she stands, brush in hand, her song suspended ; then

she recovers herself, flashes a glance at the others, and goes on with her little part. Other personages appear, the comic valet among them, who make the sort of love comic valets do make to singing chambermaids. Dolly does her part well—if she did not she would not be here; but through the whole of it her eyes are fixed every other instant on the Nolan box. Not on Mrs. Nolan, but on the face behind—her husband's—with an intensity that may be surprise, recognition, dislike—it is hard to define what. She takes so little pains to conceal at whom she stares, that they all, perforce, notice it.

" Is that little soubrette an old acquaintance of yours, Nolan?" inquires old Vanderdonck, with an unctuous chuckle. " She doesn't seem able to take her eyes off you."

" She does watch you, Lewis," says Sydney, in wonder.

" I have seen her before," Lewis answers, quietly.

" To be sure you have," says old Vanderdonck. " Don't be jealous, my dear Mrs. Nolan ; we have all been acquainted with pretty little actresses in our day."

" What a horrid old man," thinks Mrs. Nolan, disgusted. " *I* jealous of Lewis—absurd ! "

But suddenly there returns the words, half-spoken by Dick Macgregor—she could hardly recall them, but something of a *grande passion* once entertained by Lewis for somebody. Was it for this actress, with whom Bertie Vaughan and Ben Ward used to flirt ? Lewis himself had owned to a former attachment —was it for Dolly De Courcy ? It seemed odd, indeed, if Dolly could twice cross her path as rival. She certainly did watch him in a very marked manner.

During that act and the next, the chambermaid was off and on in several of the scenes. Perhaps none in the house paid as much attention to the dashing little coquette as the party in that particular box. Mrs. Nolan looked and listened to her with a growing, and, very likely, unjust sensation of dislike. She *was* coarse, bold, vulgar ; what could men see in her ? what could Lewis, whose every instinct was fastidious and refined, see to attract him in a creature like this ? In the annoyance of the bare thought, gentle Sydney absolutely called poor Dolly a *creature*, than which there exists no word of more bitter contempt from one woman to another.

The play ended delightfully ; everybody was dismissed to happiness, the singing chambermaid and comic valet among the rest, and even the critics to whom gall and bitterness are the wines of life, went home and only mildly abused it. The two

16

gentlemen made their adieus ; Miss Macgregor went to Madison Avenue, and Mr. and Mrs. Nolan entered their carriage, and were driven home.

It was an exquisite October night, moonlight, mild, even the streets of New York looked poetical under the crystal rays. It was still early, the city clocks were only striking eleven as they crossed their own threshold.

"I must run and have a peep at my boy," says Madame Sydney, tripping away.

In the last month she has become the abject slave and adorer of Master Teddy, spoiling him as thoroughly and completely as any doting mamma.   With the fine discrimination of his years and sex, Teddy, on the other hand, is loftily indifferent to all Auntie Sydney's kisses and caresses, and has bestowed his juvenile heart on Uncle Lewis, at the first sound of whose footstep he precipitates himself down the stairs and into his legal coat sleeves with jubilant shrieks of welcome.

Ted is in his crib asleep, rosy, plump, lovely, a very cherub in outward seeming—alas ! in outward seeming only, as his victimized nurse but too well knew.   She kisses him, throws off her wraps, and hastens to the apartment where she is pretty sure of finding her husband—a little gem of a room that is called the master's study by the household, and where he answers letters, etc., that he does not find time for during the day.   He is there now, the gas is lit over the green table, but turned down to one minute point.   It is the moonlight streaming between the curtains that lights the room, and Mr. Nolan sits near one of the windows gazing out.

"Oh ! wise young judge ! of what is your honor dreaming ? " his wife exclaims, standing behind him and clasping her fingers across his breast.   "To-morrow's business, I am certain.   Whoever heard of a lawyer looking at the moon ? "

Nolan smiles.

"I was neither thinking of to-morrow's business nor of the moon.   I was thinking—will you wonder ?—of the strangeness of your knowing Dolly De Courcy."

"*You* know her, Lewis."

It is not a question, it is an assertion, and as such he answers :

"Yes, well—too well, years ago.   But this Bertie Vaughan " (how pat he has the name, Sydney thinks) " what friend of yours was he ?

She perches herself lightly on his knee, and lays her pretty golden head against his shoulder.

" Lewis," she says, caressingly, " you will not care, will you ?
You will not mind. He was the person I was to marry."

There is a pause. The shadow of the curtain throws that
immobile expression over her husband's face, perhaps, but in
the half light it looks as if it were cut in stone.

" Tell me about it, Sydney," he says.

" I would have told you long ago, Lewis—I often wished to
—but I was afraid it might pain you ever so little, dear, to know
that once before my wedding-day was named, my wedding dress
on, and that I was ready and waiting to become the wife of
another man. I was only fond of him as a brother, Lewis, but
still, to please my father, I would have married him."

And then, her arm around his neck, her hand on his shoulder,
she tells him all that strange, tragical story of the past—the
mystery still unravelled of that night.

" Whoever killed Bertie, if he were killed, committed a double
murder, for he killed papa as well. But I cannot think he was
murdered ; he had no enemies, poor Bertie, and what motive
could any one have for so dreadful a deed ? It has changed my
whole life—it brought on papa's death, as I say ; it broke up
our home. Papa certainly believed he had been thrown over
the cliff, and on his death-bed, Lewis, made me promise to bring
the assassin to justice, if it ever was in my power. I promised,
and that promise troubles me sometimes, for I do nothing, of
course, to discover the guilty person. If papa had lived he
would never have given up until he had done it."

" But if you ever do meet him "—how hollow a sound has
Lewis Nolan's voice—" you will keep that promise—you will
deliver up this murderer of Bertie Vaughan ! "

" Lewis ! how hoarse you are ! " She lifts her head, but she
can only see the rigid outline of his face.

" Well—what else can I do ? My promise to my father
binds me, and it would be only just. Still it would be a very
dreadful thing to have to do. I hope I never may find him—
it would be hard indeed to let him go unpunished. Do you
remember, Lewis, how deeply I felt about Mrs. Harland, how
indignant I was with you for defending her? Well, I was not
thinking of her at all, but of poor Bertie ; thinking how I would
abhor the lawyer who would stand up and defend his assassin.'

" Even if he were thrown over the cliff, as Harland was shot
in a moment of reckless passion ? "

" Even so. To give way to reckless passion is in itself ɩ
sin—how can a lesser crime stand as excuse for a greater ɩ "

What right has any one to give way to reckless passion and lift his hand against his brother's life, taking that gift which God gave, and which all the power of earth cannot restore ? "

"You are quite right, Sydney. If ever you find the man who killed Bertie Vaughan, you will be fully justified in giving him up to the punishment he has so richly earned."

"You think he was killed, then ? "

" I think so."

She remains still, her eyes fixed on the glory of moonlight on earth and sky, her mind vaguely troubled.

" I hope I may never meet him," she says. " I do not want to be an avenger.   I wish papa had not made me give that promise. I believe I could not keep it after all—it would haunt me all my life to bring punishment on another."

He sits silent. She lifts her head and looks at him once more.

" Lewis," she says, uneasily, "it has not vexed you, this story I have told, or my keeping it from you so long ? "

" Vexed me ?   You vex me, my Sydney ? "

Then he suddenly rises and gently puts her from him.

" It is almost twelve, and time you were asleep. You were dancing all last night, remember.   Don't sit up any longer."

He turns up the gas, floods the room with light, and begins assorting letters and papers on the table.

"And you, Lewis? You are going to burn the midnight oil, as usual, I suppose, and have everybody telling you how badly you are looking, and that you are working yourself to death.   People will begin to think your married life is so miserable that you are wearing away to a shadow."

He smiles, but he does not look at her.

" No one will ever think that, my princess, but I promise not to write long to-night."

Mr. Nolan has retained a bad habit of answering a dozen or more letters every night, when he should be virtuously asleep. With his countryman, Tom Moore, he believed that

> "The best of all ways to lengthen your days
> Is to steal a few hours from the night, my dear ; "

and all expostulations to combat this vicious custom were futile.

She lingers a moment at the door to watch him as he begins work.   It is a picture she recalls, with what pain and bitterness it would be vain to tell, in later days.

The cozy room, rich in every costly and elegant appointment, the well-filled book-cases surmounted by busts of eminent lawyers and statesmen, portraits of sundry fathers of their country, a carpet like moss, the tube of gas pulled down to the table, and the rapid hand dashing over the sheet. It is a scene that stands out vividly to the day of her death.

He knows that she is lingering there, but he neither pauses nor looks round. Only when she is gone the pen drops from his fingers, and he takes it up no more. His elbows on the table, his face bowed in both hands, so he sits, heedless of time. The mellow morning hours pale and pass, the little brown English sparrows in the trees outside twitter and talk as the pink dawn breaks, and up-stairs Sydney lies asleep, an innocent smile on her lips. But Lewis has not slept, has hardly stirred, the night through.

CHAPTER XIV.

A VISIT AND A GOLDEN WEDDING.

IVE days after this, on Wednesday the eleventh of October, an event of very considerable importance in certain circles was to transpire—the golden wedding celebration of the famous Mr. and Mrs. Ten Eyck. Mr. Ten Eyck (so let us call him, although of course we dare take no such liberty with his highly respectable name as to introduce it into these pages) is a man whose invitations, like those of royalty, are equivalent to commands. No one dreams of refusing. Lewis Nolan even, who is indifferent to most invitations, and rarely cared to court favor, does not consider it derogatory to accept promptly and with pleasure this card for Wednesday night. In certain political dreams which this aspiring young man has dreamed, Mr. Ten Eyck's favor and patronage may be of immense advantage, for among the rulers who sit at the gates and administer wisdom and equity, his name has been a tower of might. A mighty sachem in the wigwams of the pale faces ; an old-time Democrat as to politics, ex-governor of a State, owner of a line of ocean steamers, and whose millions no man presumes to count—that is Mr. Ten Eyck.

"You really will go then, Lewis?" says Mrs. Lewis, with

pleasure, when the cards arrived, for Lewis had an adroit way of slipping out of unwelcome invitations at the eleventh Lour. "I may count upon you for the golden wedding?"

"Who refuses Ten Eyck? Not I!" laughs Nolan. "Little men must bow down before great ones. I expect to ask a favor or two of the great T. E. before very long."

This had passed on the day preceding the theatre-going, and no mention had been made of the subject since that night when Mr. Nolan had still further recklessly risked his health by falling asleep over his odious papers, as Mrs. N. indignantly found out. He had been more absent, more silent, more serious, more preoccupied, than she had ever seen him since. Once or twice— quite a new thing—he had not come home to dinner, and when he did return, he looked so haggard, so weary, that Sydney was growing seriously alarmed. His was a countenance that told but little of what was passing within; but something more than ordinary, something more than mere press of business, was weighing upon him now.

"Do you still intend to go to the Ten Eyck's, Lewis?" she asked on Wednesday morning at breakfast.

She asked it half timidly, for something in her husband's looks and manner of late almost awed her. She was growing bewildered and frightened, poor child, by the change in him; in spite of her clinging affection he seemed slipping away from her; there were places in his life, it seemed, and thoughts in his heart, she could not share, and her cup of felicity was not quite without alloy, at last.

"Do you still intend to go?" she repeats. "You have accepted, you know."

He looks across from the morning paper he holds, with eyes whose depth of tenderness she cannot doubt, and yet with something beside she does not understand.

"I will go, Sydney—I shall not fail you to-night."

The answer is simple enough, surely, but somehow it makes Sydney vaguely uneasy. "I shall not fail you to-night." It sounds oddly as though he had added, "It is for the last time." She looks wistfully at him, but he has gone gravely back to his paper. How worn that dear face grows! Oh! *what* is this that is coming between them, this dark vague cloud that has neither shape nor name? She goes with him to the door, lingering beside him as he puts on his light overcoat, still silent, still wistful, still troubled. Is it a presentiment that this is the last time she will ever so linger? Does he feel it, too, or is it some secret knowledge that makes his parting embrace so tender?

"Good-bye, my princess," he says, and is gone

She wanders about the house, that vague, restless trouble still haunting her. *What* is the matter with Lewis—what secret has he from her? Is he ceasing to love her? No, she does not doubt that, whatever she doubts. Has he had trouble with Mr. Graham?—losses, disappointments in business? Oh, how foolish to trouble about such trifles, and they so rich. She tries to read and fails; attempts fancy work and throws it aside in disgust; sits down to practise a new song Lewis has brought her, and fancies she can't sing. She goes to the nursery and proposes a game of romps; but Teddy is going out in his goat-carriage with his *bonne*, and loftily declines. Shall she go down town and see Lucy, and so pass the dragging hours? No, she is too listless to go out of doors—she must dawdle about as best she may until dinner hour brings Lewis, and dressing time. An intense longing to see him again takes possession of her; she will put her arms around him, and beg him to tell her the trouble between them. Her entreaties, her tears, he can never resist; whatever the cloud is, it shall be dispelled. Why has she not thought of this before?—how silly to go on wondering and fretting when a few words would have broken down the barrier of reserve. So strong does this longing grow, that once she rises and stretches forth her hand to order the carriage and drive down to the office immediately. But she stops and laughs at her own impatience. Mr. Graham will be there, and the clerks; and Lewis' look of silent wonder and disapprobation would be terrible. No, she would wait until evening and drive down for him then.

"I grow worse and worse every day," muses Mrs. Nolan. "One would think I was married yesterday, and could not bear Lewis out of my sight. I will do nothing so ridiculous; I will wait; only I *wish* it were five instead of eleven o'clock."

Half-past twelve is luncheon hour. As Mrs. Nolan sits down with Teddy to that mid-day refection, a boy from the office comes with a buff envelope, addressed in Mr. Nolan's none too legible hand:

"MY DEAREST: Do not wait for me this evening; I shall be detained, and will probably not reach the house until after eleven. Go at your own hour—we will meet there. Affectionately, LEWIS."

Will it be believed?—she has been married nearly half a year,
remember—Mrs. Nolan actually cried over this note! She had
made up her mind to have that explanation, to go to the golden
wedding in a golden glow of peace, proud and happy on her
husband's arm, and now she must go alone, and he would put
in an appearance after midnight, or perhaps not at all.

"Was the matter, Auntie Syd?" pipes Teddy, opening his
brown solemn eyes. "Was you cwying 'bout? Gimme some
more chicken pie. Was you cwying for? I ain't done nossin,
has I?"

Auntie Syd wipes away those rebellious tears, and laughs and
helps Ted to chicken-pie.

"Was I cwyin' 'bout,—what, indeed? Auntie Syd is only an
overgrown baby, after all, Master Ted, not half as much of a
hero as yourself. Auntie won't cry any more."

She keeps her word, but the afternoon is utterly spoiled.
She takes a book, lies down in her own room, darkens it, and
tries to read herself to sleep. She succeeds, and the slanting
yellow lances of sunshine that make their way in, tell her when
she wakes that it is late. She looks at her watch—past five.
She sits up refreshed, and buoyant once more, for the troubles
of her waking life have not followed her into dreamland. She
goes down-stairs at once towards the dining-room, and at the
hall-door hears bell-boy Jim in magisterial discussion with somebody who wants admission.

"Master ain't home, I tell yer; and if he was, why don't you
go 'round to the airy door. He ain't home, and I dunno when
he will be, and you can leave your name, and call again."

"I can't call again—what's more I won't," replied, a shrill
feminine voice. "I want to see Mr. Nolan, and I'll wait till
I do. Area door, indeed! I knew Mr. Lewis Nolan when he
had neither areas, nor hifalution houses, nor impudent little
niggers like you."

"What is this?" says the gentle tones of Mrs. Nolan, and
bell-boy Jim, "clothed in a little brief authority," falls back
before his mistress.

"It's a young woman, missis, wants to see master. I've
told her he ain't home yet, but she won't go."

Sydney looks, then recoils with a strange shrinking; for the
young woman, pert of aspect, loud of dress, is Dolly De
Courcy.

There is a moment's silence; even audacious Dolly seems
taken aback, but not for long.

" I want to see Mr. Nolan," she says, with a defiant toss.
" He lives here, don't he? I've had trouble enough hunting
him up, Lord knows ; I ain't going back without seeing him now."

" Mr. Nolan is not coming home to dinner—will not return
until eleven, probably. If it is anything I can do in his place—"

" V.'il; *you* see me ? " says Dolly, with a certain incredulity
in her tone.

" Undoubtedly, if it is anything I can attend to as well."

" I don't know but that you can," says Miss De Courcy,
with a disagreeable little laugh ; "perhaps better than Lewis—
oh, beg pardon ! I mean Mr. Nolan."

Something in the tone of the speech brings the blood to
Sydney's cheeks, and her manner changes from gentleness to
cold formality.

" Will you walk this way ? And I must beg you to make
your business brief, for I am very much occupied this evening."

" I won't keep you long," is Dolly's answer.

She follows Mrs. Nolan into one of the smaller reception
rooms, and gazes in undisguised wonder and admiration at the
stately magnificence.

" Ain't this just splendid !" Dolly says, half-audibly ; " and
all his ! Well, it's better to be born lucky than rich. I guess
he ain't sorry, when he looks at all this, that I didn't marry him
when he wanted me to."

The color deepens in Sydney's face. Can it be, indeed, that
Lewis—her Lewis—has ever loved, and wished to marry, this
woman ? In the thought there is unutterable pain and humiliation. In the pure, piercing light of day, withou. stage paints
or powders, the actress looks haggard and repulsi·e, on her un-
blushing front a brand there's no mistaking.

Sydney shrinks a little, but she waits quietly.

" What is it you want ? " she asks.

They both still stand ; Mrs. Nolan cannot quite ask her to
sit down.

" You know who I am ?" demands Dolly De Courcy.

" I saw you at the theatre last week."

" *He* saw me, too, didn't he ?—Lewis, you know. Oh ! I
beg pardon again : of course I mean *Mister* Nolan." A toss
of the head, an insolent giggle. The Dolly De Courcy of to-
day, it is evident, has sunk pitifully below the Dolly of five years
ago.

" Mr. Nolan saw you, and recognized you, I believe. He
said he had known you before."

16*

" Did he say he wanted me to marry him—that he was dead
in love with me—that he was madly jealous of—no matter
who—that he prayed and begged me to marry him, and
that I wouldn't? Did he tell you that?" insolently demands
Dolly.

"Will you tell me your business here?" says Mrs. Nolan,
with a stately coldness. "I have no time to waste."

"With such as me, I understand. But mind, you offered to
see me yourself—I didn't come to see you. I never expected
to speak to you. But it's queer—oh, 'good Lord!' it's the
queerest thing I have ever heard of—that you, *you* of all people, should go and marry *him!*"

Sydney stands silent looking at her—the color fading from
her face.

"I knew you the minute I set eyes on you," pursues the
actress, "and, I declare, it almost knocked me over. I had
heard Lewis had married a New York heiress, but never heard
her name; and if I had I wouldn't have thought it was *that*
Miss Owenson. Why, it's horrid of him to deceive you so, because, if you knew, I don't believe you would have married
him."

What is this? Sydney stands quite rigid, holding a chair,
her eyes on Dolly's face, her own fixed and white.

"Of course *he* knew," pursues Miss De Courcy, "and it's
what I wouldn't have expected of him, because, with all his
fiery temper and jealousy, he usn't to like that. But I suppose
he thought it a great thing to carry off a beauty, and an heiress, and a fine lady. He doesn't think I know as much as I
do, and the minute I heard he had married rich, I made up my
mind to hunt him up and just scare him a little; but I didn't
think," cries Dolly, with a tragic air, I didn't think he would
have dared to marry *you*."

Still Mrs. Nolan stands fixed, white, every faculty of mind
and body seeming to be absorbed and gazing at Dolly, and
listening to Dolly.

"What I want is money," pursues the actress, coming
briskly back to business. "It's what I've come after, and what
I must have. I am going to leave New York, and I want two
or three thousand for a suitable wardrobe, and that Mr. Lewis
has got to give me, or—well, never mind what, *now*. If you'll
let me wait, I'll wait till he comes; he won't refuse so old a
friend," Dolly laughs again. "And besides, I want to congratulate him. Why, it's like one of our pieces exactly, *his doing*

what he has done, and then marrying you, and me turning up, knowing everything. But he ought not to have married you— it wasn't the square thing, and that I mean to tell him."

Sydney wakes from her trance. Whatever horrible meaning lies beneath this wretched woman's words : one thing she feels that for some misdemeanor of the past she intends to annoy and torment Lewis—Lewis, who is sufficiently annoyed by business already. She takes out her pocket-book.

" If you are poor," she says, " I will help you. If you have any claim upon my husband's kindness, it will not be disregarded. I will tell him you have been here, and he will know what is right to be done. Meantime take this from me, and do not return. Leave your address, and you shall hear from us."

Dolly looks at her curiously, but she takes the bills, counts them over, and puts them in her pocket.

"What did you marry him for, I wonder?" she says, as if to herself, with a puzzled look at Sydney. " You're awfully pretty —I never saw any one prettier—and rich, and respectable, and everything. He isn't handsome—at least I don't think so. Never could hold a candle to Bertie Vaughan."

Sydney recoiled at the sudden sound of that name.

" You never found out who killed him, did you ? He was thrown over the bank, you know, and they suspected me." Here Miss De Courcy laughs, with a certain savage light in her black eyes. " He was a sneak and a liar anyway. It was good enough for him—telling lies to you and lies to me. " Didn't you ever tell your husband you were going to be married to him."

" I don't know what you mean."

" He has deceived you, then ; men are all alike—liars every one of them. Well, when he comes home to-night ask him if he ever knew Bertie Vaughan ; ask him how they parted last ; tell him I told you, and that I can tell you more. Don't forget. I'll be back to-morrow."

Miss De Courcy turns with the words, and goes out of the room. Mrs. Nolan makes no attempt to follow her, to bring her back, to ask an explanation. She stands feeling that the room is going round, and that if she lets go her hold of the chair she will fall. But the giddiness passes in a moment, and she gropes for a chair, and sits down, and lays her head upon the cushion, feeling sick and faint.

What does this dreadful woman mean ? Her words are all

confused in Sydney's mind; only one thing stands clear, and that—that he has known Bertie Vaughan, and knows who killed him. But that is impossible. Has she not told her husband the whole story, and has he said he ever heard the name before, ever met Bertie in his life? The creature must be crazy or drunk, or both; her story is absurd on the face of it. But what a shock even an absurd story can give. She laughs weakly at her own folly in being so overcome, and then a glow of indignation fills her, and lends her strength. How shameful that she should have listened while her husband was defamed, called a liar and deceiver by this vulgar actress—her beloved husband, with the glance of a prince, honored and respected of all men. Excitement follows indignation—no more lassitude now. She tries to dine, but finds eating a delusion.

An artist in hair comes to dress those flowing blonde tresses, greatly admired, and she is nearly an hour under his professional hands. Night has fallen, gas is lit, and she is leaving, dressed for the ball. She wears white and rich laces, and bridal pearls,- and looks lovely. There is a streaming light in her eyes, a deep, permanent flush on her cheeks that makes her absolutely brilliant to-night. After eleven she will see Lewis; that is the one thought, the one desire uppermost in her mind, as she is driven to the town house of the Ten Eycks. A lengthy file of carriages block the avenue, policemen keep order, two large private lamps burn before the house, which is lit from roof to basement. A red carpet is laid across the pavement—colored men in snowy shirt fronts, kid gloves, black broadcloth and beautiful manners, stand in waiting. It is a long time before Mrs. Nolan finds her way to the lofty and superb saloon where Madame Ten Eyck receives her guests. Flowers bloom everywhere, literally everywhere, gaslight floods every corner; it is a picture all light and no shadow, German dance music fills the air, and there are crowds of elegant women in magnificent toilets. All are making their way to where Mrs. Ten Eyck, a little old lady in creamy satin, yellow point, priceless diamonds, with a severe silvery face, snow-white hair, combed back *à la* Washington, stands in state. She looks like a large doll, or a little duchess—Sydney hardly, knows which—and she receives Mrs. Nolan with distinction.

"I was an heiress myself, my dear," the little old lady said to her, on the occasion of their first meeting; "only not half so great an heiress as they tell me you are, and not quarter as great a beauty. I ran away with Ten Eyck, my dear—he didn't run away with me, in nd—when I was only seventeen. My father cut me off with a shilling, and we began housekeeping on eighty dollars. I fell in love with you, my dear, the moment I heard what you had done. I don't understand the young women of the present day—they believe in marriage but not in love. In my time we believed in love, if we never were able to marry."

It was Sydney's good fortune to attract elderly people. Men worn and gray in life's long battle looked after the lissome shape, and frank, sweet face, with a gravely tender smile. Mr. Ten Eyck, a patriarchal old gentleman, greeted her with unwonted cordiality, inquired for her husband, hoped he would be here, had heard great things predicted of him, hoped he would prove worthy of the wife he had won, and verify these predictions.

Mrs. Nolan found herself at once surrounded and engaged for every dance before supper. People remembered afterward that never had she seemed so fair or so brilliant as to-night.

It was ten when Sydney entered the house; eleven came, twelve, and still no Lewis. A fever of expectation, impatience, longing, filled her. In half an hour supper would be commenced—surely he would be here to take her down.

She made her escape from her latest partner, and took shelter in the curtained recess of an open bay window. How cool and fresh seemed the sharp night air; imprudent perhaps to sit in a draught, but darkness and solitude were tempting. Excitement had made her head ache, and her cheeks burn. She leaned her forehead against the cool glass, and looked up at the million stars keeping watch over the great city. Some men were talking in the piazza just outside, their voices blended with the music within, and the fragrance of the cigars they were smoking came to her as she sat. They were talking, in a desultory way, of the ball, of the ladies, of the war; all at once she heard her own name pronounced—some one was saying she was the prettiest woman present. Some one else spoke of her husband's absence, a third made some campaigning remark, and the subjects seemed to connect themselves in his mind.

Why doesn't Nolan try it, I wonder?" said this gentleman in a dissatisfied tone. "He's as likely a mark for a bullet as any of us; a tall and proper fellow like that."

"Ah! why?" retorts No. 1, with a satirical laugh. "He is the only son of his mother, and she is a widow.'

" He has married a wife, and therefore cannot come," says No. 3.

" All wrong, you fellows," cuts in a fourth voice ; "he is going—I happen to know. He has been offered the captaincy in his old regiment, *vice* Wendall, shot, and has accepted. He has kept it quiet—the fact is three days old ; but I can't stand by and hear you old women abuse him. You envy him naturally—I do myself. Lovely girl, that wife. He starts in two days. As good a fellow as ever lived, is Nolan."

" And as plucky," supplements another; "he was out the first year, as you know. We served together. Got a bullet in the lung, and came home invalided. There's fight enough in Nolan—being an Irishman, that is understood. But as to his going out, by George, if I were in his place I would think twice before I left a wife like that, only married yesterday, or thereabout. There's the *"Soldaten Lieder"*—let's go back. This is a great night ; Mrs. Ten Eyck expects every man to do his duty."

They go ; but Sydney, long after their voices cease, sits frigid. Is she in a dream ? Lewis going to join the army, without a word to her—going in two days ! She sits for a while so stunned that movement or thought is impossible. Then she rises slowly and stiffly, feeling chilled to the heart by the frosty night wind, and parts the curtains and step out. Almost the first person she sees is her husband, talking to one or two other men.

" Then you're really going back, Nolan ? " one says ; "it is an accomplished fact ? Well, we need such men as you, and we all must make sacrifices at our country's call."

" Day after to-morrow, is it ? " asks a second, and Nolan nods a little impatiently, his eyes wandering about in search of some one.

Sydney comes forward. The color has left her face—it is white as her dress ; her eyes look blank and bewildered with sudden terror. The men stare at her—her husband with an alarmed look is instantly at her side.

" Sydney, you are ill ! "

" Yes—no," she answers, incoherently, grasping his arm. " Oh ! Lewis, take me home."

" Sit down for a moment," he says.

He knows she has heard what he meant to break to her himself. She obeys and he leaves her, but he is back directly with a glass of iced champagne.

" Drink this."

She obeys once more, looking at him with imploring eyes.

"Will you not take me home, Lewis? My head aches and burns—this glare and music is torture. Take me home at once."

"Certainly, my dearest ; but will you not wait for——"

"No, no—I will wait for nothing. Take me home at once —at once !"

But "at once " is not so easy. Mr. Nolan must see his hostess, and explain that his wife has been taken suddenly ill. Then another half hour passes before their carriage can come into line and she is safely seated in it, her head on Lewis' shoulder, his arm holding her to him, and scarcely a word interchanged the whole way.

CHAPTER XV.

"NO SUN GOES DOWN BUT THAT SOME HEART DOES BREAK."

IT is the supreme hour of his life—he feels that. He has not meant that a *denouement* shall come in this way ; he has intended to break to her the news of his departure ; and when far away write to her the story he knows he must tell now. All the way home he is nerving himself for the ordeal—the self-repression, the self-command, that have been the study of his life for the past five years stand him in good stead now. Except that the face on which the lamps shine is deadly pale, there is no change. The eyes he fixes on his wife are dark with unutterable sadness and compassion. For her, she trembles and clings to him, and when they reach her own room, to which he leads her, she clasps her hands and speaks for the first time.

"Lewis, is this true ? "

"Sit down, Sydney," he says gently, and places her in a chair. "Is what true, my wife ? "

"That you are about to rejoin your regiment—that you go the day after to-morrow ? I heard it all at the ball."

She is thinking of this strange fact alone, that she is about to lose him, and that he has never told her. It pierces her heart like a knife—it has driven all thought of Dolly De Courcy and her suggestion out of her mind.

"It is quite true."

"And you never told *me!*"

The passionate reproach of the eyes that look at him—those gentle blue eyes that never had for him other than infinite tenderness—move him to the soul.

"My darling, I meant to explain—I meant to have told you to-morrow. You know I have often spoken of this to you since our marriage. After all, it is only my duty. You would not listen, and I—Heaven help me!—was not strong enough to break from the gentle arms that held me back—might nevre have broken but for what passed between us the other night.

"'The other night!" She repeats, in vague wonder. Then recollection flashes upon her, and her eyes dilate incredulously. "Lewis," she exclaims, "you do not mean to say that the story I told you the other night has forced you to do this?"

"I am only doing my duty, Sydney. Still, but for that story my duty might never have been done."

She gazes at him silently, seemingly lost in wonder and incredulity.

"Did you feel the fact of my former engagement so deeply, then? Because I was once before on the verge of marriage you leave me to rejoin the army? Oh! Lewis, pardon me, but I cannot believe this."

"That was the cause, but not as you think. Sydney, love, do you remember, in telling me of your previous engagement before our marriage, you never told me the man's name? Had you done so," he stops a moment, "we would never have been man and wife."

She sits quite still, her hands clasped, her dilated eyes, looking almost black with vague terror, fixed on his face.

"Do you recall," he goes on, "that moonlight January night when we walked home together, and I told you there was a secret in my life, that if told might separate us forever? Your answer was, that with my past life you had nothing to do—you only required perfect truth and fidelity for the future. Oh! love, why did you not bid me speak? I would have told you then, when it was not yet too late, the miserable story I must tell you to-night. Truth and fidelity were all you asked in your noble trust and generosity, and these I could give you without stint or measure. If I had ever heard the name of Bertie Vaughan——"

He shudders as he says it, and looks ff, and all at once there flashes back upon her bewildered mind the memory of the afternoon's visit, and the dark hints dropped by the actress

"Lewis," she suddenly exclaims, "a very strange person came to see me this afternoon—I meant to tell you, and forgot —and she said very strange things. The person was the actress we saw the other night—Dolly De Courcy—and the things she said were about you and Bertie Vaughan."

"Dolly De Courcy!" he repeats, in wonder. "What was it she said?"

"She told me to ask you"—Sydney puts her hand to her head in a dazed way, trying to recall—"how you last parted from Bertie Vaughan."

He stood stricken speechless, it would seem, by her words.

"How, in Heaven's name, does she know?" he says, speaking as if to himself. "Was she there, and has she all this time kept the secret? Surely not—she never kept a secret in her life—she would be the first to tell. It must be that she only suspects. But to come here—to force herself upon you!"

His face flushes angrily, his eyes indignantly flash.

"She came in search of you, Lewis," his wife interposes, in a broken voice. "She said she had a claim upon you, and I saw her in your stead. I had no wish to pry into any secret of your life, Lewis."

Her voice breaks altogether for a moment in a great sob. Then she starts to her feet, and holds out both hands piteously.

"Lewis, *what* is this?" she cries. "I feel as if my heart were breaking; I am afraid of—I don't know what. Something stands between us, and keeps me from you. If you ever loved me, tell me it is no crime of yours that is parting us now. One word of denial will be enough; I will believe you, though all the world stood up and accused you with one voice."

She sees the strong frame quiver from head to foot; she sees the desperate gesture with which he stops her.

"Cease!" he says, hoarsely. "I cannot bear it; for it is a crime that stands between us—one that should have held us asunder forever."

She drops back into her chair, and puts one trembling hand over her eyes. And Lewis Nolan, leaning against the mantel, regains his wonderful self-restraint after a moment, and rapidly and concisely begins the dark record he has to tell.

"I knew Dolly De Courcy. 'Tis ten years ago now, when I was a lad of eighteen, that I knew her first. She was an actress at the time, and her black eyes and coquettish ways captured my romantic boyish fancy at sight. In those days I was an inveterate play-goer. Uncle Grift's good nature kept me always supplied with sufficient money for that dissipation. My mother remonstrated about my late hours and doubtful associates ; but I was absolutely self-willed in those days, had ideas about joining the theatrical profession myself, and went on in my own way. Dolly and I soon became warm friends—lovers, perhaps, I should say—for she was an arrant little flirt even then, and willing to fool me to the top of my bent. We were engaged, after an absurd boy-and-girl fashion, when I was twenty. I left off play-going, began to work hard, save money, and look forward to marriage and house-keeping. It was all profoundest earnest and good faith on my part. The girl had bewitched me. I believed her to be everything that was good, and warm-hearted, and honorable ; and in those days I believe she was an honest girl, and really fond of the infatuated young simpleton who ran after her about New York, and was furiously jealous of every man who looked at her—of her stage lovers, and the fellows about the theatre generally. She laughed at my jealousy, ridiculed my rages, for in those days I had a furious temper, quite uncurbed. She would not marry me, made game of my poetical ideas of love in a cottage, and I believe in her heart was tired of my too exacting devotion.

" My mother and sister knew very little of all this—they certainly were aware that I had formed some absurd attachment for an actress, but I was moody and sullen about it all. My jealous fears were always up in arms ; it was a wretched time for myself, and a supremely wretched one for all the family.

" It was about this time that Dolly went to Wychcliffe. It was not the first occasion she had gone out of New York, but I seemed to feel her absence more deeply this time than ever before. It is of no use looking back now, and wondering at the infatuation that chained me to such a woman—of no use thinking how supremely wretched my life would have been if she had taken me at my word and married me. I urged her to, before she went to Wychcliffe, and she actually promised to do so as soon as she returned, and I believe meant to keep her word.

" In the company was a man with whom I occasionally corresponded, and who kept a watchful eye upon my fickle *fiancee*. It was from him I first heard of her new lover, Bertie Vaughan. He haunted her like her shadow, it appeared ; his sudden devotion was the laughter of the whole company. Dolly, it seemed, was deeply smitten, too ; they were almost inseparable. Had I not better come on and look after my property? wrote my friend. I could not go on, but I wrote fine, furious letters to Dolly, which Dolly did not answer. Poor soul! flirtation was more in her line than letter-writing. Finally an epistle did come. 'Would I break off? She was tired of being scolded; I was too cross and hateful for any-thing. Please not to trouble her with any more jealous letters, and she would give me back my ring when she returned to New York."

"I could laugh now, even in all the bitterness of despair, as I look back and recall the effects this letter had upon me. Insane as I was, fool as I was, I still kept my rage to myself, but my mind was made up. I would go to Wychcliffe, I would see this man, this young aristocrat who was fooling Dolly, and force *him* to hear reason, if I could not force her. I knew he was fooling her, for my actor acquaintance had informed me that he was engaged to a young lady residing in the town, the only daughter of a very rich man, and, in fact, about to be married to her. Not once was your name men-tioned—it was always as a young lady of Wychcliffe you were spoken of; his name alone, Bertie Vaughan, I knew.

"Fortune seemed to favor me. While I was meditating upon some plan of making my way to Wychcliffe, Mr. Graham, on the point of starting for Minnesota upon some important business, was taken very ill. Some one must go in his place. He had limitless confidence in my integrity and business capabilities, and I was to go in his stead. It was the very opportunity I was seeking. I left home ostensibly to start West, but in reality to go first to Wychcliffe, force Vaughan to give up his pretensions, whatever they were, to Dolly, by fair means or foul.

"I reached Wychcliffe in the middle of a whirling snow-storm, and the first news I heard was that the theatre people, Dolly included, had left the town a whole week before. This was startling intelligence, and I half-resolved to go back to New York, seek out Dolly, and reproach her with her vile infidelity. I heard, too, without asking any questions, that a fashionable marriage was to take place next day, and that the name of the bridegroom was Vaughan, also that Vaughan had been courting the actress all the while he was courting the heiress, and liked the actress best.

"Men laughed, and cracked jokes about it at the hotel bar, while I listened, devoured with silent jealousy and rage. Even then your name was not mentioned—if it was, I paid no attention to it ; my only thoughts were of him who had dared to supplant me.   Still listening, I learned that he was stopping at this very house, and would be along about half-past ten. That determined me.   I would wait and meet him, as I had come so far to do it ; I would force him, if he ever met Dolly again, to drop her acquaintance ; for an engaged flirt, as I knew, was ready to prove a married flirt.   I would force this promise from him, then take the night train for New York, seek out Dolly the first thing in the morning, and have a final settlement with her before going to Minnesota for an indefinite time.   I had no other thought but that—I say it before Heaven.

"I started about half-past nine, ostensibly to take the train back to New York, in reality to take the path by which I had heard Vaughan returned to the hotel, and meet him somewhere on the way.   You may remember that night.   The snow-storm had ceased, the moon and stars were shining on the white, glistening ground ; it was mild and windless as I walked along the steep path above the shore.   The talk of the men about this man I was going to meet and Dolly, had thrown me into one of my black, silent rages ; their laughter implied more than their words, and had maddened me.   I took my stand at what I judged to be about half-way, and leaning against a large rock, looked out at the sea creeping up so far below, and waited."

Lewis Nolan pauses.   In a low, suppressed voice, full of intensest feeling, he has narrated all this.   In her chair, her eyes upon him, her face stony—his wife listens.   But now she starts up, and puts out both arms blindly.

"Lewis !" she cries, in a voice that pierces his very soul, "don't tell me that it was you who killed Bertie Vaughan !"

"God help me !   God forgive me !" he answers in a stifled voice—"it was I !"

CHAPTER XVI.

"A FOND KISS, AND THEN WE SEVER."

HE stands, almost paralyzed, looking at him, her arms held out in that blind agony, her eyes fixed and dark with horror.   He thinks she is going to faint, and takes a step towards her ; but as he attempts to touch her, she

shrinks suddenly back. It is the slightest of movements, but it holds him from her, as a wall. He turns abruptly and resumes his former place. She drops back into her chair, lays her white face on the table beside her, and neither speaks nor moves again.

"Shall I finish?" he huskily says, after a moment, and as there is no reply, he goes on : "I waited for him there. I had not long to wait. Presently he came along in the moonlight whistling as he came, as if he had not a care in the world —this man who was betraying two women. I knew him instantly in the clear moonlight—I heard him described often enough ; and as he was about to pass the place where I stood, I started out into the light, and said :

"Stay !"

"He stopped at once, ceased his whistling, and looked at me, a little startled, I could see, but he spoke coolly enough.

"'Well,' he said, 'who are you?'

"'You are Bertie Vaughan!' was my answer.

"'And who the devil are you that makes so free with my name? Get out of my way and let me pass.'

"'Not just yet,' I said ; 'I have a little account to settle with you, Mr. Bertie Vaughan, before we part, and I have come all the way from New York to settle it.'

"'Who *are* you?' he asked, curiously.

"I am Lewis Nolan, the man to whom Dolly De Courcy is engaged, and I demand of you to resign all acquaintance with her from this moment.'

He laughed.

"'So,' he said, 'you're the fellow Dolly's to marry. Well, when I am ready to give her up she may marry you, you understand? Now move aside.'

"There was something so insufferably insulting and sneering in his tone and laugh that I lost the last remnant of self-control. I sprang at his throat ; he darted back, and lifting a cane he carried, he broke it across my shoulders. Then we grappled, and the struggle began. Not a word was spoken, as we held each other there in that narrow path. At all times I must have been the stronger of the two ; now, beside myself with fury, he was no more match for me than a child. Unconsciously we had wrestled near to the edge of the cliff, and all at once I freed myself and threw him from me with all my might. I threw him from me—as Heaven hears me, I had no thought of throwing him over, no thought of the precipice at all.

"There was a cry that has rung in my ears ever since, a cry

of horror and despair that I will hear when I am dying, a glimpse
of a white, agonized face, and then——"

He breaks off. There is agony in his own face, agony in his
voice, great drops on his forehead, and the hand that hangs by
his side is clenched. The picture is before him ; if he would, he
could not keep back the words that paint it. It has lain locked
in his bosom so long—he has seen that face, heard that death-cry
so often, asleep and awake, all these years, that, now the hour
has come, he must speak all or nothing. For his wife, she neither
gives word nor sign, and yet he knows she hears all.

" Well," he says, in a hurried, breathless sort of voice, and
looking up again, " I don't know how long I stood there—paralyzed by the deed I had done. I knew the depth of that precipice—I had seen the jagged bed of rocks, like black spikes,
projecting in the moonlight eighty feet below. I knew what I
would see if I looked over. And I *could not* look over. Something of the horror of the awful sight that would meet me, held
me back. I had done a murder—that thought filled me, body
and soul. There was neither word nor cry, and turning suddenly, without one backward look I walked away.

" Perhaps, in reality, I had not stood there five seconds—five
hours could not have seemed longer. Like a man who walks in
his sleep, hardly conscious of what I did, or where I went, I hurried on ; I neither feared nor cared for detection ; I never thought
of it, in fact, I had but one feeling—the brand of Cain was upon
me for all time—I had slain my brother. I walked all night. I
was too late for any train back ; but early in the morning I found
myself, foot-sore and weary, at another town some eighteen miles
from Wychcliffe, and made inquiries of the men I met going to
work. A train started at seven ; I found it, got on board, returned to New York, breakfasted, and in a few hours was speeding along westward by express.

" ' The first intense horror had by this time faded from my
mind ; I saw now how insanely I had acted ; I was not guilty of
murder—I had no thought of taking his life. That I had thrown
him over the cliff, instead of on the ground, was purely accidental. What I should have done was to have found a path
down to the beach, and seen if he were really killed. But I
shuddered as I thought it—no, I could not have looked upon
that. And if I gave myself up for the deed I had done, who
was to prove it was not premeditated ? He was my rival ; I
had deliberately come to Wychcliffe in search of him, waylaid
and assaulted him—the circumstantial evidence would be against

me, and crushing. It would break my mother's heart, and kill my sister. Besides, I thought, with sullen doggedness, he had deserved his fate ; he was a scoundrel—why should I suffer for what was an accident after all ? I would think no more about it, it was done, and could not be undone. It was an accident, and he had brought it on himself—I kept repeating that over and over again.

"But it would not do—it never has done—judge and jury have never tried me ; but my own conscience has, and I stand condemned. It has spoiled my life, changed my nature—a nature better changed, perhaps, and I have held myself and my passions and my temper, with the higher help, for which I have prayed, better, I trust, in hand. I have suffered for what I have done, I have repented. Heaven knows there has been no time since when I would not have given my own life to have brought his back. When I pleaded for Mrs. Harland, I saw a parallel in our two cases, and it was for myself I pleaded ; when she was sentenced, as still guilty, in that sentence I read my own condemnation.

"I remained in Minnesota nearly seven months—so busy I scarcely had time to glance even at the daily papers. Once or twice I saw a brief account of the murder or accident, no one seemed able to determine which ; no one was suspected, no one arrested, all was well. If any one had been, of course there would be no alternative but to go at once and speak out. But no one was, and when I returned to New York the whole matter was a thing of the past. I went back to the office and resumed my old routine, with a secret, like Eugene Aram's, in my heart. And yet knowing that I had never meant to kill, that I would have shrunk appalled, even in the hour of my fiercest passion, from the thought, I could feel altogether guilty, altogether unhappy. And as years went on, and as I strove to atone by a better life, by fidelity to all duties, as ambitious thoughts and hopes absorbed me, I gradually grew—not to forget—that was impossible, but to look back only with remorseful sorrow to that dark night of my life, and look humbly for pardon to Him who has said, ' Though your sins be as scarlet they shall become white as wool.'

"Dolly De Courcy I never saw again—not once—until that night last week when I saw her on the stage, and we mutually recognized each other. It brought back so vividly all that was past and gone, all my wrong-doing, that it cost me an effort to sit the play out. From that night my insane infatuation for her

died a natural death ; it seemed as if my horror of my own act
had killed it. I could not think of her without a feeling of repulsion. I felt it unjustly, no doubt, as I looked at her then.
How she comes to know anything about it is a mystery to me.
I do not believe she really does know. She may suspect,
knowing my jealousy—she can know nothing beyond.

"I had ceased to care for her—I cared for no one else. I
had made up my mind to my own satisfaction, never to marry
Law should be my love, ambition my bride, honors my children
the praise of men my home. A woman, and my own madness,
had spoiled my life, no other should ever come into it;
and then, at the height of all these fine resolves, my wife, my
love, I met *you.* I met you by chance—if anything in this
world does happen by chance—and all melted before your blue
eyes and radiant smile, as snow before the sun. Did I fall in
love with you, as I saw you standing, tall and graceful, and fair
as a lily, before Von Etté's picture ? I don't know. I know
that the words you spoke stabbed me like a knife—haunted me
with incessant pain until I sat beside you in Mrs. Graham's
home, and tried to bring you to my way of thinking. You were
remembering Bertie Vaughan. Ah, Heaven ! so was I, and
neither knew it. Your face was with me incessantly—came
between me and my books, and lit the dingy office with its
sweet memory. You were unlike any one I had ever known—
you were my ideal woman, half-angelic, half-womanly, and—
I lost my head again. I had no hope of ever winning you, no,
not the faintest. I saw you surrounded by such suitors as Van
Cuyler, admired wherever you went, rich, beautiful, well-born.
What was I—what had I—that I should presumptuously hope
for anything beyond a kind smile, a friendly word ? Your
choice surprised every one—my wife, it surprised no one more
than it did myself. I struggled with my ever-growing insanity,
as I called it, more insane in a different way even than the first,
and thought I had strength of will sufficient to master it. But
I found it was every day mastering me—that each time I saw
you I grew more helplessly powerless and enslaved, that my
only hope was in flight. I had long meditated this trip to California ; the chances were better there, success more rapid and
assured—now seemed my time. I was telling all to Lucy that
night, my love and my struggles ; you came and—you know
the rest. It was as if an angel had stooped to love as mortals
love, and I could only wonder at the great joy that had come
to me and accept.

"The only thought that marred my happiness was the thought that I ought to tell you all, to lay bare my secret, and let you say whether it was sufficient to hold us asunder forever. I tried one night and you stopped me. With matchless confidence and generosity, you said that with my past life you had nothing to do, that you refused to listen, that love and fidelity were all you asked, and I was weak, and grasped at my reprieve as a sentenced man, never dreaming of the terrible truth.

"You had once lived in Wychcliffe, you had once before been engaged to be married, and the man had died—that told little or nothing. The man's name was never mentioned between us—but why go on? You will believe me when I say, had I known that day when we met in the studio what I know now we should never have met again unless I came to you and confessed the truth. Even had I loved you, I would have dreaded such a marriage as much as you could have done, but there is a retribution in these things that works its own way, and we are husband and wife, and five of the happiest months that ever mortal man enjoyed have been mine. All the parting and the expiation of the future can never dim the bliss of their memory. I may be most miserable, but I *have* been most happy."

His voice, low and husky, and hurried through it all, breaks, and he bows his forehead on the arm resting on the chimney-piece, and there is silence.

"The blow that killed Bertie Vaughan killed also your father you have told me," he resumes. "I thought that I had suffered in the past, but I never knew what suffering was until that night when you sat on my knee, your head on my shoulder, and innocently told me your story. I sat that night long after you were asleep, love, and thought of what I should do. That we must part was certain, that you must know the truth was certain, and what I have thought of long, I did at last. I meant to have told you then, and once fairly away to write you all, It seemed to me I could never look in your face and break your heart. But even that has been forced upon me ; it is part of my punishment, and a very hard one to bear."

Once more silence—she never moved nor looked up.

"You bound yourself by a promise - beside your father's death-bed," Lewis Nolan goes on, "to bring to justice the man who caused his adopted son's death. If you feel that promise must be kept——"

She lifts her head and looks at him, such agony in her face as it breaks his heart to see.

17

"Oh, forgive me !" he cries, "I know that you cannot, my own wife. I would give my life for you, and I have crushed every hope out of yours forever."

She drops her head again, and once more there is silence. The clock on the mantel strikes three, and he starts up.

"I am going at once," he says hurriedly; "every moment I linger is an added torture. There are some papers in my study that I must attend to before I leave."

He goes with the words.

Papers, letters, lie strewn over his writing-table; he turns up the gas, sits down, and for half-an-hour is busy. He fills all his pockets, and then still rapidly exchanges his full-dress evening suit for street wear, buttons up an overcoat, and hat in hand, returns to his wife's room. She is lying as he left her, she looks as if she never cared to lift her head again.

"Sydney," he says, "I am going. Will you try not to hate me for what I have done? You have always been generous— will you not be generous enough now to say one good-bye?"

She rises with a low, sobbing sort of cry, and flings herself upon his breast. Her arms cling round his neck as though they would never loosen their hold, but she does not, cannot speak a word. His kisses fall on her lips; her bewildered eyes full of an agony he can never forget, look up in his face.

"My wife! my wife! my wife!"

No word of farewell passes, he holds her strained hard for one long moment, then places her gently back in her chair; her arms fall loosely, her eyes follow him, her white lips are incapable of uttering a word. She sees him leave the room, hears him go out of the house, hears the door close behind him, and still sits motionless, speechless, staring straight before her, blankly, at the open door.

CHAPTER XVII.

"AS ONE WHOM HIS MOTHER COMFORTETH."

UCY NOLAN was ailing that night; those dreadful spasms of racking spine complaint, aggravated by her ceaseless hacking cough, were back to torture her. All night long, while suffering of another kind, infinitely harder to bear than the most torturing physical pain, was rend-

ing the heart of Lewis Nolan's wife, Lucy lay on her bed and
endured. All night the shaded lamp burned, all night her
mother watched unweariedly by her bedside, and it was only
when the chill October dawn was breaking that pain ceased,
and sleep came to the patient eyes. Then her mother, pale
and fagged, stole down-stairs to begin her duties of the day.
She threw open the shutters, unbolted the door, and stepped
out into the crisp, sparkling coldness of the early morning.
The sharp, fresh air was like an exhilarating draught. She lingered on the doorstep watching the city sky flush and grow
warm, before the coming of the red round sun. Some laborers
went straggling by to their work ; one or two grimy Dutch-
women with bags passed, raking, as they went, the offal of the
streets. As she was about to turn into the house, she espied a
man coming toward her, with something oddly familiar about
him.

The tall figure was Lewis ; but surely that downcast head
and lagging walk were strangely unlike her son's erect carriage
and quick, firm step. And yet it was Lewis ; she saw that with
wonder, and some alarm. He raised his eyes at the same moment, and came forward at a rapid pace.

"Lewis!" she exclaimed, startled strangely as she looked at
him.

Haggard, bloodless, with something of wildness in the steadfast dark eyes, he seemed almost like an apparition, in the gray
of the early morning.

"Go in, mother," he said ; "I have something to tell you."

She obeyed him. They entered the little parlor, into which
the first rays of the sun were shining.

"Speak low," she said, remembering even in her anxiety for
one child the illness of the other. "Lucy has had one of her
bad turns all night, and has just fallen asleep. What is it,
Lewis? Sydney——"

He made a sudden, almost fierce gesture, that stayed the
name on her lips, and walked to the window. The glow of the
eastern sky, all rose-red, threw a fictitious flush upon the face
that seemed to have grown worn and aged in a night.

So, standing with his back to her, his eyes on that lovely radiance, he spoke :

"Mother," he said abruptly, "I am going away."

"My son!"

"I have rejoined my old company—I leave at once—to-day.
If when the war ends there is an end of me also, well and

good ; it will be far the easiest way of solving all difficulties.
If there is not, I will start at once for Sacramente, and begin
the world anew.   In any case I shall not return to New York,
so that this is my leave-taking, perhaps for all time."

She dropped into a chair—speechless.   He had spoken with
recklessness, bitterness ; he had suffered almost beyond endurance in the hours that had intervened, hours spent in wandering through the lonely, melancholy streets.   But now, at the
exceeding bitter cry of his mother, he turned quickly around,
himself once more.

"Mother, forgive me," he said, shocked at his own words.
"I have been too abrupt—I ought not to have spoken in this
way.   But it has all come so suddenly upon myself, that I feel
half dazed.   After all, my rejoining the army ought not to
shock you very greatly.   It is only what I have contemplated
long, what I would to Heaven I had done a year ago."

"Lewis, my son," his mother said, looking at him with wondering, terrified eyes, "what is this ?   What is the meaning of
this sudden resolution ?   For it *is* sudden ; a week ago you had
no idea of forsaking your wife.   What has come between you
now ?

She saw the drawn look of torture that flashed across his face,
saw his teeth set, and his hand clench.

"A secret that will part us forever.   A crime ! "

"A crime ? "

" Yes, one of the darkest of crimes, blood-guiltiness, mother.

Her face blanches, her lips tremble, her eyes are riveted in
amaze and horror upon him.

"You thought I had no secret from you—that my life was an
open record for all men to read, that no hidden sin lay at my
door.   That was your mistake.   Five years ago I killed a man,
and to-day retribution has come home to me."

He has a vague feeling that those things should be broken
to her gently, but he cannot do it.   As he feels them, they
must come out, or not at all.   For his mother, she sits half-
stunned, half-bewildered, dumb.

"I shall tell you the story, mother ; but first let me tell you
Sydney's.   You may not know, perhaps, that once before she
was a bride—her bridal dress on, and she waiting for the bridegroom, who never came.   The man could not come, he had
been killed in a paroxysm of jealous rage the night before.
The shock, the shame, the horror of it all, brought on her father's
death.   On his death-bed his last injunction to her was,

to bring to justice, if she ever met him, the slayer of her lover. The promise was made, and promises to the dying are binding. And last night, for the first time, she met and knew this man."

Mrs. Nolan sits with her hands clasped, listening breathlessly to this rapid, almost incoherent story, which she but half comprehends.

"Last night she met him, mother—to *know* him. I, her husband, am the man whom she stands pledged to deliver up to the justice of the law. It was I who killed her lover, the night before he was to have been her husband."

Mrs. Nolan rises up, an angry flush on her face, an excited gleam in her eye.

"Lewis, I do not understand one word of what you are saying. Have you been drinking, or are you going mad? How can you stand there and tell me such shocking and false things?"

"They are not false, mother—there is no such hope for me as that."

His steady tone staggers her. She shrinks back into her chair, and puts her hand in a lost way to her head.

"Will you tell me again, Lewis, and more clearly, please. I do not seem able to understand you. *My* son a murderer! Surely I have misunderstood all you have been saying."

"Yes, it is hard to realize, is it not? It is hard to think that one sin, done years ago in a moment of passion, atoned for, as I had hoped, should break so many innocent hearts. But it is true, and it has parted me and my wife forever—it sends me an outcast from home for all time. My fate is deserved—hers, poor innocent child, is not. I ought to break those things to you, I suppose, but I never learned how to break things; I can tell you in no other way than this."

He drops into a seat, for he is dead tired, and begins, as collectedly as he can, the whole most wretched narrative of misplaced love, of insane jealousy, of ungovernable passion, and of the result. She sits listening with strained and painful attention, comprehending at last the whole sad history of passion and sin, remorse and retribution. And when the story is done, there is silence again. Mrs. Nolan sits weeping, without a word, such tears as in all her life she has never shed before, and she has been a woman of trouble, acquainted with sorrow.

"May God forgive you, my son!" is what she says at last.

"Am I indeed a murderer?" he drearily asks; "have I all these years been deluding myself with sophistries?"

"A murderer!—no, a thousand times no!" his mother cries

out, "Heaven forbid ! The sin is in the intention, and you had no intention of taking this man's life. All the same, it has been taken, and here at least it seems you must expiate your sin. Oh, my son ! my son ! what can I say to comfort you ?"

"It is past all that, mother—say you forgive me, before I go, and try and comfort my wife—I ask no more."

He breaks utterly down at the words, at the thought of that beloved, that most wretched wife, and turns away and bows his face on his arm.

"My Lewis, my boy, it is the first real sorrow you have given me in your life. I forgive you, and I know that forgiveness, higher and greater, will not be refused. I will care for your wife. Oh, poor child, what a blow for her who has loved you beyond the love of woman !"

"Hush !" he hoarsely exclaims, "I am almost mad already —do you want to drive me quite."

"Will you tell me your plans, dear ?" she asks gently, infinite compassion, infinite yearning mother-love in her eyes.

"I have none. I join my regiment, as I have told you, at once ; beyond that, the future will take care of itself. If things end as I wish, there will be no need of further plans. If they do not, I shall go to California, and there begin again. Our parting is for life, that you must see. I must write a letter to Graham explaining, without telling the real cause of my abrupt departure. There need be no scandal ; I have simply gone to the war, as is all men's duty nowadays. For my wife," —a pause to command himself—"I commit her to your care. She has youth, she has strength, and she has limitless wealth ; she need not mourn forever. Persuade her to travel, mother, to go abroad again to her English friends, or to the Continent. You will know what to say to her better than I can tell you. I am not worth one tear from those pure eyes. There are some things I would like to say to her ; I will write them here before I go."

He sits down and begins to work, resolutely summoning all his self-control. He writes his letter to Mr. Graham, answers the many documents he has brought with him from the house, and makes all into a neat parcel for the post. Then he begins that other letter. He writes " My Dear Wife," and sits staring at the words as if they held some spell for him that he could not break. But once he begins, his pen flies over the paper, page after page. It is the last he ever intends to write, and he pours out his whole heart in it, as even his wife has never seen it before. It is a voluminous epistle before it is done, folded, sealed and addressed. Then he holds it with wistful, yearning eyes, looking at the name his hand has written, "Sydney Nolan," the last link of all that binds him and his wife together now. His mother comes in, and stoops and kisses him tenderly as he sits. With homely, motherly care that is better than sentiment, she has been preparing breakfast for her boy, a breakfast he used to like when he was all her own. He sits down to please her, with the knowledge that a journey lies before him, and the loss of strength will help no man to bear trouble. But Mrs. Nolan sighs over his performance, and gazes at him anxiously as he rises. "You eat nothing, my son."

"Your coffee has done me good. Post the package to Graham, mother, and take the letter to Sydney yourself. I will go up and look at Lucy before I leave."

He ascends the stairs without noise. The little dainty room is darkened, and Lucy lies tranquilly asleep after her exhausting night of pain. How placid, how pure, how passionless is that wan face. He stoops gently and touches his lips to her thin cheek. She stirs restlessly, but does not awaken, and he goes, as he has come, unheard.

His mother is crying below. She has striven heroically to keep up, but nature is stronger than will. He takes her in his arms and kisses her.

"Good-bye, mother. Forgive me and pray for me. I will write to you regularly, and you will tell me all that there is to tell. Everything, you understand."

"I understand." She sobs audibly, in a heart-broken way and clings to him. "Oh, my boy, my boy! it is hard to let you go."

"It is hard for me ; do not make it any harder, mother," he says, in a tortured voice, and she opens her arms and lets him go."

"The only son of his mother, and she was a widow," and the last time she may ever see him this side of the grave. Her eyes are blinded with tears as she watches him out of sight. The son who has been her hope, her pride, her gladness for seven-and-twenty years. She watches him out of sight as women do watch the men they love, and may never see again, and then sits down and cries as she has never cried in all her troubled life.

CHAPTER XVIII.

"THE LIGHT IN THE DUST LIES DEAD."

YING motionless against the cushioned back of her chair, white and still ; so, when morning comes, and a servant enters, she finds Lewis Nolan's wife   She has not fainted, she has not been insensible for one moment ; she lies here stunned.   Over and over in her mind the weary hours through, the words he has said keep repeating themselves—the words that divorce them forever.

He has killed Bertie Vaughan ; her husband is the man she stands pledged to her dying father to deliver over to justice ; he has left her, never to return.   These three things follow each other ceaselessly through her dazed brain, until the very power of thinking at all becomes numb.

She opens her eyes at the girl's cry of consternation, and rises with an effort.   The servant speaks to her, but she is unconscious of what she says.   She goes into her bedroom—it is dark and still here—and lies down with a dull sense of oppression and suffering upon her, and buries her face in the pillows.

If she could only sleep, if she could only for an hour cease to think.   But she cannot.   Like a machine that has been wound up to its utmost tension, and must go on until it runs itself down, so she thinks, and thinks, and thinks.   Where is Lewis now ?   Will it be wrong for her to think of him after this, to love him, to pray for him ?   If so, she will do wrong all her life long.   Is she committing a sin in disobeying her father's last command ?   How strange, how strange that Lewis should have been the one to throw Bertie over the cliff.   Poor Bertie ! how fond and proud they all were of him once—her father, and mother, and she too.

He rises before her, the blonde, boyish beauty of his face, his fair curling hair and merry eyes.   It was a dreadful fate ; and Lewis, her Lewis, whom she has revered and honored as something more than man, his hand is red with Bertie's blood. Thought becomes such torture that she presses both hands upon her temples, striving by main force to shut it out.   She is still lying here when Mrs. Nolan reaches the house and goes up to her room.

" My own dear child ! "

The white face lifts, the eyes look at her so full of infinite misery that tears spring to those of the elder woman. She puts her arms about her and kisses the blanched lips.

"Sydney, my dearest child, what shall I say to you? How shall I comfort you? May Heaven help you—you must look for your comfort there."

"Has he gone?" Sydney says, in an odd, hollow voice that startles even herself.

"Yes, dear—Heaven help him! He came to me at daybreak this morning and told me all. Are you angry with him, Sydney? Oh, if you knew how he suffers you would not be."

"Angry with him?" she repeats, in a dreary sort of wonder. "Angry with Lewis? Oh, no!"

"It was a terrible thing. Do you not think, my dearest daughter, that it is almost as bitter a blow to me as to you? I have been so proud of my boy, of his talents, of the praise men gave him; he was such a good son always, so free from the vices of most young men. And now——"

But her voice breaks, and the tears gush forth again, none the less heart-rending for being so quiet.

But Sydney does not cry. She looks at her in the same drearily dry-eyed way, in a sort of wistful wonder and envy at her tears.

"I cannot cry," she says, wretchedly, with her hand on her heart. "I seem to ache here, but I don't feel like crying at all. It was the same when Bertie was killed, and papa lay dying and dead. They thought I was hard and cold, because when all wept I sat like a stone. I feel the same now. And mostly I cry for such little things."

She sighs heavily, and lies, in a tired way, back among the pillows. She recalls how she sat and wept when poor mamma died, lonely and sorrowing, but without this miserable, unendurable aching of the heart.

"Have you had breakfast?" Mrs. Nolan asks, more troubled by this apathetic despair than by any hysterical outburst of grief.

"No, I was not hungry. Is it past breakfast-time?"

"It is two o'clock, and you have fasted a great deal too long. We will be having you sick on our hands, and that won't help matters." Mrs. Nolan rings the bell, and wipes away all traces of tears, and orders strong coffee and toast. "I cannot nurse two invalids at once," she says, forcing a smile, "so I must keep you up. Poor Lucy was in wretched pain all night."

17*

"Ah! poor Lucy! dear Lucy! patient, gentle Lucy! does *she* know?"

"Yes, dear. I told her just before I came away. She was asleep when Lewis left, and he kissed her good-bye without awakening her."

A quiver passed over Sydney's face. She was thinking of their own last parting.

"How does she bear it?"

"As she bears all things—with angelic patience. In long suffering my child, Lucy has learned resignation, that virtue which some one beautifully calls 'putting God between ourselves and our troubles.' You must learn it, Sydney. That, and that alone, will enable you to bear this, and all the other sorrows of life."

"Life can have no other sorrow like this, mother."

"The lesson we must all learn, dear child, sooner or later, is endurance. You must lay your sorrows at the feet of Him who bore our sorrows, and look for help and comfort there. Here is a letter Lewis left for you this morning; you will read it when I am gone."

She draws back for a second, with a startled look, and gazes at it.

"May I?" she says. "Will it be right?"

"Right! Right to take your husband's letter! My child, is your mind wandering? Does your duty as a wife cease because you have discovered a sin in your husband's life?"

"But it was like no other," Sydney says, wildly, "and it must part us forever."

"I am very sorry to hear it. But that is a question of the future, for thought, and humble prayer. Just now you can decide nothing. Here come your coffee and toast. Now, Sydney, I shall expect you, for my sake, to eat and drink."

"I will try to," Sydney says, submissively. She rises in bed; Mrs. Nolan bathes her face and hands, and places the tray before her. She is thirsty, and drinks the coffee eagerly, but she cannot eat. With difficulty she swallows a mouthful or two, and looks beseechingly up in the other's face. "I cannot," she says; "at least, not now; later, I will try."

"Very well, my dear. I wish I could stay with you, but I cannot. Would you not like to come with me, and see Lucy? She asked me to bring you back if you were able to come. Will you not, my child? Order the carriage and come and stay with us for a few days."

But Sydney shakes her head, and turns away.

"No, mother. Do not feel hurt—but I cannot go, cannot leave home. I am better here, better alone. I *must* be alone for a while. No one, not even Lucy, can help me bear my trouble yet."

"Poor child!" Lewis Nolan's mother stands and looks at her with infinite mother pity in her kind old face. What can she say—what can she do for this stricken heart? And only yesterday life seemed to hold all of happiness one life can ever hold.

"I am half afraid to leave you," she says, in a troubled voice. "You ought not to be left alone. And it is so difficult for me to come often."

Sydney flings her arms about her with a tearless sob.

"Dear mother—dear, thoughtful mother, do not fear for me. I am not so weak as you think. Only leave me to myself for a little. Indeed I am better alone."

Mrs. Nolan goes, and Sydney has her desire; she is alone. The hours pass, the evening falls. Teddy, who has been clamoring for her all day, makes his way at lamp-light time into her room, but she neither hears nor heeds him. The servants look at each other, and whisper and wonder. Something has happened between master and missis, and master has gone, and missis isn't fit to rise off her bed.

The night passes, another day breaks. Sydney rises and dresses, dry-eyed, and ghastly pale. When breakfast time comes she sits down with Teddy to that meal.

"Was the matter wiz you, Auntie Sydney?" is the burden of Teddy's wondering cry; "and where's Uncle Lewis? I wants Uncle Lewis. Say, Auntie Syd, where's Uncle Lewis?" The child's reiterated question grows so torturing that she is forced to send him away at last.

An hour or two later brings once more her mother-in-law, looking wretchedly worried and anxious. Sydney is sitting listlessly in the chair in which she sat when her life was crushed out, as it seems to her, by that dreadful story; her hands folded loosely in her lap, her eyes fixed on a portrait of her husband on the wall. She has not read his letter—she feels no desire to read it; she is still striving, and still unable, to realize all the horror of the past forty-eight hours. She lifts two listless, apathetic eyes to the mother's face.

"Is Lucy better?" she asks.

"Lucy is better in body, but suffering naturally in mind—

suffering more for you than for any one else. Will you not come with me to-day, Sydney?"

But still Sydney wearily shakes her head.

"Give me a little longer, mother, to think it out by myself. It is *so* hard to realize it all. The blow was so sudden that I feel crushed—stunned."

She is firm in her resolve, and once more Mrs. Nolan leaves her, sadly troubled. What a miserable business it all is. How terrible to think that the ungoverned passion of a moment should wreck two lives forever.

The news spreads that Mr. Nolan has rejoined the army, and that Mrs. Nolan is inconsolable over his departure. Mrs. and Miss Macgregor call, and Mrs. Nolan is at home. Her sorrow she cannot forget is also her secret; Lewis' honor and safety are in her hands. Whatever she may suffer, though she never meet him more, no one must suspect that other than natural grief at parting is in her heart. She comes down as carefully dressed as usual, to meet them, but at sight of her both ladies utter a simultaneous exclamation.

" My dear Sydney, surely you have been ill!"

She is so worn, so wasted, so white, so changed in three days, that both sit and look at her, honestly shocked.

"No," Sydney answers, "I have not been ill."

She leans her head against the blue satin back of her chair, as if even to sit upright were a painful effort.

"We were *very* much surprised to hear of Mr. Nolan's de- . parture, my dear Sydney," says Mrs. Macgregor, smoothly, and watching her with a cat-like gleam. "A very sudden decision, was it not?"

"Not at all. He has been talking of it from the first."

"Ah! we all know what it is to have our dear ones in dan- ger. Poor Dick!" sighs Dick's mother, with real feeling.

"I wish my dear one—meaning, of course, Mr. Vanderdonck —would take it into his head to go three hours after the cere- mony. With what Spartan generosity would I not offer up my bridegroom upon the altar of my country," says the vivacious Katherine.

The call is short, for Sydney's responses are monosyllabic; she looks cold, and wretched, and ill, through it all, the very ghost of her own bright self.

"And this is to be in love!" says Katherine, with her most contemptuous shrug. "Thanks and praise be that I never felt the tender passion. She looks as if she might safely go into her coffin and the lid by screwed down. After six months of matrimony, too !"

" I believe there is something more under this than meets the eye," says mamma, oracularly. " I never liked the looks of that young man. In the ordinary course of things she might grieve for his departure ; but there is something more than wifely grief in that face, or I am mistaken."

Mrs. Graham came too, full of sympathy for Mrs. Nolan, and of pride and praise for Lewis. Sydney listened drearily to it all, tried to answer, and was glad when it was over, and she was left alone once more.

On the fifth day she went out for the first time, and made her way to the cottage to see Lucy. Without a word Lucy opened her arms, and Sydney went into them and lay still. The mother left them alone—if any one could help this dumb torpor of pain, it was Lucy—she would not interfere.

She was right. Seated on a hassock beside Lucy's chair, Lucy softly touching the fair head that drooped on her knee, Lucy lovingly and sweetly speaking, the first ray of light seemed to pierce the darkness of Sydney's despair. For it was despair, tearless, speechless despair, an agony of loss, or bewildered misery too great for tears or words.

" I want you to stay with me all night," Lucy said, entreatingly. " Remember you have never passed a night here yet. It is so lonely for you in that great empty house."

Lonely ! A spasm crossed the widowed wife's face. Ay, lonely indeed ; lonely forever more.

She consented, and with Lucy's gentle words still soothing her troubled soul, the first unbroken sleep that had come to her since that night refreshed her. She had knelt by the bedside with clasped hands and bent head, with no words on her lips, but bowing down body and soul at the foot of the Cross, her heart crying out in its anguish for help to that great love " that never fails, when earthly loves decay." And with next day's awakening some of Lucy's own patience and resignation seemed to awake in her soul.

" Have you read the letter Lewis left for you, Sydney ?" Lucy asked before they parted.

Sydney's lips quivered.

" Not yet," she said. " I could not. I was not able."

" Read it to-day, dear. See what he says, and if there is any-thing he asks you to do for him, you will be the happier for doing it. And keep Teddy with you—poor little fellow ; it is cruel to neglect him and make him suffer. A child is the best companion in the world, too."

Sydney goes, feeling strengthened and lightened somehow, and obeys all orders. She goes to see Teddy, who is in trouble on his own account, his frisky "wocking-hoss" having just pi:ched him heels over head. He is kissed, and comforted, and set right side up again, and then Sydney wanders away to her husband's study, and, in the room sacred to his use, reads the letter.

It is very long, and inexpressibly tender. It shows her his heart as she has never known it before. And all at once, at some loving, pathetic words, at the old pet name, "my princess," she breaks down ; and a very tempest of tears and sobs washes away the darkness of despair. The worst is over, the blow has fallen, and she knows he is dearer to her a hundred-fold than ever before. She sits there for hours, and an uplifted, sublimated feeling comes in place of the tearless, hopeless apathy that has held her so long. She will begin her life anew, apart from him in this world if it must be, and yet united more closely than before in heart. In helping others she will forget her own sorrow—in doing good, peace may return even to her. She will learn to say, "Thy Will be done," and kiss the rod that smites her. She will possess her soul in patience, and wait ; and if never here, at least in the true Fatherland, where all are forgiven, where parting and pain come not, her husband will be hers once more.

CHAPTER XIX.

"IT IS GOOD TO BE LOYAL AND TRUE."

EARLY in the December of that year, some who read this may recall a fashionable wedding, with which the papers of that day rang. It was a magnificent affair, quite regal really. For once in his life, old Vanderdonck did the handsome thing, came down regardless of expense, and awoke to find himself famous—for one day at least. The beauty of the bride, the wedding-robe, wreath, and veil, imported from Paris, the great wealth of the bridegroom, combined to make it an event of profound interest in certain circles. Outsiders might note the

trifling disparity of years, some half a century, more or less, between the happy pair—might sneer about May and December,
make cynical allusions to selling and buying—but these sarcastic
people were mostly people who knew nothing at all about it. To
the initiated it was the bridegroom who was sold, not the bride.
Poor old Vanderdonck—in snowy front and waistcoat, a small
koh-i-noor ablaze on his aged breast, with his long white hair
and wrinkled, white face—looked beautifully clean and idiotically
happy. A senile chuckle was on that old face, as he waited for
his bride at the chancel-rail; and Katie, tall and magnificent, in
one of Worth's *chefs-d'œuvre*, swept superbly up the broad nave,
with Mendelssohn's "Wedding March" thundering from the
organ-loft, and the peal of the bridal bells outside.

The church was a jam; and as the bride floated by in "gleam
of satin and glimmer of pearls," an audible murmur of "How
lovely!" ran through the house. These are the hours in which
we are made indeed to feel that virtue is its own reward, and
that "Patient waiters are no losers." Long and unweariedly
had this wise virgin angled for her prize; long had it hung
tantalizingly just within and just without her grasp; but the fish
was hooked at last, and brought safe and gasping upon the
matrimonial shore. Perhaps these pious thoughts were
Katherine's own, as—a soft flash of exultation in her eyes, a
glow of triumph on her cheeks—she heard that swelling murmur, and felt she was repaid for the toil of many a weary year.

There were present a great throng of the friends and
relatives of the bride. Her mamma among them, with her expensive wedding handkerchief to her hard old eyes, not used to
moisture. If they were wet now, the tears were crystal drops
of purest gratitude and joy.

What mother would not have wept to see her darling, her
one ewe lamb, safely sheltered from the storms of life in manly
and marital arms, and with five thousand a year pin-money settled on her for life? Uncle Grif gave the bride away, and
trembled more than she did when doing it, and wiped the drops
of moisture from his poor bald brow. Captain Dick had been
bidden, but Captain Dick had sent back a grumbling, misanthropic, and altogether unfeeling refusal. He had never had any
taste for farces or foolery; poor old Vanderdonck wasn't a bad
sort of old duffer, as old duffers went. He didn't care about
taking a journey of so many miles to witness his misery. Dick
was in the reprobate state of mind concerning these delicate
matters of sentiment and settlements, rude young men do at

times get into. His good mother's training had been thrown away upon him; he had refused point blank to make up to Emmy Vinton, who was an heiress too, just before his departure; he even went so far, in his coarse camp language, as to designate the whole affair as a "beastly sell."

It was a painful letter, very painful, and was rendered none the less so to Mrs. Macgregor by Katherine informing her coolly there was nothing to be angry at, Dick was perfectly right.

So Dick was not there; but everybody else was—among them Mrs. Lewis Nolan, cousin of the bride, whose own marriage, in a different way, had been equally sensational, and whose beauty and wealth had been so much talked of. People looked at her eagerly on this occasion, and those who saw her for the first time were apt to be disappointed.

"*That* the beautiful Mrs. Nolan—that pale, almost sickly-looking girl? Absurd! She is no more a beauty than—than I am."

Young ladies said this, and scoffed forever after at the legend of her refusing the peerless Van Cuyler. Matrons shook their heads, and whispered ominously: "Consumption, or perhaps heart disease; these transparent complexions always foretell speedy death." But men looked at, and admired that frail, spirituelle loveliness, that soft-cut youthful mouth, around which lines of pain were drawn, a mouth that seemed to have forgotten how to smile, at those deep blue eyes, from whose sad depths some abiding sorrow looked out.

"I never saw any one so changed, many people said. "I attended a ball she gave, shortly after her marriage, and you would scarcely know her for the same creature. That was a face of radiant beauty and happiness; this, why this is the face of a corpse almost, tricked out in jewels, and laces, and a silk shroud."

"My dear sir, you have heard of the youth who loved and who rode away? well, that is precisely the case here. Her knight has gone to the wars," gayly says the bride, at the break-fast half an hour later to one of these wondering inquirers; and the old sarcastic shrug of the bare plump shoulders accents the words.

"But surely that is not the reason of so great a change," says the gentleman incredulously, looking across and through a stack of cut flowers that stands between him and that fair, pale face.

"The only reason," answers Mrs. Vanderdonck, with her most caustic laugh. "Oh, you may wear that unbelieving face if you please, but it is perfectly true! Quite a pastoral, a New York idyll, a bit of Arcadia, a love sonnet, this marriage of my cousin Sydney's. I remember long ago," runs on the bride, who is in high spirits, "reading the story of a certain French Chevalier and his lady, who were so devoted to one another that when monsieur went out a hunting early in the morning, madame fell into a swoon, and stayed in a swoon—from pure agony at his absence, mind—until he came back. And the best of this story is, that it is no legend, but is related as a grave historical fact. Take it as an illustration of the present wilted lily look of Mrs. Lewis Nolan." '

Her listener joins in her satirical laugh, but there is no satire in his.

"Mr. Nolan is a fortunate man," he says, a certain earnestness underlying his laugh. "It is only the second time I have seen this lady, but it is the sort of face one does not see often, nor easily forgot, once seen."

Katherine lifts her eyebrows sceptically, and turns away. He is a rather distinguished personage this, who holds a place of honor at her right-hand, but these talented people, who make a stir in the world, are sadly lacking in tact too. Think of his moaning aloud over another woman, to the Lady Fair of the feast, the bride who deigns to flirt with him in her bridal hour.

"*Can* there be anything more than her husband's going away, the matter?" Katherine thinks, curiously. "She is greatly changed, half her good looks are gone. But no—such a pattern pair couldn't quarrel. It is a case of 'two hearts that beat as one,' and all that. How does it feel, I wonder, to love any human being to the verge of lunacy like that? If Lewis gets a bullet through his heart out there, they may order the coffin big enough for both——

"'And out of her bosom there grew a red rose,
And out of Lord Lovell's a brier!'"

hums Mrs. Vanderdonck under her breath, as she goes up to her maiden bower to change her dress. But there is a touch of envy in her mockery, too. After all, it must be pleasant to love and look up to one's husband, if one has not to buy that pleasure at the cost of all the rest of life's golden gifts.

Mrs. Vanderdonck, accompanied of course by Mr. Vander

donck, takes the steamer at noon and starts on her bridal tour
to Europe. Where can she not, in these first demented days,
drag her old millionaire ?

For Mrs. Nolan, she goes back to her lonely life. An inexpressibly lonely life ; days that are one long heart-ache, and " tears
o' nights instead of slumber." All the first passion of anguish
and despair has passed, and a hopeless night of sorrow seems
closing in. In her heart there is no anger against him, no touch
of blame ; it is simply that a gulf has opened between them,
which must forever hold them apart. If his sin had been the
same, and the victim any other among all the men of earth, it
would not have parted them for a moment. She would have
grieved, and pitied, and prayed, and loved him with a deeper
tenderness. If the sin itself had been any other—ay, any—
she could have forgiven almost without an effort, though the sin
itself broke her heart. Let his guilt have been what it might,
she would have clung to him through reproach and disgrace ;
though all the world stood up and reviled him, she would have
stood proudly by his side, more happy to share shame with him,
than glory with another. But this was different. It was her
'brother' he had killed, her father whose death he had
hastened ; to that dead father she stood pledged to see justice
done for the deed. It seemed to her that that father must rise
up and denounce her, if she took him back. And his crime had
been terrible ; a crime not to go unpunished either by heaven
or earth. "Whoso sheddeth man's blood, by man shall his
blood be shed ; for in God's image made He man."

The sentence stood clear. Murder had not been intended,
but murder had been committed, and the innocent must suffer
with the guilty. Could she ever bear to be caressed by the
hand that had flung Bertie Vaughan to his death? No—their
sentence was spoken—held asunder their lives long.

Seven weeks had elapsed since his departure, and no letters
had passed between them. What was there for either to say ?
She carried the solemn farewell letter close to her heart ; she
read it again and again, with eyes blinded in tears ; but she
never answered. He wrote to his mother, and those brief
notes his mother brought to her at once. The wife kept them
all, as we keep relics of the dead. Her name was not mentioned in them—he was only urgent for news of them all—all,
even the most minute. His mother and sister answered, and
complied ; Sydney was the burden of their replies. She was
well—that is to say, not ailing—and bore up better than they

had at first expected. But the mother's heart ached as she wrote; and the image of her son's wife arose before her, pallid, wasted, smileless, the shadow of her former self. A widow without the weeds; the deeper mourning of the heart stamped on the face for all who ran to read. But she was very quiet, pathetically quiet, no duty was undone, no daily task neglected. She read to Lucy, played with Teddy, and was bountiful to the poor at her gates, giving to all who asked with both hands, and keeping her heart-break for the night, and the solitude of her own room.

It was close upon Christmas. The days were short, cold, and dark, as Sydney Nolan's own life. Teddy was clamoring about " presents," and propounding unanswerable conundrums as to what that mythical saint, Santa Claus—no myth, but a jovial reality to Master Ted—might bring. The child was the one bright spot in Sydney's life; it is impossible to stagnate, even in the profoundest grief, with a jolly, romping, shouting, noisy, bouncing " human boy," as Mr. Chadband hath it, in the house, whose lusty yells ring from mansard to cellar.

Mrs. Nolan was very busy; there was no end of surprises to buy for him, a package to send to mamma out in her Chicago school, mamma who had promised to come and spend New Year's week with her boy. There were mother's presents, and Lucy's; there were hosts of poor people to supply with turkeys, and coals, and blankets, and beef; and last, but oh! not least, there was a box to go to Virginia, to one whose Christmas it wrung the wife's heart to think of—something to let him know that, although separation was written between them, love would last the same to the end.

The day before Christmas eve Mrs. Nolan, with Teddy as attendant cavalier, drove down Broadway, shopping. Master Frederick Carew delighted in this sort of thing; the shops and the people were never-ending sources of jubilee. He had but one unsatisfied ambition, and that was to mount the perch beside coachman Thompson, in top boots and gilt hat-band, and sit with his small arms folded across his small chest, à la footman William. But this Auntie Sydney would in no wise allow, and Teddy glued his diminutive nose to the glass, while auntie got out and went into the big stores on Broadway.

On one of these occasions the carriage was standing in front of a milliner's establishment; Mrs. Nolan, who had been for half an hour in the place, was crossing the pavement to re-enter, when one of two gentlemen, sauntering up arm-in-arm,

stopped suddenly with a look of startled recognition. Instantly
an eye-glass went up to two handsome, short-sighted blue eyes,
in a long surprised stare.

"Home, Thompson," said the lady's clear voice ; and the
carriage flashed past on the instant.

The lady had not seen him, and the hero of the eye-glass was
left blankly staring.

, "Well!" his companion laughed, "this is something new for
you, isn't it? I thought you belonged to the *nil admirari*
class, my dear fellow, and did *not* lose your head at sight. A
very pretty woman, no doubt, but a trifle too pale and fragile
for my English taste. Do you know her?"

"Do I know her?" repeats the knight of the eye-glass
blankly. Then a sudden inspiration seems to seize him.
"Wait here one moment, my dear Somerset," he exclaims, "I
must go into the shop and ask."

"By Jove!" says his companion, and laughs again; "this *is*
something new."

The other enters the great millinery emporium, advances to
a shop girl—I beg her pardon—sales-lady, and removes his
hat.

"Will you have the great kindness, madam," he says, with
that rising inflection, that flattening of the vowels, that instantly
bespeaks the Englishman to American ears, "to tell me the
name of the lady who has just left—the lady in black and
sealskins."

The sales-lady, a pretty, piquant girl, as most New York
sales-ladies are, looks at him, a certain mischievous sparkle in
her bright black eyes. But the gentleman is perfectly serious
and respectful. He is a slender man of medium height, an
unmistakably military air, with a handsome, light-complexioned
face, slightly bronzed, and a beautiful blonde beard and mustache of most silken softness.

"That lady is Mrs. Nolan, sir," responded the girl, her
sharp, quick accent contrasting with his slow, gentle manner of
speech. "Her address is No. 126 West ——th street."

"Ah, thank you very much," says the gentleman, replacing
, his hat with a slight bow, and the sharp young Yankee sales-
lady sees a look of disappointment pass over the Englishman's
face as he leaves the store.

His friend is waiting, and resumes his arm, and their walk.

"Well," he says, "I hope your curiosity has been gratified.
Who is she?"

"She is Mrs. Nolan; but, before she was Mrs. Nolan, 1 am almost positive she was Miss Owenson. She has changed con·siderably; it is five or six years since I saw her last, but surely it is the same."

He says this musingly, more to himself than to his com·panion.

"I have her address," he goes on, producing his tablets. "I think I will call upon her at once. The matter which has brought me to New York is one in which I think she may help me. If you will excuse me, I will take an omnibus and try my luck."

"Certainly, my dear fellow," responds his friend, politely, but with a puzzled look; and the owner of the eye-glass hails an up-town stage, gets in, and is jolted toward 126 West ——th street. He finds the number and rings the bell. Jim—shiny and black, an eruption of buttons all over his sable breast, a beaming smile on his ebony face—admits him, and takes his card. His mistress has just returned, has removed her bonnet and jacket, and is sitting, tired and listless, before the fire. She takes the proffered card, with a half-weary, half-impatient sigh, but the moment she looks at it all listlessness vanishes. She sits upright and stares at it as blankly as half an hour before its owner had stared at herself; for the name she reads is " Frederic Denraith Carew."

She sits stunned. Mr. Carew here! She has never thought of that. Has he discovered that Teddy—but, no; he is not aware of Teddy's existence. Rare chance has driven him to her. No doubt he is in search of his wife, and what is she to say to him? Tell the truth she cannot, tell an untruth she will not. She stands pledged to Cyrilla to keep the secret of her hiding-place a secret from all; and yet if Cyrilla's husband has forgiven her and has come back in search of her, how is she to send him away disappointed?

She sits still, blankly looking at the card, not in the least knowing what she shall say or do.

"Gen'elman's in the drawing room, missis," hints black Jim, thinking his mistress has studied that card long enough.

She rises, with a bewildered feeling, and goes down. Mr. Carew, hat in hand, stands up and bows, and in spite of the golden tan, in spite of the profuse blonde beard, she recognizes him instantly.

"Mr. Carew," she says, and comes forward, holding out her hand.

"I have not been mistaken," he rejoins, smiling; "I thought I was not, although your new name puzzled me for a moment. That you are married was news to me; and, late in the day although it may be, permit me to offer my felicitations."

She bows, and the faint flush that his coming has brought into her face fades into sad paleness.

"I saw you, not an hour ago, on Broadway," continues Mr. Carew, "and took the liberty of inquiring your address, and of following you at once. Need I say, my dear Mrs. Nolan, that my errand to New York is to find my wife?" ·

She plays nervously with her watch-chain, and again a faint color flickers and fades in her face. The serious blue eyes fixed upon her note it.

"You were always her best friend. She never cared to make many friends, poor Cyrilla! but she loved and trusted you. If any one could help me in my search, I knew you were that one; and I am sure, if you have the power, you also have the will."

But Mrs. Nolan, looping and unlooping that slender cable of dull gold, does not reply.

"During the past four years," pursues Mr. Carew, with a grave earnestness of manner that becomes him, "I have been in India. I do not deny that I left Canada in a very reckless and desperate frame of mind——"

A faint smile flickers, in spite of herself, over Sydney's lips, at the thought of placid Freddy Carew, "reckless and desperate."

"I exchanged and went to India," goes on the gentleman, who does not notice the smile, and who is in profound earnest himself. "I had made up my mind to forget my wife, to banish her from my heart, to see her no more, come what might. In the first heat of anger this seemed easy; when anger cooled, and I found myself fairly in for it, I discovered that forgetfulness was impossible. I saw my folly, my wrong, even, when it was too late, in deserting her, in throwing her on the world, a forsaken wife, and I would have given worlds to undo it. But it could not be undone—all I could do I did. I wrote to Montreal, and found out she had been disinherited by her aunt, had quitted Canada, had been sick in Boston hospital, had been provided with funds by the kindness of Mr. McKelpin, and had then disappeared. All my efforts to learn further have been useless. I would have written to you, but your address I did not know. I will not try to tell you what I have suffered in those years, thinking of my poor girl, deserted, friendless, alone.

It half maddened me at times. Then a sudden change in my
fortunes came. My uncle, the late Lord Denraith, died, and
remembered me in the most handsome manner in his will. I
immediately sold out, returned to England, and from thence
here. I only landed two days ago, and it seems as if Providence
had interposed in my behalf, in our signal rencontre on Broadway. If Cyrilla would go to any one in her loneliness, it would
be to you. Tell me where to find her ; I have long ago forgiven
all, and I will owe you a debt I can never repay."

What shall she say ? His earnestness, his loyalty, his un-
changed love, have touched her to the heart ; she can gauge the
measure of his feeling and his longing by her own. Will it indeed be a breach of faith if she tells ? Will Cyrilla be angry ?
In any case she has promised, and cannot break her word. She
sits silent, distressed. She knows he can read in her face her
reluctance to speak, and a great and sudden fear blanches his.

" You do not answer," he says. " You look troubled. Mrs.
Nolan, my wife is not dead ? "

" Oh, no, no, no ! " she cries out. " Heaven forbid ! She
is alive, and safe, and well——"

She does not finish. Fate is coming to the front, and taking
the matter in her own hands. There is a shout outside, the
door flies open, and there bounces in briskly Master Teddy, all
azure velvet, white ruffle, and gold curls, calling as he comes :

"Auntie Sydney ! "

Auntie Sydney sits with clasped hands, her breath taken away
by this dramatic *dénouement.* Teddy espies the stranger, comes
to a stand-still, and surveys him with two dauntless black eyes.

Mr. Carew smiles in a friendly way, but something in the lustrous black eyes seems to disconcert him too.

" Come here," he says, and extends the hand of acquaint-
anceship.

Teddy, never averse to adding to his list of friends, comes
promptly, and permits himself to be lifted upon the gentleman's
knee. Sydney sits motionless, perfectly pale.

" What is your name ? " asks Mr. Carew, the inevitable first
question always, to a child.

The dark, bright eyes look up at him with an answering smile,
and the prompt response comes,

" Teddy Carew ! "

CHAPTER XX.

A NEW YEAR GIFT.

O need of one word further—no need of more than one startled glance at Mrs. Nolan's agitated face. Frederic Carew comprehends that it is his son he holds on his knee. He grows quite white for a moment ; then he stoops and kisses the bright, pretty face. It is a moment before he speaks, and then with a tremor of the voice that Sydney detects. Her own eyes are full of tears.

"How old are you, Teddy?" he asks.

"Five years," promptly responds Teddy? "ain't I, Auntie Syd?"

"And where is mamma all this time?"

"Oh ! mamma's away—ever so far away," replies Teddy, with a vague wave of his arm ; " out there, where the cars come from. Me and mamma came to New York in the cars." Master Carew's powers of speech, as you may perceive, have improved. "And I have got a wockin-hoss, and a goat-carriage, and a gun ; and Santa Claus is going to bring me heaps of things on Christmas Eve—ain't he, Auntie Sydney? To-morrow's Christmas Eve," runs on Teddy, imparting all this information without once drawing his breath, " and I'se goin' to hang up my ftockin' and Santa Claus will come down the chimbly and fill it. Ain't it hunky?"

"Santa Claus has brought you something already, Teddy, that you didn't expect."

"What?" demands Teddy, opening his ebon eyes.

"Your father. I think you must be my little boy, Teddy Hasn't mamma told you you had a papa somewhere?"

"Yes," says Teddy, with an intelligent nod ; "papa's away in England—ain't it England, Auntie Syd? and mamma don't know when he's comin' back. I say, ' Bless papa, and mamma and Auntie Sydney, and Uncle Lewis,' every night, don't I, Auntie Syd? Is you my papa?" asked Ted, calmly, looking up in his new friend's face.

"I am your papa, Teddy. Won't you give me a kiss for the news?"

Teddy gives the kiss, and receives the information without

any undue excitement. He accepts his long-lost parent with
composure, and as a matter of course ; and proceeds to inform
him that Uncle Lewis has gone to the war, and how greatly
that untoward event has put him (the informant) out. This,
and a great deal more varied and miscellaneous information, Fred Carew, junior, pours into the listening ear of Fred
Carew, senior, until Sydney finds that the first shock, half-
painful, half-pleased, is over, and that there is nothing for it but
a frank confession of the whole.

" That will do, Teddy," she interposes. " Kiss papa again
and run away. Auntie Sydney wants to talk to him, and it is
time for Teddy's supper."

The last clause of this address is effective. Teddy is a frank
gourmand—is he not a man-child ?—any one might win his
heart through his stomach. He slips like an eel off papa's
knee, and darts away in search of the commissariat.

Mr. Carew and Mrs. Nolan are left alone, the lady visibly
embarrassed, the gentleman with a smile on his lips, and a look
in his eyes that makes Sydney's whole sympathetic heart go
out to him.

"'There is not much for you to confess," he says ; " that
much I know you *will* confess. Need I tell you that if I had
known this, nothing would have held me away. I owe you
more than I can say ; thanks I will not attempt. My wife
has, indeed, found that rare treasure, a true friend, in you."

" Oh, nush ! " Sydney exclaims; "I have done nothing—
nothing. The favor has been done me in giving me Teddy
Yes, Mr. Carew, I will tell you what I may, not where Cyrilla
is at present, for that I have promised not to tell, but everything else as she has told it to me."

Then Sydney, in that agitated voice, begins and relates the
episode of Cyrilla's unexpected coming with Teddy, and repeats
the story Cyrilla has told. Of her intense longing for the stage,
and of her conquering that longing because he had once said
it was no fitting life for her, or rather, that she was not fitted
for the life.

" I will not betray trust," she says ; "you shall not go to her,
but she shall come to you. As you have waited so long, Mr.
Carew, you shall wait one week more. Cyrilla has promised
to come and spend New Year with me and see Teddy, whom
she has not seen for three months. You shall wait, Mr. Carew.
Meantime, I shall expect you to come and see Teddy very constantly, and if by chance *you* should happen in some day when

18

Mrs. Carew is here—why I shall not be to blame—you under stand?"

She gives him her hand, with a reflection of Sydney's own bright, saucy smile, and Fred Carew lifts that little hand, and kisses it.

"I cannot thank you," he says, his low voice husky, his honest, blue eyes dim; "you are, indeed, a friend. I will do whatever you say, but it will be the longest week of my life."

So Mr. Carew departs, and Mrs. Nolan goes upstairs, and surprises Master Ted by suddenly catching him in her arms, and kissing and crying over him.

"Oh! my Teddy—my Teddy," she says, "am I to lose you, too?"

This performance on the part of Auntie Syd does not surprise Teddy—indeed nothing ever does surprise that youthful philosopher very greatly—but it discomposes his feelings and dampens his ruffle, and he cavalierly cuts it short.

"I isn't goin' to get lost," says Teddy, eying Auntie Sydney's tears with extreme disfavor; "what's you cryin' 'bout *now*. 'Cause my papa's gone?"

"Not exactly, but because I am afraid your papa will take you, Teddy."

"Will he take me to Uncle Lewis?" demands Teddy, brightening up, "'cause I want to go to Uncle Lewis. Auntie Syd, why don't Uncle Lewis come back?"

It is a daily question on the child's lips, and it wrings the wife's heart to hear it. Teddy's one grand passion, outside of sweetmeats, is Uncle Lewis; never once has that devotion flinched. He has even howled at times over his prolonged absence, and tears and howling are weaknesses sturdy little Ted, as a rule, disdains. Mr. Carew accepts Mrs. Nolan's invitation, comes every day, and spends many hours with her and his boy. Ted fraternizes with his father in an off-hand, indignant sort of way—he is very well, this new papa of his, Teddy seems to consider, his presents are many and handsome, but he is not to be compared to Uncle Lewis. To sit, while Mrs. Nolan's needle flies, and talk to her of the old days, and "Beauty," and their runaway honeymoon, their brief married life, and the still older vagabond days in London, when Jack Hendrick's dingy lodgings were brightened and glorified by the sunshiny presence of "Little Beauty Hendrick," is the delight of Frederic Carew's present life. Of that dreadful day when they parted, he says little—that little to make excuses for Cyrilla, not very logical perhaps, but whi :h do Sydney good to hear. In the intervals, for he cannot always sit at Mrs. Nolan's side and talk "Beauty," he goes forth with his little son, drives him through the park and the city streets, and becomes a frequenter of toy stores and bakeries to the most alarming extent ; and Teddy is in a fair way of being killed by kindness and confectionery.

A new interest has been added to Sydney's Christmas, fortunately for herself, for the great troubles of life come most keenly home to all of us on this joyful anniversary of " Peace on earth, good-will toward men." All the presents are bought, two packages are sent—one to Virginia, without word or message, for if she speaks at all she will say too much—the other to Chicago, with a cheerful little letter, which ends thus :

" I send you a little Christmas token which I know you will value for my sake, and I have something here you will value far more, for a New Year gift. Do not fail to come, let *nothing* detain you. Ted longs to see mamma "—this last a pure fiction, for Ted has expressed no desire whatever on the subject—" and Sydney longs to kiss Cyrilla."

This was enigmatical. Mrs. Carew knit her handsome black brows over Mrs. Nolan's Christmas letter.

" Something you will value far more for a New Year gift "—it was not Sydney's way to allude in that manner to her own generous gifts. She *was* generous—the little packet contained a cable chain, with a large locket suspended, set with rubies, and within Ted's picture, and a curl of his amber hair. Cyrilla kissed the fair child's face, and the black, brilliant eyes grew soft and dewy. " Dear little Syd," she said, " it is a heart of gold."

Her present came on Christmas Day. The school had broken up until the second week of January, and on the third day after, Cyrilla Carew, ·looking handsome, and stately, and elegant, with much more the air of a grand dame than a poor governess, took the train for New York. Cyrilla's splendid vitality was something to marvel at ; her health was perfect, her five years of trouble and toil had altered her character but not her beauty. That had but grown ripe and perfect ; maturity had but a charm and sweetness of its own. Cyrilla Carew, the teacher, was a far nobler and more beautiful woman than Cyrilla Hendrick, Miss Dormer's wayward, wilful heiress and niece.

She tried to read as the train flew along, but in vain. The old, wild love of freedom was strong still, and for a week she was free—free to see her boy, to be with Sydney, and talk of

the dear old days forever gone.   Where was he this Christmas ?
she thought, with a sharp contraction of the heart.   Did he ever
think of her now?   Was she remembered only in cold, slow,
pitiless anger? or worse, not remembered at all?   Slow ro
wrath, Fred Carew was slow also to forgive, and hers had been
an offence few men would have found easy to pardon.   Oh, if
the past could but come over again, and she were free once
more to choose between Miss Dormer's money and Fred Carew's
love.

Men looked at her as she sat there quite alone, her book lying
unopened in her lap, her dark, brooding eyes fixed on the
flitting, wintry landscape, and turned and looked again.   She
was the sort of woman men always look at, but the coquettish
spirit was dead within her, with many other evil things.

The long, dreary, weary railway journey ended at last, the
train rushed thunderously into the New York depot.   There on
the platform, as she had once before awaited her in the Wychcliffe station, stood Sydney.   Then her attendant had been Bertie Vaughan ; now she stood alone.

"Darling Cy !"

"Dearest Sydney !"   Kisses, smiles, ejaculations, etc., etc.

"How well you are looking, Cyrilla !" Sydney cries out in
admiration.   "You are a perfect picture of health and happiness."

"I am perfectly well in health," Cyrilla answers, gravely ;
"and yes—in a way—I am happy, too.   But you, dear child,
how changed *you* are since last September."

"Changed—yes," Sydney says, and the anguish of memory is
in face and voice.

"Your husband has joined the army?" says Cyrilla, looking at her with those far-seeing, thoughtful, dark eyes.   She
makes a motion of assent ; not even to Cyrilla can she speak
of him.

"I would have brought Ted," she observes, as they fly along
through the twilight streets, "but—well, the fact is, the little ingrate was so taken up with a gentleman friend of mine, who has
lately won his fickle affections, that he declined to come.   Ah !
Cy, you don't know what a blessing Teddy has been to me.
What shall I do when you take him away?"

"It may be years before that catastrophe happens," says Mrs.
Carew, with a half smile, half sigh.   "I seem to be as far off a
home as ever."

They reach the house ; Sydney's heart is beating fast with

excitement. Cyrilla is eager, but calm. She leads her to an upper room.

"Ted is here," she says; "go in," and flits past and away.

Cyrilla enters. One pale star of gas alone lights the apartment, and in the middle of the room, a huge Noah's ark between his sturdy legs, and about a million, more or less, it seems to his mamma, birds and beasts around him, sits Master Teddy absorbed.

"My boy! my Teddy!" cries Teddy's mamma, and Ted is suddenly caught up and hugged. "Oh, my darling, how good it seems to see you again!"

"There!" exclaims Teddy; "you'se upset my fellafant and broke his trunk. Has you brought me anysing in your pocket, mamma?"

"Little gourmand! Something in my pocket is all *you* care for. Are you not glad to see mamma at all?"

"Oh, yes, I'se glad," Teddy responds, in his calmest accents, and all the while with a regretful eye upon the prostrate ele-phant. "Will you help me put my beastseses in the ark again? I can get 'em out easy, but I can't get 'em in."

Cyrilla laughs, and goes down on her knees and assists this new Noah to stow away his beasts; then in the midst of it she seizes him again, and a fresh shower of kisses are inflicted on long-suffering and victimized Teddy.

"Oh, my baby, my baby!" she says; "what would I do if it were not for you!"

The door behind her has opened, and some one comes in, pauses a second, and looks at mother and son. Then:

"Are they *all* for your boy, Beauty?" says a quiet voice; "have you none left for Teddy's father?"

There is a wild cry that rings even to the room where Sydney sits, and thrills her to her heart's core. Cyrilla springs to her feet, recoils, and, pale as death, with dilated eyes, stands look ing at her husband.

"It is I, 'Rilla," he says, a quiver in the familiar voice. "Life was not worth living witnout you. My fault has been that I ever left you. My darling, come to me and say you forgive me."

"Forgive *you*!" she cries, with a great joyful sob; and then, as the arms of her lover fold about her, Cyrilla Carew knows that her expiation is at an end.

CHAPTER XXI.

"TWO HANDS UPON THE BREAST AND LABOR PAST."

T is the hour for your medicine, dear Lucy; will you take it?"

Sydney Nolan slips one hand gently under the invalid's head, and with the other holds the medicine-glass to her lips. Lucy drinks it with the grateful smile that has grown habitual, and lies wearily back among her pillows.

"What hour is it?" she asks.

"Nearly'six, dear. How do you feel?"

"Oh, so free from pain, so peaceful, so content. It is like Heaven. Sydney, has Sister Monica come?"

"Sister Monica is down stairs with your mother; she will be here presently. Is there anything else you want, Lucy?"

"Nothing else. You have been here all day, Sydney? Dear, how good you are, how patient, how unwearied in nursing me. All these weeks you have hardly left my bedside to take needful rest."

"You must not talk, Lucy; you are far too weak. *I* good, *I* patient! Oh, you don't know! you don't know!"

She says it with a stifled sob, and lays her face against the pillow. She good, whose heart is one wild, rebellious, ceaseless longing for what may never be. She patient, whose life is one long cry of loss and despair.

"Oh," she says, in that stifled voice, "what shall I do when you are gone?"

"I will still be with you, my sister," Lucy Nolan's faint voice replies, "loving you, helping you, praying for you. Sydney, I have something to say to you, and I want to say it to-night. Is it you or mother who is to watch to-night with Sister Monica?"

"It is I. Last night was mother's night, you know, Lucy?"

"Yes, I know—poor mother," sighs Lucy. "I am a dreadful trouble; I always have been, but she will miss me when I am gone. And Lewis, too. Oh," she cries out, and a spasm crosses her white face; "if I could only see Lewis once before I die."

Sydney clenches her hands. That cry, wrung from Lucy's soul, is but the echo of that which never ceases in her own.

"But it is not to be," she goes on, the old patient look of

perfect resignation returning. *"He* knows best. I will try
and sleep now, and by-and by, when I am stronger, I will talk
to you, Sydney. Dear little sister, what a comfort you have
been to me from the first. Kiss me, please."

Something besides the kiss falls on her face. Sydney's tears
flow fast. She has lost Lewis, lost little Teddy, lost Cyrilla,
and now Lucy is gliding out on that dark and lonely sea that
leads to the Land of Life. She stills her heart-wrung sobs lest
they may disturb her, and softly Lucy glides away into painless,
tranquil sleep.

For Lucy Nolan, whose life has been one long death, is dying
at last. Nay, death is ending, life is dawning; pain, and tears,
and bodily torture are drawing to their end. She lies here white
and still, dead, you might almost think her, but for the faint
breath that stirs the night-dress.

The windows stand wide and the June sunset slants through
the thick, glossy leaves of her pet ivy. Over the other the curtains are drawn, but Lucy likes to lie and watch that glory of
ruby and golden light in the western sky. The voices of children at play arise from the quiet street, but they do not disturb
the sleeper. . With her forehead against the head of the bed,
Sydney sits in an attitude of utter dejection, as motionless as
the slumberer herself, and thinks of another death-bed by which
she sat, over seven years ago.

Many months, long, dragging, aimless months, have passed
since that evening when Cyrilla Carew took her New Year gift
to her heart; a winter, a spring, a summer, an autumn, another
winter and spring, and now once more summer is here. It has
been a time full of changes, but it has brought no change in
Sydney's life. Fred Carew took his wife and son home. Lord
Dunraith *had* remembered him handsomely—all the more
handsomely, perhaps, that he had married Phillis Dormer's
niece, and so in part atoned for his father's wrong. There was
a heavy-chimneyed and many-gabled old house in the green
heart of Somersetshire, with five hundred a year in the three
per cents, and to this ancestral homestead Mr. and Mrs. Carew
had gone.

That was one change. The second great event was the ending of the war, many months after. Captain Nolan, as recklessly brave as that other Captain Nolan who led the great
charge at Balaklava, had been in more than one engagement;
but death, the best boon life held, passed him by—he was not
even wounded. But to the last day of her life Sydney will re-

call the sensation of deathly terror with which she used to take
up the papers after some bloody battle, and go over the list of
wounded, missing and killed. In those sickening lists that
name was never to be read, and then falling on her knees, her
face bowed in her hands, such grateful prayers would ascend as
might indeed pierce the heavens.

All this time no word passed directly between them. What
was there to say? What was done was done—nothing could
undo it. What could Sydney Nolan have to say to the husband
who had directly caused the death of Bertie Vaughan, indirectly
the death of her father? What could Lewis Nolan have to say
to the wife he had unintentionally wronged beyond reparation?
Nothing was to be said, nothing to be done, it seemed to them
both, but go on to the end apart.

"I saw her shrink from me in horror once," Lewis said in
one of his letters, in answer to an urgent appeal from his sister;
"I saw a look in her eyes that it would kill me to see again.
Could my hand ever touch hers without her recalling that her
brother's blood stained it? No, Lucy, the dead cannot arise.
I cannot restore the life I took away, and my wife and I can
never meet."

And Sydney knew it, and made no effort to span the chasm.
But how empty, how hollow, was her life! She tried to pray,
to be patient, to do good to others, to keep busy and useful, to
relieve all the misery she met that mere money can relieve; to
become, if not a happy woman, at least a good and charitable
one. In this she could not fail to succeed; the poor at her
gates arose and called her blessed; into the homes of the sick
and the wretched she came as an angel of light, but to her own
heart peace never came. Always that waiting, hungrily expectant look, always that restless craving for the life that had
once been one with her own.

Then came the end of the war.

Would love that never reasons, that is reckless and selfish,
too, it may be, fling conviction and atonement to the winds?
Would impulse sway his heart as it did hers, and Lewis return
to her? Her heart beat with wild, inconsistent hope—if he
came she would never let him go! Inconsistent indeed; but
when are women consistent? For a month or more, a fever
of fear, of hope, of restless impatience held her—then a letter
came.

It was dated San Francisco, and was calm, almost cold, it
seemed to poor expectant Sydney, in its steady, impassive, un-

shaken will. Surely she had been insane ever to dream that a
strong heart, fixed in its conviction of what must be, could ever
be swayed hither and thither as hers. Once Lewis Nolan,
listening to unreasoning passion and impulse, had committed a
wrong he could never repair; for all his after-life he would rein
in passion and impulse with a steady hand. He would remain
in San Francisco, he said, for good and all, unless something
imperative called him back. Whatever happened at home, as
usual, they were to let him know. Mrs. Nolan, senior, put this
letter in her daughter in-law's hand, without a word, and hastily
left the room. For three days Sydney did not come to the
cottage, then one evening, just as they were growing seriously
uneasy, she paid them a visit. She came gliding in, so unlike
herself, so like a spirit, that Lucy's heart ached for her as it had
never ached before.

And so hope had died and was buried decently out of sight,
and life went on without it.

That winter Lucy failed, sickened, took to her bed, and when
April came began to die daily. Now it was June, and death at
last in mercy was here.

The yellow gleams of the sunset pale, fade, grow crystal gray,
but the sleeper sleeps, and the watcher watches, both without
stir or sound. Presently the chamber door opens softly, and
there comes in a Sister of Charity, in long rosary and white
"cornette." The church to which Lucy belongs, infinitely rich
in comfort for her passing children, sends one of her vestal
daughters daily, to watch, and read, and pray in the sick-room.
Sydney lifts her face, such a pale, spent face in the silvery dusk,
and smiles a faint greeting to Sister Monica.

"How is our patient?" the nun asks, as she stoops and
touches the transparent cheek with her lips.

"Easy—free from pain—sleeping like a child."

The answer is infinitely weary, the blue eyes full of infinite
mournfulness.

"Dear child," Sister Monica says, and takes that colorless,
tired face between her soft palms, "she is freer from pain, I
fear, than you are. What a sorrowful face you wear, my
child."

She is scarcely older than Sydney's self, this young nun, not
yet five-and-twenty; but the motherly "my child" comes very
sweetly and naturally from her lips. Sydney looks up, and
thinks, as she has often thought before, what a pure, serene,
passionless face it is, with eyes of untold placidity, and mouth

18*

and brow of indescribable peace, that "peace wh:ch the
world cannot give." She lays her head once more against the
pillow, with a feeling of wistful envy for that serene peace,
which has passed from her forever.

"Dear Sister Monica," she says, "how happy you are. It
rests me only to look at you. Ah! why cannot we be all nuns,
and have done with the wretched cares of this most wretched
world ?"

Sister Monica laughs.

"I am afraid, my dear, when you present yourself as a
novice, they may object if you tell them *that* is your motive
in coming. We do not cut off all the 'cares of this most
wretched world,' with our hair, I assure you ; nor do we put on
perfect exemptions from trouble, with our habits. Our good
Father sends us our trials and our joys, in the cloister as in the
world, and we must kiss the rod that strikes, as well as the
beneficent hand that gives. I don't know what *your* special
trouble may be, Mrs. Nolan, but I think I can guess, and what
is still more, I think you are doing wrong."

"Sister !"

"No need to look so startled, my child ; I am not going to
scold ; neither do I know what your trouble is, as I have said.
Only this I know, that it has parted you and your husband ;
and husbands and wives should not part."

"You don't know, you don't know !" says poor Sydney.

"No, dear, I don't know—I don't wish to know—it is something very hard to bear, I am sure ; and it is breaking your heart.
Your husband has committed some offence against you which
you cannot forgive. Is not that it ?"

"Oh, no, no, sister ! not that. I have forgiven from my
heart of hearts."

"No," Sister Monica retorts, energetically, "that cannot be.
He is there—you are here. If you forgave you would be
together. There can be no forgiveness like that."

"You do not understand, and I cannot tell you," is Sydney's
helpless reply.

"I understand this much, that in marriage, it is for better for
worse, till death doth ye part. God has joined you, and you
put yourselves asunder. Nothing can make that right. When
duties clash, or we think they clash, then the duty that lies
nearest is the duty to be done. Your duty as a wife is to forgive your husband's wrong, if wrong he has done, and go to
him at once. We all · have a cross to bear, a great deal to for-

give others. If *your* cross has come to you as a wife, as a wife you must bear it."

"Oh!" Sydney passionately cries out, "if I only thought *that* was my duty, what an infinitely happy woman I would be!"

"I have known your husband," says Sister Monica. "I have met him two or three times, and have heard of him often; and from what I have seen, and all I have heard, I should take him to be an exceptionally good man—as men go!" adds Sister Monica, a sudden, half-satirical smile dimpling her pretty mouth. "He has been a good son and brother, a young man of fixed principles and steadfast will. I cannot believe but that you exaggerate his fault, whatever that may be. But suppose you do not—has he sinned, do you think, beyond divine forgiveness?"

"Oh, no, no!" Sydney cries again, Heaven forbid! If he has done wrong, he has bitterly suffered, and repented, and atoned."

"Then, if he is forgiven of Heaven, what are you, that you should withhold pardon and reconciliation on earth? 'Though a man's crime be murder, if the Lord hath compassion on him, shalt not thou?'"

Sydney looks up with a faint cry; but in the sister's gentle compassionate eyes, there is only the holy light of tender pity. She stoops in her impulsive way and kisses the nun's hand.

"Pray for me, sister," she says. "Oh I pray that I may know the truth."

"Lucy!" exclaims Sister Monica; "dear child, are you awake?"

"Awake and listening," Lucy answers, with a smile, "thinking how good it is of you to anticipate the sermon I meant to preach. Sydney, sister, come here and let me look at you. Dear, what a pale, sad face, so different from the bright fair face I first saw in this room. Sister Monica is right; your martyrdom has lasted long enough; you must go to Lewis."

Sydney kneels by the bedside and buries her face.

"You must go to Lewis," pursues Lucy, "because I do not think he will come. He is terribly steadfast in his notions of duty, and he thinks it is his duty to keep away; but once you are with him all will be well. It seems to me I see the things of time more clearly by the light of eternity, and I know, I KNOW it is your duty to return to your husband."

She still kneels, with clasped hands, parted, breathless lips, pale as ashes, listening to the *fiat* from dying lips, that is new life to her.

" If your father were alive, and knew all as we know it, do you think, dearly as he loved his adopted son, he would consign you to a life of misery because an accident had been done ? For, after all, Sydney, it was as much an accident as anything else. Would he have forbidden your return ? "

" No, no—oh, no ! My happiness was nearer to my father's heart than anything else in this world."

" Then do as he would have permitted you. Forget the past, and begin life anew. Tell Lewis it was Lucy's dying wish. Tell him I send him my dearest love, and that I ask him to come back and make mother happy until I see her again. Sydney, you promise this ? "

" I promise."

Once before, kneeling by a bedside, she made a promise to the dying—that, of stern justice and retribution—this, of pardon and peace.

A look of great content falls upon the dying face. She turns, and holds out a feeble hand to sister Monica.

" Read to me," she says, softly smiling. " My last trouble is at an end."

The sister obeys, and her sweetly solemn voice alone breaks the stillness ; and presently, her hand still clasped in the sister's, she drops asleep once more, quietly as a child.

The evening wears on ; a priest comes and goes ; Mrs. Nolan steals in to take one last look at Lucy before retiring. Nine, ten, eleven, strike from the city clocks ; the street is perfectly quiet. Faint and far off come the night noises of New York, the " car rattling o'er the stony street," the dulled roll of many wheels. Sister Monica, wearied with a long, hot day's teaching, folds her hands inside her sleeves presently, lays her head against the side of her chair, and sleeps. Only Sydney watches, her eyes never leaving Lucy, except to rest for a moment on the placid face of the other sleeper. Then, all at once —it is close upon twelve—Lucy Nolan's eyes fly open, her lips part in a radiant smile, they turn for a second upon Sydney, then close, and in this world open no more. With the striking of that most solemn hour, which links the night and the day, the stainless soul has gone.

CHAPTER XXII.

DOLLY.

 SULTRY summer night. A great city bathed in amber haze, its towers, its steeples, its tall chimneys, piercing the misty, yellow air, sits throned like a queen, with the sea at its feet. A windless, breathless, midsummer night, with all life lying languorous under its sultry spell.

In a quiet room, in a quiet street, a man lies, looking out at the shining stars that pierce the blue air like eyes. He lies on a low lounge wheeled beneath the open window, his hands clasped under his head, quite still, as he has lain for nearly an hour. He is in his shirt sleves, trying to catch a breath of salt air from the distant ocean. A man whose long length, as he lies here, is beyond that of most men ; a man upon the colorlessness of whose clear, calm face trouble has scored its inevitable lines ; a man from the gray darkness of whose eyes profound thoughtfulness looks out.

Yet it is not a stern face, nor a sombre face, not the face of a man whose life trouble has spoiled. It is rather that of one who has greatly suffered, who may have greatly sinned, but who also has learned to endure. Sorrow either takes all or gives more than it takes. It has refined and purified him, given a quick, almost womanly sympathy with all who suffer ; given him a spur to live down private grief in public work ; given a new and nobler color to his whole life.

He lies here, looks out at the yellow winking stars, and dreams. In his full and rapidly rising life, there is little time for idle dreams or vain regrets. This hour "between the lights" is the hour sacred to memory, when the heat and labor of the day are at an end, and the occupation or relaxation of the night have not begun. The street in which his office is, is retired and removed from the turmoil of the city. Two or three lamps blink through the yellow sleepy air ; the voices of little children arise in shout and laughter now and then. In the trees some belated birds are twittering, mosquitoes chant their deadly song, the sharp chirp of the grasshopper and cricket is audible, and fire-flies flash in myriads over the grass-plots. Down at the corner some Italian harpers, a little brown boy and a girl, are playing and singing the Marseillaise :

"Ye sons of France, awake to glory! "

Across the way, a girl in a white dress is sitting in the hot darkness at a jingly piano, and she is also singing :

"'Mid pleasures and palaces though we may roam,
Be it ever so humble, there's no place like home.
A charm from the sky seems to hallow us there."

It all blends harmoniously together with the dull roar of the distant city heart for an accompaniment, and soothes him as he listens. Even the pain the girl's song gives him is not without its alloy of sweetness and rest. It is a tender, little voice, and sings the dear old words with feeling. She has long light hair, too, and blue eyes—he has seen her many evenings lying wearily here, and it gives him a sort of comfort to watch the light glittering on those fair tresses, so like a coil of pale gold, he wears over his heart.

The harpists move away ; the girl closes the piano, lights her lamp, and draws the curtain. His hour of idleness has ended ; he rises, puts on his coat and hat, locks his door, and saunters slowly away toward his hotel and his supper. The streets are filled, are brilliant with light and color, animation and restless life. Men from every nation under Heaven jostle each other on the *pavé*, all the tongues that clanged at Babel seem to make discord here. It is a panorama he is well used to, but one that never loses its interest for him, a student of his kind.

All at once the steady flow of this human tide is broken ; there is a sudden rush, and commotion, and uproar, and from a dozen hoarse voices there arises the cry :

" Fire ! "

At all times, by night or by day, it is a thrilling word. People turn and rush pell-mell in the wake of the fire engines, and he follows the crowd. The fire is some half dozen blocks off, and the sultry air is stifling with black rolling smoke. There is more smoke than flame, thick, choking volumes from along the street, that half smother the eager crowd. · Now and then an orange tongue of flame, like a fiery serpent-head, darts forth, licks the blackened bricks, and disappears. It is a large, shell-like house, and though there is little to be seen, the fire has already gutted it. It originated in the cellar, some one says, and has made such headway unnoticed that those in the upper rooms are entirely cut off. It is a boarding-house, and is packed with people. Faces, wild with terror, appear at every window, women's shrieks rend the air, the engines play in steady streams, the firemen dart up and down their ladders, and men, women, and children are drawn forth from the burning building. There is no fire-escape, it seems ; the only means of exit is by the firemen's ladders.

The man who has interestedly followed the crowd helps with might and main ; not the firemen themselves work harder, or help more than he. It is growing desperate work—the imprisoned flames all at once break their boundaries and burst forth in sheets and volumes of fire. In five minutes the whole blazing shell will fall in. The firemen draw back. Have all been saved ? Only a few minutes have passed since they came. No ! As the question is asked, at a third story window a woman's face gleams through the lurid "gilt-edged hell," and a woman's frenzied scream thrills every heart with horror.

"The ladders ! the ladders !" is the hoarse roar. "Quick, for Heaven's sake !"

But the woman neither hears, nor heeds, nor stops. As they clutch the ladders for the desperate venture, with a second cry of fear and despair, the pursuing flames close behind her, she throws up the sash and leaps headlong among the spectators. There is an indescribable groan from the multitude, a dull, heavy, sickening *thud*, then for a second blank stillness.

The flames roar and crackle triumphantly, the firemen rush to save the adjoining buildings, as with a tremendous crash the roof falls in and the air is afire with flying sparks and cinders.

The woman who leaped lies in a motionless heap on the pavement. They lift her up, and the lurid blaze falls full on her death-white countenance. She is a young woman, and a pretty woman, for the face is uninjured, and masses of dark hair fall and trail over the arms of the men who raise her. One of them speaks :

"Great Heaven ! Dolly !"

"You know her, stranger ?" half a dozen voices ask.

It is the man who has worked with the firemen. He is bending over the senseless woman, pity and horror in his eyes.

"She is an actress. Yes, I know her. For Heaven's sake, men, let us take her where she can be cared for at once !"

"No use," somebody made answer; "all the doctors in

'Frisco won't do *her* any good.   She passed in her checks when
she took that jump."

It seems so.   She lies awfully limber and corpse-like in their
arms.   An ambulance comes and she is taken away, and the
man who has recognized her, follows, and waits in painful expectation for the verdict of the surgeons.   It comes.

" Not dead.   Compound fracture of right leg.   Shoulder dis-
located.   Bruises on head and side.   May die.   Impossible to
be positive yet."

" She is a person I once knew.   May I beg you to take even
more than ordinary care?   Any extra attention——"

" All right, sir," the gentlemanly physician says.   He knows
the man who speaks for a rising young lawyer, who has made
considerable stir in the city by his conduct of a recent popular
divorce suit.

The young woman does not die, but life has a sharp tussle
for the victory.   She has youth and a vigorous constitution on
her side, and three weeks after that sweltering night all danger
is over, and she lies, unable to move, suffering intensely, but
still wrested from the grasp of grim King Death.   As convales-
cence fairly sets in, the hours begin to drag, and she amuses herself in a dreary way by watching all that goes on in the ward
A hospital is not half a bad place, this patient thinks, as she
swallows with gusto fruity old wines, and devours her chickens, and peaches, and ice-cream, and grapes.   But gradually it
dawns upon her that these are luxuries the other patients are
not fed on.   Oranges, pears, pineapples, fruits of all kinds come
for her, fresh and crisp, every morning in a basket—so do the
chickens and the wines.   Now, colored boys and baskets don't
come of themselves—some one must send them.   Who is that
some one ?   She has not a friend in San Francisco who cares
a straw whether she lives or dies—who, then, takes all this trouble
and expense ?   Her nurse is more attentive to her than to any
other patient in the ward ; has her palm been anointed with gold,
too ?   She debates this question two whole days, then she calls
the nurse, a fat old Englishwoman, and demands an explanation.

" Say," she begins, " who is it sends me all these things ?
Nobody else gets 'em—wine, fowl, fruit, all that.   Who is it ?"

" A very nice gentleman indeed, my dear," responds the
nurse ; " a friend of yours that came with you here, and has
behaved most 'andsome about you in hevery way.   *Most* 'andsome," repeats the nurse, with emphasis.

" A friend of mine !" says the patient, bewildered, opening

wide two black eyes. "Nonsense! I haven't a friend in California. I have only just come."

"Which I think you must be mistook, my dear. I only 'ope, if hever I comes to grief, I may find such a friend as him."

A sudden, eager flush reddens the young woman's pale face.

"What is his name?" she demands.

"His name it is Mr. Nolan, and a scholar and a gentleman he is if I ever see one. A young lawyer, my dear—which, hold or young, they ain't mostly tender-'earted, from all I have 'eard, but if you was his own sister or sweetheart he couldn't be more concerned than he is. He spoke to the doctor, he spoke to me in the most 'andsome way; he sends you these things; there ain't a day he don't come, or send, to inquire."

"Nolan!" repeated the patient, and the hopeful, eager flush faded out, and a spasm of painful surprise took its place. "Lewis Nolan?"

"Which his Christian name I do not know, but Nolan it is. A tall, fine-looking young gentleman as you ever might wish to see, and spoke most high of in all the papers."

"Dark?" the silk girl cries, eagerly, "with large, piercing looking eyes, and a stern sort of face."

"Dark it is," responds the nurse; and his heyes, now that you put it to me, I do not know the color of, but quite dark and 'andsome. About the stern look I don't know—he smiles most sweet at times, but he certinly do look like a gentleman as has seen trouble."

"Lewis Nolan here!" the invalid mutters; that is strange. Does his wife come with him, nurse? A pretty, fair-haired young lady, with a soft voice and blue eyes?"

"No, my dear; no lady has ever come with him here, from first to last."

There is a pause; she lies with her brows knit, her lips twitching in nervous pain.

"You say he comes to see me, nurse?" she says, at last. "How is it I have never got a glimpse of him?"

"Well, you see, first of all you was out of your poor dear 'ead of course, and didn't know nothin' or nobody. Then when you got right in your 'ead, he would only come and look at you when you was asleep, and stop at the door if you was awake. You would not care to see him, he said, and he would not disturb you. Will you 'ave some wine or broth now, my deary?"

"No, not now," Dolly De Courcy answers, and turns away her face.

So! Lewis Nolan is here, and it is he who cares for her when all the world has forsaken her. Lewis Nolan cares for her and spends his money upon her; and she, two years ago, she betrayed him to his wife. That was her hour—this is his, and it seems he likes a noble revenge. Dolly, little benighted heathen that she is, has never read or heard, of heaping coals of fire on an enemy's head, but she feels it keenly now. There dawns upon her untaught soul a glimpse of something nobler than life has ever shown her yet. She broods over it all day, and in the restless vigil of bodily torture in the night, and comes to a resolution. Next morning, when the nurse visits her bedside, Dolly speaks abruptly:

"When was Mr. Nolan here last?"

"Day before yesterday, deary. He don't come so often now that you are getting nicely, but he never forgets to send the things."

"The next time he comes, tell him I want to see him—that I *must* see him," says Dolly.

The nurse promises, and goes, and Dolly lies and thinks and thinks. Softened and subdued thoughts they must be; for by and by tears well up in the hard black eyes and roll silently over the wasted cheeks. Touched by kindness, weakened by pain, Dolly will rise from that bed a better little woman than she lay down.

He does not come that day; but the next, Saturday, brings him. He comes early in the afternoon, and Dolly's message is delivered. For a moment he hesitates in irresolute thought: she can have nothing to say that it will not be intensely painful for him to hear. He bears her no ill-will, has never done so, for the part of informant she played. Since the truth was as it was, it is much better it should be known; but the sight of her recalls memories that are the slow torture of his life. But he will not refuse. Self-sacrifice grows easy by practice. He goes to her bedside and looks down kindly upon her.

"You are better, Dolly," he says. "I am glad of that."

She seizes the hand he holds out—she has ever been a creature of impulse—and covers it with passionately grateful kisses.

"Lewis Nolan," she says, "you are a good man. I have not deserved this from you."

"Hush, Dolly," he answers, in a troubled voice. "I have done nothing. When will you be up, and about?"

"I don't know: I don't care! The best thing I can do is to die. I am of no use in the world; nobody wants me;

nobody cares for me. I am not going to talk of myself. I want to hear something about *you.* When did you come to San Francisco?"

" Over a year ago."

" You were in the army until the end of the war ? "

" Yes."

" Then you came straight out here ? "

" I did."

" You joined the army a week after I went and told your wife—*that ?* "

His face whitens, but his grave eyes look at her kindly; his voice keeps its gentle tone.

" I did."

" Was that the cause ? "

" That was the cause."

"What I said parted your wife and you ? "

" Yes, Dolly."

" And keeps you parted still ? "

He bends his head, a flush of intensest pain darkening his face.

" Lewis, your wife is lovely and sweet, and like a queen. You love her, don't you ?"

" With all my heart."

" And she you ? "

" Yes," he says. " Dolly, you must cease. I can't bear this."

" Wait a minute," she cries, almost triumphantly. " You stay apart because I told her you killed Bertie Vaughan, and you are both breaking your hearts because you *are* apart. Is that it ? "

She sees that she is torturing him, but she still grasps his hand, and looks with eager eyes into his.

" I thought so," she says ; exultation in her tone, " when I heard you were here. Now, then, Lewis Nolan, you have done a good turn for me, and I am going to do a good turn for you. You may go back to your wife as soon as you please, if *that* is all that holds you asunder ; for Bertie Vaughan is no more dead than you are."

CHAPTER XXIII.   •

"HE WHO ENDURES CONQUERS."

HE stands speechless, looking down at her, every trace of color slowly leaving his face.

Dolly laughs aloud in her triumph.

"I was afraid you might have found it out, but I see you haven't. I am glad that I am the first to tell you! it seems like making up for the past and thanking you for the present. If you had not been good to me I would never have told you. Nobody ever treated me well—that was how I thought—why should I treat anybody well? But now it is different. I did you harm, all the harm I could; and you do me good when your turn comes. That is being a Christian; but I don't think there are many out-and-out Christians. No; you needn't stand and look at me as white as a sheet, there's nothing to be scared about. You thought you killed Bertie Vaughan when you threw him over the bank, but you didn't. I've often wished since you had; but people that are born to make other people miserable don't go off the hooks so easy. That's what I sent for you to tell you. Now sit down here; it ain't a long story, and I'll tell you all about it."

She points to a chair by the bedside, still holding his hand fast in hers, and with her round black eyes shining upon him, begins in a rapid voice her story.

"You remember that night? Yes, of course you do. Well, do you know I felt sure you would go to Wychcliffe, and I didn't care, because I meant to make a fuss myself, and never let that wedding come off. Oh! how fond I was of him! He was awfully good-looking, you know, and his aristocratic airs, and all the rest of it, fairly turned my head. I'd never seen anybody like him, and never have since, for that matter. I couldn't have let him marry Miss Owenson, no I couldn't. I would rather have killed him than let him. So I watched and waited, and went down to Wychcliffe as you did, the night before. I knew he was staying at the hotel, and I made up my mind to see him before he slept, and make him hear to reason; but when I spied *you* on the train I changed my plans. I would watch you instead. I knew what a horrid temper you had—beg your par-

don, Lewis—and how jealous you were, and I didn't want you
to hurt him. I've often wondered since how a man like you,
clever, and educated, and serious, and all that, came to care
about a girl like me. I wasn't worth it, but I was good enough
for Bertie Vaughan, for he is a scoundrel, with all his airs and
graces, if there ever was one.

" You didn't know me ; I had on a thick brown veil, and I
kept away in a corner. But I never lost sight of you. I followed you to the hotel ; I waited outside until you left it, and
then I went after you along the cliff-path. I saw you stop behind the big boulder, and then I knew you meant to wait there
for Bertie. Very well, I stopped and waited, too. By-and-by
he came whistling along quite cheerful and bridegroom-like, and
you stalked out like a ghost and said : ' Stay !' I was hiding
behind some spruces a little way off, and could see and hear
quite comfortable. I was curious to know what you would do
or say—I had no idea you would heave him over—and I kept
quiet and waited. Lor' bless you ! I don't think two minutes
passed before you clinched, and the next thing you gave him a
plunge from you and over he went.

" Well ! I was so stunned, turned so dead sick, that for a
while I could neither move nor open my mouth. You looked
stunned, too—*such* a face as you had in the moonlight ! Then
you turned and walked away. That roused me up, and I started
out and made for the edge of the cliff. You might have seen
me easy if you had looked back, but you kept straight on as if
you didn't care. I can't tell you how I felt as I looked over
that horrid place expecting to see him all mashed to a jelly
down on the rocks.

" Bless you, no ! the Old Boy's good to his own. There was
Bertie, half way down, clinging for dear life to a cedar bush, and
staring up, froze stiff with terror, and not able to say a word.

" Well, I gave a gasp at that, and nearly went over myself,
so glad was I at the sight.

" ' Bertie,' I said, ' don't be afraid. It's me, it's Dolly, and
I'll save you if I break my own neck doing it.'

" ' Dolly !' he cried out, in, oh ! such a voice of agony and
fear. ' Dolly, save me, and I'll never leave you again as long
as I live.'

" You see he was a coward, as all traitors are, and was pretty
well scared to death. All my wits came back at once.

" ' Wait,' I said ; ' let me think. I can't go down to you, and
you can't reach the bottom without killing yourself. I have it

I'll make a rope. I'll fasten it up here to this rock, and I'll throw the other end to you. Wait, Bertie—wait.'

"'Hurry, then,' he says, in that same dreadful voice, 'for this bush is breaking, and won't hold my weight five minutes more. Dolly, save me, and I swear I'll marry you before morning.'

"I didn't need that to make me work, but I worked as I never did before. I had a penknife in my pocket, and a broché shawl around me. These broché things are strong, you know; no, perhaps you don't, but they are; and I set to work and cut it into seven strips. I knotted them together, and stood on every knot, and pulled with all my might. I threw it down and it was just long enough. Then I twisted one end round the rock, and braced myself, and held on with both hands. If the knots had slipped, Lord a' mercy on him—his brains would have been knocked out—but they didn't. He caught it, and it held, and when he got to the top, he just fell down, all in a heap, and, if you'll believe it, fainted away like a frightened girl.

"Well, I didn't mind that; I rubbed him with snow, and loosened his collar, and slapped his hands, and by-and-by he came to. But he was white as a corpse, and so weak at first with scare he could hardly stand. He just let me do as I pleased with him; he had no more pluck left than a chicken. We went to the station, but the train was gone, and you with it, I suppose, in a fine state, thinking you had killed him. I can't say I was angry with you, for you had made matters smooth and easy for me; but Bertie was furious. His face and hands were all scratched and bleeding, and after awhile, as we walked along, he got silent and sulky. He must go with me, he knew; but you and the Owenson family, and everybody else, must believe he was killed; that was better than they should know he had run away with me—no, that I had run away with him. We could walk to the next station and take a later train there for New York. He would change his name, and he would have the satisfaction of making the ruffian who threw him over, think himself a murderer. I encouraged him in all this. Well, the end of it is, we got to New York unnoticed and were married the very next day."

Dolly pauses. Retrospective memories seem for a moment too many for her, but she rallies and goes on.

"We kept quiet for a while. He called himself Hamilton, and did not stay with mother and me. How we both enjoyed it when the detective came to pump me about the murder. For my part, I was glad you were out of the way, Lewis, and that no one suspected you. If you had been arrested, you may be sure I would have come forward and told the truth. I think Bertie felt the death of Captain Owenson and the loss of his fortune, but it was too late now; and I did my best to make up to him, but he was sullen and dissatisfied from the very first. I worked for both. I got an engagement with a company going to Texas, and Bertie, of course, went along. All that winter and the following summer we spent in Galveston; then we returned to New York, and made our next winter trip to Cuba. The succeeding summer we passed in Canada, the last we ever passed anywhere together. All this time Bertie was getting more and more surly, and cross, and dissatisfied—it wasn't what he was used to—and he kept nag, nag, nagging at me until I was nearly wild. Actresses like me don't make fortunes. What I did make he spent faster than it was earned. He was sick of our strolling life, he wished a dozen times a day I had never saved his life, any death was better than this sort of existence ; he hated being perpetually pinched, and forever with low company and a vulgar, uneducated wife—that is what he called me. After that, I got reckless too, nothing I did could please him, and after a while I stopped trying. We led a regular cat-and-dog life of it ; but all the while, mind you, there was this difference—I was as fond of him as ever, while he got fairly to hate me. He took to drink and to gamble ; things went on from worse to worse, until at last jealousy was added, and then all was over between us.

"We were playing that third year in Northern Indiana, and it was there he fell in with a Mrs. Morgan, a widow, who had had two husbands, and buried 'em, and was ready for a third. She was very rich—Morgan had been an army contractor—she was fifteen years older than Bertie, she was fat and ugly, and coarse and common ; she was called a Tartar by every one who knew her ; she had jawed the army contractor to death, but she fell in love with my husband. She saw him on the stage—he went on in minor parts—and that he had a wife already made no difference to a woman like Mrs. Morgan, nor a State like Indiana. She let him know it too, and he began to go to her house, and escort her to places just as if he was a single man. You may guess the sort of row I raised when I first found it out, but he only laughed in my face ; and all at once, before I knew it, he had instituted a suit for divorce, and *she* gave him the money to carry it on. Incompatibility of temper—'the devil couldn't live with me'—was what he told them, and he got his divorce,

for he had no trouble in proving the sort of life we led. Before
the decree was granted they had left the place ; and two weeks
after, their marriage was in the papers.   He had taken back his
own name, and there it was 'Albert Vaughan, Esq., and Caroline, relict of the late Peter Morgan of this city.'

"After that, I don't care to tell or think how I felt or how I
went on.   I was reckless and mad, and didn't care for anything.
But I kept decent looks, and decent clothes, and by a fluke of
fortune got an engagement in the theatre where I saw you and
your wife.   It was only temporarily to fill the place of an
actress who had suddenly been taken ill.   I think the devil got
into me at the sight.   The world prospered with everybody but
me.   Bertie Vaughan was rolling in riches—so were you.   I
had made up my mind to shoot him if I ever met him, and
that night I made up mind to do *you* all the mischief I could.
I was struck of a heap to see you had married Miss Sydney
Owenson of all women, and I felt sure she couldn't know what
you had done to Bertie.   I had found out that he was in California—I wanted money to come after and hunt him down ;
you would give me that money to keep your secret, I was sure.
So I went to your house to see you, and saw her instead.   You
know what I told her—a little truth and a little lie.   Between
both the work was done, and you and she parted.   I heard you
went to the war, and guessed the reason.   But I never went
back.   There was something in your wife's look that, bad
as I was, I couldn't face again. . I stayed away, and let her
all alone.

"All this time I had kept track of Bertie Vaughan.   He and
the Morgan woman went to Europe ; tremendous swells, both of
them ; and he was proud of her money, if he was ashamed of
her.   When they came back—and with a French nurse and a
baby, if you please !—they went off to California before I could
set eyes on them.   If I had, the Morgan woman would have
been looking out for number four by this time.   I followed
them here as soon as I could, and I was only here two days
when the house I boarded in took fire, and I jumped from the
window, and smashed myself.   You've been good to me, and
I've told you this story to pay you back.   Bertie Vaughan's alive
and well, and in this city, if he hasn't left it since I came here."

She stops, still clasping closely the hand that has grown cold
in hers.   He has not spoken a word ; he has sat and listened
to all, his face rigid with surprise, and perfectly colorless.

"You ain't angry, Lewis ?" she asks, wistfully.   "I know it was horrid mean of me, but I'm awful sorry now. I can't say any more than that."

"Angry, Dolly? No. You have done me the greatest service to-day any human being could do. I never was a murderer in intention; I find I am not one in fact. No words of mine can tell how grateful, how thankful I am."

"Well, I'm glad," says Dolly. "I've done mischief enough; it is pleasant to help make somebody happy. I had just got Bertie's address that very afternoon. He and the Morgan woman were stopping at the ———— House."

"At the ———— House!" exclaims Nolan, in amaze. "That is my hotel for the past six months."

"It is odd, then, you never saw him; for that's where he was with the rest of his caravan, three weeks ago."

"No, not so odd either; I always leave early in the morning, before most people are up, and do not return, as a rule, until late. But I shall ascertain at once. Let me thank you once more, Dolly; and believe me, I will remember you with gratitude and affection forever."

So he goes, and Dolly's heathen heart is full of the after-glow that comes from a good deed done. And Lewis Nolan, like a man who walks in a dream, as Atlas, with the load of a world lifted off his shoulders, with a soul full of silent thanksgiving and great joy, walks back to his hotel.

Excepting Sundays, he has hardly ever been in it, during his sojourn, at this time of day. Half the States might come and go, and he be none the wiser. Bertie Vaughan might be his next door neighbor for all he knew. Alive! thank Heaven! thank Heaven for that! His first act is to examine the hotel register. Yes, it is there.

"Albert Vaughan, Esquire, lady, nurse, and child."

His heart gives a great leap at the confirmation; but his quiet face, except that it flushes slightly under his dark skin, tells nothing.

"How long have this family been here?" he asks.

"Well, off and on, nine months or more. They travel about, and make this their headquarters in San Francisco. Know Mr. Vaughan, sir?"

"I think I have met him. A very blonde, British-looking young fellow?"

"With a drawl! and an eye-*gloss*, a half a quarter of an inch of brain," says the smart clerk, throwing himself into an attitude and mimicking Mr. Vaughan:

19

" ' Aw, I say, my good fellah, just mix me a sherry cobbler,
will you—it's so blawsted 'ot to-day !'   Uncommon fond of
crooking his elbow, is Mr. Vaughan.   And he ain't hen-pecked
neither.   Oh, no, not at all."

Mr. Nolan does not wait for the conclusion of these sarcastic
remarks, but springs with elastic lightness up the stairs to his
own room on the third floor.   He will write to his wife and tell
her all.   No, he will send her a telegram ; he cannot wait,   A
telegram just to apprise her that Bertie Vaughan is alive, and a
letter afterward to explain how he comes to know.   Nothing
need stand between them now.   Such a rush of hope and joy
comes over him as he realizes it that he can do nothing but sit,
the pen idle in his hand, in a happy dream.

He begins his letter at last :

SAN FRANCISCO, August 28th.

"My DEAR WIFE."

Again he pauses, the words he has written seem to hold his
hand by some charmed spell, and he can get no further.   " My
dear wife."   With what different feelings he wrote these very
words last, sitting in his mother's cottage, while the dull dawn
broke, beginning that letter of saddest farewell.   He has never
written them since, never sent her word, or note, or line.   Between them stood the red shadow of murder, the dead, menacing
face of Bertie Vaughan.   But Bertie Vaughan is alive and well,
and beneath this very roof—how strange, how strange—once
more the sweet familiar address, so long unwritten, looks up at
him from the paper.   He could see her as she received this
letter, the tears, the joy, the prayer of almost speechless
gratitude, the loving, eager reply.

" My dear wife ! "—what shall he say—how begin ?   He is
not usually at a loss for words, either in writing or speaking ;
but this is the supreme moment of a life, and it is not so easy
either to break the news of great sorrow or joy.   He sits so
absorbed that a faint tap at the door fails to reach him.   He
neither hears nor knows, when the handle is gently turned and
some one comes in.

Five minutes previously, there had been an arrival.   A lady,
youthful and elegant, though slightly travel-worn, has driven up
to the hotel and inquired for Mr. Nolan.   Yes, Mr. Nolan is
there, and up in his room, says the smart clerk, with a look of
mingled surprise, curiosity, and admiration.   In the six months
of his stay, Mr. Nolan has had no ladies to ask after him before.

This young lady, despite her gray veil, the clerk can see, is exceptionally handsome and "high-toned." "The sort of missis *I* should like to swell down Montgomery street any day in the week with, and I ain't easy to please neither, I ain't," is what the clerk says afterward, relating the occurrence.

"Shall I send for Mr. Nolan, madame?" in his most suave manner, says the smart clerk.

"I am Mrs. Nolan," the young lady answers, with quiet dignity and a vivid blush. "If you will show me to his room I will not trouble you."

"You Pete," calls the clerk, and "You Pete," a colored boy, bounces forward. "Show this lady to seventy-three, and look sharp."

The lady follows "You Pete," and the sprightly clerk blows after her an enthusiastic kiss.

"Beauteous creature! 'She's all my fancy painted her, she's lovely, she's divine; but her heart it is another's, and it never can be mine.' Didn't know Nolan had a wife. Close mouthed fellow, Nolan. Such a stunner, too. Just from the States. Steamer in an hour ago. Wonder if he expects her? Never went to the pier. But then she's his *own* wife. If she was any other fellow's——"

Pete escorts her to No. 73—points it out with a grin, ducks his woolly head, and disappears. She taps lightly, her heart beating so fast that she grows faint. There is no response; she opens and goes in. He is seated, his back to her, writing. She throws off her veil, clasps her hands, and looks at him for a moment—the husband unseen so long. Then there is a waft of perfume, the flutter of a woman's dress, and she is kneeling before him, her face bowed on his knee.

"Lewis!"

He starts with a violent recoil, and looks at her. She has been so vividly before him, that for a moment he thinks it is a hallucination, conjured up by his own intense longing. But she speaks again brokenly, in Sydney's own soft voice:

"Lewis—husband—I have come to you! I could not stay away longer. Oh! Lewis, say you are glad I am here."

"Sydney!" he says in a dazed voice, and sits and looks at her, almost afraid to touch this kneeling figure, lest it should vanish, "*is* it Sydney, or am I dreaming?"

She lifts her face, all pale and wet with passionate tears, and throws her arms about him.

"Lewis! Lewis! Lewis!"

"It is real then ; it is Sydney !"

While he sat here trying to get beyond the words that charmed him, she was on her way to him. Once more he looks on Sydney's fair, sweet face ; once more Sydney's tender arms clasp him.

"My wife ! my wife !"

He holds her for a little, and no words are spoken. She still kneels, and he makes no attempt to raise her. So intense is the surprise that he is almost stunned. Then a sudden startling thought strikes him—why has she come! Does she know? He draws back and looks down into the face that is dearer to him than all earth beside—that he has seen only in dreams for two long years.

"Sydney," he asks, "*why* have you come ? How is it that what parted us once does not part us still ? "

" Because it should never have parted us," she says with a great sob ; "because my life away from you was one long death. I could not stay. Whether you want me or not, Lewis, I had to come. Do what you may, I can never have any life apart from you more."

She knows nothing. She has come to him because she loves him too well to let even guilt stand between them. And he bows his head, and from his full heart come the words, sublime beyond all others to speak the utter joy of human souls :

"Thank God !"

CHAPTER XXIV.

"INTO MARVELLOUS LIGHT."

THE first shock of glad meeting, of joyful surprise is past, and they sit side by side, and it is Sydney who talks. She has much to tell. First and chief is Lucy's death, of which as yet he has not heard, and he covers his eyes for a moment as he hears it. It is well perhaps that some dimness should shadow the radiance of too much light—this is the dark spot in his picture. He has long known she must die ; but let death be ever so long expected, it is none the less a shock when it comes. He has loved and venerated that tender, patient sister, even in the most thoughtless days of his youth ; but it seems to him he has never known how dear she was to him before. Looking up in his face, his hands clasped in hers, Sydney tells him all. How Sister Monica and Lucy pointed out the path of duty, that has led her here. She tells him, too, the story of Teddy's loss, and the happy reunion, after long parting and pain, of Teddy's father and mother.

"So you lost all," he says to her, looking down into the fair earnest face with a tender smile, "your friend and your boy. It must have been very lonely for you, my princess."

"Lonely !" She makes a little passionate gesture ; "I had lost *you*, Lewis—it could not matter who came or went after that."

"Still you would never have come to me if it had not been for Sister Monica ;" he answers. "By-the-by, if ever I meet that best of little sisters, I must thank her for sending me my wife. You never would have come of yourself, would you, Sydney ?"

"Ah ! I don't know," Sydney says sorrowfully ; "it was such a miserable, miserable time, Lewis. It gives me the heartache even now that I sit beside you and look back upon it—the long desolate months of waiting, and hoping, and fearing, and longing. Lewis, I thought you would have returned when the war ended. I so hoped you would have come ; I would never have let you go again, if you had. Duty—as I thought it then—my promise to the dead—all would have been flung to the winds at the sight of your face. But you did not come, you did not seem to care to come. You had your work and your ambition. Men do not feel these things as women do. My life has been one long wretchedness ; and yours—has your profession kept sorrow and loneliness altogether at bay ? Has your life not been so full and so busy that you have had little time to grieve for your wife ? "

There is a smile on his face as he listens to the impassioned reproach, but his eyes are tender and grave.

"What do you think about it ? " he asks.

"Your work has *not* filled your life ;" she answers, "Look here, Lewis," she lifts his dark hair, and with a touch that is a caress, "there are gray hairs here, my dearest, and when I saw you last it was all raven dark. You have not changed much, but I can see that you have suffered. My husband, I should never have let you go."

She lays her face on his shoulder, and there is silence for a little ; her heart full of the loneliness and loss of these two past years.

"It was such a hard conflict between duty and love," she goes on, "my duty, it seemed to me, forbade my ever seeing again the man who had caused Bertie Vaughan's death—forgive me that I speak of it, Lewis, I never will again—and my love called always for my husband's return. Many, many times, when half wild with thinking of you, alone and wretched as I was, have I begun letters imploring your return, telling you the past was forgiven and forgotten ; but when they were finished and the impulse was past, I could not send them. My promise to my father seemed to rise before me and appal me. To ask you to return seemed to me like a crime, and these letters went into the fire, one and all."

"And yet, my wife, you are here."

"Yes, Lewis, it all seemed so clear that night. Sister Monica and Lucy were nearer heaven than I ; they knew best. All was dark with me ; I could not decide what was right or what was wrong. I was like one shipwrecked, tossing about on a troubled sea without rudder or compass or pilot to guide. But they knew, and my heart, hungry for the sight of you, echoed every word they said. And so I am here, and I know at last my first earthly duty is to the husband I love and venerate above all men, and to whom I have pledged to cleave until death. And never—no never, Lewis, shall the shadow of the past come to darken my life. I want you to know and feel *that*, to believe that I love and honor you as greatly as though the past had never been."

She flings her arms about him with a great sob as she ceases, and they sit in silence. Presently he reaches over and takes up the sheet of paper on which he has been writing.

"Look here, Sydney."

She looks and reads, " My Dear Wife," and lifts her surprised eyes to his face.

"Were you writing to me, Lewis ? "

"I was writing to you. Does it not strike you as strange that after a silence of two years I should to-day begin a letter to you ? I could get no further than these three words ; they hold a charm for me. I thought I had written them for the last time that morning in my mother's house. Do you not wonder what I was going to say ? "

She laughs and blushes in the old charming way that Sydney Owenson was wont to do, under Lewis Nolan's eyes.

" You were going to tell me what I have come all the way from New York to San Francisco to tell you—that .ife apart was impossible any longer."

" Well, not exactly, although I think it is highly probable I might have said that too. But I had something to tell you. Do you recall the message Dolly De Courcy gave you for me, the afternoon she came to you? Do you remember the words? You look puzzled : let me help you. She said, 'Ask your husband how he last parted with Bertie Vaughan?' Was that not it?'"

" Y-e-s ; I think so. "

" Recall the story I told you. You may recollect I said that after flinging Vaughan from me, and seeing him fall over, I took it for granted he was smashed to atoms, and never looked to confirm the supposition. Now does it not strike you that there may have been a mistake? That he may not have been killed after all?"

" Lewis, what is this? I—I do not understand you!"

She lifts a white startled face, and he smiles down upon her a smile she does not understand.

" I do not believe Bertie Vaughan was killed. Indeed I have excellent reason for believing he is very much alive at this moment. 1 believe that he is in California ; more, that he is in San Francisco ; still more, that he is in this very hotel at this very hour ! Beneath the same roof with you, Sydney—think of it—Bertie Vaughan !"

She is trembling from head to foot ; she is clinging to him with a terrified face.

"Lewis, what are you saying! Oh ! you would not jest about this. If you have any pity, speak out—what do you mean?"

" My dear little wife, what I say. All my remorse, all our suffering, all our parting have been for nothing. On that long-gone wedding day of yours, when the bridegroom did not come and you mourned for him as dead, he was the bridegroom of another bride. On the day he was to have married you, my Sydney, he married Dolly De Courcy. "

She utters a gasping cry, clasps both hands together, and sits breathlessly waiting.

" Oh !" she cries out, "he was not killed after all ! Thank Heaven, thank Heaven !"

" Amen. No, he was not killed. He was but a poor creature to suffer for at the Lest, but your suffering was in vain.

Had your father known the truth, proud, high spirited, as you told me he was, the shock of the reality would have been worse to him than the shock of the delusion. Dolly De Courcy saved his life that night, and he married her next day. Married her and deserted her, and is now under this roof the husband of another woman. Don't tremble so, Sydney; I will tell you the whole story?

He tells it; the story of that sultry night, of Dolly, of the services he was able to render, and of her return. And Sydney listens, dazed, in a dream. Bertie Vaughan alive and here! She has thought him dead so long that it is impossible to realize it. And Lewis's hand is unstained by blood, not the shadow of a shadow need stand between them. She turns so white, so deathly faint and sick, that he thinks she is going to swoon, and springs to his feet in consternation.

"Good Heaven! Sydney, the shock has been too much for you. Don't faint, I beg!" cries Lewis with a man's comical horror, "wait! I'll get a glass of wine—of water."

He rushes off, despite Sydney's gasping protest. Under the open window there is a marble stand and a crystal jug of ice-water. He is hastily filling a goblet, when the stentor tones of "You Pete," on the sidewalk below arrest his hand.

"Look-a-heah! you darn black nigger!" is what "You Pete" is vociferating; "does you mean to loaf up dar all day? Jest fotch along Missy Vaughan's tother Sairytogy, and look alive 'bout it, will yer!"

It is the name that arrests his attention. At the curbstone stands a hack, the driver busily strapping on trunks. Within, upon the front seat sits a nurse and a baby; upon the back, a lady, her head thrust out of the doorway giving directions. She is a woman of forty or more, fat and yellow, with an unpleasantly bilious look, a wide thin mouth, a sharply pointed nose, small fierce black eyes, and shrew and vixen in every acrid tone of her piercing voice.

"Say, you darkey!" she shrieks to "You Pete," "just go and see what Mr. Vaughan's about, will you. I can't wait here for him all day."

"All right, missis, he ain't doin' nuffin, missis," briskly responds Pete; "jest a wettin' his whistle in de bar. Now den, old whip, here's dat ar Sairytogy at last."

"Wetting his whistle!" repeats the lady vindictively. "*Will* you go, you black boy, and tell him to come here this very minute. I shall drive on if he isn't here when that trunk is strapped."

" All right 'm," says Pete with a grin, and an intense appreciation of the situation, and dives into the hotel.

"Sydney," says Mr. Nolan, with what can be called nothing less than diabolical malice, "come here. The air will do you good."

There is a wicked laugh in his eyes as he draws her hand through his arm. His windows "give" on the piazza, like doors, and he throws this wide, and leads her out.

"I am better, Lewis," she says, "it was nothing. It was only——"

She suddenly stops. In flaring painted capitals, on the canvas cover of the "Sairytogys" there is the name VAUGHAN.

" Well," cries the owner of the vinegar face, in a most vinegary voice, to " You Pete," who reappears : " *is* Mr. Vaughan coming or is he not ? Does he mean to keep me here all day, or—— Oh ! really, Mr. Vaughan, here you are at last ! " (this in accents of scathing politeness.) " How very good of you to condescend to come at all ! "

" What a devil of a hurry you're in, Caroline," says a sulky, masculine voice ; " it wants twenty minutes of train-time yet, and it isn't a ten-minute drive. Can't you let a man——"

He pauses and looks up. For from the piazza there comes a low, irrepressible cry of " *Bertie !* " And the words die on his lips, and the deep, permanent flush fades into sickly pallor on his face, and he stands like a man whom every power is leaving but the one power of sight. And Bertie Vaughan and Sydney are face to face.

He recognizes her instantly and she him. She has changed but little, and that little for the better ; he has changed much, and that much for the worse ; but they know each other instantaneously. Grown stout and somewhat bloated, indeed, all that delicacy of figure and complexion that once made Bertie Vaughan beautiful, with a woman's beauty, forever lost, it is yet Bertie Vaughan who stands there and looks at Captain Owenson's daughter.

He has turned dead white to the very lips ; he stands paralyzed, and for ten seconds they look straight into each other's eyes.

Then Mrs. Vaughan comes to the rescue in tones of smothered fury.

"Mr. Vaughan, for the last time, will you or will you not get into this carriage? What are you standing there gaping like a fool for ? Driver, don't wait another minute ; drive on."

19*

It arouses him from his trance. Alas! those tones of ver-
juice arouse him often. He turns and leaps in.

" Drive and be ——— !" is the awful expression he makes use
of, in his recklessness, to his wealthy wife.

He pulls his hat over his eyes, shuts his lips, folds his arms,
and is driven to the station.   But all the while the ruddy color
does not return, all the while the ceaseless nag, nag, of a nagging woman falls like the harmless buzzing of a summer fly.
Whatever this woman whom he has married may know of his
career, there is one episode she does not know, never will know ;
one name she will never hear, and that Sydney Owenson.

The husband and wife on the piazza stand and watch the carriage that bears the other husband and wife out of sight.   Then
she turns to him with a sort of sobbing cry———

" Oh, Lewis, take me in."

He obeys, almost sorry for what he has done, and she leans
her face against him, and he knows that she is crying.   Not for
the man she has just seen, may never see again, and has so long
mourned as dead, but for the memory of that other Bertie
Vaughan, the brother of her youth, the pet of her father and
mother—a memory that is dead and buried forever.

" Don't cry, my princess," her husband says, smiling, yet
looking sympathetic, too ; "he never was worth one of those
tears ; and, poor fellow, my deepest sympathies go with him."

" That wife !" Lewis Nolan laughs, in spite of his concern
at these falling tears.   "I knew you could never realize the
fact of his being alive so vividly as if you saw him face to face.
Mrs. Nolan, cease immediately ! I object to your crying for
another man."

It is the briefest of summer showers.   She lifts her face and
dashes away the lingering tear-drops, indignant at herself.

" Oh !" she says, with a great gasp, and clasping both hands
tightly around Mr. Nolan's gray coat-sleeve, "to think I might
have been his wife to-day if you had not thrown him over the
cliff.   I never want to think of Bertie Vaughan again."

" Then my rising jealousy is allayed. Blame him not, my
princess—awful retribution has befallen him—an avenging Nemesis has overtaken him in the person of that appalling Mrs.
Vaughan.   Even Dolly De Courcy is avenged."

" Let us talk of something else," says Mrs. Nolan, with a little distasteful look, as if Mr. and Mrs. Vaughan left a bad taste
in her mouth—" yonder sunset, for instance. I did not think

you got up such gorgeous coloring in the land of gold. It equals Venice."

For the sun is going down behind the myriad city roofs and steeples, in a glory of color we call golden and crimson, but which no hue of earth ever approaches. Fleecy clouds all palest rose or vividest red, faintest amber and deepest orange, go before like heralds, and in his royal purples, like any other monarch, the king of day is sinking from sight.

"How lovely ! how lovely !" Sydney murmurs. "What a glorious sky !"

"Ye-e-s," Mr. Nolan says, in the critical tone of a connoisseur in sunsets. "When we do this sort of thing in San Francisco, we do do it. A very fine celestial illumination, my dear Mrs. Nolan, got up for your special delectation, no doubt, to convince you that painted skies are home as well as foreign products. It *is* beautiful."

She smiles, but says nothing—her swelling heart too full for words. It seems to her as if the great new happiness that has come to her were but reflected in that lovely western radiance. She still clasps his arm, and so, side by side, to part no more, they stand together, the rose light on their faces, the "light that never shone on sea or land," in their hearts, and watch the sun go down.

THE END.

www.ingramcontent.com/pod-product-compliance
Lightning Source LLC
Chambersburg PA
CBHW020900130726
47900CB00014B/1167

* 9 7 8 3 3 3 7 0 2 7 5 0 6 *